P9-AZV-030

THE HEROES OF OLYMPUS

Book One

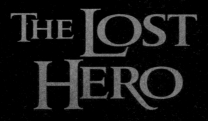

THE LOST HERO

THE GRAPHIC NOVEL

by

RICK RIORDAN

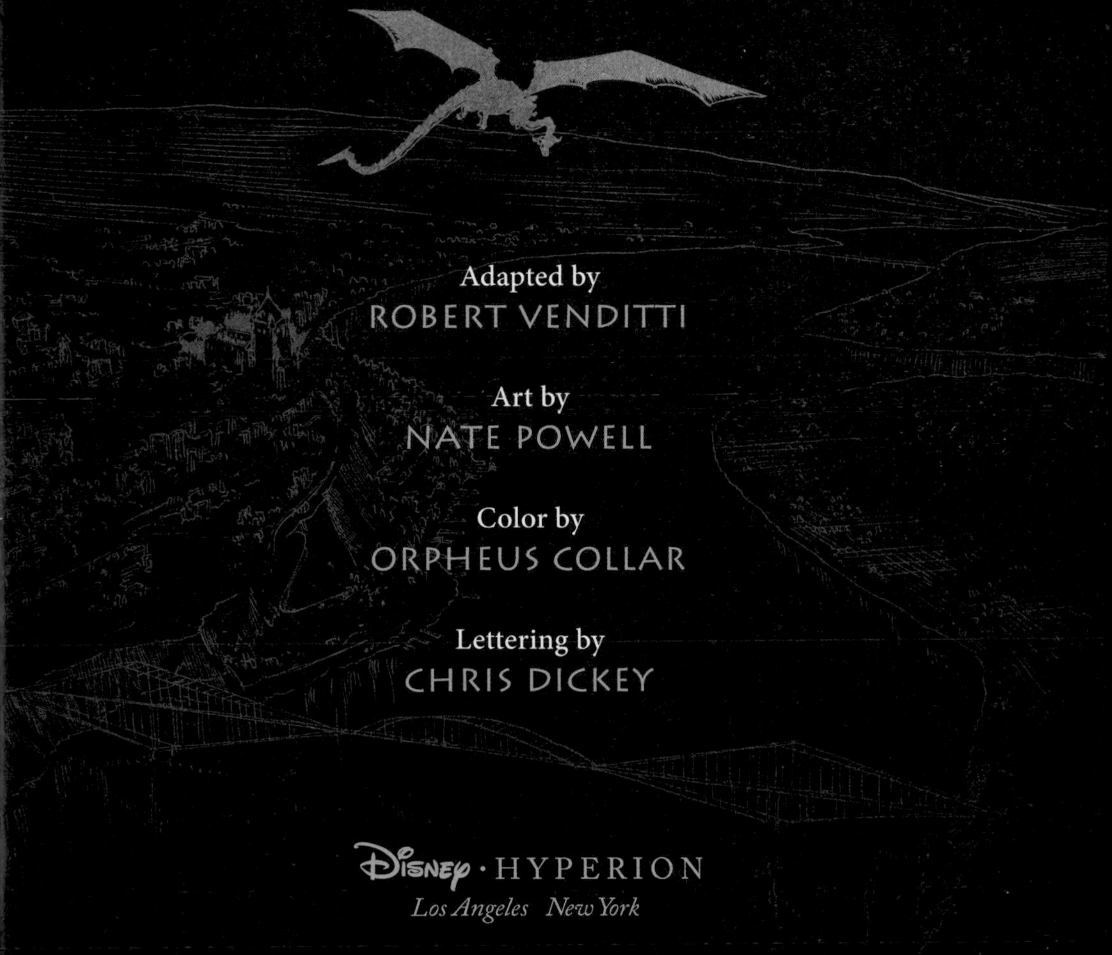

Adapted by

ROBERT VENDITTI

Art by

NATE POWELL

Color by

ORPHEUS COLLAR

Lettering by

CHRIS DICKEY

Disney · HYPERION

Los Angeles New York

Adapted from the novel
The Heroes of Olympus, Book One: *The Lost Hero*

Designed by Jim Titus
Printed in the United States of America
V381-8386-5-14196

First Edition
1 3 5 7 9 10 8 6 4 2
ISBN (hardcover) 978-1-4231-6279-7
ISBN (paperback) 978-1-4231-6325-1
Visit www.RickRiordan.com
And www.DisneyBooks.com

Library of Congress Cataloging-in-Publication Data
Venditti, Robert.
The lost hero : the graphic novel / by Rick Riordan ; adapted by Robert Venditti ; art by Nate Powell ; color by Orpheus Collar ; lettering by Chris Dickey. — First edition.
pages cm. — (The heroes of Olympus ; book 1)
"Adapted from the novel The Heroes of Olympus, Book One: The Lost Hero"— Copyright page.
Summary: Jason, Piper, and Leo, three students from a school for "bad kids," find themselves at Camp Half-Blood, where they learn that they are demigods and begin a quest to free Hera, who has been imprisoned by Mother Earth herself.
ISBN 978-1-4231-6279-7 (alk. paper) — ISBN 978-1-4231-6325-1 (alk. paper)
1. Graphic novels. [1. Graphic novels. 2. Mythology, Greek — Fiction. 3. Camps — Fiction. 4. Hera (Greek deity) — Fiction. 5. Gaia (Greek deity) — Fiction. 6. Monsters — Fiction. 7. Riordan, Rick. Lost hero — Adaptations.] I. Powell, Nate, illustrator. II. Riordan, Rick. Lost hero. III. Title.
PZ7.7.V48Lo 2014
741.5'973 — dc23 2013013559

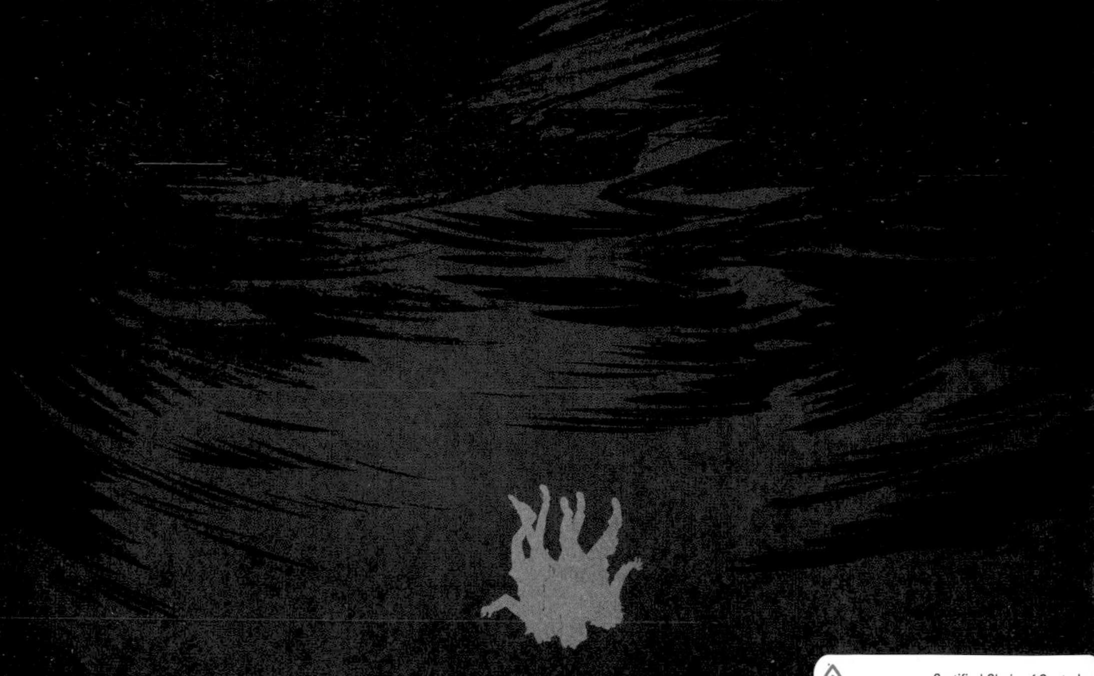

SUSTAINABLE FORESTRY INITIATIVE
Certified Chain of Custody
At Least 20% Certified Forest Content
www.sfiprogram.org
SFI-00993

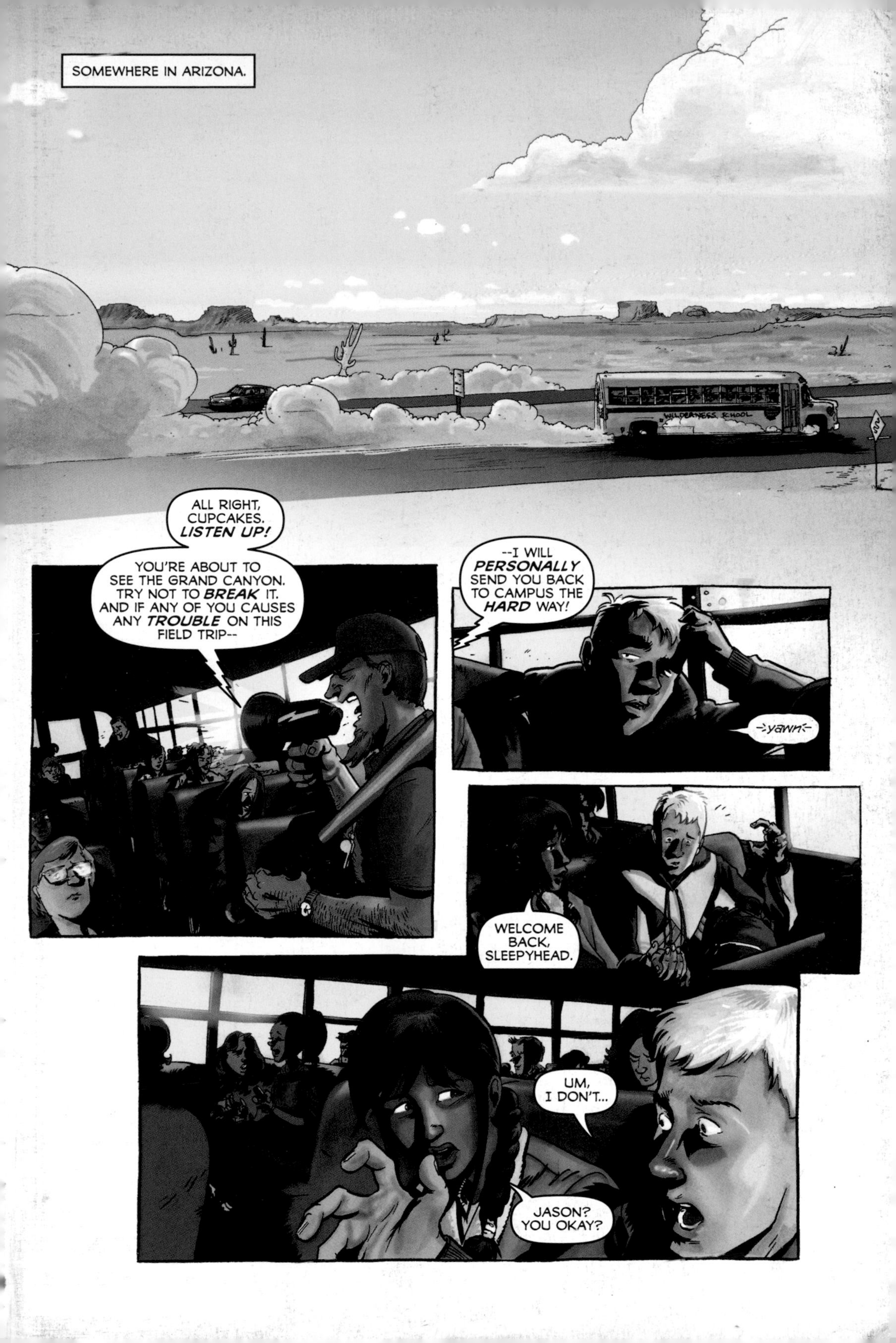
SOMEWHERE IN ARIZONA.
WILDERNESS SCHOOL
ALL RIGHT, CUPCAKES. LISTEN UP!
YOU'RE ABOUT TO SEE THE GRAND CANYON. TRY NOT TO BREAK IT. AND IF ANY OF YOU CAUSES ANY TROUBLE ON THIS FIELD TRIP--
--I WILL PERSONALLY SEND YOU BACK TO CAMPUS THE HARD WAY!
yawn
WELCOME BACK, SLEEPYHEAD.
UM, I DON'T...
JASON? YOU OKAY?

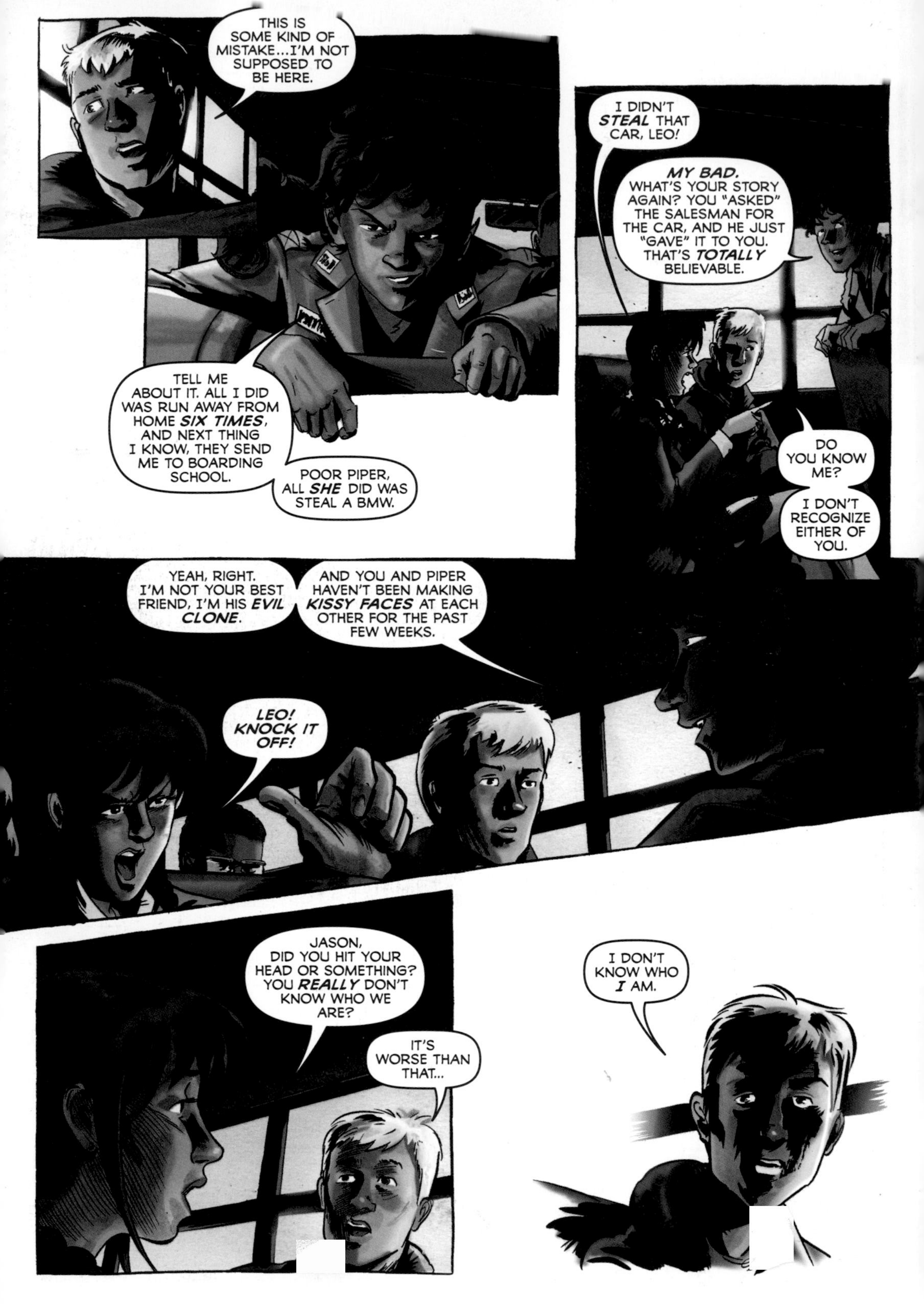
THIS IS SOME KIND OF MISTAKE...I'M NOT SUPPOSED TO BE HERE.
TELL ME ABOUT IT. ALL I DID WAS RUN AWAY FROM HOME SIX TIMES, AND NEXT THING I KNOW, THEY SEND ME TO BOARDING SCHOOL.
POOR PIPER, ALL SHE DID WAS STEAL A BMW.
I DIDN'T STEAL THAT CAR, LEO!
MY BAD. WHAT'S YOUR STORY AGAIN? YOU "ASKED" THE SALESMAN FOR THE CAR, AND HE JUST "GAVE" IT TO YOU. THAT'S TOTALLY BELIEVABLE.
DO YOU KNOW ME?
I DON'T RECOGNIZE EITHER OF YOU.
YEAH, RIGHT. I'M NOT YOUR BEST FRIEND, I'M HIS EVIL CLONE.
AND YOU AND PIPER HAVEN'T BEEN MAKING KISSY FACES AT EACH OTHER FOR THE PAST FEW WEEKS.
LEO! KNOCK IT OFF!
JASON, DID YOU HIT YOUR HEAD OR SOMETHING? YOU REALLY DON'T KNOW WHO WE ARE?
IT'S WORSE THAN THAT...
I DON'T KNOW WHO I AM.

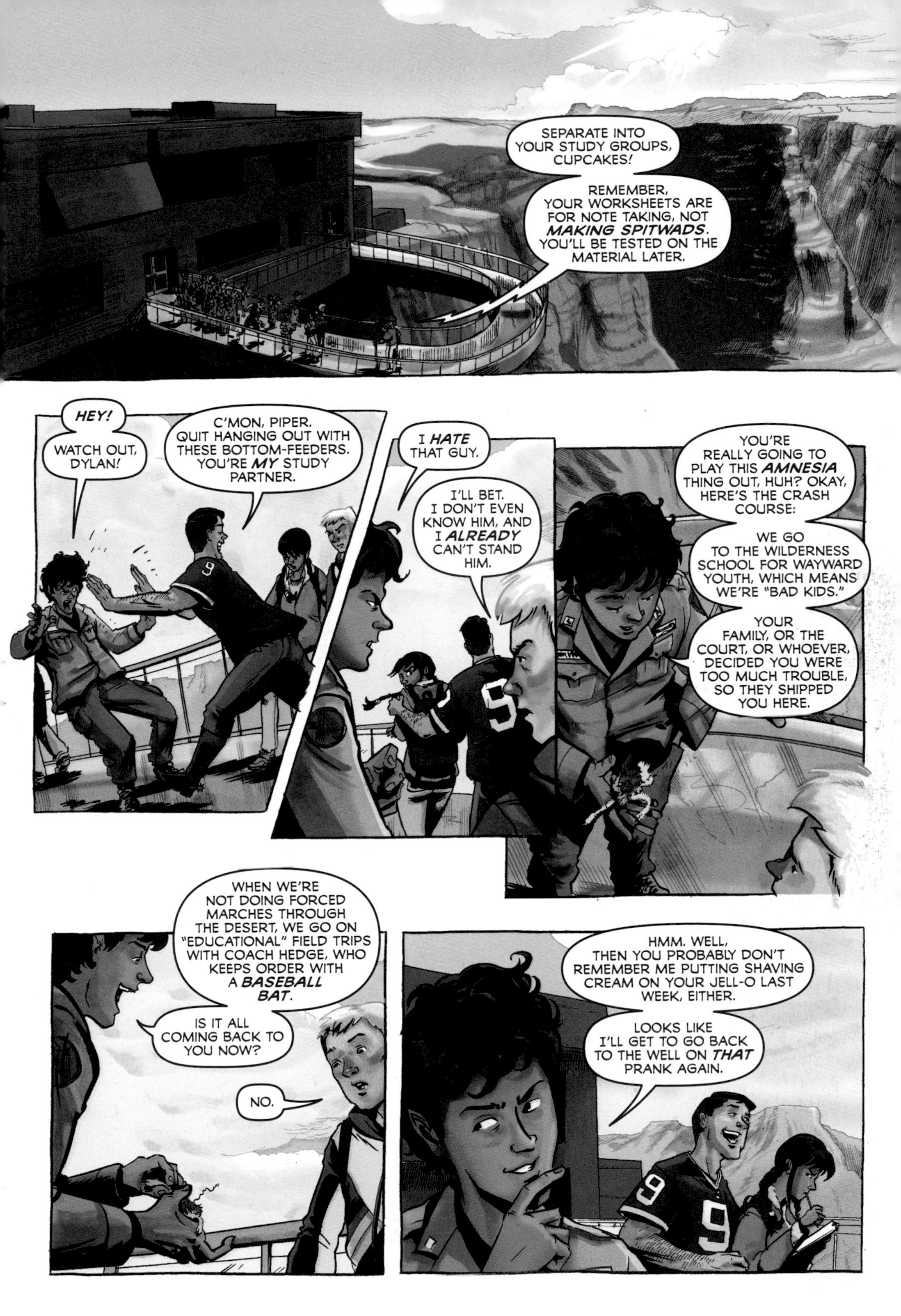

SEPARATE INTO YOUR STUDY GROUPS, CUPCAKES!
REMEMBER, YOUR WORKSHEETS ARE FOR NOTE TAKING, NOT *MAKING SPITWADS*. YOU'LL BE TESTED ON THE MATERIAL LATER.
HEY!
WATCH OUT, DYLAN!
C'MON, PIPER. QUIT HANGING OUT WITH THESE BOTTOM-FEEDERS. YOU'RE *MY* STUDY PARTNER.
I *HATE* THAT GUY.
I'LL BET. I DON'T EVEN KNOW HIM, AND I *ALREADY* CAN'T STAND HIM.
YOU'RE REALLY GOING TO PLAY THIS *AMNESIA* THING OUT, HUH? OKAY, HERE'S THE CRASH COURSE:
WE GO TO THE WILDERNESS SCHOOL FOR WAYWARD YOUTH, WHICH MEANS WE'RE "BAD KIDS."
YOUR FAMILY, OR THE COURT, OR WHOEVER, DECIDED YOU WERE TOO MUCH TROUBLE, SO THEY SHIPPED YOU HERE.
WHEN WE'RE NOT DOING FORCED MARCHES THROUGH THE DESERT, WE GO ON "EDUCATIONAL" FIELD TRIPS WITH COACH HEDGE, WHO KEEPS ORDER WITH A *BASEBALL BAT*.
IS IT ALL COMING BACK TO YOU NOW?
NO.
HMM. WELL, THEN YOU PROBABLY DON'T REMEMBER ME PUTTING SHAVING CREAM ON YOUR JELL-O LAST WEEK, EITHER.
LOOKS LIKE I'LL GET TO GO BACK TO THE WELL ON *THAT* PRANK AGAIN.

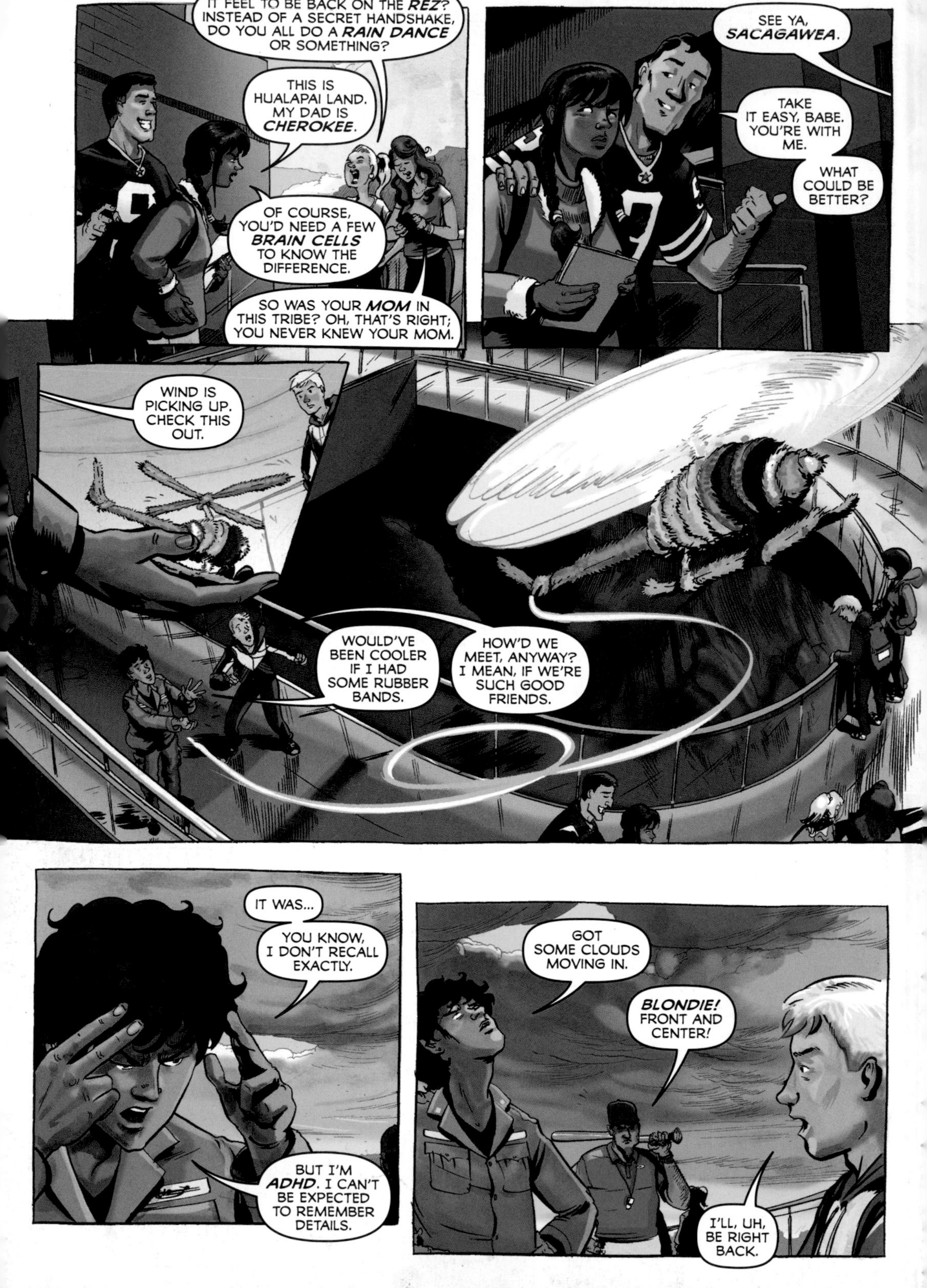
HEY, PIPER, HOW'S IT FEEL TO BE BACK ON THE *REZ*? INSTEAD OF A SECRET HANDSHAKE, DO YOU ALL DO A *RAIN DANCE* OR SOMETHING?
THIS IS HUALAPAI LAND. MY DAD IS *CHEROKEE*.
OF COURSE, YOU'D NEED A FEW *BRAIN CELLS* TO KNOW THE DIFFERENCE.
SO WAS YOUR *MOM* IN THIS TRIBE? OH, THAT'S RIGHT; YOU NEVER KNEW YOUR MOM.
SEE YA, *SACAGAWEA*.
TAKE IT EASY, BABE. YOU'RE WITH ME.
WHAT COULD BE BETTER?
WIND IS PICKING UP. CHECK THIS OUT.
WOULD'VE BEEN COOLER IF I HAD SOME RUBBER BANDS.
HOW'D WE MEET, ANYWAY? I MEAN, IF WE'RE SUCH GOOD FRIENDS.
IT WAS...
YOU KNOW, I DON'T RECALL EXACTLY.
BUT I'M *ADHD*. I CAN'T BE EXPECTED TO REMEMBER DETAILS.
GOT SOME CLOUDS MOVING IN.
BLONDIE! FRONT AND CENTER!
I'LL, UH, BE RIGHT BACK.

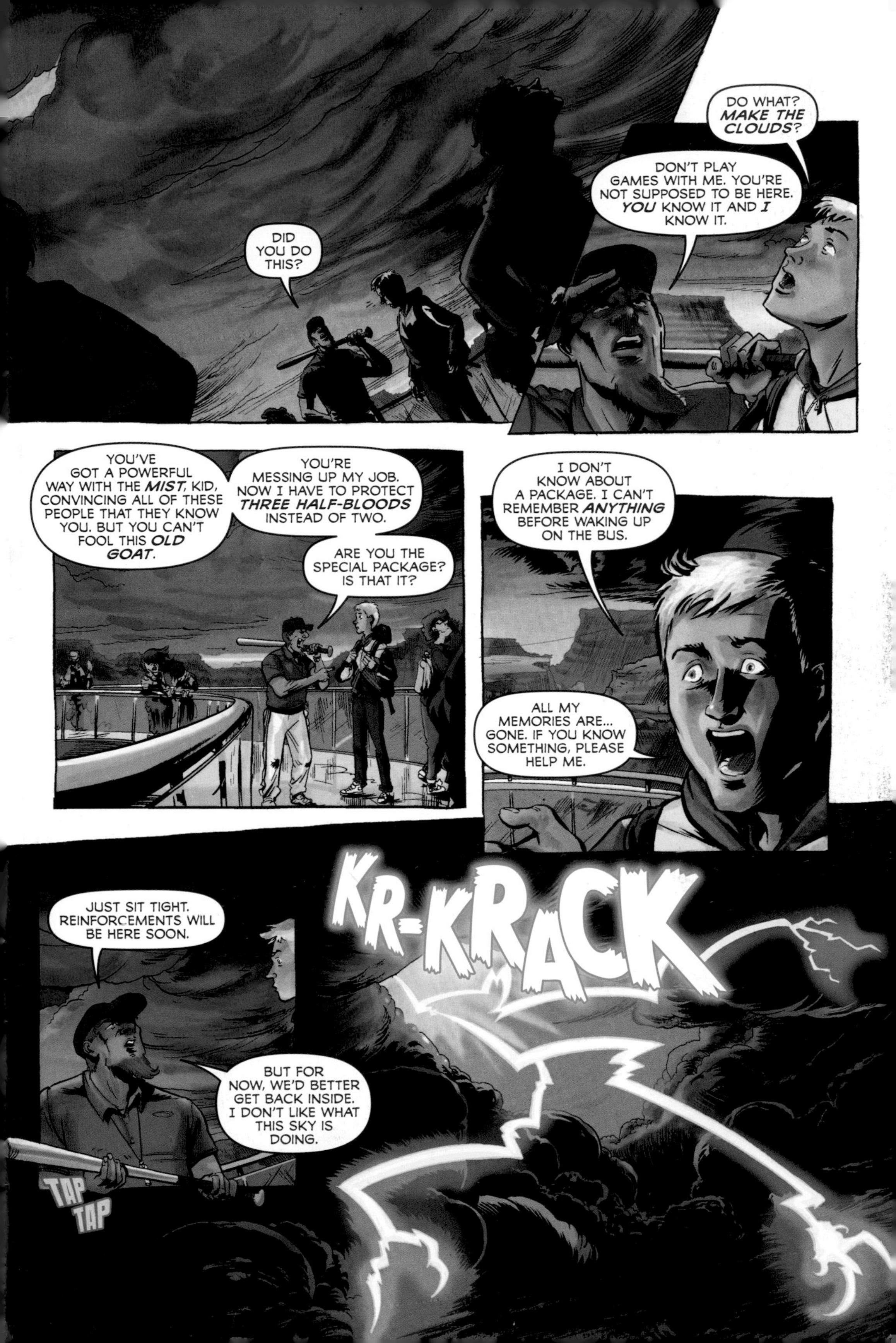
DID YOU DO THIS?
DO WHAT? MAKE THE CLOUDS?
DON'T PLAY GAMES WITH ME. YOU'RE NOT SUPPOSED TO BE HERE. YOU KNOW IT AND I KNOW IT.
YOU'VE GOT A POWERFUL WAY WITH THE MIST, KID, CONVINCING ALL OF THESE PEOPLE THAT THEY KNOW YOU. BUT YOU CAN'T FOOL THIS OLD GOAT.
YOU'RE MESSING UP MY JOB. NOW I HAVE TO PROTECT THREE HALF-BLOODS INSTEAD OF TWO.
ARE YOU THE SPECIAL PACKAGE? IS THAT IT?
I DON'T KNOW ABOUT A PACKAGE. I CAN'T REMEMBER ANYTHING BEFORE WAKING UP ON THE BUS.
ALL MY MEMORIES ARE... GONE. IF YOU KNOW SOMETHING, PLEASE HELP ME.
JUST SIT TIGHT. REINFORCEMENTS WILL BE HERE SOON.
BUT FOR NOW, WE'D BETTER GET BACK INSIDE. I DON'T LIKE WHAT THIS SKY IS DOING.
TAP TAP
KR-KRACK

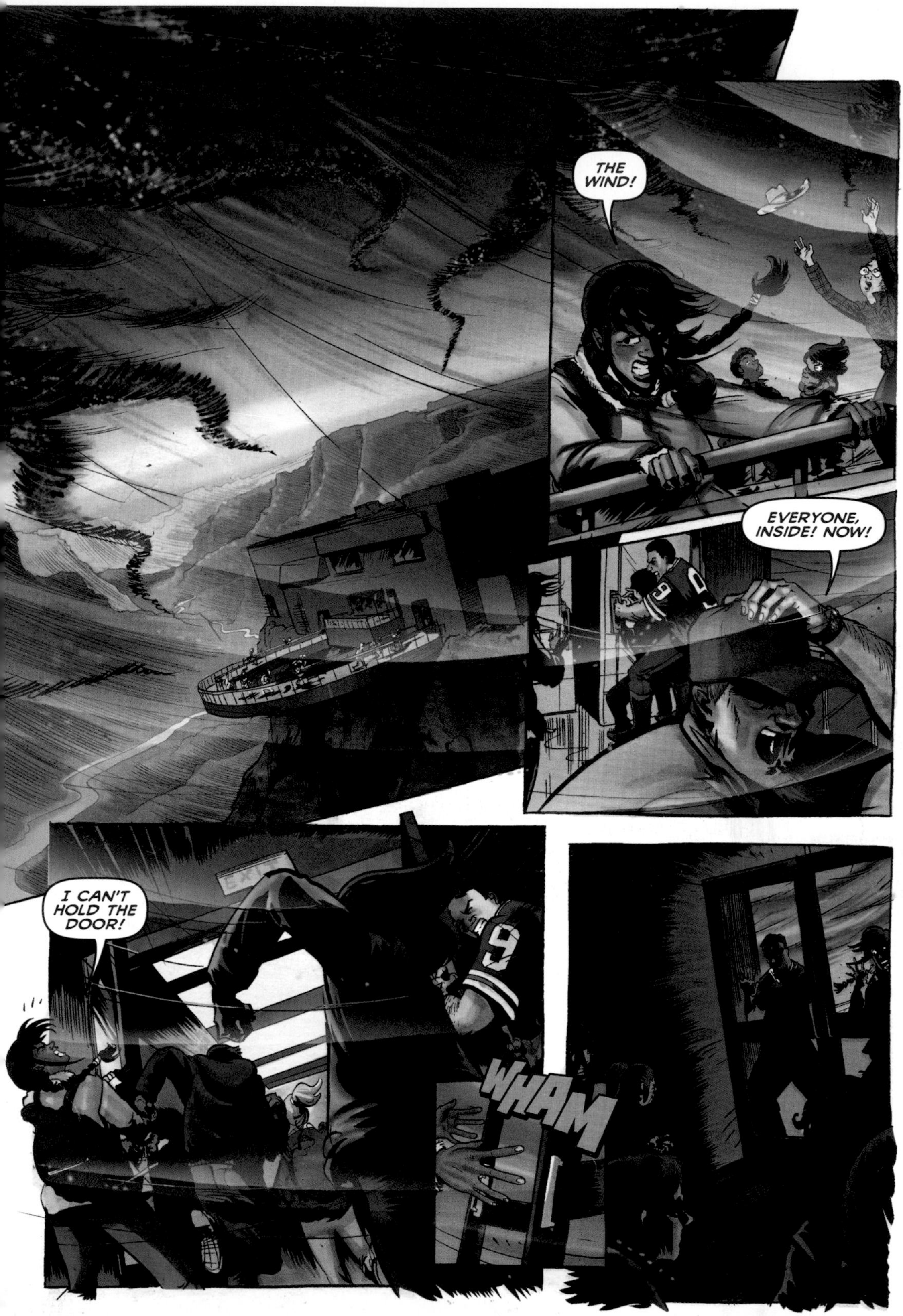
THE WIND!
EVERYONE, INSIDE! NOW!
I CAN'T HOLD THE DOOR!
WHAM

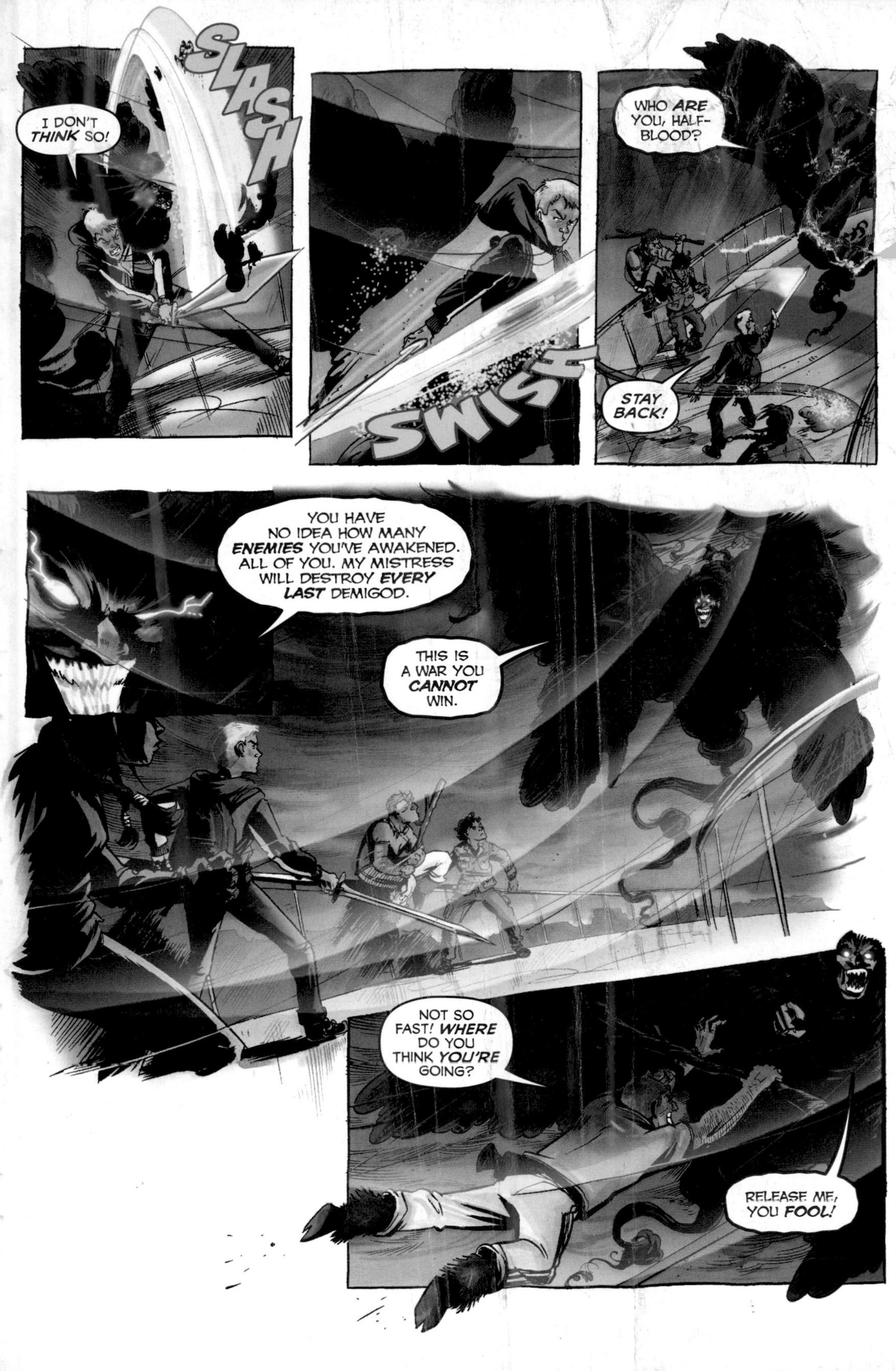

I DON'T THINK SO!
SLASH
SWISH
WHO ARE YOU, HALF-BLOOD?
STAY BACK!
YOU HAVE NO IDEA HOW MANY ENEMIES YOU'VE AWAKENED. ALL OF YOU. MY MISTRESS WILL DESTROY EVERY LAST DEMIGOD.
THIS IS A WAR YOU CANNOT WIN.
NOT SO FAST! WHERE DO YOU THINK YOU'RE GOING?
RELEASE ME, YOU FOOL!

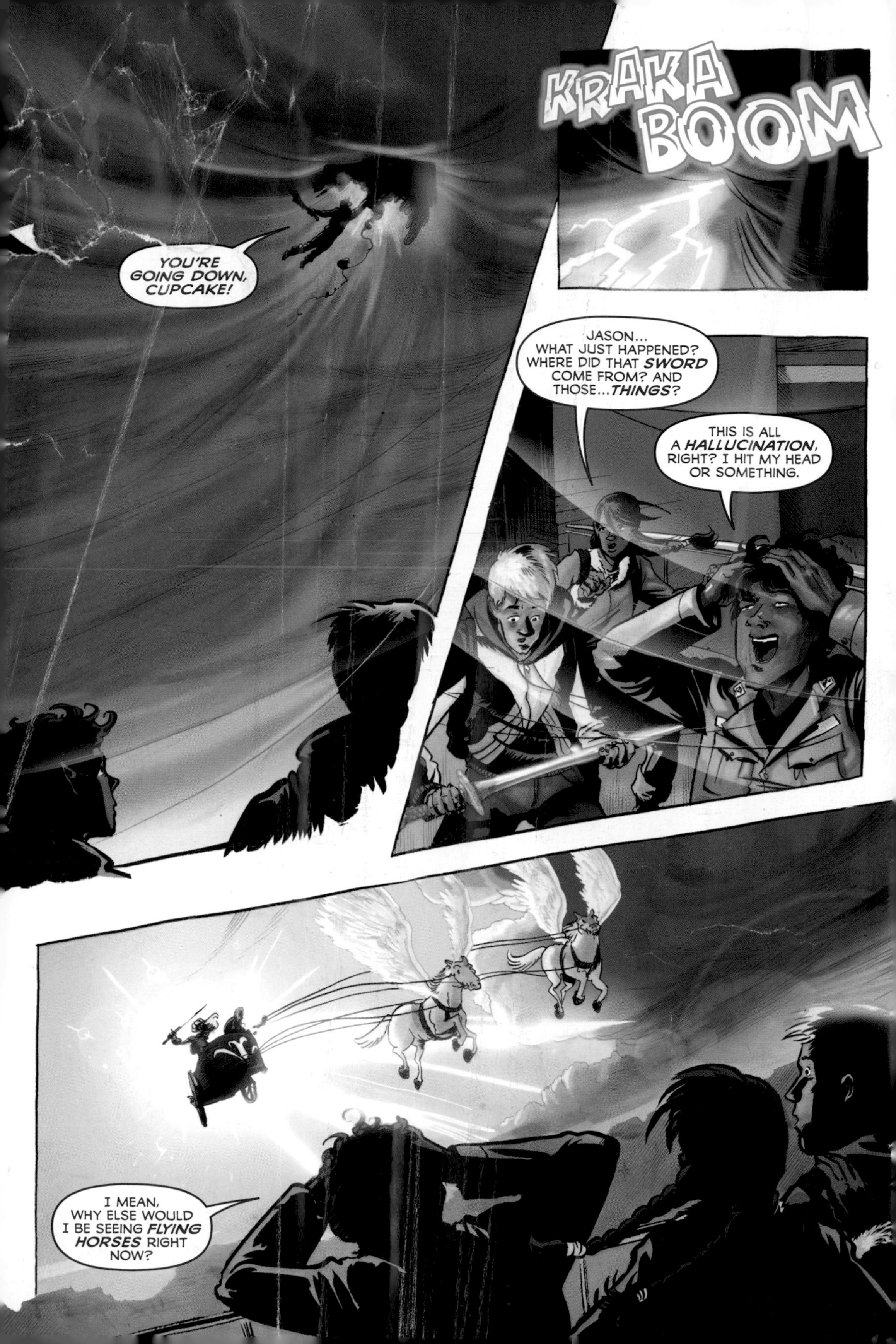
KRAKA BOOM
YOU'RE GOING DOWN, CUPCAKE!
JASON... WHAT JUST HAPPENED? WHERE DID THAT SWORD COME FROM? AND THOSE...THINGS?
THIS IS ALL A HALLUCINATION, RIGHT? I HIT MY HEAD OR SOMETHING.
I MEAN, WHY ELSE WOULD I BE SEEING FLYING HORSES RIGHT NOW?

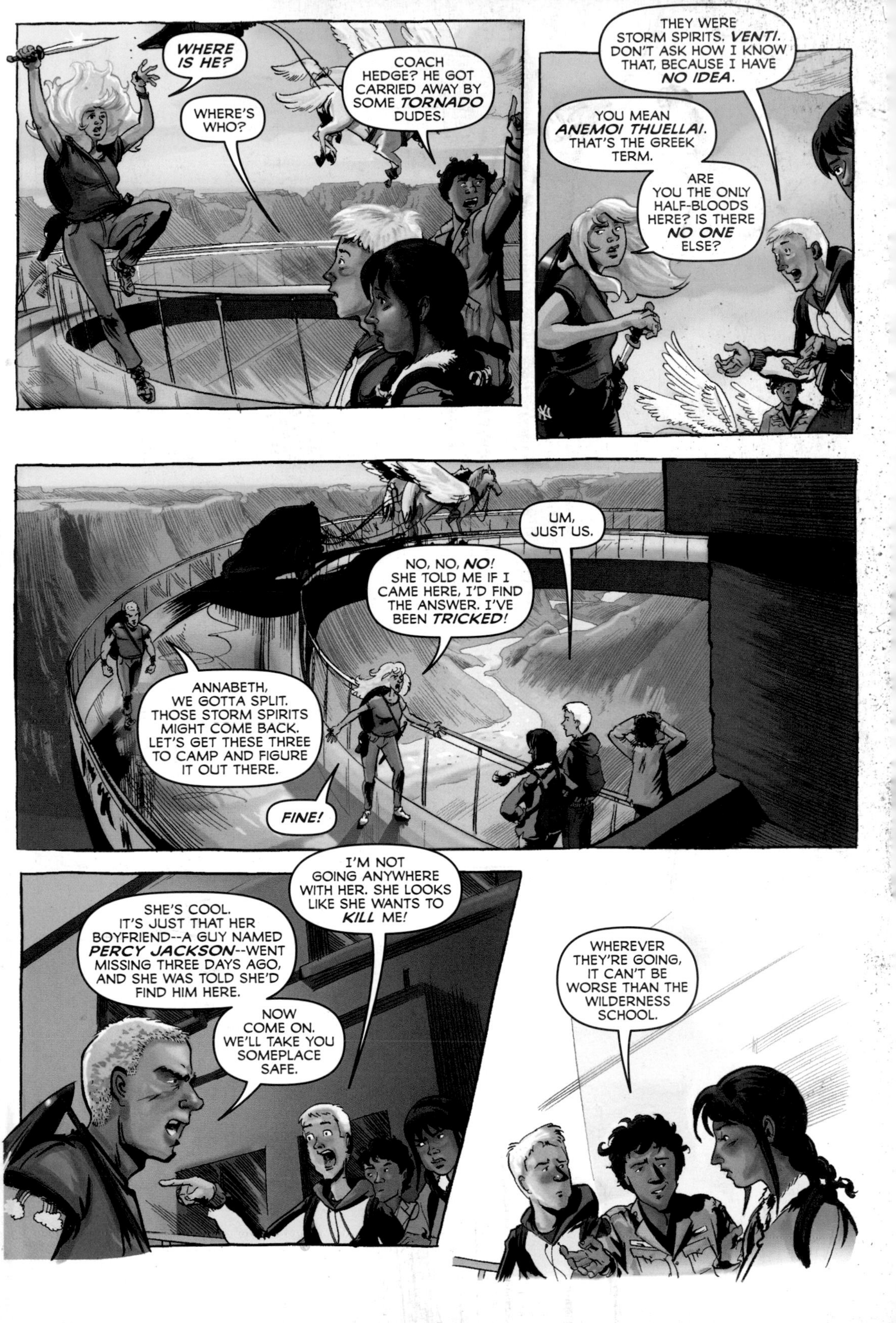
WHERE IS HE?
WHERE'S WHO?
COACH HEDGE? HE GOT CARRIED AWAY BY SOME TORNADO DUDES.
THEY WERE STORM SPIRITS. VENTI. DON'T ASK HOW I KNOW THAT, BECAUSE I HAVE NO IDEA.
YOU MEAN ANEMOI THUELLAI. THAT'S THE GREEK TERM.
ARE YOU THE ONLY HALF-BLOODS HERE? IS THERE NO ONE ELSE?
UM, JUST US.
NO, NO, NO! SHE TOLD ME IF I CAME HERE, I'D FIND THE ANSWER. I'VE BEEN TRICKED!
ANNABETH, WE GOTTA SPLIT. THOSE STORM SPIRITS MIGHT COME BACK. LET'S GET THESE THREE TO CAMP AND FIGURE IT OUT THERE.
FINE!
I'M NOT GOING ANYWHERE WITH HER. SHE LOOKS LIKE SHE WANTS TO KILL ME!
SHE'S COOL. IT'S JUST THAT HER BOYFRIEND--A GUY NAMED PERCY JACKSON--WENT MISSING THREE DAYS AGO, AND SHE WAS TOLD SHE'D FIND HIM HERE.
NOW COME ON. WE'LL TAKE YOU SOMEPLACE SAFE.
WHEREVER THEY'RE GOING, IT CAN'T BE WORSE THAN THE WILDERNESS SCHOOL.

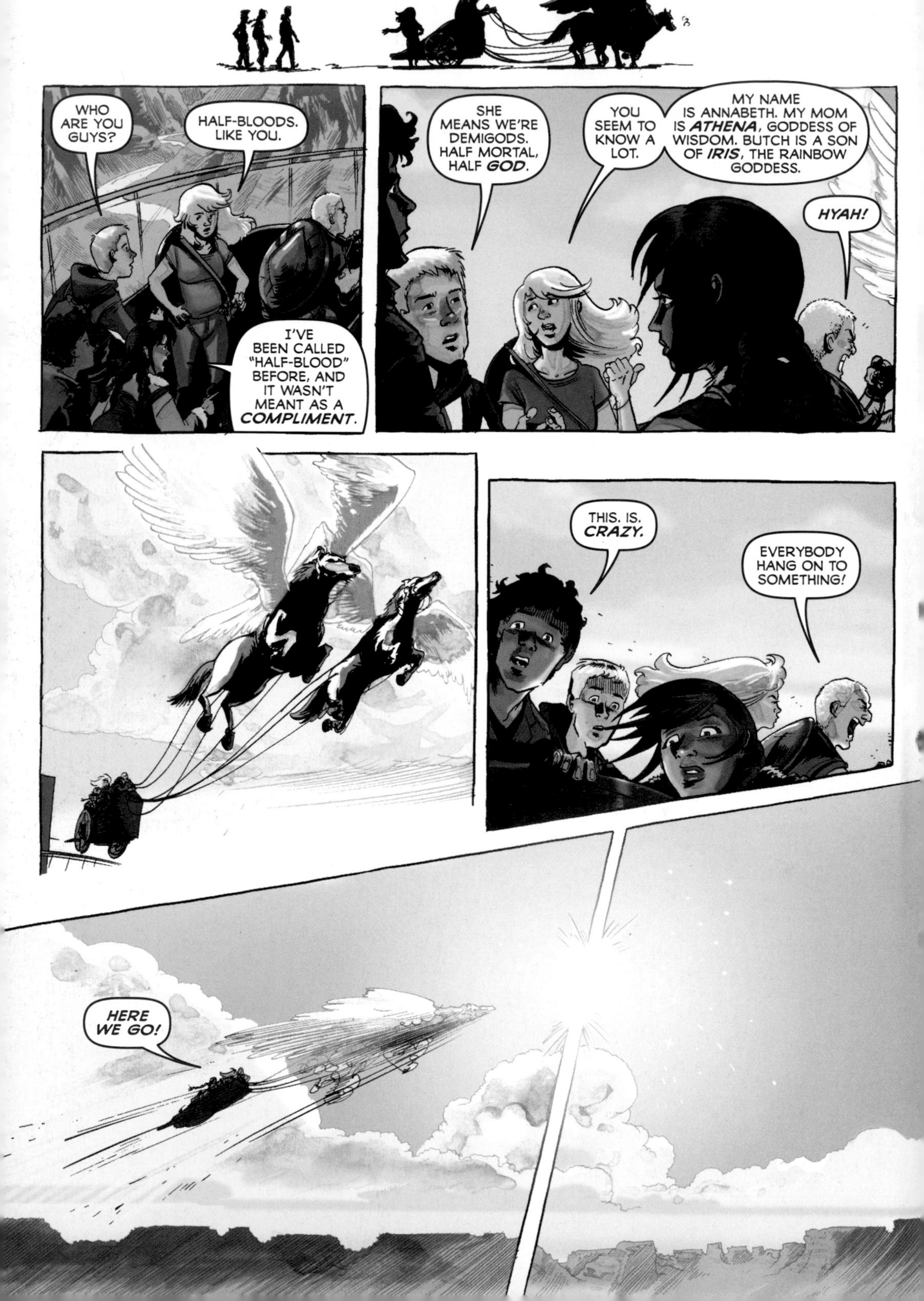
WHO ARE YOU GUYS?
HALF-BLOODS. LIKE YOU.
I'VE BEEN CALLED "HALF-BLOOD" BEFORE, AND IT WASN'T MEANT AS A COMPLIMENT.
SHE MEANS WE'RE DEMIGODS. HALF MORTAL, HALF GOD.
YOU SEEM TO KNOW A LOT.
MY NAME IS ANNABETH. MY MOM IS ATHENA, GODDESS OF WISDOM. BUTCH IS A SON OF IRIS, THE RAINBOW GODDESS.
HYAH!
THIS. IS. CRAZY.
EVERYBODY HANG ON TO SOMETHING!
HERE WE GO!

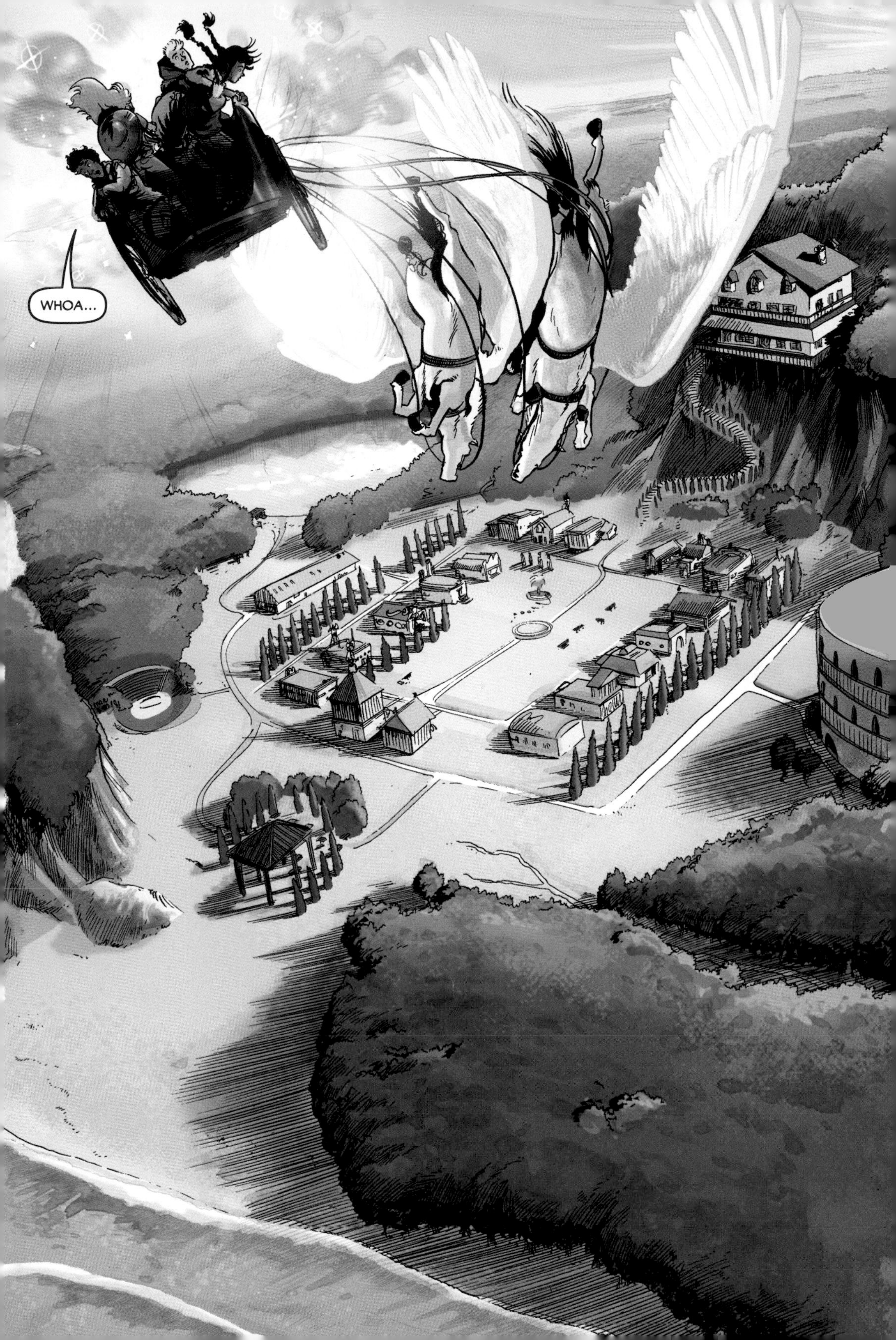
WHOA...

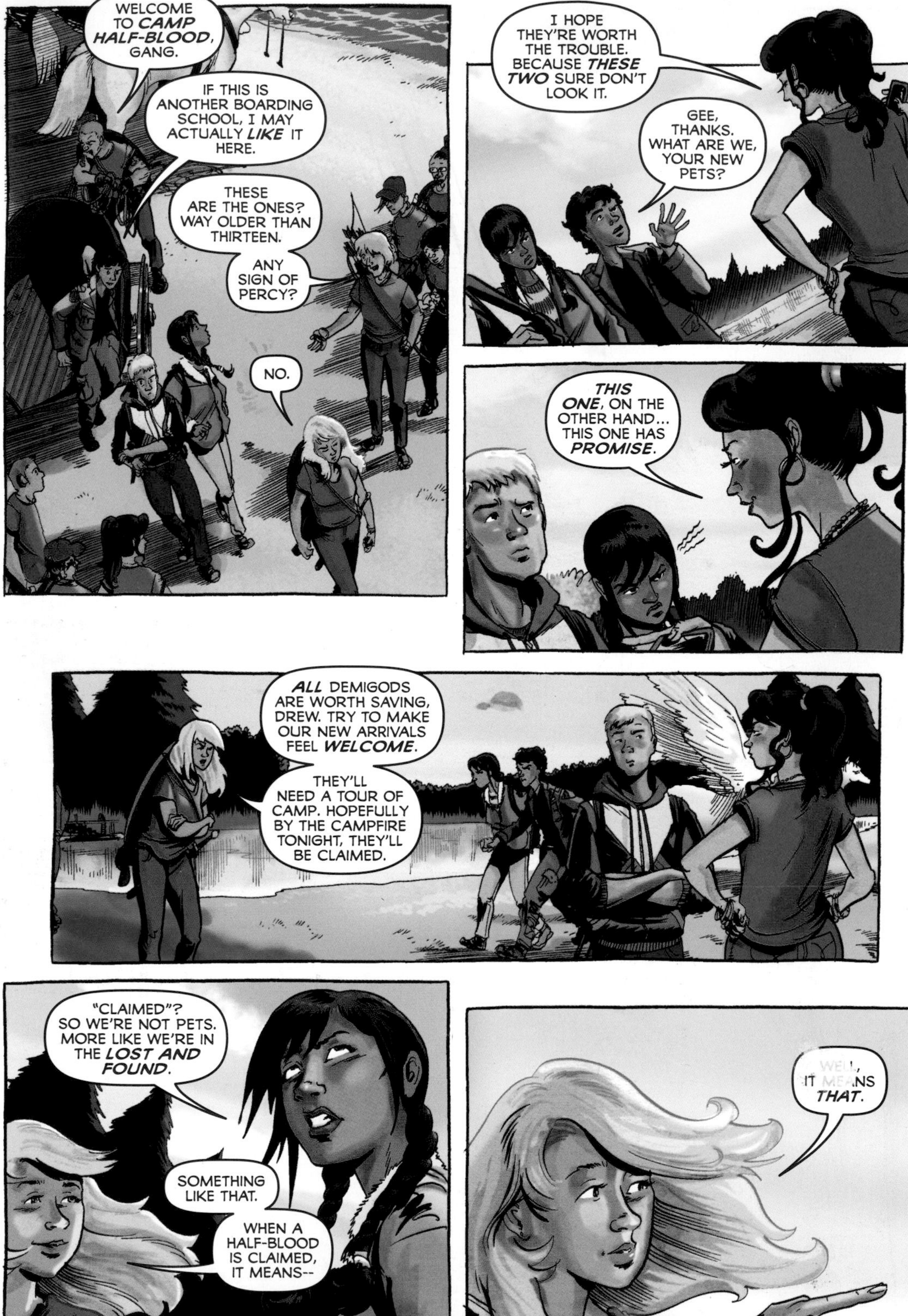
WELCOME TO CAMP HALF-BLOOD, GANG.
IF THIS IS ANOTHER BOARDING SCHOOL, I MAY ACTUALLY LIKE IT HERE.
THESE ARE THE ONES? WAY OLDER THAN THIRTEEN.
ANY SIGN OF PERCY?
NO.
I HOPE THEY'RE WORTH THE TROUBLE. BECAUSE THESE TWO SURE DON'T LOOK IT.
GEE, THANKS. WHAT ARE WE, YOUR NEW PETS?
THIS ONE, ON THE OTHER HAND... THIS ONE HAS PROMISE.
ALL DEMIGODS ARE WORTH SAVING, DREW. TRY TO MAKE OUR NEW ARRIVALS FEEL WELCOME.
THEY'LL NEED A TOUR OF CAMP. HOPEFULLY BY THE CAMPFIRE TONIGHT, THEY'LL BE CLAIMED.
"CLAIMED"? SO WE'RE NOT PETS. MORE LIKE WE'RE IN THE LOST AND FOUND.
SOMETHING LIKE THAT.
WHEN A HALF-BLOOD IS CLAIMED, IT MEANS--
WELL, IT MEANS THAT.

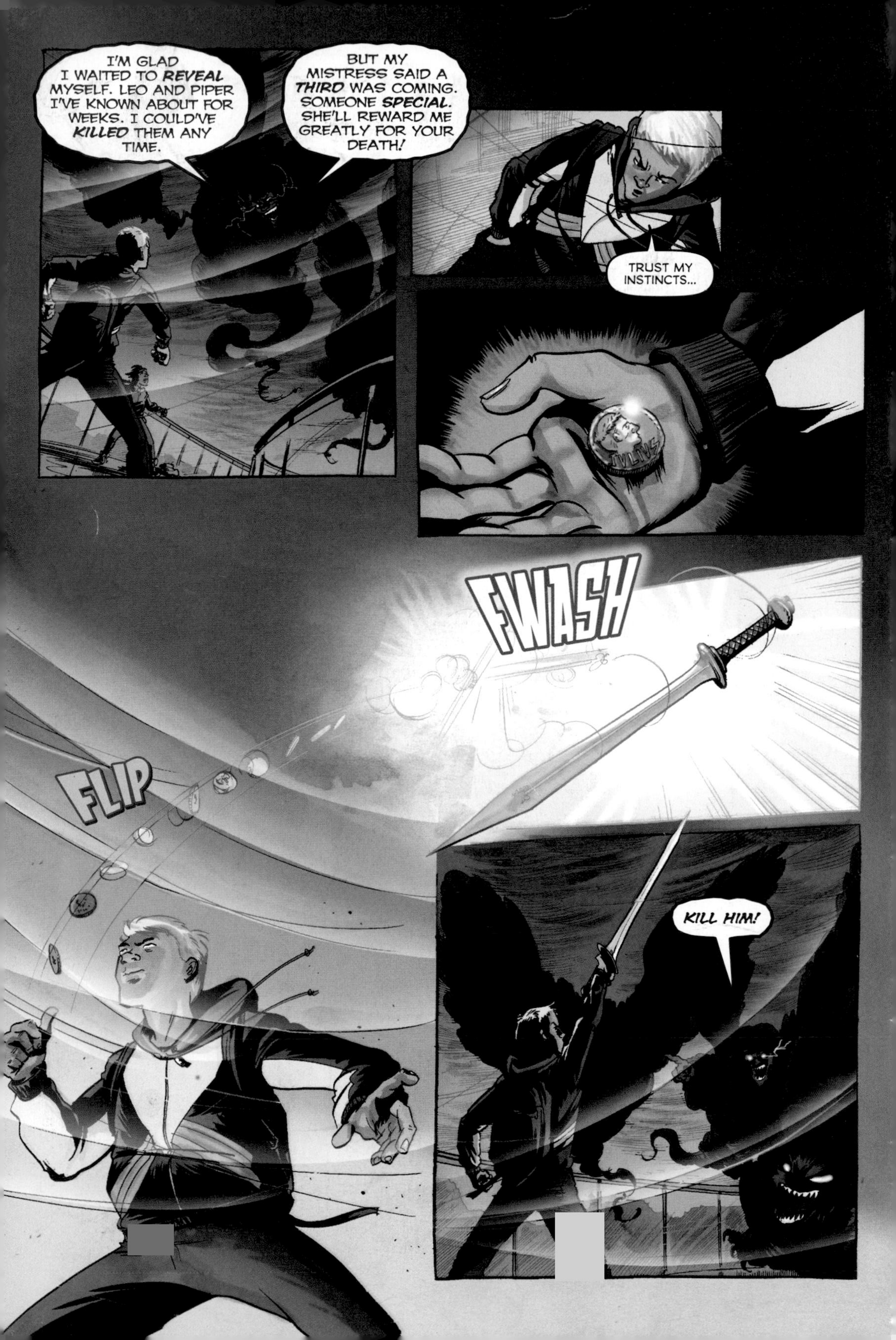
I'M GLAD I WAITED TO REVEAL MYSELF. LEO AND PIPER I'VE KNOWN ABOUT FOR WEEKS. I COULD'VE KILLED THEM ANY TIME.
BUT MY MISTRESS SAID A THIRD WAS COMING. SOMEONE SPECIAL. SHE'LL REWARD ME GREATLY FOR YOUR DEATH!
TRUST MY INSTINCTS...
IVLIVS
FWASH
FLIP
KILL HIM!

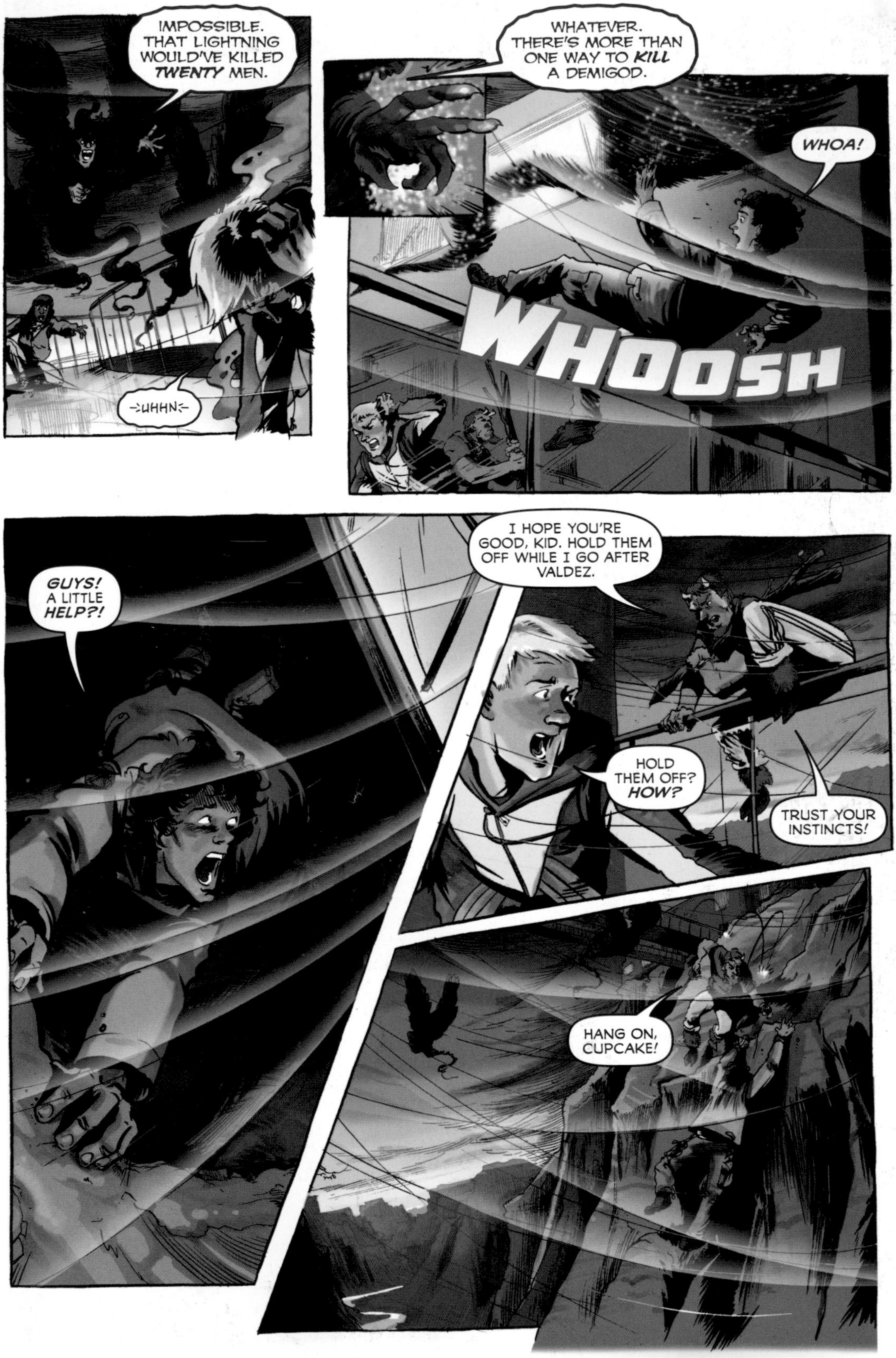
IMPOSSIBLE. THAT LIGHTNING WOULD'VE KILLED TWENTY MEN.
-UHHN-
WHATEVER. THERE'S MORE THAN ONE WAY TO KILL A DEMIGOD.
WHOA!
WHOOSH
GUYS! A LITTLE HELP?!
I HOPE YOU'RE GOOD, KID. HOLD THEM OFF WHILE I GO AFTER VALDEZ.
HOLD THEM OFF? HOW?
TRUST YOUR INSTINCTS!
HANG ON, CUPCAKE!

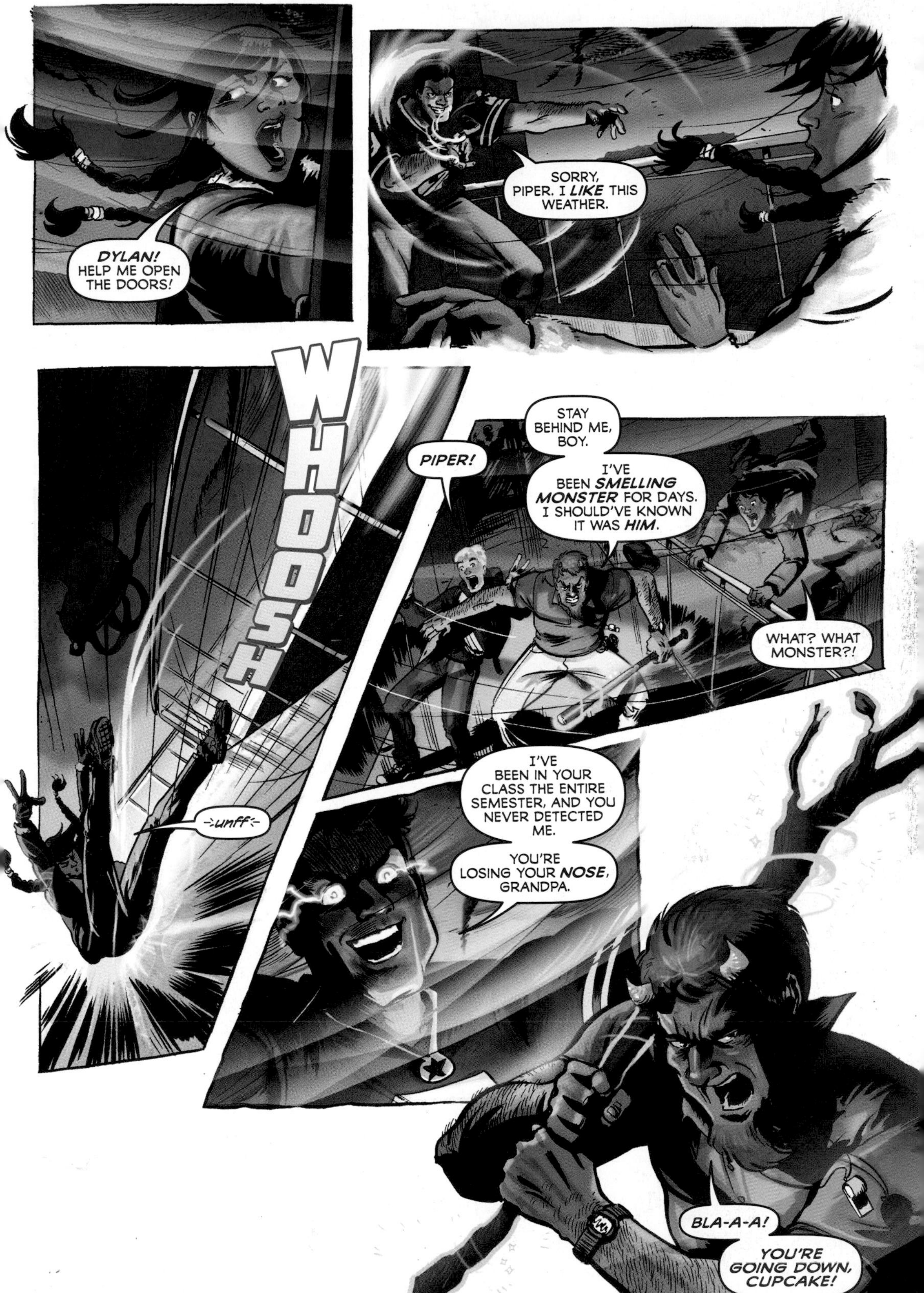
DYLAN! HELP ME OPEN THE DOORS!
SORRY, PIPER. I LIKE THIS WEATHER.
WHOOSH
PIPER!
STAY BEHIND ME, BOY.
I'VE BEEN SMELLING MONSTER FOR DAYS. I SHOULD'VE KNOWN IT WAS HIM.
WHAT? WHAT MONSTER?!
unff
I'VE BEEN IN YOUR CLASS THE ENTIRE SEMESTER, AND YOU NEVER DETECTED ME.
YOU'RE LOSING YOUR NOSE, GRANDPA.
BLA-A-A!
YOU'RE GOING DOWN, CUPCAKE!

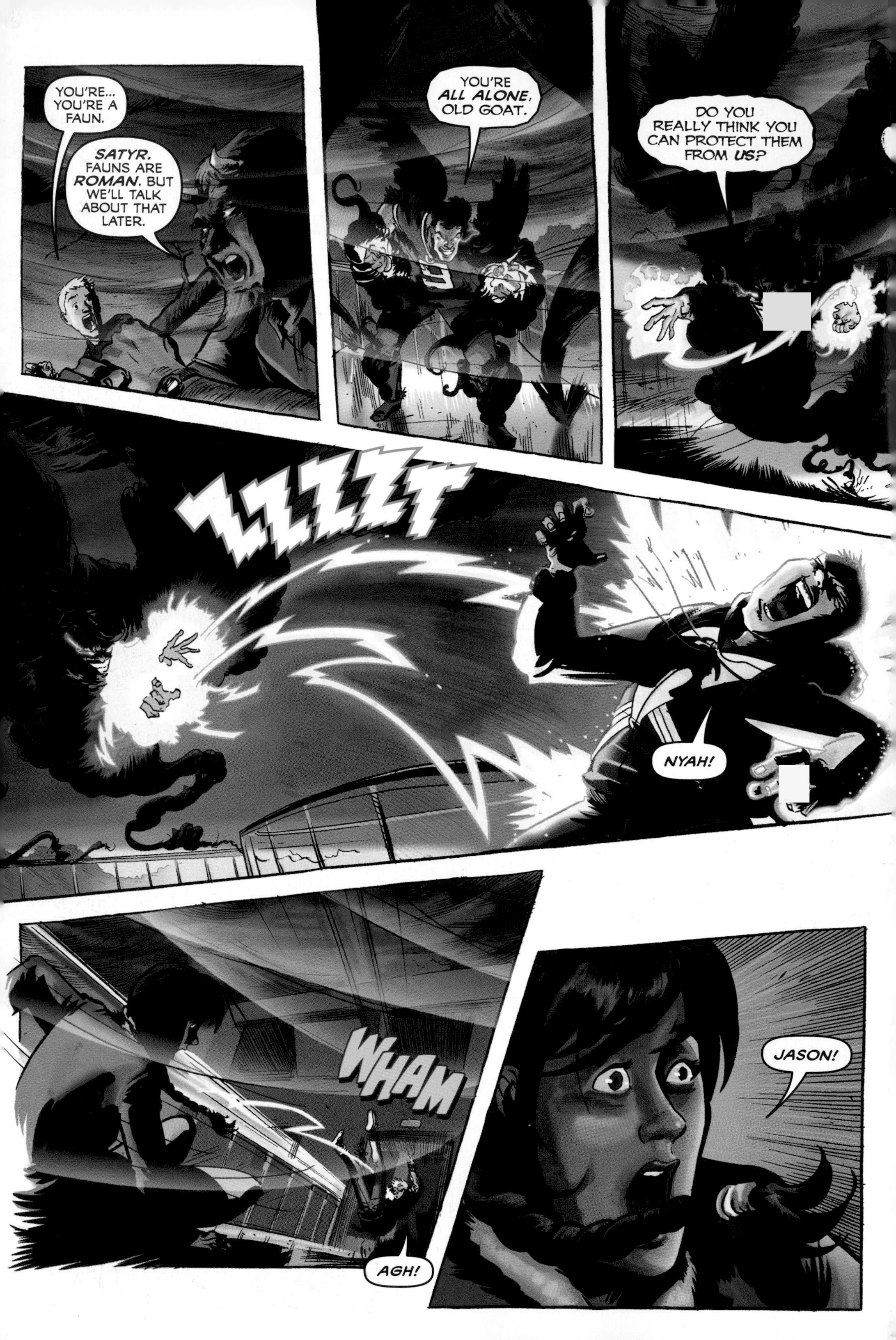

YOU'RE... YOU'RE A FAUN.
SATYR. FAUNS ARE ROMAN. BUT WE'LL TALK ABOUT THAT LATER.
YOU'RE ALL ALONE, OLD GOAT.
DO YOU REALLY THINK YOU CAN PROTECT THEM FROM US?
ZZZZZT
NYAH!
WHAM
AGH!
JASON!

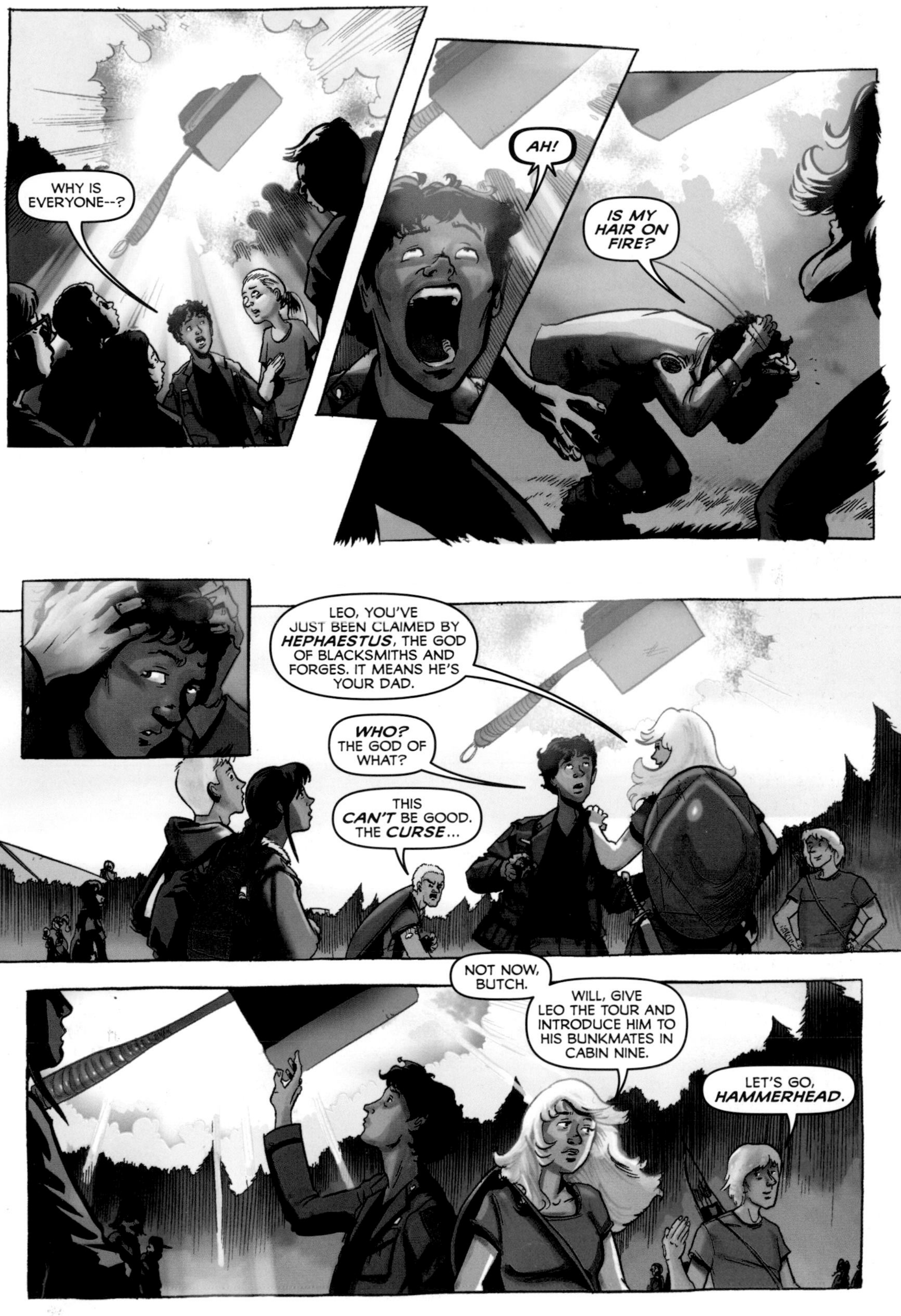
WHY IS EVERYONE--?
AH!
IS MY HAIR ON FIRE?
LEO, YOU'VE JUST BEEN CLAIMED BY HEPHAESTUS, THE GOD OF BLACKSMITHS AND FORGES. IT MEANS HE'S YOUR DAD.
WHO? THE GOD OF WHAT?
THIS CAN'T BE GOOD. THE CURSE...
NOT NOW, BUTCH.
WILL, GIVE LEO THE TOUR AND INTRODUCE HIM TO HIS BUNKMATES IN CABIN NINE.
LET'S GO, HAMMERHEAD.

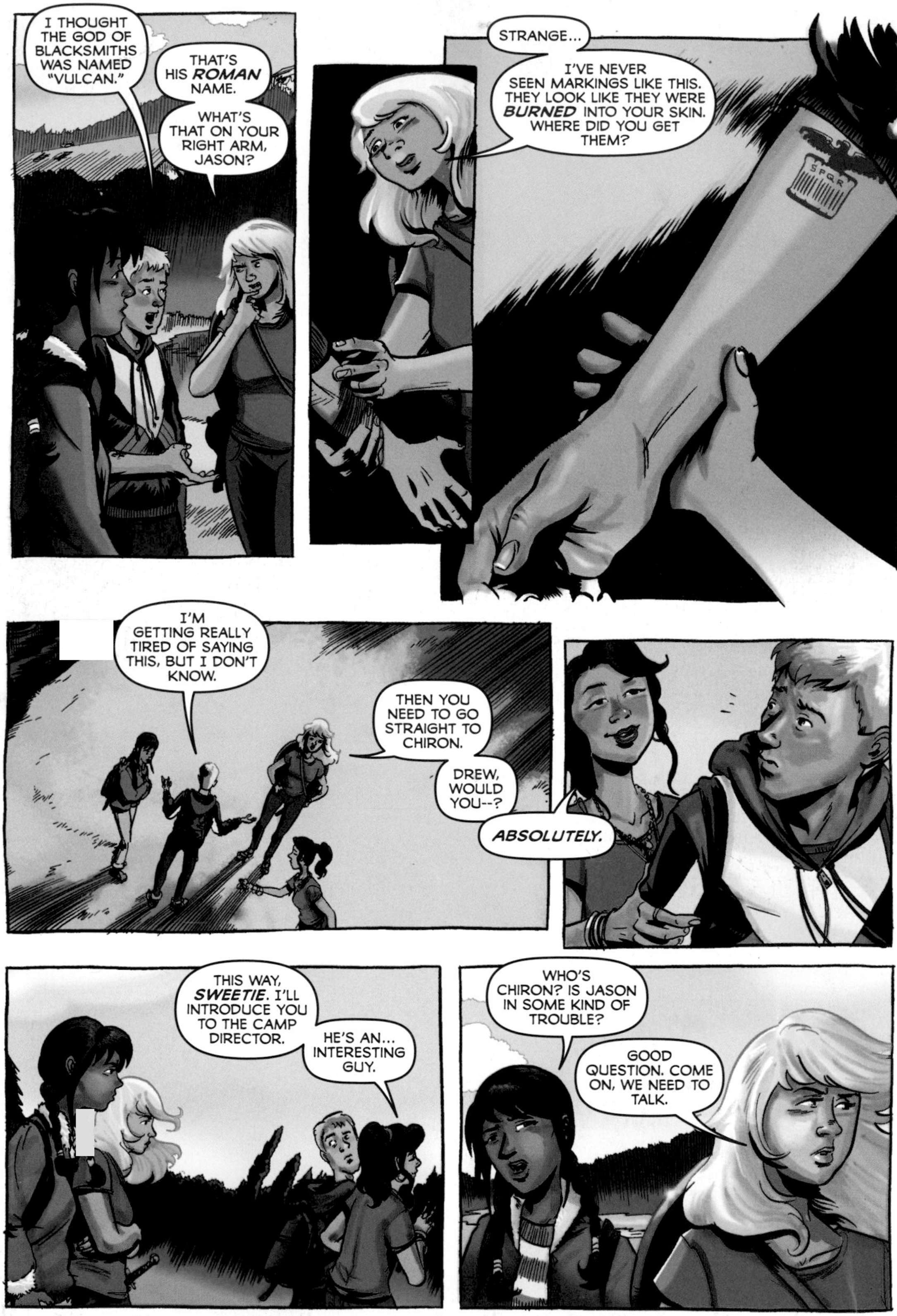
I THOUGHT THE GOD OF BLACKSMITHS WAS NAMED "VULCAN."
THAT'S HIS *ROMAN* NAME.
WHAT'S THAT ON YOUR RIGHT ARM, JASON?
STRANGE...
I'VE NEVER SEEN MARKINGS LIKE THIS. THEY LOOK LIKE THEY WERE *BURNED* INTO YOUR SKIN. WHERE DID YOU GET THEM?
SPQR
I'M GETTING REALLY TIRED OF SAYING THIS, BUT I DON'T KNOW.
THEN YOU NEED TO GO STRAIGHT TO CHIRON.
DREW, WOULD YOU--?
ABSOLUTELY.
THIS WAY, *SWEETIE*. I'LL INTRODUCE YOU TO THE CAMP DIRECTOR.
HE'S AN... INTERESTING GUY.
WHO'S CHIRON? IS JASON IN SOME KIND OF TROUBLE?
GOOD QUESTION. COME ON, WE NEED TO TALK.

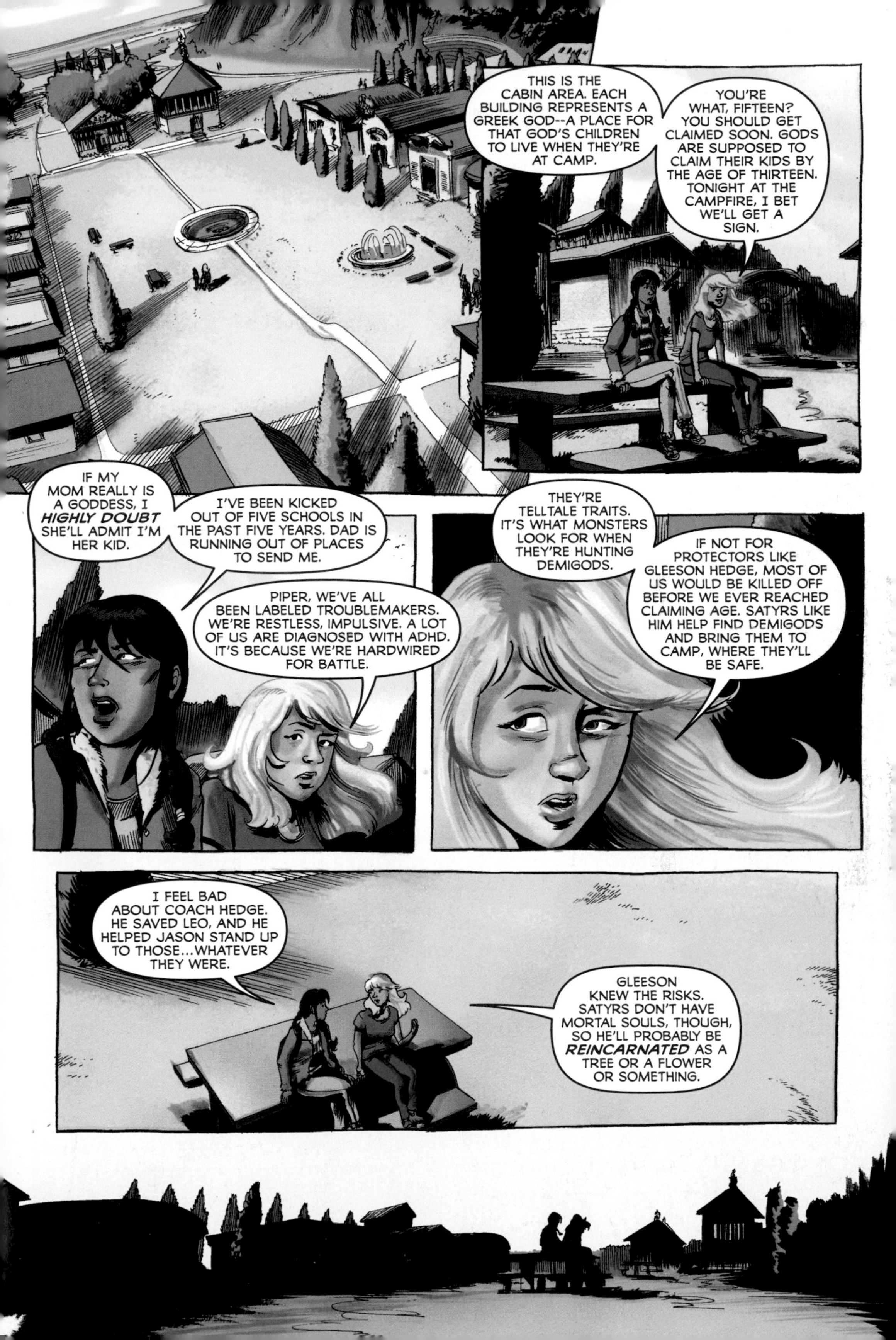
THIS IS THE CABIN AREA. EACH BUILDING REPRESENTS A GREEK GOD--A PLACE FOR THAT GOD'S CHILDREN TO LIVE WHEN THEY'RE AT CAMP.
YOU'RE WHAT, FIFTEEN? YOU SHOULD GET CLAIMED SOON. GODS ARE SUPPOSED TO CLAIM THEIR KIDS BY THE AGE OF THIRTEEN. TONIGHT AT THE CAMPFIRE, I BET WE'LL GET A SIGN.
IF MY MOM REALLY IS A GODDESS, I HIGHLY DOUBT SHE'LL ADMIT I'M HER KID.
I'VE BEEN KICKED OUT OF FIVE SCHOOLS IN THE PAST FIVE YEARS. DAD IS RUNNING OUT OF PLACES TO SEND ME.
PIPER, WE'VE ALL BEEN LABELED TROUBLEMAKERS. WE'RE RESTLESS, IMPULSIVE. A LOT OF US ARE DIAGNOSED WITH ADHD. IT'S BECAUSE WE'RE HARDWIRED FOR BATTLE.
THEY'RE TELLTALE TRAITS. IT'S WHAT MONSTERS LOOK FOR WHEN THEY'RE HUNTING DEMIGODS.
IF NOT FOR PROTECTORS LIKE GLEESON HEDGE, MOST OF US WOULD BE KILLED OFF BEFORE WE EVER REACHED CLAIMING AGE. SATYRS LIKE HIM HELP FIND DEMIGODS AND BRING THEM TO CAMP, WHERE THEY'LL BE SAFE.
I FEEL BAD ABOUT COACH HEDGE. HE SAVED LEO, AND HE HELPED JASON STAND UP TO THOSE...WHATEVER THEY WERE.
GLEESON KNEW THE RISKS. SATYRS DON'T HAVE MORTAL SOULS, THOUGH, SO HE'LL PROBABLY BE REINCARNATED AS A TREE OR A FLOWER OR SOMETHING.

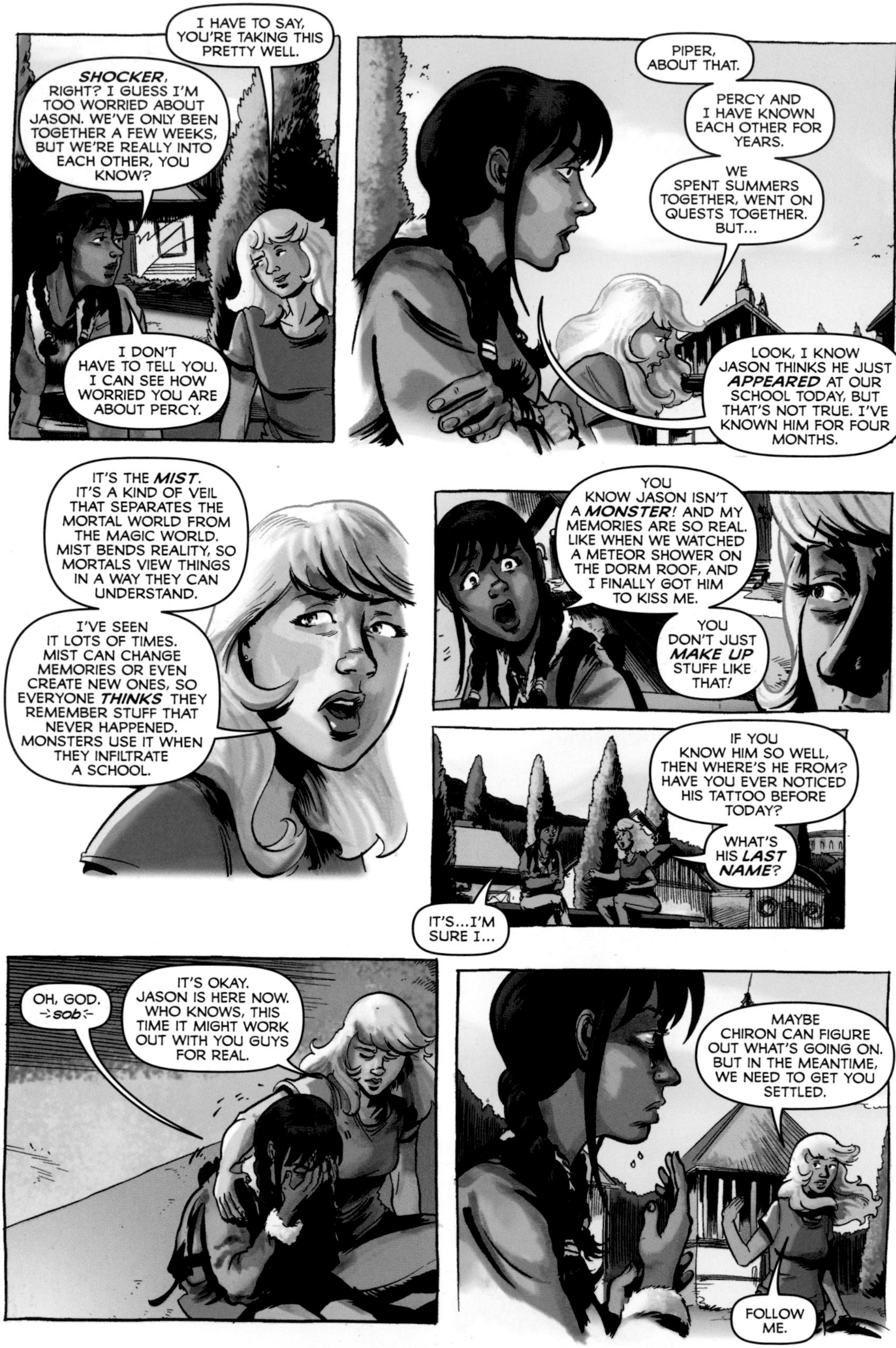
I HAVE TO SAY, YOU'RE TAKING THIS PRETTY WELL.
SHOCKER, RIGHT? I GUESS I'M TOO WORRIED ABOUT JASON. WE'VE ONLY BEEN TOGETHER A FEW WEEKS, BUT WE'RE REALLY INTO EACH OTHER, YOU KNOW?
I DON'T HAVE TO TELL YOU. I CAN SEE HOW WORRIED YOU ARE ABOUT PERCY.
PIPER, ABOUT THAT.
PERCY AND I HAVE KNOWN EACH OTHER FOR YEARS.
WE SPENT SUMMERS TOGETHER, WENT ON QUESTS TOGETHER. BUT...
LOOK, I KNOW JASON THINKS HE JUST APPEARED AT OUR SCHOOL TODAY, BUT THAT'S NOT TRUE. I'VE KNOWN HIM FOR FOUR MONTHS.
IT'S THE MIST. IT'S A KIND OF VEIL THAT SEPARATES THE MORTAL WORLD FROM THE MAGIC WORLD. MIST BENDS REALITY, SO MORTALS VIEW THINGS IN A WAY THEY CAN UNDERSTAND.
I'VE SEEN IT LOTS OF TIMES. MIST CAN CHANGE MEMORIES OR EVEN CREATE NEW ONES, SO EVERYONE THINKS THEY REMEMBER STUFF THAT NEVER HAPPENED. MONSTERS USE IT WHEN THEY INFILTRATE A SCHOOL.
YOU KNOW JASON ISN'T A MONSTER! AND MY MEMORIES ARE SO REAL. LIKE WHEN WE WATCHED A METEOR SHOWER ON THE DORM ROOF, AND I FINALLY GOT HIM TO KISS ME.
YOU DON'T JUST MAKE UP STUFF LIKE THAT!
IF YOU KNOW HIM SO WELL, THEN WHERE'S HE FROM? HAVE YOU EVER NOTICED HIS TATTOO BEFORE TODAY?
WHAT'S HIS LAST NAME?
IT'S...I'M SURE I...
OH, GOD. -sob-
IT'S OKAY. JASON IS HERE NOW. WHO KNOWS, THIS TIME IT MIGHT WORK OUT WITH YOU GUYS FOR REAL.
MAYBE CHIRON CAN FIGURE OUT WHAT'S GOING ON. BUT IN THE MEANTIME, WE NEED TO GET YOU SETTLED.
FOLLOW ME.

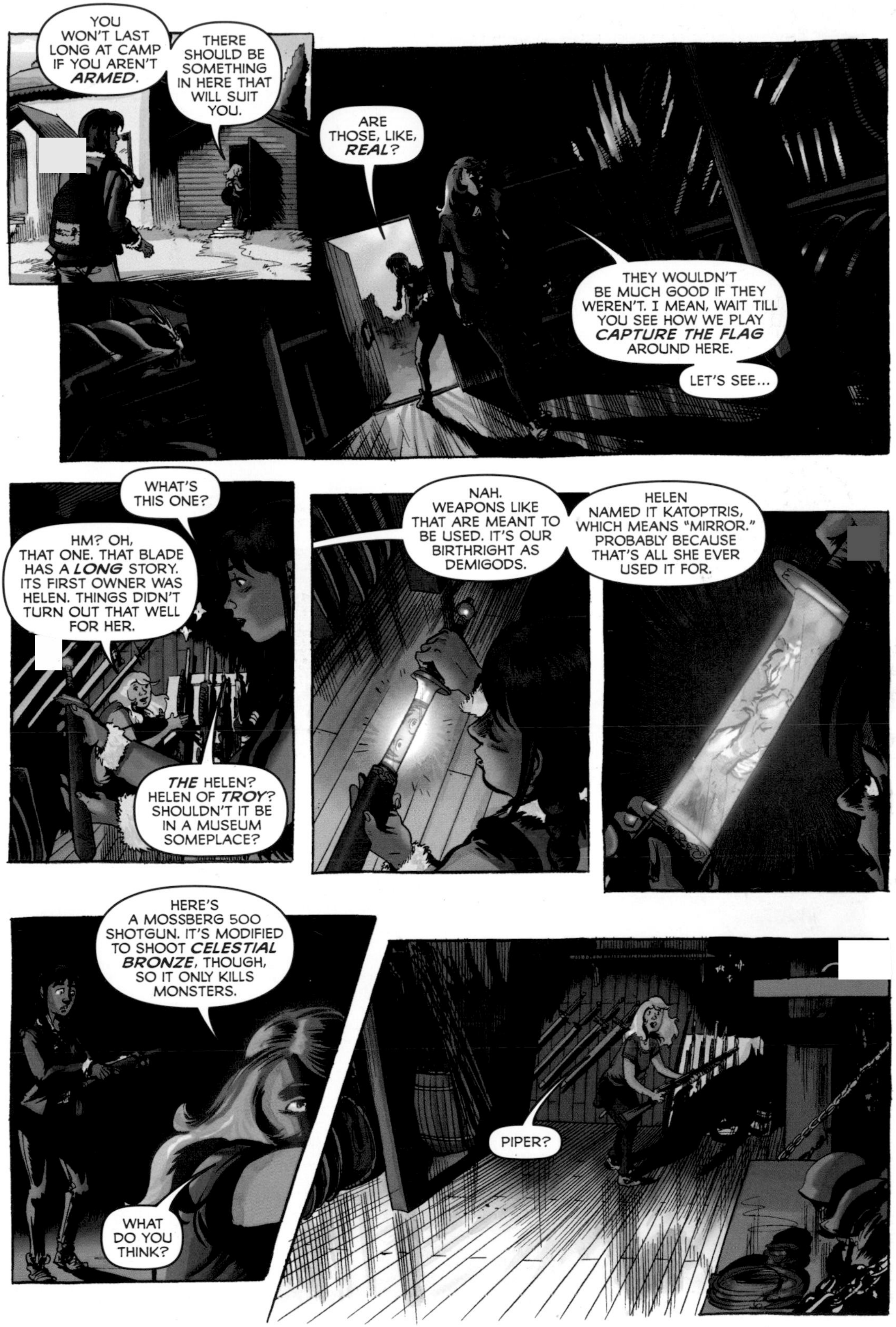
YOU WON'T LAST LONG AT CAMP IF YOU AREN'T ARMED.
THERE SHOULD BE SOMETHING IN HERE THAT WILL SUIT YOU.
ARE THOSE, LIKE, REAL?
THEY WOULDN'T BE MUCH GOOD IF THEY WEREN'T. I MEAN, WAIT TILL YOU SEE HOW WE PLAY CAPTURE THE FLAG AROUND HERE.
LET'S SEE...
WHAT'S THIS ONE?
HM? OH, THAT ONE. THAT BLADE HAS A LONG STORY. ITS FIRST OWNER WAS HELEN. THINGS DIDN'T TURN OUT THAT WELL FOR HER.
THE HELEN? HELEN OF TROY? SHOULDN'T IT BE IN A MUSEUM SOMEPLACE?
NAH. WEAPONS LIKE THAT ARE MEANT TO BE USED. IT'S OUR BIRTHRIGHT AS DEMIGODS.
HELEN NAMED IT KATOPTRIS, WHICH MEANS "MIRROR." PROBABLY BECAUSE THAT'S ALL SHE EVER USED IT FOR.
HERE'S A MOSSBERG 500 SHOTGUN. IT'S MODIFIED TO SHOOT CELESTIAL BRONZE, THOUGH, SO IT ONLY KILLS MONSTERS.
WHAT DO YOU THINK?
PIPER?

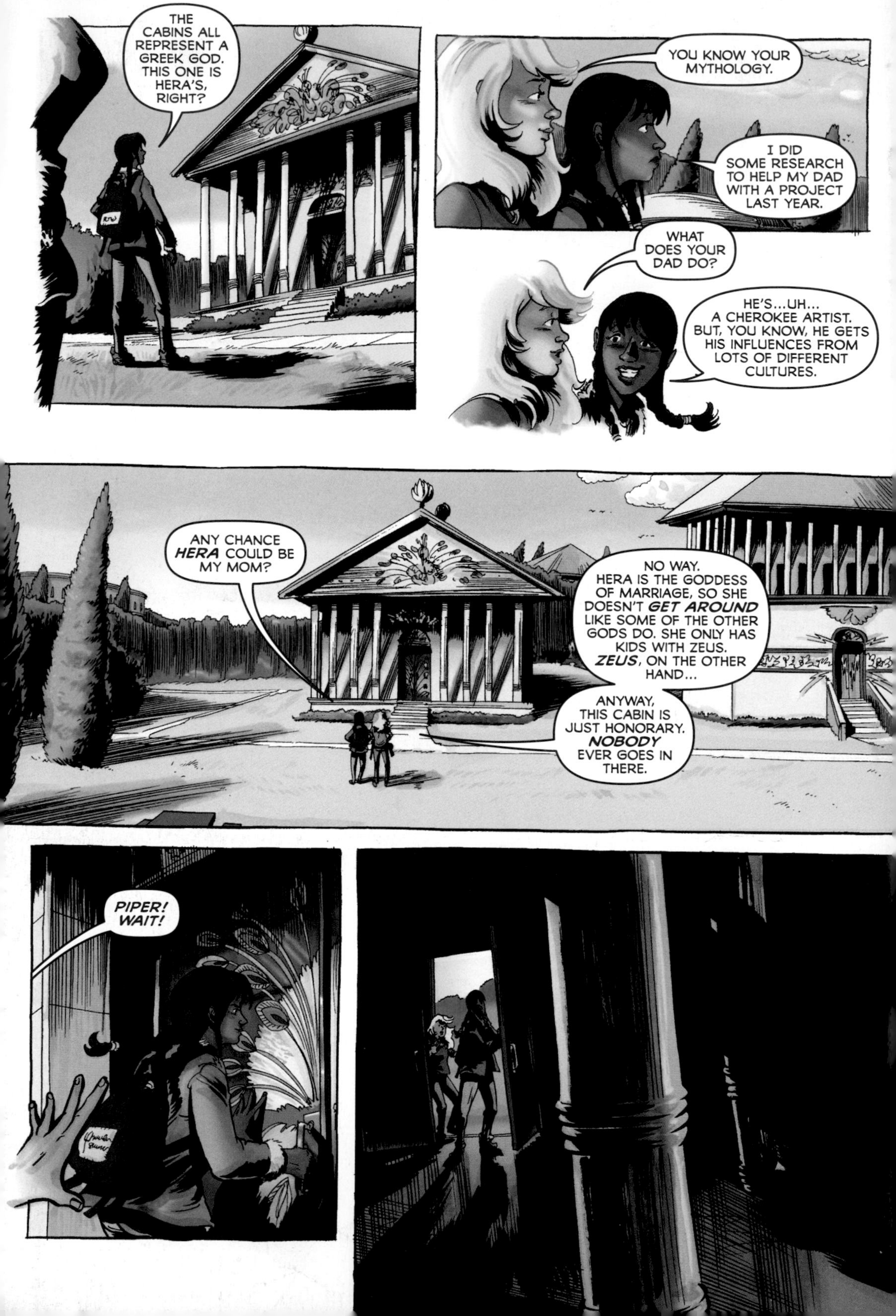
THE CABINS ALL REPRESENT A GREEK GOD. THIS ONE IS HERA'S, RIGHT?
YOU KNOW YOUR MYTHOLOGY.
I DID SOME RESEARCH TO HELP MY DAD WITH A PROJECT LAST YEAR.
WHAT DOES YOUR DAD DO?
HE'S...UH... A CHEROKEE ARTIST. BUT, YOU KNOW, HE GETS HIS INFLUENCES FROM LOTS OF DIFFERENT CULTURES.
ANY CHANCE HERA COULD BE MY MOM?
NO WAY. HERA IS THE GODDESS OF MARRIAGE, SO SHE DOESN'T GET AROUND LIKE SOME OF THE OTHER GODS DO. SHE ONLY HAS KIDS WITH ZEUS. ZEUS, ON THE OTHER HAND...
ANYWAY, THIS CABIN IS JUST HONORARY. NOBODY EVER GOES IN THERE.
PIPER! WAIT!

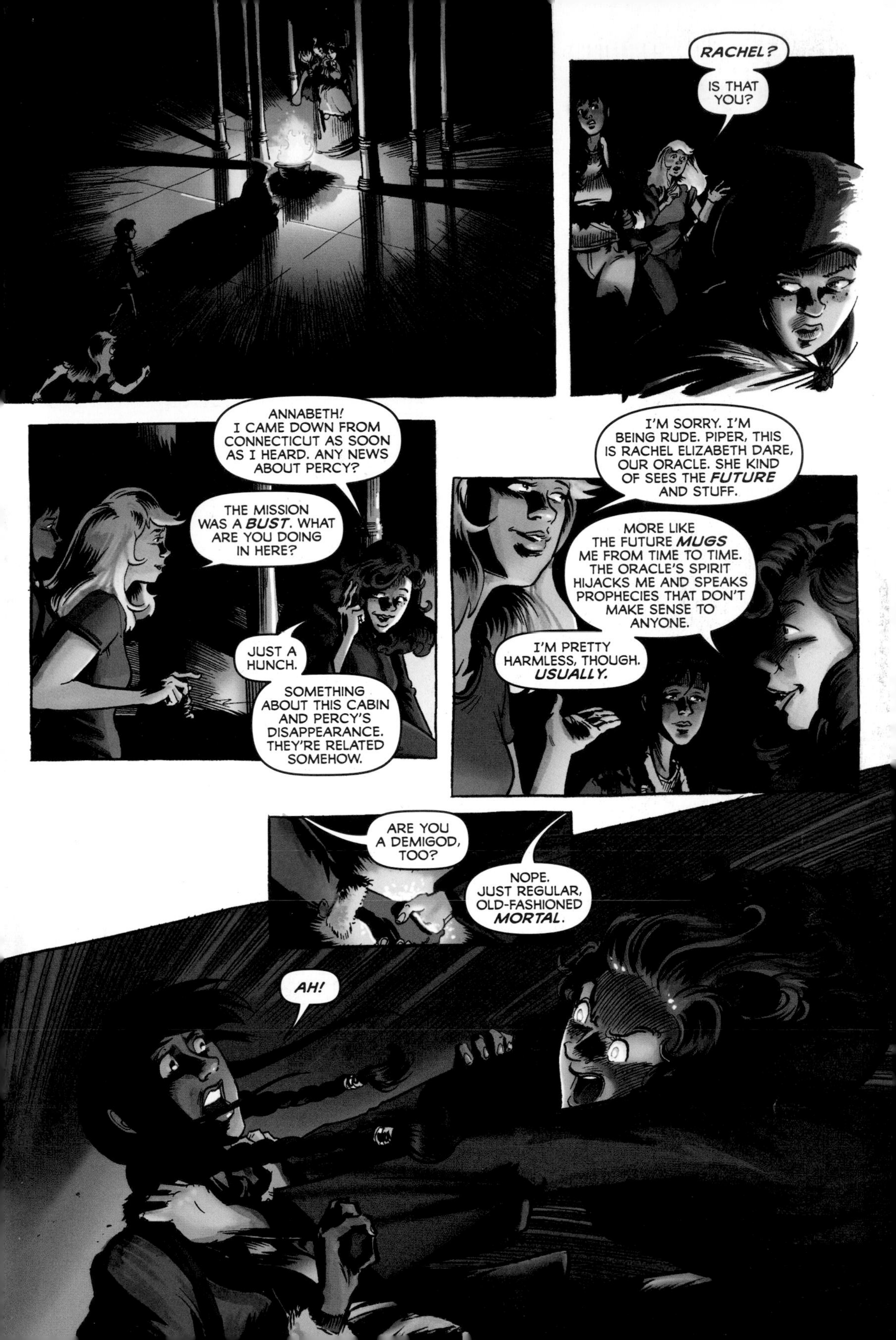
RACHEL?
IS THAT YOU?
ANNABETH! I CAME DOWN FROM CONNECTICUT AS SOON AS I HEARD. ANY NEWS ABOUT PERCY?
THE MISSION WAS A BUST. WHAT ARE YOU DOING IN HERE?
JUST A HUNCH.
SOMETHING ABOUT THIS CABIN AND PERCY'S DISAPPEARANCE. THEY'RE RELATED SOMEHOW.
I'M SORRY. I'M BEING RUDE. PIPER, THIS IS RACHEL ELIZABETH DARE, OUR ORACLE. SHE KIND OF SEES THE FUTURE AND STUFF.
MORE LIKE THE FUTURE MUGS ME FROM TIME TO TIME. THE ORACLE'S SPIRIT HIJACKS ME AND SPEAKS PROPHECIES THAT DON'T MAKE SENSE TO ANYONE.
I'M PRETTY HARMLESS, THOUGH. USUALLY.
ARE YOU A DEMIGOD, TOO?
NOPE. JUST REGULAR, OLD-FASHIONED MORTAL.
AH!

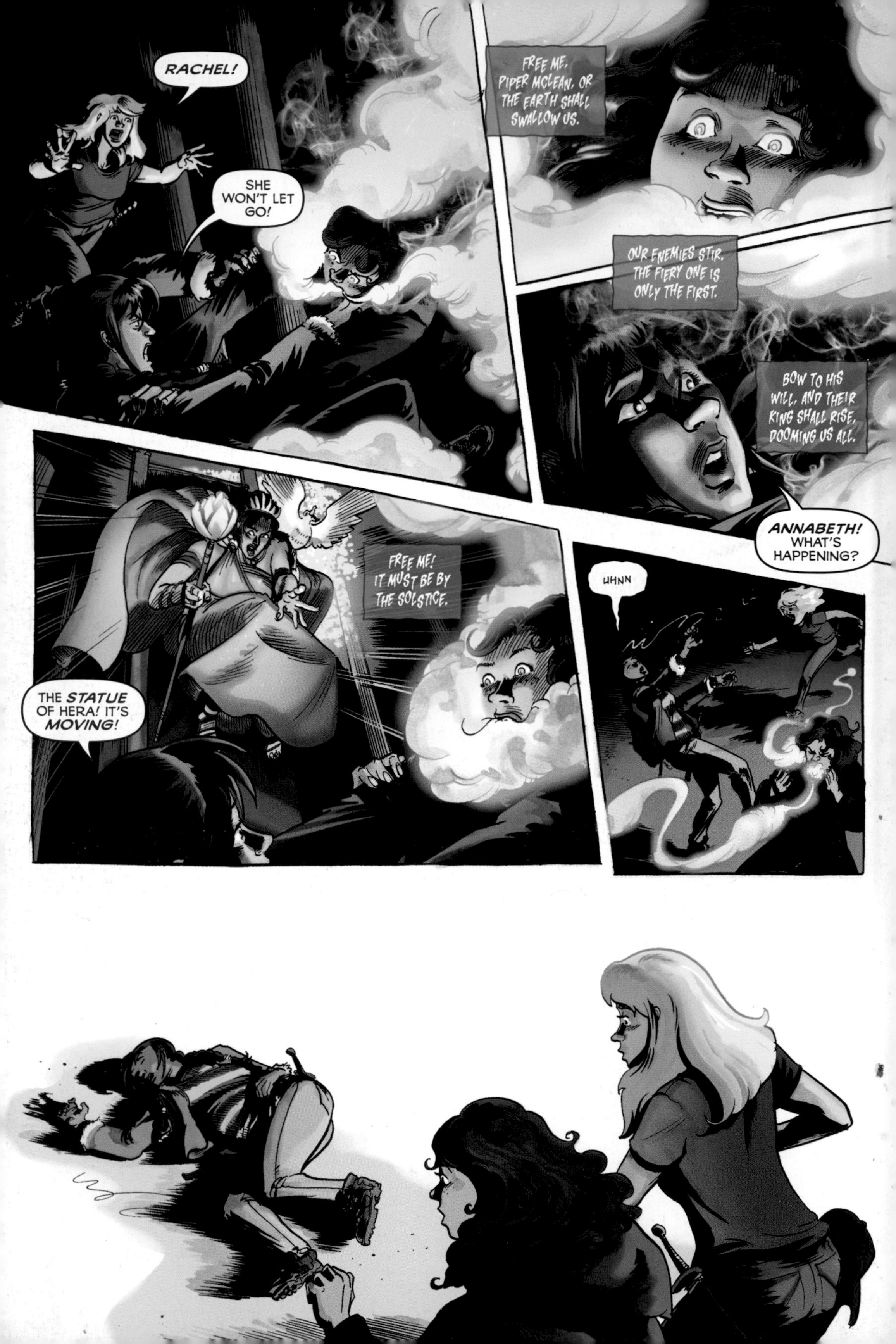
RACHEL!
SHE WON'T LET GO!
FREE ME, PIPER MCLEAN, OR THE EARTH SHALL SWALLOW US.
OUR ENEMIES STIR. THE FIERY ONE IS ONLY THE FIRST.
BOW TO HIS WILL, AND THEIR KING SHALL RISE, DOOMING US ALL.
ANNABETH! WHAT'S HAPPENING?
FREE ME! IT MUST BE BY THE SOLSTICE.
THE STATUE OF HERA! IT'S MOVING!
UHNN

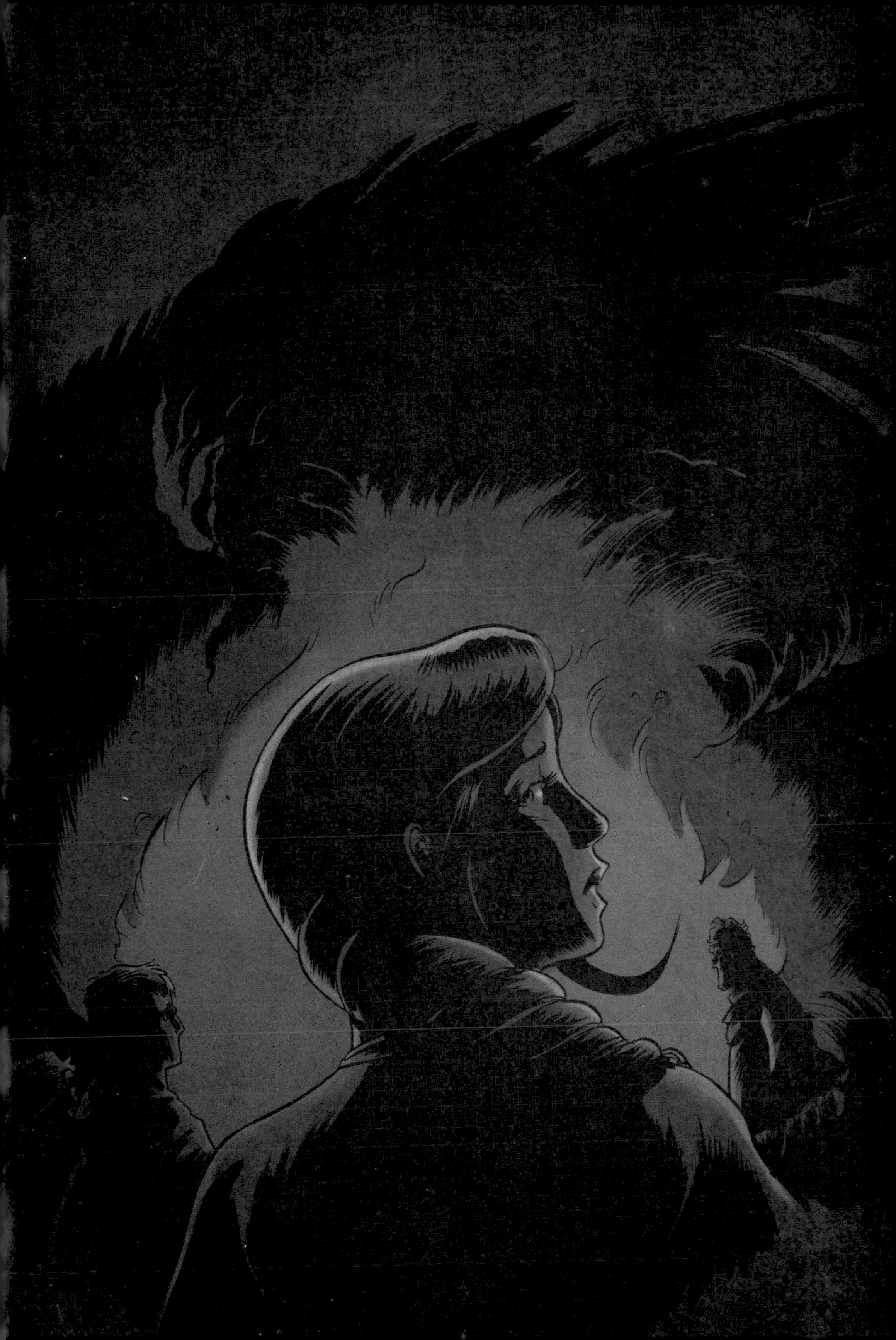

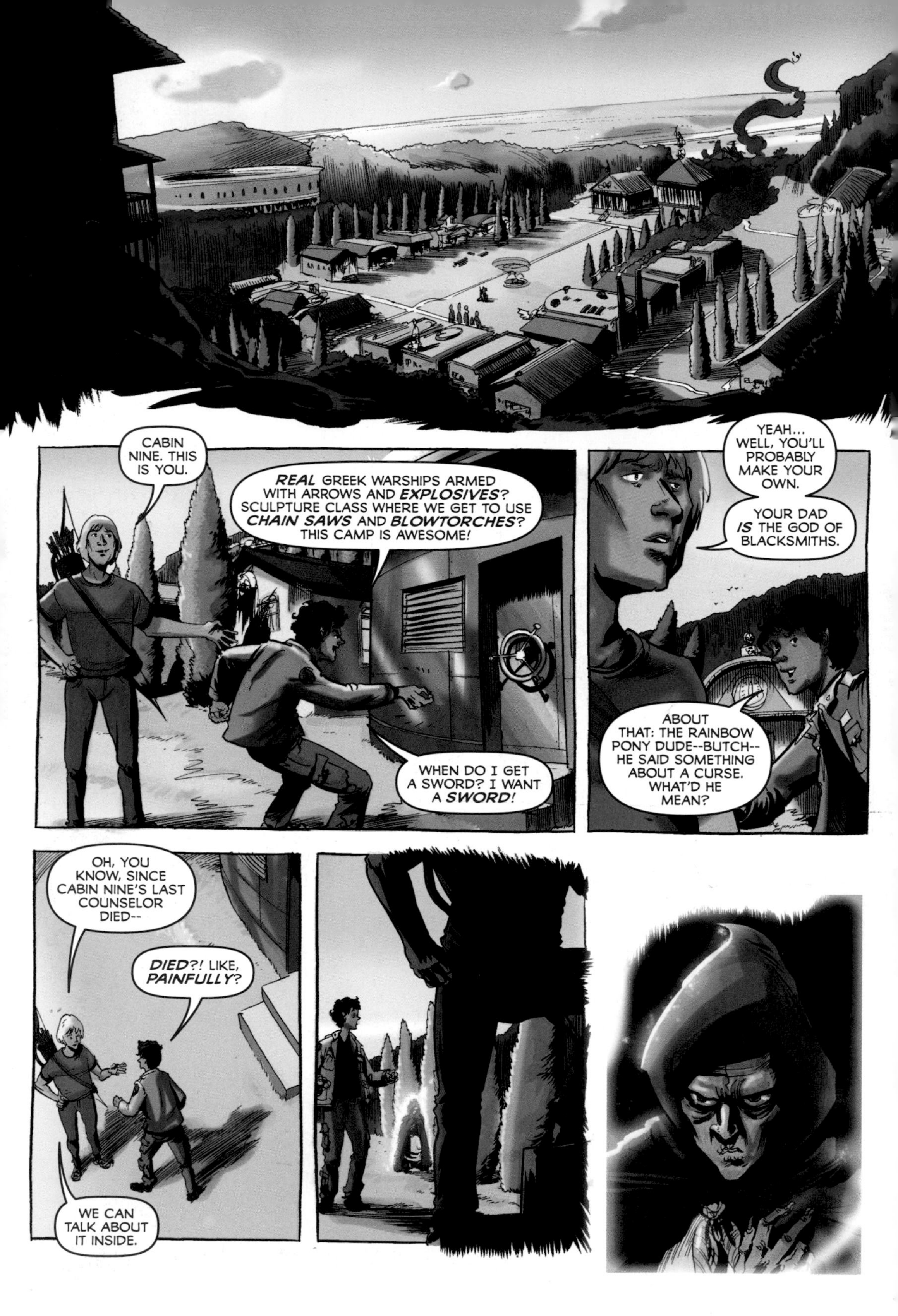
CABIN NINE. THIS IS YOU.
REAL GREEK WARSHIPS ARMED WITH ARROWS AND EXPLOSIVES? SCULPTURE CLASS WHERE WE GET TO USE CHAIN SAWS AND BLOWTORCHES? THIS CAMP IS AWESOME!
WHEN DO I GET A SWORD? I WANT A SWORD!
YEAH... WELL, YOU'LL PROBABLY MAKE YOUR OWN.
YOUR DAD IS THE GOD OF BLACKSMITHS.
ABOUT THAT: THE RAINBOW PONY DUDE--BUTCH--HE SAID SOMETHING ABOUT A CURSE. WHAT'D HE MEAN?
OH, YOU KNOW, SINCE CABIN NINE'S LAST COUNSELOR DIED--
DIED?! LIKE, PAINFULLY?
WE CAN TALK ABOUT IT INSIDE.

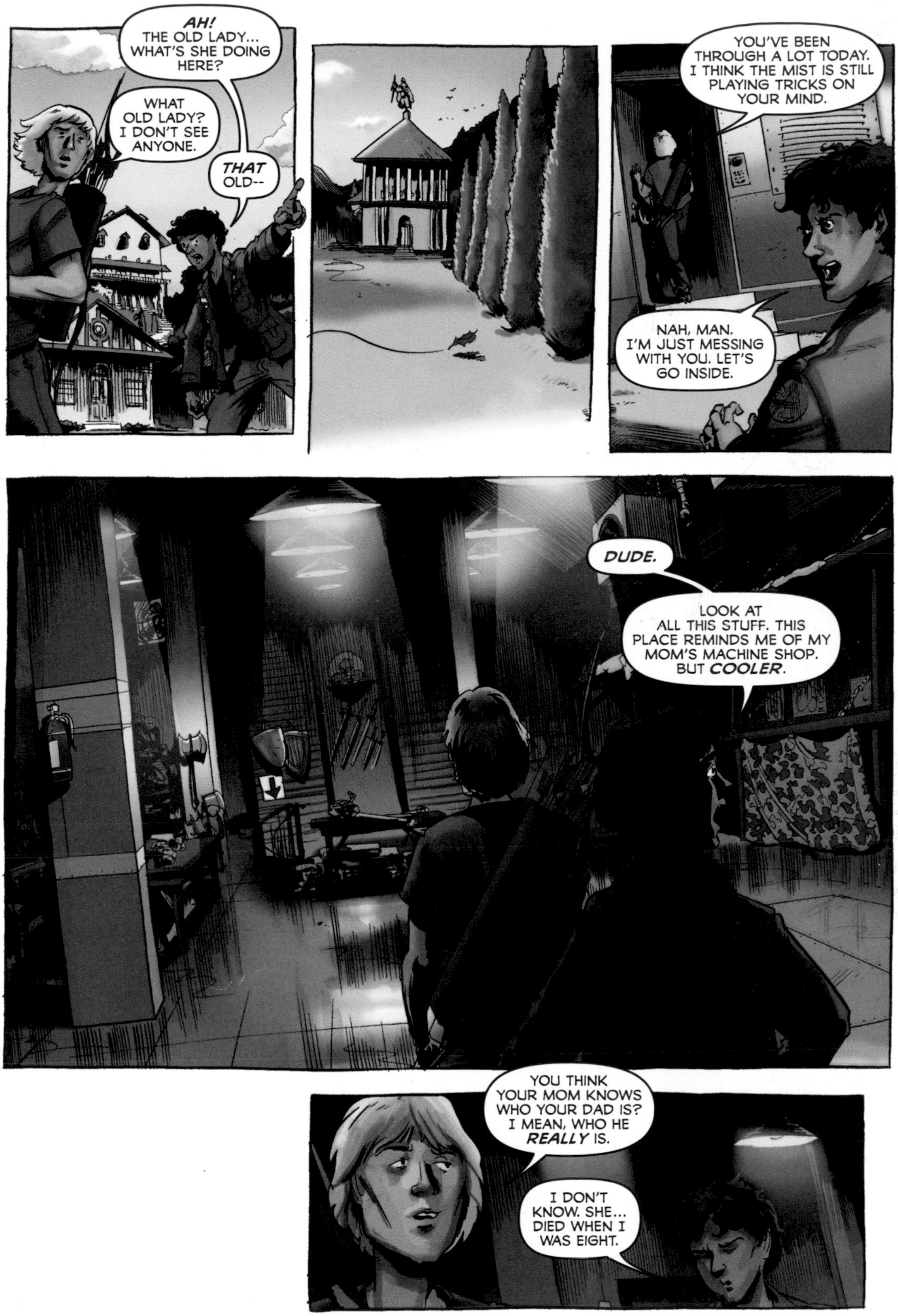
AH! THE OLD LADY... WHAT'S SHE DOING HERE?
WHAT OLD LADY? I DON'T SEE ANYONE.
THAT OLD--
YOU'VE BEEN THROUGH A LOT TODAY. I THINK THE MIST IS STILL PLAYING TRICKS ON YOUR MIND.
NAH, MAN. I'M JUST MESSING WITH YOU. LET'S GO INSIDE.
DUDE.
LOOK AT ALL THIS STUFF. THIS PLACE REMINDS ME OF MY MOM'S MACHINE SHOP. BUT COOLER.
YOU THINK YOUR MOM KNOWS WHO YOUR DAD IS? I MEAN, WHO HE REALLY IS.
I DON'T KNOW. SHE... DIED WHEN I WAS EIGHT.

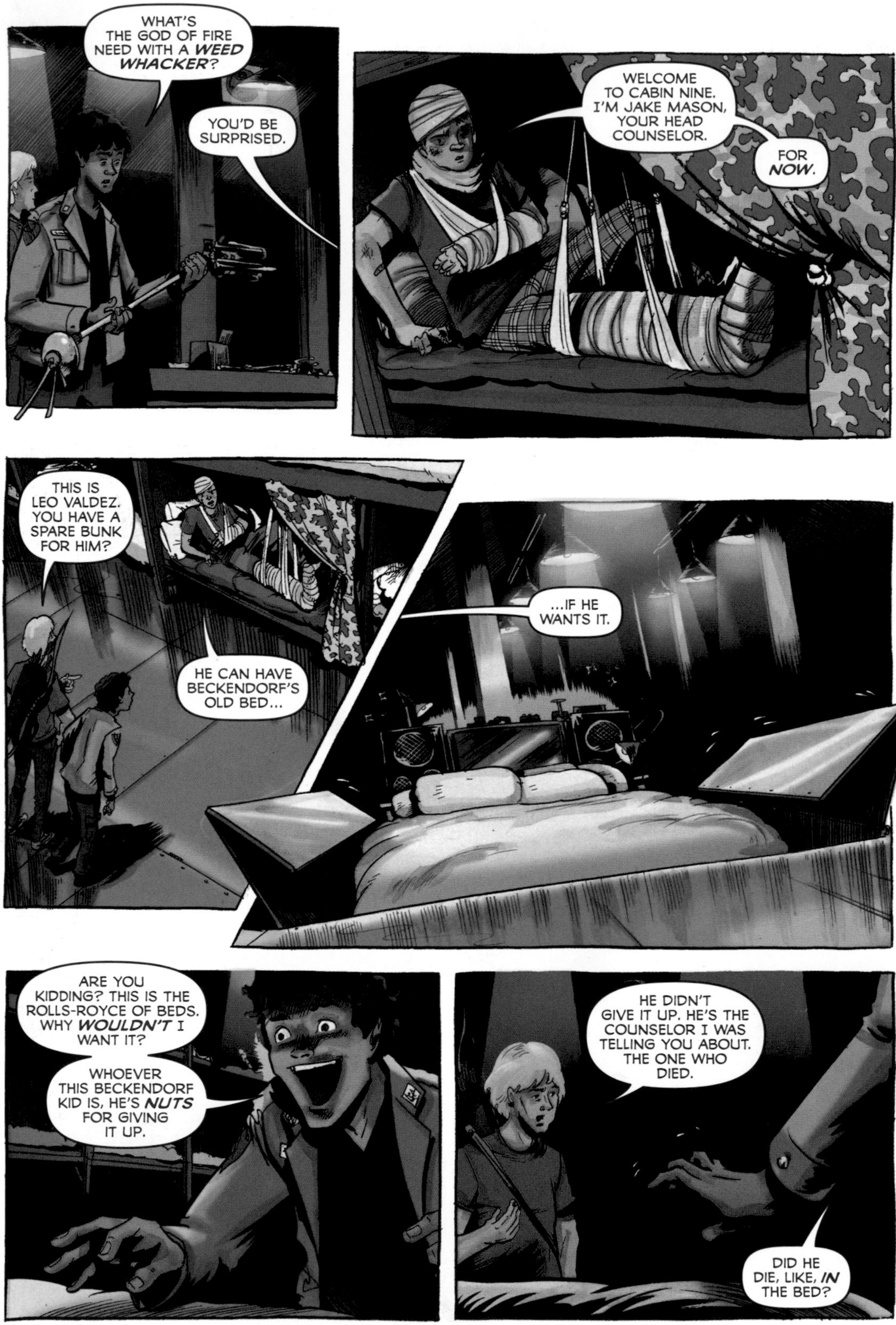
WHAT'S THE GOD OF FIRE NEED WITH A *WEED WHACKER*?
YOU'D BE SURPRISED.
WELCOME TO CABIN NINE. I'M JAKE MASON, YOUR HEAD COUNSELOR.
FOR *NOW*.
THIS IS LEO VALDEZ. YOU HAVE A SPARE BUNK FOR HIM?
HE CAN HAVE BECKENDORF'S OLD BED...
...IF HE WANTS IT.
ARE YOU KIDDING? THIS IS THE ROLLS-ROYCE OF BEDS. WHY *WOULDN'T* I WANT IT?
WHOEVER THIS BECKENDORF KID IS, HE'S *NUTS* FOR GIVING IT UP.
HE DIDN'T GIVE IT UP. HE'S THE COUNSELOR I WAS TELLING YOU ABOUT. THE ONE WHO DIED.
DID HE DIE, LIKE, *IN* THE BED?

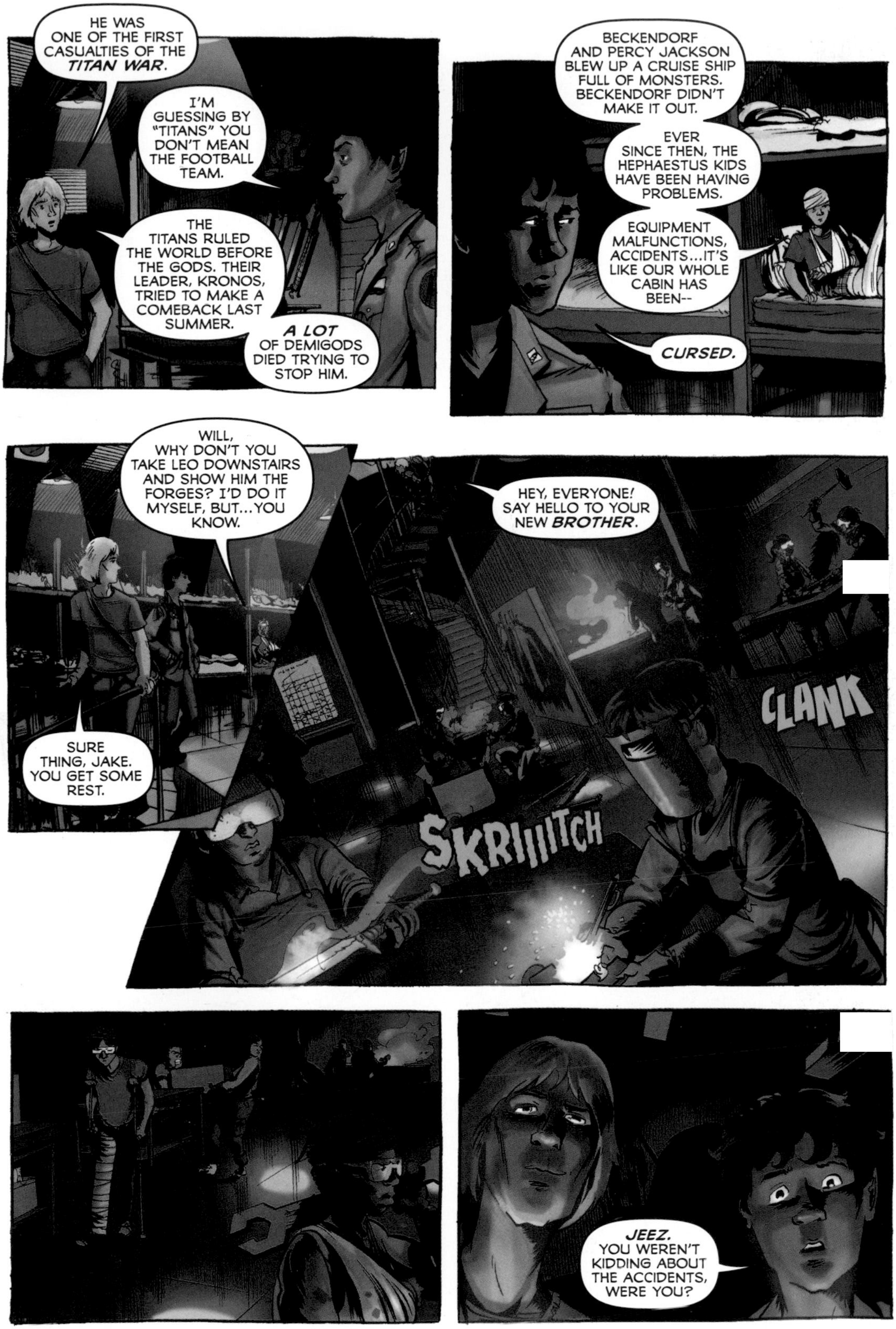
HE WAS ONE OF THE FIRST CASUALTIES OF THE *TITAN WAR*.
I'M GUESSING BY "TITANS" YOU DON'T MEAN THE FOOTBALL TEAM.
THE TITANS RULED THE WORLD BEFORE THE GODS. THEIR LEADER, KRONOS, TRIED TO MAKE A COMEBACK LAST SUMMER.
A LOT OF DEMIGODS DIED TRYING TO STOP HIM.
BECKENDORF AND PERCY JACKSON BLEW UP A CRUISE SHIP FULL OF MONSTERS. BECKENDORF DIDN'T MAKE IT OUT.
EVER SINCE THEN, THE HEPHAESTUS KIDS HAVE BEEN HAVING PROBLEMS.
EQUIPMENT MALFUNCTIONS, ACCIDENTS...IT'S LIKE OUR WHOLE CABIN HAS BEEN--
CURSED.
WILL, WHY DON'T YOU TAKE LEO DOWNSTAIRS AND SHOW HIM THE FORGES? I'D DO IT MYSELF, BUT...YOU KNOW.
SURE THING, JAKE. YOU GET SOME REST.
HEY, EVERYONE! SAY HELLO TO YOUR NEW *BROTHER*.
CLANK
SKRIIIIITCH
JEEZ. YOU WEREN'T KIDDING ABOUT THE ACCIDENTS, WERE YOU?

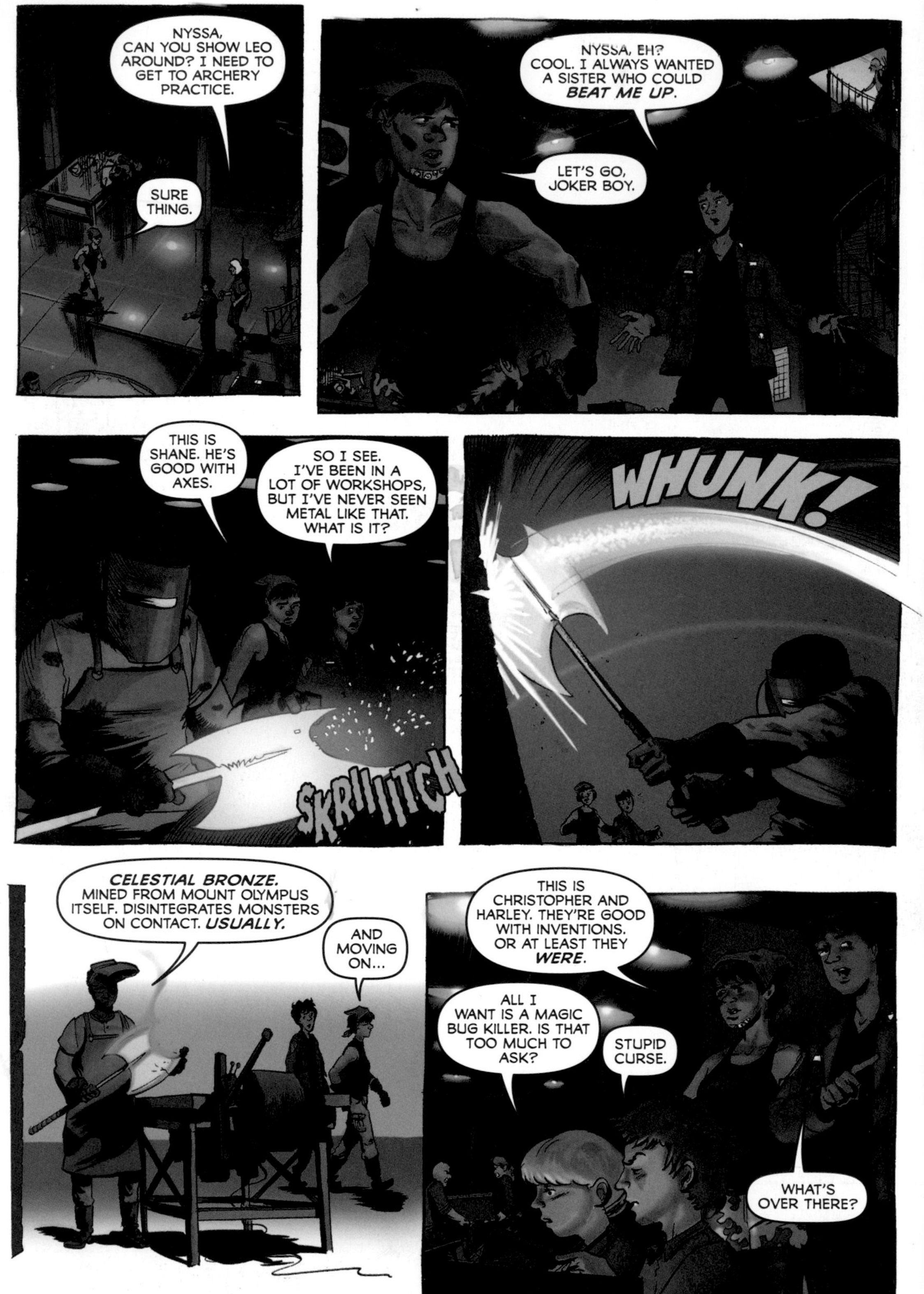
NYSSA, CAN YOU SHOW LEO AROUND? I NEED TO GET TO ARCHERY PRACTICE.
SURE THING.
NYSSA, EH? COOL. I ALWAYS WANTED A SISTER WHO COULD *BEAT ME UP*.
LET'S GO, JOKER BOY.
THIS IS SHANE. HE'S GOOD WITH AXES.
SO I SEE. I'VE BEEN IN A LOT OF WORKSHOPS, BUT I'VE NEVER SEEN METAL LIKE THAT. WHAT IS IT?
SKRIIIITCH
WHUNK!
CELESTIAL BRONZE. MINED FROM MOUNT OLYMPUS ITSELF. DISINTEGRATES MONSTERS ON CONTACT. *USUALLY.*
AND MOVING ON...
THIS IS CHRISTOPHER AND HARLEY. THEY'RE GOOD WITH INVENTIONS. OR AT LEAST THEY *WERE*.
ALL I WANT IS A MAGIC BUG KILLER. IS THAT TOO MUCH TO ASK?
STUPID CURSE.
WHAT'S OVER THERE?

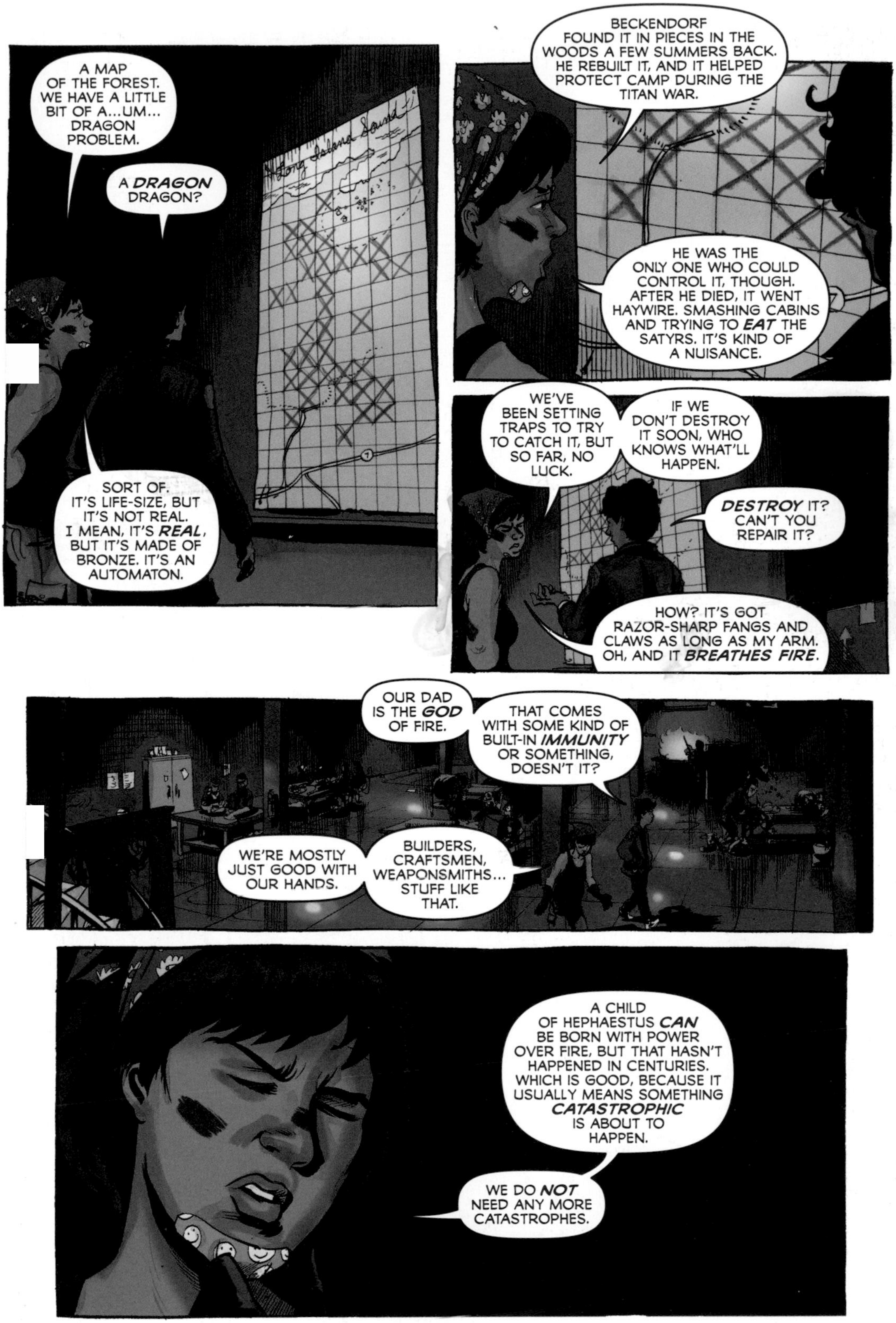
A MAP OF THE FOREST. WE HAVE A LITTLE BIT OF A...UM... DRAGON PROBLEM.
A DRAGON DRAGON?
Long Island Sound
SORT OF. IT'S LIFE-SIZE, BUT IT'S NOT REAL. I MEAN, IT'S REAL, BUT IT'S MADE OF BRONZE. IT'S AN AUTOMATON.
BECKENDORF FOUND IT IN PIECES IN THE WOODS A FEW SUMMERS BACK. HE REBUILT IT, AND IT HELPED PROTECT CAMP DURING THE TITAN WAR.
HE WAS THE ONLY ONE WHO COULD CONTROL IT, THOUGH. AFTER HE DIED, IT WENT HAYWIRE. SMASHING CABINS AND TRYING TO EAT THE SATYRS. IT'S KIND OF A NUISANCE.
WE'VE BEEN SETTING TRAPS TO TRY TO CATCH IT, BUT SO FAR, NO LUCK.
IF WE DON'T DESTROY IT SOON, WHO KNOWS WHAT'LL HAPPEN.
DESTROY IT? CAN'T YOU REPAIR IT?
HOW? IT'S GOT RAZOR-SHARP FANGS AND CLAWS AS LONG AS MY ARM. OH, AND IT BREATHES FIRE.
OUR DAD IS THE GOD OF FIRE.
THAT COMES WITH SOME KIND OF BUILT-IN IMMUNITY OR SOMETHING, DOESN'T IT?
WE'RE MOSTLY JUST GOOD WITH OUR HANDS.
BUILDERS, CRAFTSMEN, WEAPONSMITHS... STUFF LIKE THAT.
A CHILD OF HEPHAESTUS CAN BE BORN WITH POWER OVER FIRE, BUT THAT HASN'T HAPPENED IN CENTURIES. WHICH IS GOOD, BECAUSE IT USUALLY MEANS SOMETHING CATASTROPHIC IS ABOUT TO HAPPEN.
WE DO NOT NEED ANY MORE CATASTROPHES.

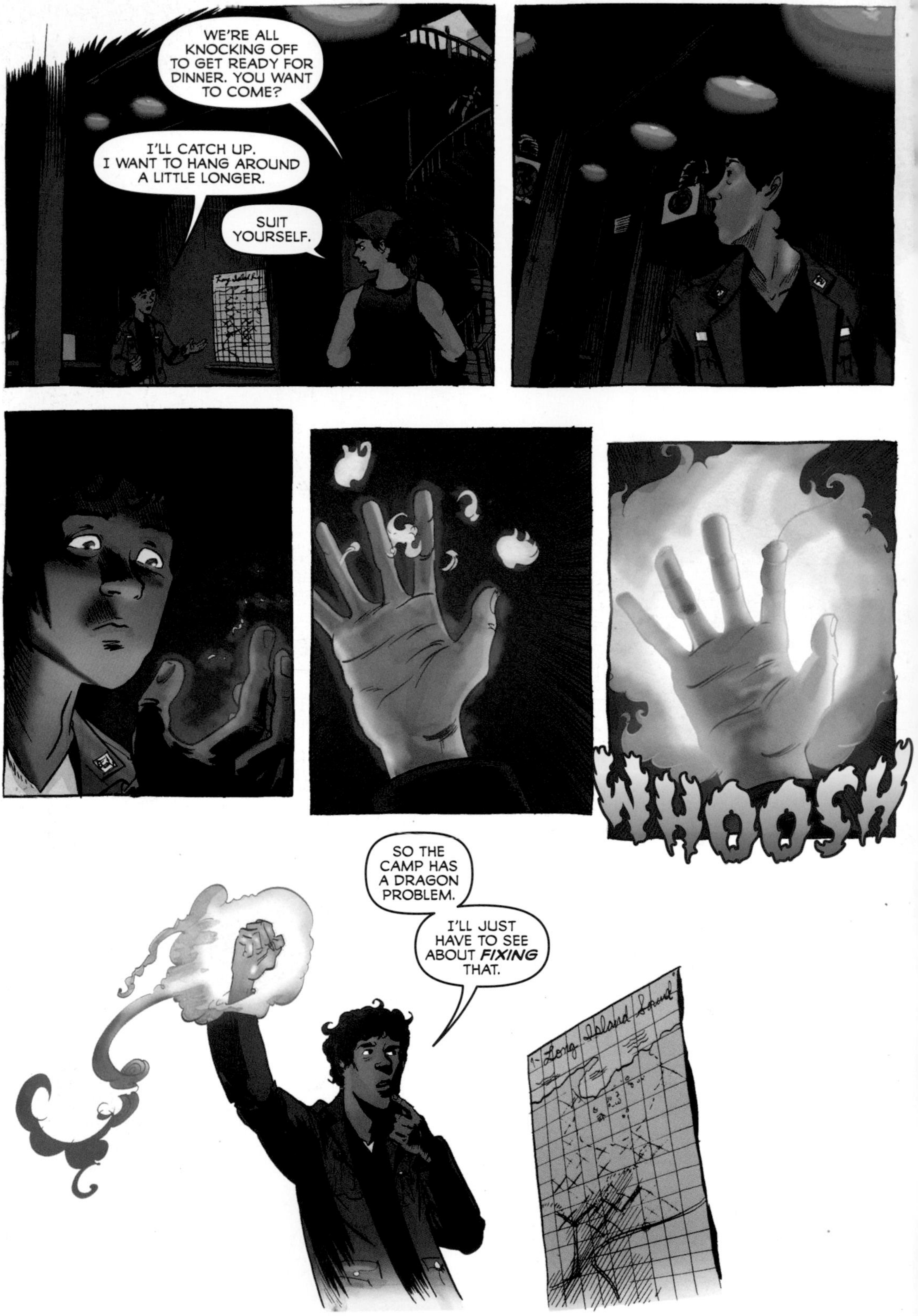
WE'RE ALL KNOCKING OFF TO GET READY FOR DINNER. YOU WANT TO COME?
I'LL CATCH UP. I WANT TO HANG AROUND A LITTLE LONGER.
SUIT YOURSELF.
WHOOSH
SO THE CAMP HAS A DRAGON PROBLEM.
I'LL JUST HAVE TO SEE ABOUT *FIXING* THAT.

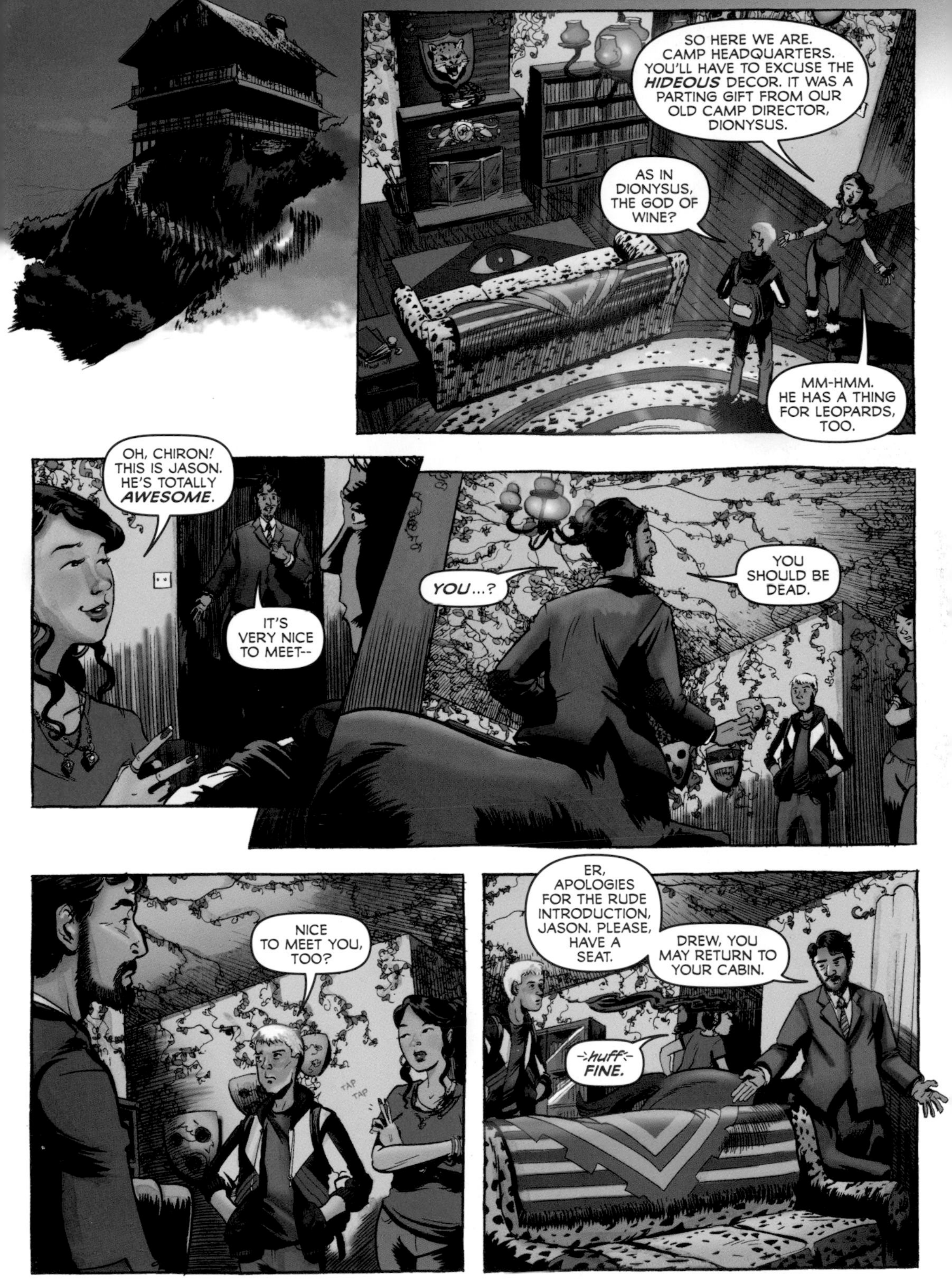
SO HERE WE ARE. CAMP HEADQUARTERS. YOU'LL HAVE TO EXCUSE THE HIDEOUS DECOR. IT WAS A PARTING GIFT FROM OUR OLD CAMP DIRECTOR, DIONYSUS.
AS IN DIONYSUS, THE GOD OF WINE?
MM-HMM. HE HAS A THING FOR LEOPARDS, TOO.
OH, CHIRON! THIS IS JASON. HE'S TOTALLY AWESOME.
IT'S VERY NICE TO MEET--
YOU...?
YOU SHOULD BE DEAD.
NICE TO MEET YOU, TOO?
TAP TAP
ER, APOLOGIES FOR THE RUDE INTRODUCTION, JASON. PLEASE, HAVE A SEAT.
DREW, YOU MAY RETURN TO YOUR CABIN.
huff FINE.

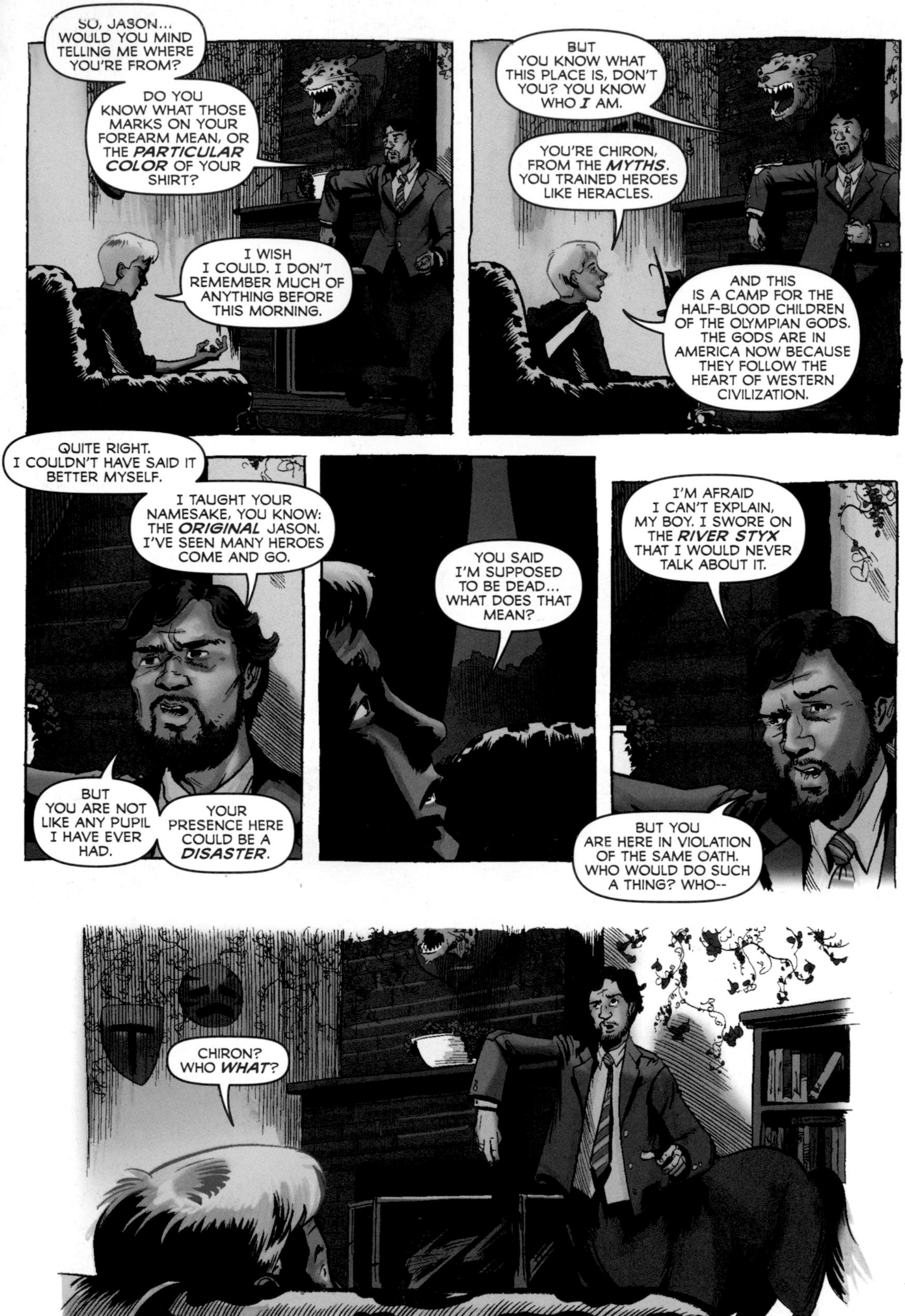
SO, JASON... WOULD YOU MIND TELLING ME WHERE YOU'RE FROM?
DO YOU KNOW WHAT THOSE MARKS ON YOUR FOREARM MEAN, OR THE PARTICULAR COLOR OF YOUR SHIRT?
I WISH I COULD. I DON'T REMEMBER MUCH OF ANYTHING BEFORE THIS MORNING.
BUT YOU KNOW WHAT THIS PLACE IS, DON'T YOU? YOU KNOW WHO I AM.
YOU'RE CHIRON, FROM THE MYTHS. YOU TRAINED HEROES LIKE HERACLES.
AND THIS IS A CAMP FOR THE HALF-BLOOD CHILDREN OF THE OLYMPIAN GODS. THE GODS ARE IN AMERICA NOW BECAUSE THEY FOLLOW THE HEART OF WESTERN CIVILIZATION.
QUITE RIGHT. I COULDN'T HAVE SAID IT BETTER MYSELF.
I TAUGHT YOUR NAMESAKE, YOU KNOW: THE ORIGINAL JASON. I'VE SEEN MANY HEROES COME AND GO.
BUT YOU ARE NOT LIKE ANY PUPIL I HAVE EVER HAD.
YOUR PRESENCE HERE COULD BE A DISASTER.
YOU SAID I'M SUPPOSED TO BE DEAD... WHAT DOES THAT MEAN?
I'M AFRAID I CAN'T EXPLAIN, MY BOY. I SWORE ON THE RIVER STYX THAT I WOULD NEVER TALK ABOUT IT.
BUT YOU ARE HERE IN VIOLATION OF THE SAME OATH. WHO WOULD DO SUCH A THING? WHO--
CHIRON? WHO WHAT?

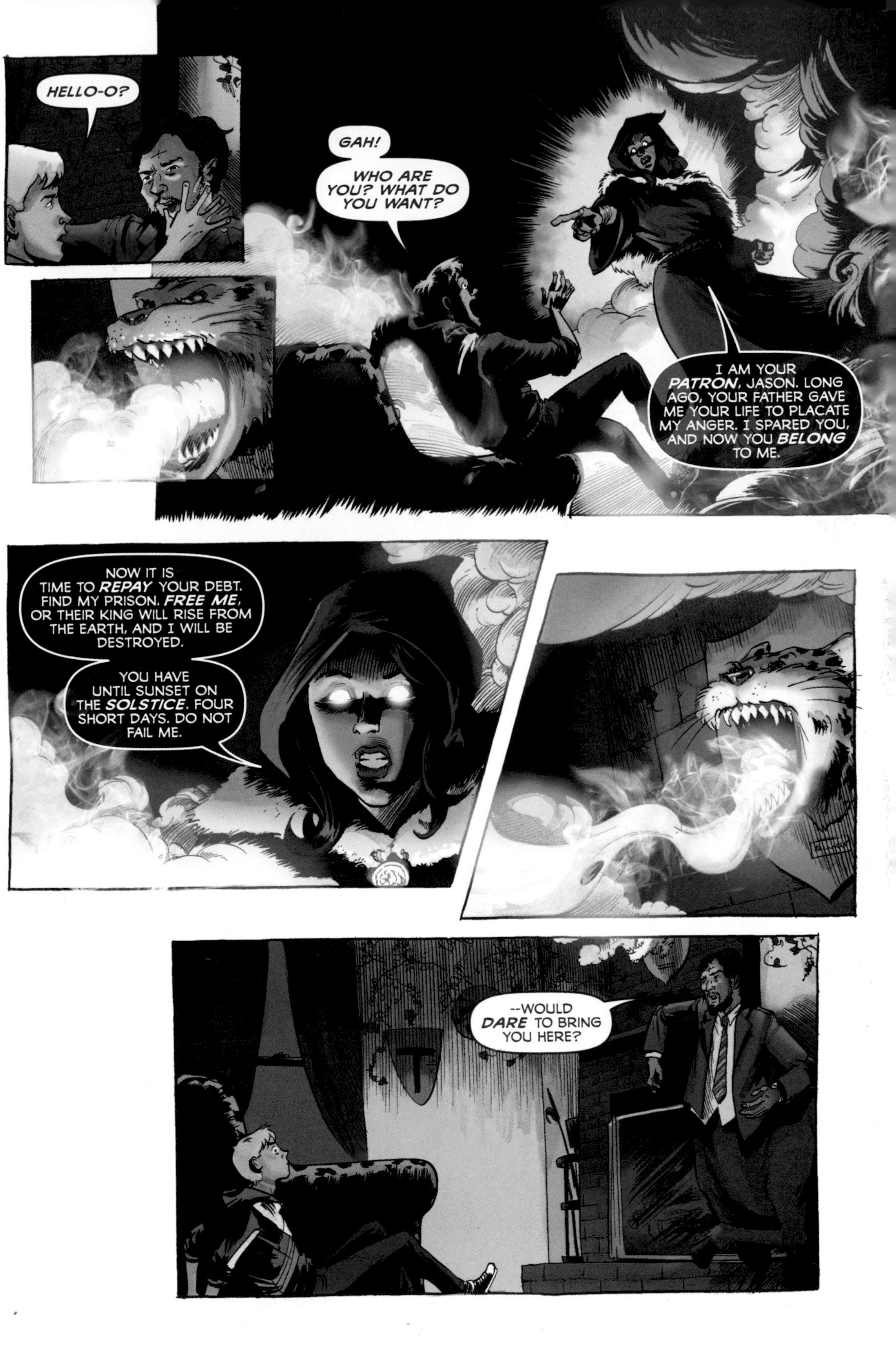
HELLO-O?
GAH!
WHO ARE YOU? WHAT DO YOU WANT?
I AM YOUR PATRON, JASON. LONG AGO, YOUR FATHER GAVE ME YOUR LIFE TO PLACATE MY ANGER. I SPARED YOU, AND NOW YOU BELONG TO ME.
NOW IT IS TIME TO REPAY YOUR DEBT. FIND MY PRISON. FREE ME, OR THEIR KING WILL RISE FROM THE EARTH, AND I WILL BE DESTROYED.
YOU HAVE UNTIL SUNSET ON THE SOLSTICE. FOUR SHORT DAYS. DO NOT FAIL ME.
--WOULD DARE TO BRING YOU HERE?

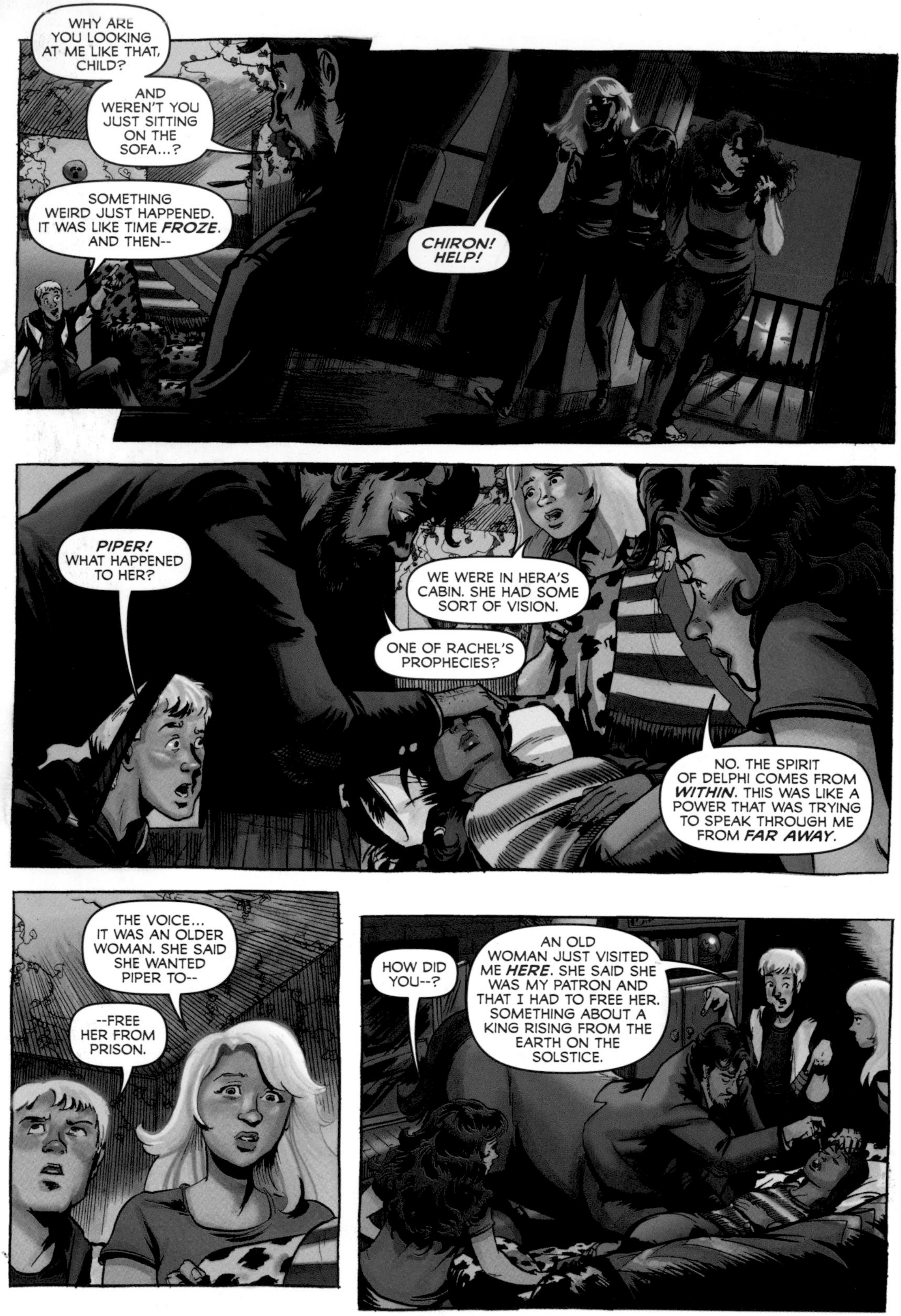
WHY ARE YOU LOOKING AT ME LIKE THAT, CHILD?
AND WEREN'T YOU JUST SITTING ON THE SOFA...?
SOMETHING WEIRD JUST HAPPENED. IT WAS LIKE TIME *FROZE*. AND THEN--
CHIRON! HELP!
PIPER! WHAT HAPPENED TO HER?
WE WERE IN HERA'S CABIN. SHE HAD SOME SORT OF VISION.
ONE OF RACHEL'S PROPHECIES?
NO. THE SPIRIT OF DELPHI COMES FROM *WITHIN*. THIS WAS LIKE A POWER THAT WAS TRYING TO SPEAK THROUGH ME FROM *FAR AWAY*.
THE VOICE... IT WAS AN OLDER WOMAN. SHE SAID SHE WANTED PIPER TO--
--FREE HER FROM PRISON.
HOW DID YOU--?
AN OLD WOMAN JUST VISITED ME *HERE*. SHE SAID SHE WAS MY PATRON AND THAT I HAD TO FREE HER. SOMETHING ABOUT A KING RISING FROM THE EARTH ON THE SOLSTICE.

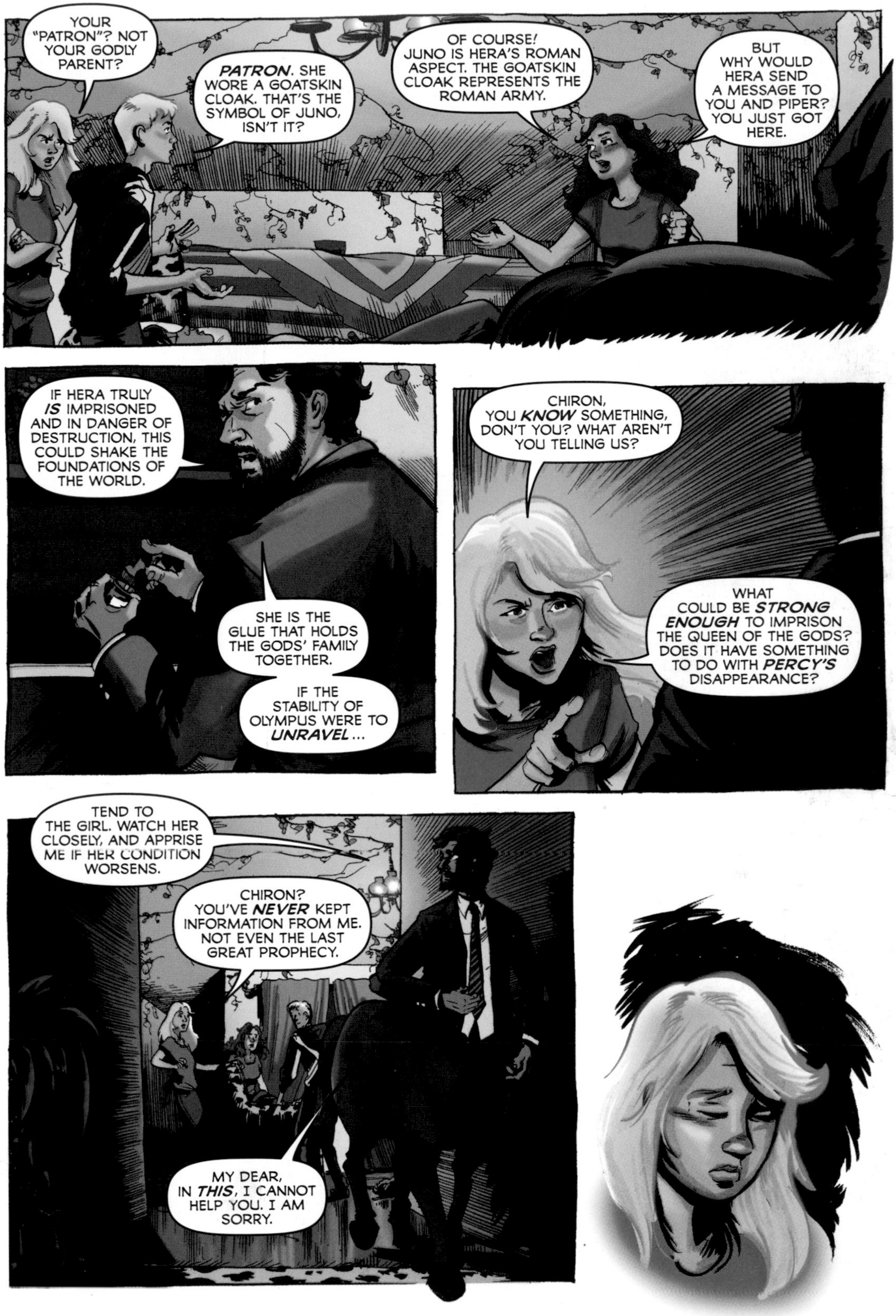
YOUR "PATRON"? NOT YOUR GODLY PARENT?
PATRON. SHE WORE A GOATSKIN CLOAK. THAT'S THE SYMBOL OF JUNO, ISN'T IT?
OF COURSE! JUNO IS HERA'S ROMAN ASPECT. THE GOATSKIN CLOAK REPRESENTS THE ROMAN ARMY.
BUT WHY WOULD HERA SEND A MESSAGE TO YOU AND PIPER? YOU JUST GOT HERE.
IF HERA TRULY IS IMPRISONED AND IN DANGER OF DESTRUCTION, THIS COULD SHAKE THE FOUNDATIONS OF THE WORLD.
SHE IS THE GLUE THAT HOLDS THE GODS' FAMILY TOGETHER.
IF THE STABILITY OF OLYMPUS WERE TO UNRAVEL...
CHIRON, YOU KNOW SOMETHING, DON'T YOU? WHAT AREN'T YOU TELLING US?
WHAT COULD BE STRONG ENOUGH TO IMPRISON THE QUEEN OF THE GODS? DOES IT HAVE SOMETHING TO DO WITH PERCY'S DISAPPEARANCE?
TEND TO THE GIRL. WATCH HER CLOSELY, AND APPRISE ME IF HER CONDITION WORSENS.
CHIRON? YOU'VE NEVER KEPT INFORMATION FROM ME. NOT EVEN THE LAST GREAT PROPHECY.
MY DEAR, IN THIS, I CANNOT HELP YOU. I AM SORRY.

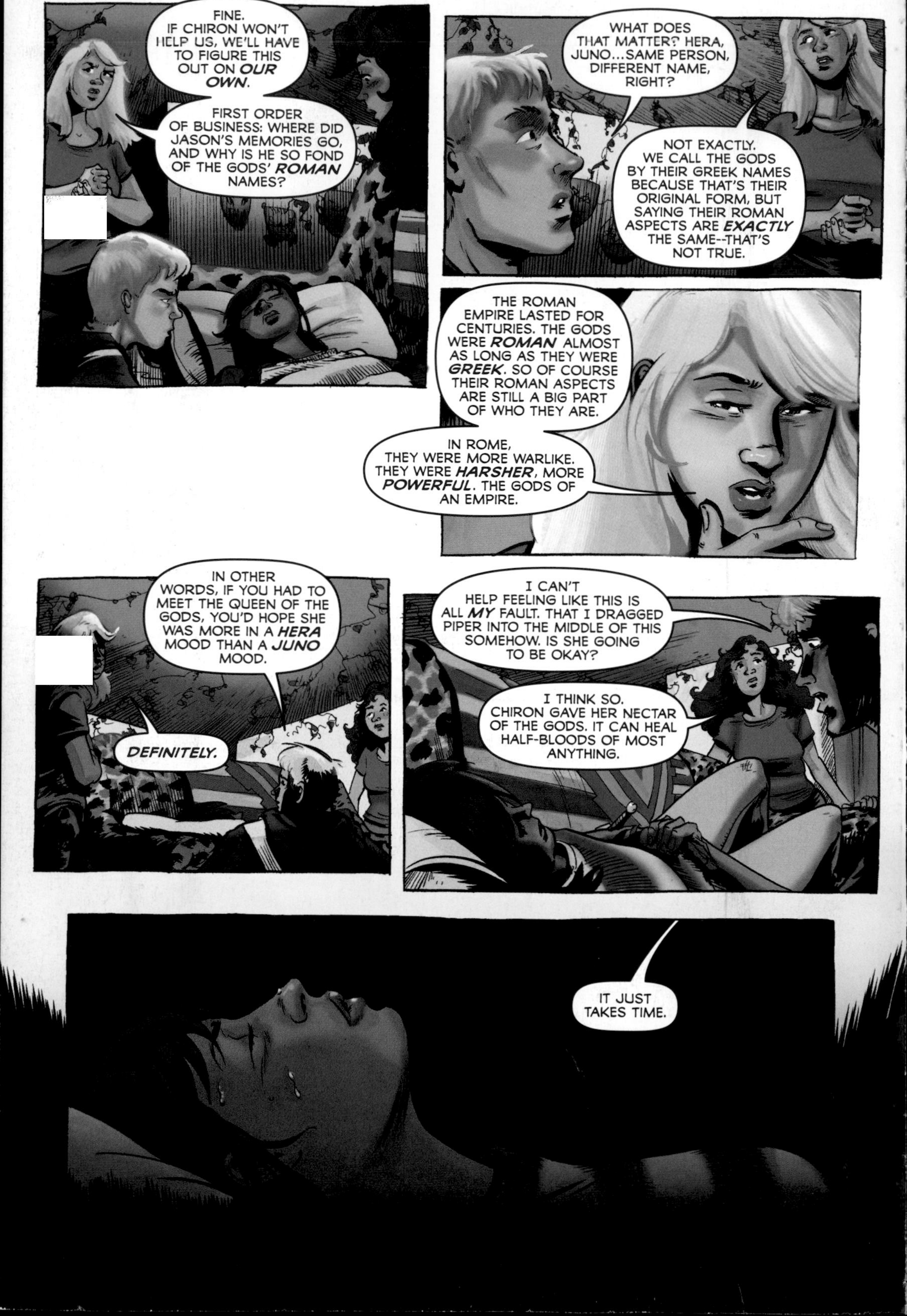
FINE. IF CHIRON WON'T HELP US, WE'LL HAVE TO FIGURE THIS OUT ON OUR OWN.
FIRST ORDER OF BUSINESS: WHERE DID JASON'S MEMORIES GO, AND WHY IS HE SO FOND OF THE GODS' ROMAN NAMES?
WHAT DOES THAT MATTER? HERA, JUNO...SAME PERSON, DIFFERENT NAME, RIGHT?
NOT EXACTLY. WE CALL THE GODS BY THEIR GREEK NAMES BECAUSE THAT'S THEIR ORIGINAL FORM, BUT SAYING THEIR ROMAN ASPECTS ARE EXACTLY THE SAME--THAT'S NOT TRUE.
THE ROMAN EMPIRE LASTED FOR CENTURIES. THE GODS WERE ROMAN ALMOST AS LONG AS THEY WERE GREEK. SO OF COURSE THEIR ROMAN ASPECTS ARE STILL A BIG PART OF WHO THEY ARE.
IN ROME, THEY WERE MORE WARLIKE. THEY WERE HARSHER, MORE POWERFUL. THE GODS OF AN EMPIRE.
IN OTHER WORDS, IF YOU HAD TO MEET THE QUEEN OF THE GODS, YOU'D HOPE SHE WAS MORE IN A HERA MOOD THAN A JUNO MOOD.
DEFINITELY.
I CAN'T HELP FEELING LIKE THIS IS ALL MY FAULT. THAT I DRAGGED PIPER INTO THE MIDDLE OF THIS SOMEHOW. IS SHE GOING TO BE OKAY?
I THINK SO. CHIRON GAVE HER NECTAR OF THE GODS. IT CAN HEAL HALF-BLOODS OF MOST ANYTHING.
IT JUST TAKES TIME.

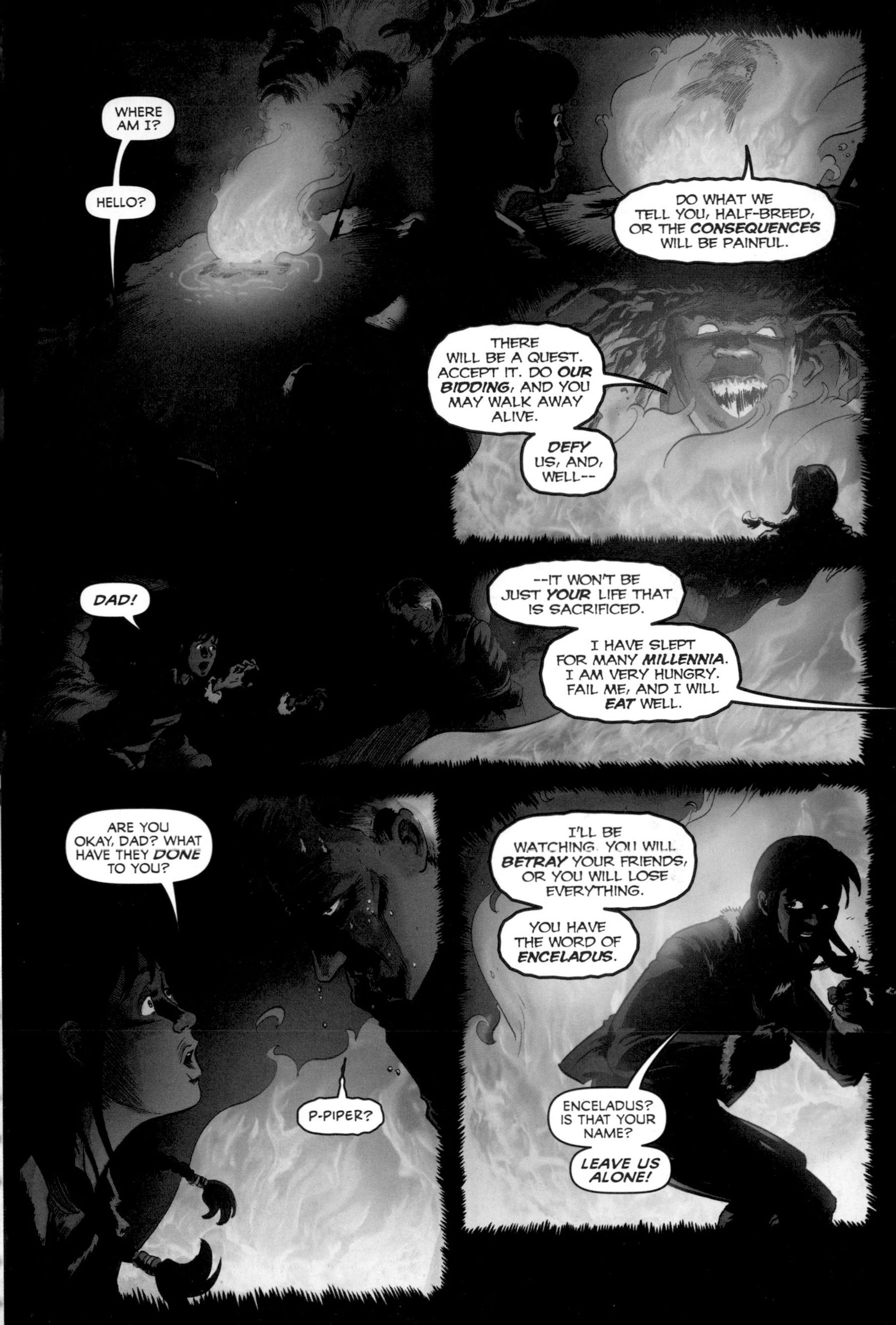
WHERE AM I?
HELLO?
DO WHAT WE TELL YOU, HALF-BREED, OR THE CONSEQUENCES WILL BE PAINFUL.
THERE WILL BE A QUEST. ACCEPT IT. DO OUR BIDDING, AND YOU MAY WALK AWAY ALIVE.
DEFY US, AND, WELL--
DAD!
--IT WON'T BE JUST YOUR LIFE THAT IS SACRIFICED.
I HAVE SLEPT FOR MANY MILLENNIA. I AM VERY HUNGRY. FAIL ME, AND I WILL EAT WELL.
ARE YOU OKAY, DAD? WHAT HAVE THEY DONE TO YOU?
P-PIPER?
I'LL BE WATCHING. YOU WILL BETRAY YOUR FRIENDS, OR YOU WILL LOSE EVERYTHING.
YOU HAVE THE WORD OF ENCELADUS.
ENCELADUS? IS THAT YOUR NAME?
LEAVE US ALONE!

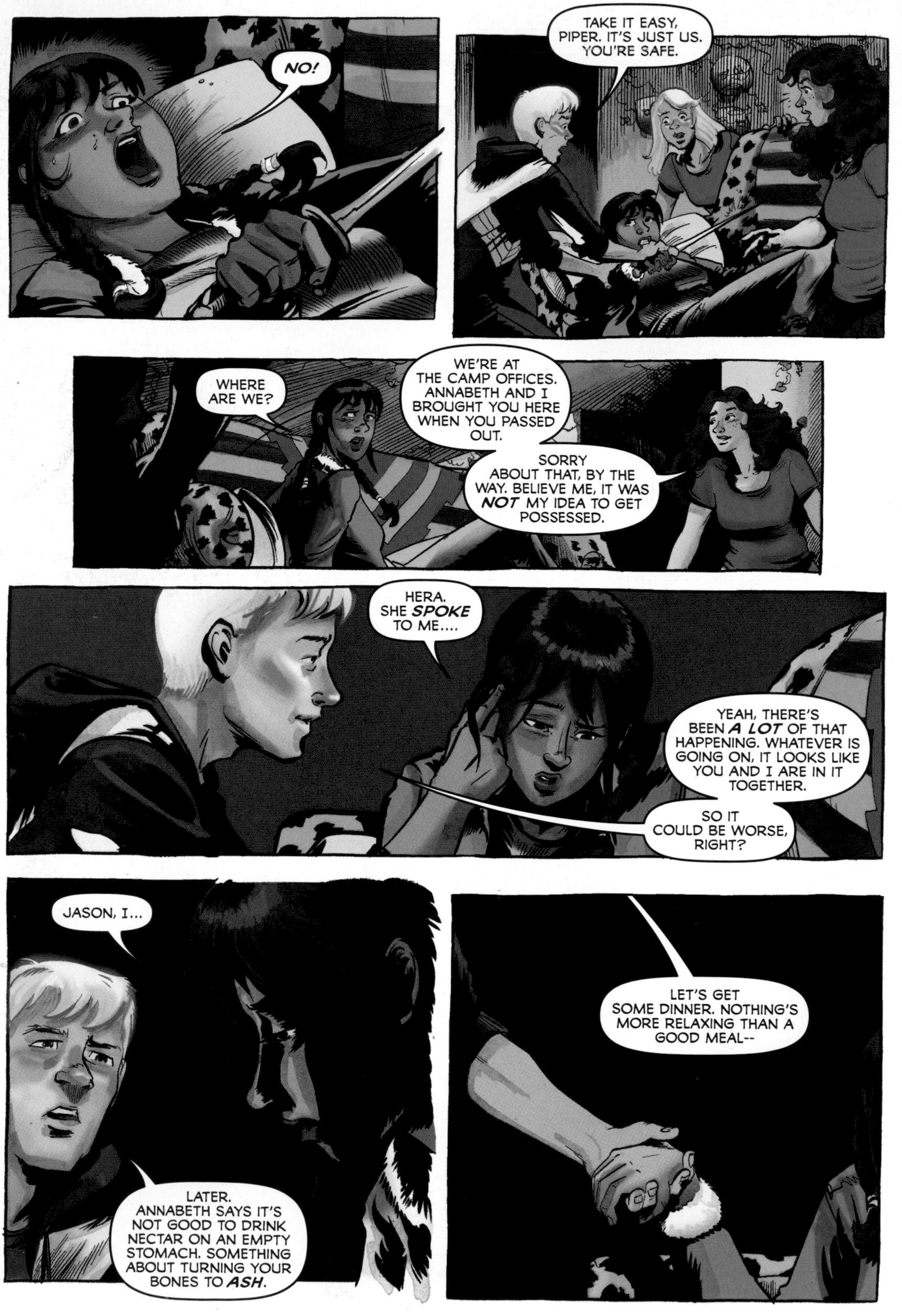
NO!
TAKE IT EASY, PIPER. IT'S JUST US. YOU'RE SAFE.
WHERE ARE WE?
WE'RE AT THE CAMP OFFICES. ANNABETH AND I BROUGHT YOU HERE WHEN YOU PASSED OUT.
SORRY ABOUT THAT, BY THE WAY. BELIEVE ME, IT WAS NOT MY IDEA TO GET POSSESSED.
HERA. SHE SPOKE TO ME....
YEAH, THERE'S BEEN A LOT OF THAT HAPPENING. WHATEVER IS GOING ON, IT LOOKS LIKE YOU AND I ARE IN IT TOGETHER.
SO IT COULD BE WORSE, RIGHT?
JASON, I...
LATER. ANNABETH SAYS IT'S NOT GOOD TO DRINK NECTAR ON AN EMPTY STOMACH. SOMETHING ABOUT TURNING YOUR BONES TO ASH.
LET'S GET SOME DINNER. NOTHING'S MORE RELAXING THAN A GOOD MEAL--

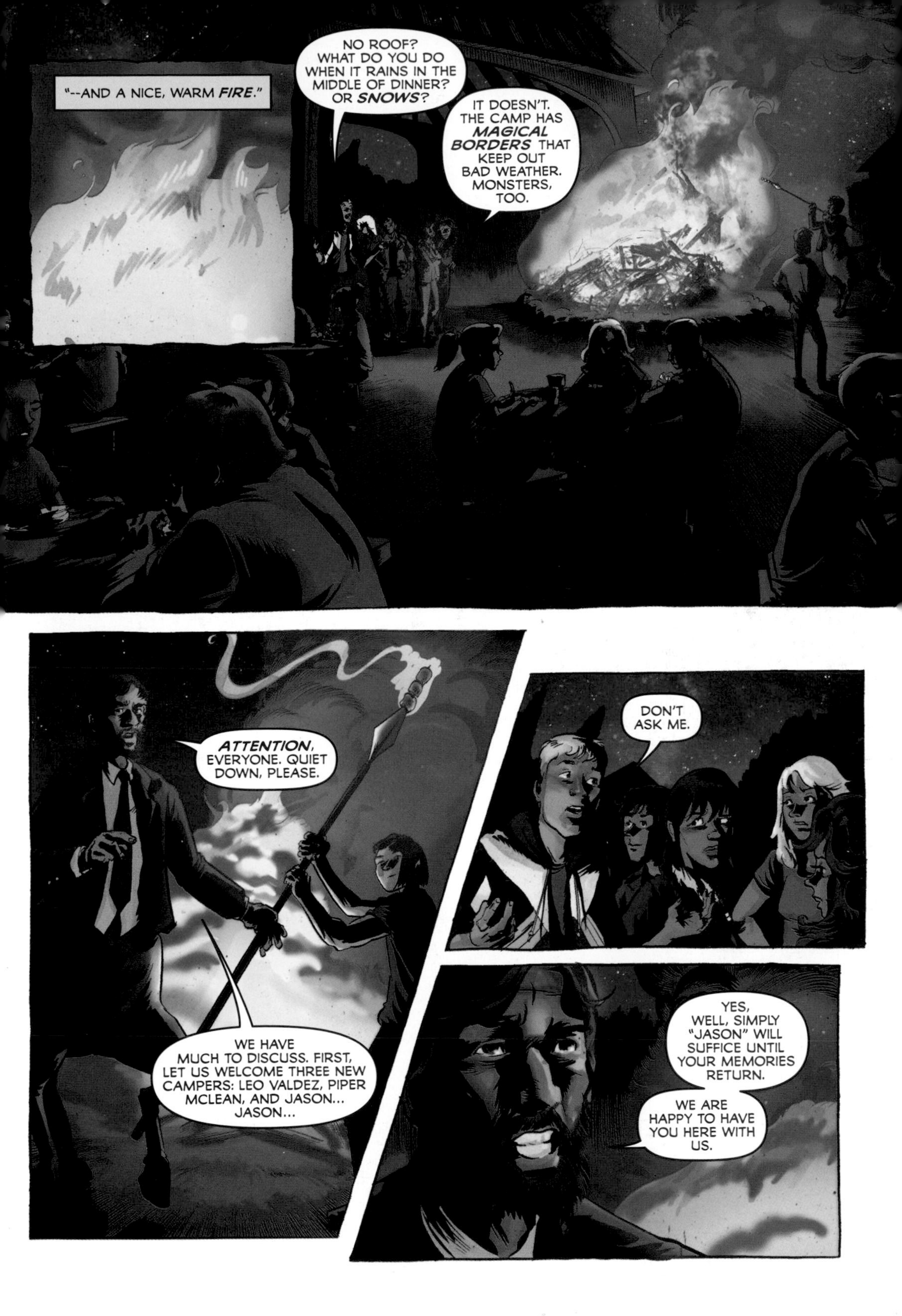
"--AND A NICE, WARM FIRE."
NO ROOF? WHAT DO YOU DO WHEN IT RAINS IN THE MIDDLE OF DINNER? OR SNOWS?
IT DOESN'T. THE CAMP HAS MAGICAL BORDERS THAT KEEP OUT BAD WEATHER. MONSTERS, TOO.
ATTENTION, EVERYONE. QUIET DOWN, PLEASE.
WE HAVE MUCH TO DISCUSS. FIRST, LET US WELCOME THREE NEW CAMPERS: LEO VALDEZ, PIPER MCLEAN, AND JASON... JASON...
DON'T ASK ME.
YES, WELL, SIMPLY "JASON" WILL SUFFICE UNTIL YOUR MEMORIES RETURN.
WE ARE HAPPY TO HAVE YOU HERE WITH US.

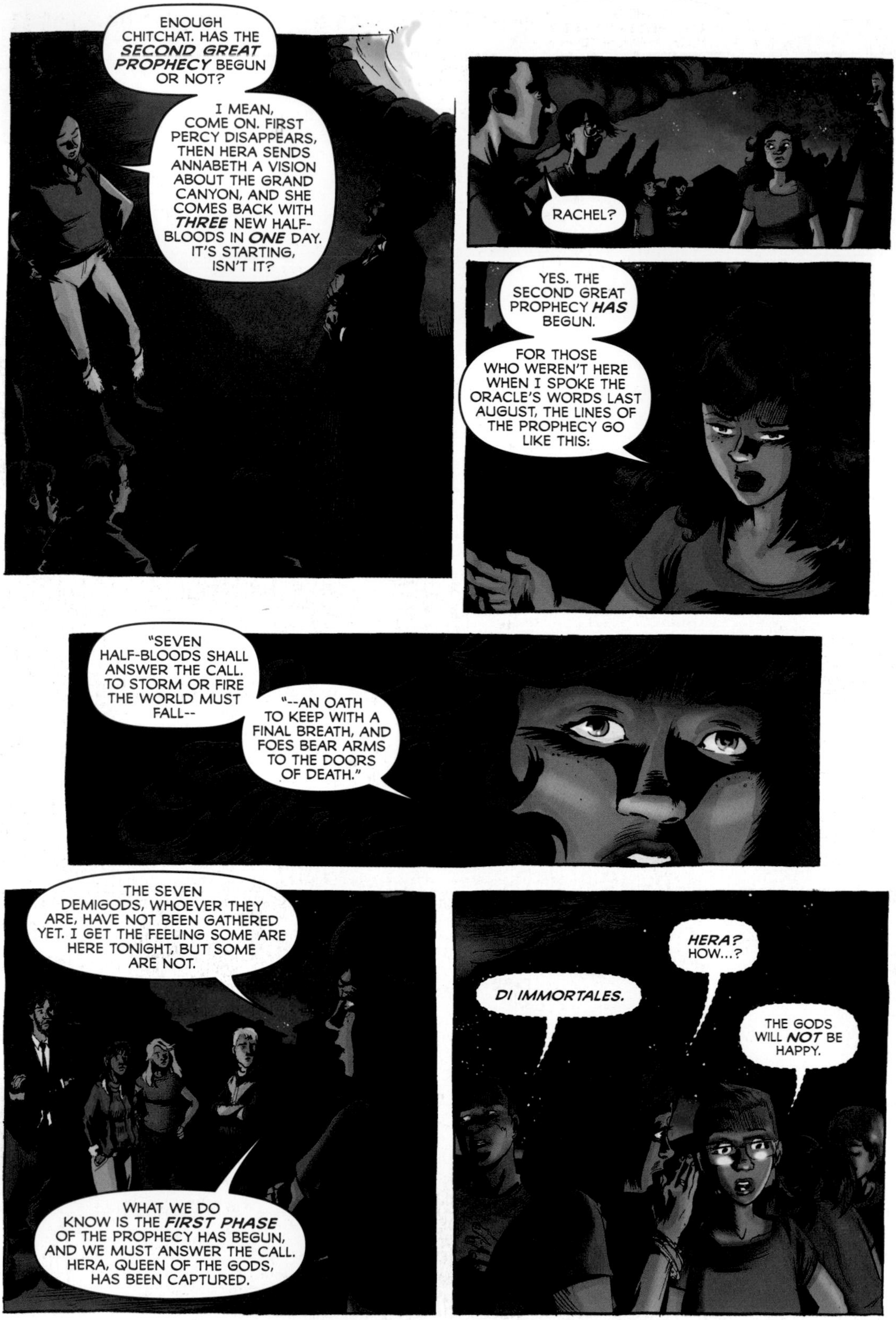
ENOUGH CHITCHAT. HAS THE SECOND GREAT PROPHECY BEGUN OR NOT?
I MEAN, COME ON. FIRST PERCY DISAPPEARS, THEN HERA SENDS ANNABETH A VISION ABOUT THE GRAND CANYON, AND SHE COMES BACK WITH THREE NEW HALF-BLOODS IN ONE DAY. IT'S STARTING, ISN'T IT?
RACHEL?
YES. THE SECOND GREAT PROPHECY HAS BEGUN.
FOR THOSE WHO WEREN'T HERE WHEN I SPOKE THE ORACLE'S WORDS LAST AUGUST, THE LINES OF THE PROPHECY GO LIKE THIS:
"SEVEN HALF-BLOODS SHALL ANSWER THE CALL. TO STORM OR FIRE THE WORLD MUST FALL--
"--AN OATH TO KEEP WITH A FINAL BREATH, AND FOES BEAR ARMS TO THE DOORS OF DEATH."
THE SEVEN DEMIGODS, WHOEVER THEY ARE, HAVE NOT BEEN GATHERED YET. I GET THE FEELING SOME ARE HERE TONIGHT, BUT SOME ARE NOT.
WHAT WE DO KNOW IS THE FIRST PHASE OF THE PROPHECY HAS BEGUN, AND WE MUST ANSWER THE CALL. HERA, QUEEN OF THE GODS, HAS BEEN CAPTURED.
HERA? HOW...?
DI IMMORTALES.
THE GODS WILL NOT BE HAPPY.

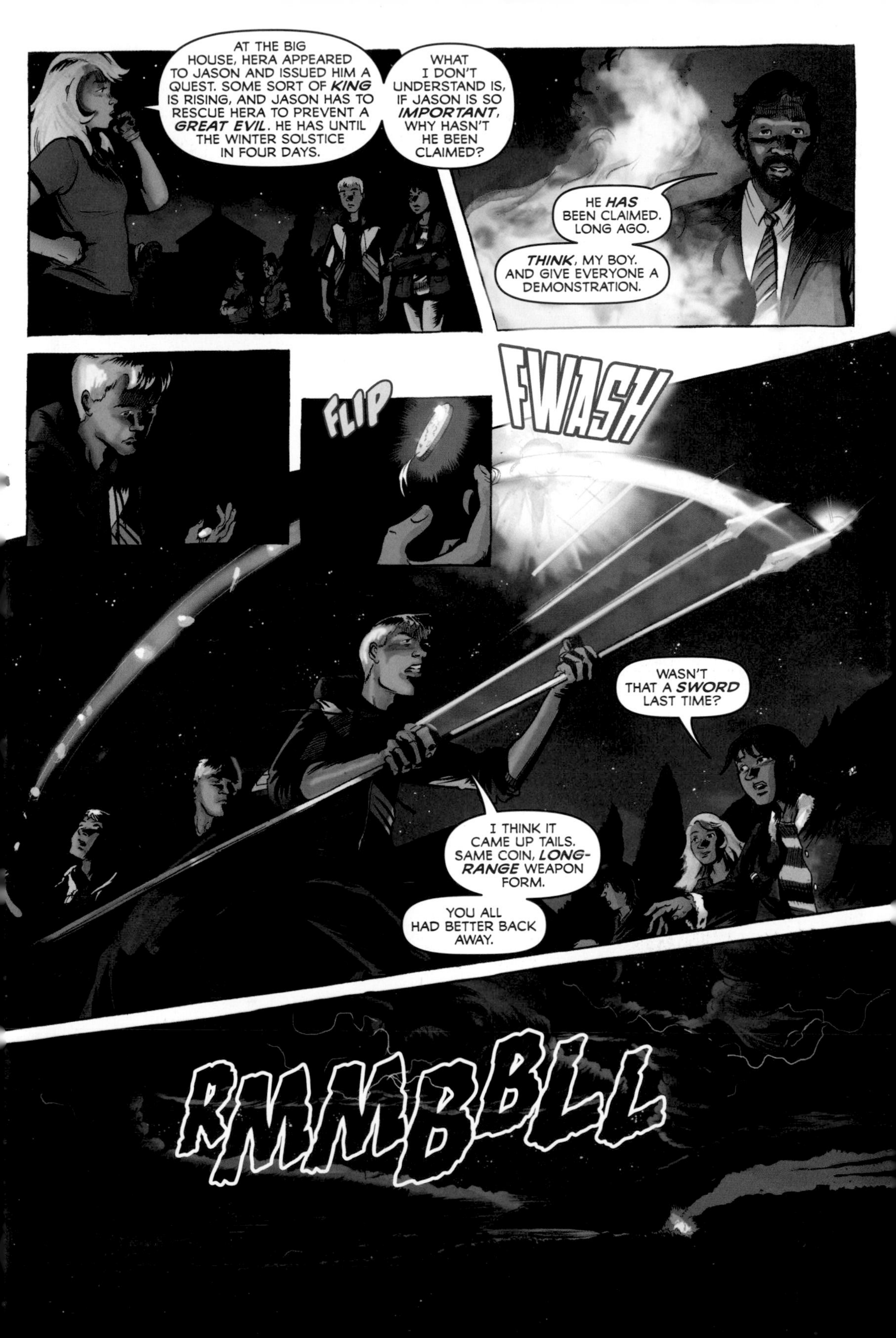

AT THE BIG HOUSE, HERA APPEARED TO JASON AND ISSUED HIM A QUEST. SOME SORT OF *KING* IS RISING, AND JASON HAS TO RESCUE HERA TO PREVENT A *GREAT EVIL*. HE HAS UNTIL THE WINTER SOLSTICE IN FOUR DAYS.
WHAT I DON'T UNDERSTAND IS, IF JASON IS SO *IMPORTANT*, WHY HASN'T HE BEEN CLAIMED?
HE *HAS* BEEN CLAIMED. LONG AGO.
THINK, MY BOY. AND GIVE EVERYONE A DEMONSTRATION.
FLIP
FWASH
WASN'T THAT A *SWORD* LAST TIME?
I THINK IT CAME UP TAILS. SAME COIN, *LONG-RANGE* WEAPON FORM.
YOU ALL HAD BETTER BACK AWAY.
RMMBLL

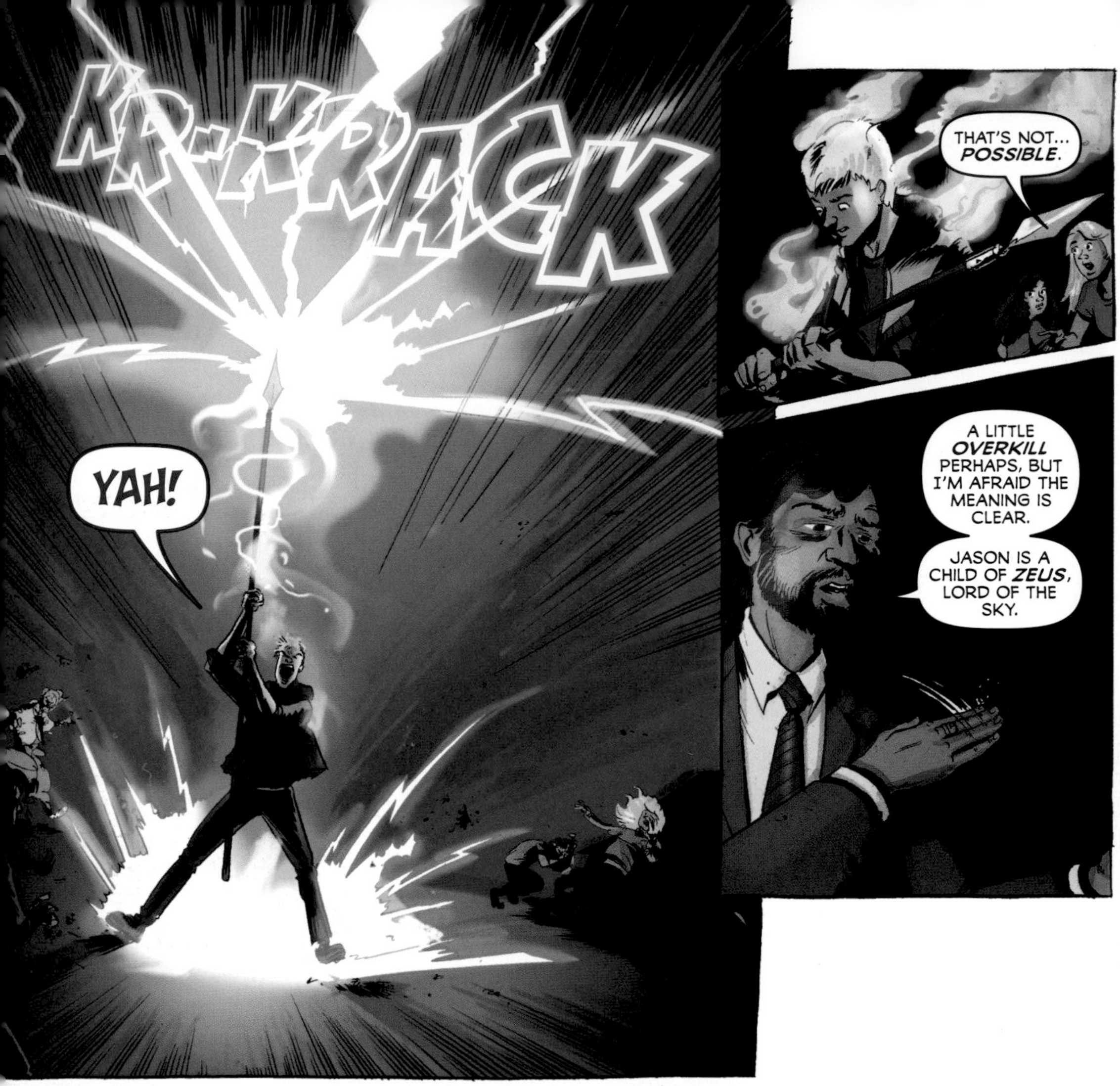
KR-KRACK
YAH!
THAT'S NOT... POSSIBLE.
A LITTLE OVERKILL PERHAPS, BUT I'M AFRAID THE MEANING IS CLEAR.
JASON IS A CHILD OF ZEUS, LORD OF THE SKY.

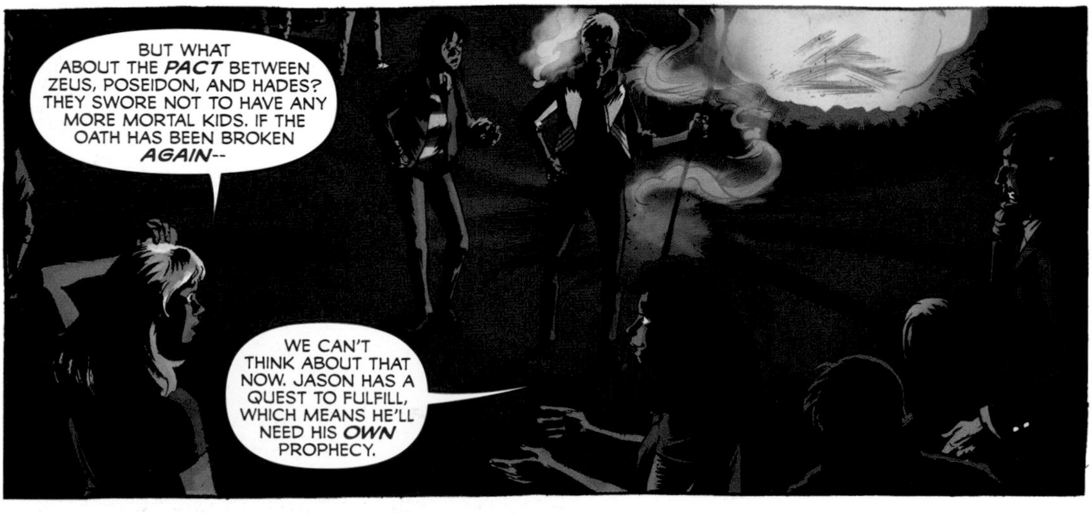
BUT WHAT ABOUT THE PACT BETWEEN ZEUS, POSEIDON, AND HADES? THEY SWORE NOT TO HAVE ANY MORE MORTAL KIDS. IF THE OATH HAS BEEN BROKEN AGAIN--
WE CAN'T THINK ABOUT THAT NOW. JASON HAS A QUEST TO FULFILL, WHICH MEANS HE'LL NEED HIS OWN PROPHECY.

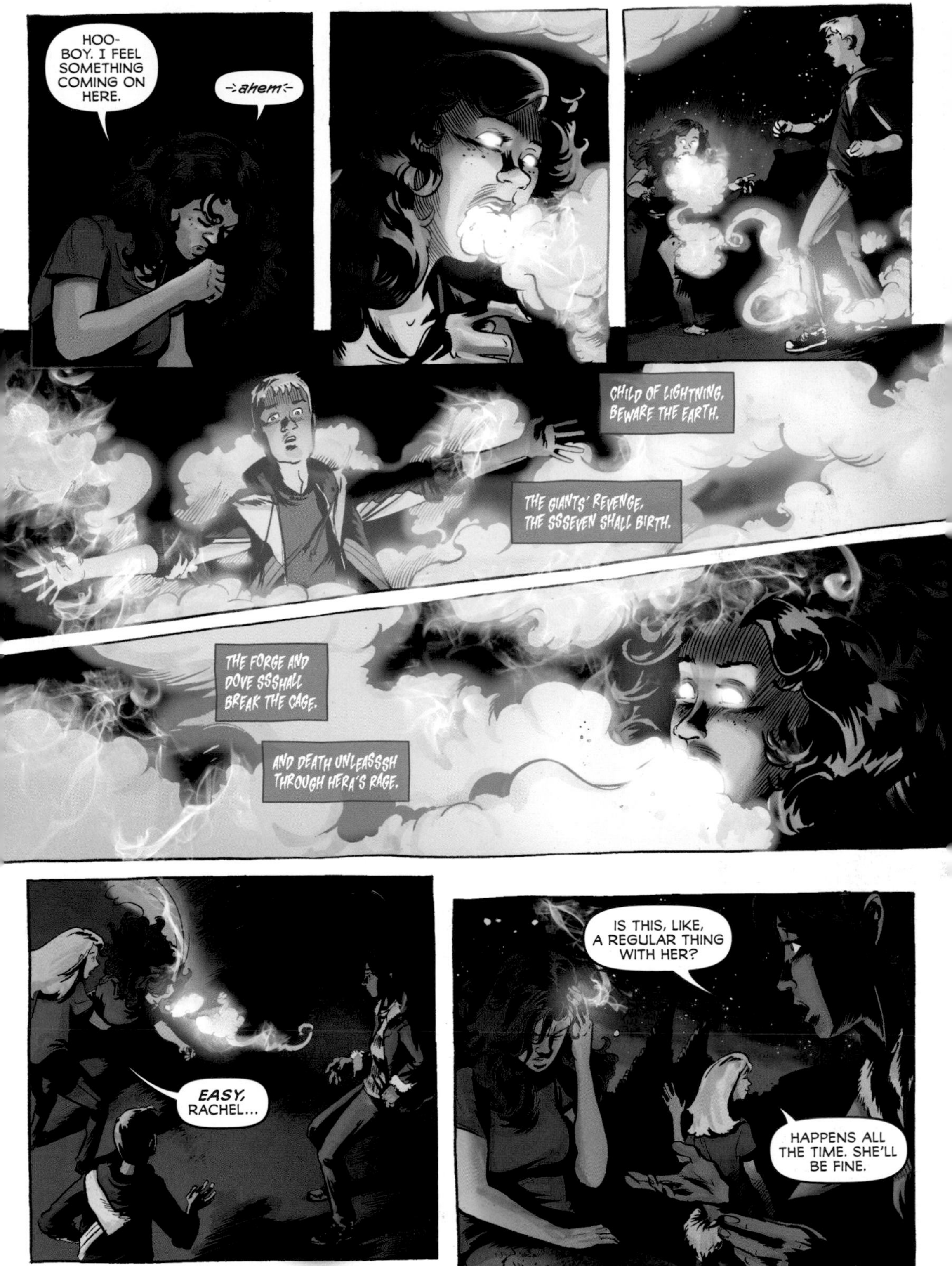

HOO-BOY. I FEEL SOMETHING COMING ON HERE.
-ahem-
CHILD OF LIGHTNING, BEWARE THE EARTH.
THE GIANTS' REVENGE, THE SSSEVEN SHALL BIRTH.
THE FORGE AND DOVE SSSHALL BREAK THE CAGE.
AND DEATH UNLEASSSH THROUGH HERA'S RAGE.
EASY, RACHEL...
IS THIS, LIKE, A REGULAR THING WITH HER?
HAPPENS ALL THE TIME. SHE'LL BE FINE.

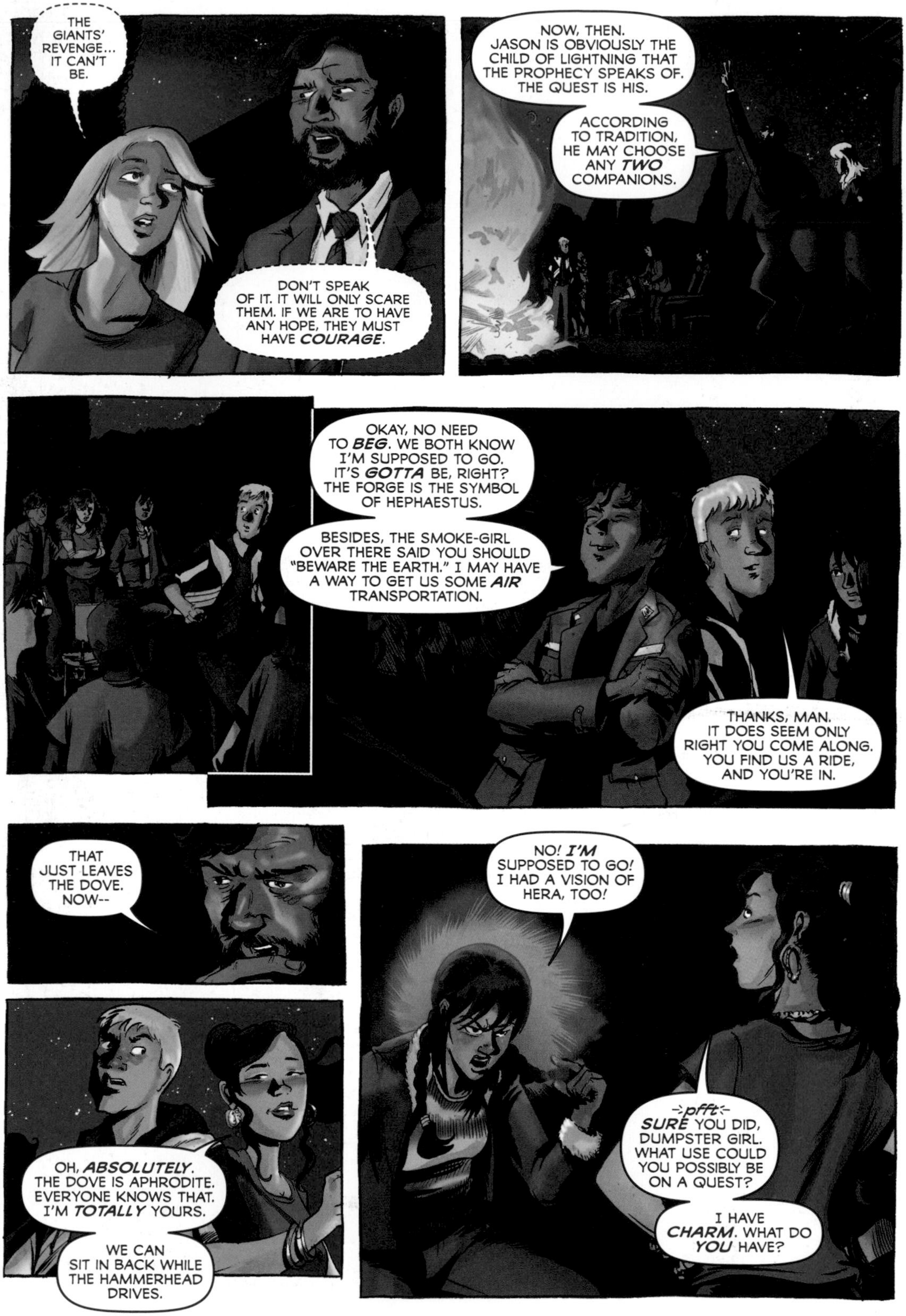
THE GIANTS' REVENGE... IT CAN'T BE.
DON'T SPEAK OF IT. IT WILL ONLY SCARE THEM. IF WE ARE TO HAVE ANY HOPE, THEY MUST HAVE COURAGE.
NOW, THEN. JASON IS OBVIOUSLY THE CHILD OF LIGHTNING THAT THE PROPHECY SPEAKS OF. THE QUEST IS HIS.
ACCORDING TO TRADITION, HE MAY CHOOSE ANY TWO COMPANIONS.
OKAY, NO NEED TO BEG. WE BOTH KNOW I'M SUPPOSED TO GO. IT'S GOTTA BE, RIGHT? THE FORGE IS THE SYMBOL OF HEPHAESTUS.
BESIDES, THE SMOKE-GIRL OVER THERE SAID YOU SHOULD "BEWARE THE EARTH." I MAY HAVE A WAY TO GET US SOME AIR TRANSPORTATION.
THANKS, MAN. IT DOES SEEM ONLY RIGHT YOU COME ALONG. YOU FIND US A RIDE, AND YOU'RE IN.
THAT JUST LEAVES THE DOVE. NOW--
OH, ABSOLUTELY. THE DOVE IS APHRODITE. EVERYONE KNOWS THAT. I'M TOTALLY YOURS.
WE CAN SIT IN BACK WHILE THE HAMMERHEAD DRIVES.
NO! I'M SUPPOSED TO GO! I HAD A VISION OF HERA, TOO!
-pfft- SURE YOU DID, DUMPSTER GIRL. WHAT USE COULD YOU POSSIBLY BE ON A QUEST?
I HAVE CHARM. WHAT DO YOU HAVE?

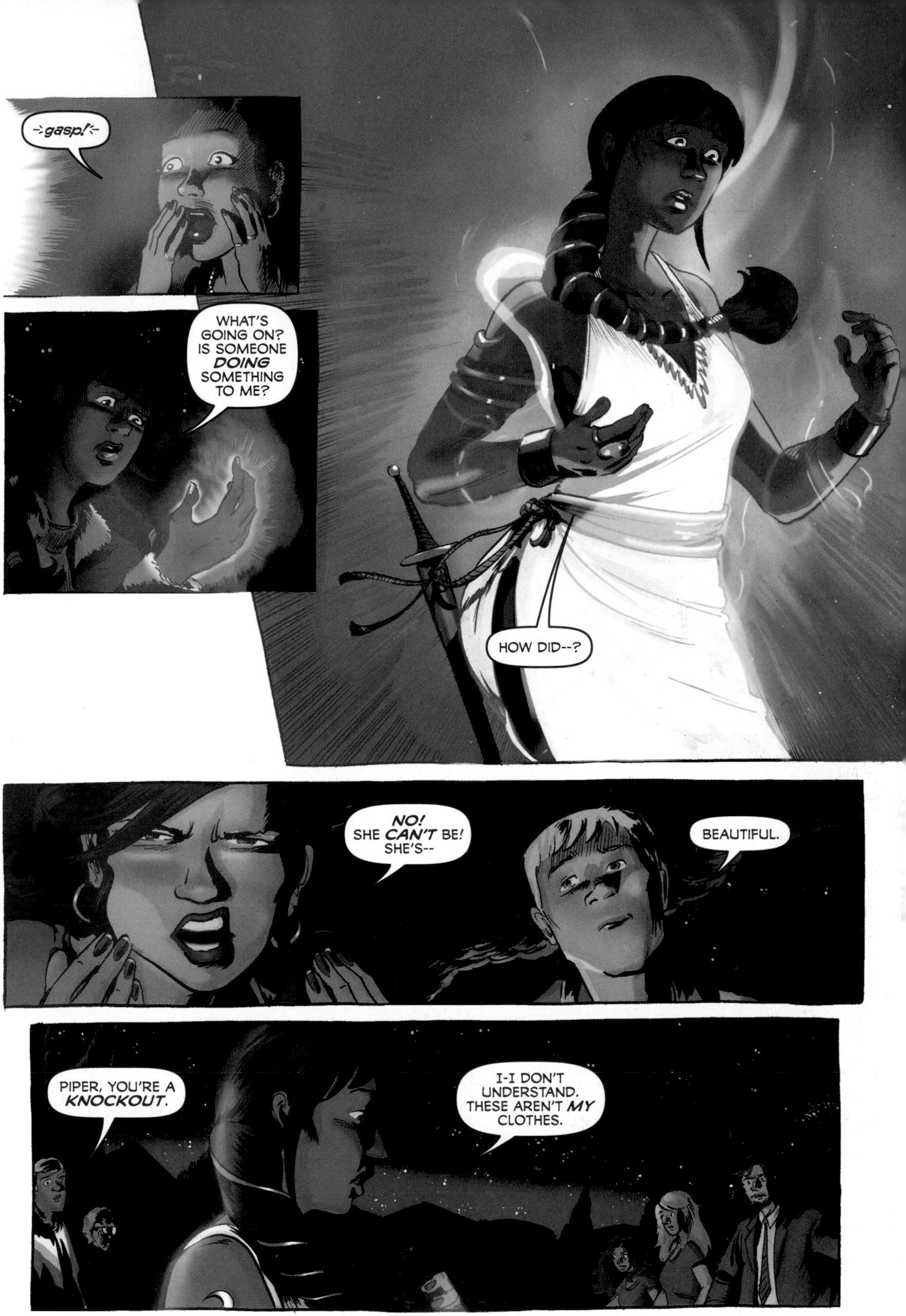
-gasp!-
WHAT'S GOING ON? IS SOMEONE *DOING* SOMETHING TO ME?
HOW DID--?
NO! SHE *CAN'T* BE! SHE'S--
BEAUTIFUL.
PIPER, YOU'RE A *KNOCKOUT*.
I-I DON'T UNDERSTAND. THESE AREN'T *MY* CLOTHES.

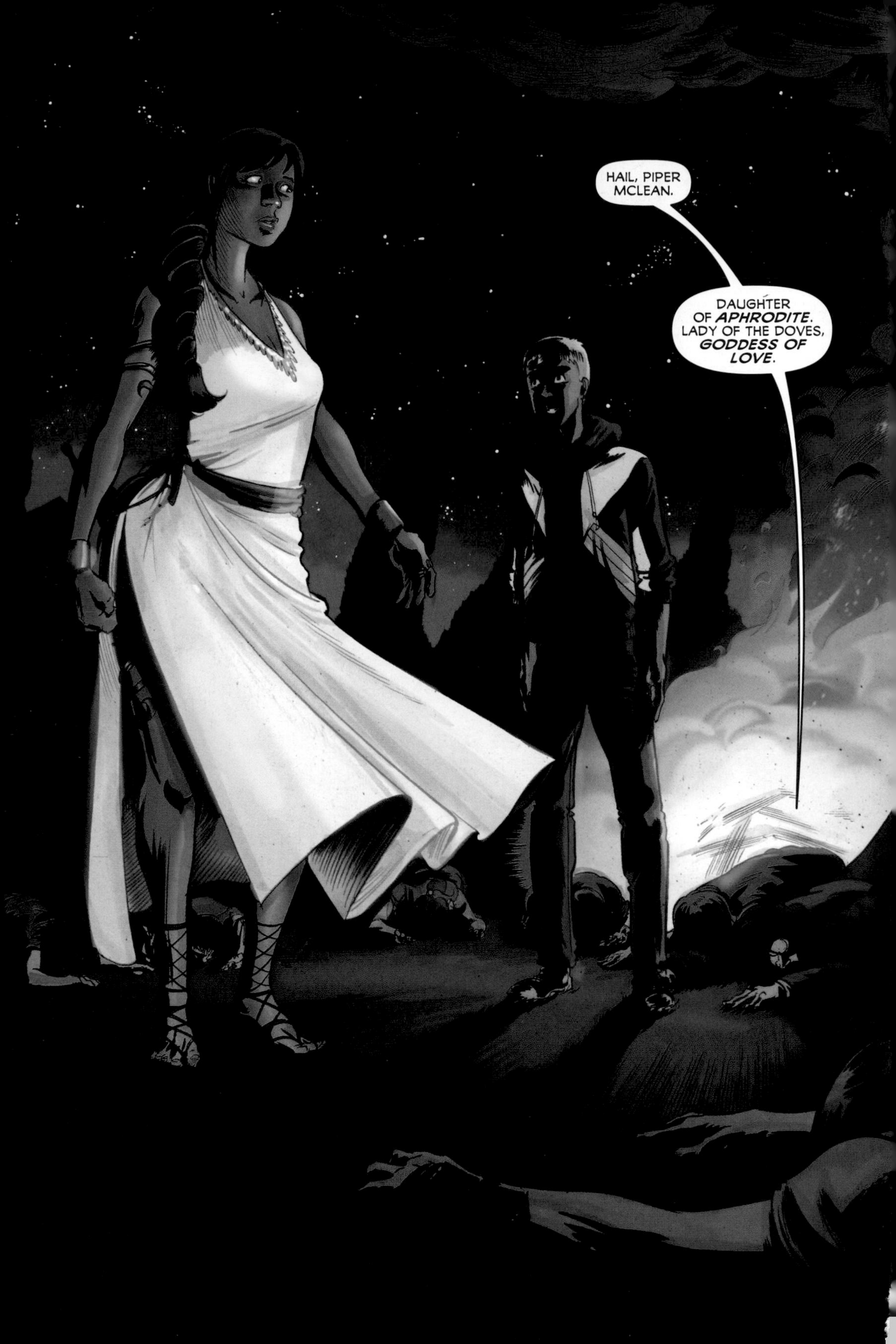
HAIL, PIPER MCLEAN.
DAUGHTER OF *APHRODITE*. LADY OF THE DOVES, *GODDESS OF LOVE*.

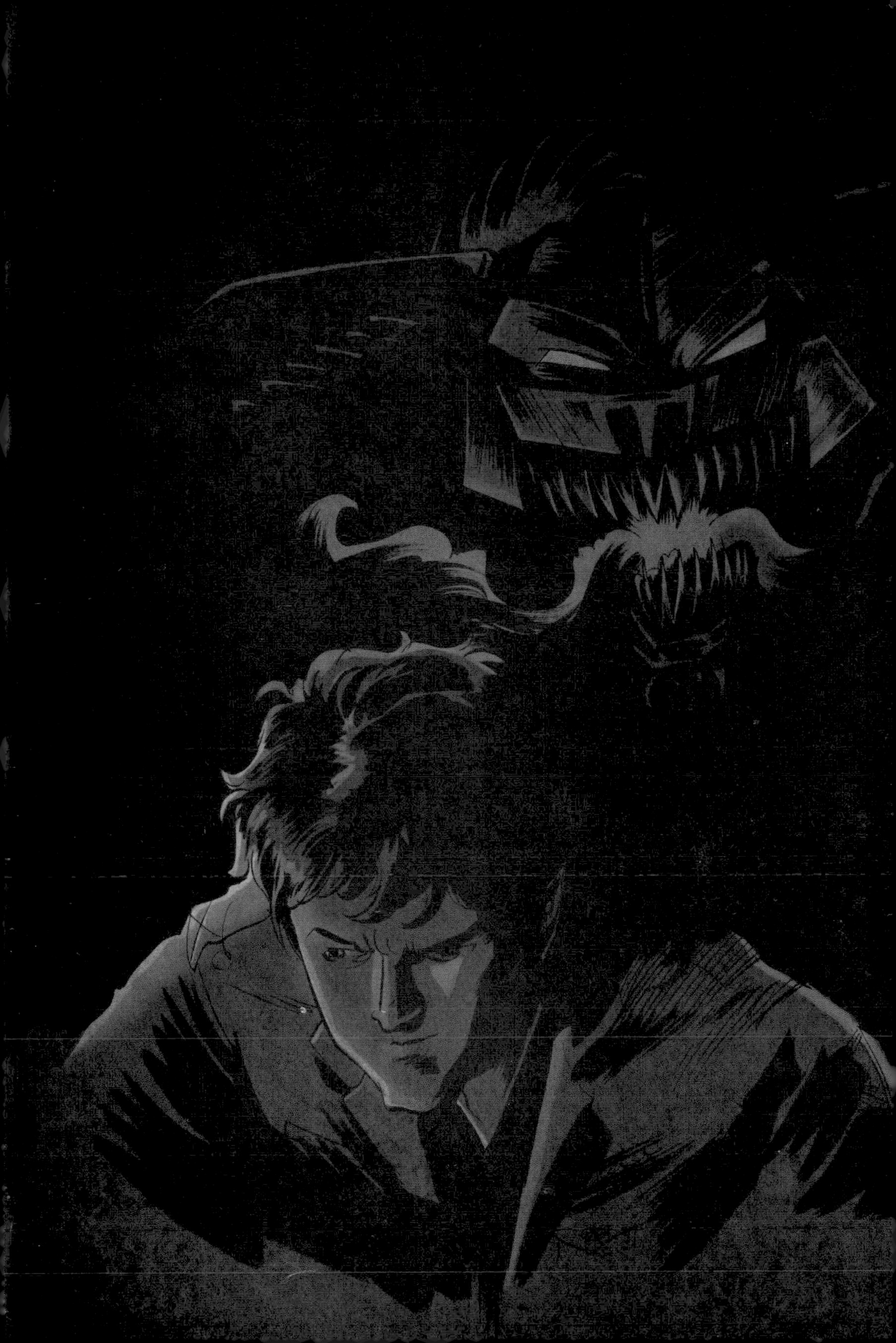

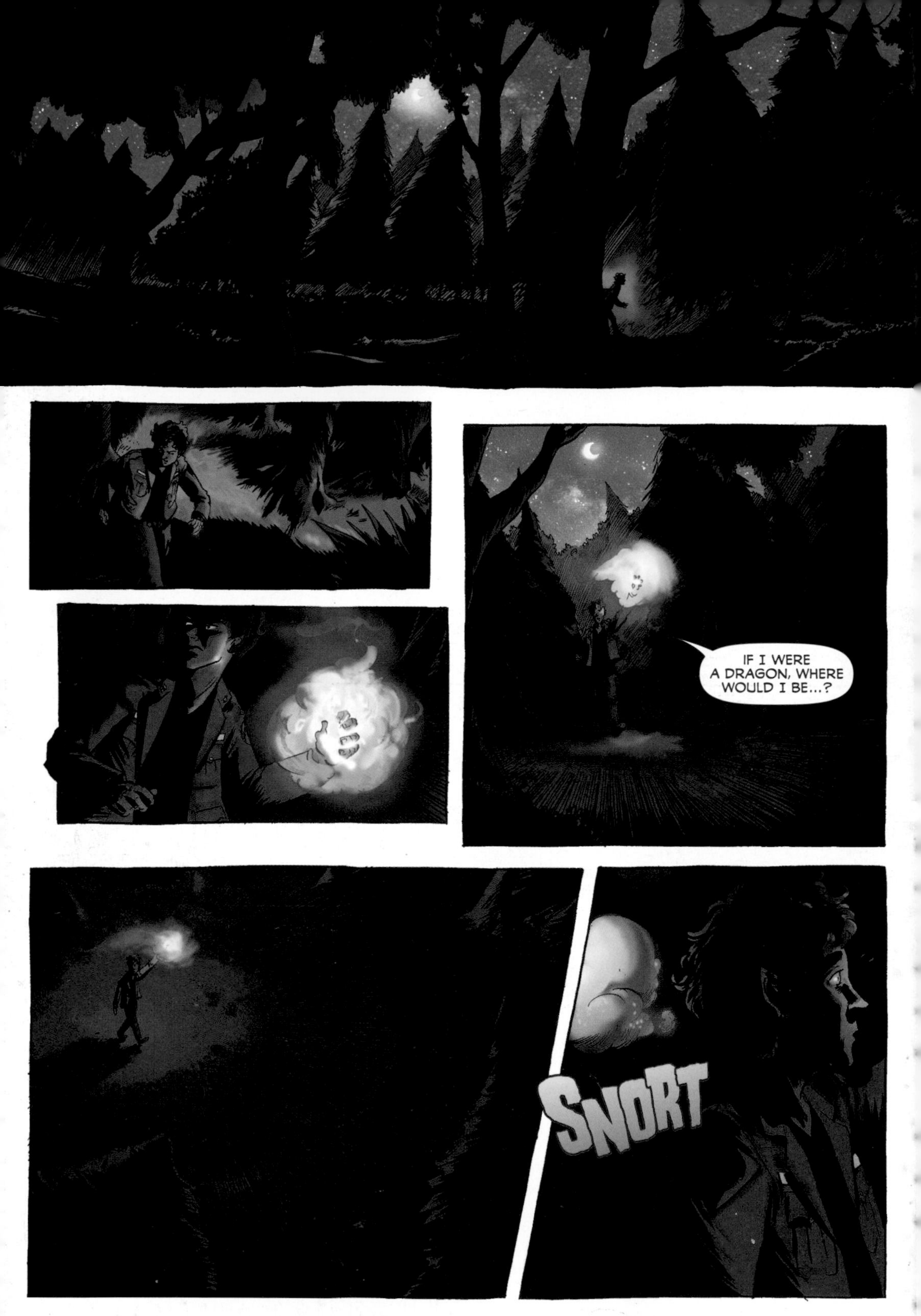
IF I WERE A DRAGON, WHERE WOULD I BE...?
SNORT

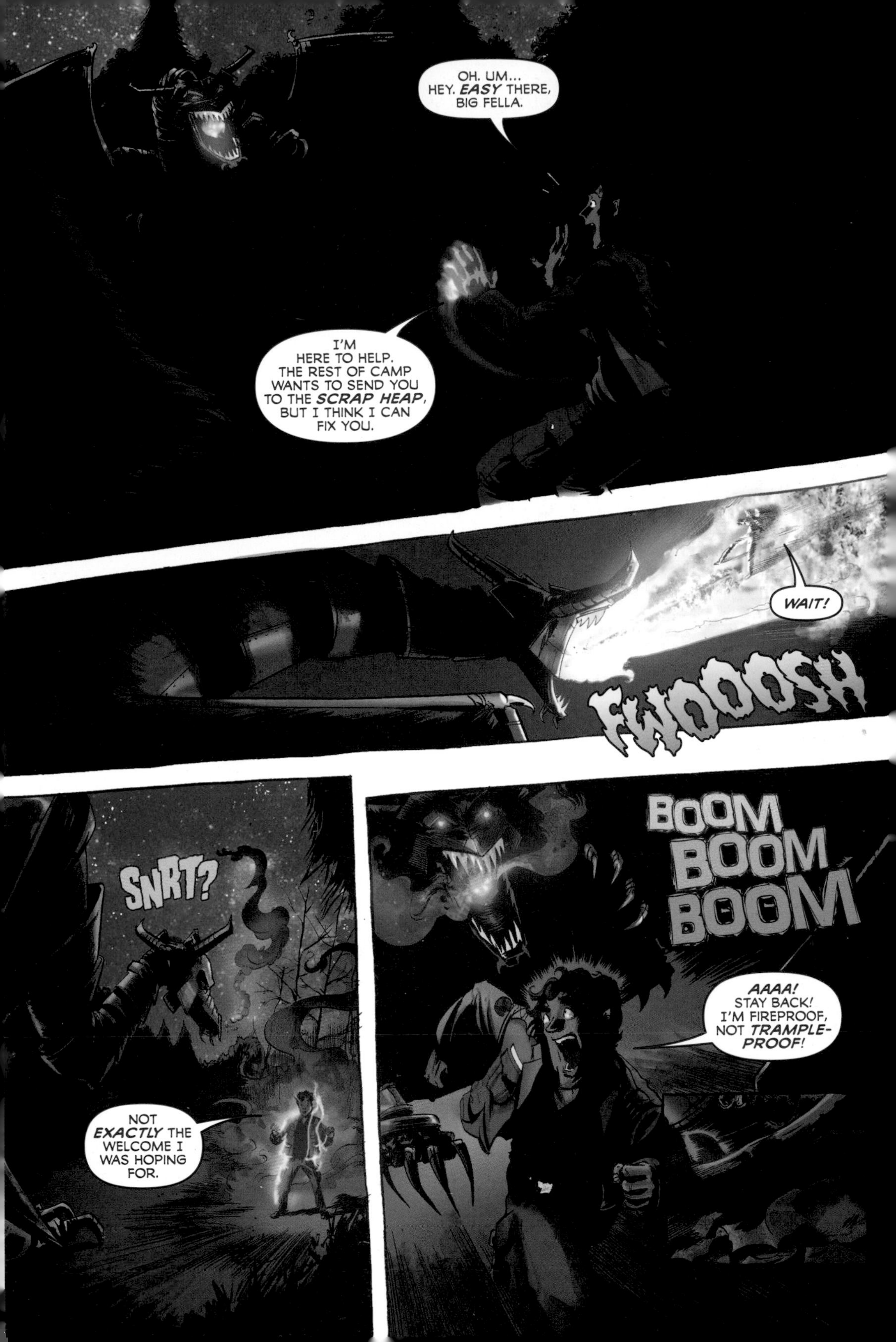
OH. UM... HEY. EASY THERE, BIG FELLA.
I'M HERE TO HELP. THE REST OF CAMP WANTS TO SEND YOU TO THE SCRAP HEAP, BUT I THINK I CAN FIX YOU.
WAIT!
FWOOOSH
SNRT?
NOT EXACTLY THE WELCOME I WAS HOPING FOR.
BOOM BOOM BOOM
AAAA! STAY BACK! I'M FIREPROOF, NOT TRAMPLE-PROOF!

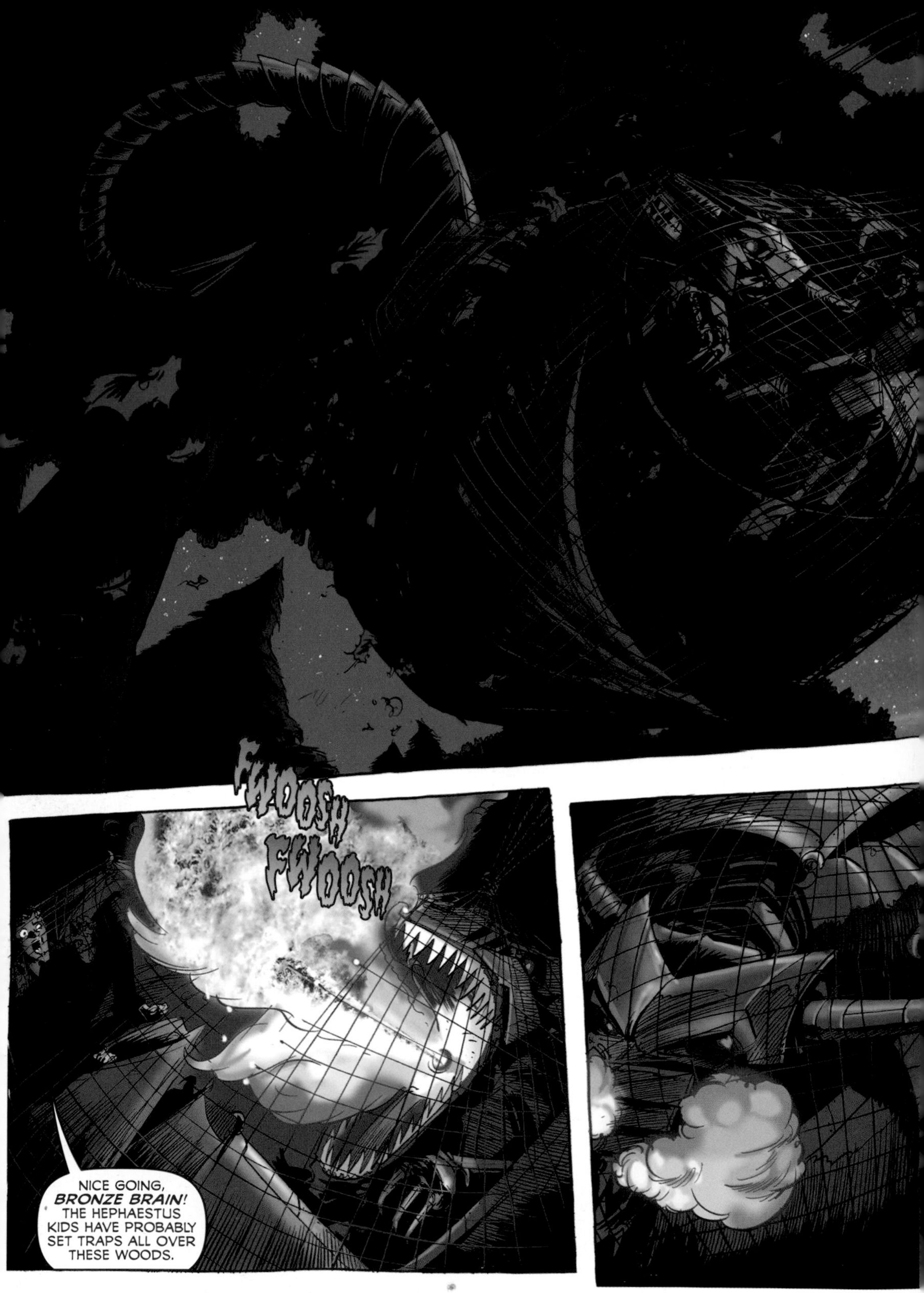
FWOOSH
FWOOSH
NICE GOING, BRONZE BRAIN! THE HEPHAESTUS KIDS HAVE PROBABLY SET TRAPS ALL OVER THESE WOODS.

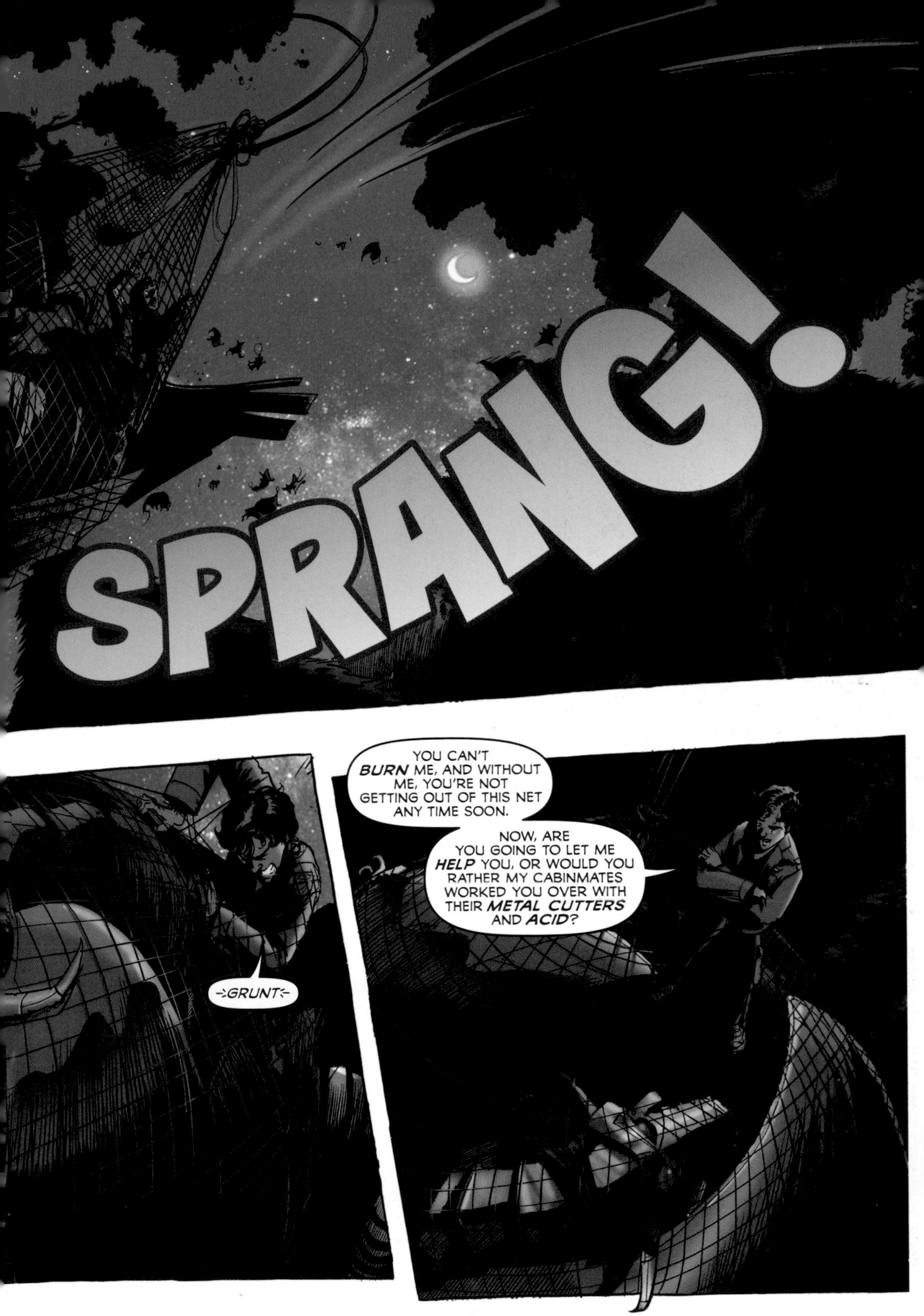
SPRANG!
-GRUNT-
YOU CAN'T BURN ME, AND WITHOUT ME, YOU'RE NOT GETTING OUT OF THIS NET ANY TIME SOON.
NOW, ARE YOU GOING TO LET ME HELP YOU, OR WOULD YOU RATHER MY CABINMATES WORKED YOU OVER WITH THEIR METAL CUTTERS AND ACID?

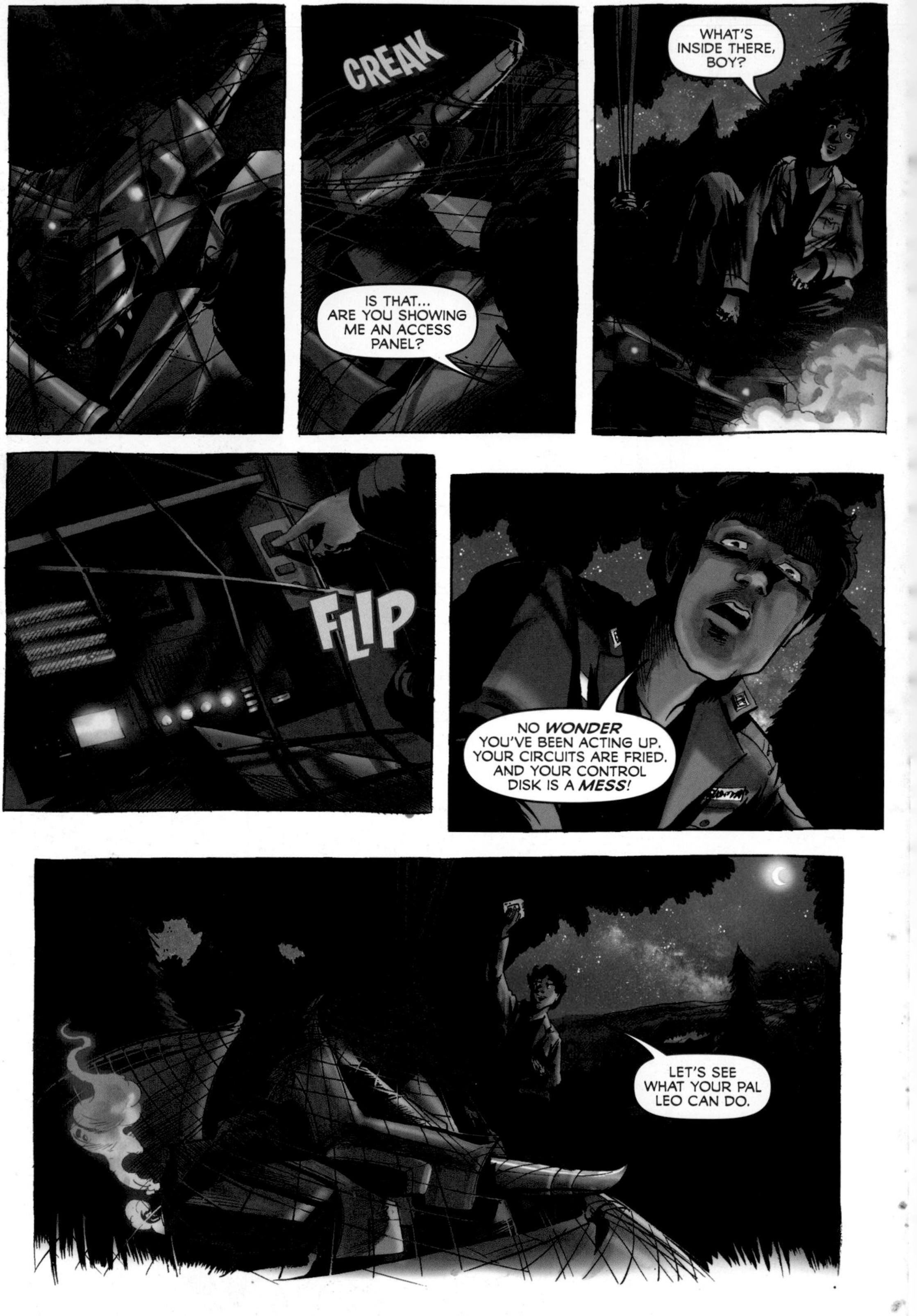
CREAK
IS THAT... ARE YOU SHOWING ME AN ACCESS PANEL?
WHAT'S INSIDE THERE, BOY?
FLIP
NO WONDER YOU'VE BEEN ACTING UP. YOUR CIRCUITS ARE FRIED. AND YOUR CONTROL DISK IS A MESS!
LET'S SEE WHAT YOUR PAL LEO CAN DO.

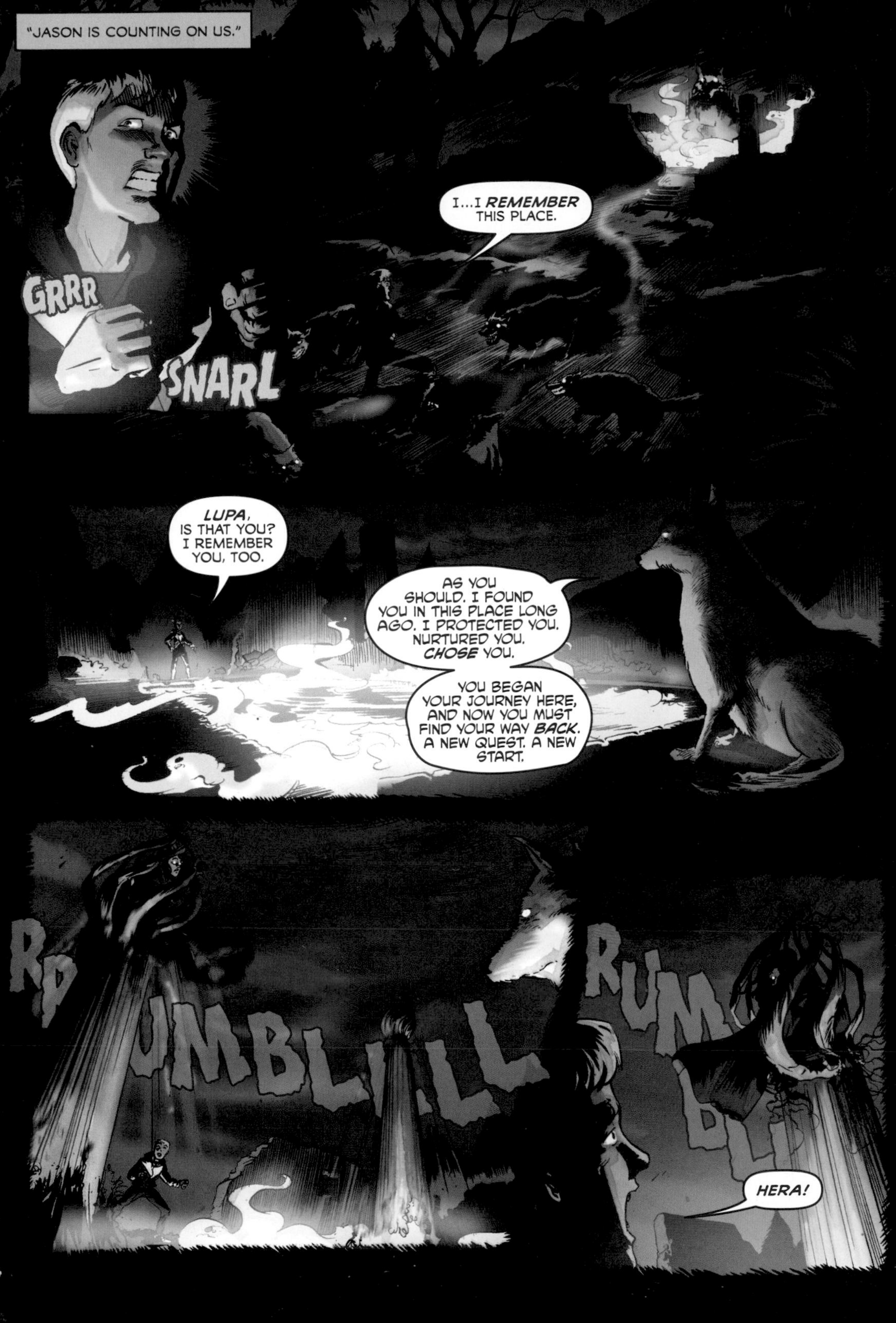
"JASON IS COUNTING ON US."
GRRR
SNARL
I...I REMEMBER THIS PLACE.
LUPA, IS THAT YOU? I REMEMBER YOU, TOO.
AS YOU SHOULD. I FOUND YOU IN THIS PLACE LONG AGO. I PROTECTED YOU. NURTURED YOU. CHOSE YOU.
YOU BEGAN YOUR JOURNEY HERE, AND NOW YOU MUST FIND YOUR WAY BACK. A NEW QUEST. A NEW START.
RUMBLLLL
RUMBLL
HERA!

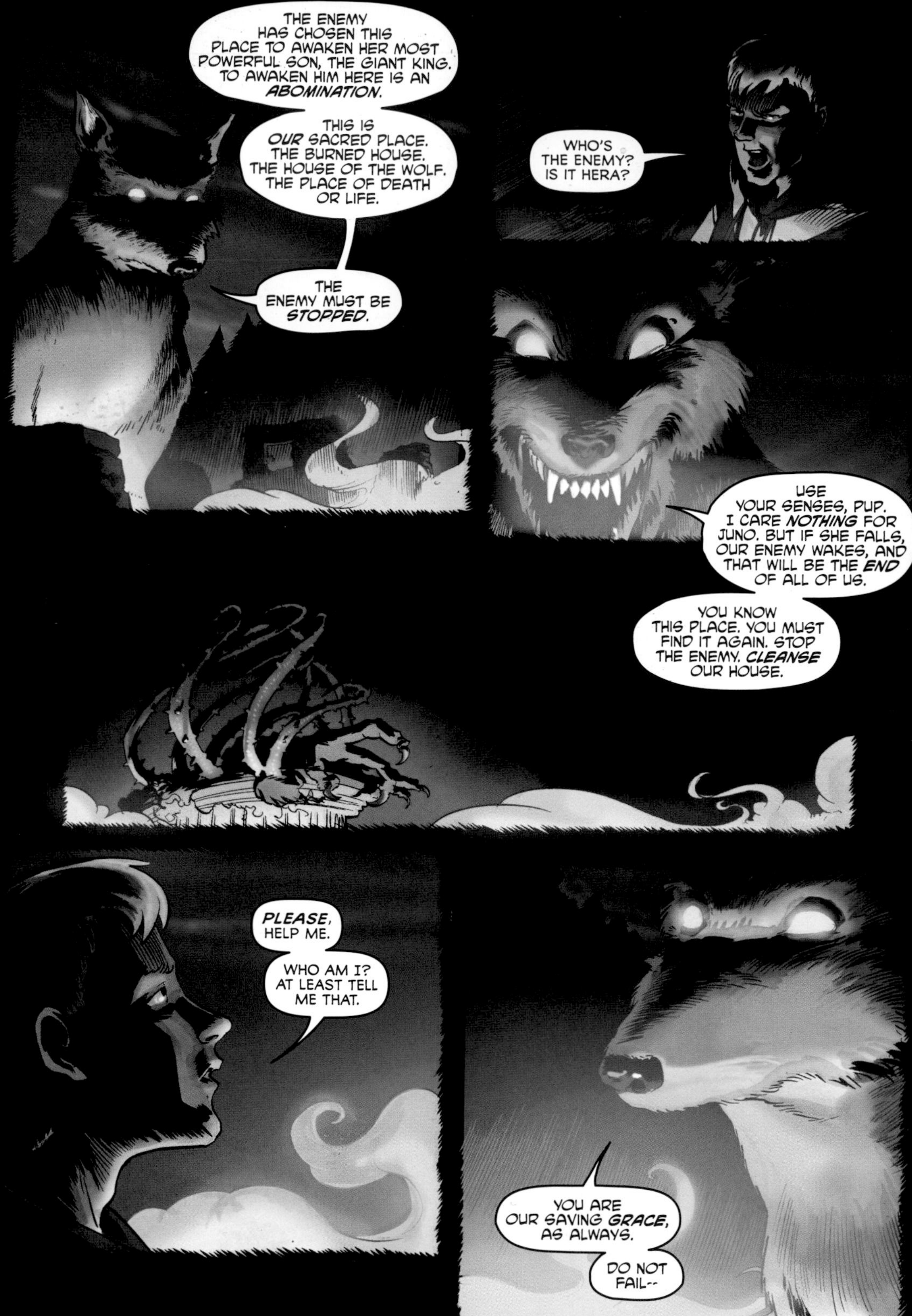
THE ENEMY HAS CHOSEN THIS PLACE TO AWAKEN HER MOST POWERFUL SON, THE GIANT KING. TO AWAKEN HIM HERE IS AN ABOMINATION.
THIS IS OUR SACRED PLACE. THE BURNED HOUSE. THE HOUSE OF THE WOLF. THE PLACE OF DEATH OR LIFE.
THE ENEMY MUST BE STOPPED.
WHO'S THE ENEMY? IS IT HERA?
USE YOUR SENSES, PUP. I CARE NOTHING FOR JUNO. BUT IF SHE FALLS, OUR ENEMY WAKES, AND THAT WILL BE THE END OF ALL OF US.
YOU KNOW THIS PLACE. YOU MUST FIND IT AGAIN. STOP THE ENEMY. CLEANSE OUR HOUSE.
PLEASE, HELP ME.
WHO AM I? AT LEAST TELL ME THAT.
YOU ARE OUR SAVING GRACE, AS ALWAYS.
DO NOT FAIL--

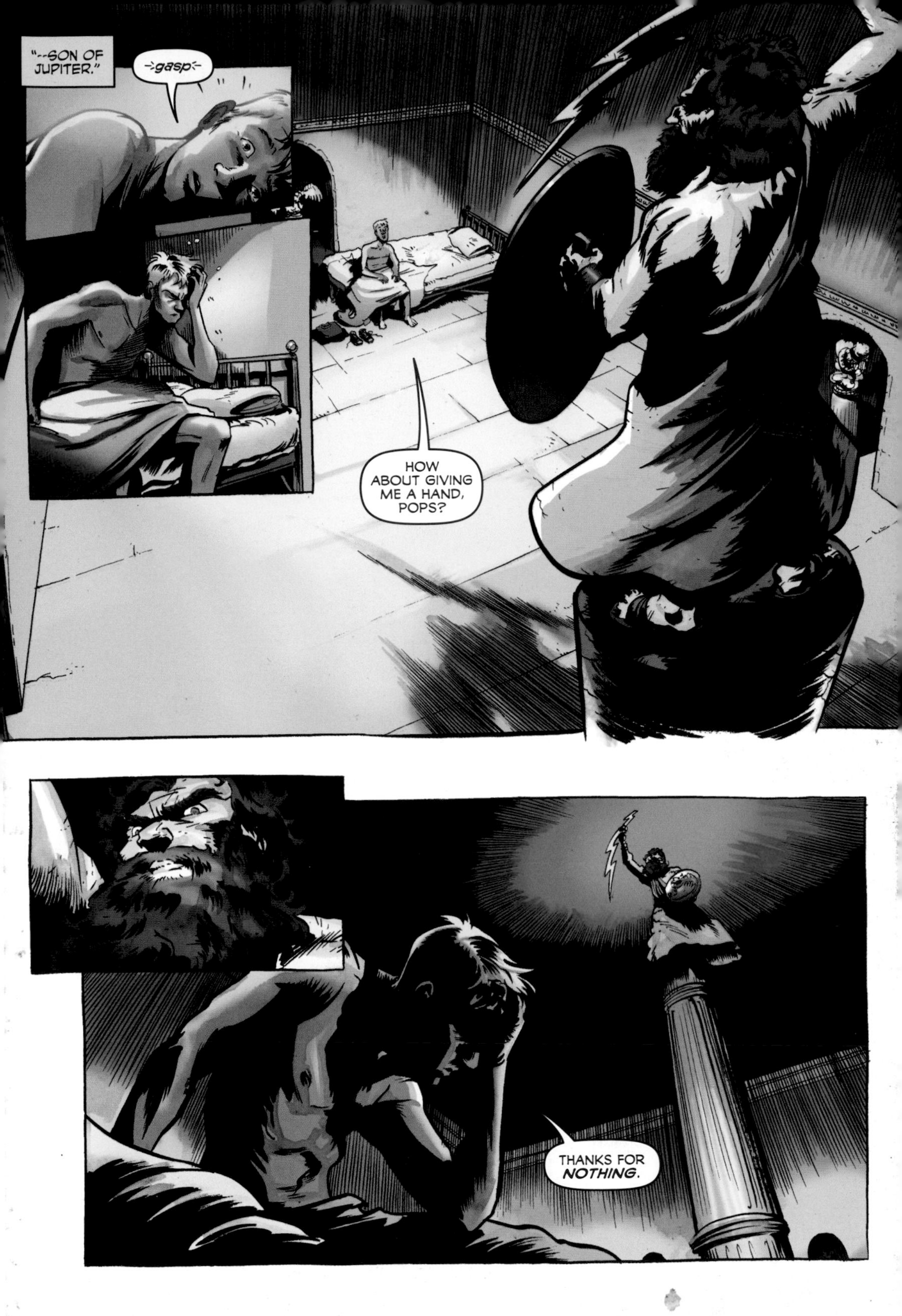
"--SON OF JUPITER."
-gasp-
HOW ABOUT GIVING ME A HAND, POPS?
THANKS FOR *NOTHING*.

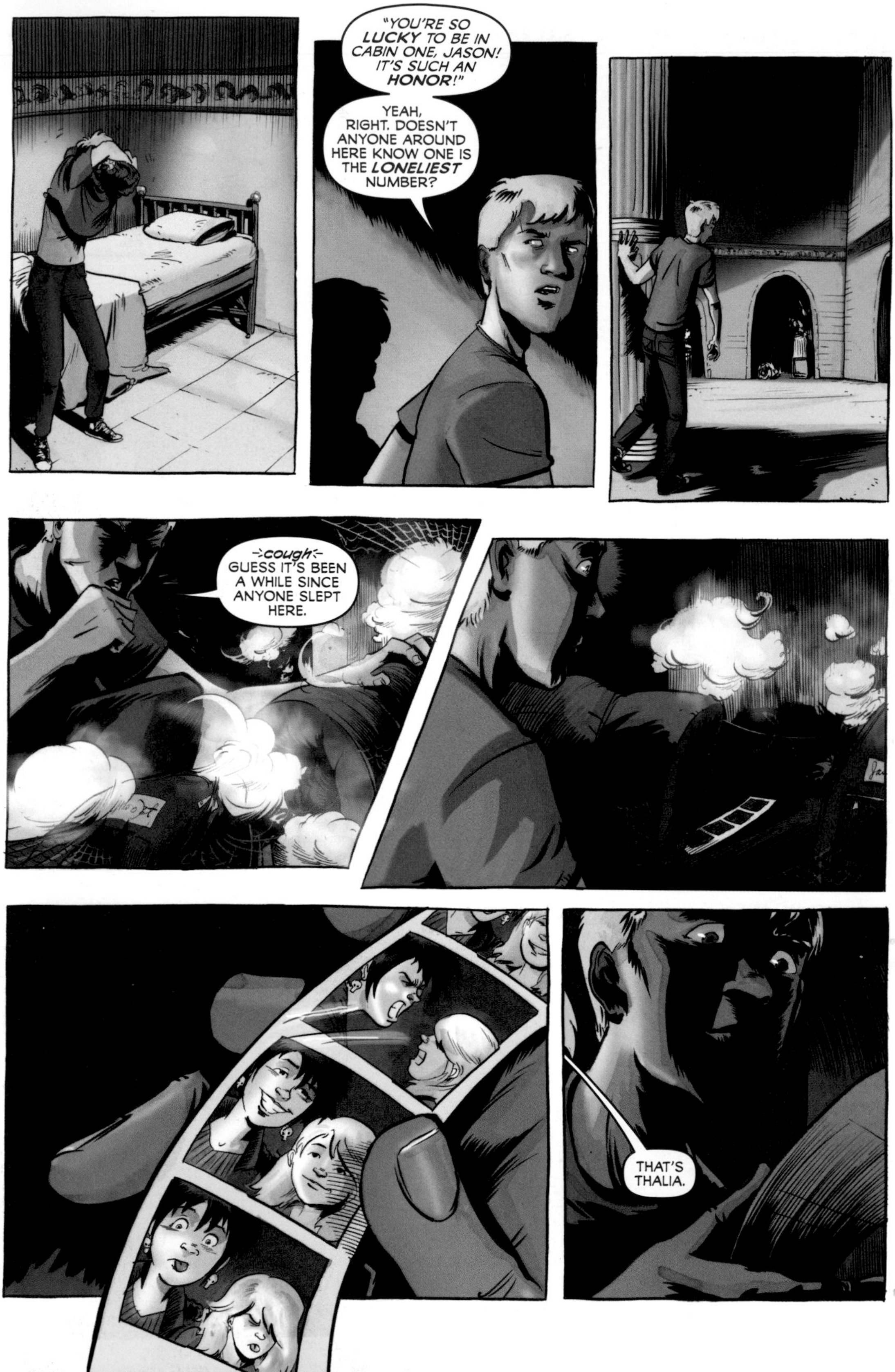
"YOU'RE SO LUCKY TO BE IN CABIN ONE, JASON! IT'S SUCH AN HONOR!"
YEAH, RIGHT. DOESN'T ANYONE AROUND HERE KNOW ONE IS THE LONELIEST NUMBER?
-cough- GUESS IT'S BEEN A WHILE SINCE ANYONE SLEPT HERE.
THAT'S THALIA.

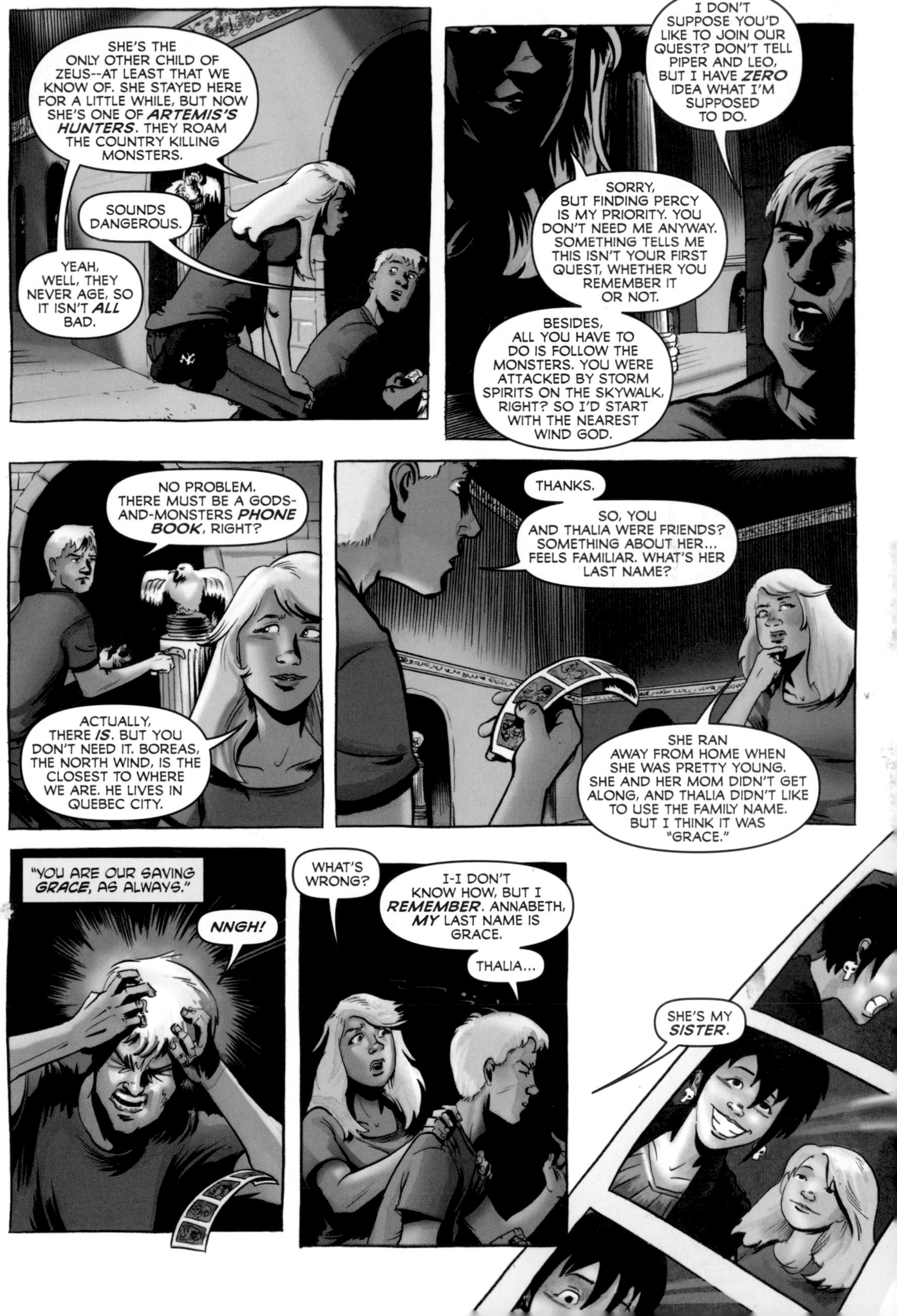
SHE'S THE ONLY OTHER CHILD OF ZEUS--AT LEAST THAT WE KNOW OF. SHE STAYED HERE FOR A LITTLE WHILE, BUT NOW SHE'S ONE OF ARTEMIS'S HUNTERS. THEY ROAM THE COUNTRY KILLING MONSTERS.
SOUNDS DANGEROUS.
YEAH, WELL, THEY NEVER AGE, SO IT ISN'T ALL BAD.
I DON'T SUPPOSE YOU'D LIKE TO JOIN OUR QUEST? DON'T TELL PIPER AND LEO, BUT I HAVE ZERO IDEA WHAT I'M SUPPOSED TO DO.
SORRY, BUT FINDING PERCY IS MY PRIORITY. YOU DON'T NEED ME ANYWAY. SOMETHING TELLS ME THIS ISN'T YOUR FIRST QUEST, WHETHER YOU REMEMBER IT OR NOT.
BESIDES, ALL YOU HAVE TO DO IS FOLLOW THE MONSTERS. YOU WERE ATTACKED BY STORM SPIRITS ON THE SKYWALK, RIGHT? SO I'D START WITH THE NEAREST WIND GOD.
NO PROBLEM. THERE MUST BE A GODS-AND-MONSTERS PHONE BOOK, RIGHT?
ACTUALLY, THERE IS. BUT YOU DON'T NEED IT. BOREAS, THE NORTH WIND, IS THE CLOSEST TO WHERE WE ARE. HE LIVES IN QUEBEC CITY.
THANKS.
SO, YOU AND THALIA WERE FRIENDS? SOMETHING ABOUT HER... FEELS FAMILIAR. WHAT'S HER LAST NAME?
SHE RAN AWAY FROM HOME WHEN SHE WAS PRETTY YOUNG. SHE AND HER MOM DIDN'T GET ALONG, AND THALIA DIDN'T LIKE TO USE THE FAMILY NAME. BUT I THINK IT WAS "GRACE."
"YOU ARE OUR SAVING GRACE, AS ALWAYS."
NNGH!
WHAT'S WRONG?
I-I DON'T KNOW HOW, BUT I REMEMBER. ANNABETH, MY LAST NAME IS GRACE.
THALIA...
SHE'S MY SISTER.

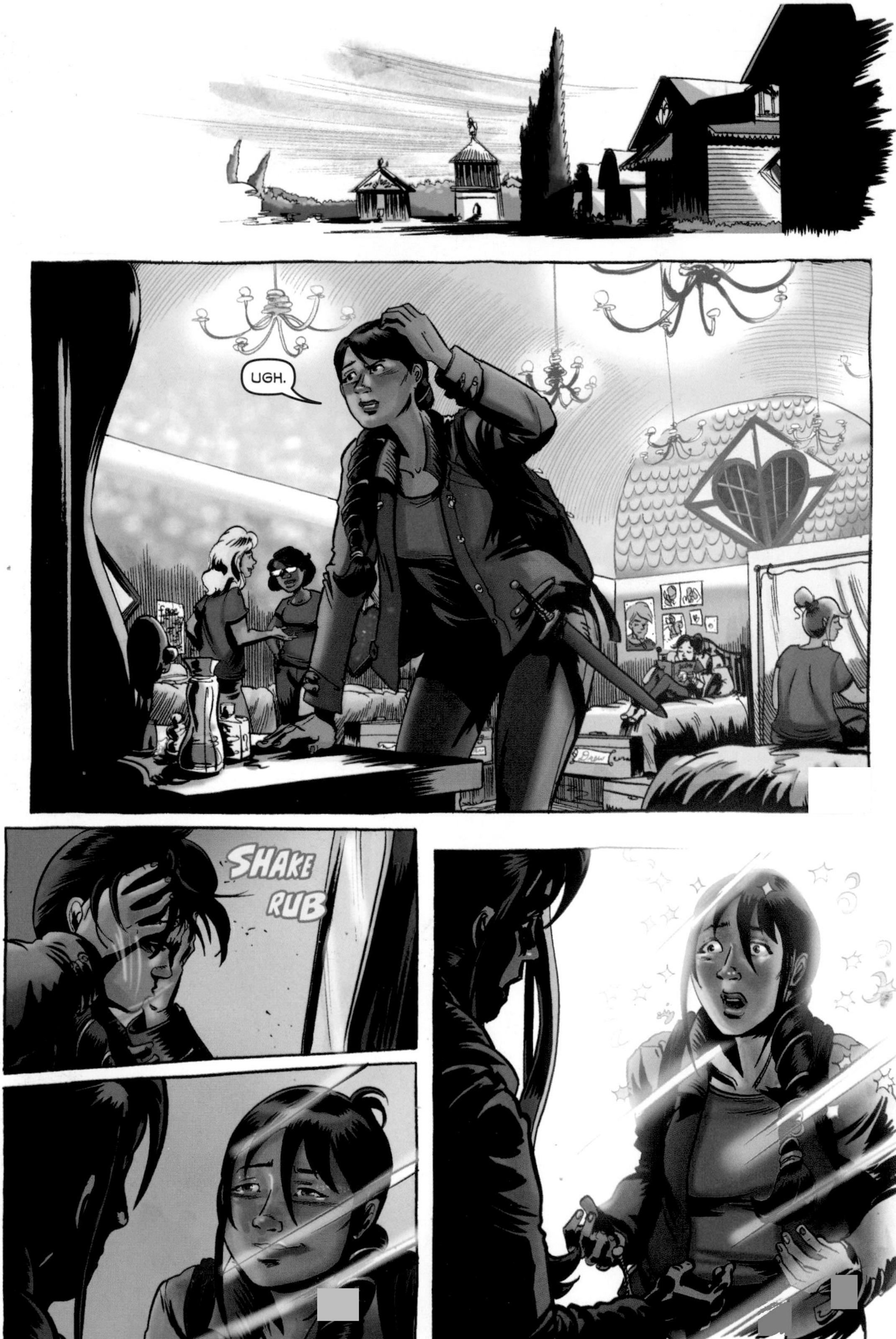
UGH.
SHAKE
RUB

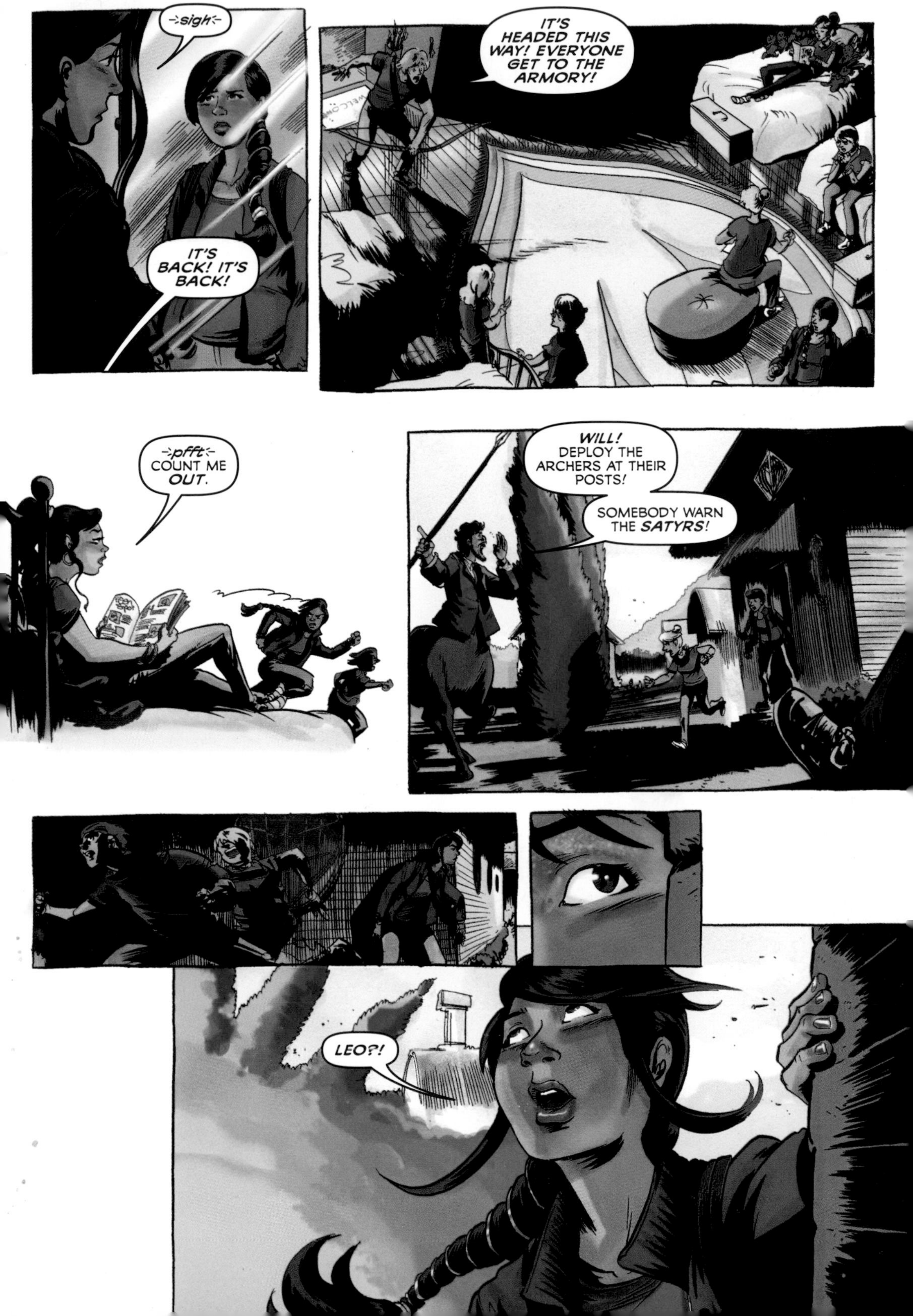

-sigh-
IT'S BACK! IT'S BACK!
IT'S HEADED THIS WAY! EVERYONE GET TO THE ARMORY!
-pfft- COUNT ME OUT.
WILL! DEPLOY THE ARCHERS AT THEIR POSTS!
SOMEBODY WARN THE SATYRS!
LEO?!

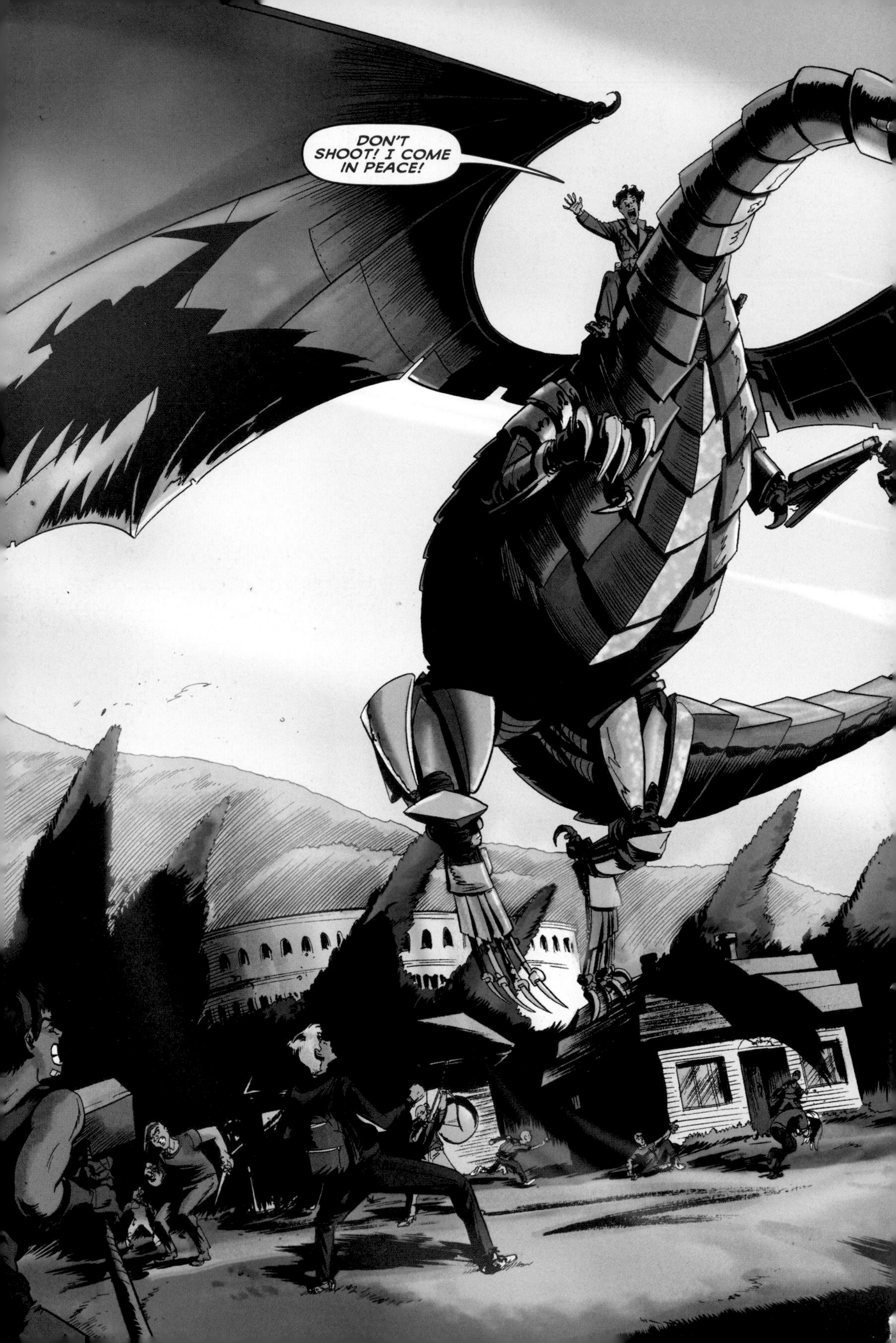
DON'T SHOOT! I COME IN PEACE!

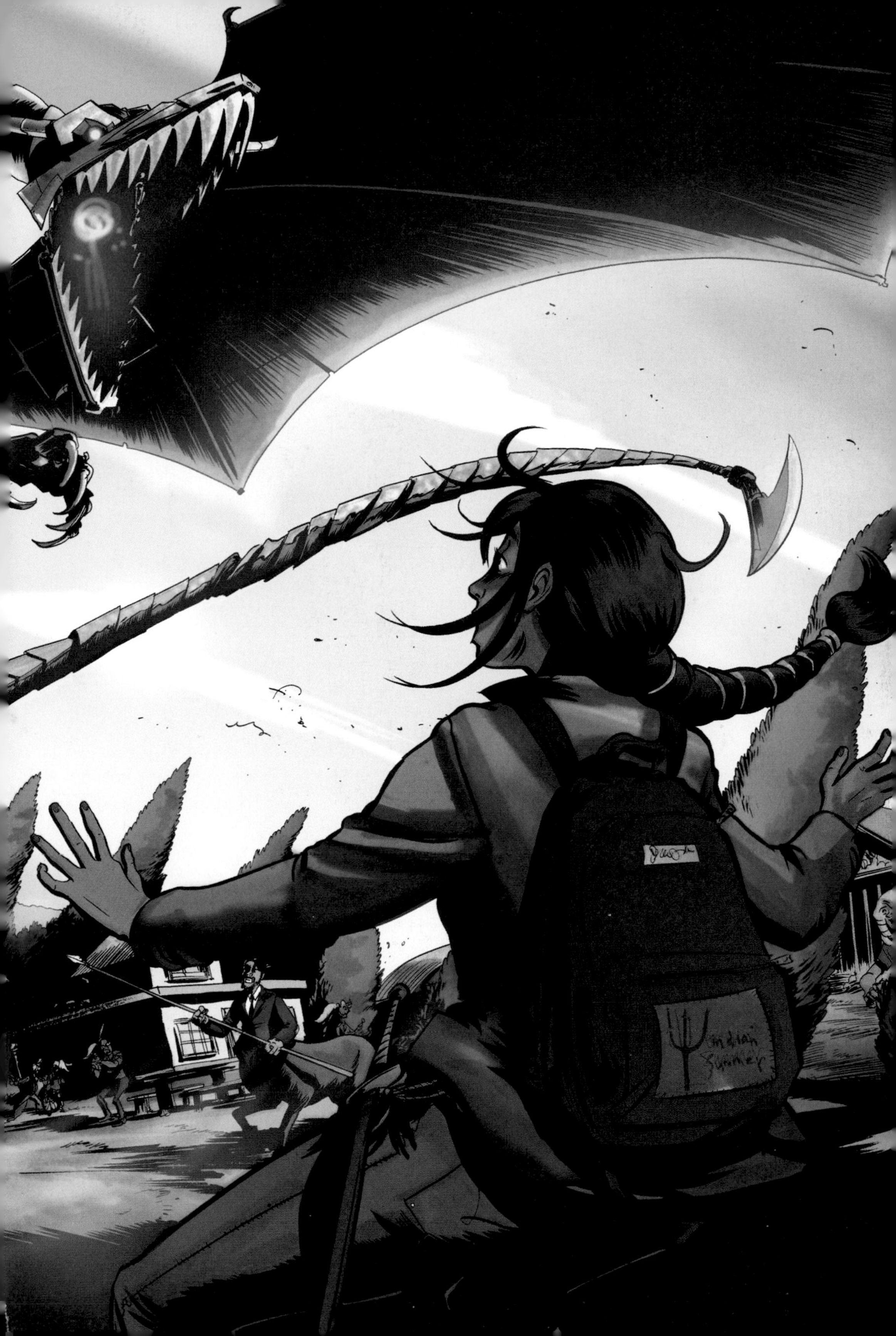

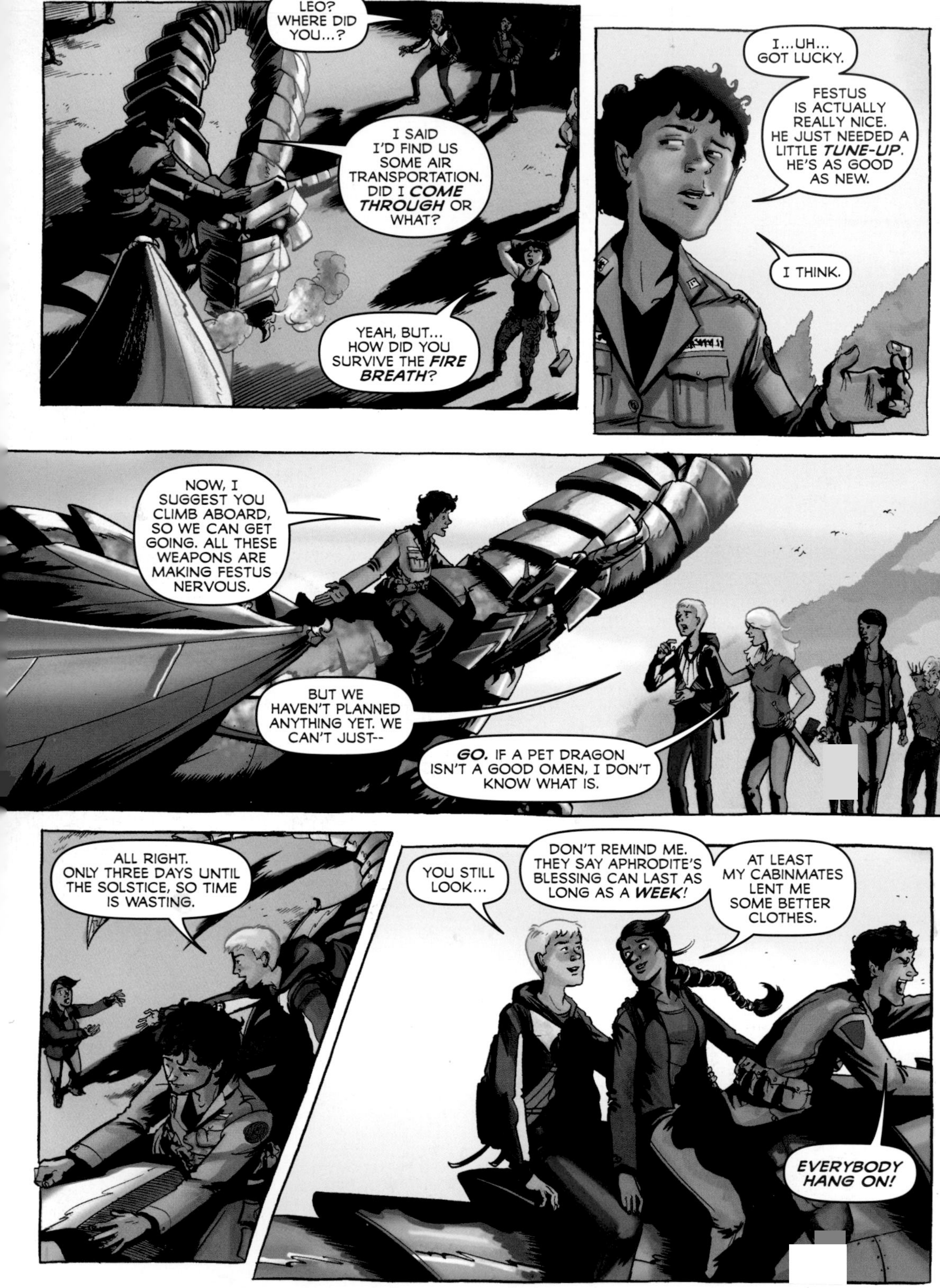
LEO? WHERE DID YOU...?
I SAID I'D FIND US SOME AIR TRANSPORTATION. DID I COME THROUGH OR WHAT?
YEAH, BUT... HOW DID YOU SURVIVE THE FIRE BREATH?
I...UH... GOT LUCKY.
FESTUS IS ACTUALLY REALLY NICE. HE JUST NEEDED A LITTLE TUNE-UP. HE'S AS GOOD AS NEW.
I THINK.
NOW, I SUGGEST YOU CLIMB ABOARD, SO WE CAN GET GOING. ALL THESE WEAPONS ARE MAKING FESTUS NERVOUS.
BUT WE HAVEN'T PLANNED ANYTHING YET. WE CAN'T JUST--
GO. IF A PET DRAGON ISN'T A GOOD OMEN, I DON'T KNOW WHAT IS.
ALL RIGHT. ONLY THREE DAYS UNTIL THE SOLSTICE, SO TIME IS WASTING.
YOU STILL LOOK...
DON'T REMIND ME. THEY SAY APHRODITE'S BLESSING CAN LAST AS LONG AS A WEEK!
AT LEAST MY CABINMATES LENT ME SOME BETTER CLOTHES.
EVERYBODY HANG ON!

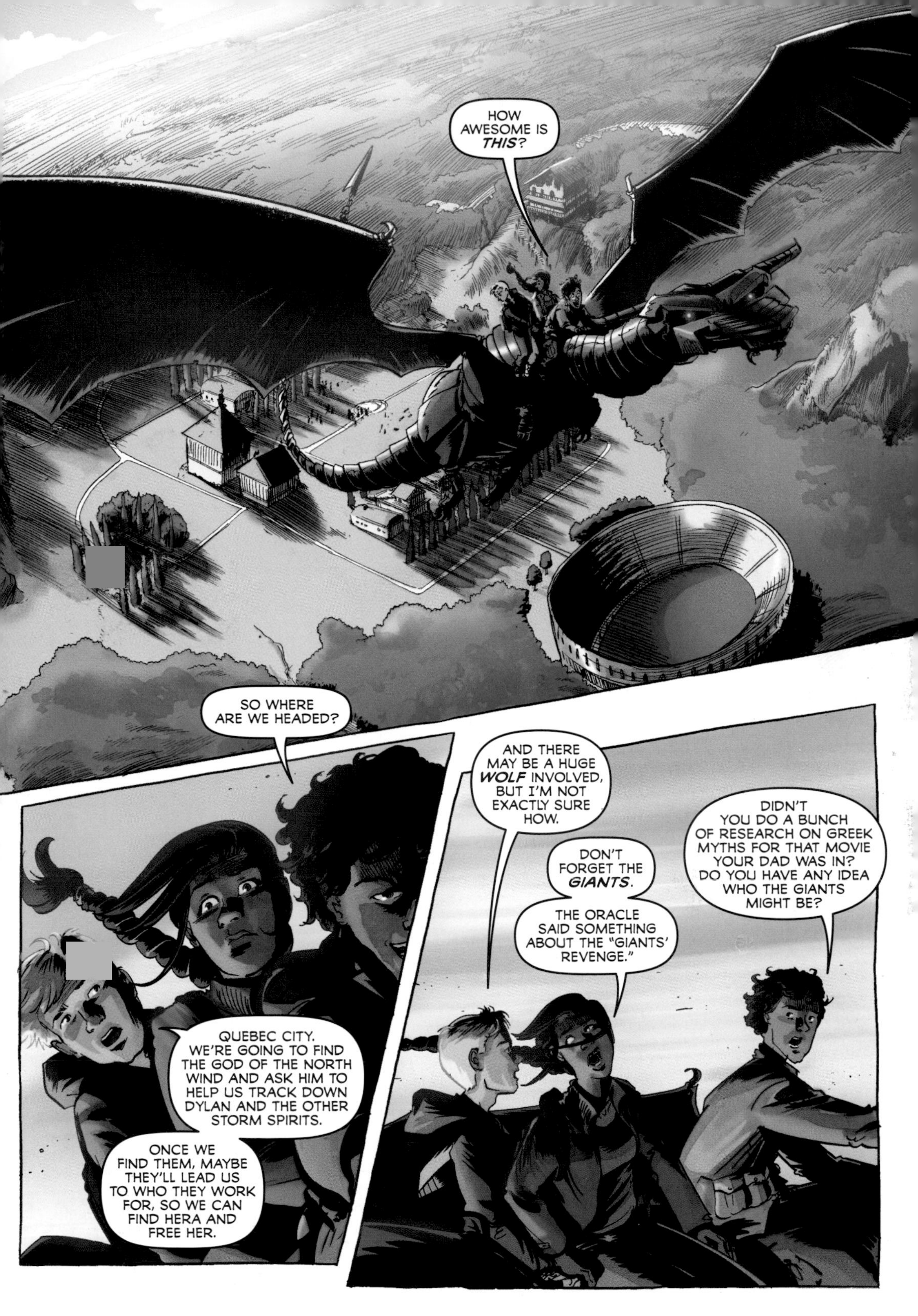
HOW AWESOME IS *THIS*?
SO WHERE ARE WE HEADED?
QUEBEC CITY. WE'RE GOING TO FIND THE GOD OF THE NORTH WIND AND ASK HIM TO HELP US TRACK DOWN DYLAN AND THE OTHER STORM SPIRITS.
ONCE WE FIND THEM, MAYBE THEY'LL LEAD US TO WHO THEY WORK FOR, SO WE CAN FIND HERA AND FREE HER.
AND THERE MAY BE A HUGE *WOLF* INVOLVED, BUT I'M NOT EXACTLY SURE HOW.
DON'T FORGET THE *GIANTS*.
THE ORACLE SAID SOMETHING ABOUT THE "GIANTS' REVENGE."
DIDN'T YOU DO A BUNCH OF RESEARCH ON GREEK MYTHS FOR THAT MOVIE YOUR DAD WAS IN? DO YOU HAVE ANY IDEA WHO THE GIANTS MIGHT BE?

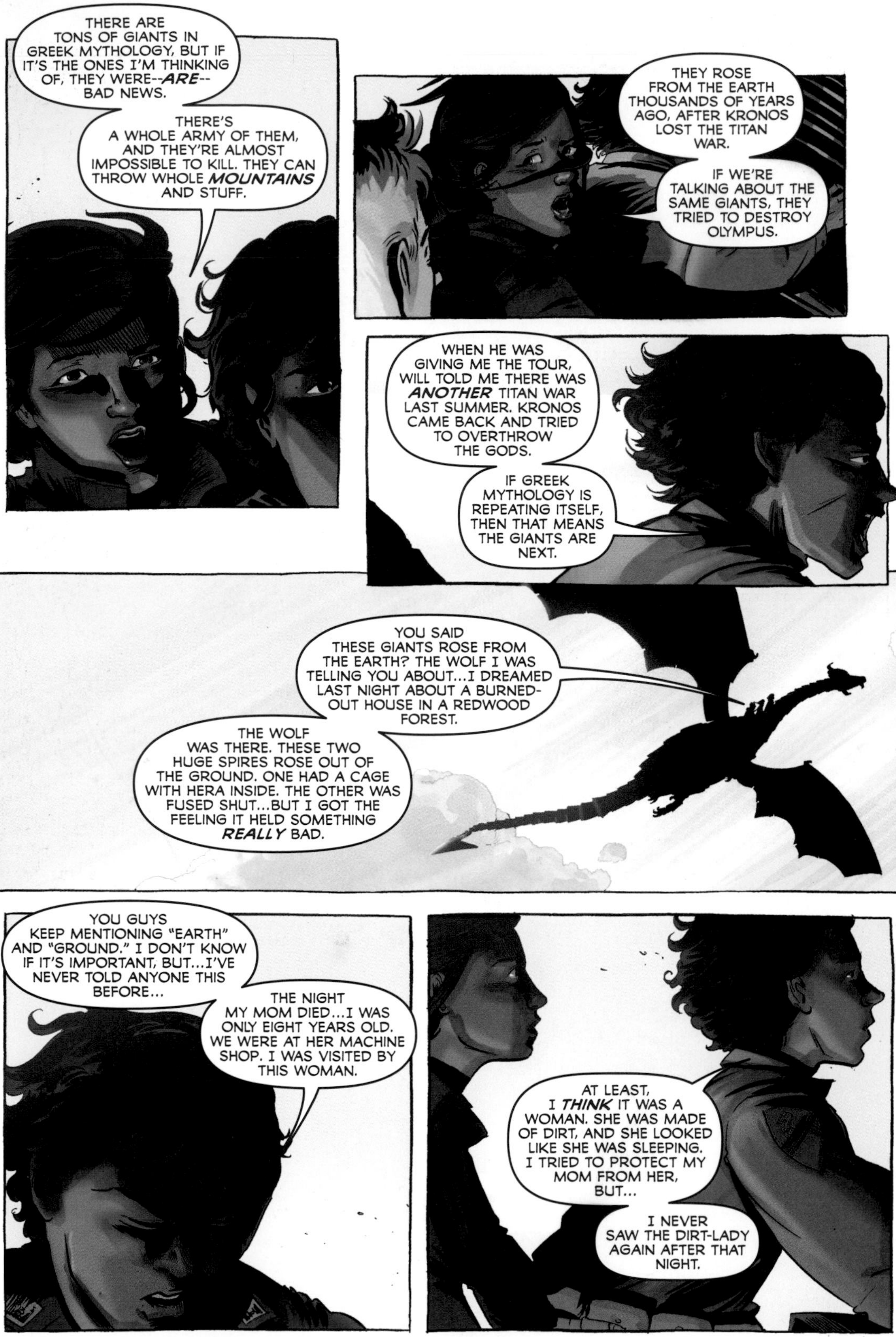
THERE ARE TONS OF GIANTS IN GREEK MYTHOLOGY, BUT IF IT'S THE ONES I'M THINKING OF, THEY WERE--ARE--BAD NEWS.
THERE'S A WHOLE ARMY OF THEM, AND THEY'RE ALMOST IMPOSSIBLE TO KILL. THEY CAN THROW WHOLE MOUNTAINS AND STUFF.
THEY ROSE FROM THE EARTH THOUSANDS OF YEARS AGO, AFTER KRONOS LOST THE TITAN WAR.
IF WE'RE TALKING ABOUT THE SAME GIANTS, THEY TRIED TO DESTROY OLYMPUS.
WHEN HE WAS GIVING ME THE TOUR, WILL TOLD ME THERE WAS ANOTHER TITAN WAR LAST SUMMER. KRONOS CAME BACK AND TRIED TO OVERTHROW THE GODS.
IF GREEK MYTHOLOGY IS REPEATING ITSELF, THEN THAT MEANS THE GIANTS ARE NEXT.
YOU SAID THESE GIANTS ROSE FROM THE EARTH? THE WOLF I WAS TELLING YOU ABOUT...I DREAMED LAST NIGHT ABOUT A BURNED-OUT HOUSE IN A REDWOOD FOREST.
THE WOLF WAS THERE. THESE TWO HUGE SPIRES ROSE OUT OF THE GROUND. ONE HAD A CAGE WITH HERA INSIDE. THE OTHER WAS FUSED SHUT...BUT I GOT THE FEELING IT HELD SOMETHING REALLY BAD.
YOU GUYS KEEP MENTIONING "EARTH" AND "GROUND." I DON'T KNOW IF IT'S IMPORTANT, BUT...I'VE NEVER TOLD ANYONE THIS BEFORE...
THE NIGHT MY MOM DIED...I WAS ONLY EIGHT YEARS OLD. WE WERE AT HER MACHINE SHOP. I WAS VISITED BY THIS WOMAN.
AT LEAST, I THINK IT WAS A WOMAN. SHE WAS MADE OF DIRT, AND SHE LOOKED LIKE SHE WAS SLEEPING. I TRIED TO PROTECT MY MOM FROM HER, BUT...
I NEVER SAW THE DIRT-LADY AGAIN AFTER THAT NIGHT.

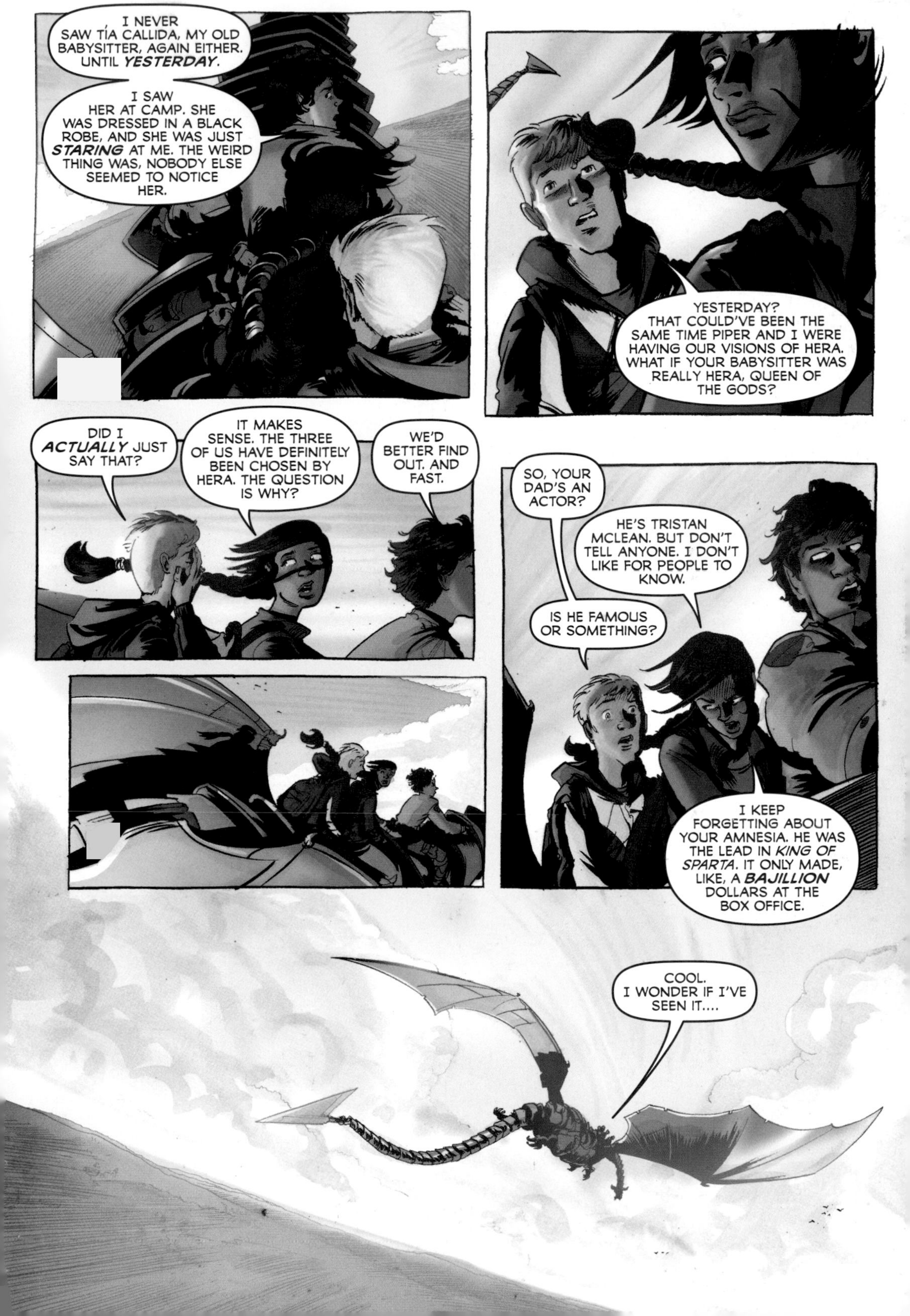

I NEVER SAW TÍA CALLIDA, MY OLD BABYSITTER, AGAIN EITHER. UNTIL *YESTERDAY*.
I SAW HER AT CAMP. SHE WAS DRESSED IN A BLACK ROBE, AND SHE WAS JUST *STARING* AT ME. THE WEIRD THING WAS, NOBODY ELSE SEEMED TO NOTICE HER.
YESTERDAY? THAT COULD'VE BEEN THE SAME TIME PIPER AND I WERE HAVING OUR VISIONS OF HERA. WHAT IF YOUR BABYSITTER WAS REALLY HERA, QUEEN OF THE GODS?
DID I *ACTUALLY* JUST SAY THAT?
IT MAKES SENSE. THE THREE OF US HAVE DEFINITELY BEEN CHOSEN BY HERA. THE QUESTION IS WHY?
WE'D BETTER FIND OUT. AND FAST.
SO, YOUR DAD'S AN ACTOR?
HE'S TRISTAN MCLEAN. BUT DON'T TELL ANYONE. I DON'T LIKE FOR PEOPLE TO KNOW.
IS HE FAMOUS OR SOMETHING?
I KEEP FORGETTING ABOUT YOUR AMNESIA. HE WAS THE LEAD IN *KING OF SPARTA*. IT ONLY MADE, LIKE, A *BAJILLION* DOLLARS AT THE BOX OFFICE.
COOL. I WONDER IF I'VE SEEN IT....

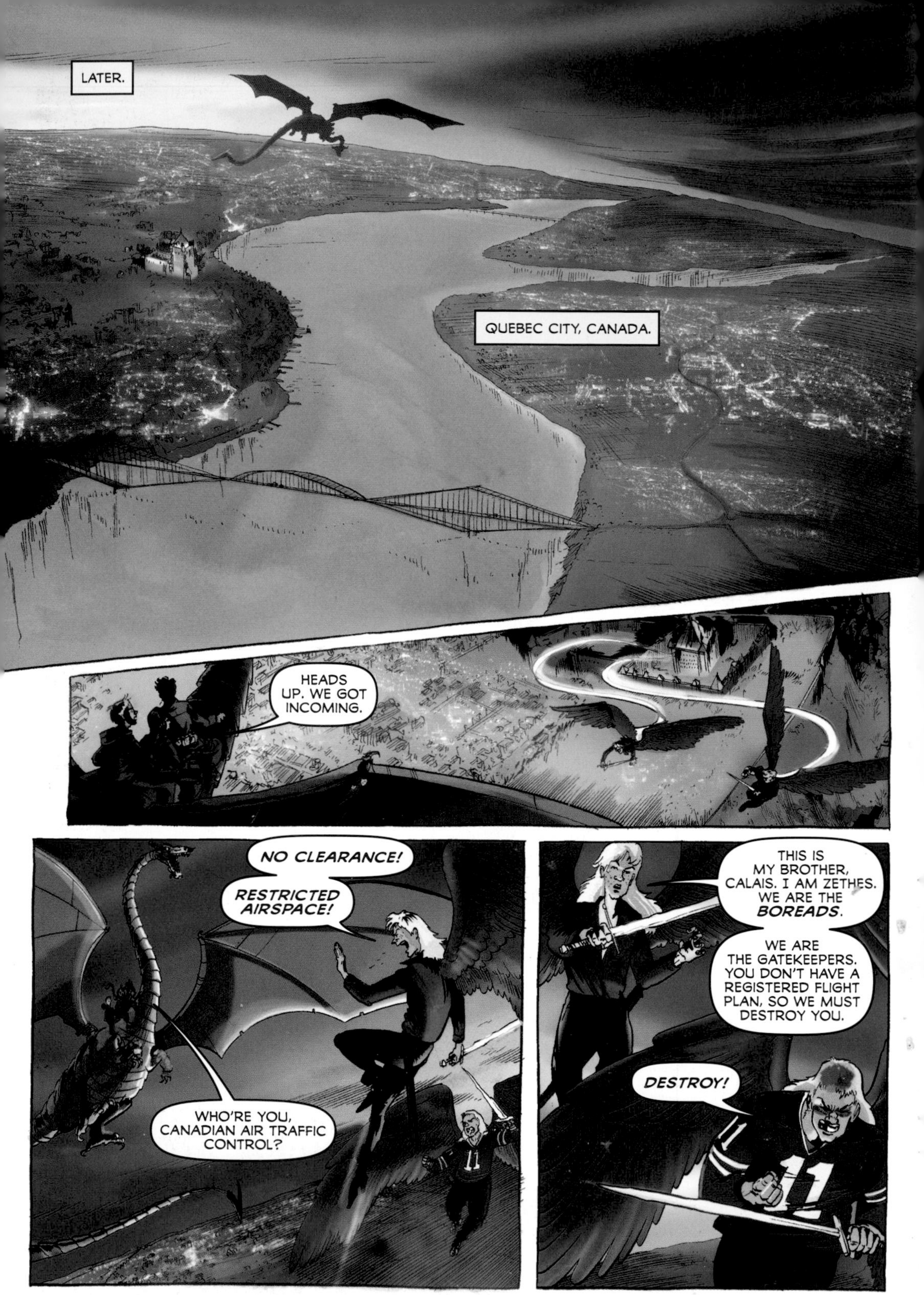

LATER.
QUEBEC CITY, CANADA.
HEADS UP. WE GOT INCOMING.
NO CLEARANCE!
RESTRICTED AIRSPACE!
WHO'RE YOU, CANADIAN AIR TRAFFIC CONTROL?
THIS IS MY BROTHER, CALAIS. I AM ZETHES. WE ARE THE BOREADS.
WE ARE THE GATEKEEPERS. YOU DON'T HAVE A REGISTERED FLIGHT PLAN, SO WE MUST DESTROY YOU.
DESTROY!

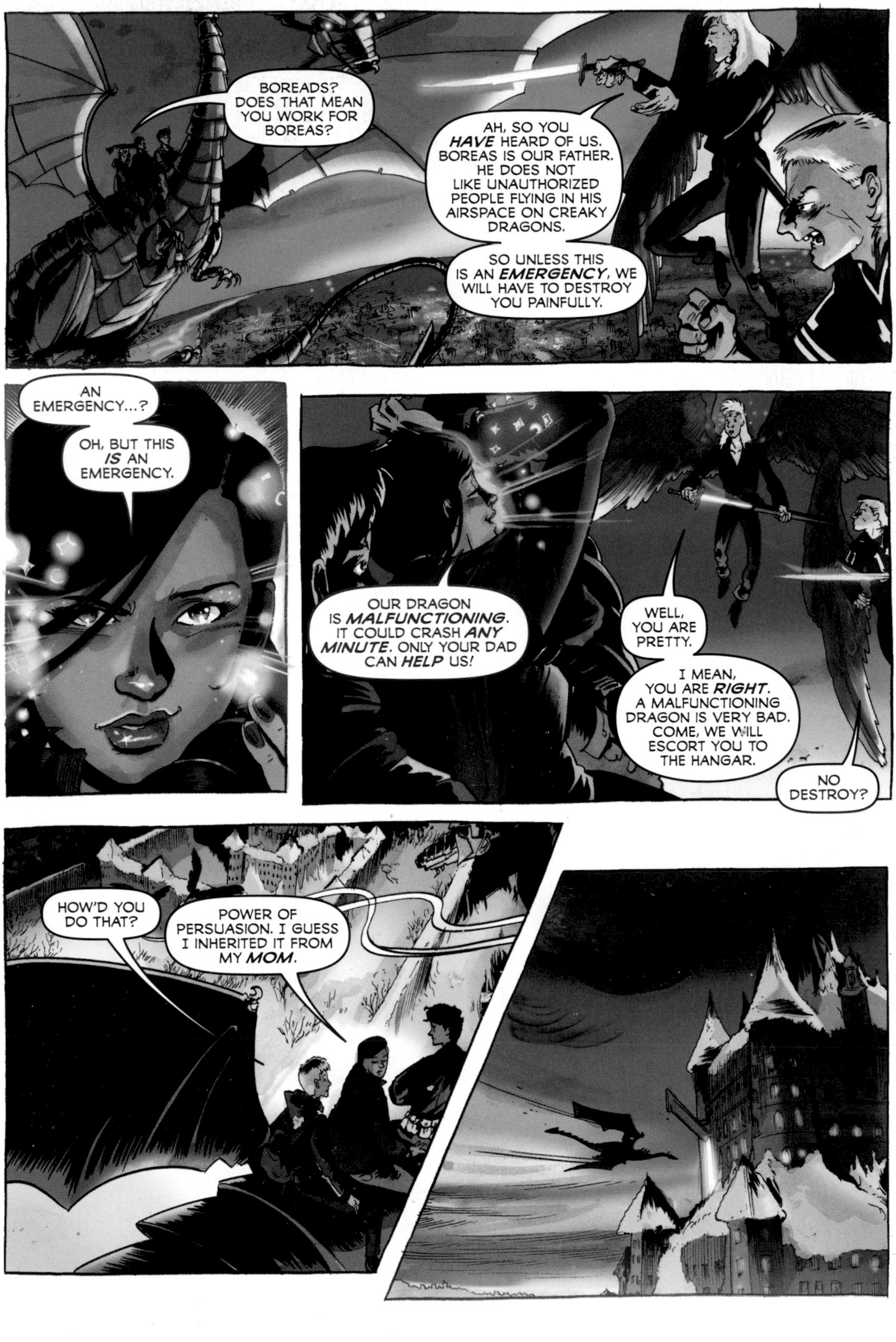
BOREADS? DOES THAT MEAN YOU WORK FOR BOREAS?
AH, SO YOU **HAVE** HEARD OF US. BOREAS IS OUR FATHER. HE DOES NOT LIKE UNAUTHORIZED PEOPLE FLYING IN HIS AIRSPACE ON CREAKY DRAGONS.
SO UNLESS THIS IS AN **EMERGENCY**, WE WILL HAVE TO DESTROY YOU PAINFULLY.
AN EMERGENCY...?
OH, BUT THIS ***IS*** AN EMERGENCY.
OUR DRAGON IS ***MALFUNCTIONING***. IT COULD CRASH ***ANY MINUTE***. ONLY YOUR DAD CAN ***HELP*** US!
WELL, YOU ARE PRETTY.
I MEAN, YOU ARE ***RIGHT***. A MALFUNCTIONING DRAGON IS VERY BAD. COME, WE WILL ESCORT YOU TO THE HANGAR.
NO DESTROY?
HOW'D YOU DO THAT?
POWER OF PERSUASION. I GUESS I INHERITED IT FROM MY ***MOM***.

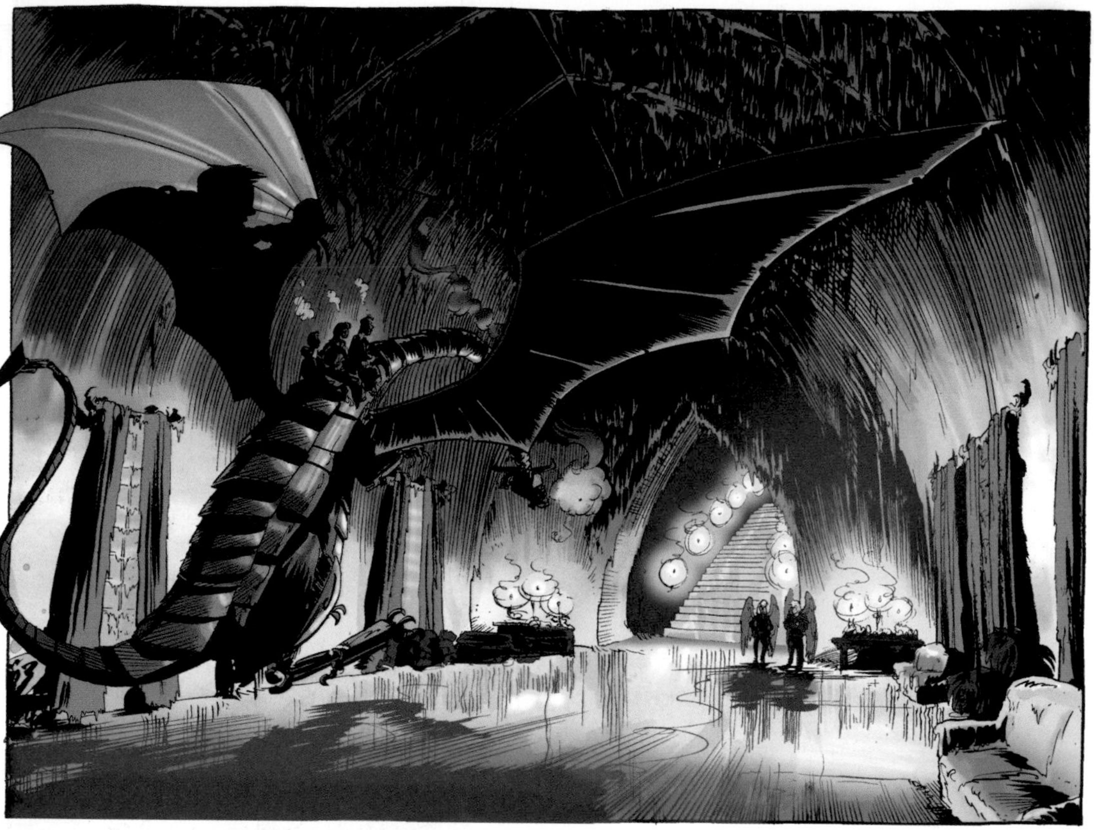

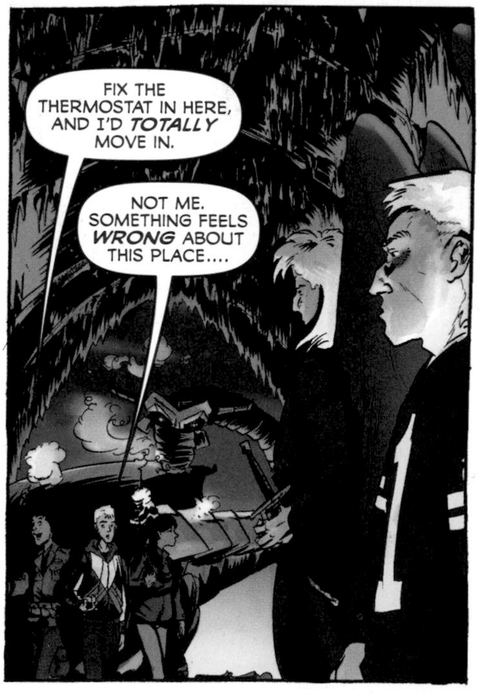
FIX THE THERMOSTAT IN HERE, AND I'D TOTALLY MOVE IN.
NOT ME. SOMETHING FEELS WRONG ABOUT THIS PLACE....

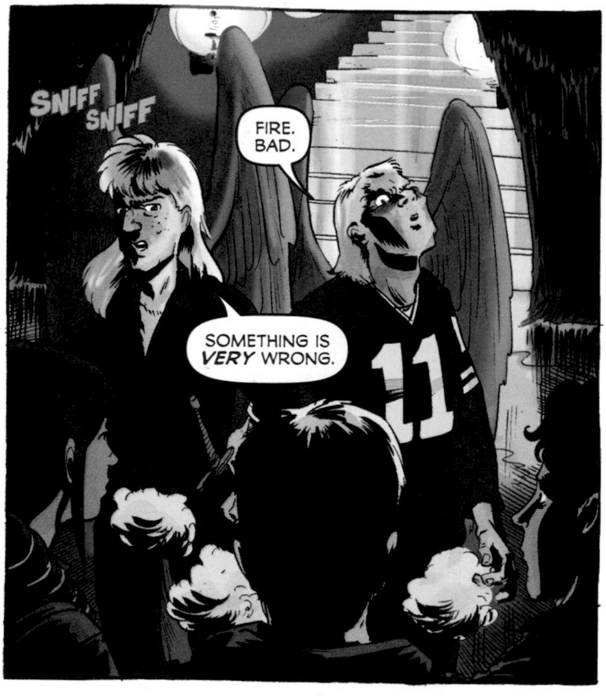
SNIFF SNIFF
FIRE. BAD.
SOMETHING IS VERY WRONG.

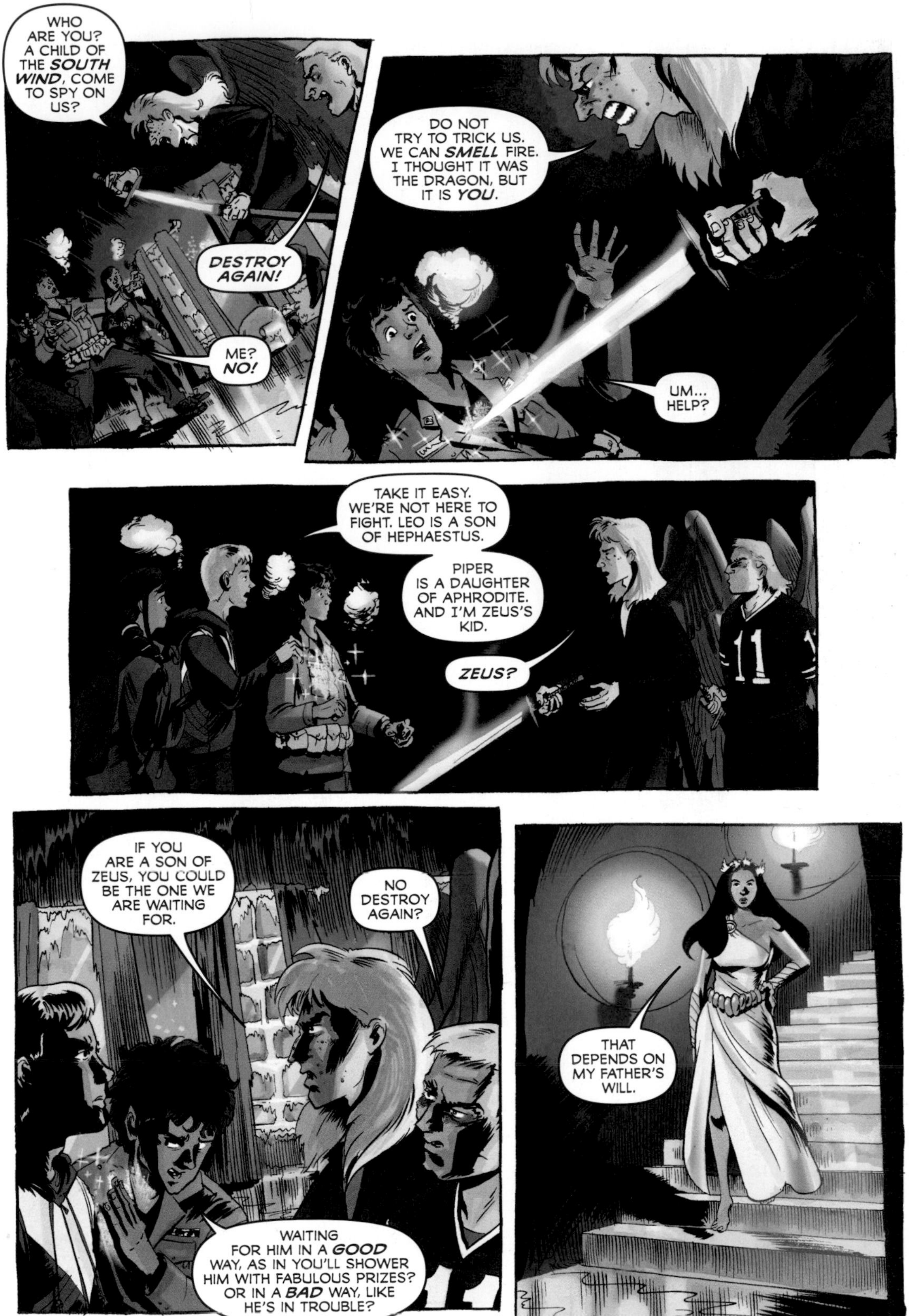
WHO ARE YOU? A CHILD OF THE SOUTH WIND, COME TO SPY ON US?
DESTROY AGAIN!
ME? NO!
DO NOT TRY TO TRICK US. WE CAN SMELL FIRE. I THOUGHT IT WAS THE DRAGON, BUT IT IS YOU.
UM... HELP?
TAKE IT EASY. WE'RE NOT HERE TO FIGHT. LEO IS A SON OF HEPHAESTUS.
PIPER IS A DAUGHTER OF APHRODITE. AND I'M ZEUS'S KID.
ZEUS?
11
IF YOU ARE A SON OF ZEUS, YOU COULD BE THE ONE WE ARE WAITING FOR.
NO DESTROY AGAIN?
WAITING FOR HIM IN A GOOD WAY, AS IN YOU'LL SHOWER HIM WITH FABULOUS PRIZES? OR IN A BAD WAY, LIKE HE'S IN TROUBLE?
THAT DEPENDS ON MY FATHER'S WILL.

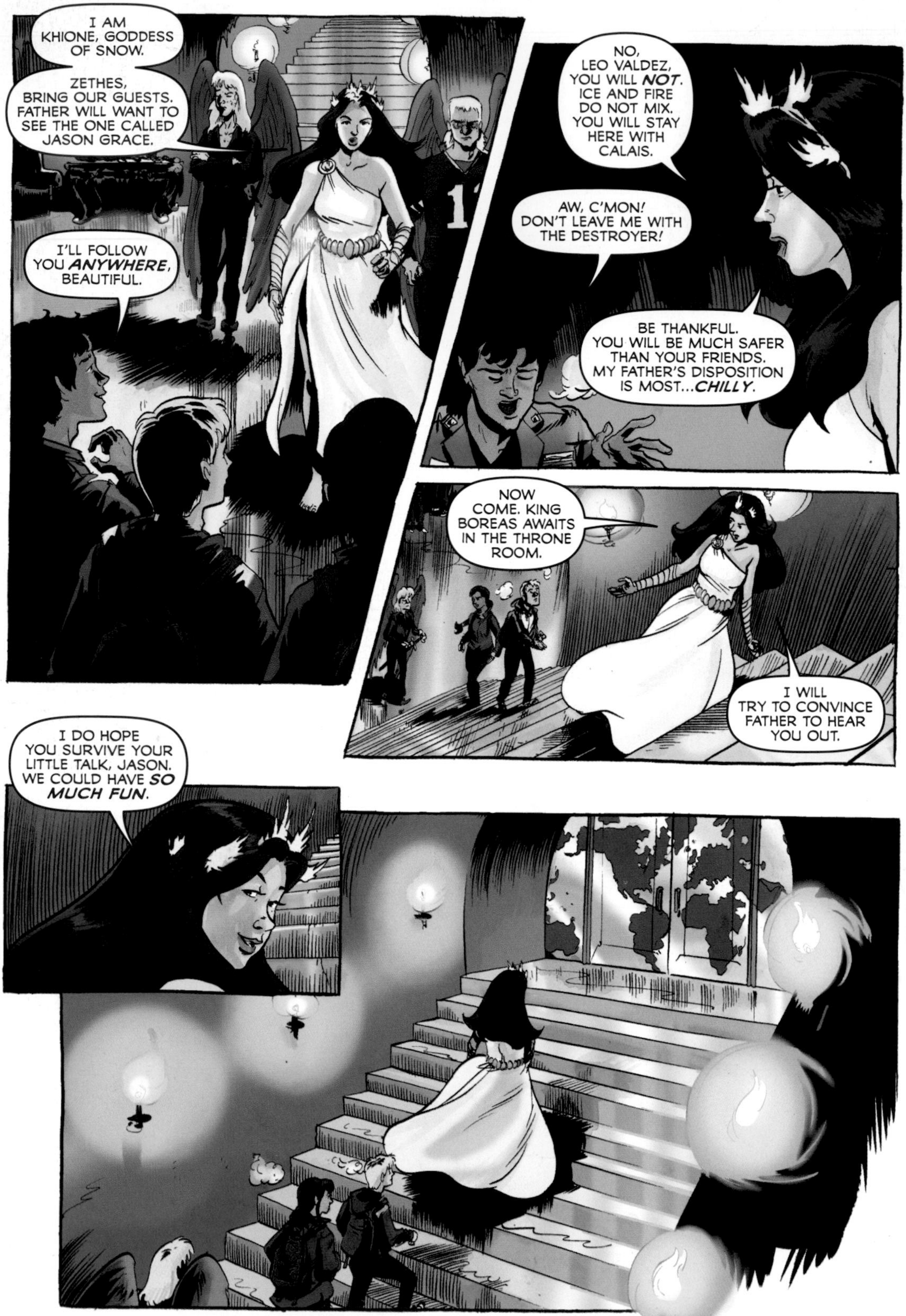
I AM KHIONE, GODDESS OF SNOW.
ZETHES, BRING OUR GUESTS. FATHER WILL WANT TO SEE THE ONE CALLED JASON GRACE.
I'LL FOLLOW YOU ANYWHERE, BEAUTIFUL.
NO, LEO VALDEZ, YOU WILL NOT. ICE AND FIRE DO NOT MIX. YOU WILL STAY HERE WITH CALAIS.
AW, C'MON! DON'T LEAVE ME WITH THE DESTROYER!
BE THANKFUL. YOU WILL BE MUCH SAFER THAN YOUR FRIENDS. MY FATHER'S DISPOSITION IS MOST...CHILLY.
NOW COME. KING BOREAS AWAITS IN THE THRONE ROOM.
I WILL TRY TO CONVINCE FATHER TO HEAR YOU OUT.
I DO HOPE YOU SURVIVE YOUR LITTLE TALK, JASON. WE COULD HAVE SO MUCH FUN.

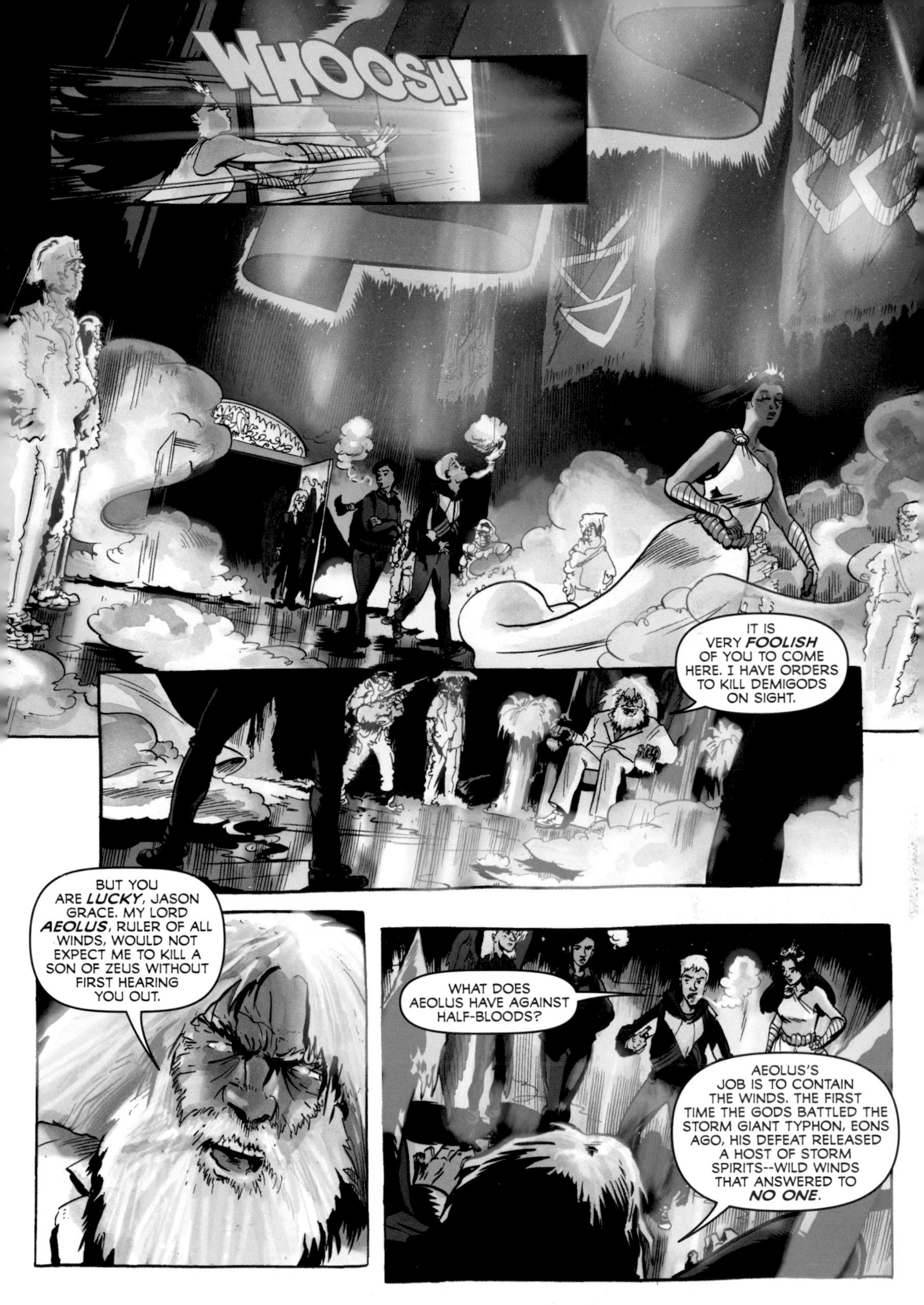
WHOOSH
IT IS VERY FOOLISH OF YOU TO COME HERE. I HAVE ORDERS TO KILL DEMIGODS ON SIGHT.
BUT YOU ARE LUCKY, JASON GRACE. MY LORD AEOLUS, RULER OF ALL WINDS, WOULD NOT EXPECT ME TO KILL A SON OF ZEUS WITHOUT FIRST HEARING YOU OUT.
WHAT DOES AEOLUS HAVE AGAINST HALF-BLOODS?
AEOLUS'S JOB IS TO CONTAIN THE WINDS. THE FIRST TIME THE GODS BATTLED THE STORM GIANT TYPHON, EONS AGO, HIS DEFEAT RELEASED A HOST OF STORM SPIRITS--WILD WINDS THAT ANSWERED TO NO ONE.

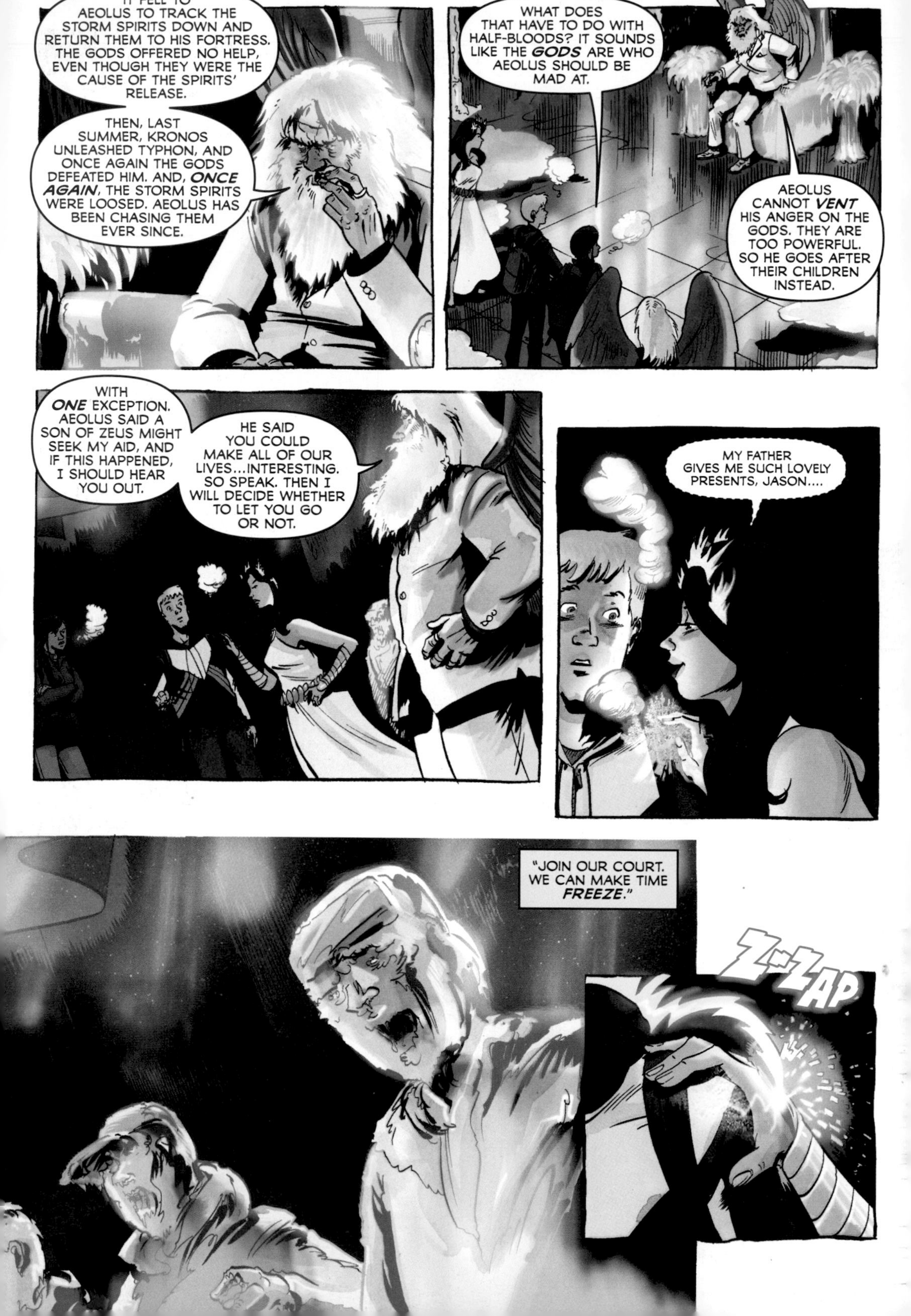
IT FELL TO AEOLUS TO TRACK THE STORM SPIRITS DOWN AND RETURN THEM TO HIS FORTRESS. THE GODS OFFERED NO HELP, EVEN THOUGH THEY WERE THE CAUSE OF THE SPIRITS' RELEASE.
THEN, LAST SUMMER, KRONOS UNLEASHED TYPHON, AND ONCE AGAIN THE GODS DEFEATED HIM. AND, ONCE AGAIN, THE STORM SPIRITS WERE LOOSED. AEOLUS HAS BEEN CHASING THEM EVER SINCE.
WHAT DOES THAT HAVE TO DO WITH HALF-BLOODS? IT SOUNDS LIKE THE GODS ARE WHO AEOLUS SHOULD BE MAD AT.
AEOLUS CANNOT VENT HIS ANGER ON THE GODS. THEY ARE TOO POWERFUL. SO HE GOES AFTER THEIR CHILDREN INSTEAD.
WITH ONE EXCEPTION. AEOLUS SAID A SON OF ZEUS MIGHT SEEK MY AID, AND IF THIS HAPPENED, I SHOULD HEAR YOU OUT.
HE SAID YOU COULD MAKE ALL OF OUR LIVES...INTERESTING. SO SPEAK. THEN I WILL DECIDE WHETHER TO LET YOU GO OR NOT.
MY FATHER GIVES ME SUCH LOVELY PRESENTS, JASON....
"JOIN OUR COURT. WE CAN MAKE TIME FREEZE."
Z-ZAP

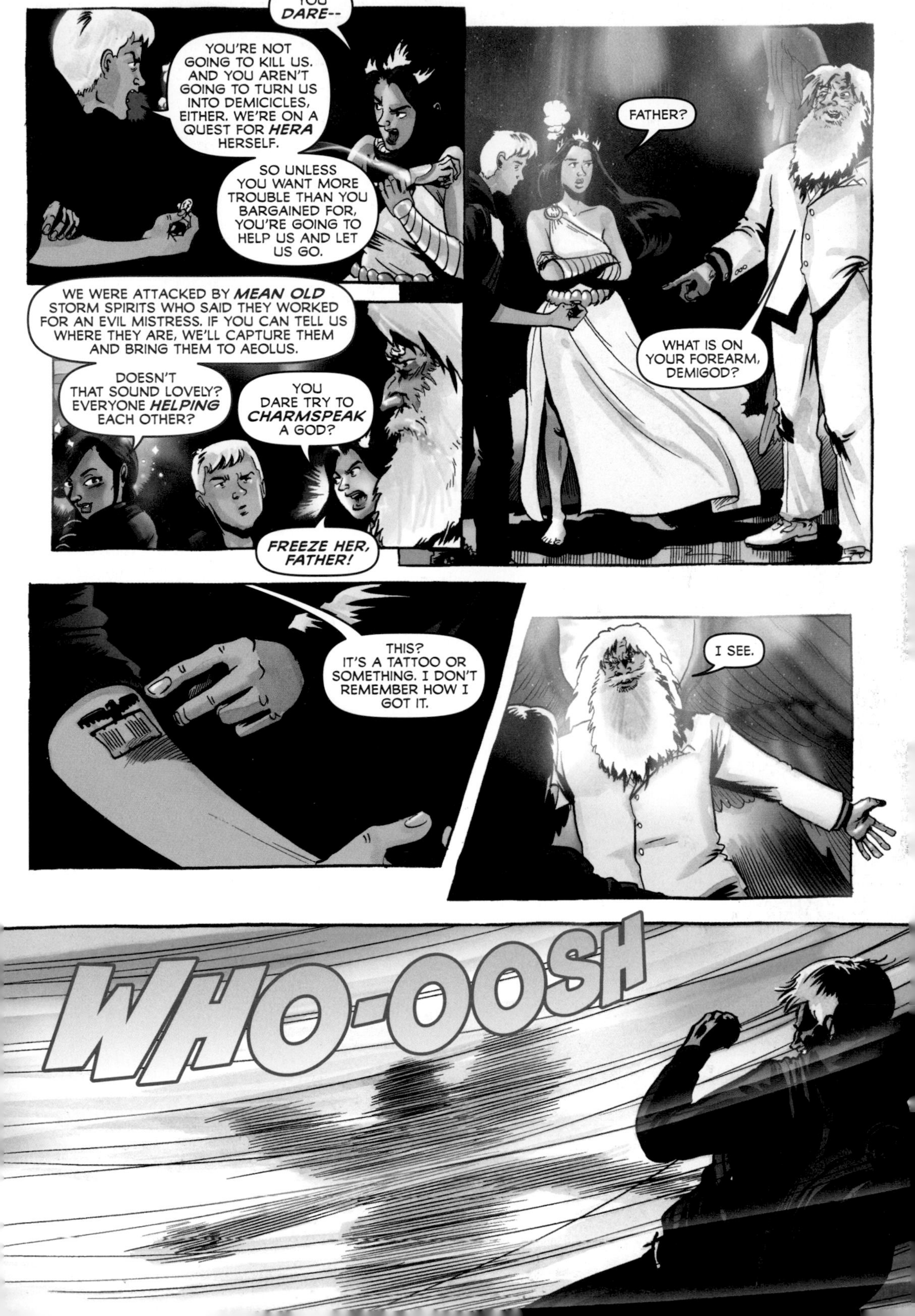

YOU DARE--
YOU'RE NOT GOING TO KILL US. AND YOU AREN'T GOING TO TURN US INTO DEMICICLES, EITHER. WE'RE ON A QUEST FOR HERA HERSELF.
SO UNLESS YOU WANT MORE TROUBLE THAN YOU BARGAINED FOR, YOU'RE GOING TO HELP US AND LET US GO.
FATHER?
WE WERE ATTACKED BY MEAN OLD STORM SPIRITS WHO SAID THEY WORKED FOR AN EVIL MISTRESS. IF YOU CAN TELL US WHERE THEY ARE, WE'LL CAPTURE THEM AND BRING THEM TO AEOLUS.
DOESN'T THAT SOUND LOVELY? EVERYONE HELPING EACH OTHER?
YOU DARE TRY TO CHARMSPEAK A GOD?
FREEZE HER, FATHER!
WHAT IS ON YOUR FOREARM, DEMIGOD?
THIS? IT'S A TATTOO OR SOMETHING. I DON'T REMEMBER HOW I GOT IT.
I SEE.
WHO-OOSH

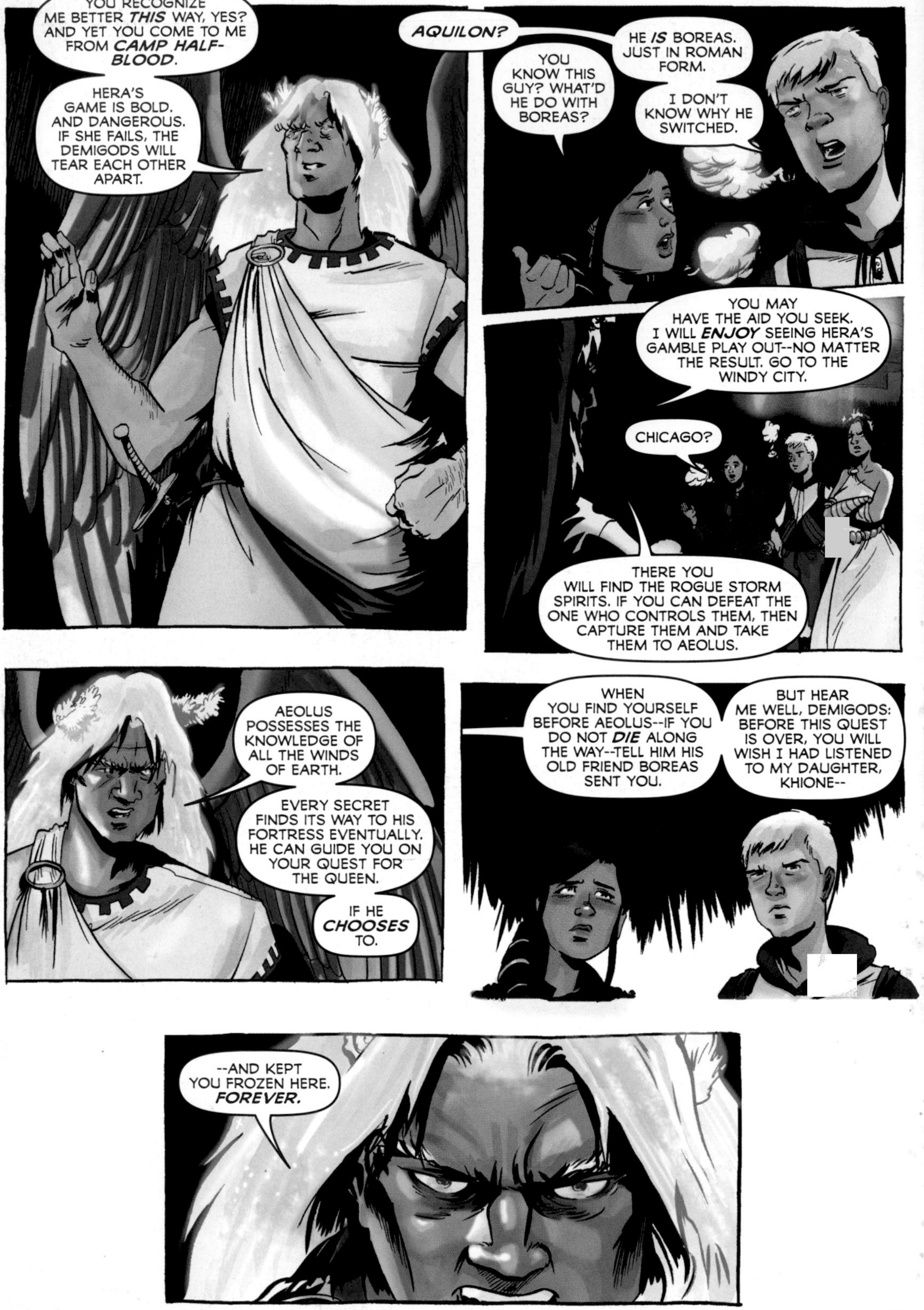
YOU RECOGNIZE ME BETTER *THIS* WAY, YES? AND YET YOU COME TO ME FROM *CAMP HALF-BLOOD*.
HERA'S GAME IS BOLD. AND DANGEROUS. IF SHE FAILS, THE DEMIGODS WILL TEAR EACH OTHER APART.
AQUILON?
YOU KNOW THIS GUY? WHAT'D HE DO WITH BOREAS?
HE *IS* BOREAS. JUST IN ROMAN FORM.
I DON'T KNOW WHY HE SWITCHED.
YOU MAY HAVE THE AID YOU SEEK. I WILL *ENJOY* SEEING HERA'S GAMBLE PLAY OUT--NO MATTER THE RESULT. GO TO THE WINDY CITY.
CHICAGO?
THERE YOU WILL FIND THE ROGUE STORM SPIRITS. IF YOU CAN DEFEAT THE ONE WHO CONTROLS THEM, THEN CAPTURE THEM AND TAKE THEM TO AEOLUS.
AEOLUS POSSESSES THE KNOWLEDGE OF ALL THE WINDS OF EARTH.
EVERY SECRET FINDS ITS WAY TO HIS FORTRESS EVENTUALLY. HE CAN GUIDE YOU ON YOUR QUEST FOR THE QUEEN.
IF HE *CHOOSES* TO.
WHEN YOU FIND YOURSELF BEFORE AEOLUS--IF YOU DO NOT *DIE* ALONG THE WAY--TELL HIM HIS OLD FRIEND BOREAS SENT YOU.
BUT HEAR ME WELL, DEMIGODS: BEFORE THIS QUEST IS OVER, YOU WILL WISH I HAD LISTENED TO MY DAUGHTER, KHIONE--
--AND KEPT YOU FROZEN HERE. *FOREVER.*

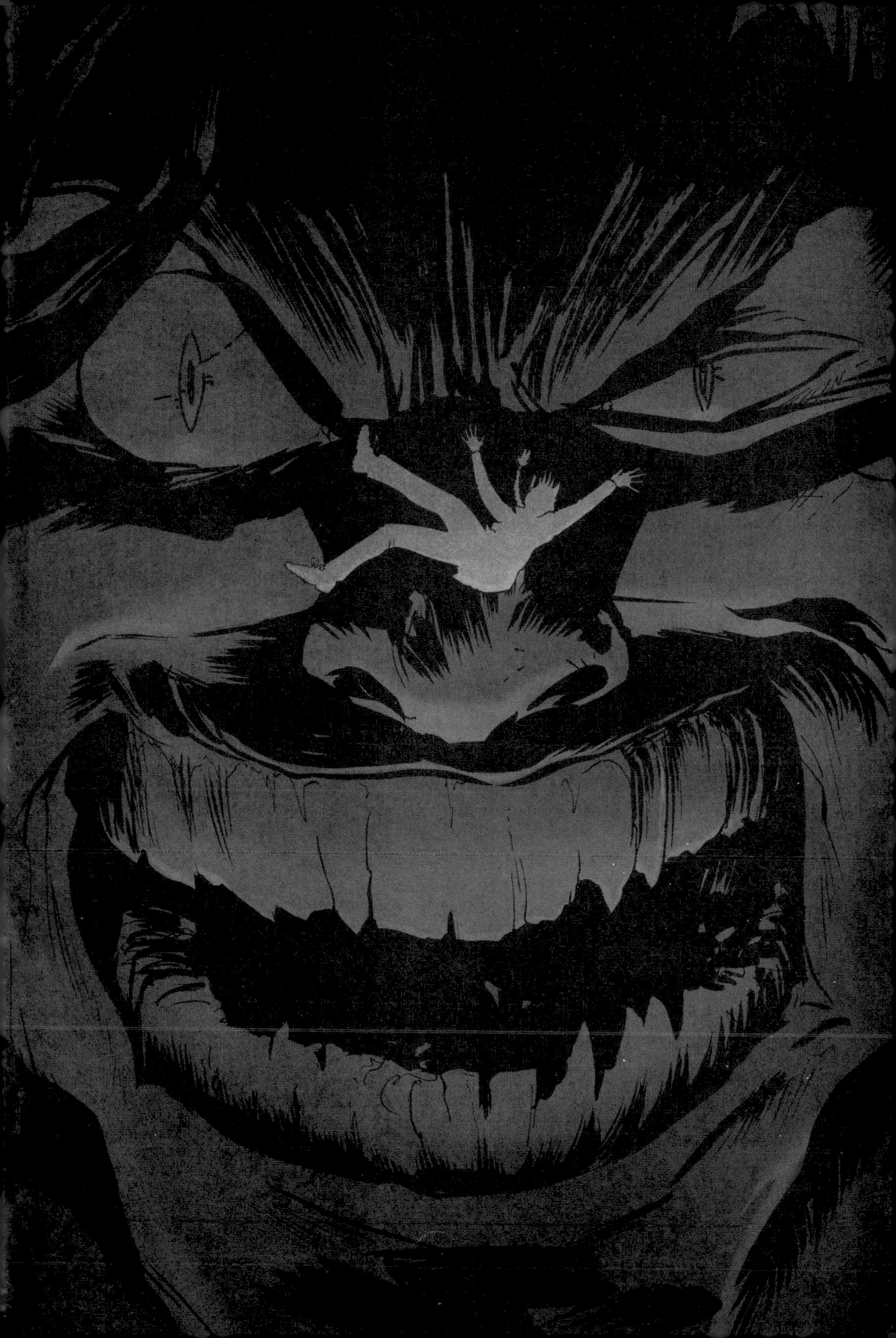

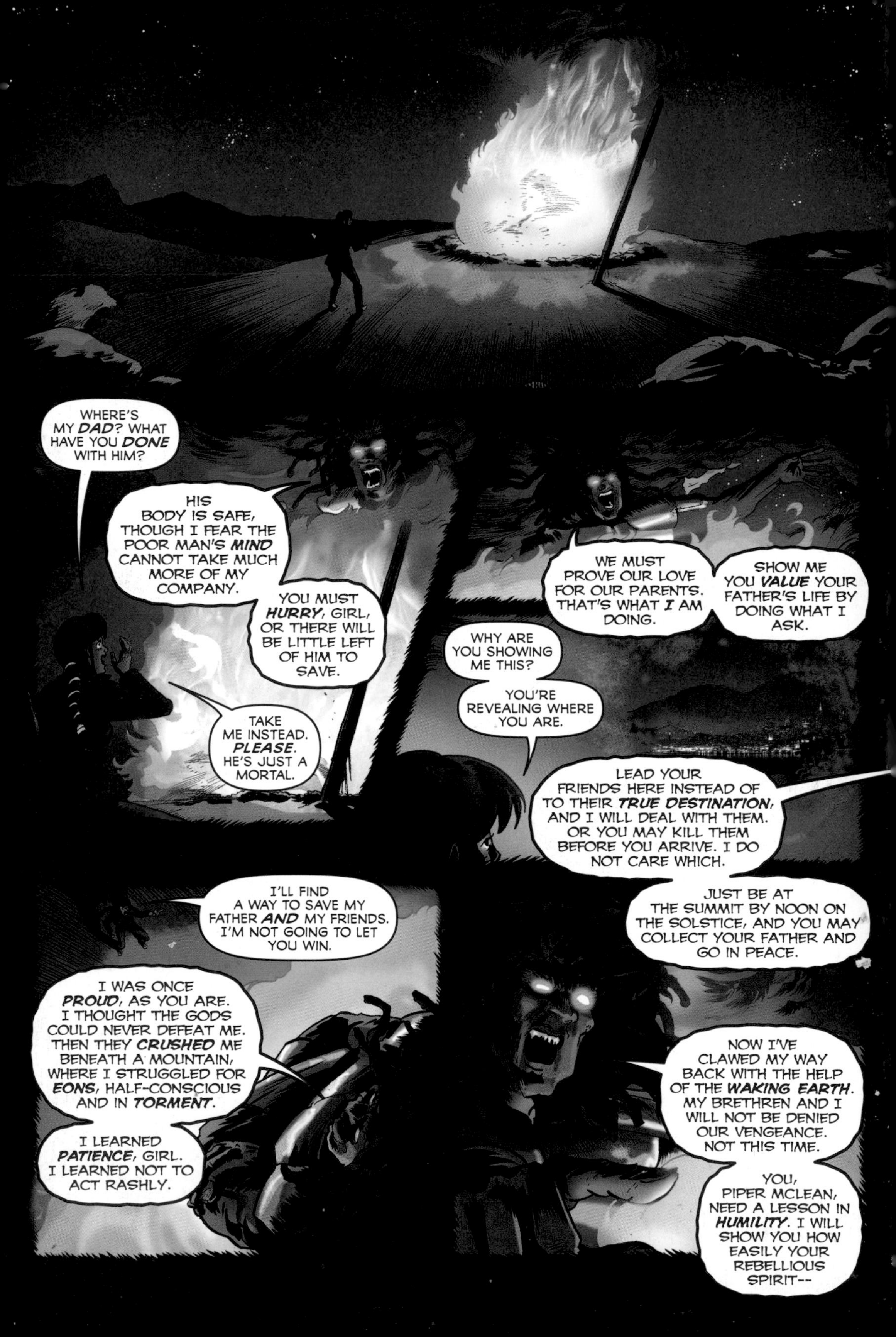
WHERE'S MY DAD? WHAT HAVE YOU DONE WITH HIM?
HIS BODY IS SAFE, THOUGH I FEAR THE POOR MAN'S MIND CANNOT TAKE MUCH MORE OF MY COMPANY.
YOU MUST HURRY, GIRL, OR THERE WILL BE LITTLE LEFT OF HIM TO SAVE.
TAKE ME INSTEAD. PLEASE. HE'S JUST A MORTAL.
WE MUST PROVE OUR LOVE FOR OUR PARENTS. THAT'S WHAT I AM DOING.
SHOW ME YOU VALUE YOUR FATHER'S LIFE BY DOING WHAT I ASK.
WHY ARE YOU SHOWING ME THIS?
YOU'RE REVEALING WHERE YOU ARE.
LEAD YOUR FRIENDS HERE INSTEAD OF TO THEIR TRUE DESTINATION, AND I WILL DEAL WITH THEM. OR YOU MAY KILL THEM BEFORE YOU ARRIVE. I DO NOT CARE WHICH.
JUST BE AT THE SUMMIT BY NOON ON THE SOLSTICE, AND YOU MAY COLLECT YOUR FATHER AND GO IN PEACE.
I'LL FIND A WAY TO SAVE MY FATHER AND MY FRIENDS. I'M NOT GOING TO LET YOU WIN.
I WAS ONCE PROUD, AS YOU ARE. I THOUGHT THE GODS COULD NEVER DEFEAT ME. THEN THEY CRUSHED ME BENEATH A MOUNTAIN, WHERE I STRUGGLED FOR EONS, HALF-CONSCIOUS AND IN TORMENT.
I LEARNED PATIENCE, GIRL. I LEARNED NOT TO ACT RASHLY.
NOW I'VE CLAWED MY WAY BACK WITH THE HELP OF THE WAKING EARTH. MY BRETHREN AND I WILL NOT BE DENIED OUR VENGEANCE. NOT THIS TIME.
YOU, PIPER MCLEAN, NEED A LESSON IN HUMILITY. I WILL SHOW YOU HOW EASILY YOUR REBELLIOUS SPIRIT--

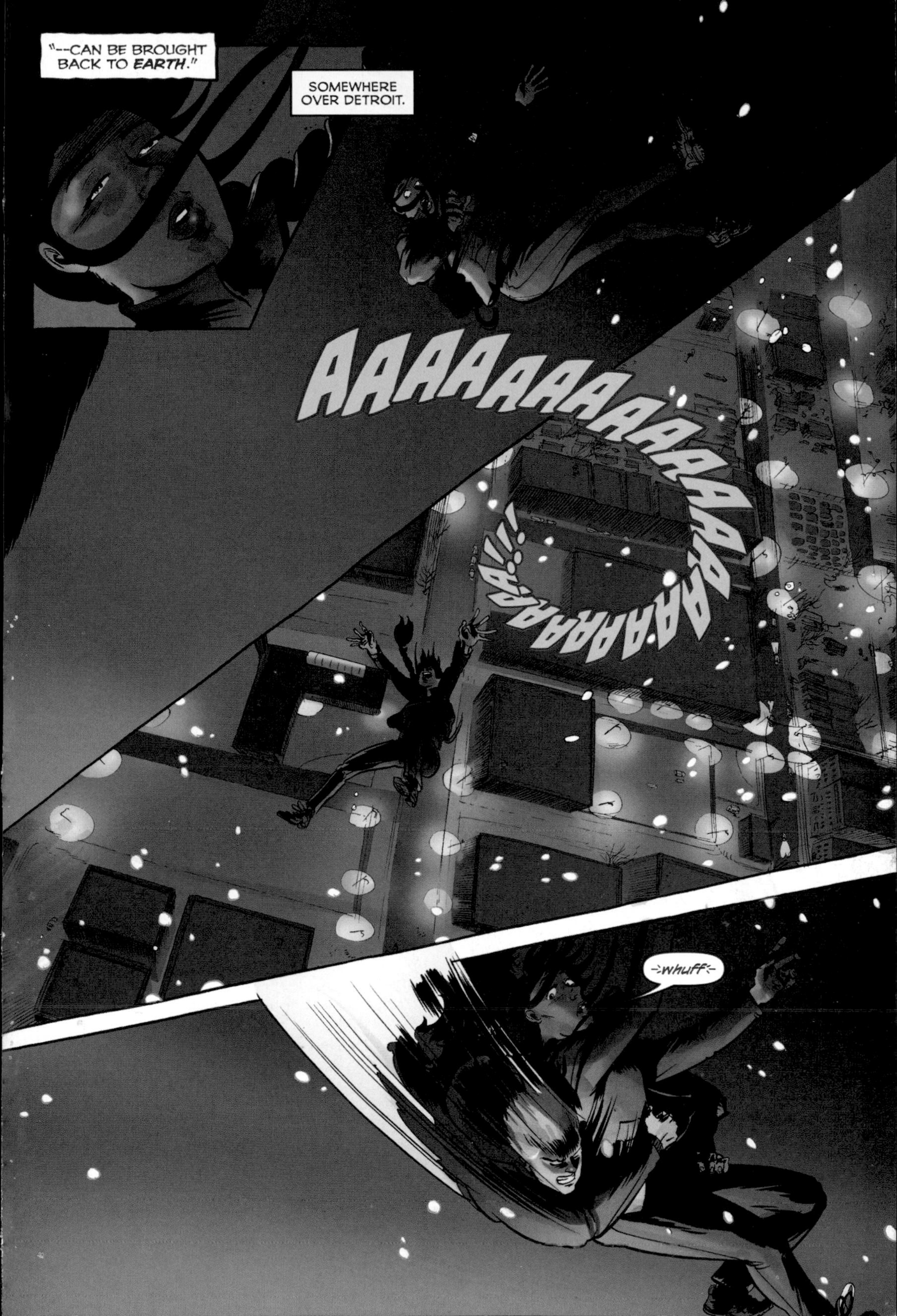
"--CAN BE BROUGHT BACK TO *EARTH*."
SOMEWHERE OVER DETROIT.
AAAAAAAAAAAAAAAAAAAAAAAGH!!!
-whuff-

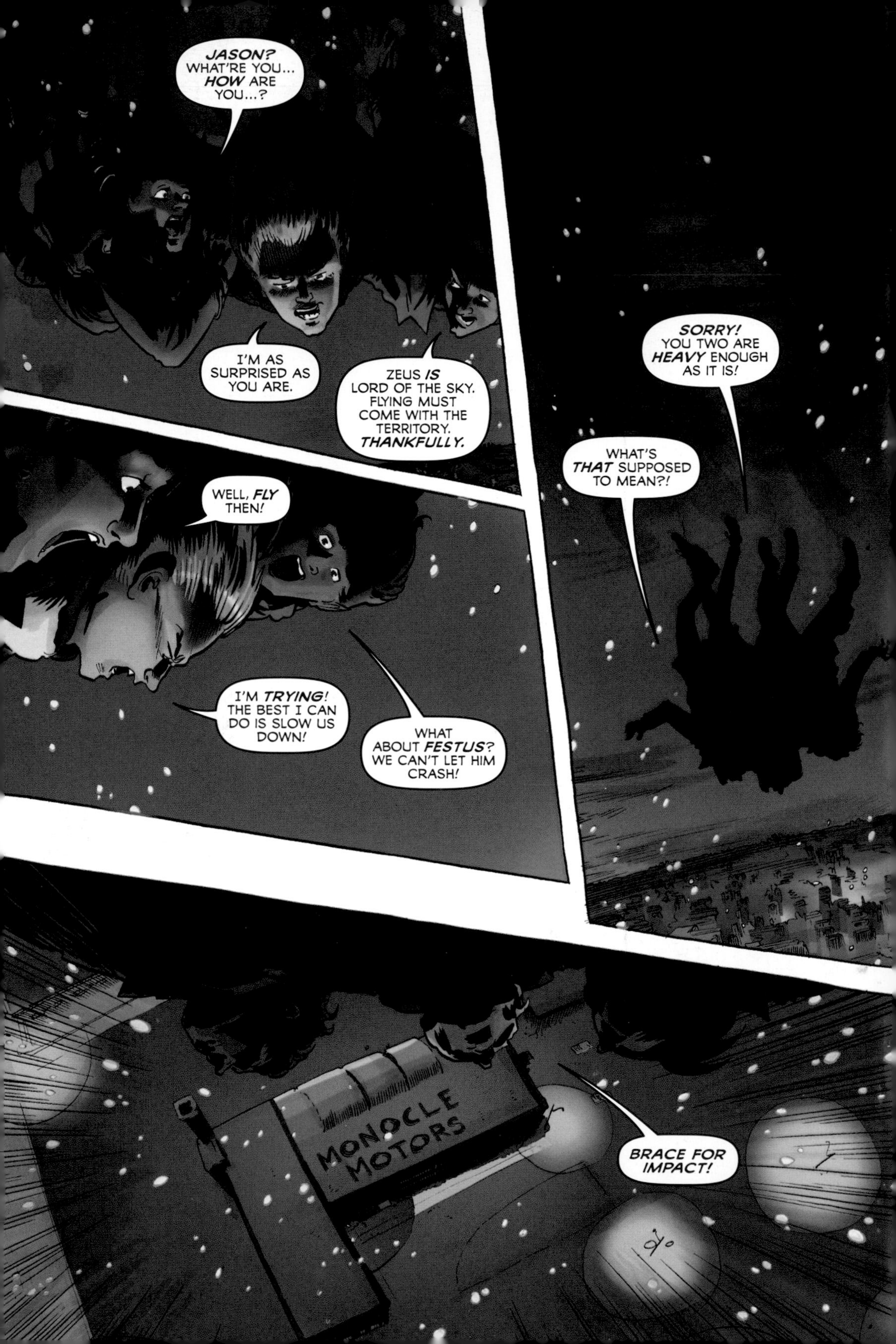
JASON? WHAT'RE YOU... HOW ARE YOU...?
I'M AS SURPRISED AS YOU ARE.
ZEUS IS LORD OF THE SKY. FLYING MUST COME WITH THE TERRITORY. THANKFULLY.
WELL, FLY THEN!
I'M TRYING! THE BEST I CAN DO IS SLOW US DOWN!
WHAT ABOUT FESTUS? WE CAN'T LET HIM CRASH!
SORRY! YOU TWO ARE HEAVY ENOUGH AS IT IS!
WHAT'S THAT SUPPOSED TO MEAN?!
MONOCLE MOTORS
BRACE FOR IMPACT!

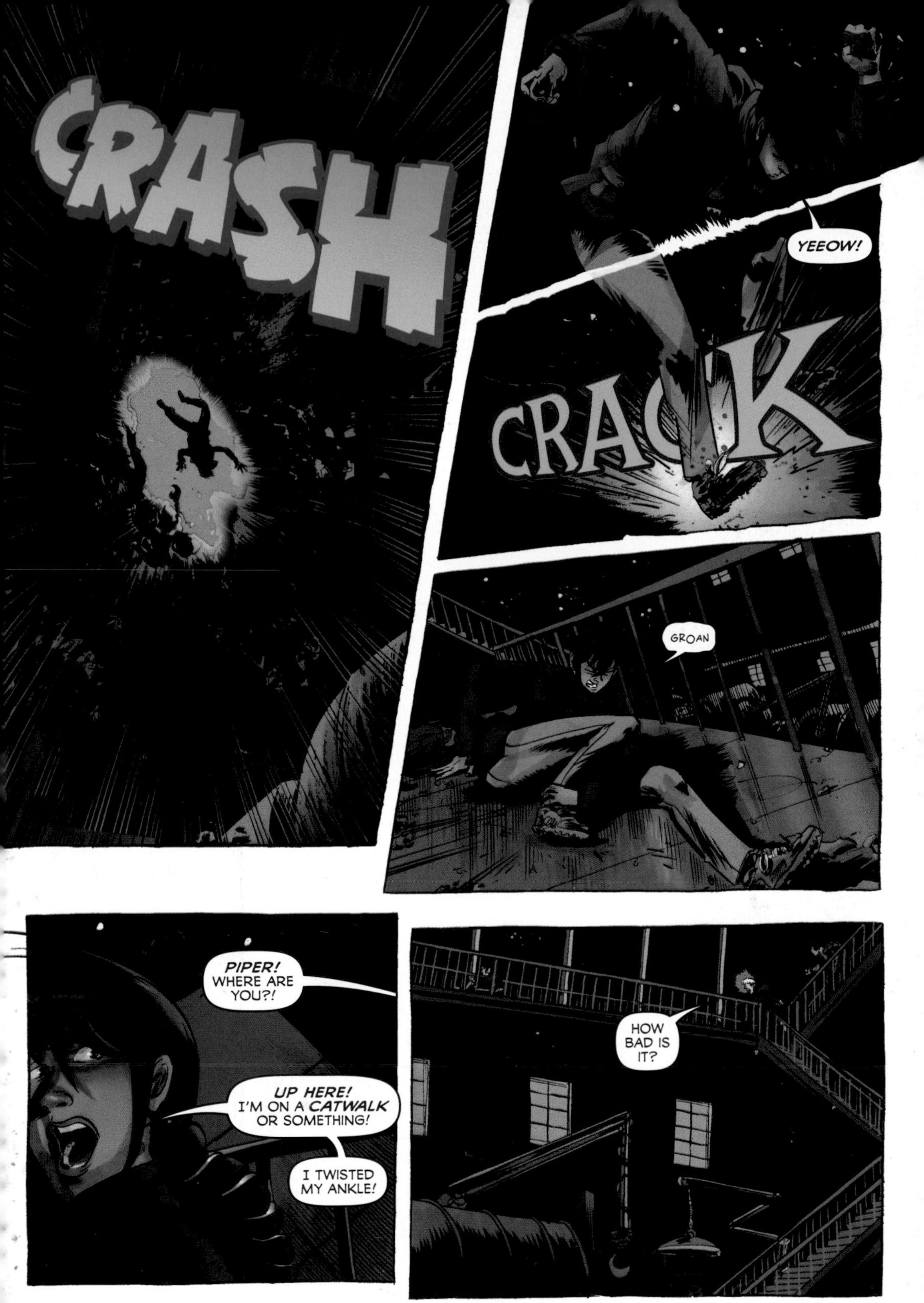
CRASH
YEEOW!
CRACK
GROAN
PIPER! WHERE ARE YOU?!
UP HERE! I'M ON A CATWALK OR SOMETHING!
I TWISTED MY ANKLE!
HOW BAD IS IT?

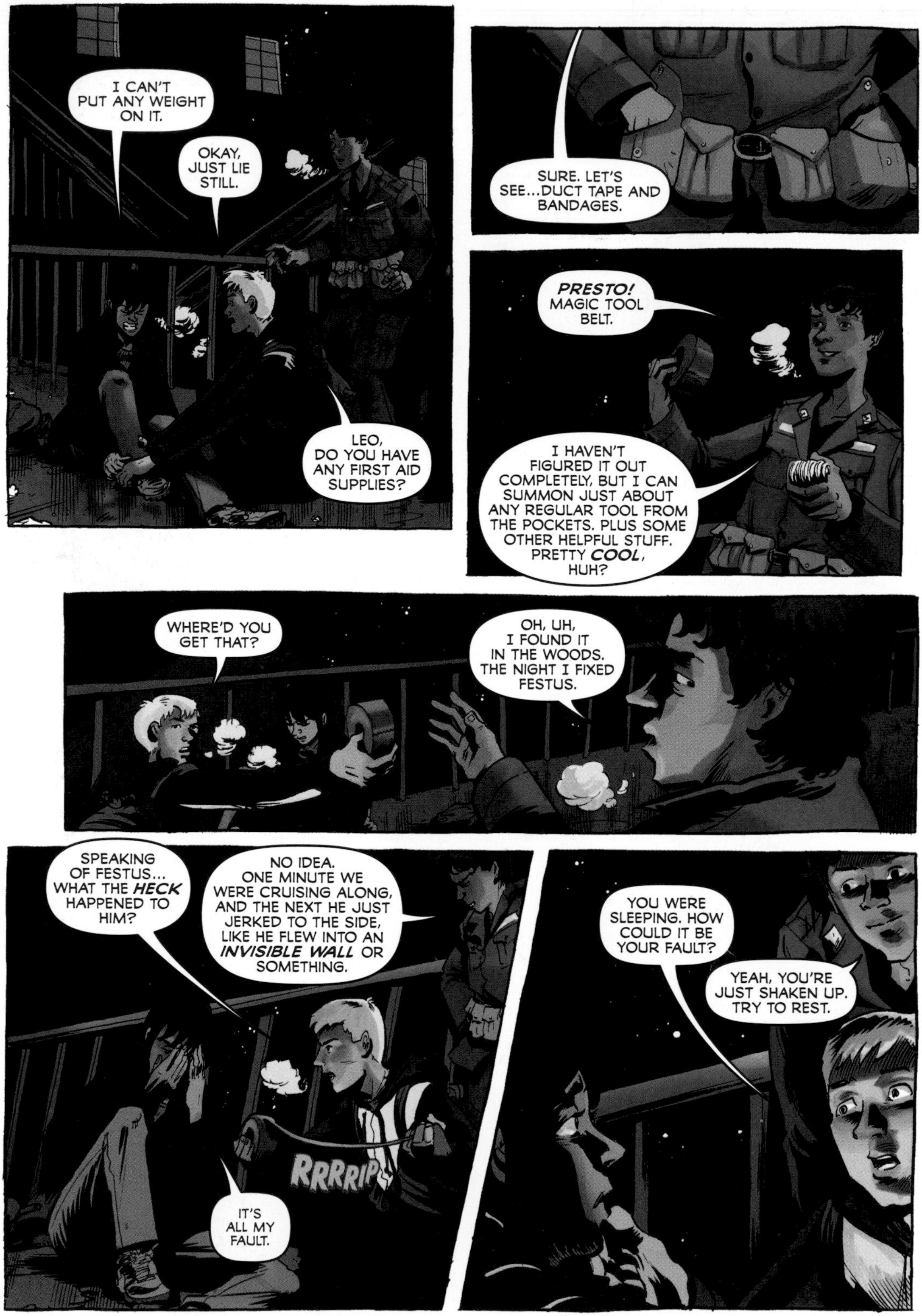
I CAN'T PUT ANY WEIGHT ON IT.
OKAY, JUST LIE STILL.
LEO, DO YOU HAVE ANY FIRST AID SUPPLIES?
SURE. LET'S SEE...DUCT TAPE AND BANDAGES.
PRESTO! MAGIC TOOL BELT.
I HAVEN'T FIGURED IT OUT COMPLETELY, BUT I CAN SUMMON JUST ABOUT ANY REGULAR TOOL FROM THE POCKETS. PLUS SOME OTHER HELPFUL STUFF. PRETTY COOL, HUH?
WHERE'D YOU GET THAT?
OH, UH, I FOUND IT IN THE WOODS. THE NIGHT I FIXED FESTUS.
SPEAKING OF FESTUS... WHAT THE HECK HAPPENED TO HIM?
NO IDEA. ONE MINUTE WE WERE CRUISING ALONG, AND THE NEXT HE JUST JERKED TO THE SIDE, LIKE HE FLEW INTO AN INVISIBLE WALL OR SOMETHING.
RRRRIP
IT'S ALL MY FAULT.
YOU WERE SLEEPING. HOW COULD IT BE YOUR FAULT?
YEAH, YOU'RE JUST SHAKEN UP. TRY TO REST.

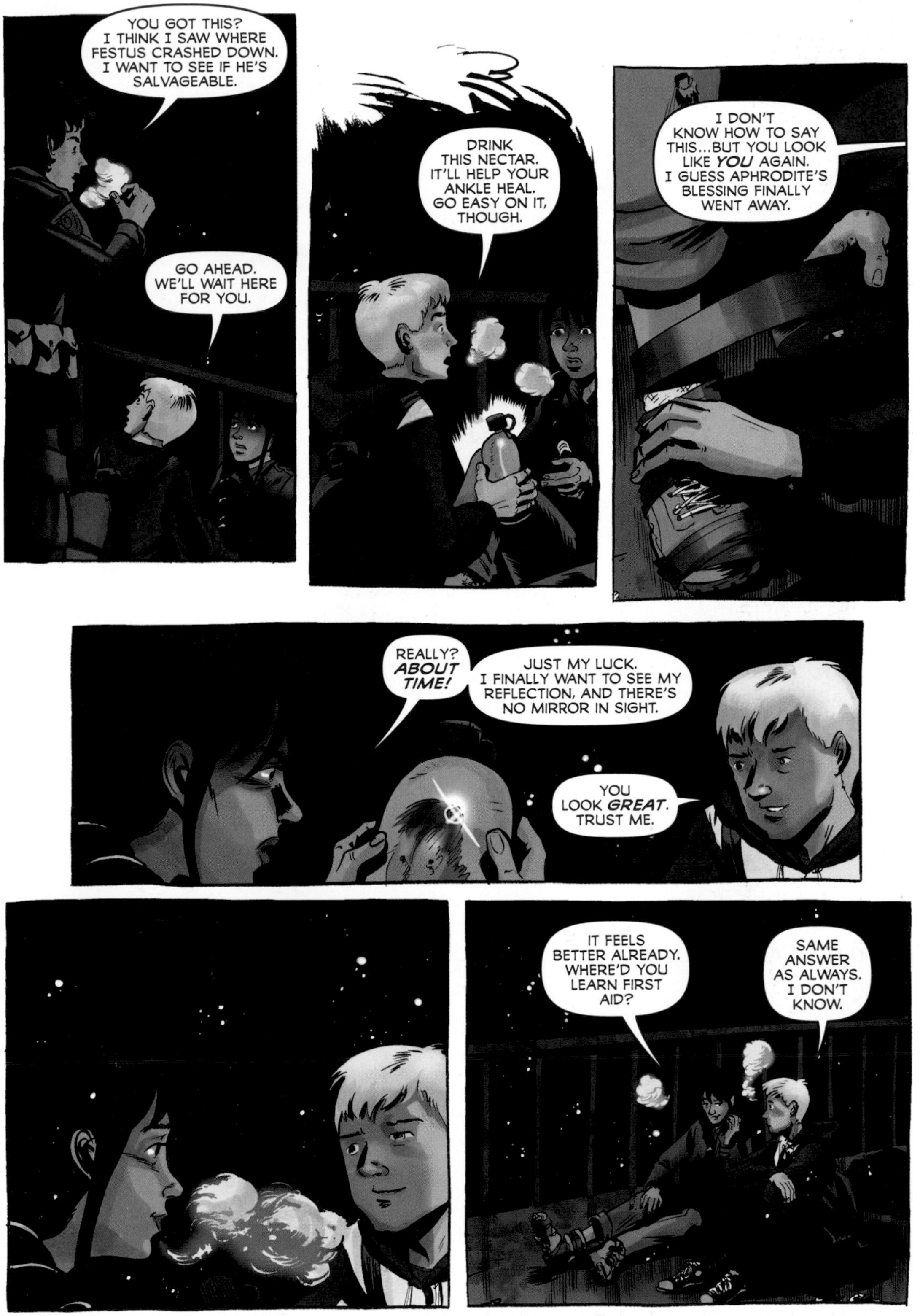
YOU GOT THIS? I THINK I SAW WHERE FESTUS CRASHED DOWN. I WANT TO SEE IF HE'S SALVAGEABLE.
GO AHEAD. WE'LL WAIT HERE FOR YOU.
DRINK THIS NECTAR. IT'LL HELP YOUR ANKLE HEAL. GO EASY ON IT, THOUGH.
I DON'T KNOW HOW TO SAY THIS...BUT YOU LOOK LIKE YOU AGAIN. I GUESS APHRODITE'S BLESSING FINALLY WENT AWAY.
REALLY? ABOUT TIME!
JUST MY LUCK. I FINALLY WANT TO SEE MY REFLECTION, AND THERE'S NO MIRROR IN SIGHT.
YOU LOOK GREAT. TRUST ME.
IT FEELS BETTER ALREADY. WHERE'D YOU LEARN FIRST AID?
SAME ANSWER AS ALWAYS. I DON'T KNOW.

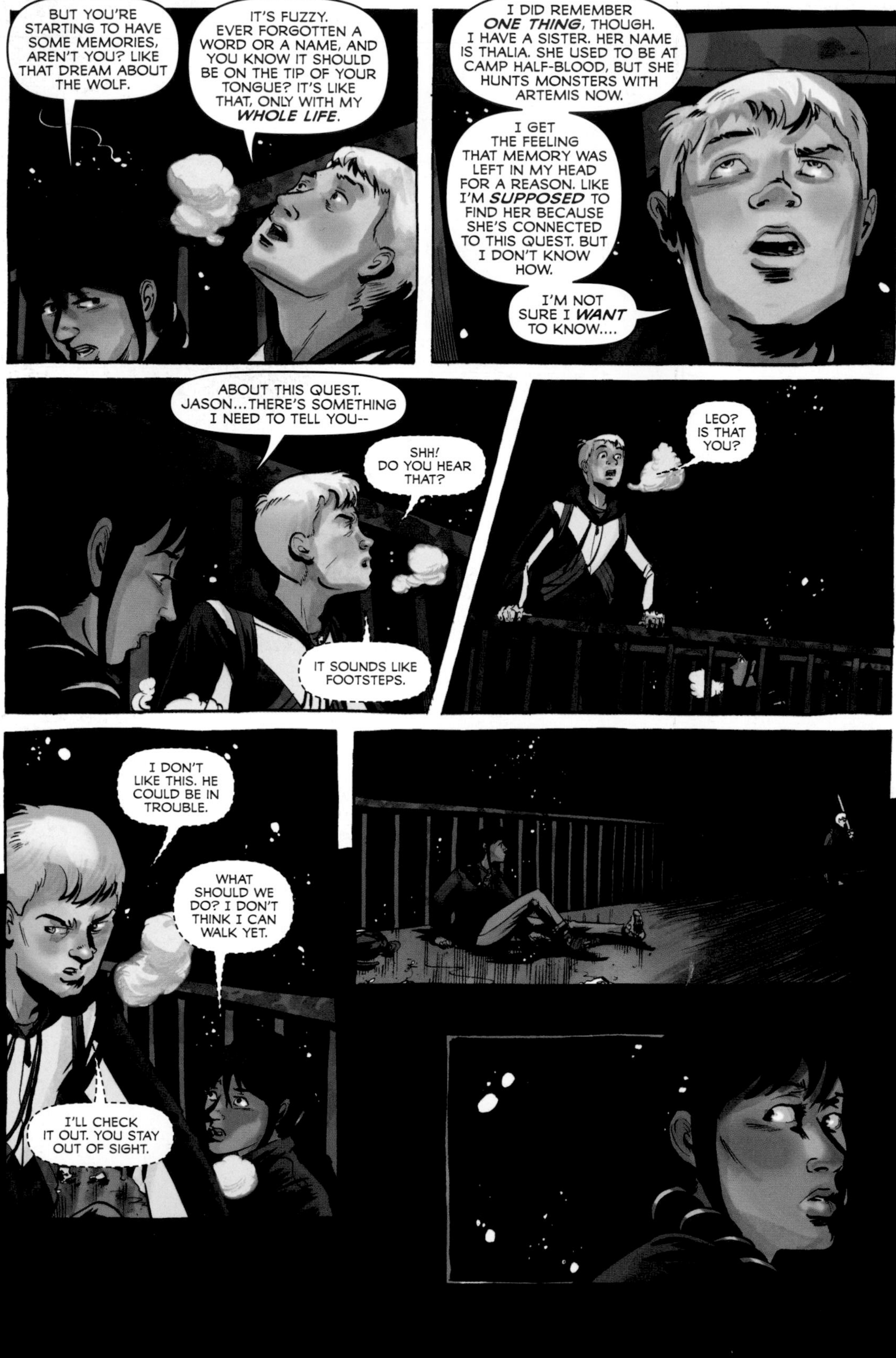
BUT YOU'RE STARTING TO HAVE SOME MEMORIES, AREN'T YOU? LIKE THAT DREAM ABOUT THE WOLF.
IT'S FUZZY. EVER FORGOTTEN A WORD OR A NAME, AND YOU KNOW IT SHOULD BE ON THE TIP OF YOUR TONGUE? IT'S LIKE THAT, ONLY WITH MY WHOLE LIFE.
I DID REMEMBER ONE THING, THOUGH. I HAVE A SISTER. HER NAME IS THALIA. SHE USED TO BE AT CAMP HALF-BLOOD, BUT SHE HUNTS MONSTERS WITH ARTEMIS NOW.
I GET THE FEELING THAT MEMORY WAS LEFT IN MY HEAD FOR A REASON. LIKE I'M SUPPOSED TO FIND HER BECAUSE SHE'S CONNECTED TO THIS QUEST. BUT I DON'T KNOW HOW.
I'M NOT SURE I WANT TO KNOW....
ABOUT THIS QUEST. JASON...THERE'S SOMETHING I NEED TO TELL YOU--
SHH! DO YOU HEAR THAT?
IT SOUNDS LIKE FOOTSTEPS.
LEO? IS THAT YOU?
I DON'T LIKE THIS. HE COULD BE IN TROUBLE.
WHAT SHOULD WE DO? I DON'T THINK I CAN WALK YET.
I'LL CHECK IT OUT. YOU STAY OUT OF SIGHT.

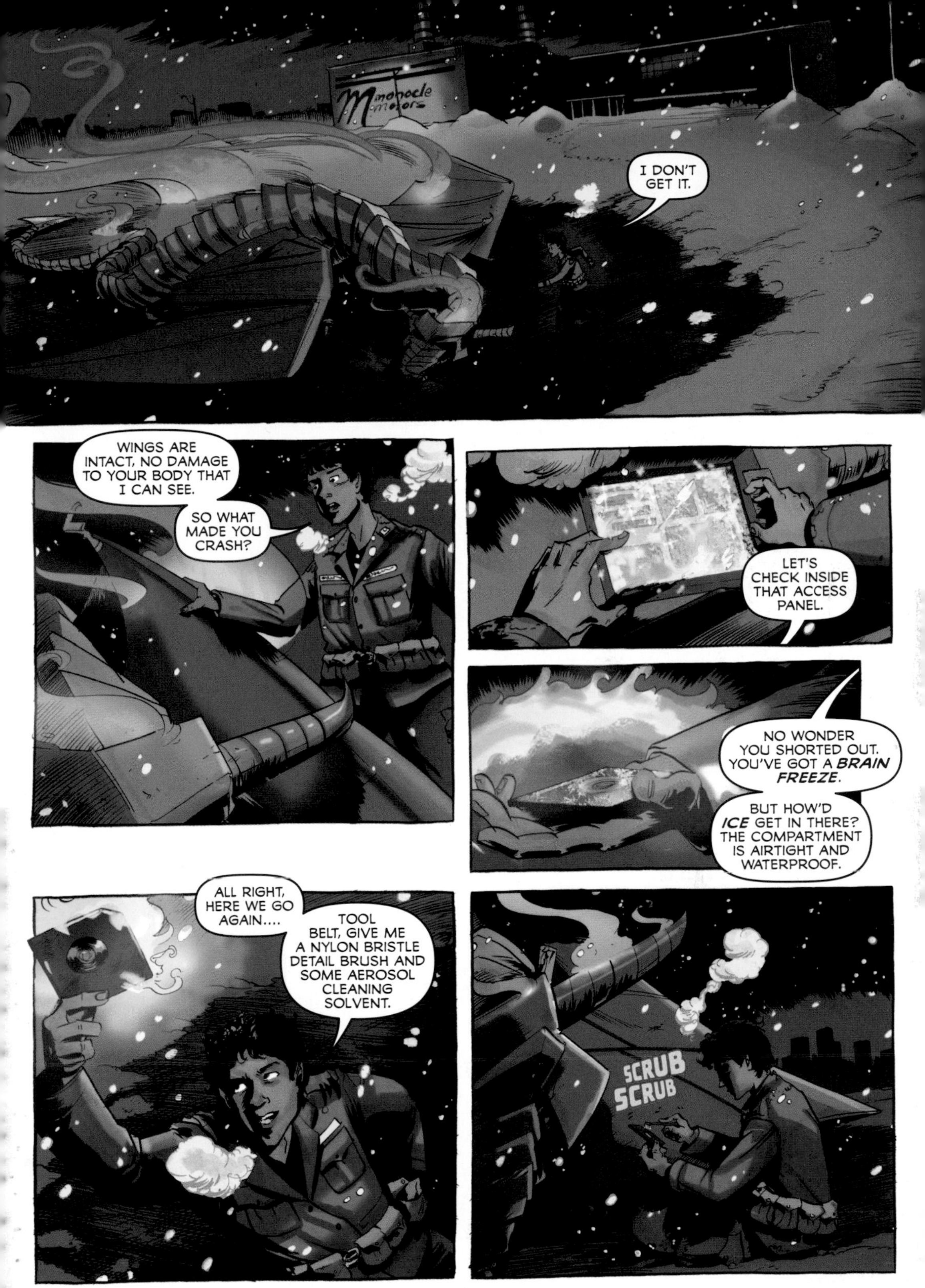
Monocle Motors
I DON'T GET IT.
WINGS ARE INTACT, NO DAMAGE TO YOUR BODY THAT I CAN SEE.
SO WHAT MADE YOU CRASH?
LET'S CHECK INSIDE THAT ACCESS PANEL.
NO WONDER YOU SHORTED OUT. YOU'VE GOT A ***BRAIN FREEZE***.
BUT HOW'D ***ICE*** GET IN THERE? THE COMPARTMENT IS AIRTIGHT AND WATERPROOF.
ALL RIGHT, HERE WE GO AGAIN....
TOOL BELT, GIVE ME A NYLON BRISTLE DETAIL BRUSH AND SOME AEROSOL CLEANING SOLVENT.
SCRUB SCRUB

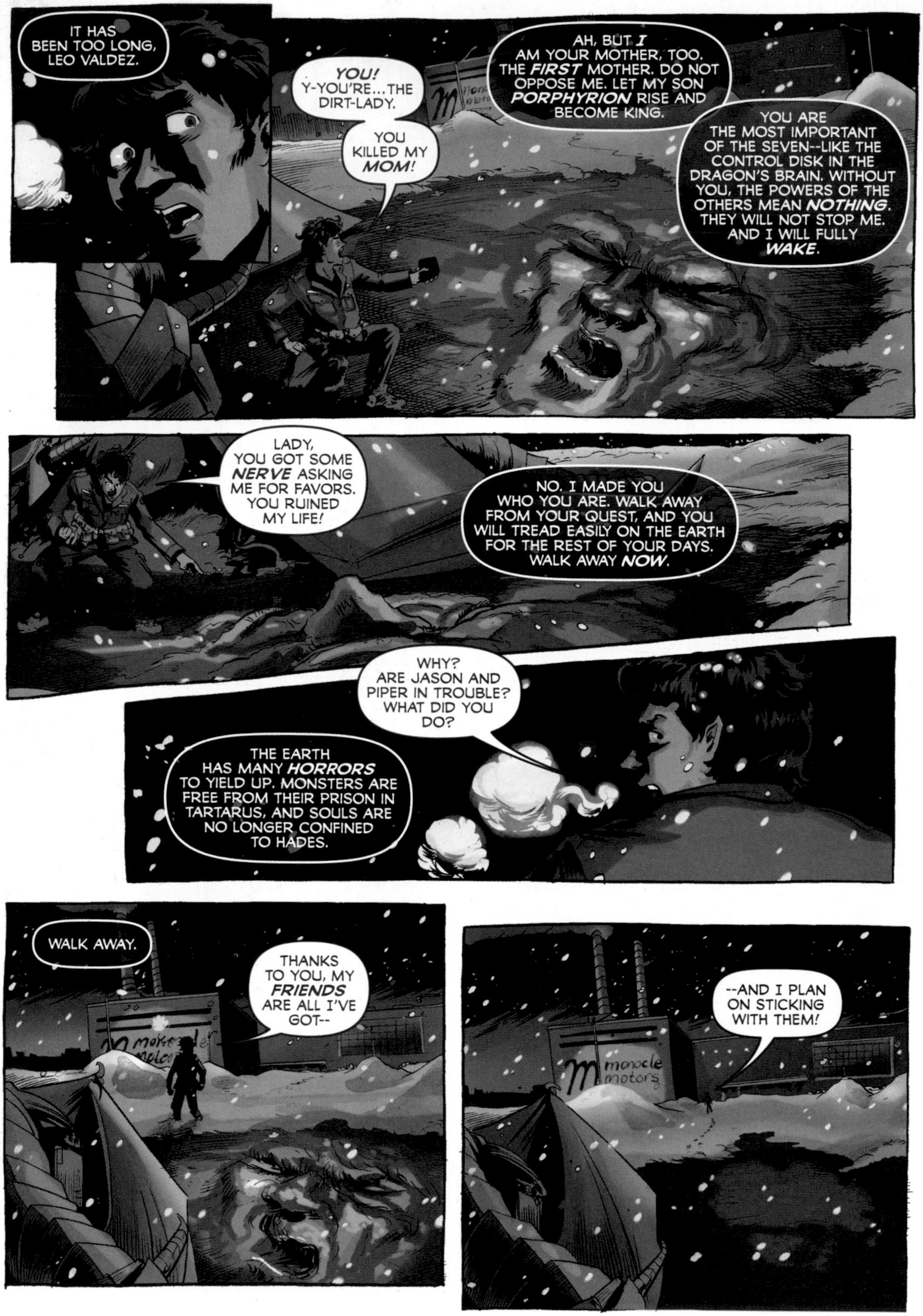
IT HAS BEEN TOO LONG, LEO VALDEZ.
YOU! Y-YOU'RE... THE DIRT-LADY.
YOU KILLED MY MOM!
AH, BUT I AM YOUR MOTHER, TOO. THE FIRST MOTHER. DO NOT OPPOSE ME. LET MY SON PORPHYRION RISE AND BECOME KING.
YOU ARE THE MOST IMPORTANT OF THE SEVEN--LIKE THE CONTROL DISK IN THE DRAGON'S BRAIN. WITHOUT YOU, THE POWERS OF THE OTHERS MEAN NOTHING. THEY WILL NOT STOP ME. AND I WILL FULLY WAKE.
LADY, YOU GOT SOME NERVE ASKING ME FOR FAVORS. YOU RUINED MY LIFE!
NO. I MADE YOU WHO YOU ARE. WALK AWAY FROM YOUR QUEST, AND YOU WILL TREAD EASILY ON THE EARTH FOR THE REST OF YOUR DAYS. WALK AWAY NOW.
WHY? ARE JASON AND PIPER IN TROUBLE? WHAT DID YOU DO?
THE EARTH HAS MANY HORRORS TO YIELD UP. MONSTERS ARE FREE FROM THEIR PRISON IN TARTARUS, AND SOULS ARE NO LONGER CONFINED TO HADES.
WALK AWAY.
THANKS TO YOU, MY FRIENDS ARE ALL I'VE GOT--
--AND I PLAN ON STICKING WITH THEM!
monocle motors

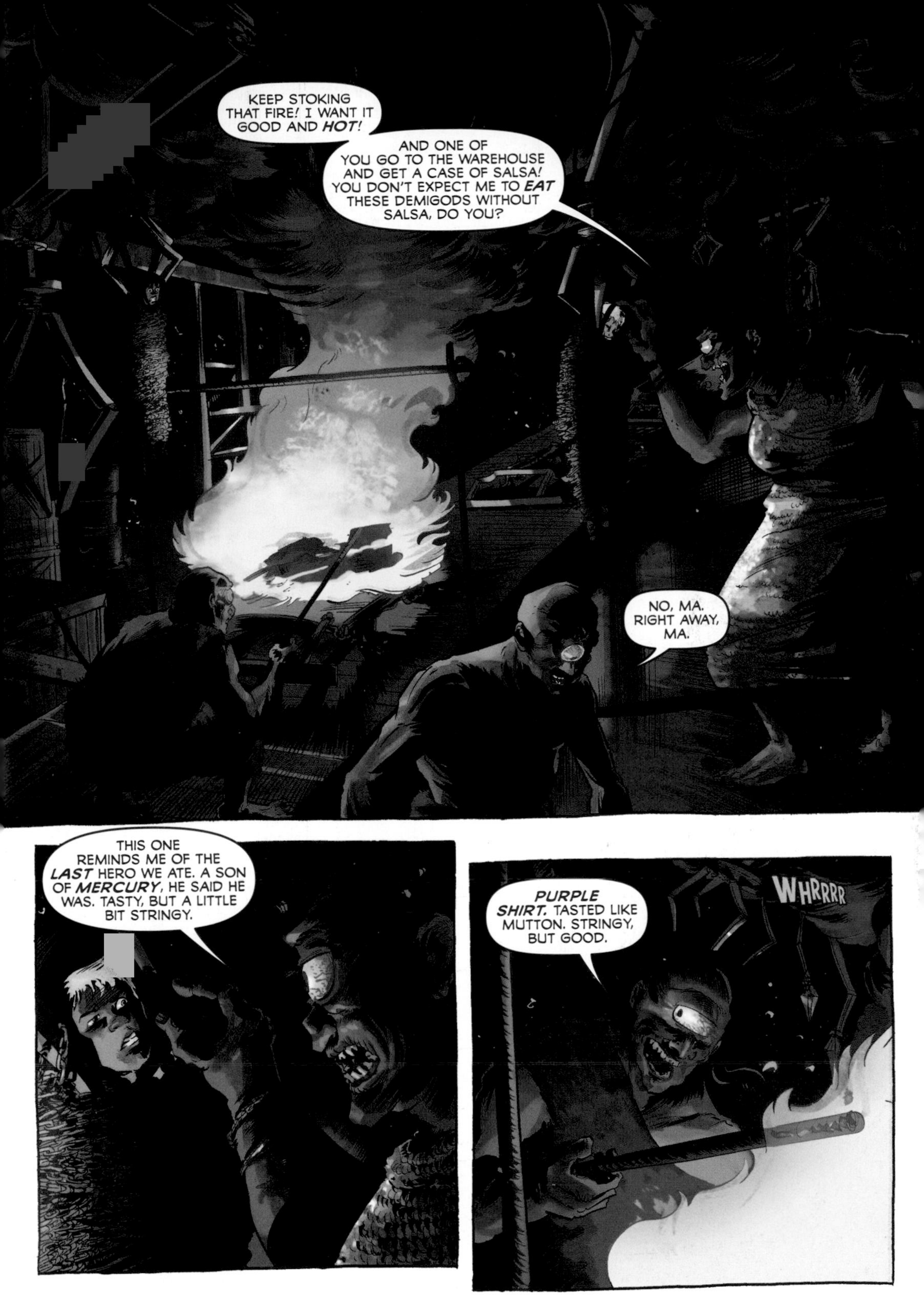
KEEP STOKING THAT FIRE! I WANT IT GOOD AND *HOT*!
AND ONE OF YOU GO TO THE WAREHOUSE AND GET A CASE OF SALSA! YOU DON'T EXPECT ME TO *EAT* THESE DEMIGODS WITHOUT SALSA, DO YOU?
NO, MA. RIGHT AWAY, MA.
THIS ONE REMINDS ME OF THE *LAST* HERO WE ATE. A SON OF *MERCURY*, HE SAID HE WAS. TASTY, BUT A LITTLE BIT STRINGY.
PURPLE SHIRT. TASTED LIKE MUTTON. STRINGY, BUT GOOD.
WHRRRR

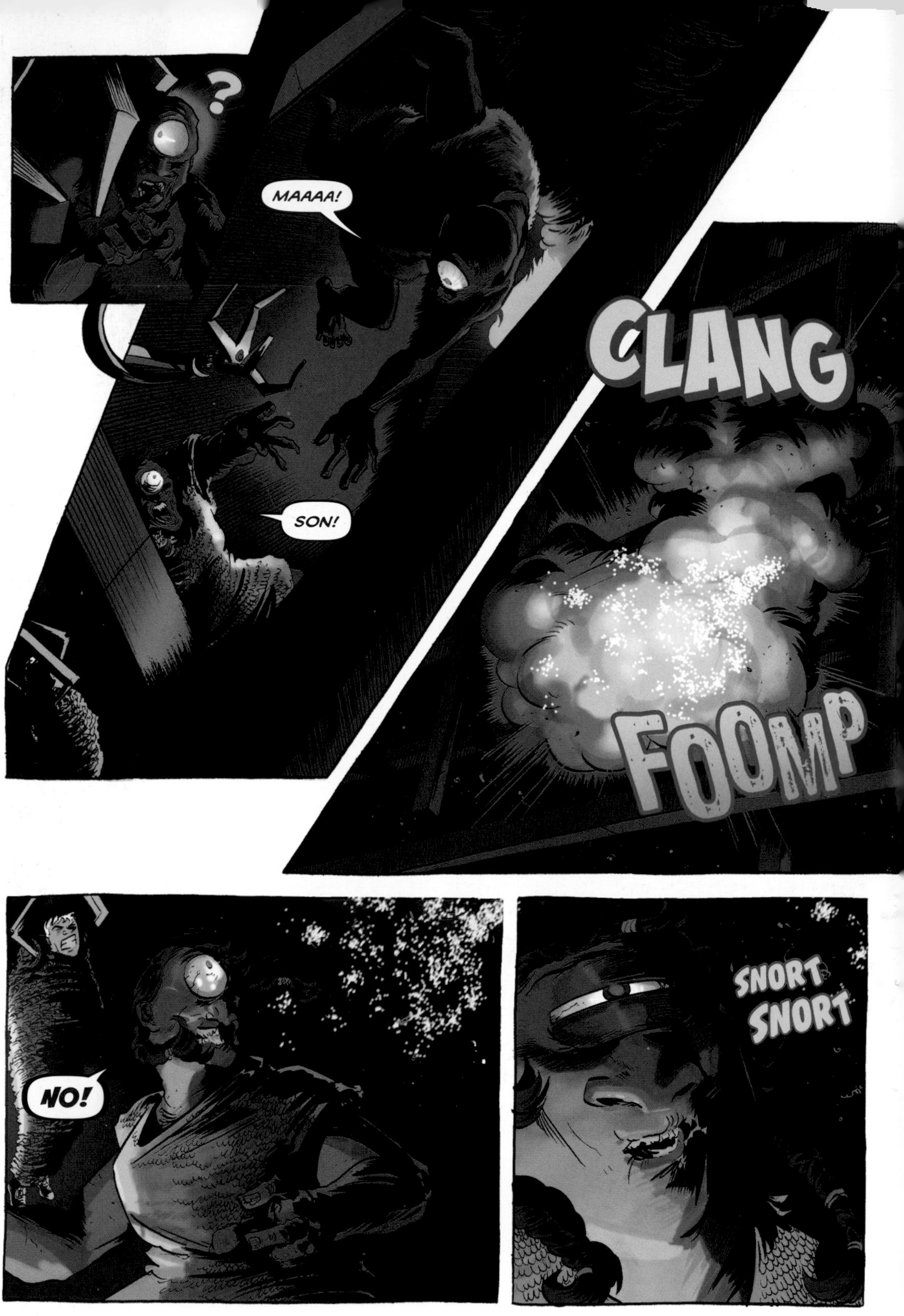
?
MAAAA!
SON!
CLANG
FOOMP
NO!
SNORT
SNORT

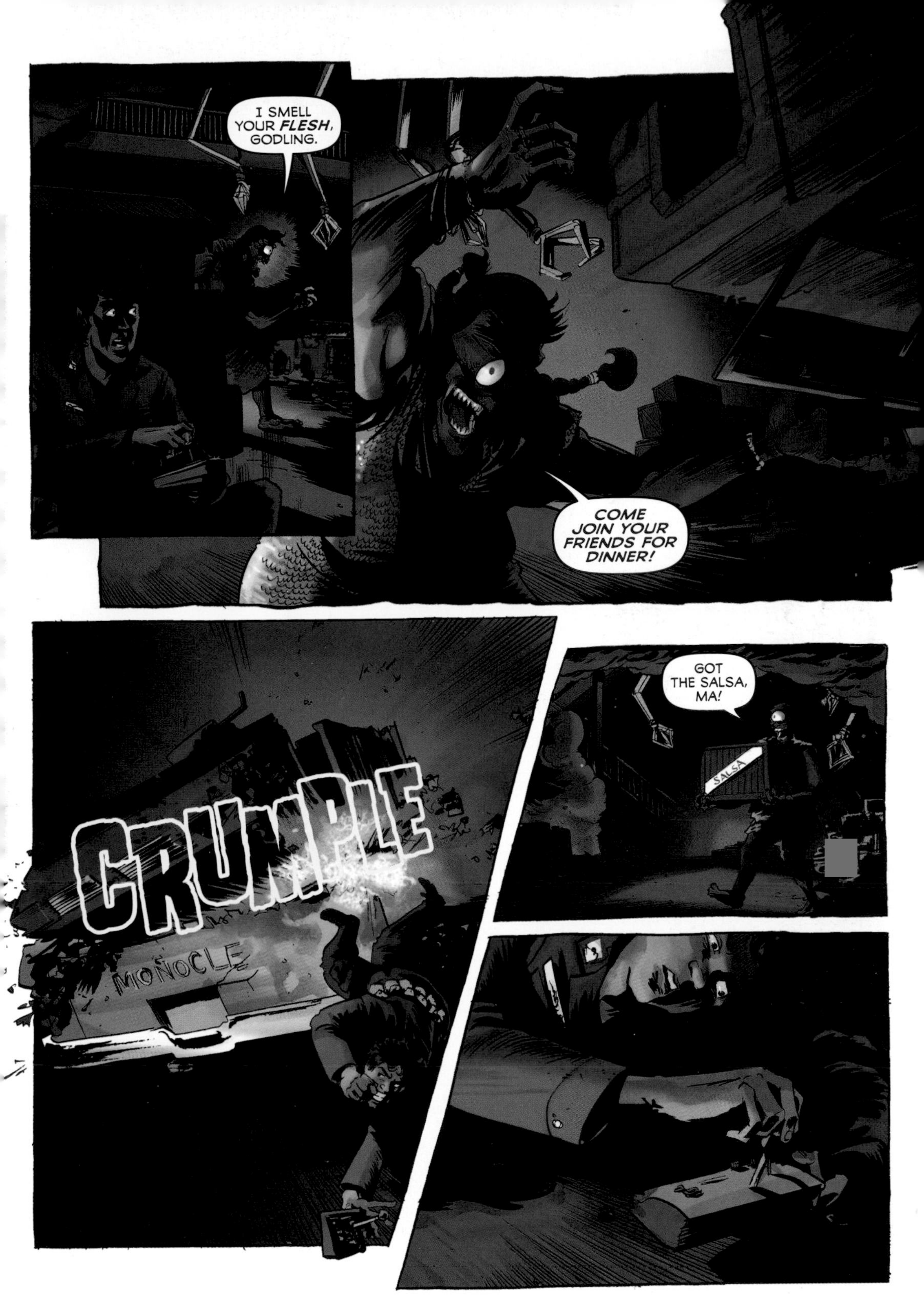
I SMELL YOUR *FLESH*, GODLING.
COME JOIN YOUR FRIENDS FOR DINNER!
CRUMPLE
MONOCLE
GOT THE SALSA, MA!
SALSA

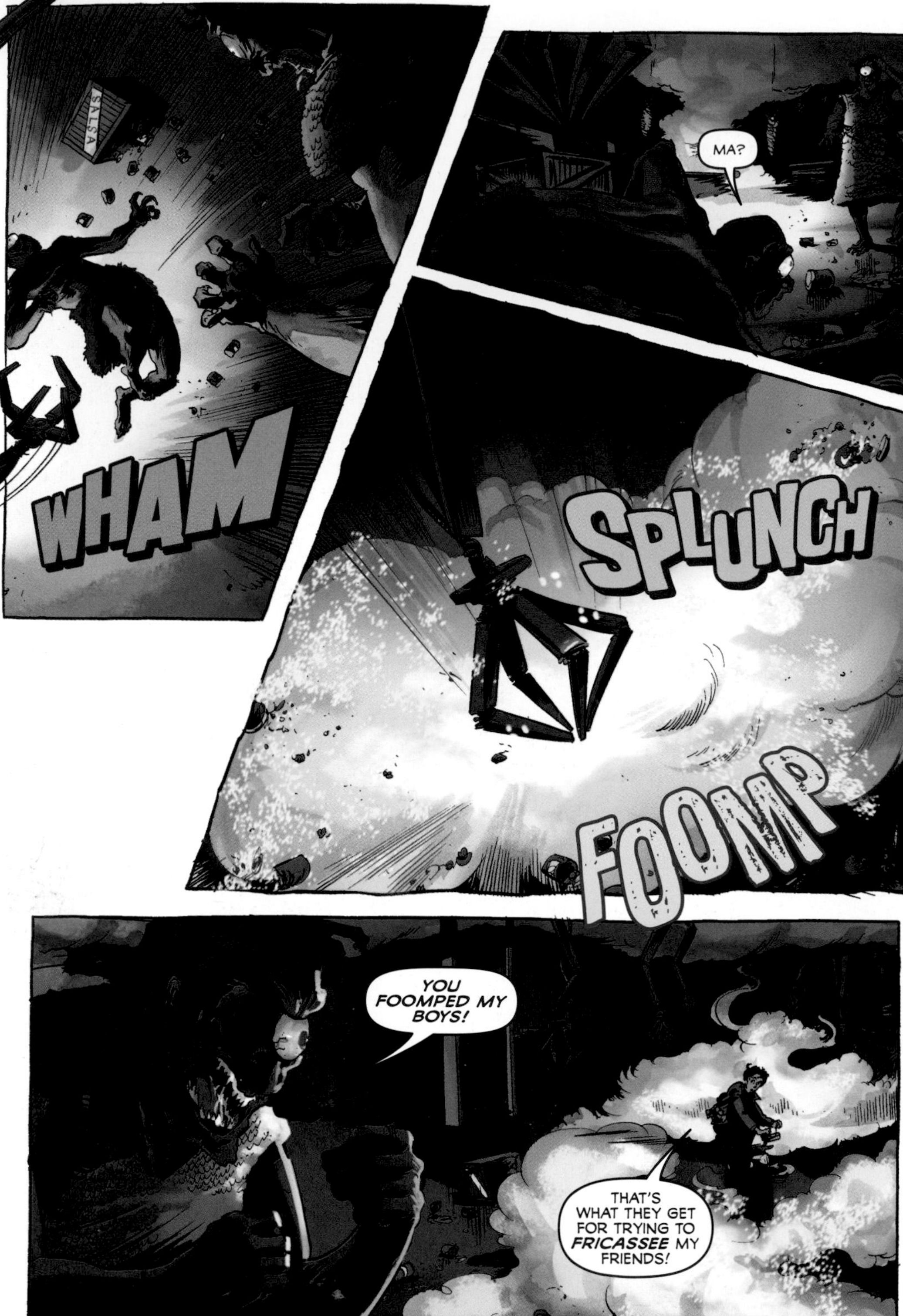
SALSA
WHAM
MA?
SPLUNCH
FOOMP
YOU FOOMPED MY BOYS!
THAT'S WHAT THEY GET FOR TRYING TO *FRICASSEE* MY FRIENDS!

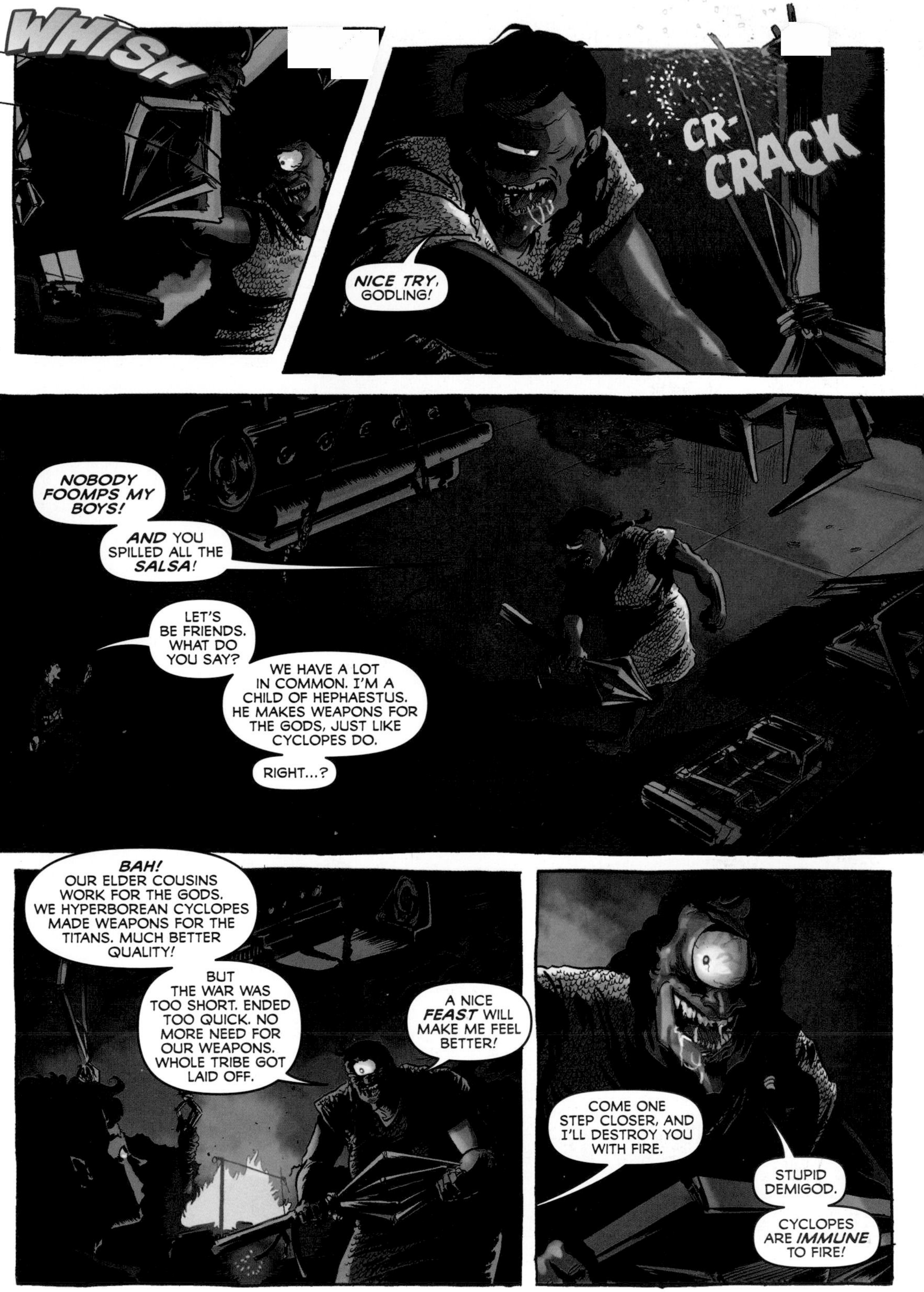
WHISH
NICE TRY, GODLING!
CR-CRACK
NOBODY FOOMPS MY BOYS!
AND YOU SPILLED ALL THE SALSA!
LET'S BE FRIENDS. WHAT DO YOU SAY?
WE HAVE A LOT IN COMMON. I'M A CHILD OF HEPHAESTUS. HE MAKES WEAPONS FOR THE GODS, JUST LIKE CYCLOPES DO.
RIGHT...?
BAH! OUR ELDER COUSINS WORK FOR THE GODS. WE HYPERBOREAN CYCLOPES MADE WEAPONS FOR THE TITANS. MUCH BETTER QUALITY!
BUT THE WAR WAS TOO SHORT. ENDED TOO QUICK. NO MORE NEED FOR OUR WEAPONS. WHOLE TRIBE GOT LAID OFF.
A NICE FEAST WILL MAKE ME FEEL BETTER!
COME ONE STEP CLOSER, AND I'LL DESTROY YOU WITH FIRE.
STUPID DEMIGOD.
CYCLOPES ARE IMMUNE TO FIRE!

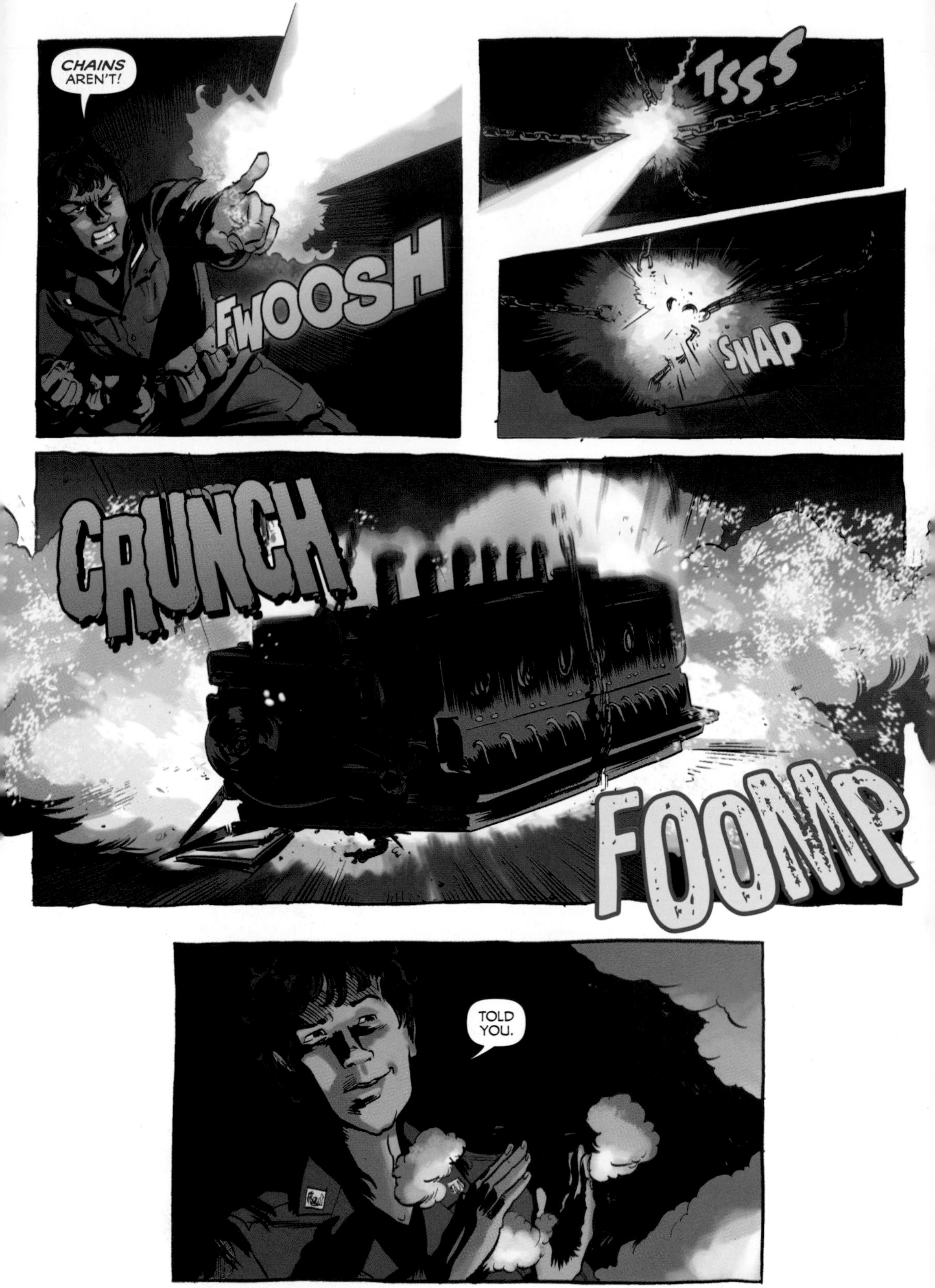
CHAINS AREN'T!
FWOOSH
TSSS
SNAP
CRUNCH
FOOMP
TOLD YOU.

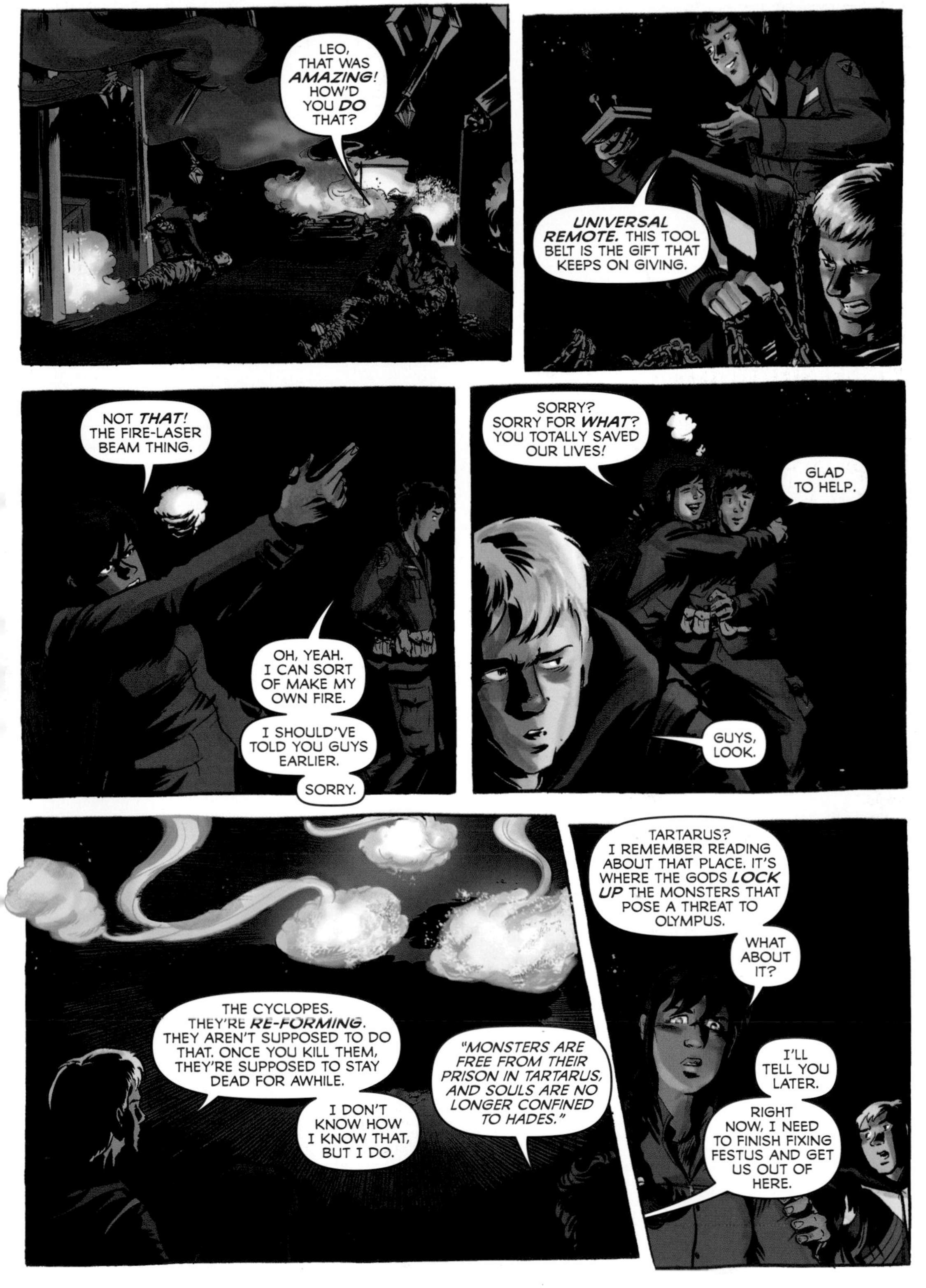

LEO, THAT WAS AMAZING! HOW'D YOU DO THAT?
UNIVERSAL REMOTE. THIS TOOL BELT IS THE GIFT THAT KEEPS ON GIVING.
NOT THAT! THE FIRE-LASER BEAM THING.
OH, YEAH. I CAN SORT OF MAKE MY OWN FIRE.
I SHOULD'VE TOLD YOU GUYS EARLIER.
SORRY.
SORRY? SORRY FOR WHAT? YOU TOTALLY SAVED OUR LIVES!
GLAD TO HELP.
GUYS, LOOK.
THE CYCLOPES. THEY'RE RE-FORMING. THEY AREN'T SUPPOSED TO DO THAT. ONCE YOU KILL THEM, THEY'RE SUPPOSED TO STAY DEAD FOR AWHILE.
I DON'T KNOW HOW I KNOW THAT, BUT I DO.
"MONSTERS ARE FREE FROM THEIR PRISON IN TARTARUS, AND SOULS ARE NO LONGER CONFINED TO HADES."
TARTARUS? I REMEMBER READING ABOUT THAT PLACE. IT'S WHERE THE GODS LOCK UP THE MONSTERS THAT POSE A THREAT TO OLYMPUS.
WHAT ABOUT IT?
I'LL TELL YOU LATER.
RIGHT NOW, I NEED TO FINISH FIXING FESTUS AND GET US OUT OF HERE.

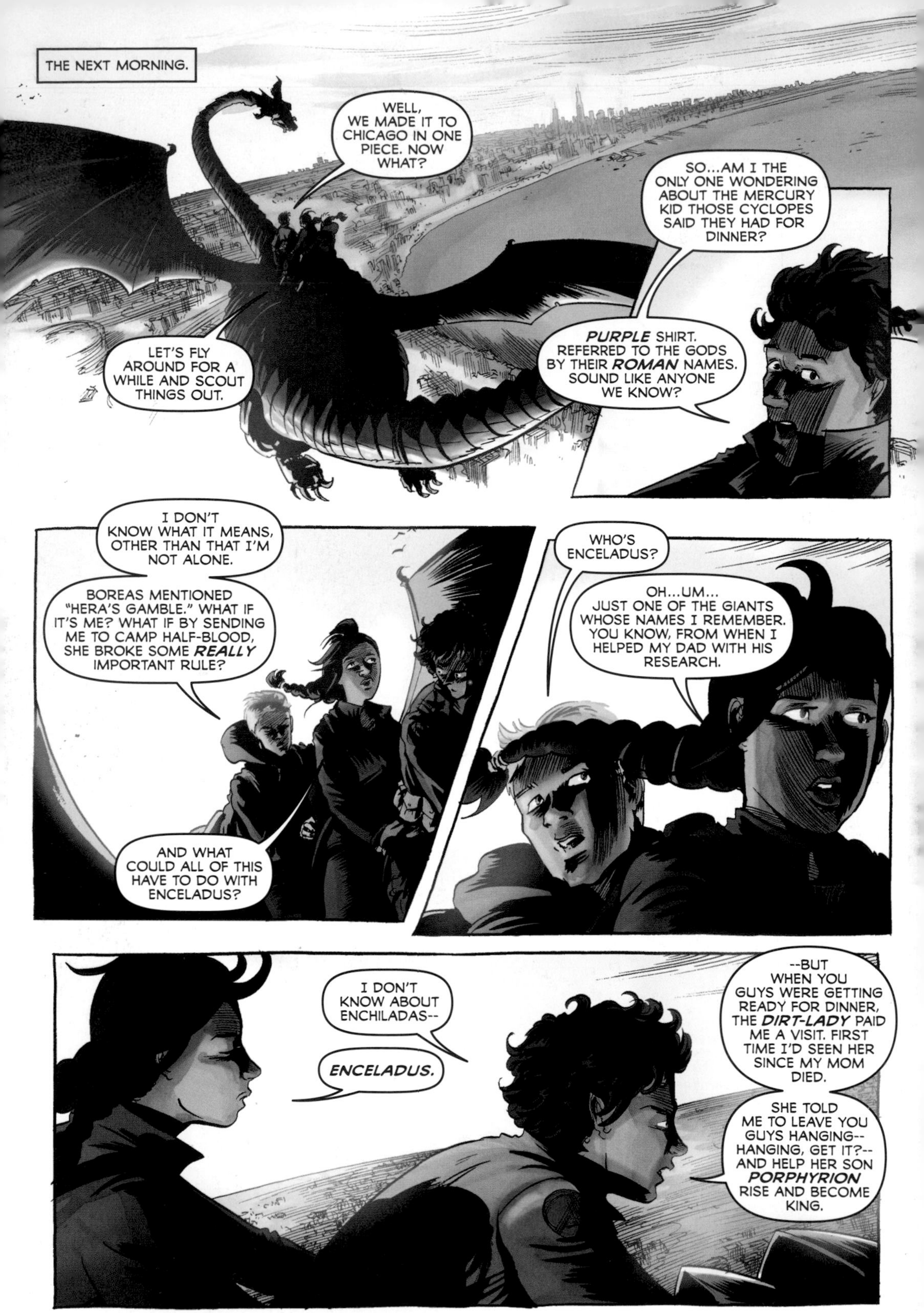
THE NEXT MORNING.
WELL, WE MADE IT TO CHICAGO IN ONE PIECE. NOW WHAT?
LET'S FLY AROUND FOR A WHILE AND SCOUT THINGS OUT.
SO...AM I THE ONLY ONE WONDERING ABOUT THE MERCURY KID THOSE CYCLOPES SAID THEY HAD FOR DINNER?
PURPLE SHIRT. REFERRED TO THE GODS BY THEIR *ROMAN* NAMES. SOUND LIKE ANYONE WE KNOW?
I DON'T KNOW WHAT IT MEANS, OTHER THAN THAT I'M NOT ALONE.
BOREAS MENTIONED "HERA'S GAMBLE." WHAT IF IT'S ME? WHAT IF BY SENDING ME TO CAMP HALF-BLOOD, SHE BROKE SOME *REALLY* IMPORTANT RULE?
AND WHAT COULD ALL OF THIS HAVE TO DO WITH ENCELADUS?
WHO'S ENCELADUS?
OH...UM... JUST ONE OF THE GIANTS WHOSE NAMES I REMEMBER. YOU KNOW, FROM WHEN I HELPED MY DAD WITH HIS RESEARCH.
I DON'T KNOW ABOUT ENCHILADAS--
ENCELADUS.
--BUT WHEN YOU GUYS WERE GETTING READY FOR DINNER, THE *DIRT-LADY* PAID ME A VISIT. FIRST TIME I'D SEEN HER SINCE MY MOM DIED.
SHE TOLD ME TO LEAVE YOU GUYS HANGING--HANGING, GET IT?--AND HELP HER SON *PORPHYRION* RISE AND BECOME KING.

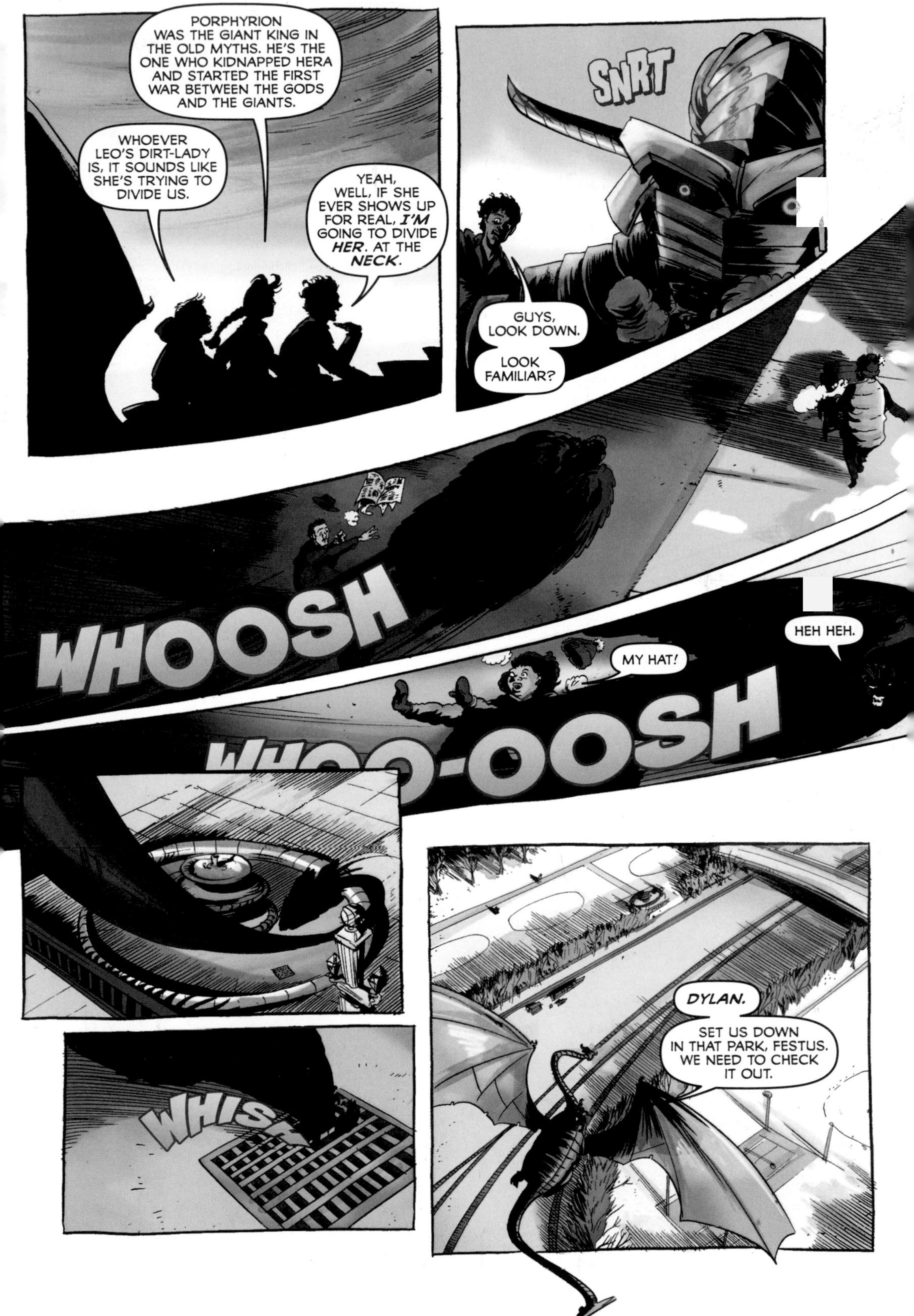
PORPHYRION WAS THE GIANT KING IN THE OLD MYTHS. HE'S THE ONE WHO KIDNAPPED HERA AND STARTED THE FIRST WAR BETWEEN THE GODS AND THE GIANTS.
WHOEVER LEO'S DIRT-LADY IS, IT SOUNDS LIKE SHE'S TRYING TO DIVIDE US.
YEAH, WELL, IF SHE EVER SHOWS UP FOR REAL, *I'M* GOING TO DIVIDE *HER*. AT THE *NECK*.
SNRT
GUYS, LOOK DOWN.
LOOK FAMILIAR?
WHOOSH
HEH HEH.
MY HAT!
WHOO-OOSH
WHISH
DYLAN.
SET US DOWN IN THAT PARK, FESTUS. WE NEED TO CHECK IT OUT.

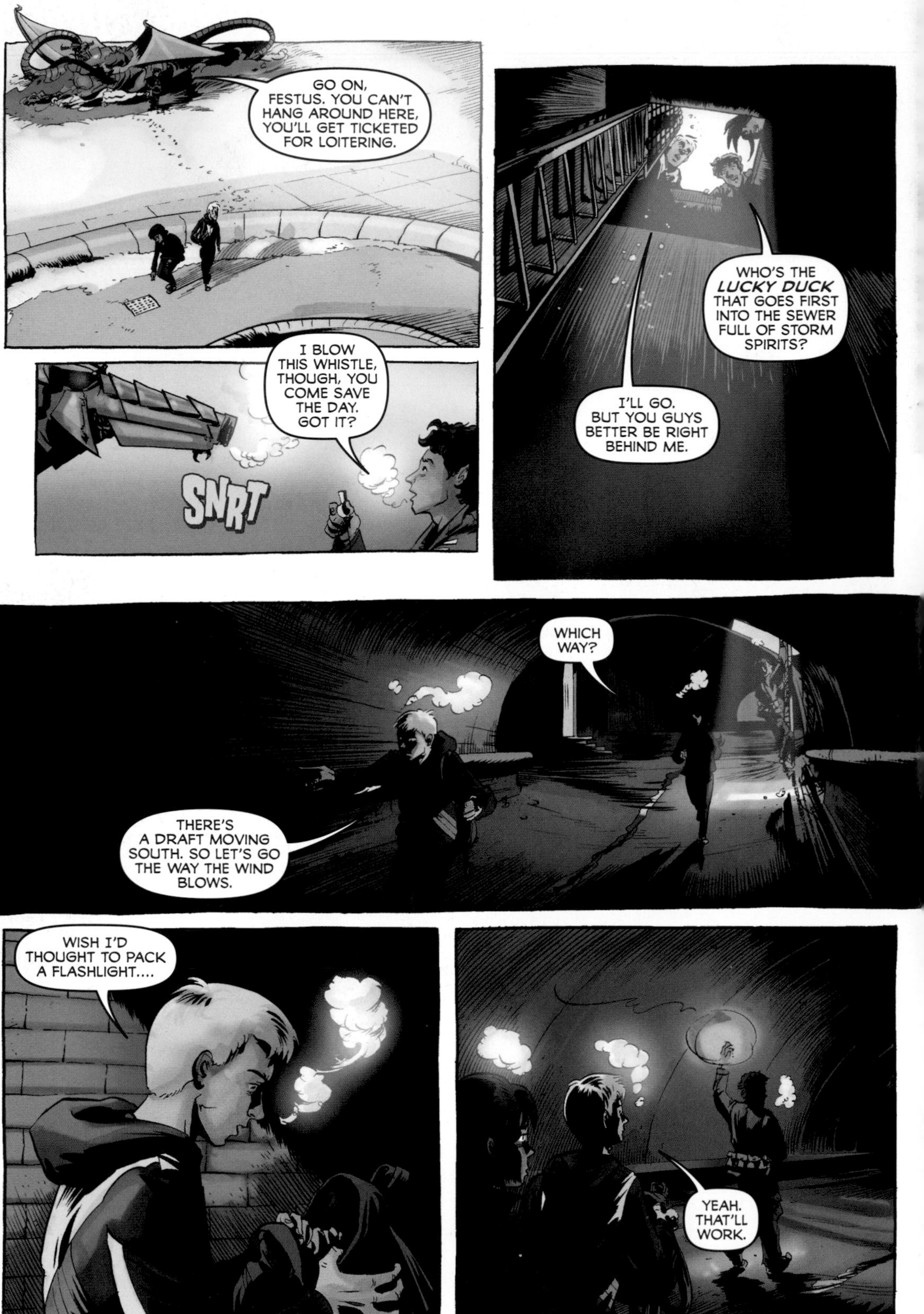
GO ON, FESTUS. YOU CAN'T HANG AROUND HERE, YOU'LL GET TICKETED FOR LOITERING.
I BLOW THIS WHISTLE, THOUGH, YOU COME SAVE THE DAY. GOT IT?
SNRT
WHO'S THE *LUCKY DUCK* THAT GOES FIRST INTO THE SEWER FULL OF STORM SPIRITS?
I'LL GO. BUT YOU GUYS BETTER BE RIGHT BEHIND ME.
WHICH WAY?
THERE'S A DRAFT MOVING SOUTH. SO LET'S GO THE WAY THE WIND BLOWS.
WISH I'D THOUGHT TO PACK A FLASHLIGHT....
YEAH. THAT'LL WORK.

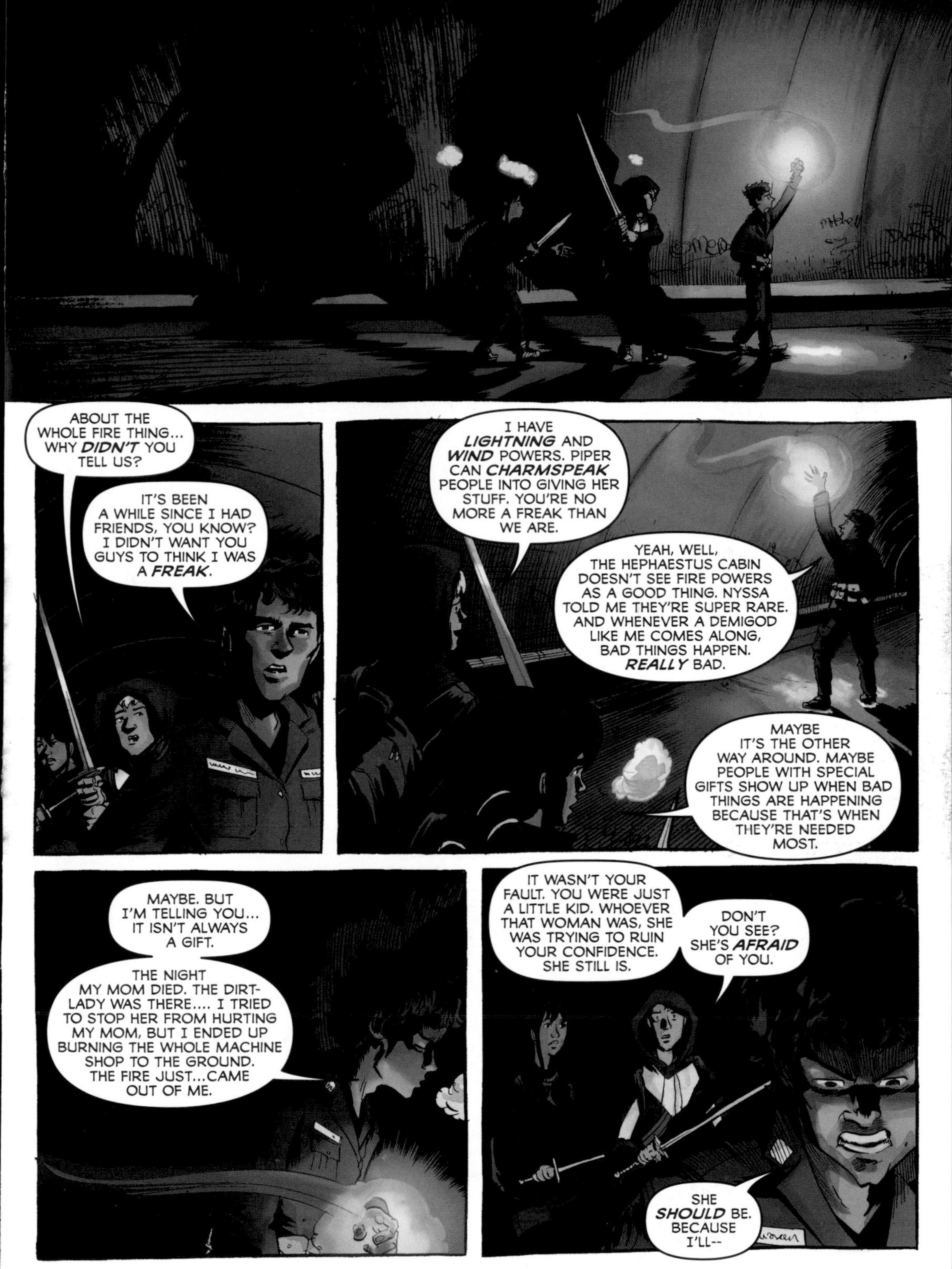
ABOUT THE WHOLE FIRE THING... WHY *DIDN'T* YOU TELL US?
IT'S BEEN A WHILE SINCE I HAD FRIENDS, YOU KNOW? I DIDN'T WANT YOU GUYS TO THINK I WAS A *FREAK*.
I HAVE *LIGHTNING* AND *WIND* POWERS. PIPER CAN *CHARMSPEAK* PEOPLE INTO GIVING HER STUFF. YOU'RE NO MORE A FREAK THAN WE ARE.
YEAH, WELL, THE HEPHAESTUS CABIN DOESN'T SEE FIRE POWERS AS A GOOD THING. NYSSA TOLD ME THEY'RE SUPER RARE. AND WHENEVER A DEMIGOD LIKE ME COMES ALONG, BAD THINGS HAPPEN. *REALLY* BAD.
MAYBE IT'S THE OTHER WAY AROUND. MAYBE PEOPLE WITH SPECIAL GIFTS SHOW UP WHEN BAD THINGS ARE HAPPENING BECAUSE THAT'S WHEN THEY'RE NEEDED MOST.
MAYBE. BUT I'M TELLING YOU... IT ISN'T ALWAYS A GIFT.
THE NIGHT MY MOM DIED. THE DIRT-LADY WAS THERE.... I TRIED TO STOP HER FROM HURTING MY MOM, BUT I ENDED UP BURNING THE WHOLE MACHINE SHOP TO THE GROUND. THE FIRE JUST...CAME OUT OF ME.
IT WASN'T YOUR FAULT. YOU WERE JUST A LITTLE KID. WHOEVER THAT WOMAN WAS, SHE WAS TRYING TO RUIN YOUR CONFIDENCE. SHE STILL IS.
DON'T YOU SEE? SHE'S *AFRAID* OF YOU.
SHE *SHOULD* BE. BECAUSE I'LL--

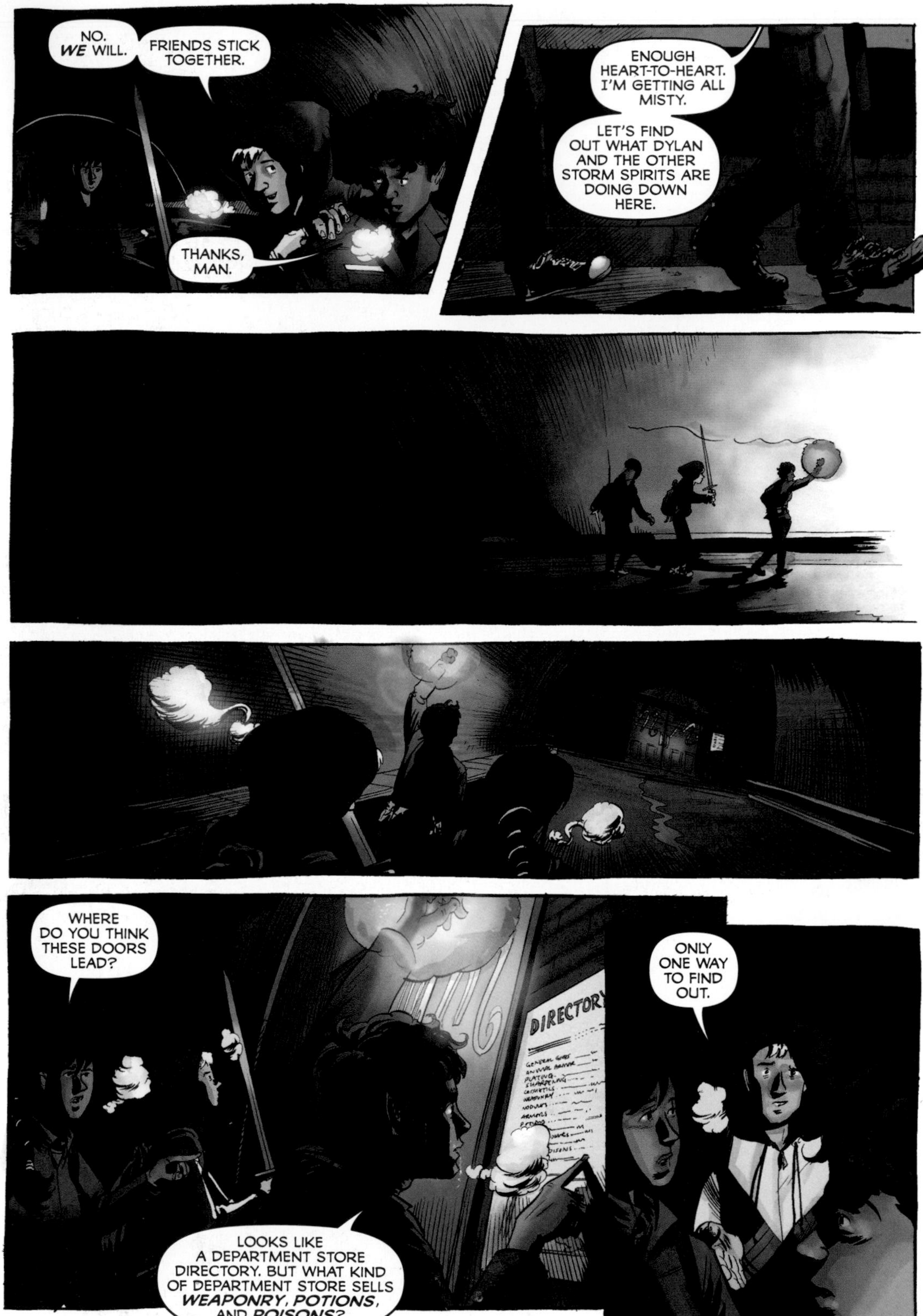
NO. *WE* WILL.
FRIENDS STICK TOGETHER.
THANKS, MAN.
ENOUGH HEART-TO-HEART. I'M GETTING ALL MISTY.
LET'S FIND OUT WHAT DYLAN AND THE OTHER STORM SPIRITS ARE DOING DOWN HERE.
WHERE DO YOU THINK THESE DOORS LEAD?
DIRECTORY
LOOKS LIKE A DEPARTMENT STORE DIRECTORY. BUT WHAT KIND OF DEPARTMENT STORE SELLS *WEAPONRY*, *POTIONS*, AND *POISONS*?
ONLY ONE WAY TO FIND OUT.

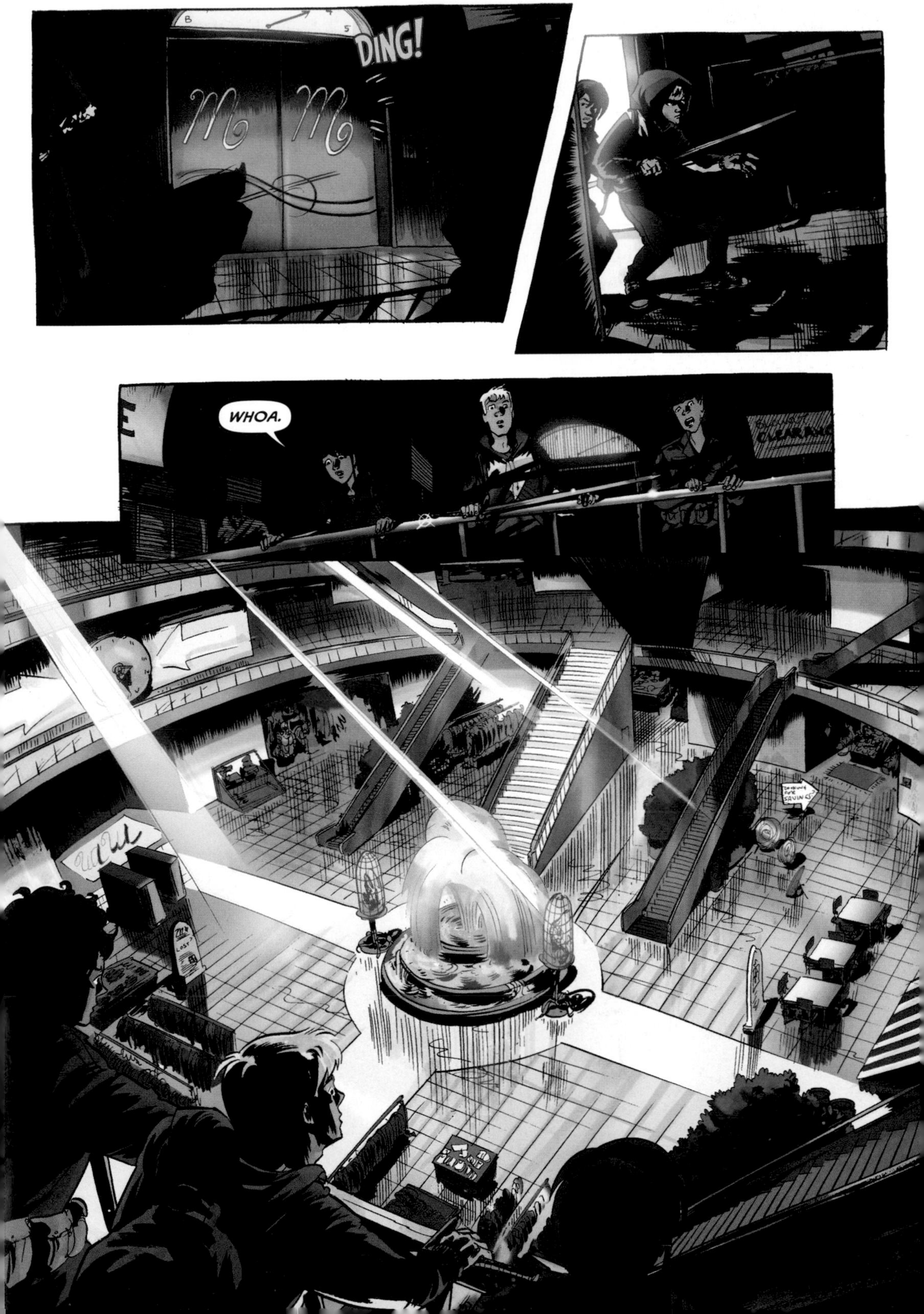
DING!
WHOA.

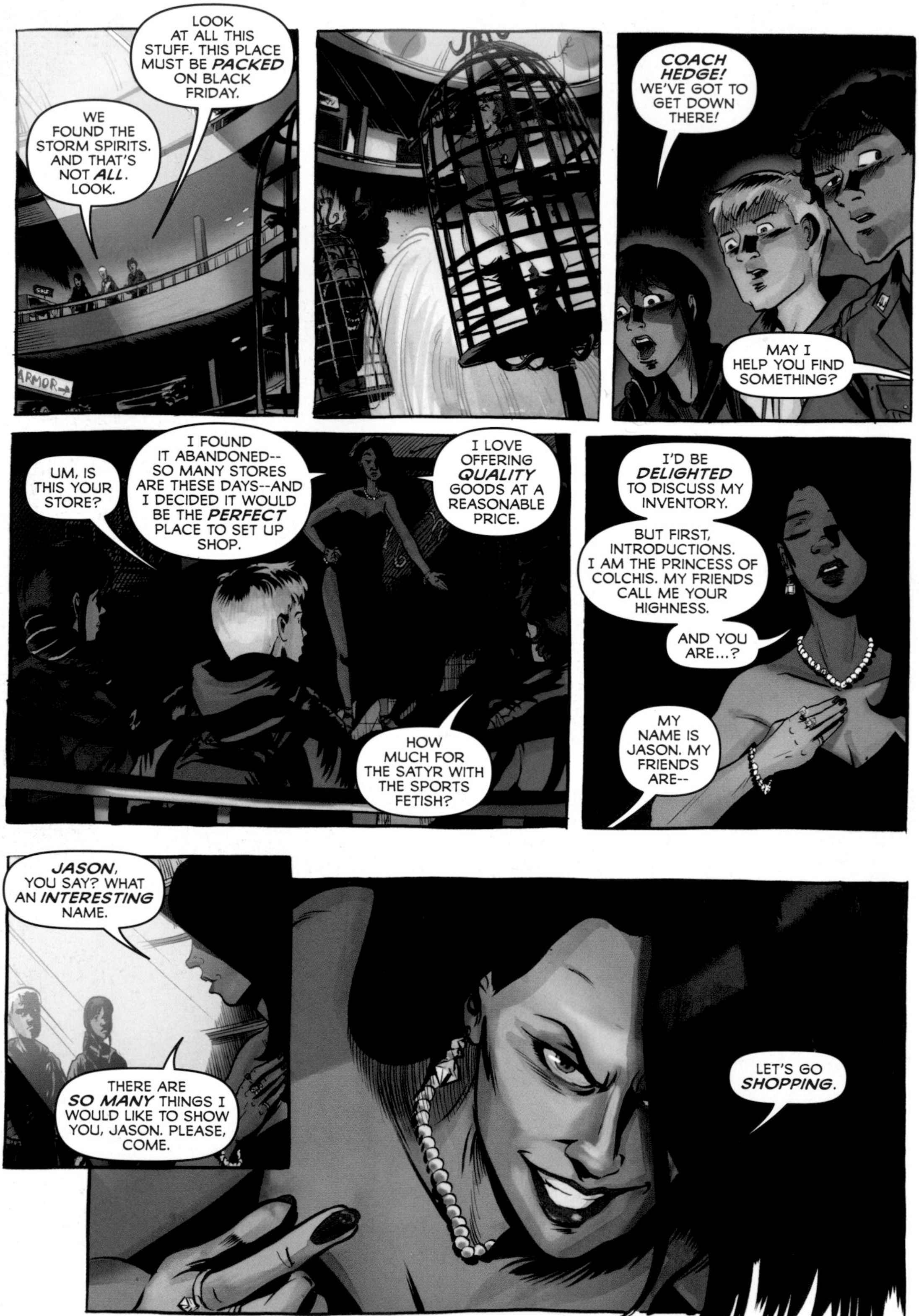
WE FOUND THE STORM SPIRITS. AND THAT'S NOT ALL. LOOK.
LOOK AT ALL THIS STUFF. THIS PLACE MUST BE PACKED ON BLACK FRIDAY.
ARMOR
COACH HEDGE! WE'VE GOT TO GET DOWN THERE!
MAY I HELP YOU FIND SOMETHING?
UM, IS THIS YOUR STORE?
I FOUND IT ABANDONED-- SO MANY STORES ARE THESE DAYS--AND I DECIDED IT WOULD BE THE PERFECT PLACE TO SET UP SHOP.
I LOVE OFFERING QUALITY GOODS AT A REASONABLE PRICE.
HOW MUCH FOR THE SATYR WITH THE SPORTS FETISH?
I'D BE DELIGHTED TO DISCUSS MY INVENTORY.
BUT FIRST, INTRODUCTIONS. I AM THE PRINCESS OF COLCHIS. MY FRIENDS CALL ME YOUR HIGHNESS.
AND YOU ARE...?
MY NAME IS JASON. MY FRIENDS ARE--
JASON, YOU SAY? WHAT AN INTERESTING NAME.
THERE ARE SO MANY THINGS I WOULD LIKE TO SHOW YOU, JASON. PLEASE, COME.
LET'S GO SHOPPING.

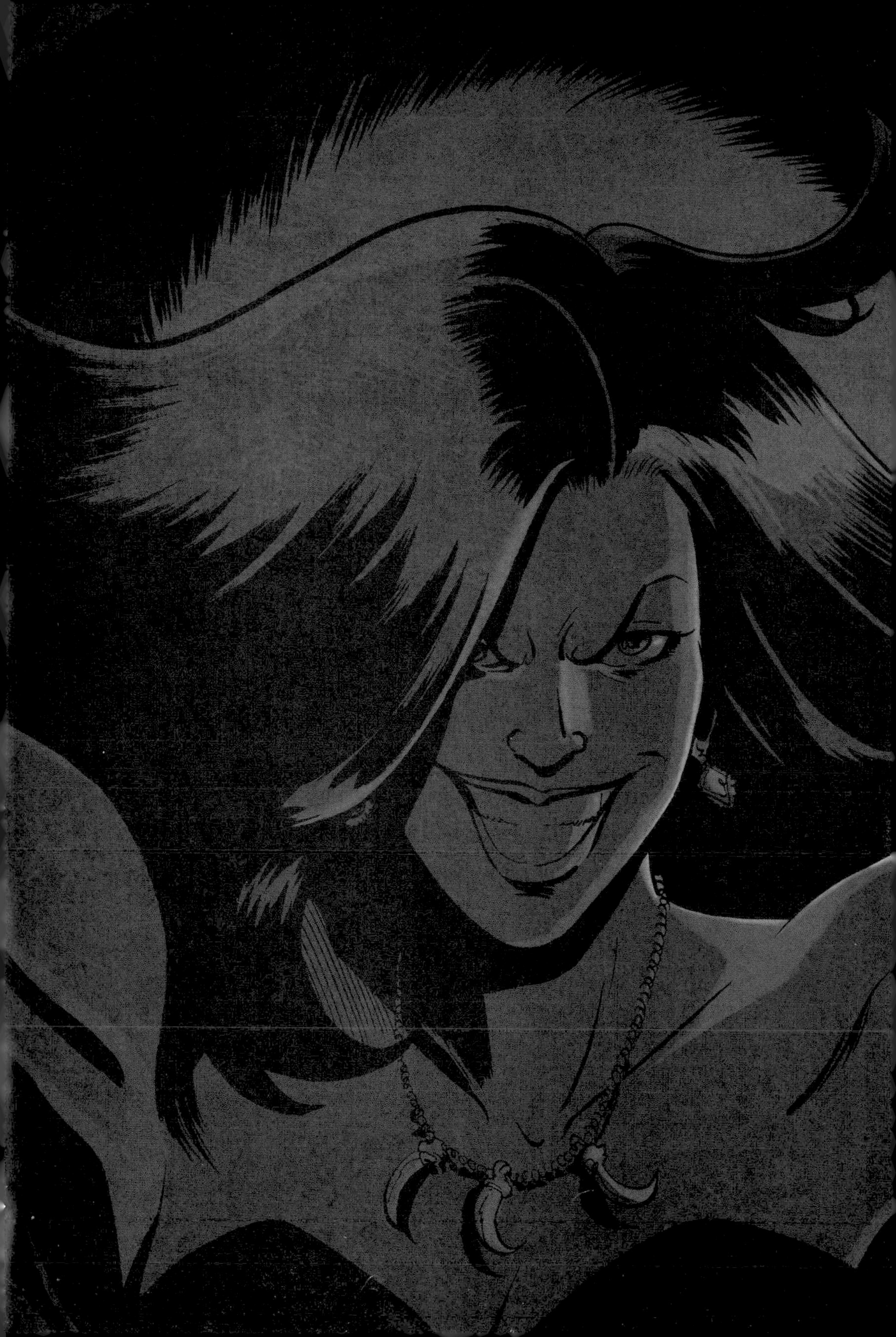

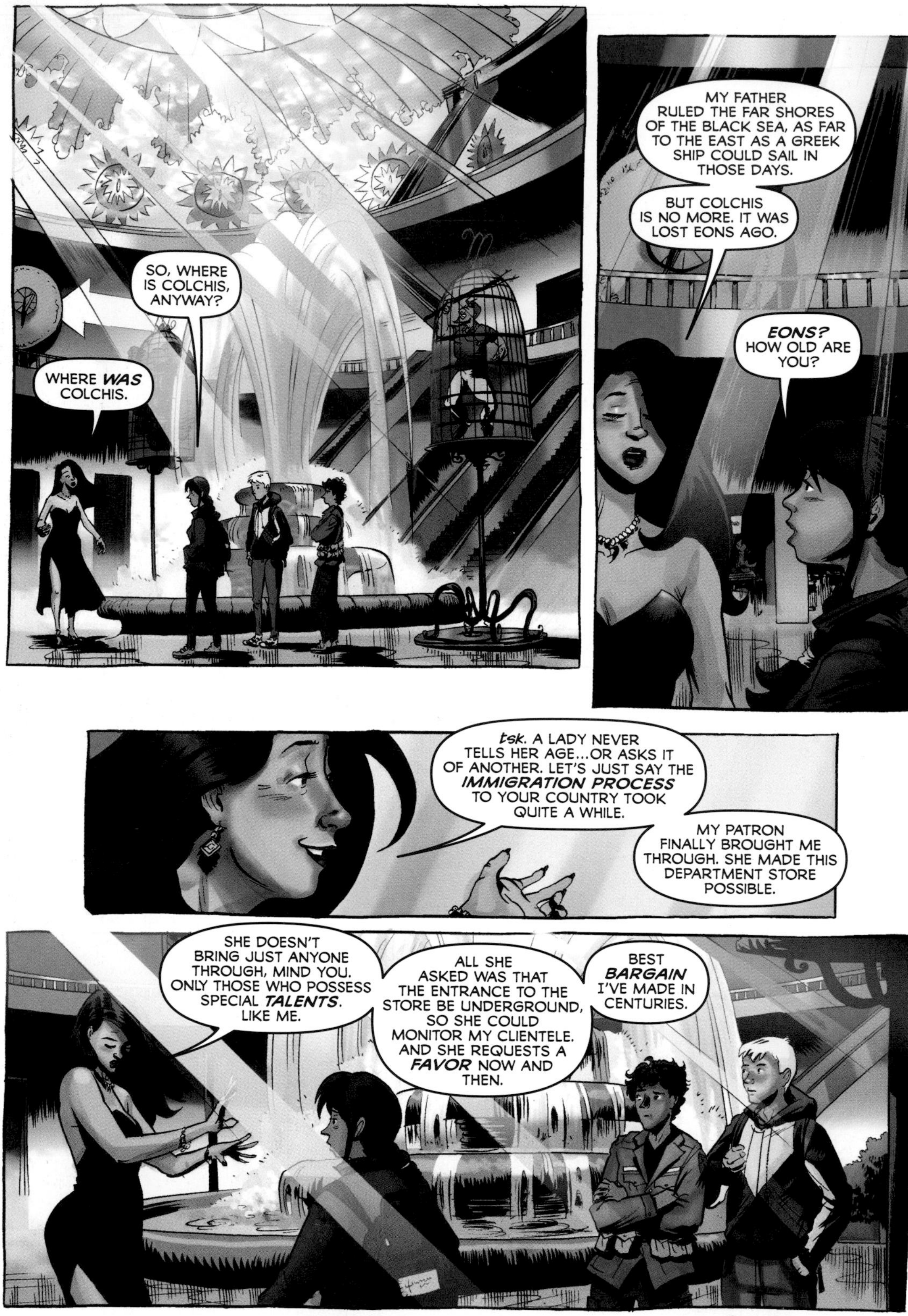
SO, WHERE IS COLCHIS, ANYWAY?
WHERE *WAS* COLCHIS.
MY FATHER RULED THE FAR SHORES OF THE BLACK SEA, AS FAR TO THE EAST AS A GREEK SHIP COULD SAIL IN THOSE DAYS.
BUT COLCHIS IS NO MORE. IT WAS LOST EONS AGO.
EONS? HOW OLD ARE YOU?
tsk. A LADY NEVER TELLS HER AGE...OR ASKS IT OF ANOTHER. LET'S JUST SAY THE *IMMIGRATION PROCESS* TO YOUR COUNTRY TOOK QUITE A WHILE.
MY PATRON FINALLY BROUGHT ME THROUGH. SHE MADE THIS DEPARTMENT STORE POSSIBLE.
SHE DOESN'T BRING JUST ANYONE THROUGH, MIND YOU. ONLY THOSE WHO POSSESS SPECIAL *TALENTS*. LIKE ME.
ALL SHE ASKED WAS THAT THE ENTRANCE TO THE STORE BE UNDERGROUND, SO SHE COULD MONITOR MY CLIENTELE. AND SHE REQUESTS A *FAVOR* NOW AND THEN.
BEST *BARGAIN* I'VE MADE IN CENTURIES.

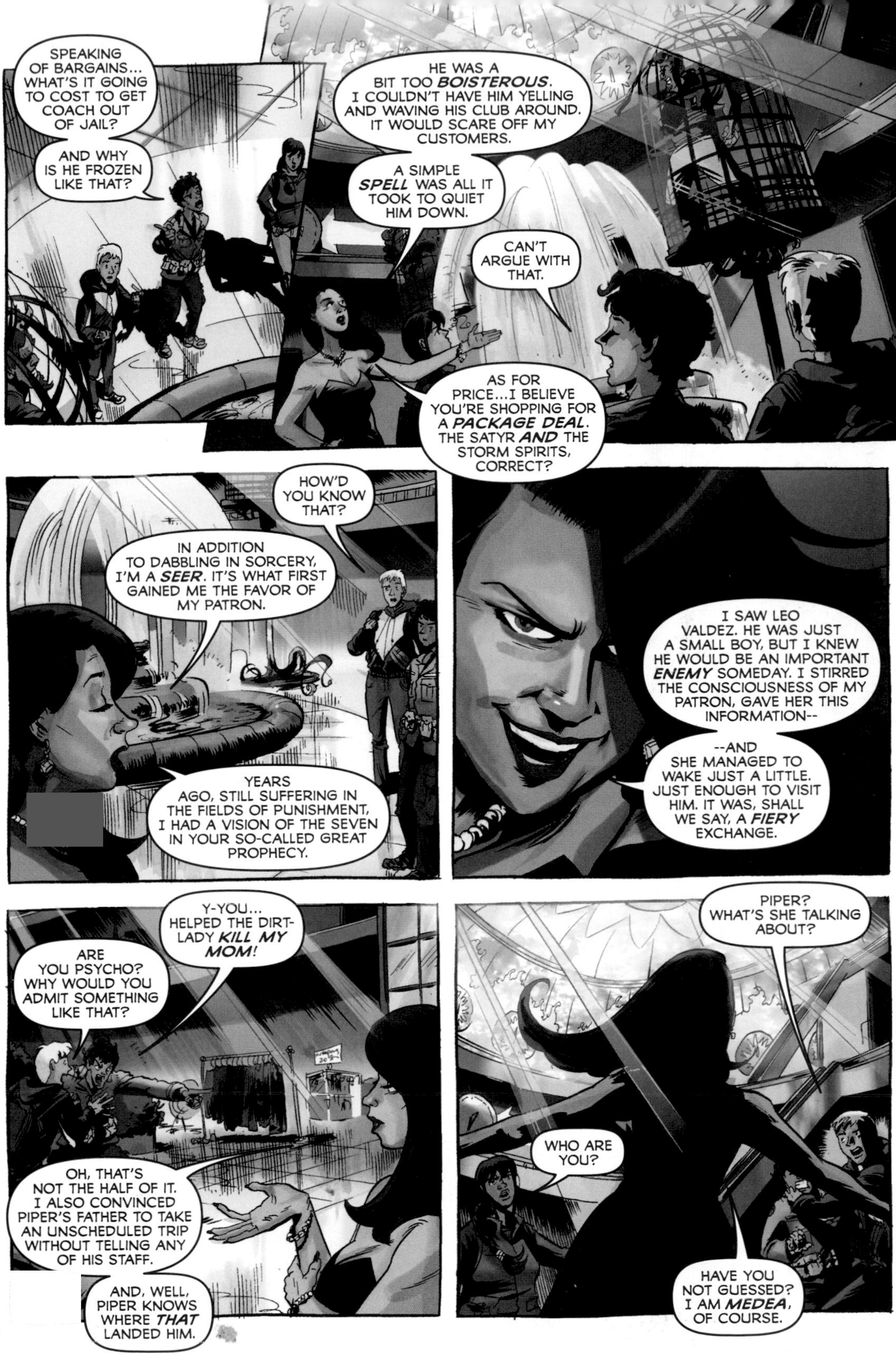
SPEAKING OF BARGAINS... WHAT'S IT GOING TO COST TO GET COACH OUT OF JAIL?
AND WHY IS HE FROZEN LIKE THAT?
HE WAS A BIT TOO BOISTEROUS. I COULDN'T HAVE HIM YELLING AND WAVING HIS CLUB AROUND. IT WOULD SCARE OFF MY CUSTOMERS.
A SIMPLE SPELL WAS ALL IT TOOK TO QUIET HIM DOWN.
CAN'T ARGUE WITH THAT.
AS FOR PRICE...I BELIEVE YOU'RE SHOPPING FOR A PACKAGE DEAL. THE SATYR AND THE STORM SPIRITS, CORRECT?
HOW'D YOU KNOW THAT?
IN ADDITION TO DABBLING IN SORCERY, I'M A SEER. IT'S WHAT FIRST GAINED ME THE FAVOR OF MY PATRON.
YEARS AGO, STILL SUFFERING IN THE FIELDS OF PUNISHMENT, I HAD A VISION OF THE SEVEN IN YOUR SO-CALLED GREAT PROPHECY.
I SAW LEO VALDEZ. HE WAS JUST A SMALL BOY, BUT I KNEW HE WOULD BE AN IMPORTANT ENEMY SOMEDAY. I STIRRED THE CONSCIOUSNESS OF MY PATRON, GAVE HER THIS INFORMATION--
--AND SHE MANAGED TO WAKE JUST A LITTLE. JUST ENOUGH TO VISIT HIM. IT WAS, SHALL WE SAY, A FIERY EXCHANGE.
Y-YOU... HELPED THE DIRT-LADY KILL MY MOM!
ARE YOU PSYCHO? WHY WOULD YOU ADMIT SOMETHING LIKE THAT?
OH, THAT'S NOT THE HALF OF IT. I ALSO CONVINCED PIPER'S FATHER TO TAKE AN UNSCHEDULED TRIP WITHOUT TELLING ANY OF HIS STAFF.
AND, WELL, PIPER KNOWS WHERE THAT LANDED HIM.
PIPER? WHAT'S SHE TALKING ABOUT?
WHO ARE YOU?
HAVE YOU NOT GUESSED? I AM MEDEA, OF COURSE.

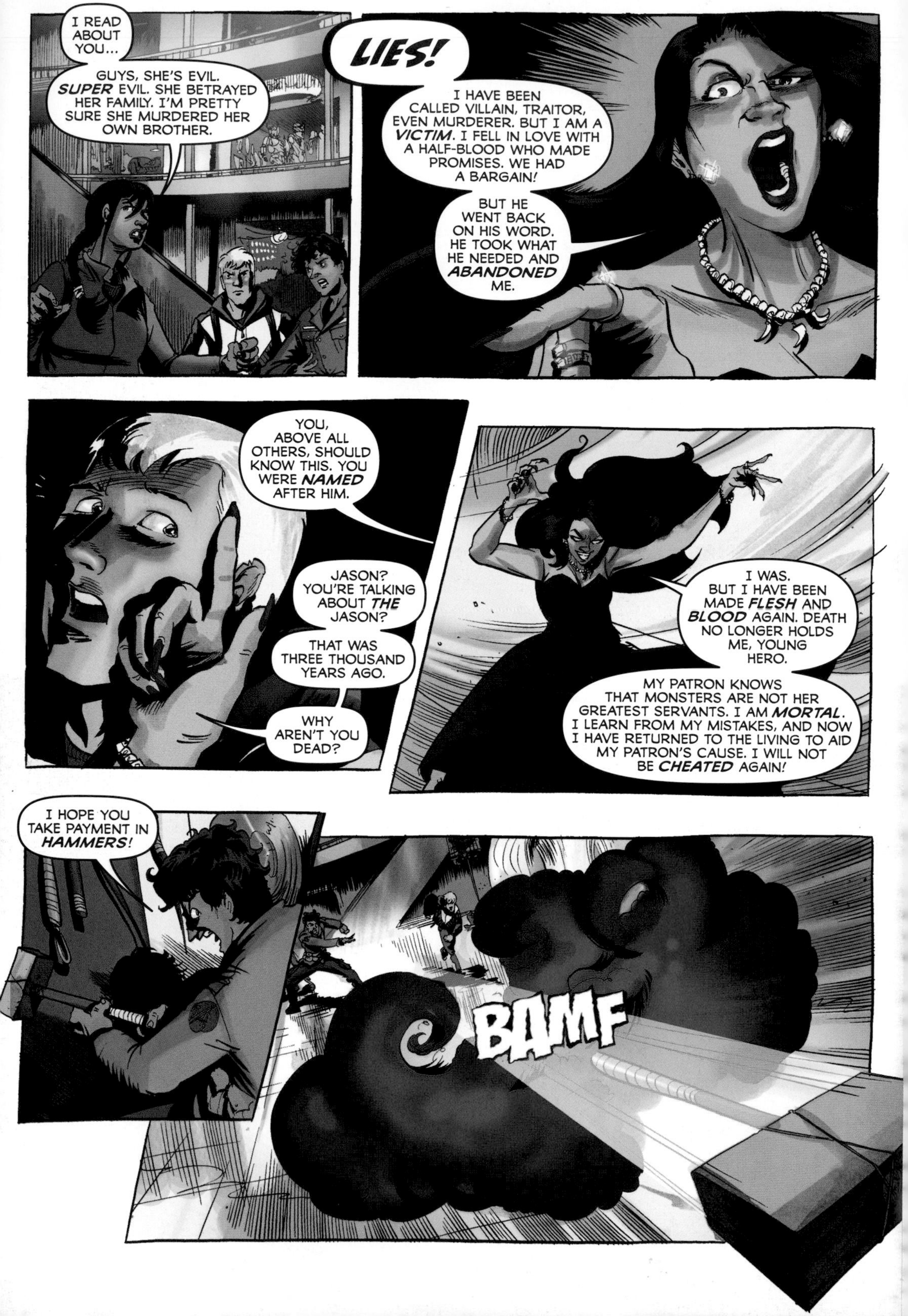
I READ ABOUT YOU...
GUYS, SHE'S EVIL. SUPER EVIL. SHE BETRAYED HER FAMILY. I'M PRETTY SURE SHE MURDERED HER OWN BROTHER.
LIES!
I HAVE BEEN CALLED VILLAIN, TRAITOR, EVEN MURDERER. BUT I AM A VICTIM. I FELL IN LOVE WITH A HALF-BLOOD WHO MADE PROMISES. WE HAD A BARGAIN!
BUT HE WENT BACK ON HIS WORD. HE TOOK WHAT HE NEEDED AND ABANDONED ME.
YOU, ABOVE ALL OTHERS, SHOULD KNOW THIS. YOU WERE NAMED AFTER HIM.
JASON? YOU'RE TALKING ABOUT THE JASON?
THAT WAS THREE THOUSAND YEARS AGO.
WHY AREN'T YOU DEAD?
I WAS. BUT I HAVE BEEN MADE FLESH AND BLOOD AGAIN. DEATH NO LONGER HOLDS ME, YOUNG HERO.
MY PATRON KNOWS THAT MONSTERS ARE NOT HER GREATEST SERVANTS. I AM MORTAL. I LEARN FROM MY MISTAKES, AND NOW I HAVE RETURNED TO THE LIVING TO AID MY PATRON'S CAUSE. I WILL NOT BE CHEATED AGAIN!
I HOPE YOU TAKE PAYMENT IN HAMMERS!
BAMF

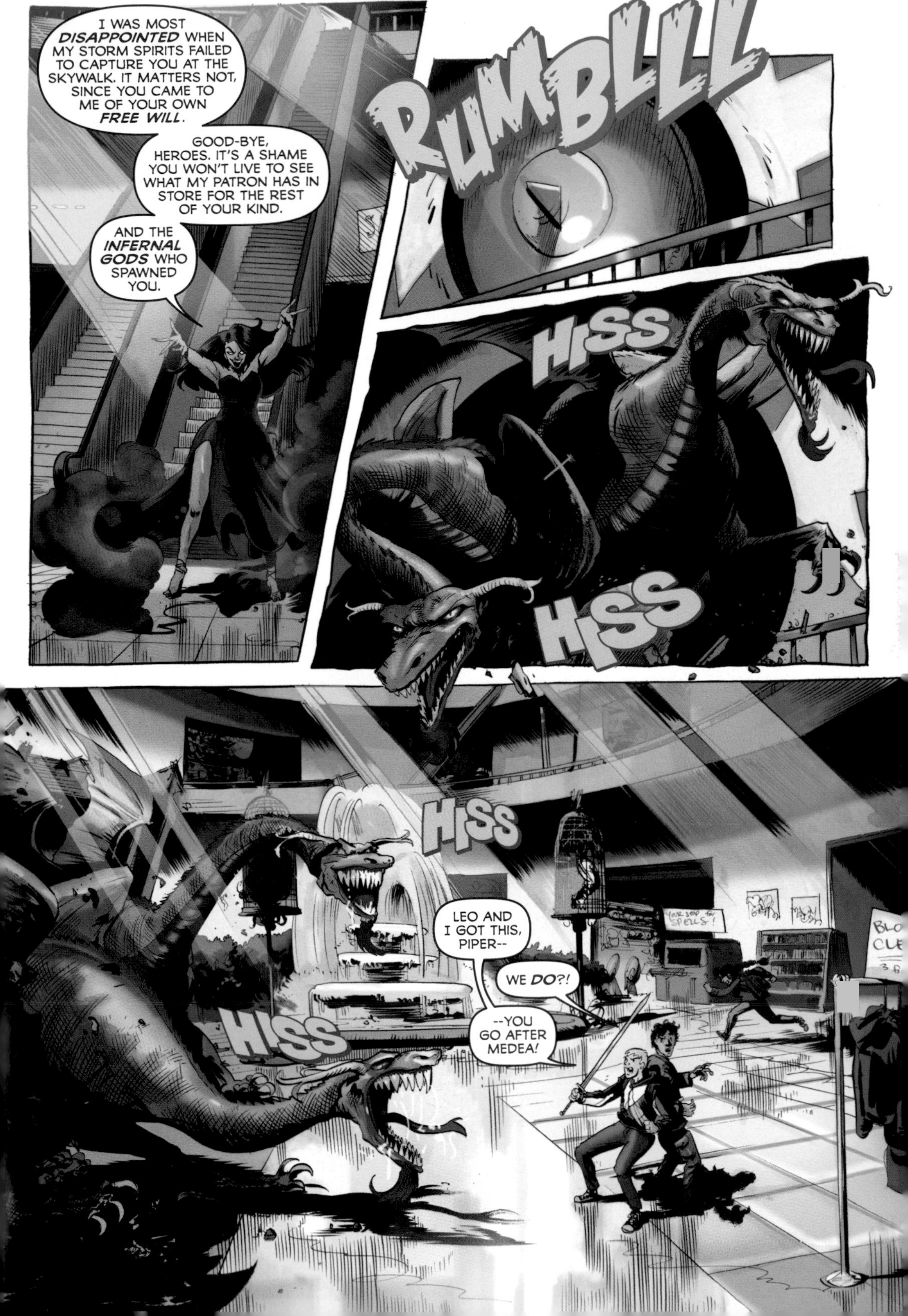
I WAS MOST DISAPPOINTED WHEN MY STORM SPIRITS FAILED TO CAPTURE YOU AT THE SKYWALK. IT MATTERS NOT, SINCE YOU CAME TO ME OF YOUR OWN FREE WILL.
GOOD-BYE, HEROES. IT'S A SHAME YOU WON'T LIVE TO SEE WHAT MY PATRON HAS IN STORE FOR THE REST OF YOUR KIND.
AND THE INFERNAL GODS WHO SPAWNED YOU.
RUMBLLL
HISS
HISS
HISS
HISS
LEO AND I GOT THIS, PIPER--
WE DO?!
--YOU GO AFTER MEDEA!

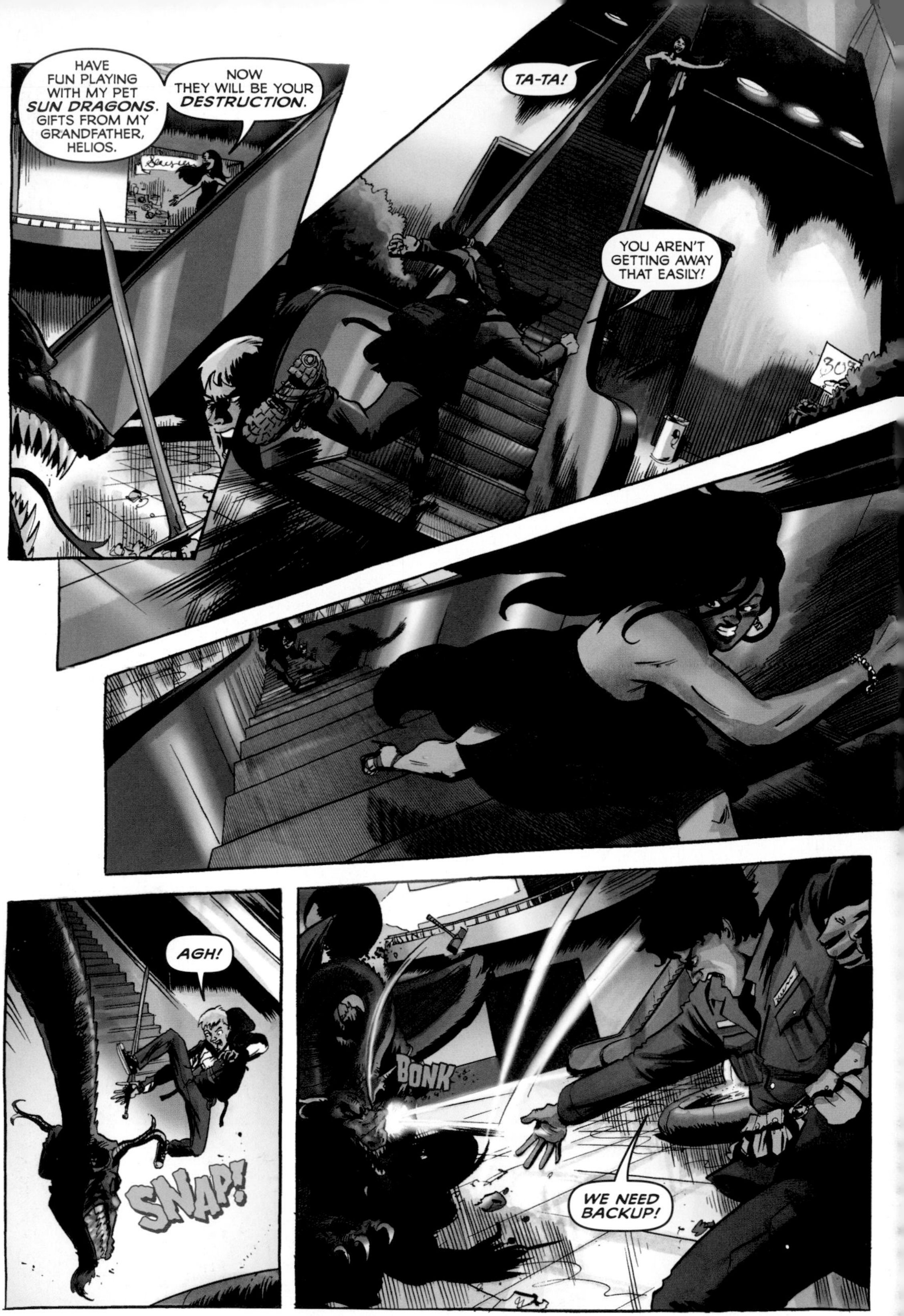
HAVE FUN PLAYING WITH MY PET SUN DRAGONS. GIFTS FROM MY GRANDFATHER, HELIOS.
NOW THEY WILL BE YOUR DESTRUCTION.
TA-TA!
YOU AREN'T GETTING AWAY THAT EASILY!
AGH!
SNAP!
BONK
WE NEED BACKUP!

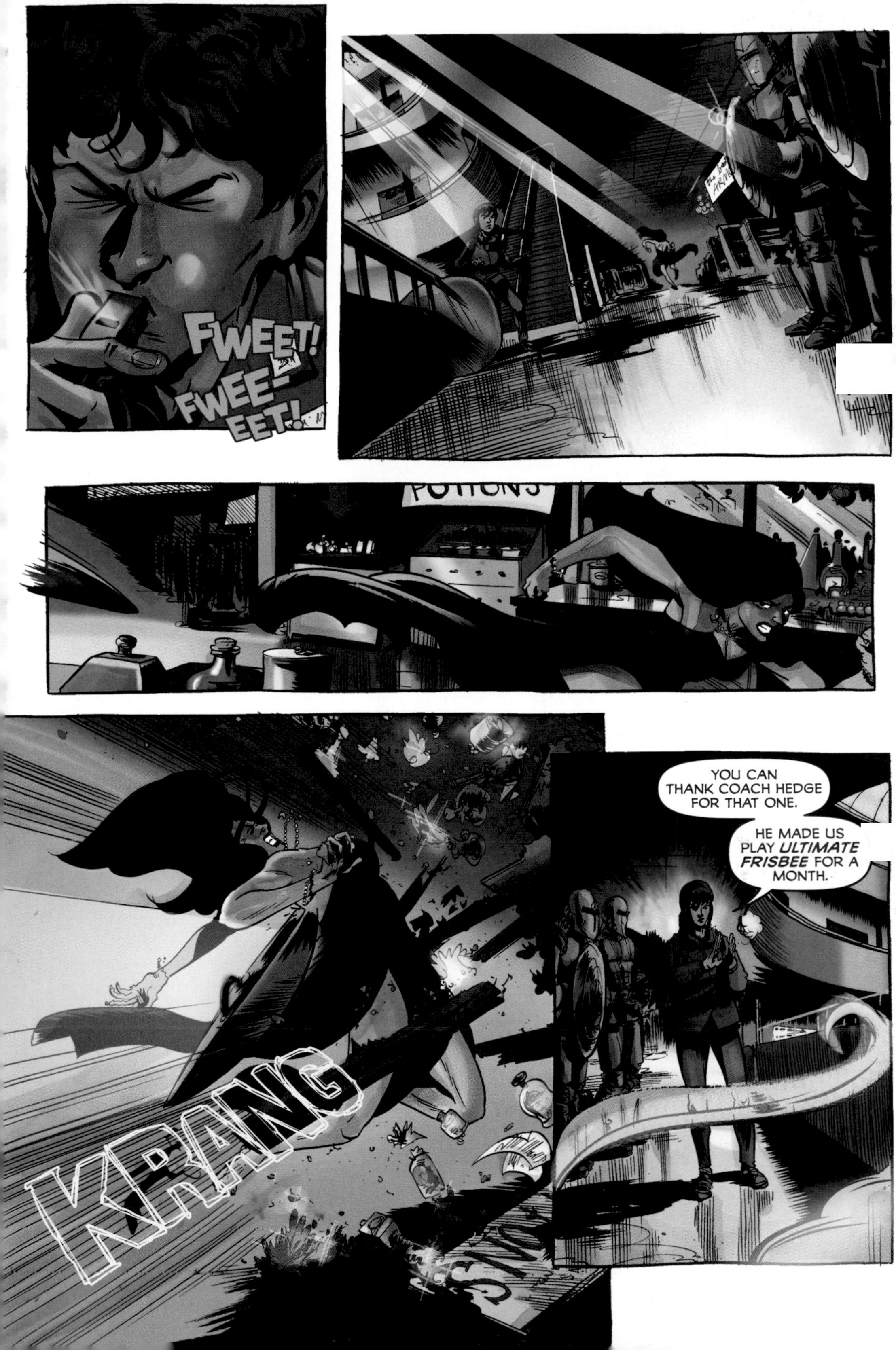
FWEET!
FWEE-EET!
POTIONS
KRANG
YOU CAN THANK COACH HEDGE FOR THAT ONE.
HE MADE US PLAY *ULTIMATE FRISBEE* FOR A MONTH.

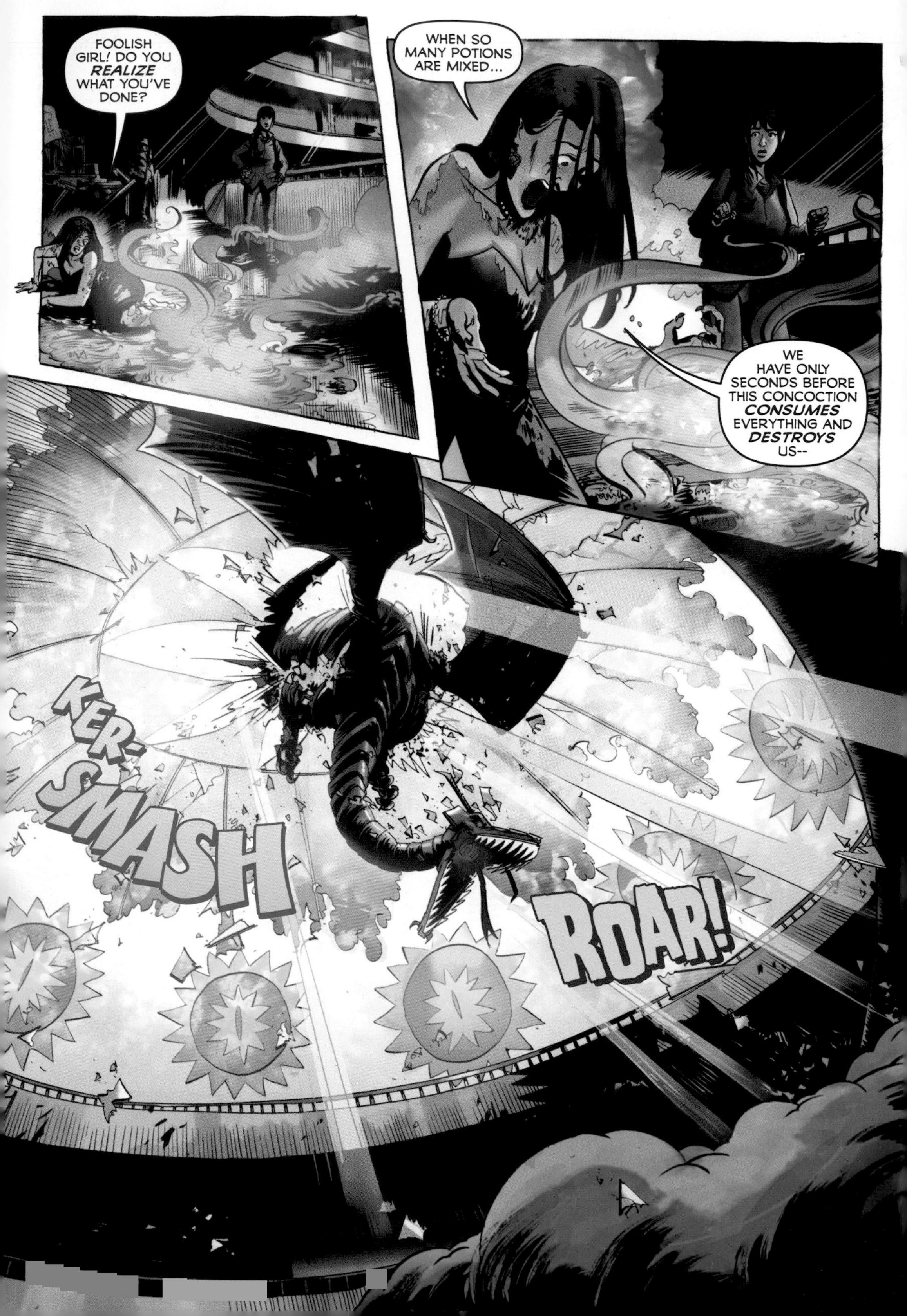
FOOLISH GIRL! DO YOU *REALIZE* WHAT YOU'VE DONE?
WHEN SO MANY POTIONS ARE MIXED...
WE HAVE ONLY SECONDS BEFORE THIS CONCOCTION *CONSUMES* EVERYTHING AND *DESTROYS* US--
KER-SMASH
ROAR!

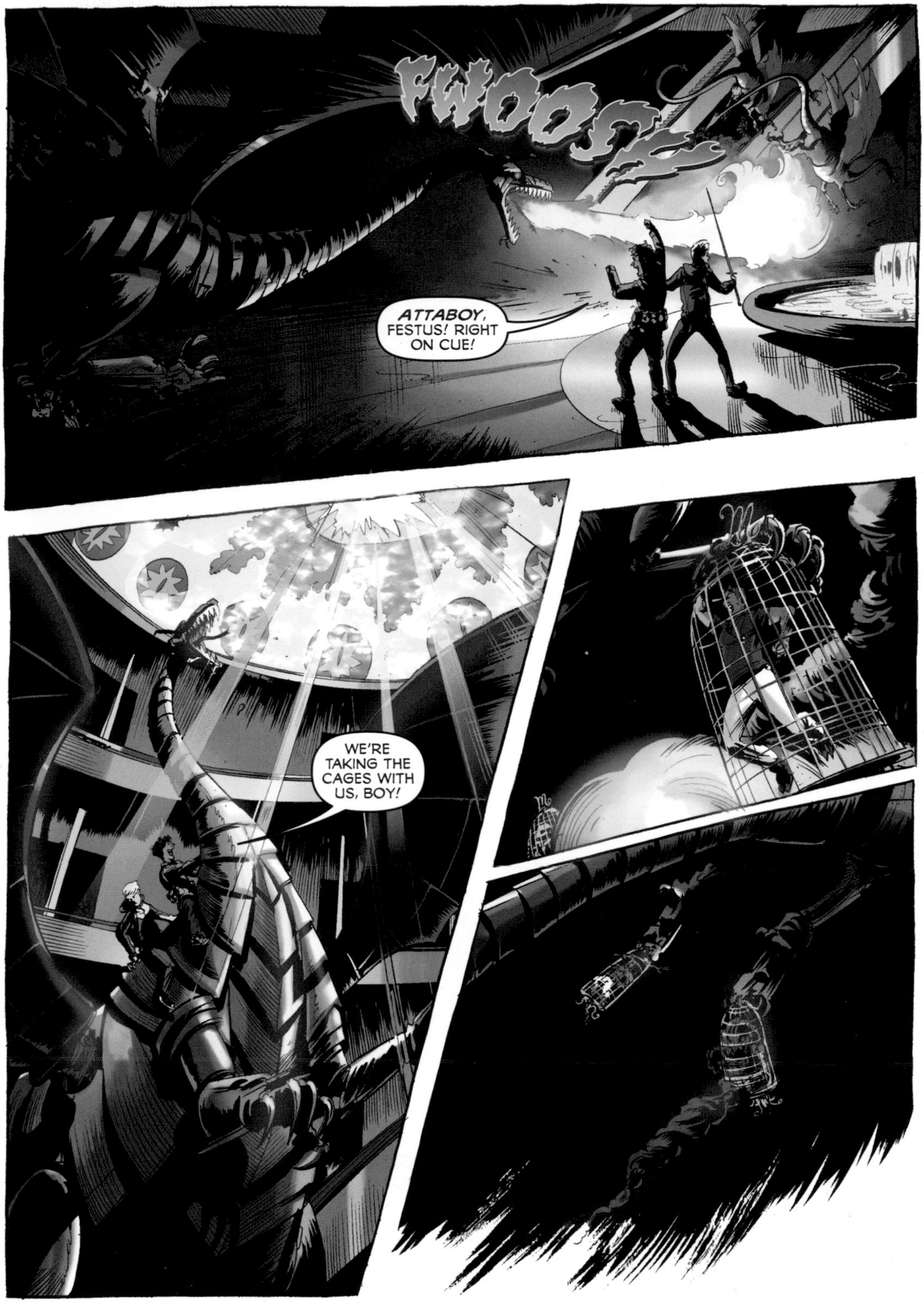
FWOOSH
ATTABOY, FESTUS! RIGHT ON CUE!
WE'RE TAKING THE CAGES WITH US, BOY!

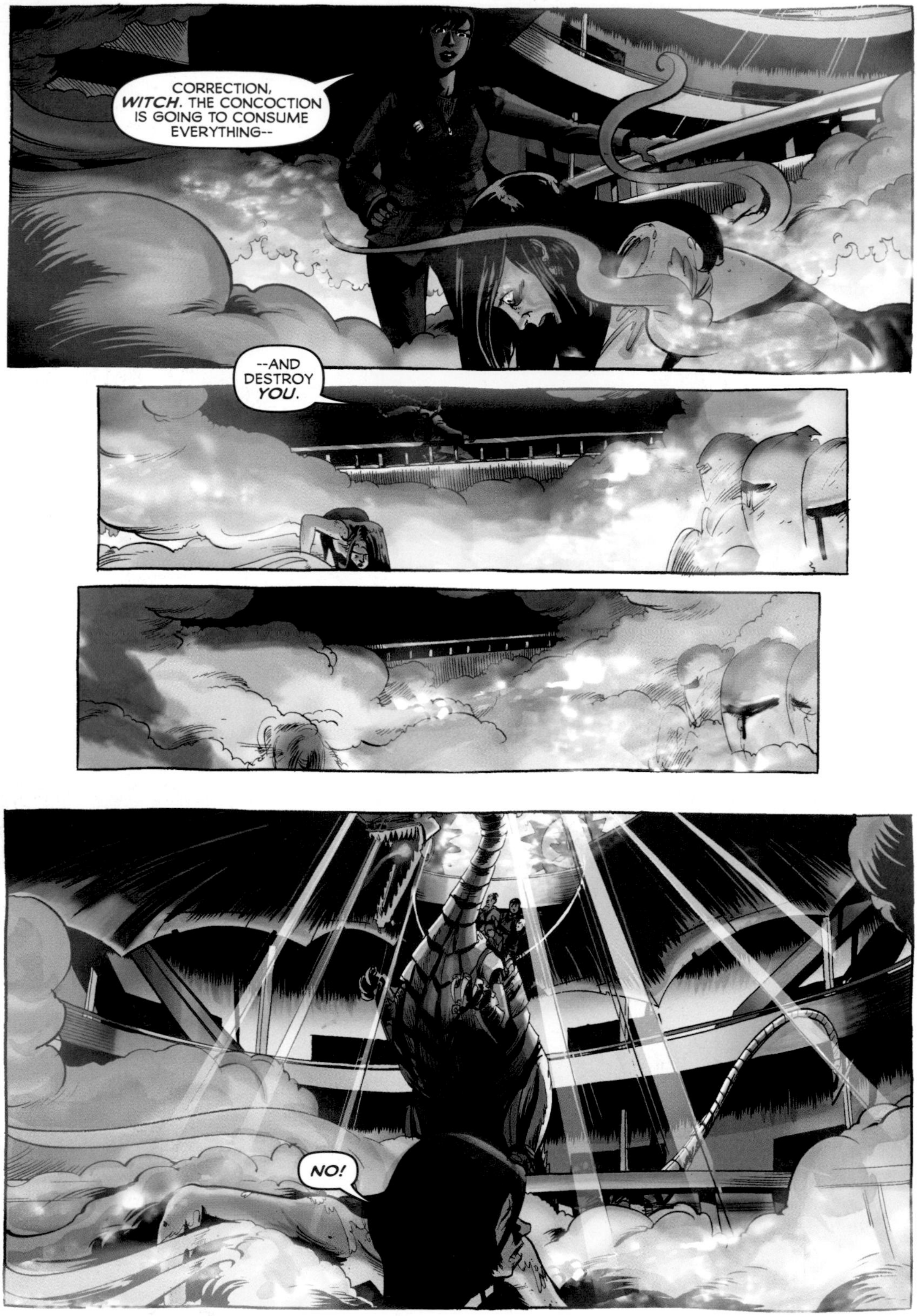
CORRECTION, WITCH. THE CONCOCTION IS GOING TO CONSUME EVERYTHING--
--AND DESTROY YOU.
NO!

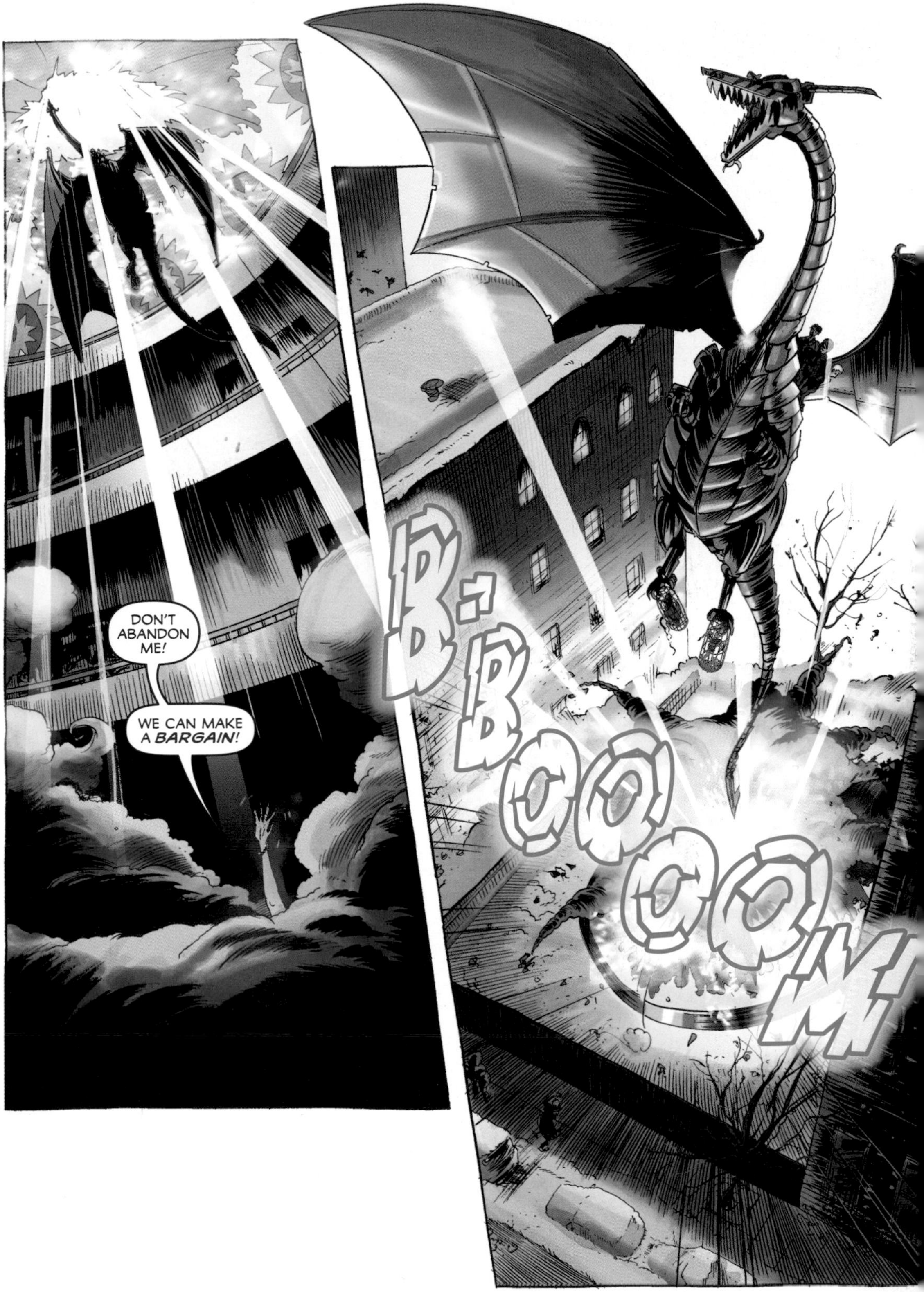
DON'T ABANDON ME!
WE CAN MAKE A BARGAIN!
B-BOOOOOM!

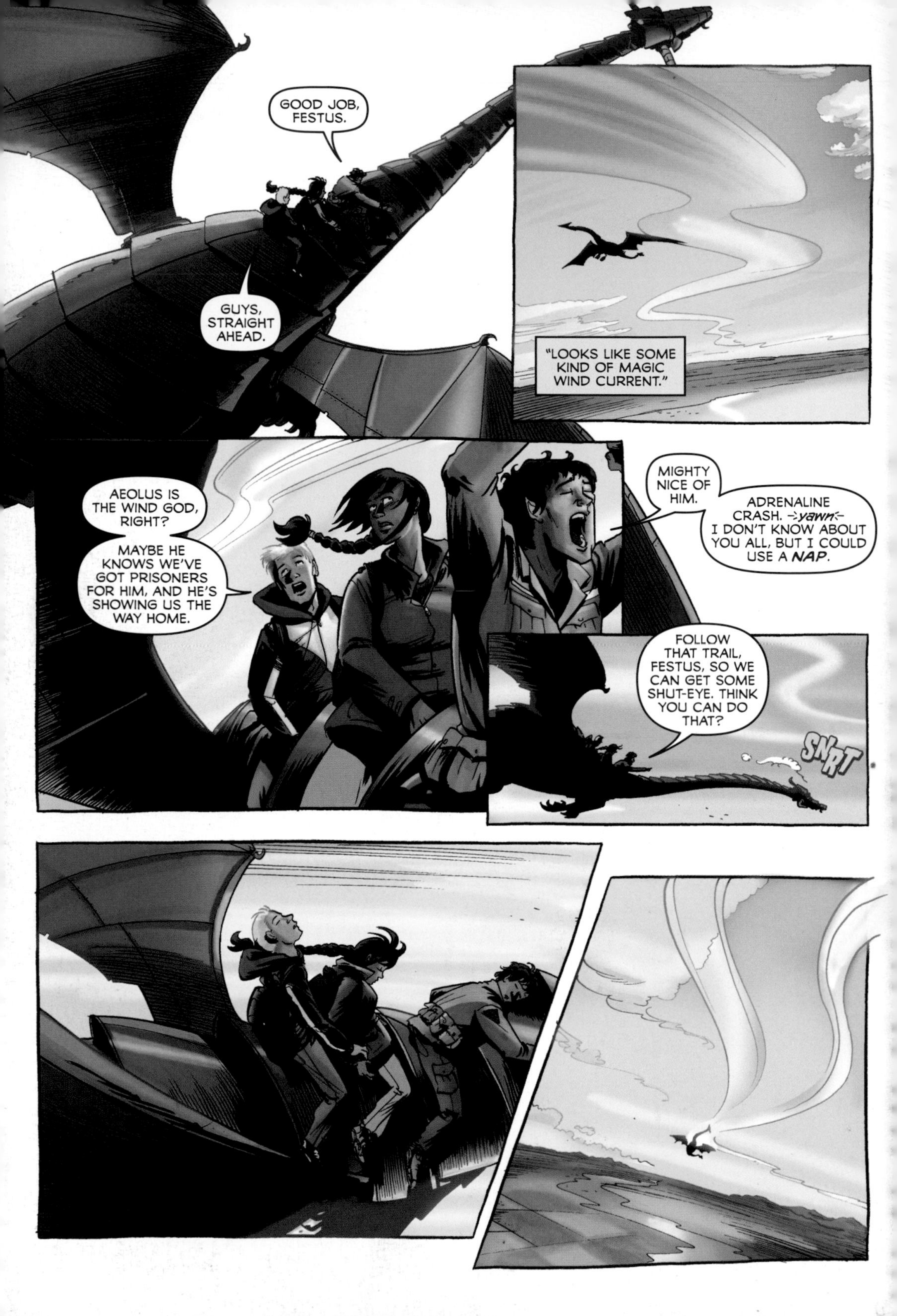
GOOD JOB, FESTUS.
GUYS, STRAIGHT AHEAD.
"LOOKS LIKE SOME KIND OF MAGIC WIND CURRENT."
AEOLUS IS THE WIND GOD, RIGHT?
MAYBE HE KNOWS WE'VE GOT PRISONERS FOR HIM, AND HE'S SHOWING US THE WAY HOME.
MIGHTY NICE OF HIM.
ADRENALINE CRASH. -yawn- I DON'T KNOW ABOUT YOU ALL, BUT I COULD USE A NAP.
FOLLOW THAT TRAIL, FESTUS, SO WE CAN GET SOME SHUT-EYE. THINK YOU CAN DO THAT?
SNRT

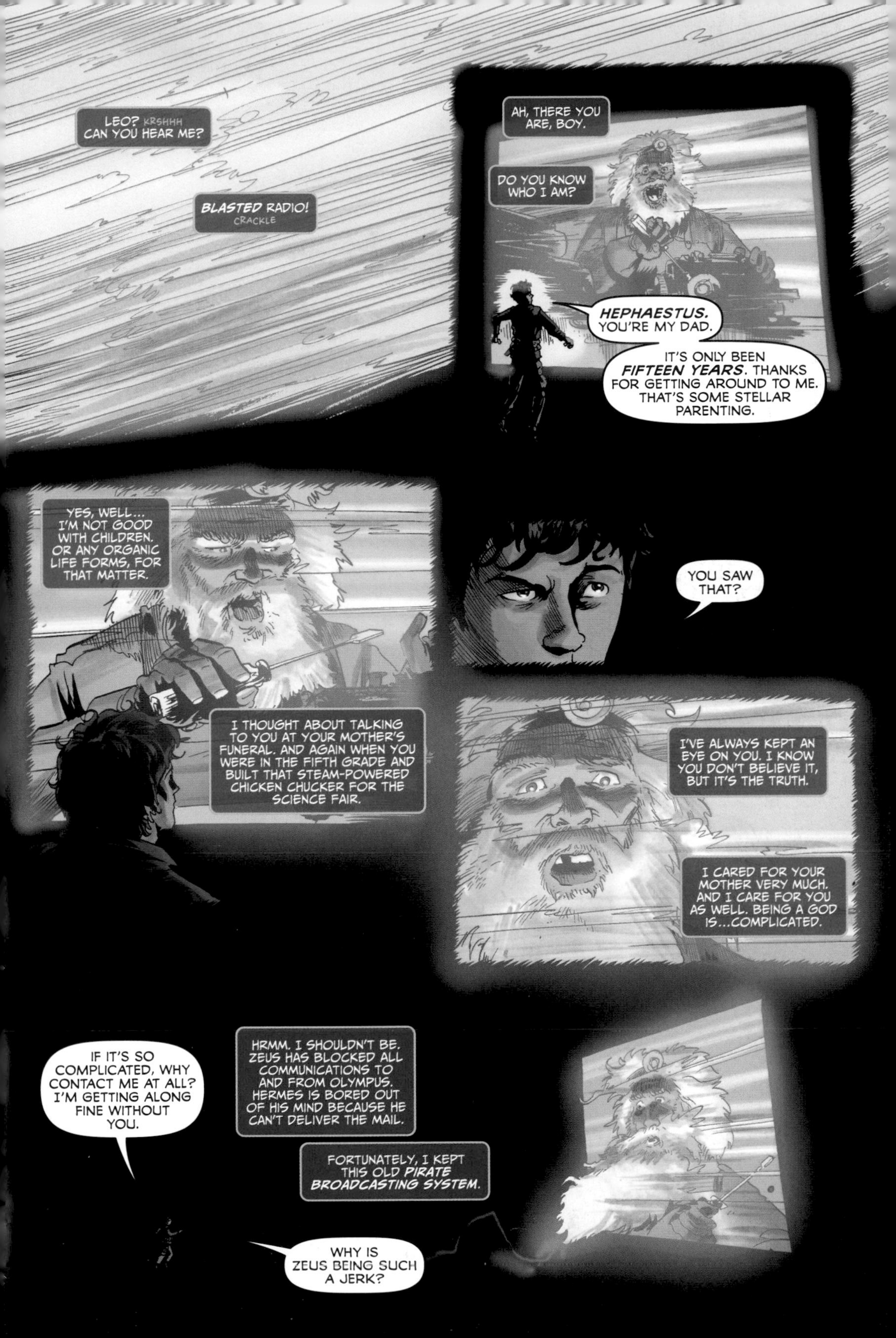

LEO? KRSHHH
CAN YOU HEAR ME?
BLASTED RADIO!
CRACKLE
AH, THERE YOU ARE, BOY.
DO YOU KNOW WHO I AM?
HEPHAESTUS. YOU'RE MY DAD.
IT'S ONLY BEEN FIFTEEN YEARS. THANKS FOR GETTING AROUND TO ME. THAT'S SOME STELLAR PARENTING.
YES, WELL... I'M NOT GOOD WITH CHILDREN. OR ANY ORGANIC LIFE FORMS, FOR THAT MATTER.
I THOUGHT ABOUT TALKING TO YOU AT YOUR MOTHER'S FUNERAL. AND AGAIN WHEN YOU WERE IN THE FIFTH GRADE AND BUILT THAT STEAM-POWERED CHICKEN CHUCKER FOR THE SCIENCE FAIR.
YOU SAW THAT?
I'VE ALWAYS KEPT AN EYE ON YOU. I KNOW YOU DON'T BELIEVE IT, BUT IT'S THE TRUTH.
I CARED FOR YOUR MOTHER VERY MUCH. AND I CARE FOR YOU AS WELL. BEING A GOD IS...COMPLICATED.
IF IT'S SO COMPLICATED, WHY CONTACT ME AT ALL? I'M GETTING ALONG FINE WITHOUT YOU.
HRMM. I SHOULDN'T BE. ZEUS HAS BLOCKED ALL COMMUNICATIONS TO AND FROM OLYMPUS. HERMES IS BORED OUT OF HIS MIND BECAUSE HE CAN'T DELIVER THE MAIL.
FORTUNATELY, I KEPT THIS OLD PIRATE BROADCASTING SYSTEM.
WHY IS ZEUS BEING SUCH A JERK?

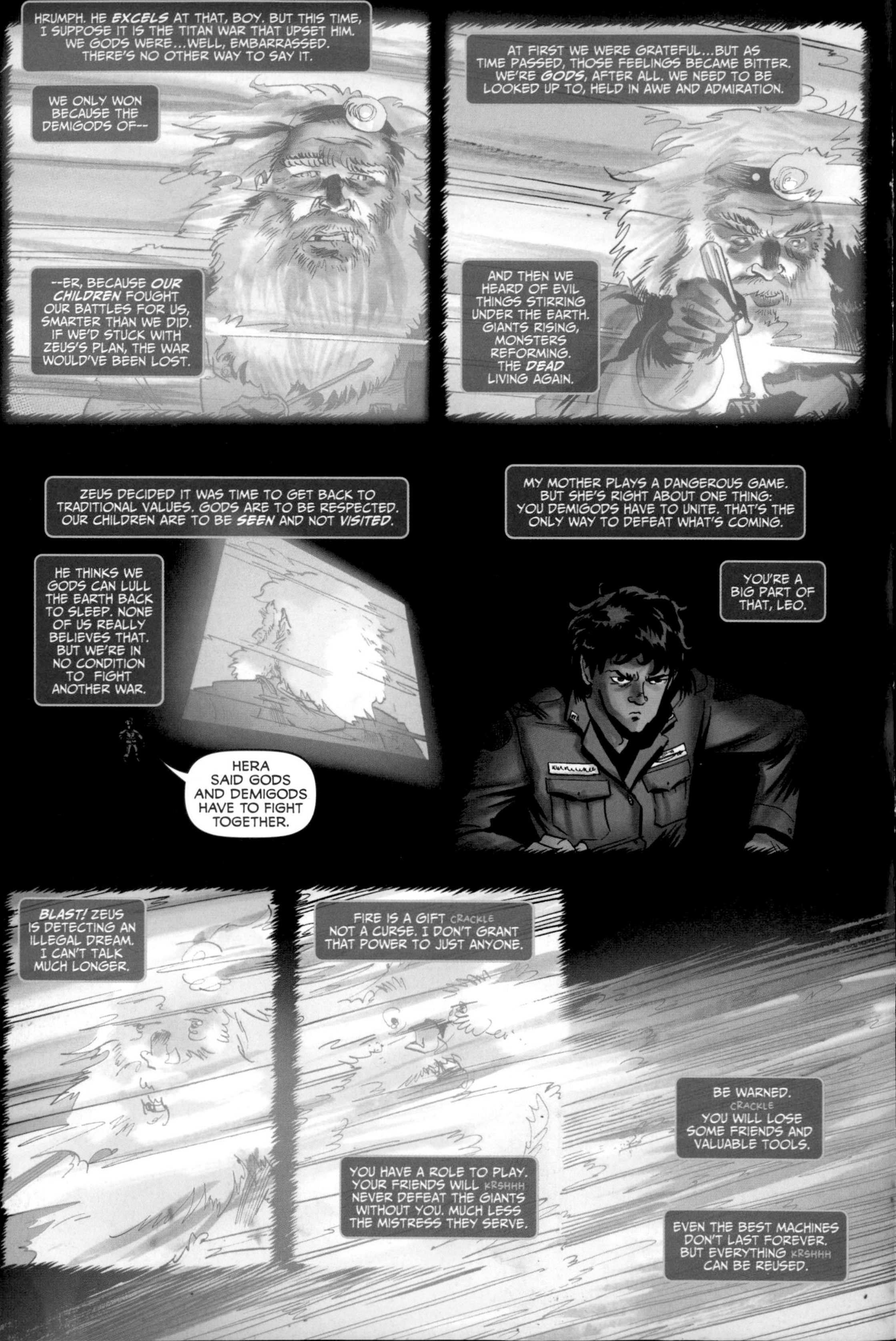
HRUMPH. HE EXCELS AT THAT, BOY. BUT THIS TIME, I SUPPOSE IT IS THE TITAN WAR THAT UPSET HIM. WE GODS WERE...WELL, EMBARRASSED. THERE'S NO OTHER WAY TO SAY IT.
WE ONLY WON BECAUSE THE DEMIGODS OF--
--ER, BECAUSE OUR CHILDREN FOUGHT OUR BATTLES FOR US, SMARTER THAN WE DID. IF WE'D STUCK WITH ZEUS'S PLAN, THE WAR WOULD'VE BEEN LOST.
AT FIRST WE WERE GRATEFUL...BUT AS TIME PASSED, THOSE FEELINGS BECAME BITTER. WE'RE GODS, AFTER ALL. WE NEED TO BE LOOKED UP TO, HELD IN AWE AND ADMIRATION.
AND THEN WE HEARD OF EVIL THINGS STIRRING UNDER THE EARTH. GIANTS RISING, MONSTERS REFORMING. THE DEAD LIVING AGAIN.
ZEUS DECIDED IT WAS TIME TO GET BACK TO TRADITIONAL VALUES. GODS ARE TO BE RESPECTED. OUR CHILDREN ARE TO BE SEEN AND NOT VISITED.
HE THINKS WE GODS CAN LULL THE EARTH BACK TO SLEEP. NONE OF US REALLY BELIEVES THAT. BUT WE'RE IN NO CONDITION TO FIGHT ANOTHER WAR.
HERA SAID GODS AND DEMIGODS HAVE TO FIGHT TOGETHER.
MY MOTHER PLAYS A DANGEROUS GAME. BUT SHE'S RIGHT ABOUT ONE THING: YOU DEMIGODS HAVE TO UNITE. THAT'S THE ONLY WAY TO DEFEAT WHAT'S COMING.
YOU'RE A BIG PART OF THAT, LEO.
BLAST! ZEUS IS DETECTING AN ILLEGAL DREAM. I CAN'T TALK MUCH LONGER.
FIRE IS A GIFT CRACKLE NOT A CURSE. I DON'T GRANT THAT POWER TO JUST ANYONE.
YOU HAVE A ROLE TO PLAY. YOUR FRIENDS WILL KRSHHH NEVER DEFEAT THE GIANTS WITHOUT YOU. MUCH LESS THE MISTRESS THEY SERVE.
BE WARNED. CRACKLE YOU WILL LOSE SOME FRIENDS AND VALUABLE TOOLS.
EVEN THE BEST MACHINES DON'T LAST FOREVER. BUT EVERYTHING KRSHHH CAN BE REUSED.

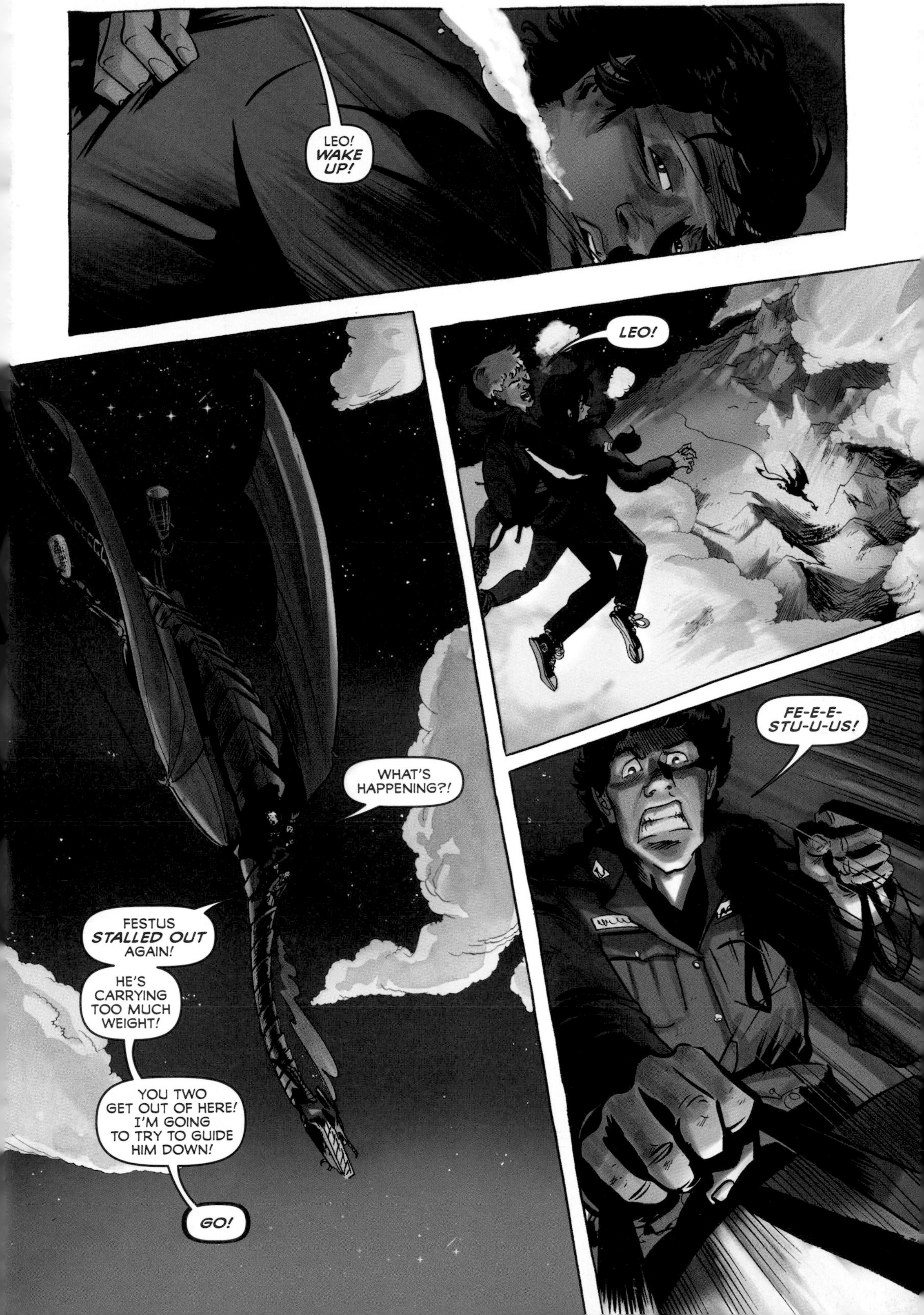
LEO! WAKE UP!
LEO!
WHAT'S HAPPENING?!
FESTUS STALLED OUT AGAIN!
HE'S CARRYING TOO MUCH WEIGHT!
YOU TWO GET OUT OF HERE! I'M GOING TO TRY TO GUIDE HIM DOWN!
GO!
FE-E-E-STU-U-US!

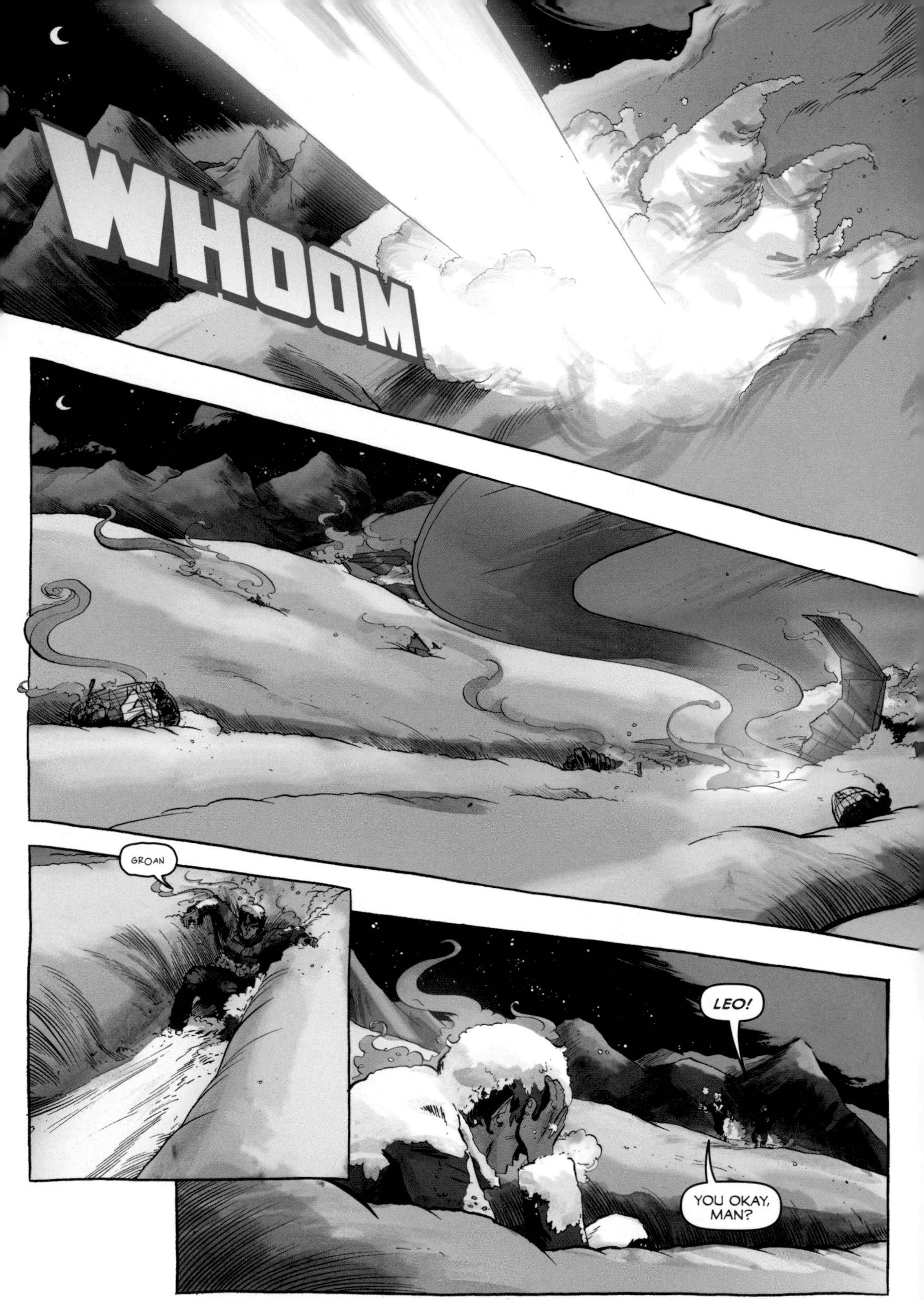
WHOOM
GROAN
LEO!
YOU OKAY, MAN?

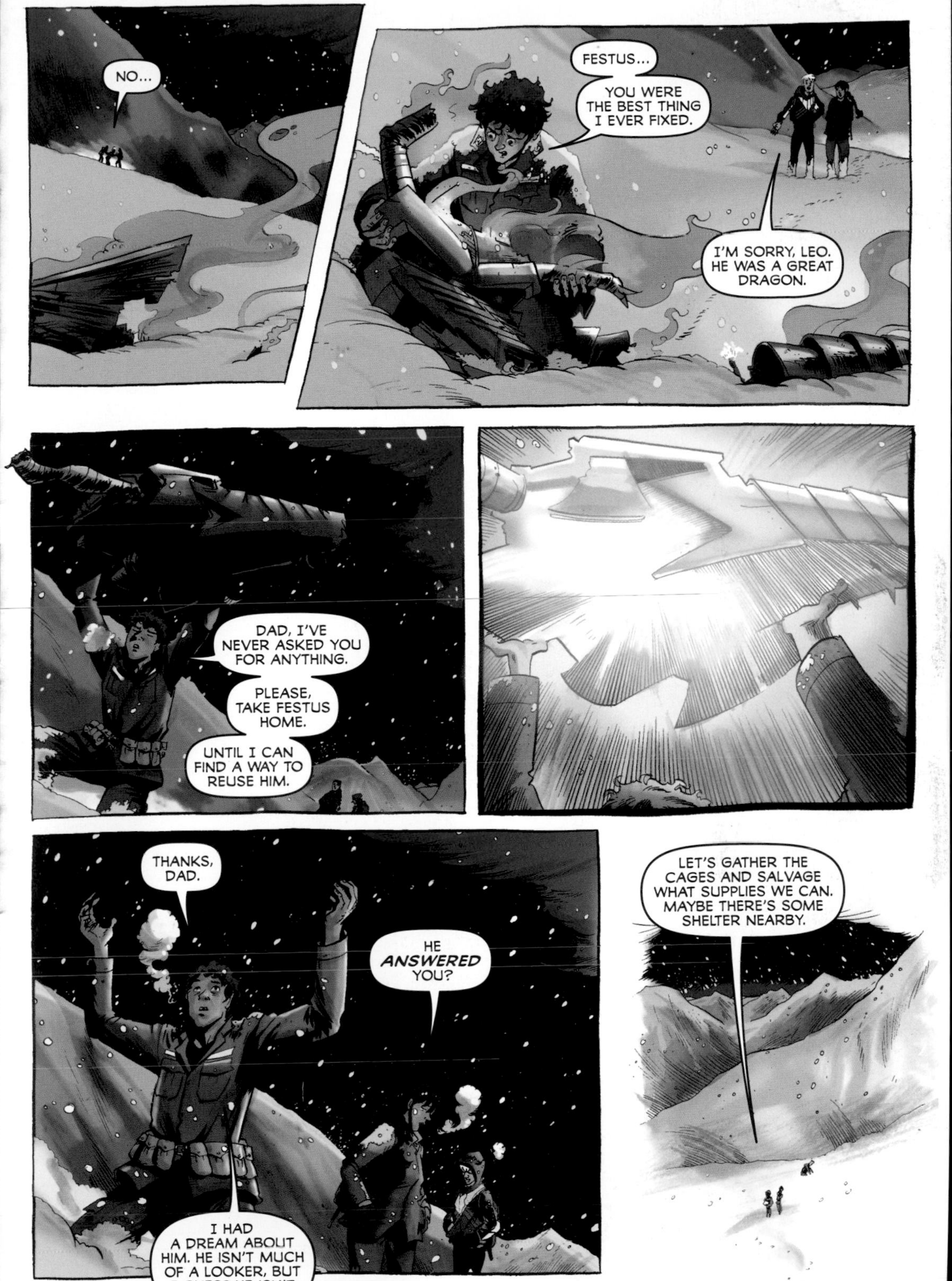
NO...
FESTUS...
YOU WERE THE BEST THING I EVER FIXED.
I'M SORRY, LEO. HE WAS A GREAT DRAGON.
DAD, I'VE NEVER ASKED YOU FOR ANYTHING.
PLEASE, TAKE FESTUS HOME.
UNTIL I CAN FIND A WAY TO REUSE HIM.
THANKS, DAD.
HE *ANSWERED* YOU?
I HAD A DREAM ABOUT HIM. HE ISN'T MUCH OF A LOOKER, BUT I GUESS HE ISN'T SO BAD.
LET'S GATHER THE CAGES AND SALVAGE WHAT SUPPLIES WE CAN. MAYBE THERE'S SOME SHELTER NEARBY.

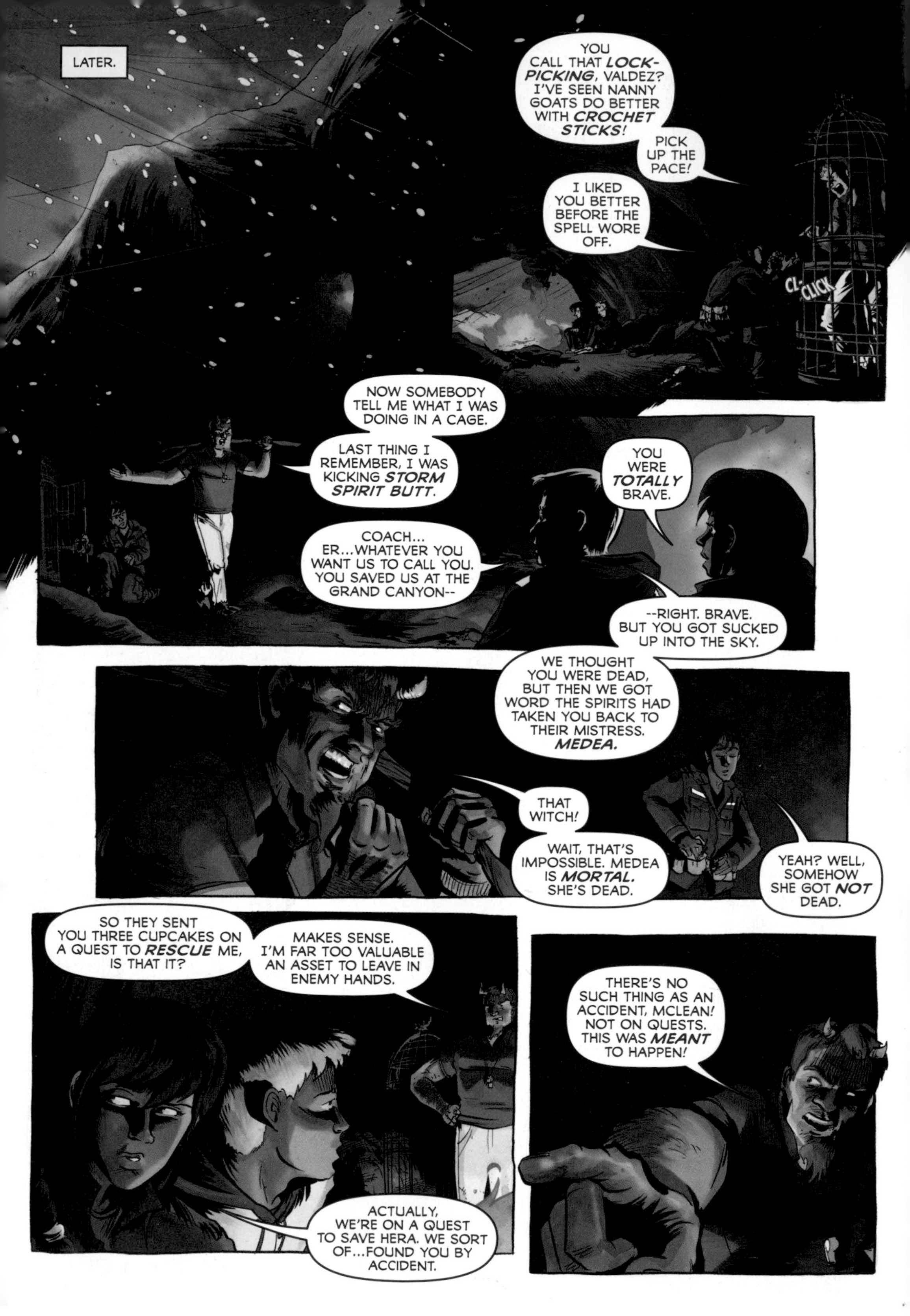

LATER.
YOU CALL THAT LOCK-PICKING, VALDEZ? I'VE SEEN NANNY GOATS DO BETTER WITH CROCHET STICKS!
PICK UP THE PACE!
I LIKED YOU BETTER BEFORE THE SPELL WORE OFF.
CL-CLICK
NOW SOMEBODY TELL ME WHAT I WAS DOING IN A CAGE.
LAST THING I REMEMBER, I WAS KICKING STORM SPIRIT BUTT.
YOU WERE TOTALLY BRAVE.
COACH... ER...WHATEVER YOU WANT US TO CALL YOU. YOU SAVED US AT THE GRAND CANYON--
--RIGHT. BRAVE. BUT YOU GOT SUCKED UP INTO THE SKY.
WE THOUGHT YOU WERE DEAD, BUT THEN WE GOT WORD THE SPIRITS HAD TAKEN YOU BACK TO THEIR MISTRESS. MEDEA.
THAT WITCH!
WAIT, THAT'S IMPOSSIBLE. MEDEA IS MORTAL. SHE'S DEAD.
YEAH? WELL, SOMEHOW SHE GOT NOT DEAD.
SO THEY SENT YOU THREE CUPCAKES ON A QUEST TO RESCUE ME, IS THAT IT?
MAKES SENSE. I'M FAR TOO VALUABLE AN ASSET TO LEAVE IN ENEMY HANDS.
ACTUALLY, WE'RE ON A QUEST TO SAVE HERA. WE SORT OF...FOUND YOU BY ACCIDENT.
THERE'S NO SUCH THING AS AN ACCIDENT, MCLEAN! NOT ON QUESTS. THIS WAS MEANT TO HAPPEN!

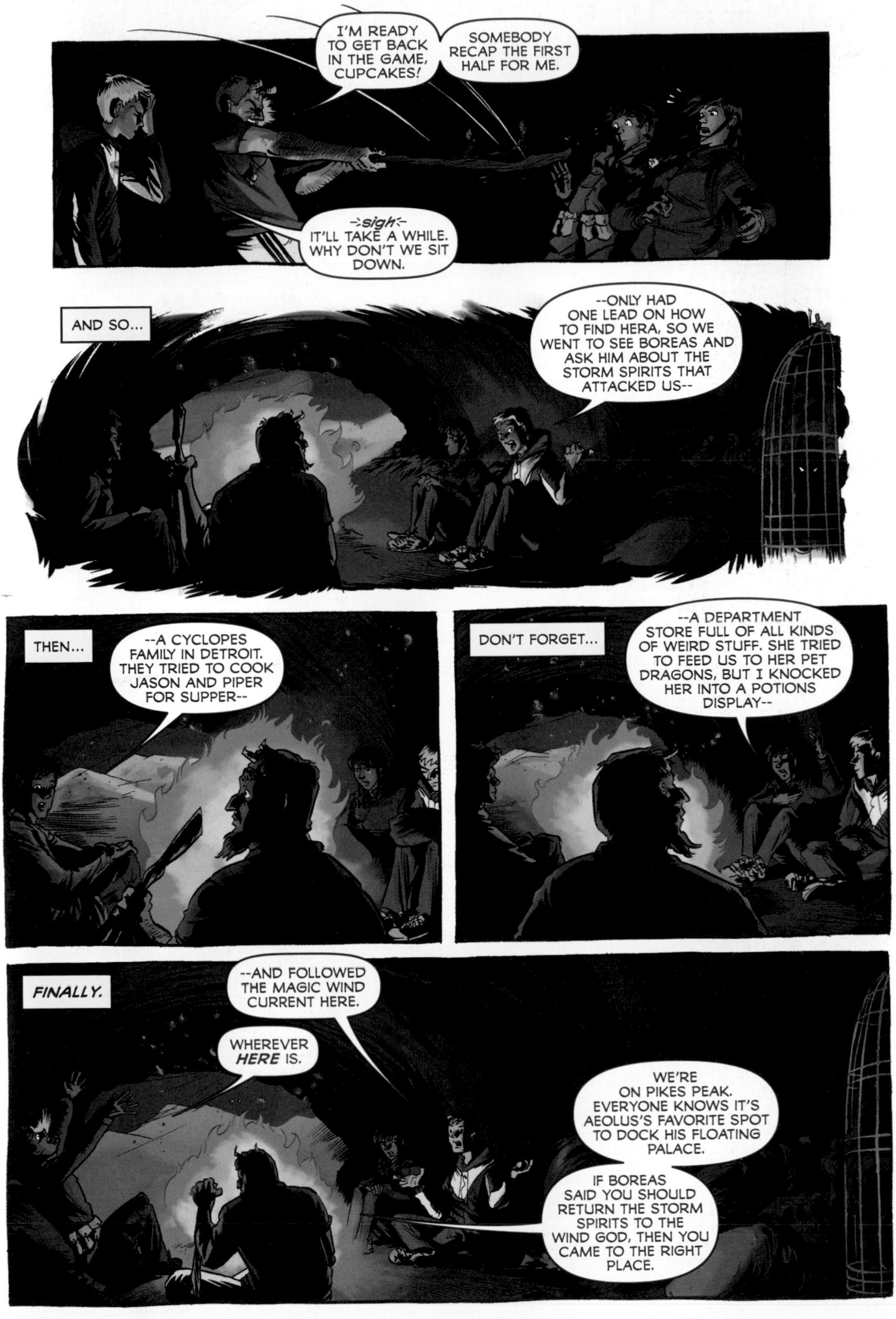
I'M READY TO GET BACK IN THE GAME, CUPCAKES!
SOMEBODY RECAP THE FIRST HALF FOR ME.
-sigh- IT'LL TAKE A WHILE. WHY DON'T WE SIT DOWN.
AND SO...
--ONLY HAD ONE LEAD ON HOW TO FIND HERA, SO WE WENT TO SEE BOREAS AND ASK HIM ABOUT THE STORM SPIRITS THAT ATTACKED US--
THEN...
--A CYCLOPES FAMILY IN DETROIT. THEY TRIED TO COOK JASON AND PIPER FOR SUPPER--
DON'T FORGET...
--A DEPARTMENT STORE FULL OF ALL KINDS OF WEIRD STUFF. SHE TRIED TO FEED US TO HER PET DRAGONS, BUT I KNOCKED HER INTO A POTIONS DISPLAY--
FINALLY.
--AND FOLLOWED THE MAGIC WIND CURRENT HERE.
WHEREVER HERE IS.
WE'RE ON PIKES PEAK. EVERYONE KNOWS IT'S AEOLUS'S FAVORITE SPOT TO DOCK HIS FLOATING PALACE.
IF BOREAS SAID YOU SHOULD RETURN THE STORM SPIRITS TO THE WIND GOD, THEN YOU CAME TO THE RIGHT PLACE.

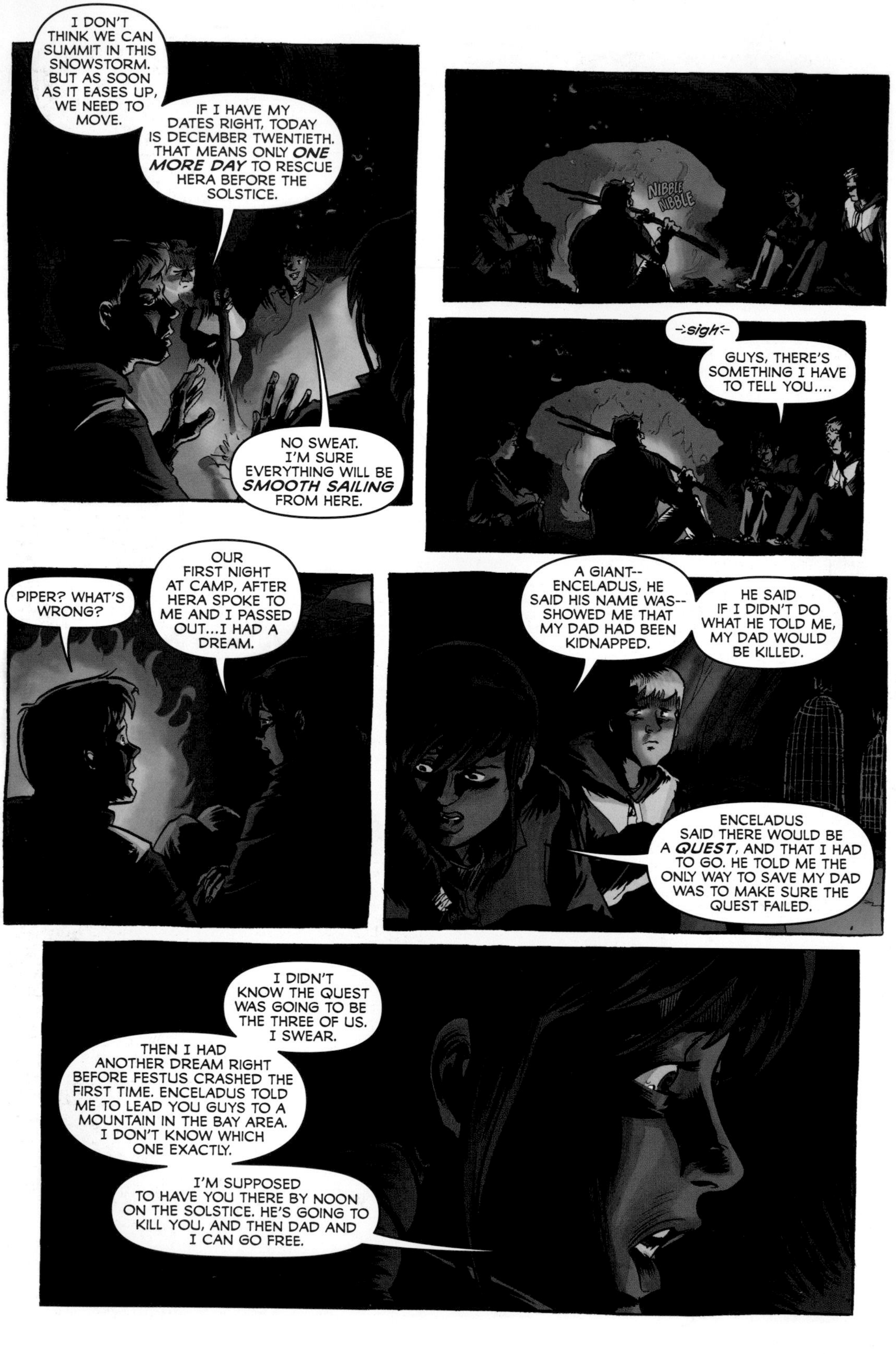
I DON'T THINK WE CAN SUMMIT IN THIS SNOWSTORM. BUT AS SOON AS IT EASES UP, WE NEED TO MOVE.
IF I HAVE MY DATES RIGHT, TODAY IS DECEMBER TWENTIETH. THAT MEANS ONLY ONE MORE DAY TO RESCUE HERA BEFORE THE SOLSTICE.
NO SWEAT. I'M SURE EVERYTHING WILL BE SMOOTH SAILING FROM HERE.
NIBBLE NIBBLE
-sigh-
GUYS, THERE'S SOMETHING I HAVE TO TELL YOU....
PIPER? WHAT'S WRONG?
OUR FIRST NIGHT AT CAMP, AFTER HERA SPOKE TO ME AND I PASSED OUT...I HAD A DREAM.
A GIANT--ENCELADUS, HE SAID HIS NAME WAS--SHOWED ME THAT MY DAD HAD BEEN KIDNAPPED.
HE SAID IF I DIDN'T DO WHAT HE TOLD ME, MY DAD WOULD BE KILLED.
ENCELADUS SAID THERE WOULD BE A QUEST, AND THAT I HAD TO GO. HE TOLD ME THE ONLY WAY TO SAVE MY DAD WAS TO MAKE SURE THE QUEST FAILED.
I DIDN'T KNOW THE QUEST WAS GOING TO BE THE THREE OF US. I SWEAR.
THEN I HAD ANOTHER DREAM RIGHT BEFORE FESTUS CRASHED THE FIRST TIME. ENCELADUS TOLD ME TO LEAD YOU GUYS TO A MOUNTAIN IN THE BAY AREA. I DON'T KNOW WHICH ONE EXACTLY.
I'M SUPPOSED TO HAVE YOU THERE BY NOON ON THE SOLSTICE. HE'S GOING TO KILL YOU, AND THEN DAD AND I CAN GO FREE.

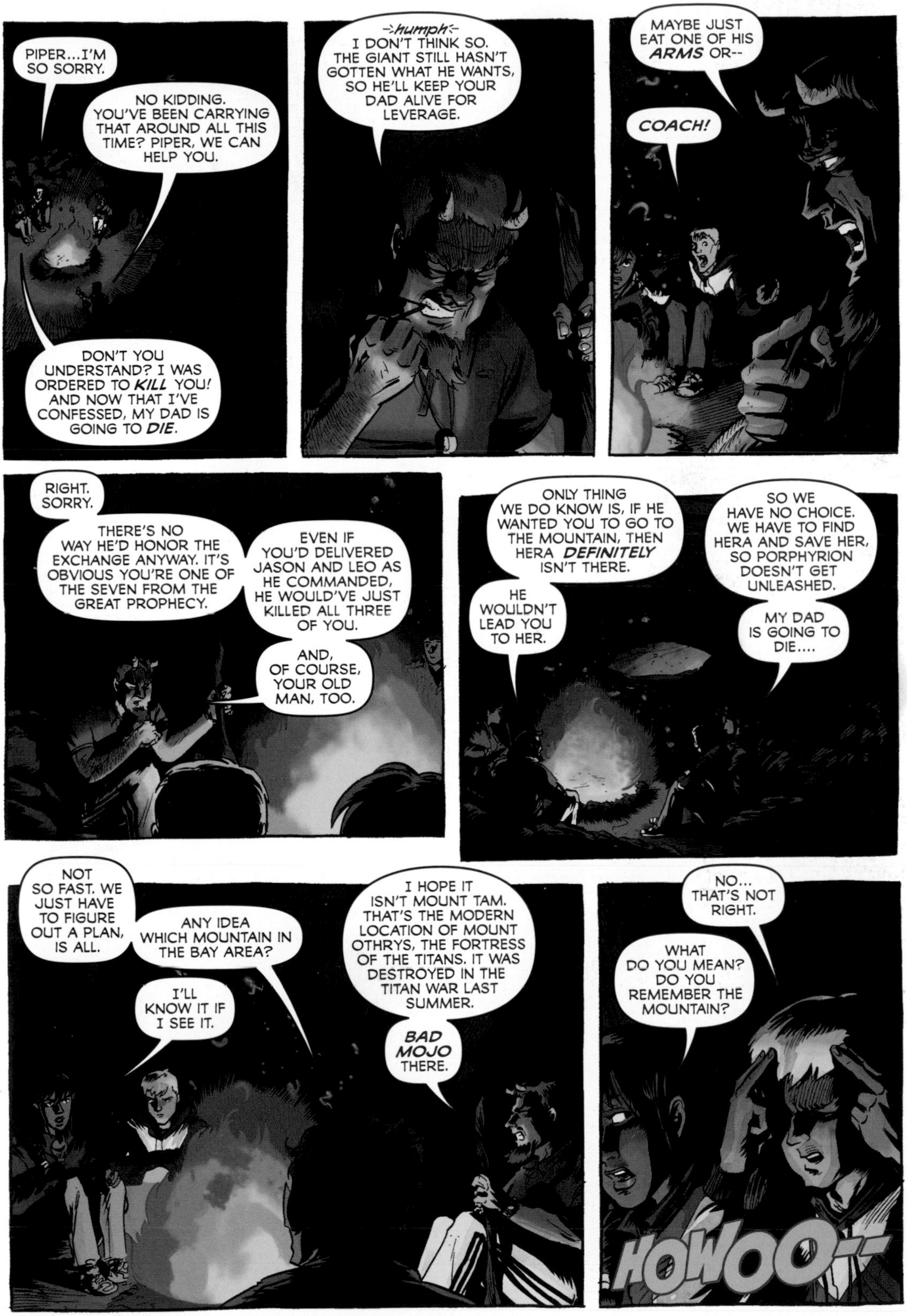
PIPER...I'M SO SORRY.
NO KIDDING. YOU'VE BEEN CARRYING THAT AROUND ALL THIS TIME? PIPER, WE CAN HELP YOU.
DON'T YOU UNDERSTAND? I WAS ORDERED TO KILL YOU! AND NOW THAT I'VE CONFESSED, MY DAD IS GOING TO DIE.
-humph-
I DON'T THINK SO. THE GIANT STILL HASN'T GOTTEN WHAT HE WANTS, SO HE'LL KEEP YOUR DAD ALIVE FOR LEVERAGE.
MAYBE JUST EAT ONE OF HIS ARMS OR--
COACH!
RIGHT. SORRY.
THERE'S NO WAY HE'D HONOR THE EXCHANGE ANYWAY. IT'S OBVIOUS YOU'RE ONE OF THE SEVEN FROM THE GREAT PROPHECY.
EVEN IF YOU'D DELIVERED JASON AND LEO AS HE COMMANDED, HE WOULD'VE JUST KILLED ALL THREE OF YOU.
AND, OF COURSE, YOUR OLD MAN, TOO.
ONLY THING WE DO KNOW IS, IF HE WANTED YOU TO GO TO THE MOUNTAIN, THEN HERA DEFINITELY ISN'T THERE.
HE WOULDN'T LEAD YOU TO HER.
SO WE HAVE NO CHOICE. WE HAVE TO FIND HERA AND SAVE HER, SO PORPHYRION DOESN'T GET UNLEASHED.
MY DAD IS GOING TO DIE....
NOT SO FAST. WE JUST HAVE TO FIGURE OUT A PLAN, IS ALL.
ANY IDEA WHICH MOUNTAIN IN THE BAY AREA?
I'LL KNOW IT IF I SEE IT.
I HOPE IT ISN'T MOUNT TAM. THAT'S THE MODERN LOCATION OF MOUNT OTHRYS, THE FORTRESS OF THE TITANS. IT WAS DESTROYED IN THE TITAN WAR LAST SUMMER.
BAD MOJO THERE.
NO... THAT'S NOT RIGHT.
WHAT DO YOU MEAN? DO YOU REMEMBER THE MOUNTAIN?
HOWOO--

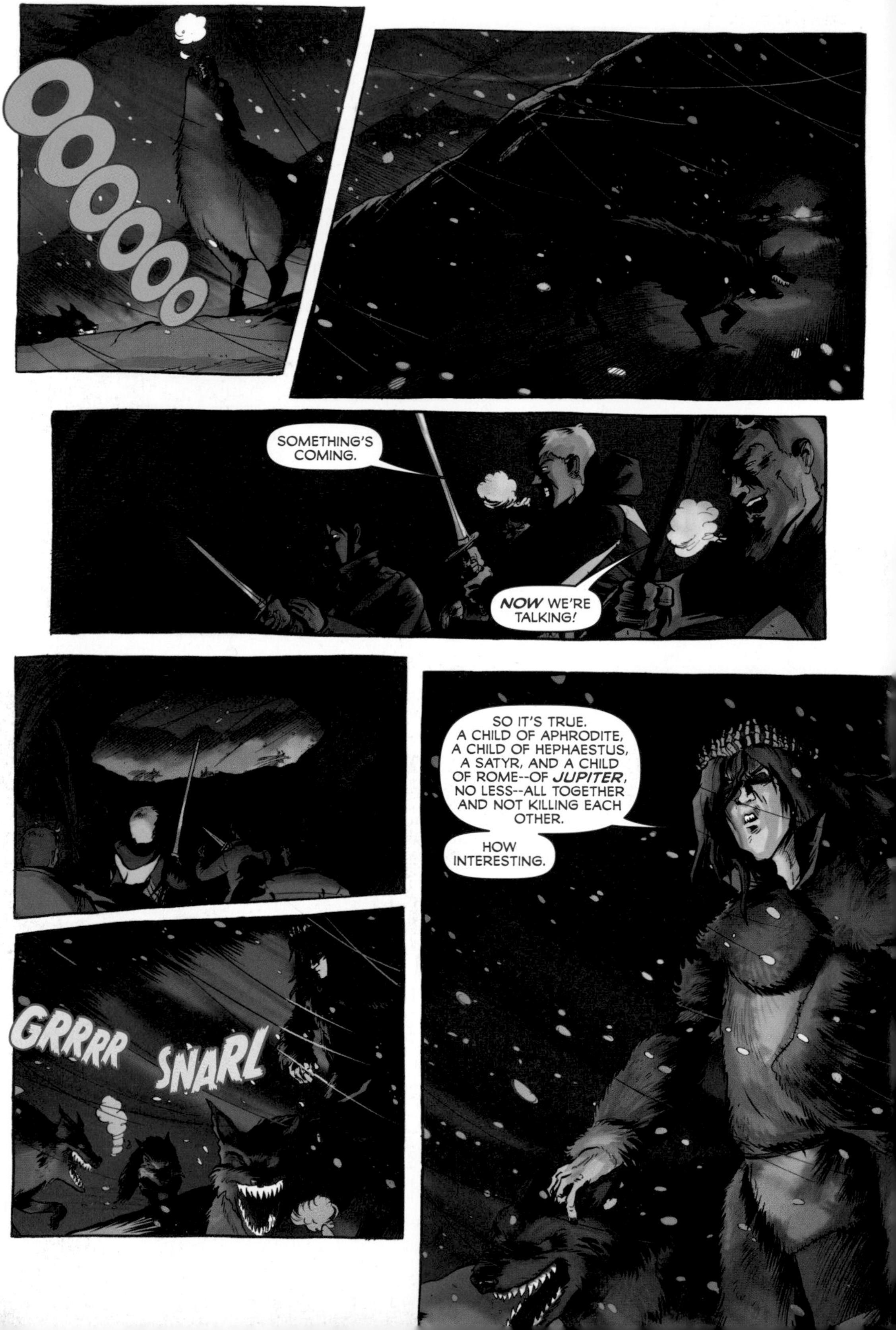
OOOOOO
SOMETHING'S COMING.
NOW WE'RE TALKING!
SO IT'S TRUE. A CHILD OF APHRODITE, A CHILD OF HEPHAESTUS, A SATYR, AND A CHILD OF ROME--OF JUPITER, NO LESS--ALL TOGETHER AND NOT KILLING EACH OTHER.
HOW INTERESTING.
GRRRR
SNARL

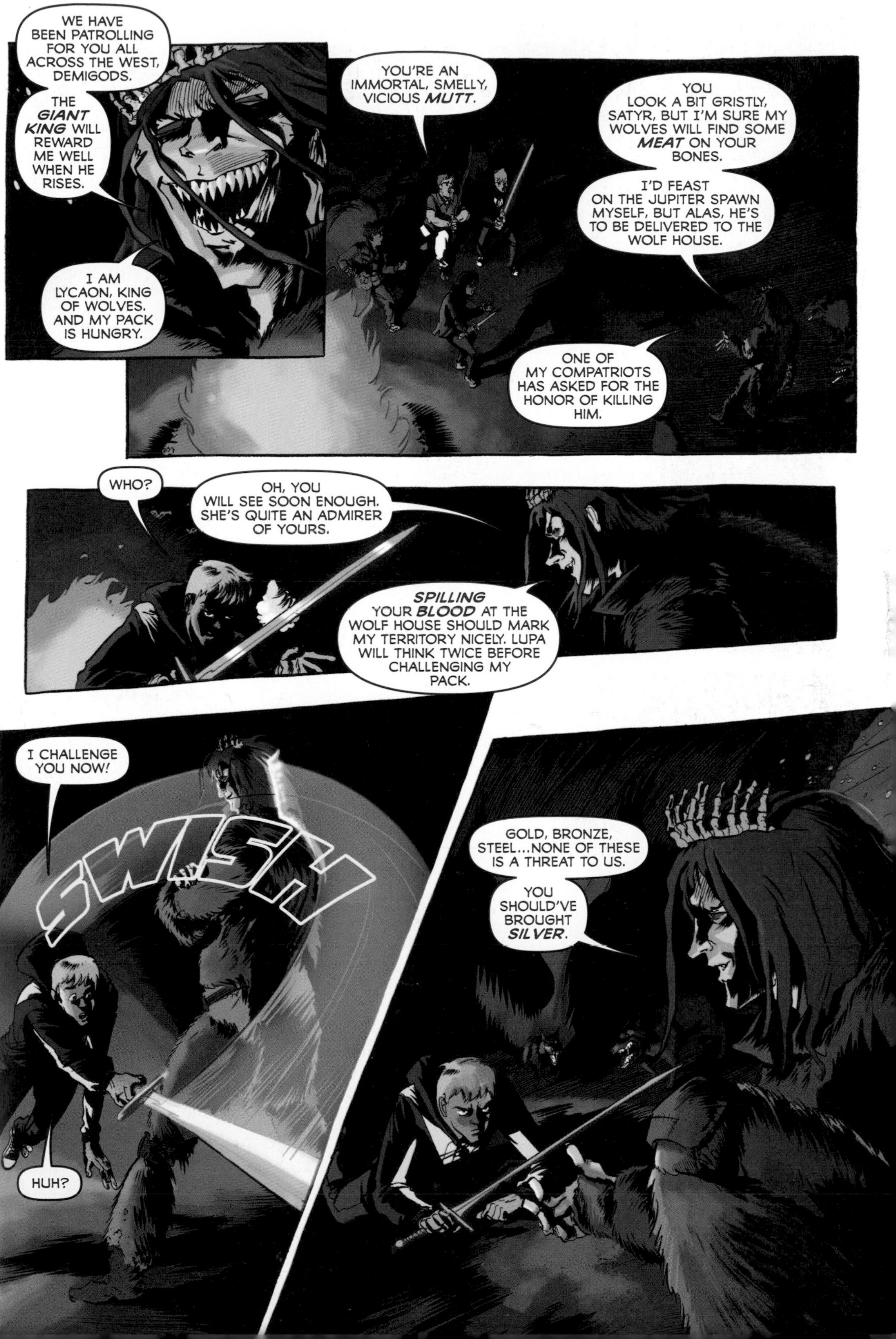
WE HAVE BEEN PATROLLING FOR YOU ALL ACROSS THE WEST, DEMIGODS.
THE *GIANT KING* WILL REWARD ME WELL WHEN HE RISES.
I AM LYCAON, KING OF WOLVES. AND MY PACK IS HUNGRY.
YOU'RE AN IMMORTAL, SMELLY, VICIOUS *MUTT*.
YOU LOOK A BIT GRISTLY, SATYR, BUT I'M SURE MY WOLVES WILL FIND SOME *MEAT* ON YOUR BONES.
I'D FEAST ON THE JUPITER SPAWN MYSELF, BUT ALAS, HE'S TO BE DELIVERED TO THE WOLF HOUSE.
ONE OF MY COMPATRIOTS HAS ASKED FOR THE HONOR OF KILLING HIM.
WHO?
OH, YOU WILL SEE SOON ENOUGH. SHE'S QUITE AN ADMIRER OF YOURS.
SPILLING YOUR *BLOOD* AT THE WOLF HOUSE SHOULD MARK MY TERRITORY NICELY. LUPA WILL THINK TWICE BEFORE CHALLENGING MY PACK.
I CHALLENGE YOU NOW!
SWISH
HUH?
GOLD, BRONZE, STEEL...NONE OF THESE IS A THREAT TO US.
YOU SHOULD'VE BROUGHT *SILVER*.

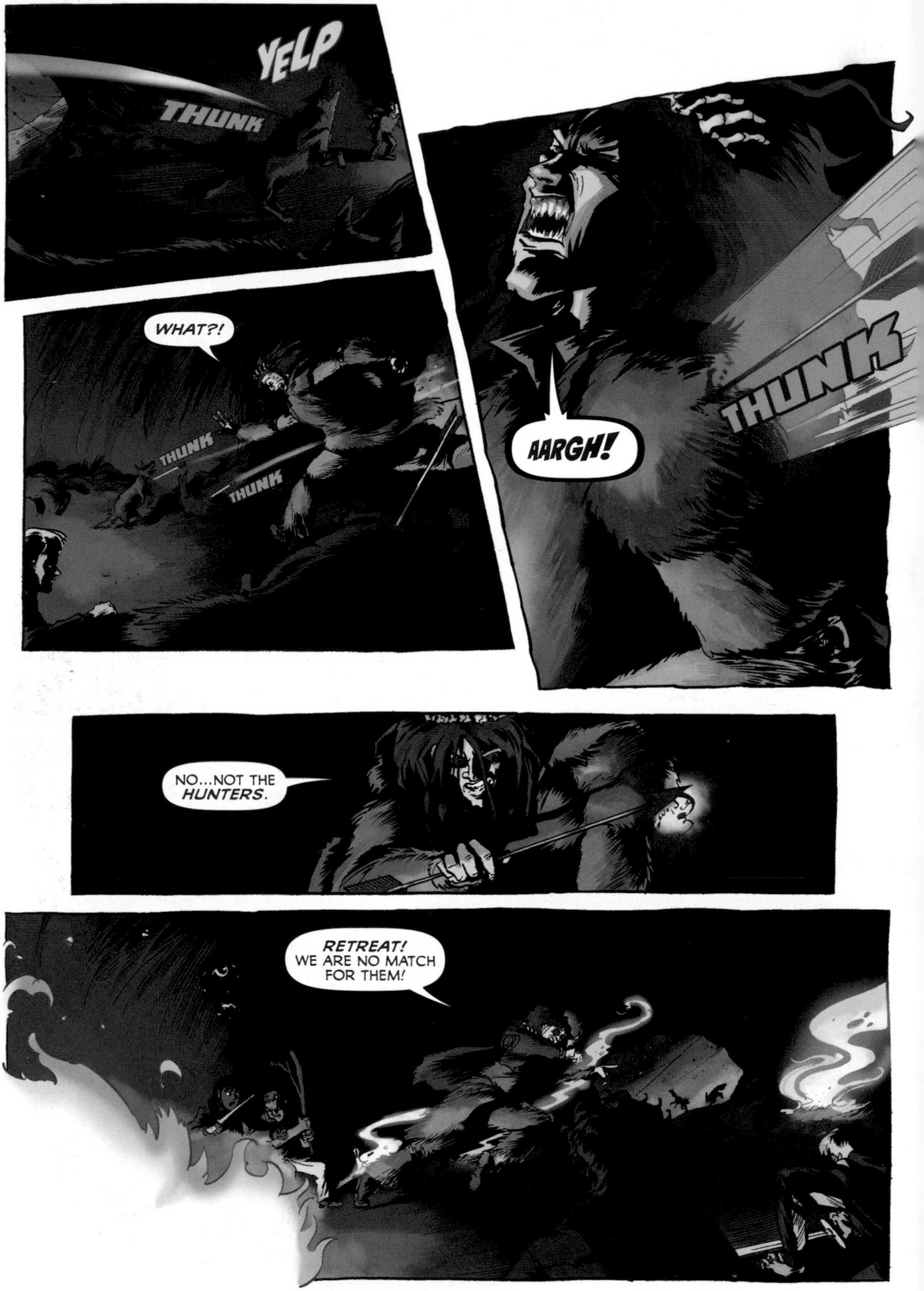
YELP
THUNK
WHAT?!
THUNK
THUNK
AARGH!
THUNK
NO...NOT THE HUNTERS.
RETREAT! WE ARE NO MATCH FOR THEM!

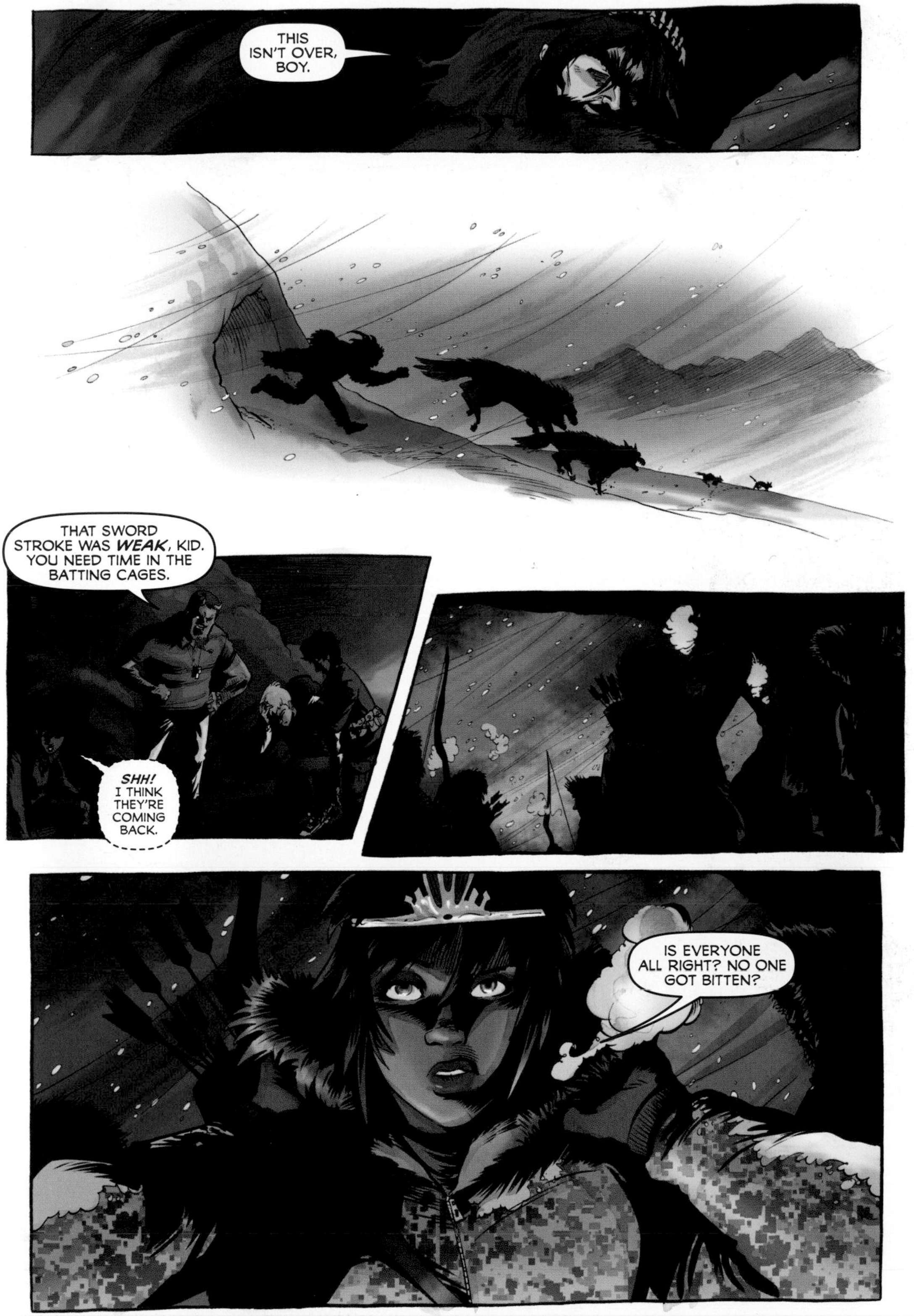
THIS ISN'T OVER, BOY.
THAT SWORD STROKE WAS *WEAK*, KID. YOU NEED TIME IN THE BATTING CAGES.
SHH! I THINK THEY'RE COMING BACK.
IS EVERYONE ALL RIGHT? NO ONE GOT BITTEN?

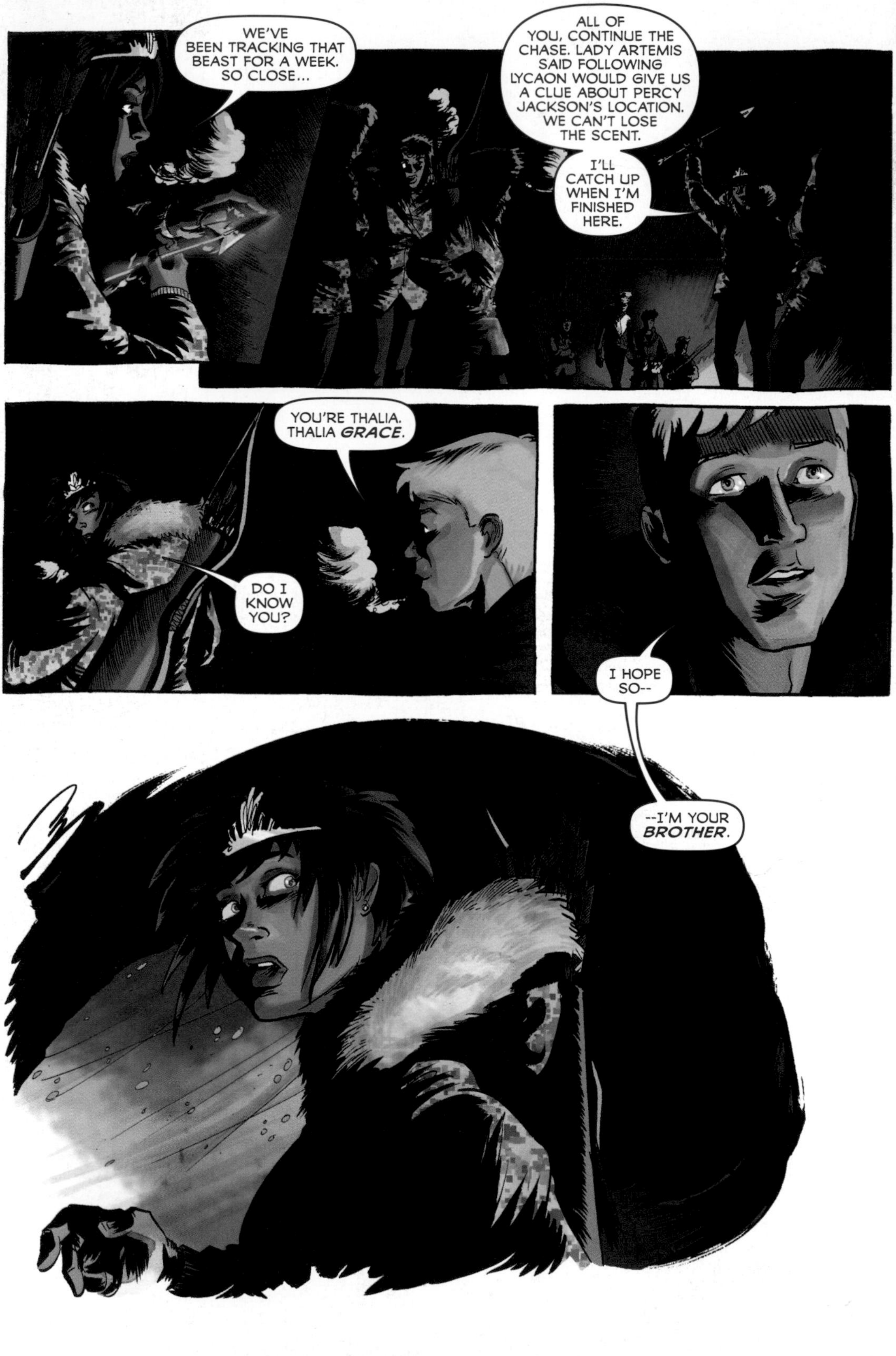
WE'VE BEEN TRACKING THAT BEAST FOR A WEEK. SO CLOSE...
ALL OF YOU, CONTINUE THE CHASE. LADY ARTEMIS SAID FOLLOWING LYCAON WOULD GIVE US A CLUE ABOUT PERCY JACKSON'S LOCATION. WE CAN'T LOSE THE SCENT.
I'LL CATCH UP WHEN I'M FINISHED HERE.
YOU'RE THALIA. THALIA *GRACE*.
DO I KNOW YOU?
I HOPE SO--
--I'M YOUR *BROTHER*.

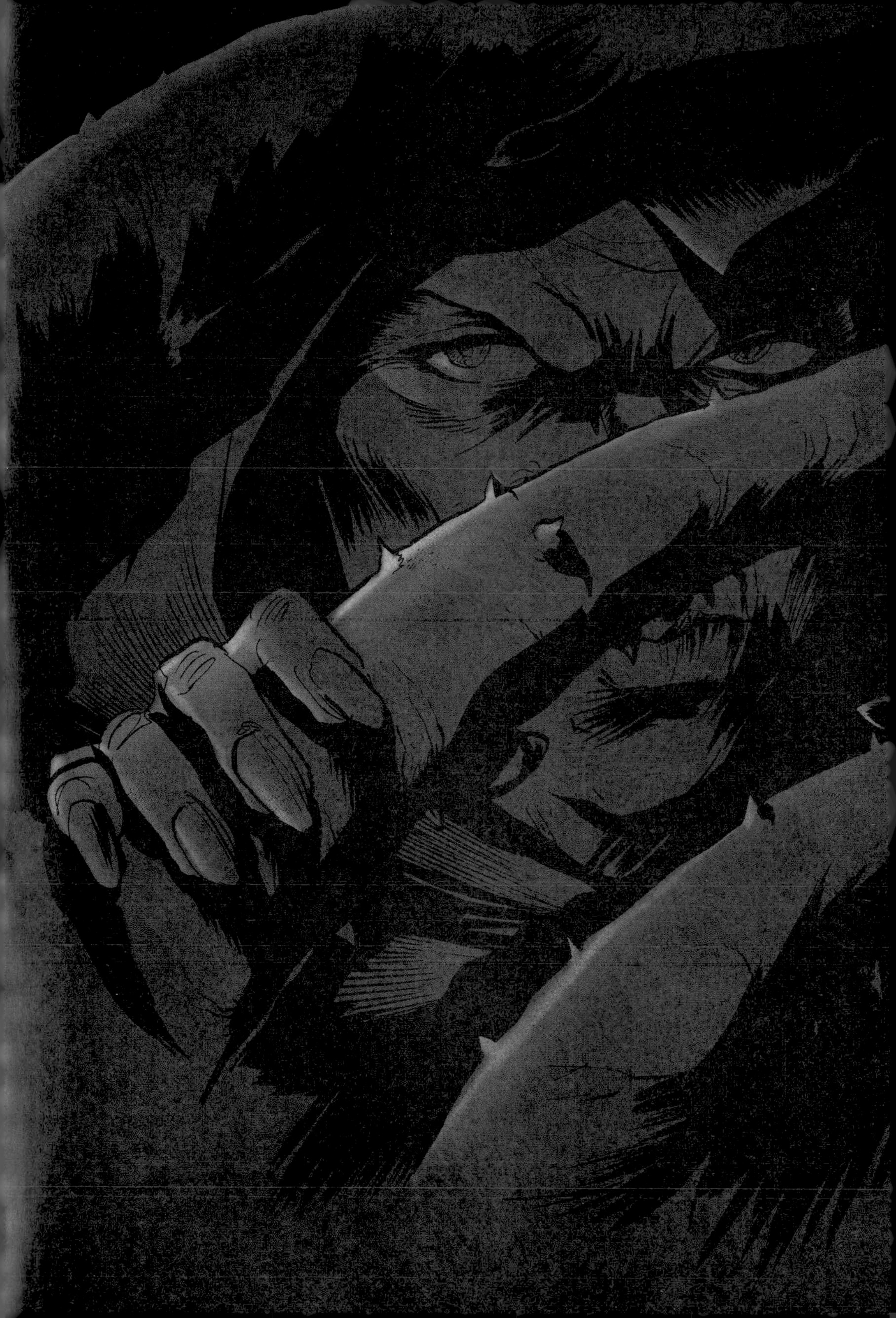

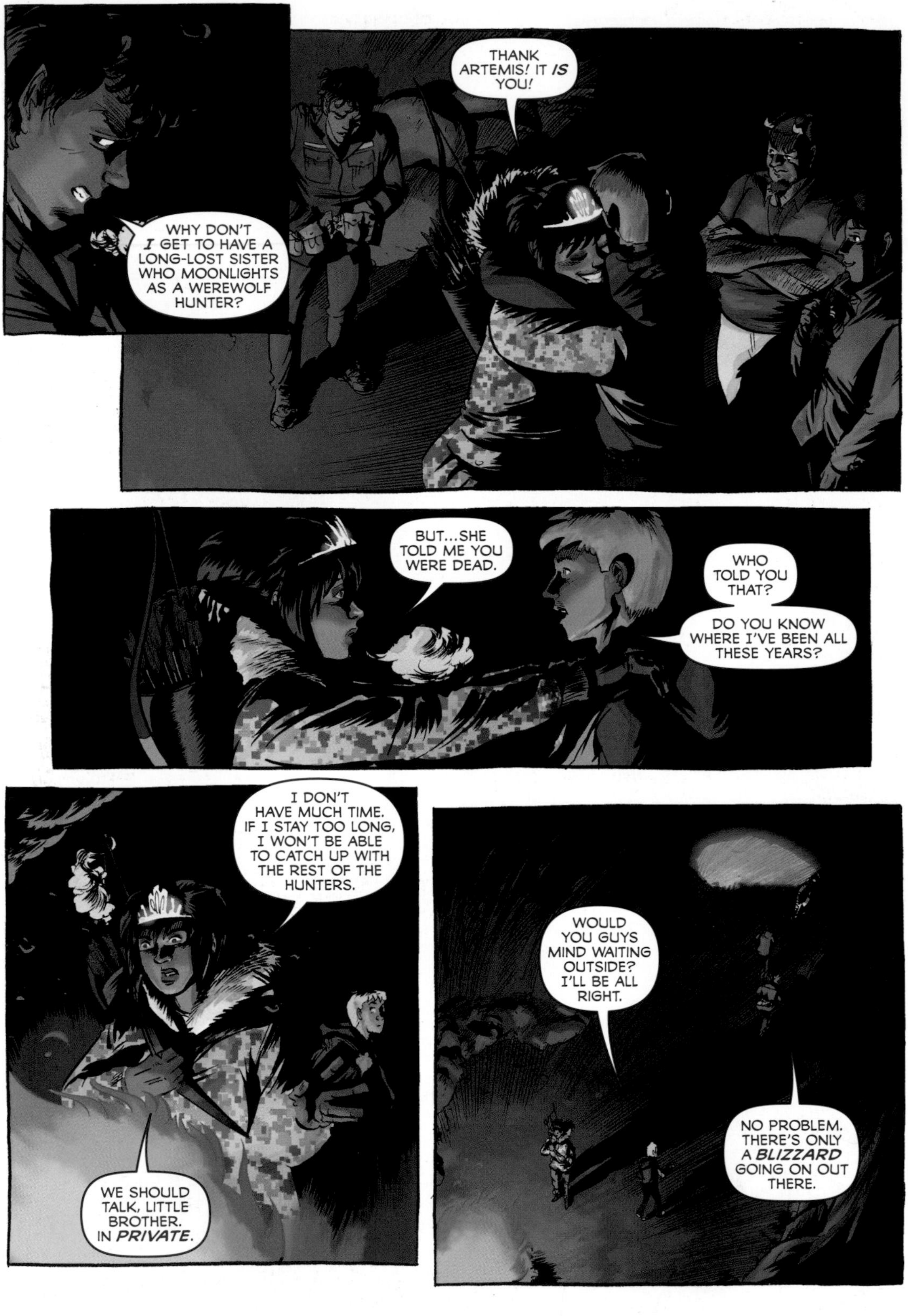
THANK ARTEMIS! IT *IS* YOU!
WHY DON'T *I* GET TO HAVE A LONG-LOST SISTER WHO MOONLIGHTS AS A WEREWOLF HUNTER?
BUT...SHE TOLD ME YOU WERE DEAD.
WHO TOLD YOU THAT?
DO YOU KNOW WHERE I'VE BEEN ALL THESE YEARS?
I DON'T HAVE MUCH TIME. IF I STAY TOO LONG, I WON'T BE ABLE TO CATCH UP WITH THE REST OF THE HUNTERS.
WE SHOULD TALK, LITTLE BROTHER. IN *PRIVATE*.
WOULD YOU GUYS MIND WAITING OUTSIDE? I'LL BE ALL RIGHT.
NO PROBLEM. THERE'S ONLY A *BLIZZARD* GOING ON OUT THERE.

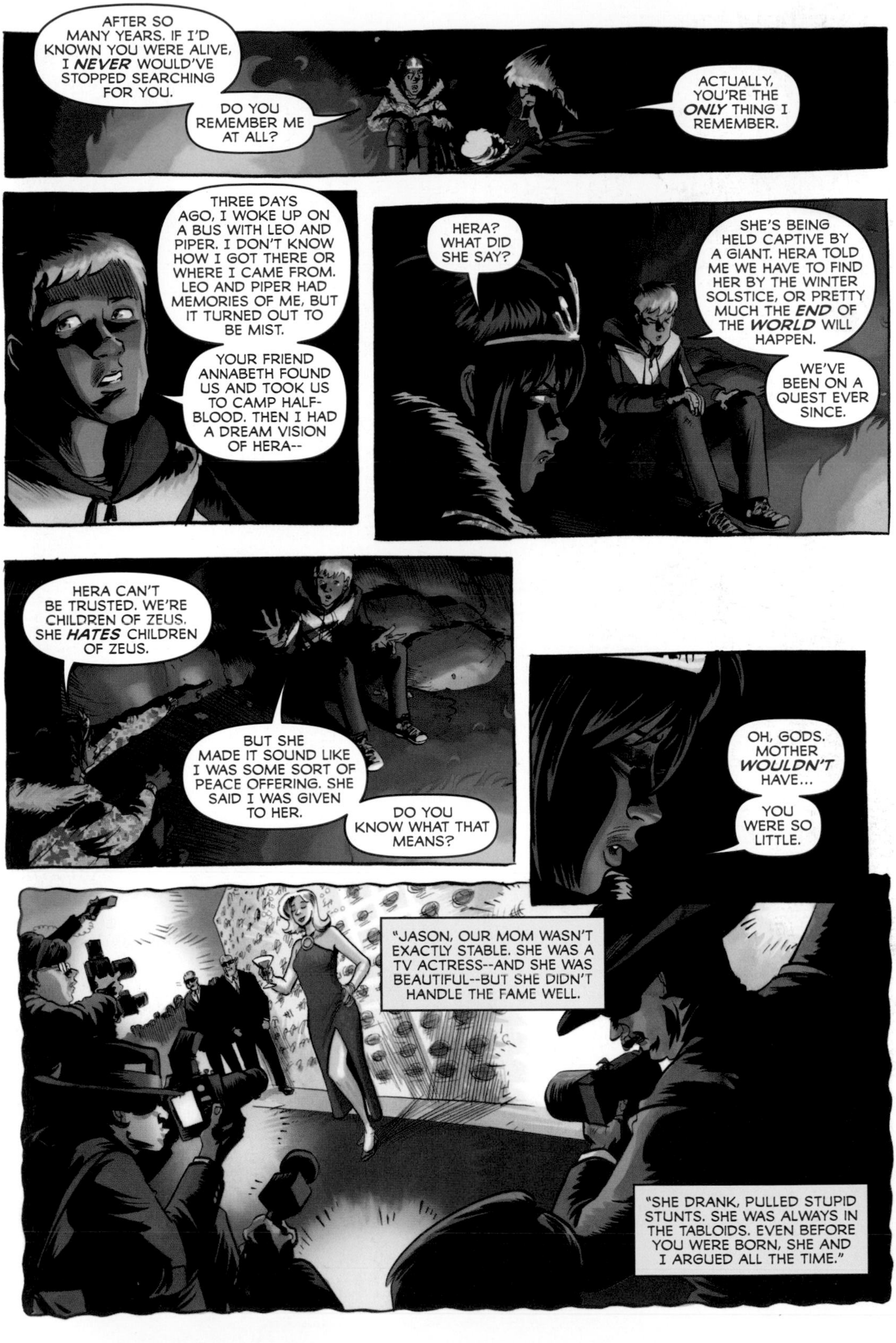
AFTER SO MANY YEARS. IF I'D KNOWN YOU WERE ALIVE, I NEVER WOULD'VE STOPPED SEARCHING FOR YOU.
DO YOU REMEMBER ME AT ALL?
ACTUALLY, YOU'RE THE ONLY THING I REMEMBER.
THREE DAYS AGO, I WOKE UP ON A BUS WITH LEO AND PIPER. I DON'T KNOW HOW I GOT THERE OR WHERE I CAME FROM. LEO AND PIPER HAD MEMORIES OF ME, BUT IT TURNED OUT TO BE MIST.
YOUR FRIEND ANNABETH FOUND US AND TOOK US TO CAMP HALF-BLOOD. THEN I HAD A DREAM VISION OF HERA--
HERA? WHAT DID SHE SAY?
SHE'S BEING HELD CAPTIVE BY A GIANT. HERA TOLD ME WE HAVE TO FIND HER BY THE WINTER SOLSTICE, OR PRETTY MUCH THE END OF THE WORLD WILL HAPPEN.
WE'VE BEEN ON A QUEST EVER SINCE.
HERA CAN'T BE TRUSTED. WE'RE CHILDREN OF ZEUS. SHE HATES CHILDREN OF ZEUS.
BUT SHE MADE IT SOUND LIKE I WAS SOME SORT OF PEACE OFFERING. SHE SAID I WAS GIVEN TO HER.
DO YOU KNOW WHAT THAT MEANS?
OH, GODS. MOTHER WOULDN'T HAVE...
YOU WERE SO LITTLE.
"JASON, OUR MOM WASN'T EXACTLY STABLE. SHE WAS A TV ACTRESS--AND SHE WAS BEAUTIFUL--BUT SHE DIDN'T HANDLE THE FAME WELL.
"SHE DRANK, PULLED STUPID STUNTS. SHE WAS ALWAYS IN THE TABLOIDS. EVEN BEFORE YOU WERE BORN, SHE AND I ARGUED ALL THE TIME."

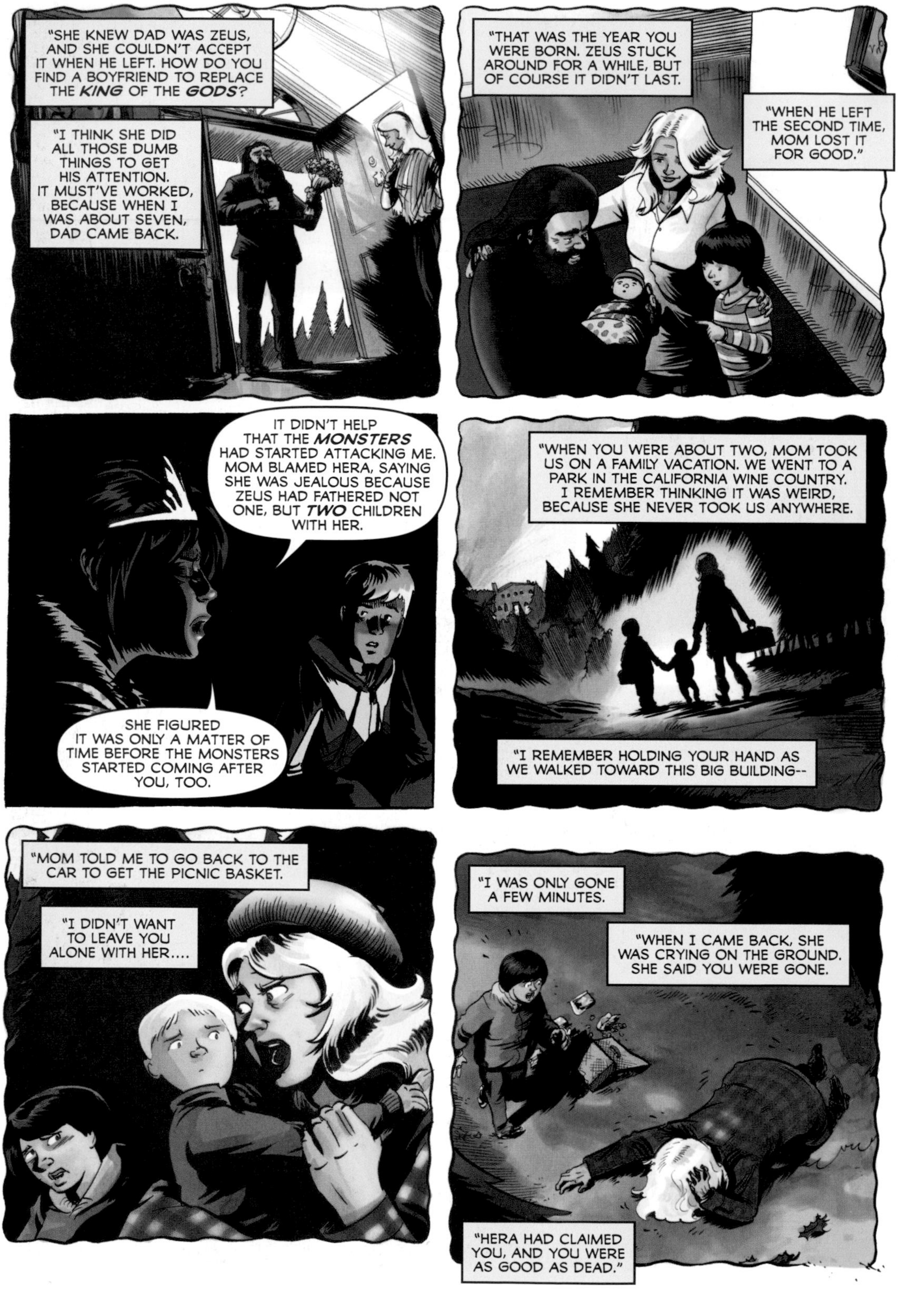
"SHE KNEW DAD WAS ZEUS, AND SHE COULDN'T ACCEPT IT WHEN HE LEFT. HOW DO YOU FIND A BOYFRIEND TO REPLACE THE *KING* OF THE *GODS*?
"I THINK SHE DID ALL THOSE DUMB THINGS TO GET HIS ATTENTION. IT MUST'VE WORKED, BECAUSE WHEN I WAS ABOUT SEVEN, DAD CAME BACK.
"THAT WAS THE YEAR YOU WERE BORN. ZEUS STUCK AROUND FOR A WHILE, BUT OF COURSE IT DIDN'T LAST.
"WHEN HE LEFT THE SECOND TIME, MOM LOST IT FOR GOOD."
IT DIDN'T HELP THAT THE *MONSTERS* HAD STARTED ATTACKING ME. MOM BLAMED HERA, SAYING SHE WAS JEALOUS BECAUSE ZEUS HAD FATHERED NOT ONE, BUT *TWO* CHILDREN WITH HER.
SHE FIGURED IT WAS ONLY A MATTER OF TIME BEFORE THE MONSTERS STARTED COMING AFTER YOU, TOO.
"WHEN YOU WERE ABOUT TWO, MOM TOOK US ON A FAMILY VACATION. WE WENT TO A PARK IN THE CALIFORNIA WINE COUNTRY. I REMEMBER THINKING IT WAS WEIRD, BECAUSE SHE NEVER TOOK US ANYWHERE.
"I REMEMBER HOLDING YOUR HAND AS WE WALKED TOWARD THIS BIG BUILDING--
"MOM TOLD ME TO GO BACK TO THE CAR TO GET THE PICNIC BASKET.
"I DIDN'T WANT TO LEAVE YOU ALONE WITH HER....
"I WAS ONLY GONE A FEW MINUTES.
"WHEN I CAME BACK, SHE WAS CRYING ON THE GROUND. SHE SAID YOU WERE GONE.
"HERA HAD CLAIMED YOU, AND YOU WERE AS GOOD AS DEAD."

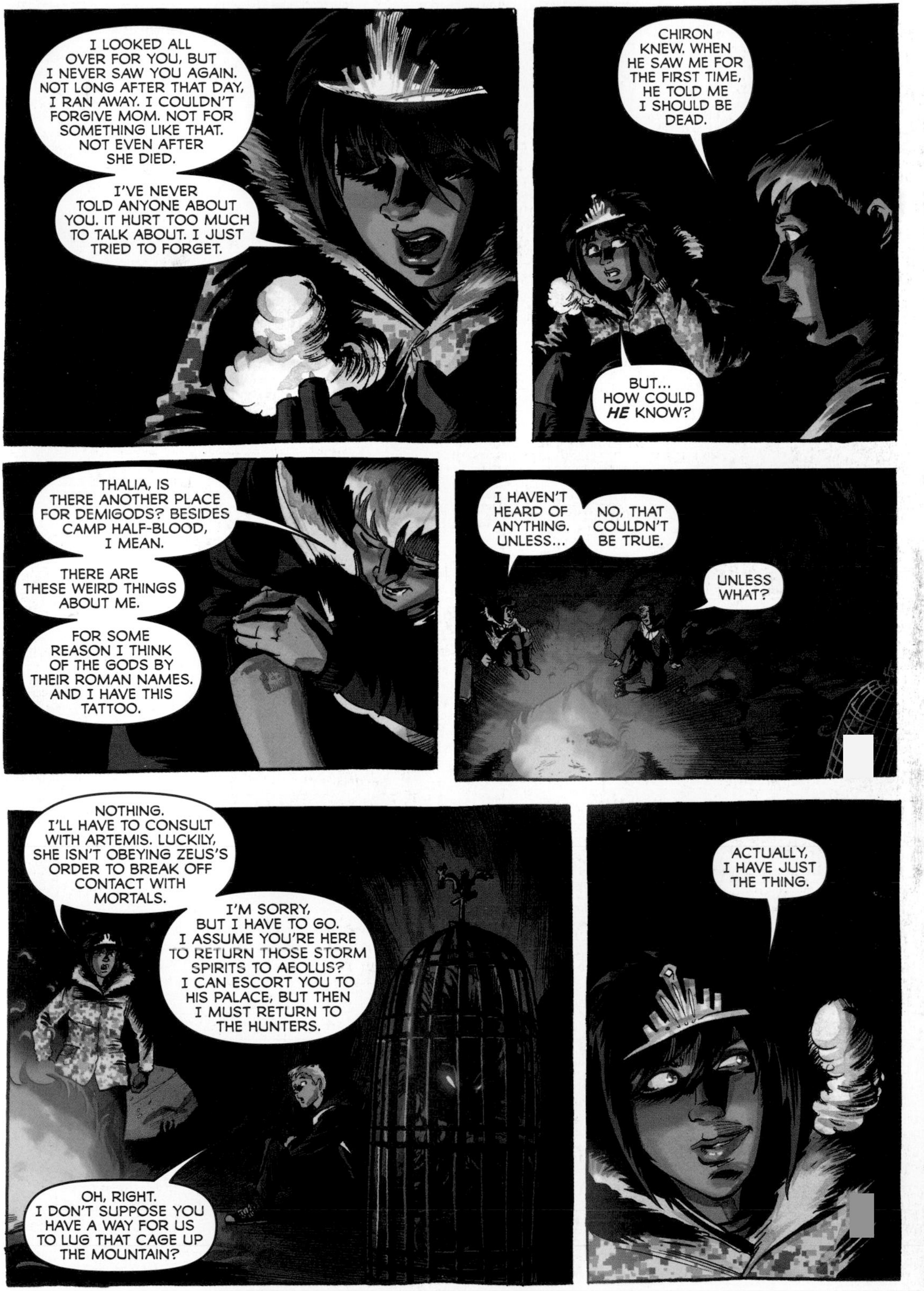

I LOOKED ALL OVER FOR YOU, BUT I NEVER SAW YOU AGAIN. NOT LONG AFTER THAT DAY, I RAN AWAY. I COULDN'T FORGIVE MOM. NOT FOR SOMETHING LIKE THAT. NOT EVEN AFTER SHE DIED.
I'VE NEVER TOLD ANYONE ABOUT YOU. IT HURT TOO MUCH TO TALK ABOUT. I JUST TRIED TO FORGET.
CHIRON KNEW. WHEN HE SAW ME FOR THE FIRST TIME, HE TOLD ME I SHOULD BE DEAD.
BUT... HOW COULD ***HE*** KNOW?
THALIA, IS THERE ANOTHER PLACE FOR DEMIGODS? BESIDES CAMP HALF-BLOOD, I MEAN.
THERE ARE THESE WEIRD THINGS ABOUT ME.
FOR SOME REASON I THINK OF THE GODS BY THEIR ROMAN NAMES. AND I HAVE THIS TATTOO.
I HAVEN'T HEARD OF ANYTHING. UNLESS...
NO, THAT COULDN'T BE TRUE.
UNLESS WHAT?
NOTHING. I'LL HAVE TO CONSULT WITH ARTEMIS. LUCKILY, SHE ISN'T OBEYING ZEUS'S ORDER TO BREAK OFF CONTACT WITH MORTALS.
I'M SORRY, BUT I HAVE TO GO. I ASSUME YOU'RE HERE TO RETURN THOSE STORM SPIRITS TO AEOLUS? I CAN ESCORT YOU TO HIS PALACE, BUT THEN I MUST RETURN TO THE HUNTERS.
OH, RIGHT. I DON'T SUPPOSE YOU HAVE A WAY FOR US TO LUG THAT CAGE UP THE MOUNTAIN?
ACTUALLY, I HAVE JUST THE THING.

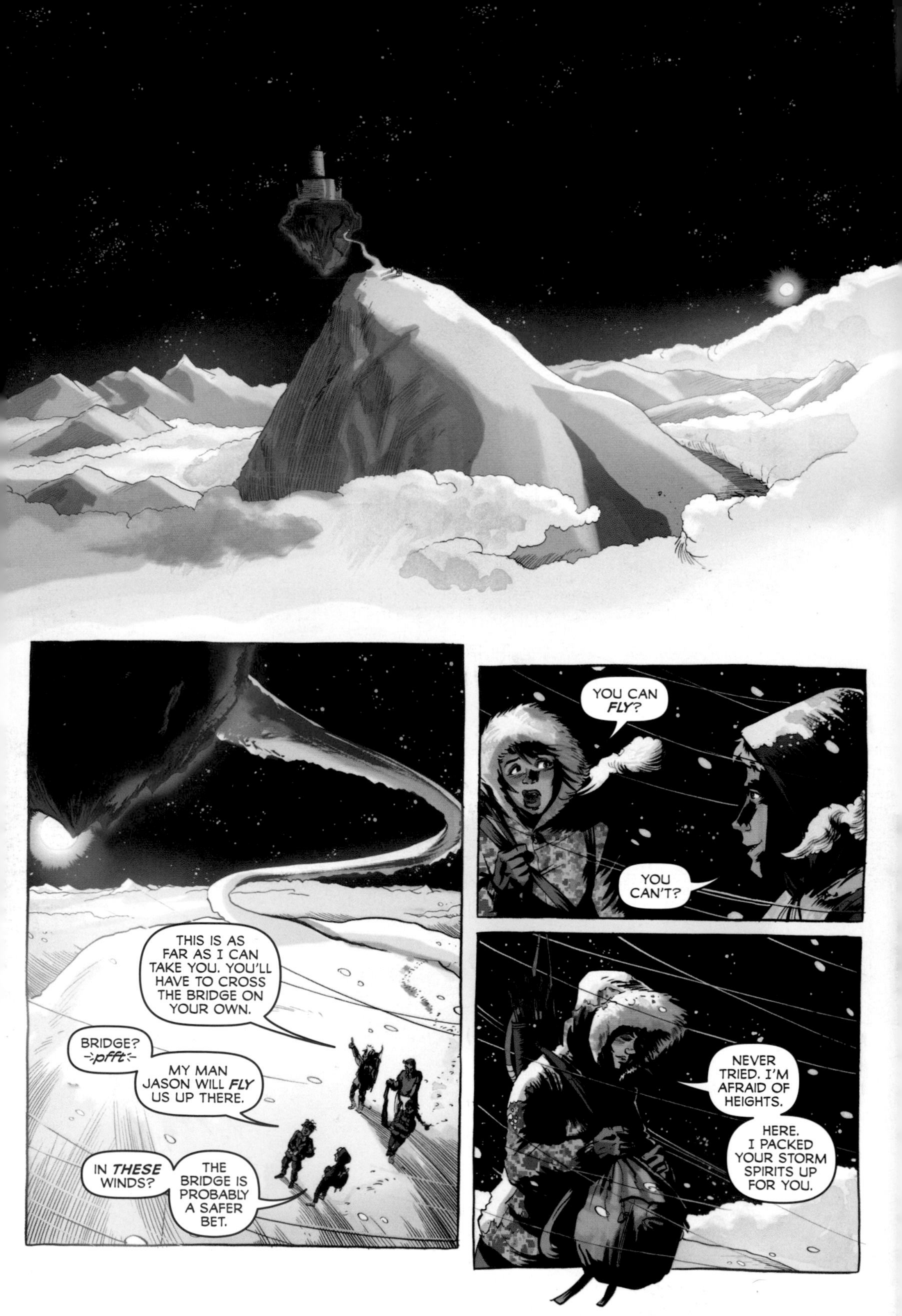
THIS IS AS FAR AS I CAN TAKE YOU. YOU'LL HAVE TO CROSS THE BRIDGE ON YOUR OWN.
BRIDGE? -pfft-
MY MAN JASON WILL FLY US UP THERE.
IN THESE WINDS?
THE BRIDGE IS PROBABLY A SAFER BET.
YOU CAN FLY?
YOU CAN'T?
NEVER TRIED. I'M AFRAID OF HEIGHTS.
HERE. I PACKED YOUR STORM SPIRITS UP FOR YOU.

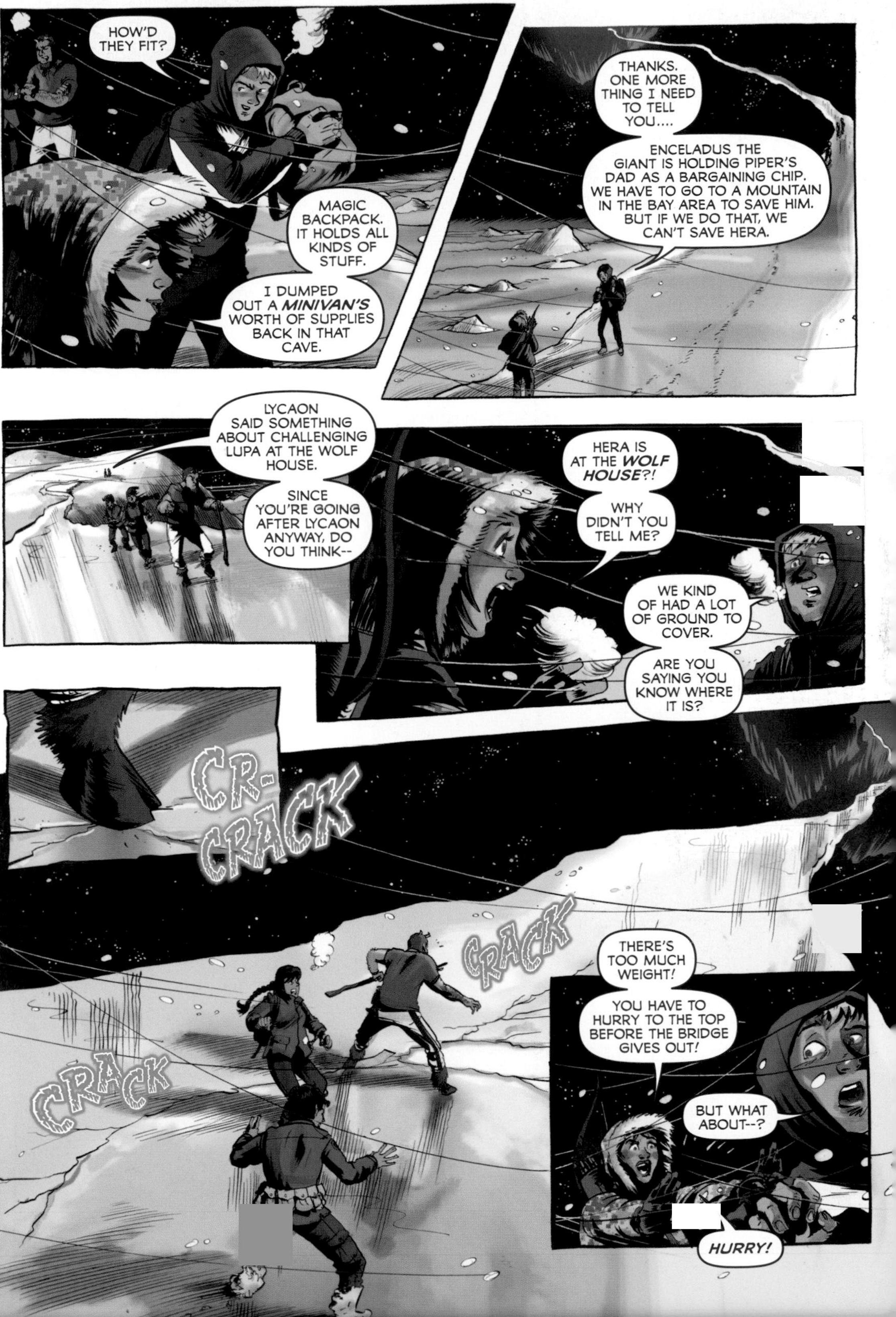
HOW'D THEY FIT?
MAGIC BACKPACK. IT HOLDS ALL KINDS OF STUFF.
I DUMPED OUT A *MINIVAN'S* WORTH OF SUPPLIES BACK IN THAT CAVE.
THANKS. ONE MORE THING I NEED TO TELL YOU....
ENCELADUS THE GIANT IS HOLDING PIPER'S DAD AS A BARGAINING CHIP. WE HAVE TO GO TO A MOUNTAIN IN THE BAY AREA TO SAVE HIM. BUT IF WE DO THAT, WE CAN'T SAVE HERA.
LYCAON SAID SOMETHING ABOUT CHALLENGING LUPA AT THE WOLF HOUSE.
SINCE YOU'RE GOING AFTER LYCAON ANYWAY, DO YOU THINK--
HERA IS AT THE *WOLF HOUSE*?!
WHY DIDN'T YOU TELL ME?
WE KIND OF HAD A LOT OF GROUND TO COVER.
ARE YOU SAYING YOU KNOW WHERE IT IS?
CR-CRACK
CRACK
CRACK
THERE'S TOO MUCH WEIGHT!
YOU HAVE TO HURRY TO THE TOP BEFORE THE BRIDGE GIVES OUT!
BUT WHAT ABOUT--?
HURRY!

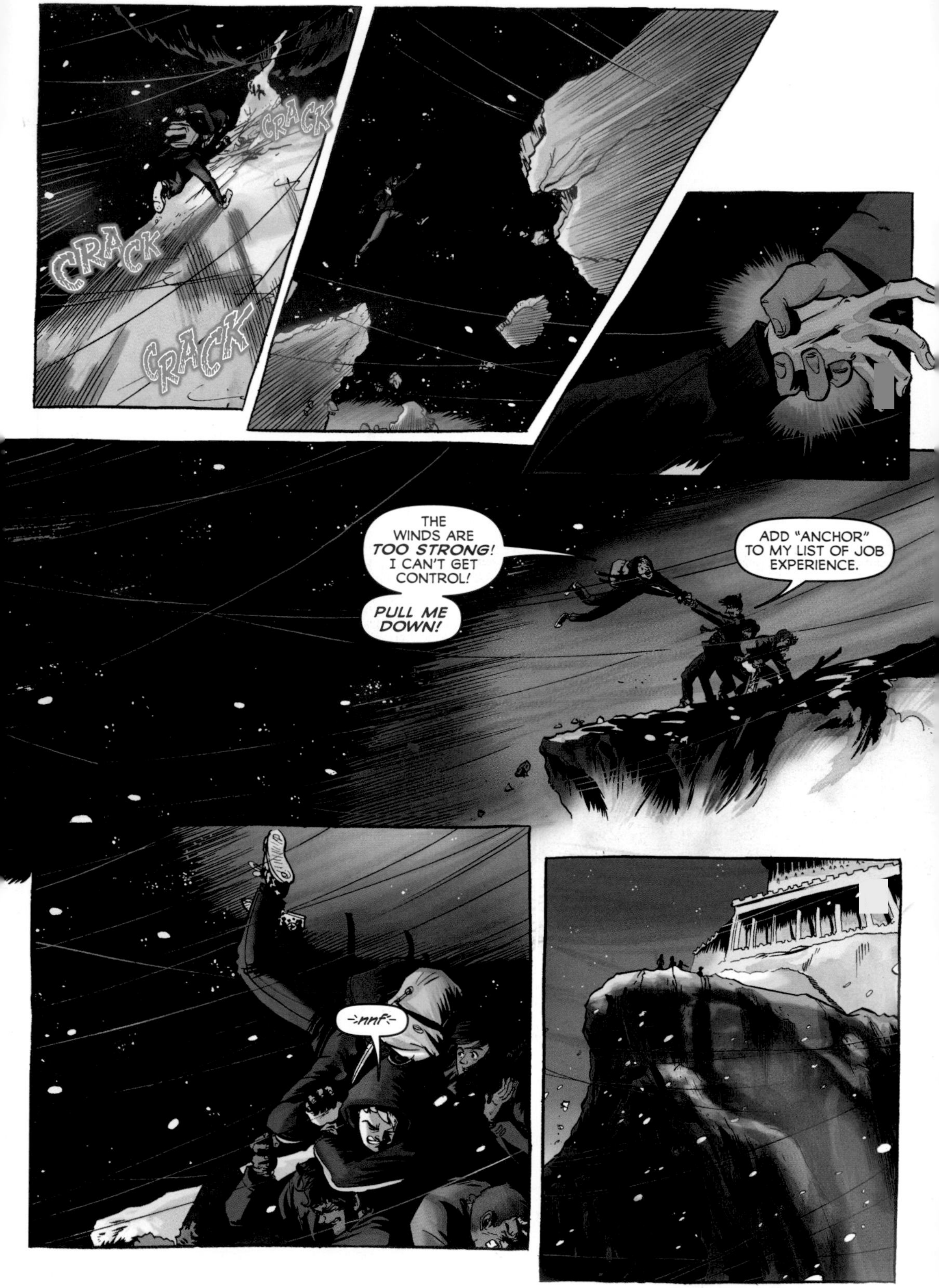
CRACK
CRACK
CRACK
THE WINDS ARE TOO STRONG! I CAN'T GET CONTROL!
PULL ME DOWN!
ADD "ANCHOR" TO MY LIST OF JOB EXPERIENCE.
-nnf-

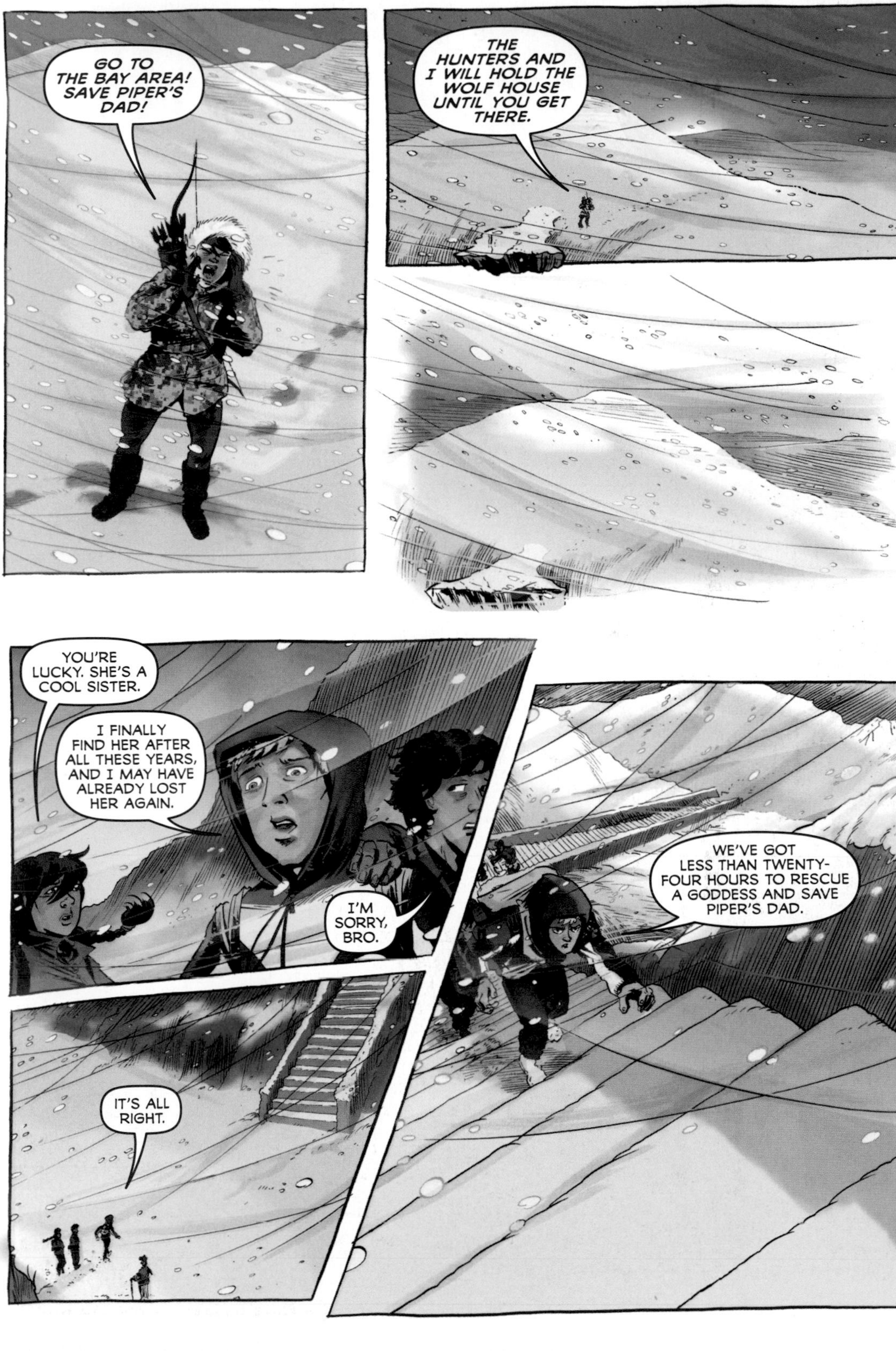
GO TO THE BAY AREA! SAVE PIPER'S DAD!
THE HUNTERS AND I WILL HOLD THE WOLF HOUSE UNTIL YOU GET THERE.
YOU'RE LUCKY. SHE'S A COOL SISTER.
I FINALLY FIND HER AFTER ALL THESE YEARS, AND I MAY HAVE ALREADY LOST HER AGAIN.
I'M SORRY, BRO.
IT'S ALL RIGHT.
WE'VE GOT LESS THAN TWENTY-FOUR HOURS TO RESCUE A GODDESS AND SAVE PIPER'S DAD.

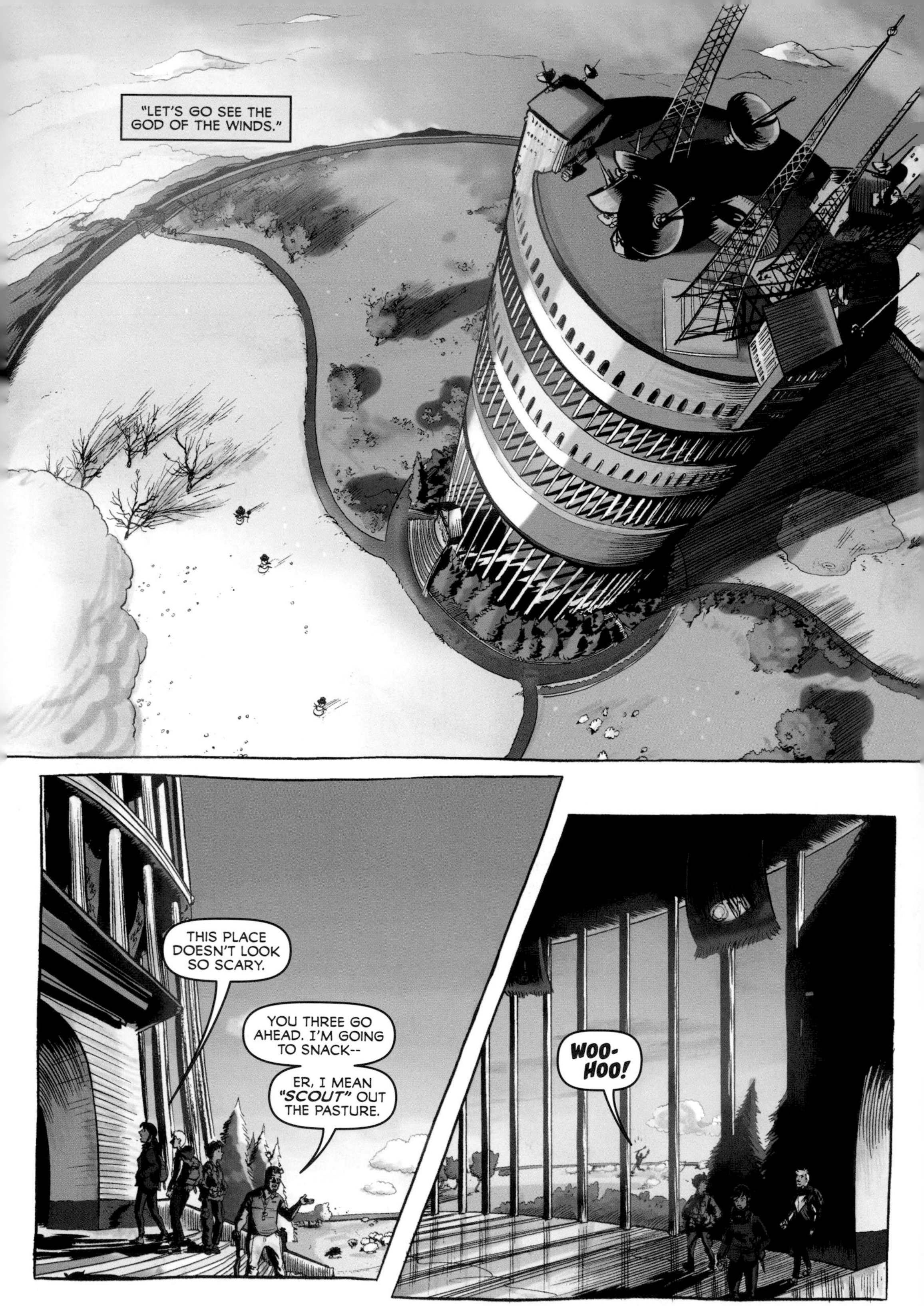
"LET'S GO SEE THE GOD OF THE WINDS."
THIS PLACE DOESN'T LOOK SO SCARY.
YOU THREE GO AHEAD. I'M GOING TO SNACK--
ER, I MEAN "SCOUT" OUT THE PASTURE.
WOO-HOO!

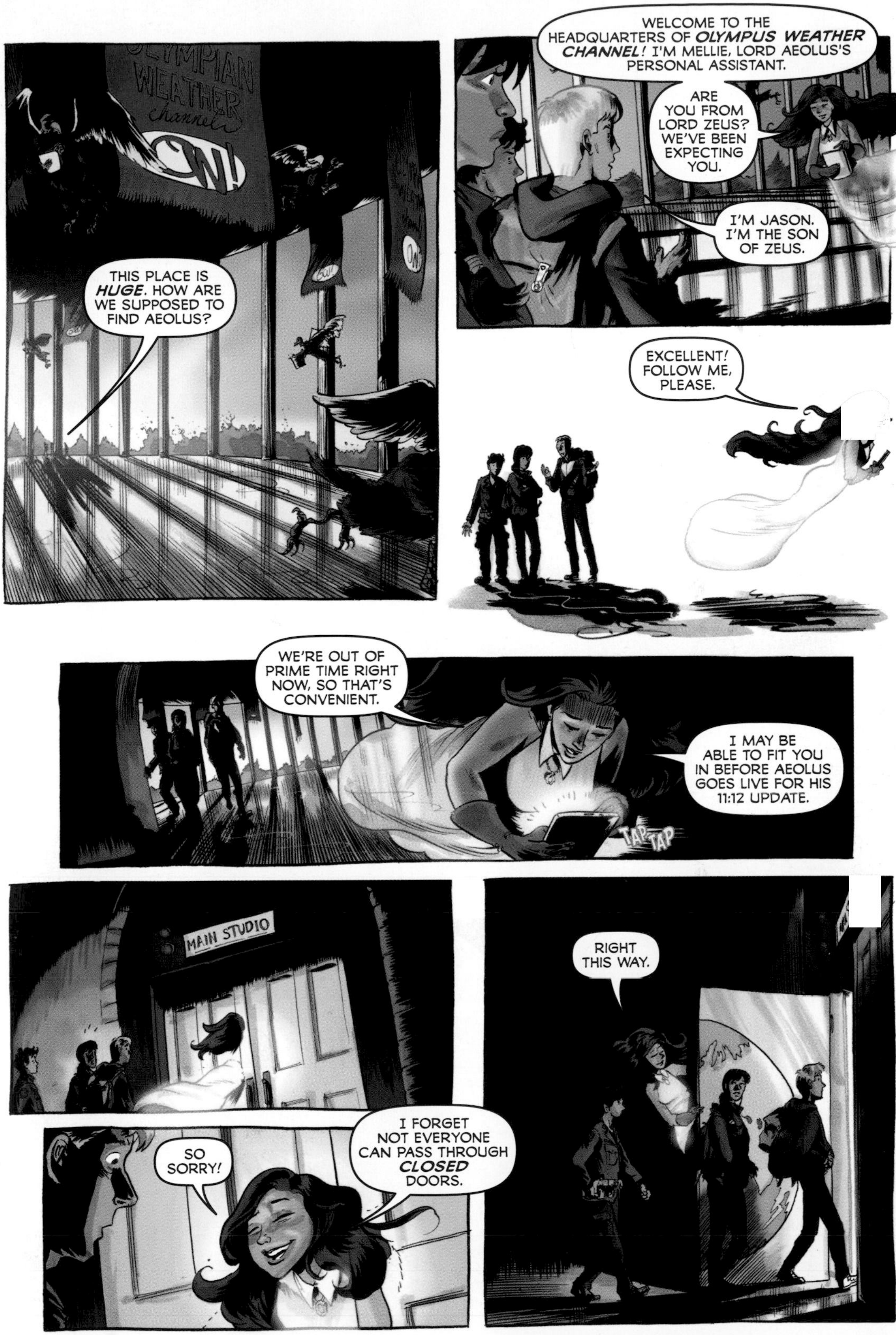
THIS PLACE IS HUGE. HOW ARE WE SUPPOSED TO FIND AEOLUS?
WELCOME TO THE HEADQUARTERS OF OLYMPUS WEATHER CHANNEL! I'M MELLIE, LORD AEOLUS'S PERSONAL ASSISTANT.
ARE YOU FROM LORD ZEUS? WE'VE BEEN EXPECTING YOU.
I'M JASON. I'M THE SON OF ZEUS.
EXCELLENT! FOLLOW ME, PLEASE.
WE'RE OUT OF PRIME TIME RIGHT NOW, SO THAT'S CONVENIENT.
I MAY BE ABLE TO FIT YOU IN BEFORE AEOLUS GOES LIVE FOR HIS 11:12 UPDATE.
TAP TAP
MAIN STUDIO
SO SORRY!
I FORGET NOT EVERYONE CAN PASS THROUGH CLOSED DOORS.
RIGHT THIS WAY.

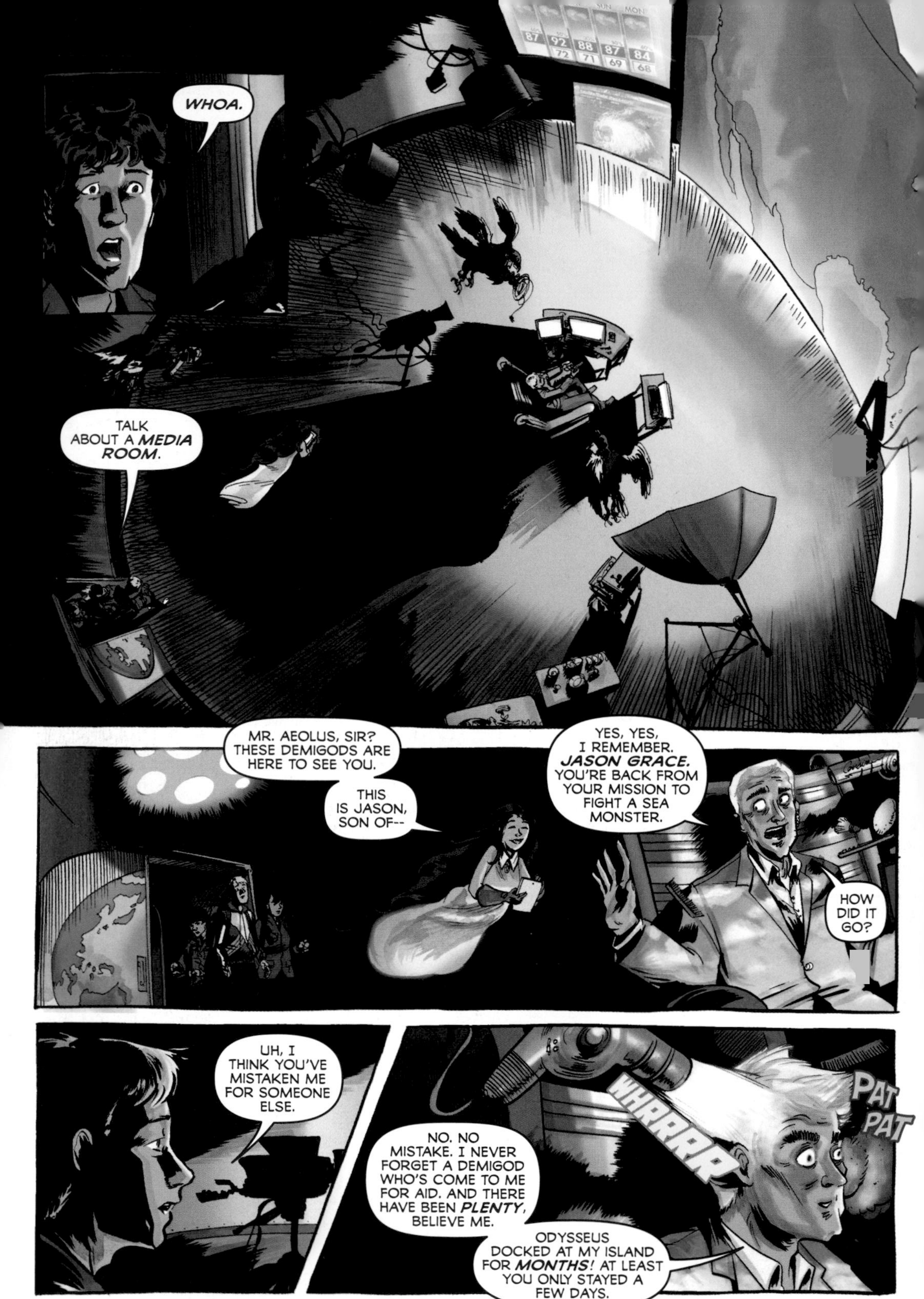

WHOA.
TALK ABOUT A *MEDIA ROOM*.
MR. AEOLUS, SIR? THESE DEMIGODS ARE HERE TO SEE YOU.
THIS IS JASON, SON OF--
YES, YES, I REMEMBER. *JASON GRACE.* YOU'RE BACK FROM YOUR MISSION TO FIGHT A SEA MONSTER.
HOW DID IT GO?
UH, I THINK YOU'VE MISTAKEN ME FOR SOMEONE ELSE.
WHRRRR
PAT PAT
NO. NO MISTAKE. I NEVER FORGET A DEMIGOD WHO'S COME TO ME FOR AID. AND THERE HAVE BEEN *PLENTY*, BELIEVE ME.
ODYSSEUS DOCKED AT MY ISLAND FOR *MONTHS!* AT LEAST YOU ONLY STAYED A FEW DAYS.

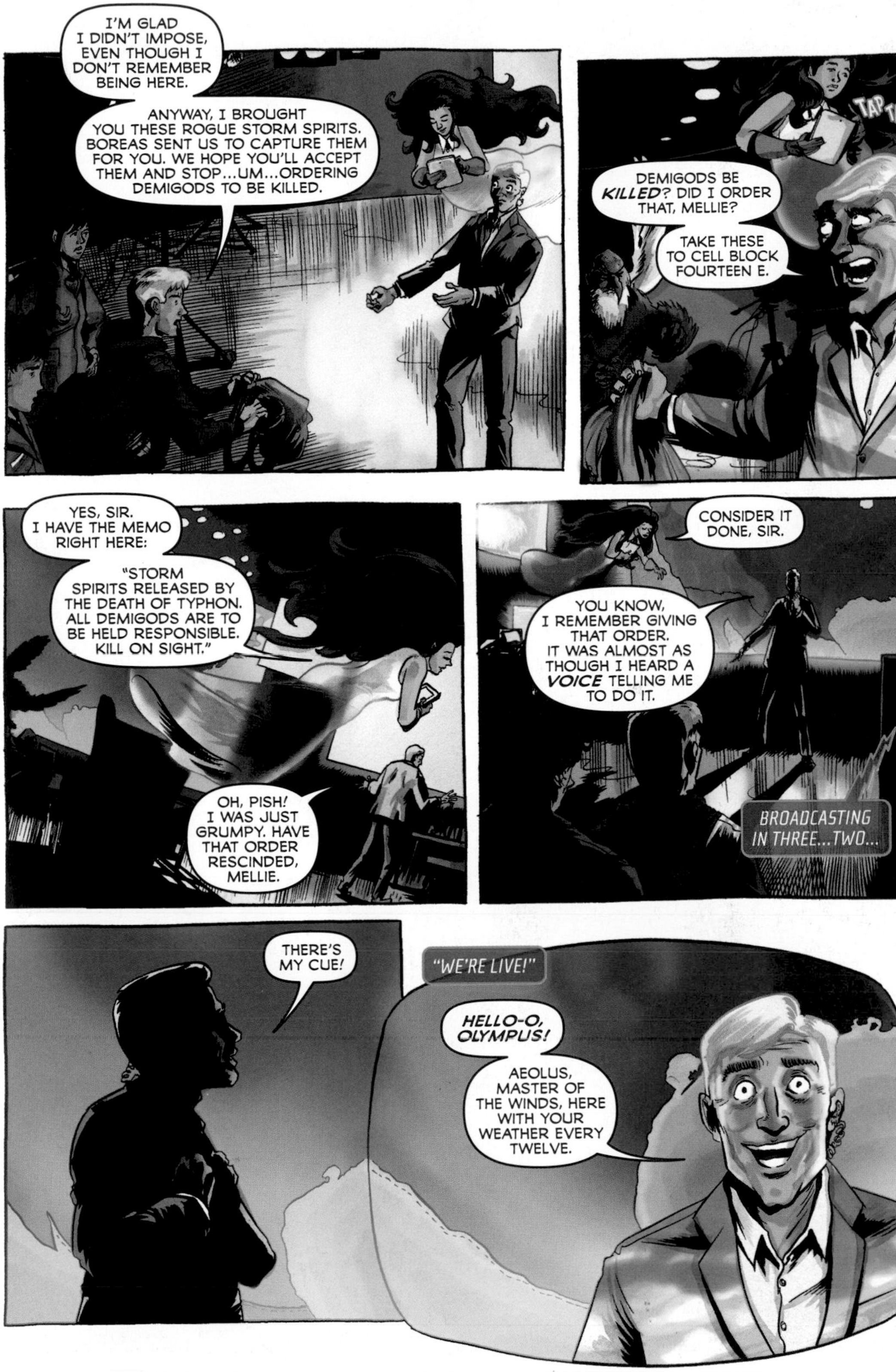
I'M GLAD I DIDN'T IMPOSE, EVEN THOUGH I DON'T REMEMBER BEING HERE.
ANYWAY, I BROUGHT YOU THESE ROGUE STORM SPIRITS. BOREAS SENT US TO CAPTURE THEM FOR YOU. WE HOPE YOU'LL ACCEPT THEM AND STOP...UM...ORDERING DEMIGODS TO BE KILLED.
TAP TAP
DEMIGODS BE KILLED? DID I ORDER THAT, MELLIE?
TAKE THESE TO CELL BLOCK FOURTEEN E.
YES, SIR. I HAVE THE MEMO RIGHT HERE:
"STORM SPIRITS RELEASED BY THE DEATH OF TYPHON. ALL DEMIGODS ARE TO BE HELD RESPONSIBLE. KILL ON SIGHT."
OH, PISH! I WAS JUST GRUMPY. HAVE THAT ORDER RESCINDED, MELLIE.
CONSIDER IT DONE, SIR.
YOU KNOW, I REMEMBER GIVING THAT ORDER. IT WAS ALMOST AS THOUGH I HEARD A VOICE TELLING ME TO DO IT.
BROADCASTING IN THREE...TWO...
THERE'S MY CUE!
"WE'RE LIVE!"
HELLO-O, OLYMPUS!
AEOLUS, MASTER OF THE WINDS, HERE WITH YOUR WEATHER EVERY TWELVE.

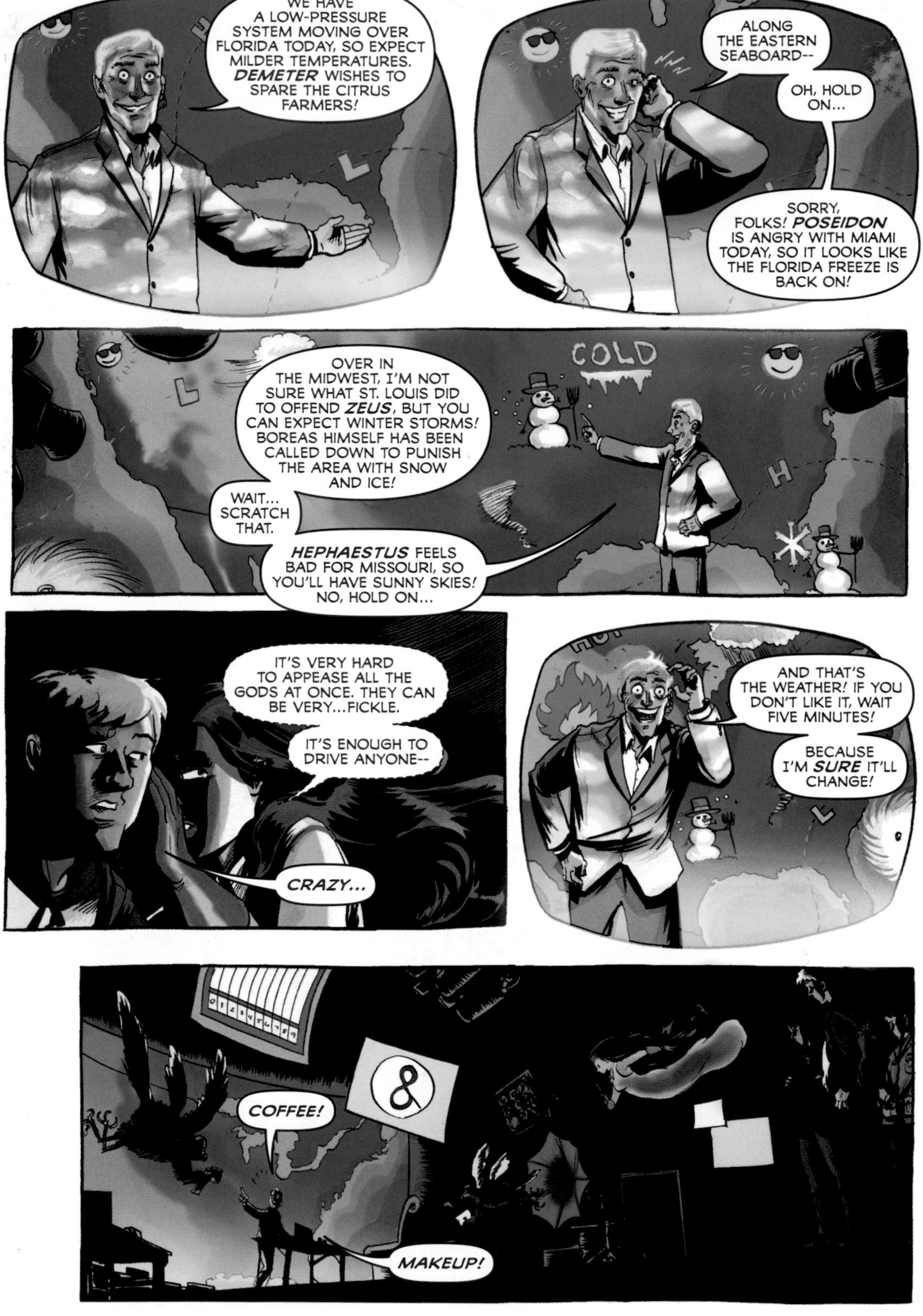

WE HAVE A LOW-PRESSURE SYSTEM MOVING OVER FLORIDA TODAY, SO EXPECT MILDER TEMPERATURES. DEMETER WISHES TO SPARE THE CITRUS FARMERS!
ALONG THE EASTERN SEABOARD--
OH, HOLD ON...
SORRY, FOLKS! POSEIDON IS ANGRY WITH MIAMI TODAY, SO IT LOOKS LIKE THE FLORIDA FREEZE IS BACK ON!
COLD
OVER IN THE MIDWEST, I'M NOT SURE WHAT ST. LOUIS DID TO OFFEND ZEUS, BUT YOU CAN EXPECT WINTER STORMS! BOREAS HIMSELF HAS BEEN CALLED DOWN TO PUNISH THE AREA WITH SNOW AND ICE!
WAIT... SCRATCH THAT.
HEPHAESTUS FEELS BAD FOR MISSOURI, SO YOU'LL HAVE SUNNY SKIES! NO, HOLD ON...
IT'S VERY HARD TO APPEASE ALL THE GODS AT ONCE. THEY CAN BE VERY...FICKLE.
IT'S ENOUGH TO DRIVE ANYONE--
CRAZY...
AND THAT'S THE WEATHER! IF YOU DON'T LIKE IT, WAIT FIVE MINUTES!
BECAUSE I'M SURE IT'LL CHANGE!
COFFEE!
MAKEUP!

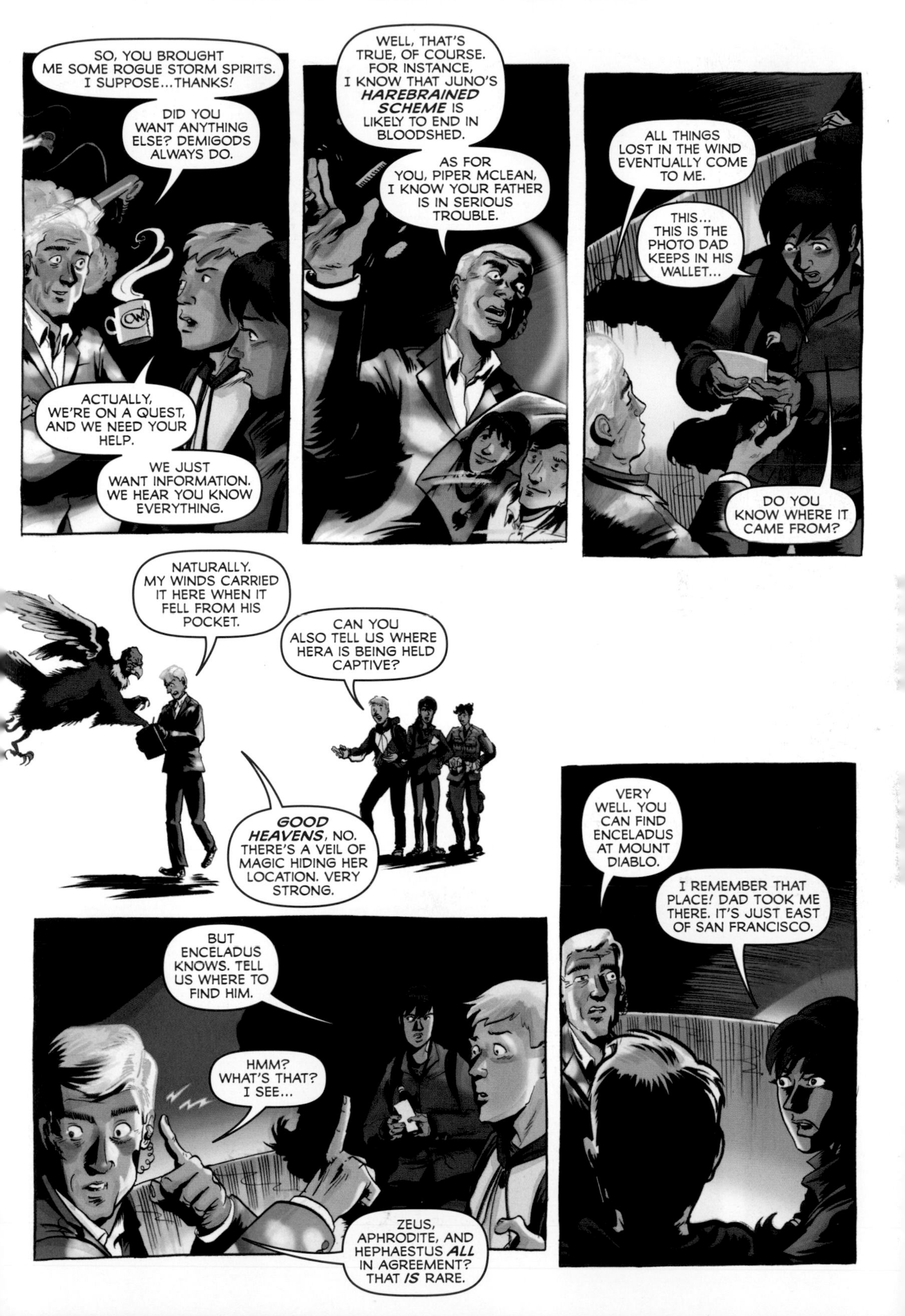
SO, YOU BROUGHT ME SOME ROGUE STORM SPIRITS. I SUPPOSE...THANKS!
DID YOU WANT ANYTHING ELSE? DEMIGODS ALWAYS DO.
ACTUALLY, WE'RE ON A QUEST, AND WE NEED YOUR HELP.
WE JUST WANT INFORMATION. WE HEAR YOU KNOW EVERYTHING.
WELL, THAT'S TRUE, OF COURSE. FOR INSTANCE, I KNOW THAT JUNO'S HAREBRAINED SCHEME IS LIKELY TO END IN BLOODSHED.
AS FOR YOU, PIPER MCLEAN, I KNOW YOUR FATHER IS IN SERIOUS TROUBLE.
ALL THINGS LOST IN THE WIND EVENTUALLY COME TO ME.
THIS... THIS IS THE PHOTO DAD KEEPS IN HIS WALLET...
DO YOU KNOW WHERE IT CAME FROM?
NATURALLY. MY WINDS CARRIED IT HERE WHEN IT FELL FROM HIS POCKET.
CAN YOU ALSO TELL US WHERE HERA IS BEING HELD CAPTIVE?
GOOD HEAVENS, NO. THERE'S A VEIL OF MAGIC HIDING HER LOCATION. VERY STRONG.
BUT ENCELADUS KNOWS. TELL US WHERE TO FIND HIM.
HMM? WHAT'S THAT? I SEE...
ZEUS, APHRODITE, AND HEPHAESTUS ALL IN AGREEMENT? THAT IS RARE.
VERY WELL. YOU CAN FIND ENCELADUS AT MOUNT DIABLO.
I REMEMBER THAT PLACE! DAD TOOK ME THERE. IT'S JUST EAST OF SAN FRANCISCO.

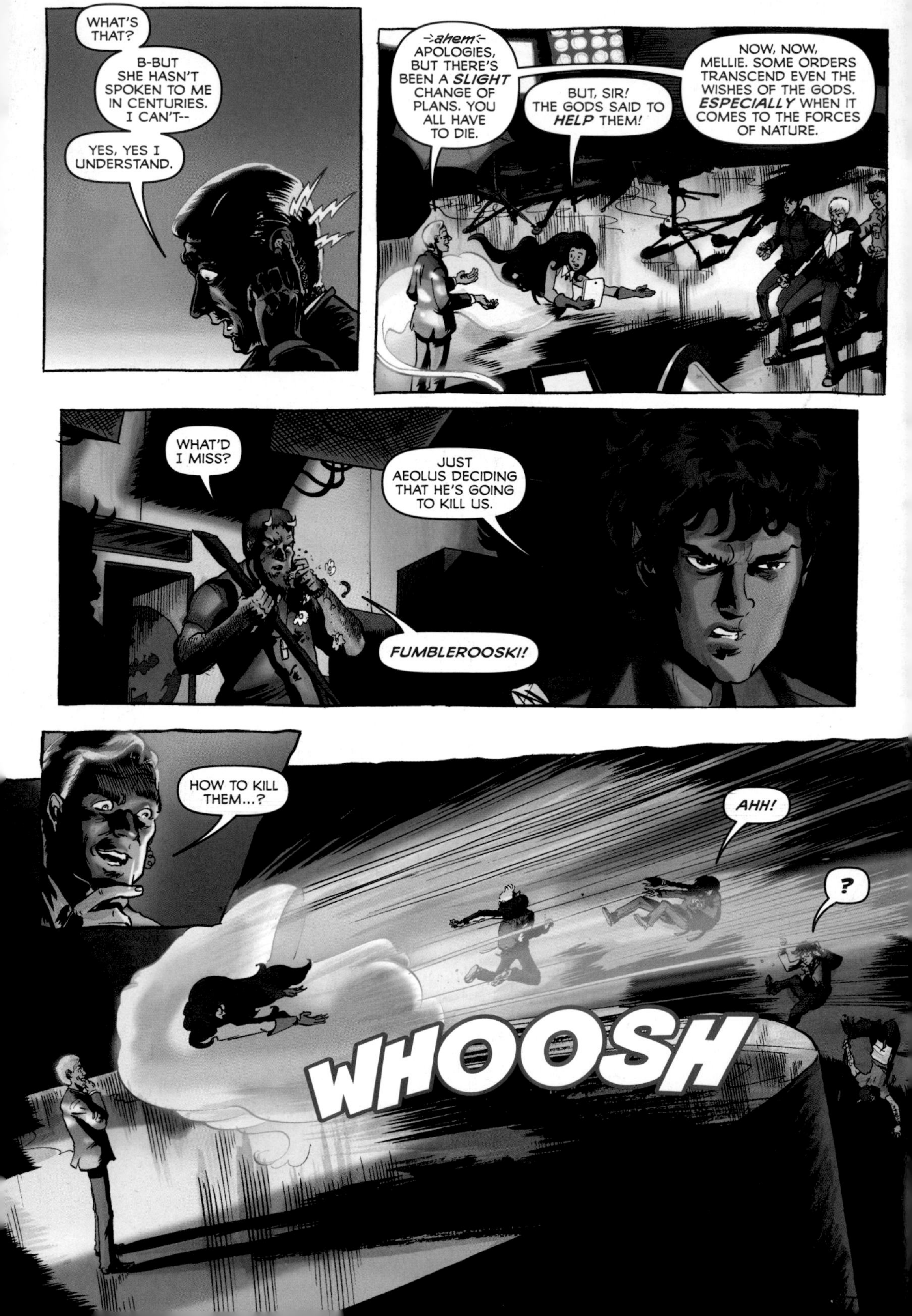
WHAT'S THAT?
B-BUT SHE HASN'T SPOKEN TO ME IN CENTURIES. I CAN'T--
YES, YES I UNDERSTAND.
~ahem~ APOLOGIES, BUT THERE'S BEEN A SLIGHT CHANGE OF PLANS. YOU ALL HAVE TO DIE.
BUT, SIR! THE GODS SAID TO HELP THEM!
NOW, NOW, MELLIE. SOME ORDERS TRANSCEND EVEN THE WISHES OF THE GODS. ESPECIALLY WHEN IT COMES TO THE FORCES OF NATURE.
WHAT'D I MISS?
JUST AEOLUS DECIDING THAT HE'S GOING TO KILL US.
FUMBLEROOSKI!
HOW TO KILL THEM...?
AHH!
?
WHOOSH

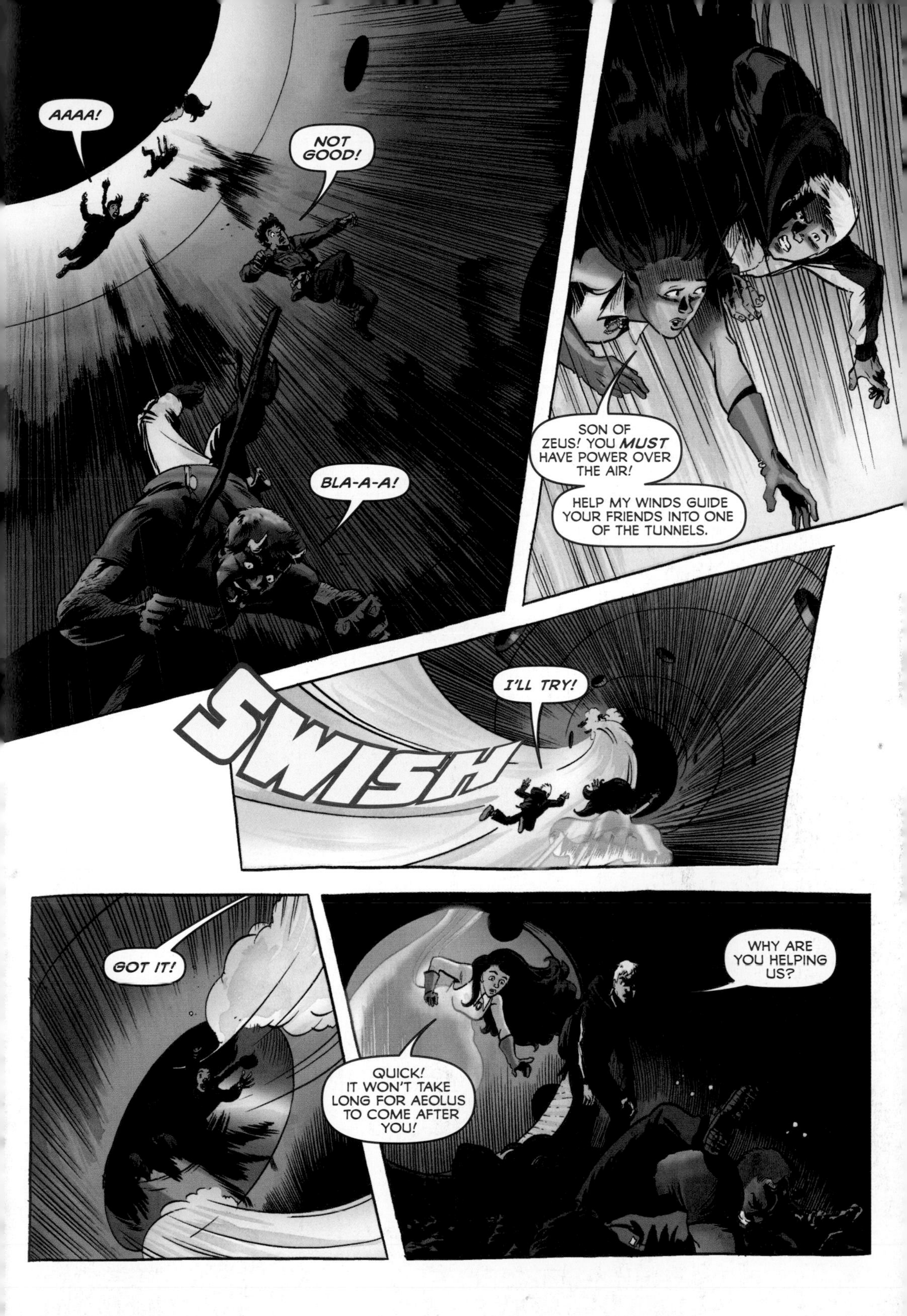
AAAA!
NOT GOOD!
BLA-A-A!
SON OF ZEUS! YOU *MUST* HAVE POWER OVER THE AIR!
HELP MY WINDS GUIDE YOUR FRIENDS INTO ONE OF THE TUNNELS.
SWISH
I'LL TRY!
GOT IT!
QUICK! IT WON'T TAKE LONG FOR AEOLUS TO COME AFTER YOU!
WHY ARE YOU HELPING US?

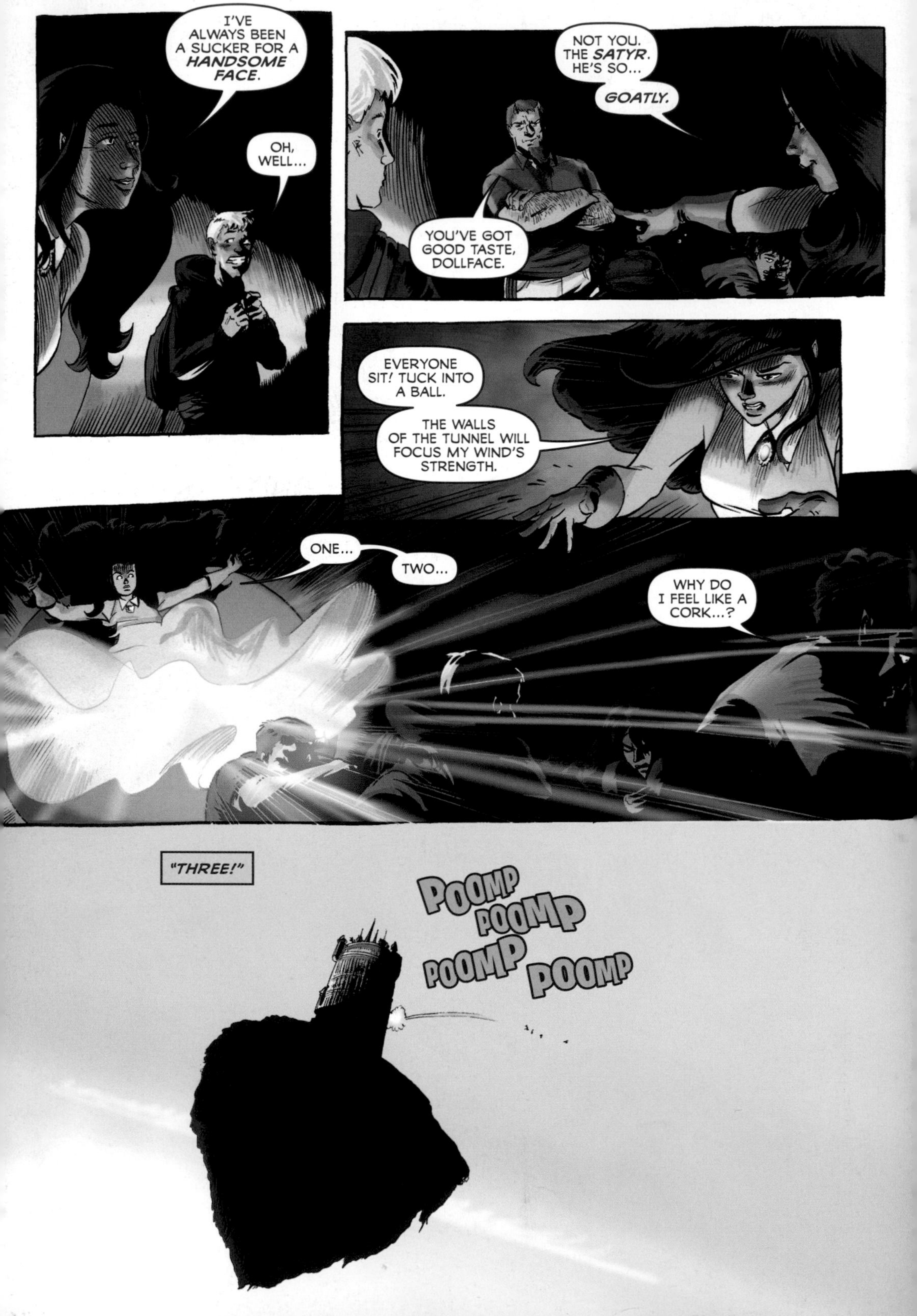
I'VE ALWAYS BEEN A SUCKER FOR A HANDSOME FACE.
OH, WELL...
NOT YOU. THE SATYR. HE'S SO... GOATLY.
YOU'VE GOT GOOD TASTE, DOLLFACE.
EVERYONE SIT! TUCK INTO A BALL.
THE WALLS OF THE TUNNEL WILL FOCUS MY WIND'S STRENGTH.
ONE...
TWO...
WHY DO I FEEL LIKE A CORK...?
"THREE!"
POOMP POOMP POOMP POOMP

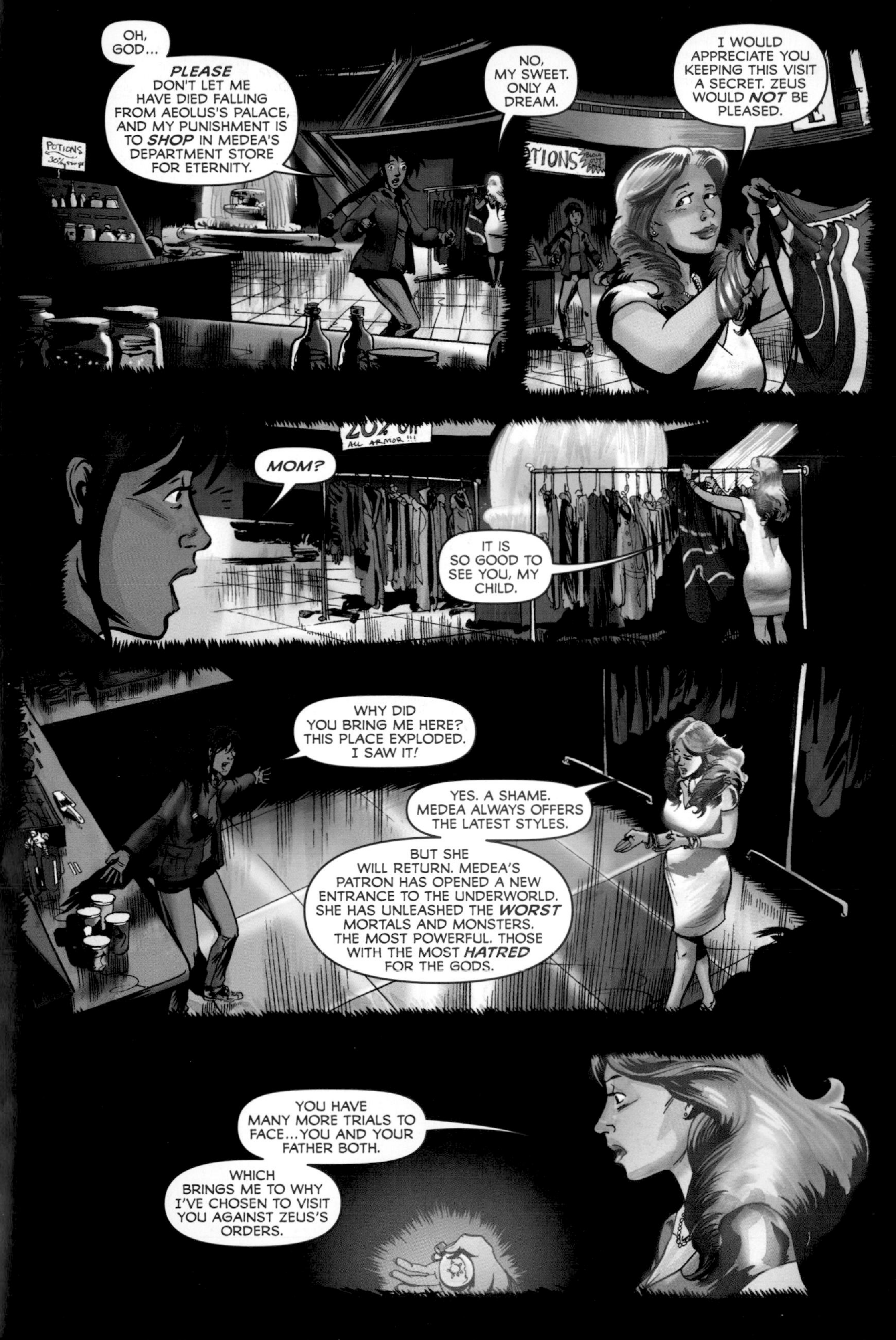

OH, GOD... PLEASE DON'T LET ME HAVE DIED FALLING FROM AEOLUS'S PALACE, AND MY PUNISHMENT IS TO SHOP IN MEDEA'S DEPARTMENT STORE FOR ETERNITY.
POTIONS
NO, MY SWEET. ONLY A DREAM.
I WOULD APPRECIATE YOU KEEPING THIS VISIT A SECRET. ZEUS WOULD NOT BE PLEASED.
MOM?
IT IS SO GOOD TO SEE YOU, MY CHILD.
WHY DID YOU BRING ME HERE? THIS PLACE EXPLODED. I SAW IT!
YES. A SHAME. MEDEA ALWAYS OFFERS THE LATEST STYLES.
BUT SHE WILL RETURN. MEDEA'S PATRON HAS OPENED A NEW ENTRANCE TO THE UNDERWORLD. SHE HAS UNLEASHED THE WORST MORTALS AND MONSTERS. THE MOST POWERFUL. THOSE WITH THE MOST HATRED FOR THE GODS.
YOU HAVE MANY MORE TRIALS TO FACE...YOU AND YOUR FATHER BOTH.
WHICH BRINGS ME TO WHY I'VE CHOSEN TO VISIT YOU AGAINST ZEUS'S ORDERS.

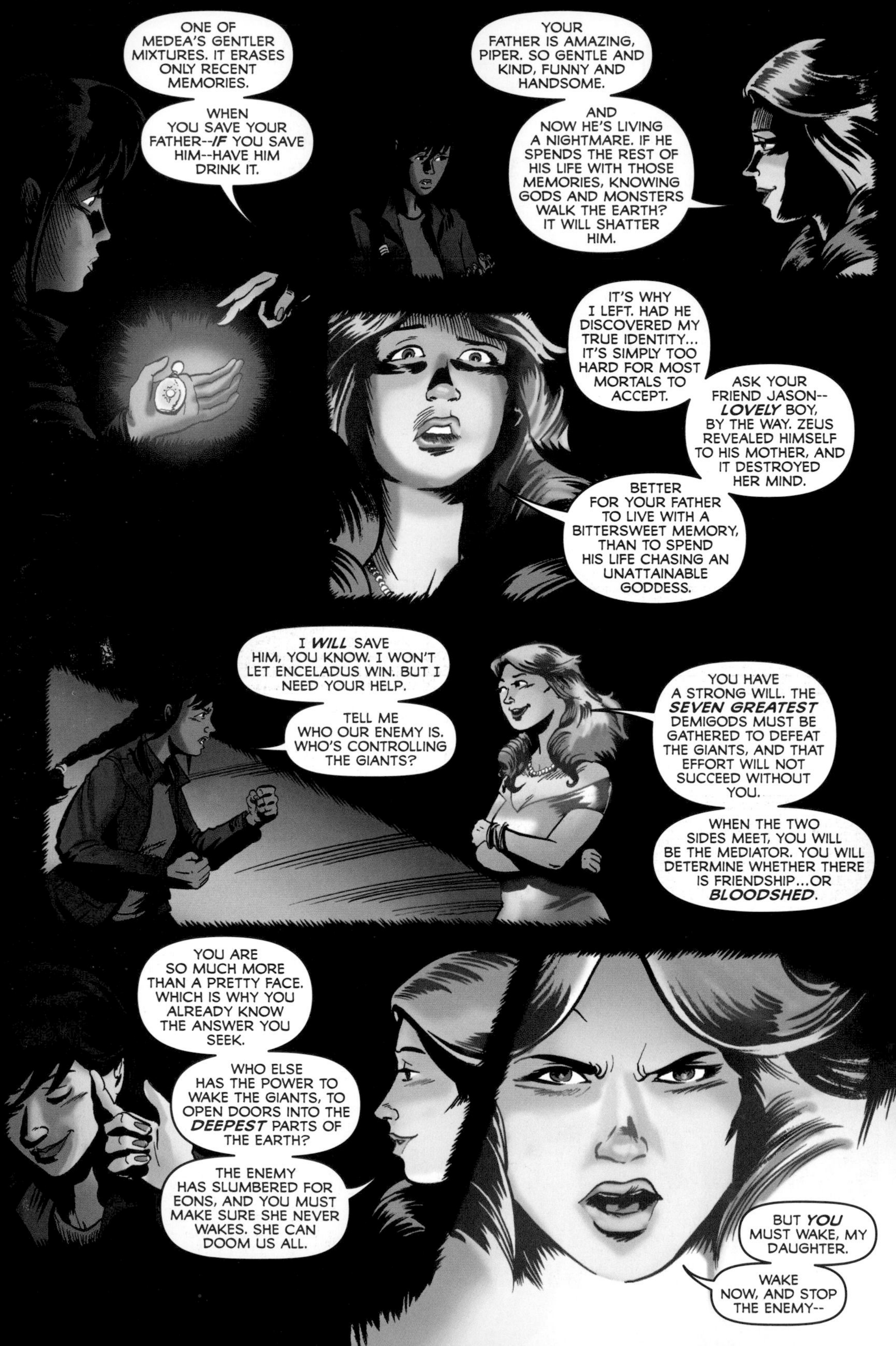
ONE OF MEDEA'S GENTLER MIXTURES. IT ERASES ONLY RECENT MEMORIES.
WHEN YOU SAVE YOUR FATHER--*IF* YOU SAVE HIM--HAVE HIM DRINK IT.
YOUR FATHER IS AMAZING, PIPER. SO GENTLE AND KIND, FUNNY AND HANDSOME.
AND NOW HE'S LIVING A NIGHTMARE. IF HE SPENDS THE REST OF HIS LIFE WITH THOSE MEMORIES, KNOWING GODS AND MONSTERS WALK THE EARTH? IT WILL SHATTER HIM.
IT'S WHY I LEFT. HAD HE DISCOVERED MY TRUE IDENTITY... IT'S SIMPLY TOO HARD FOR MOST MORTALS TO ACCEPT.
ASK YOUR FRIEND JASON--*LOVELY* BOY, BY THE WAY. ZEUS REVEALED HIMSELF TO HIS MOTHER, AND IT DESTROYED HER MIND.
BETTER FOR YOUR FATHER TO LIVE WITH A BITTERSWEET MEMORY, THAN TO SPEND HIS LIFE CHASING AN UNATTAINABLE GODDESS.
I *WILL* SAVE HIM, YOU KNOW. I WON'T LET ENCELADUS WIN. BUT I NEED YOUR HELP.
TELL ME WHO OUR ENEMY IS. WHO'S CONTROLLING THE GIANTS?
YOU HAVE A STRONG WILL. THE *SEVEN GREATEST* DEMIGODS MUST BE GATHERED TO DEFEAT THE GIANTS, AND THAT EFFORT WILL NOT SUCCEED WITHOUT YOU.
WHEN THE TWO SIDES MEET, YOU WILL BE THE MEDIATOR. YOU WILL DETERMINE WHETHER THERE IS FRIENDSHIP...OR *BLOODSHED*.
YOU ARE SO MUCH MORE THAN A PRETTY FACE. WHICH IS WHY YOU ALREADY KNOW THE ANSWER YOU SEEK.
WHO ELSE HAS THE POWER TO WAKE THE GIANTS, TO OPEN DOORS INTO THE *DEEPEST* PARTS OF THE EARTH?
THE ENEMY HAS SLUMBERED FOR EONS, AND YOU MUST MAKE SURE SHE NEVER WAKES. SHE CAN DOOM US ALL.
BUT *YOU* MUST WAKE, MY DAUGHTER.
WAKE NOW, AND STOP THE ENEMY--

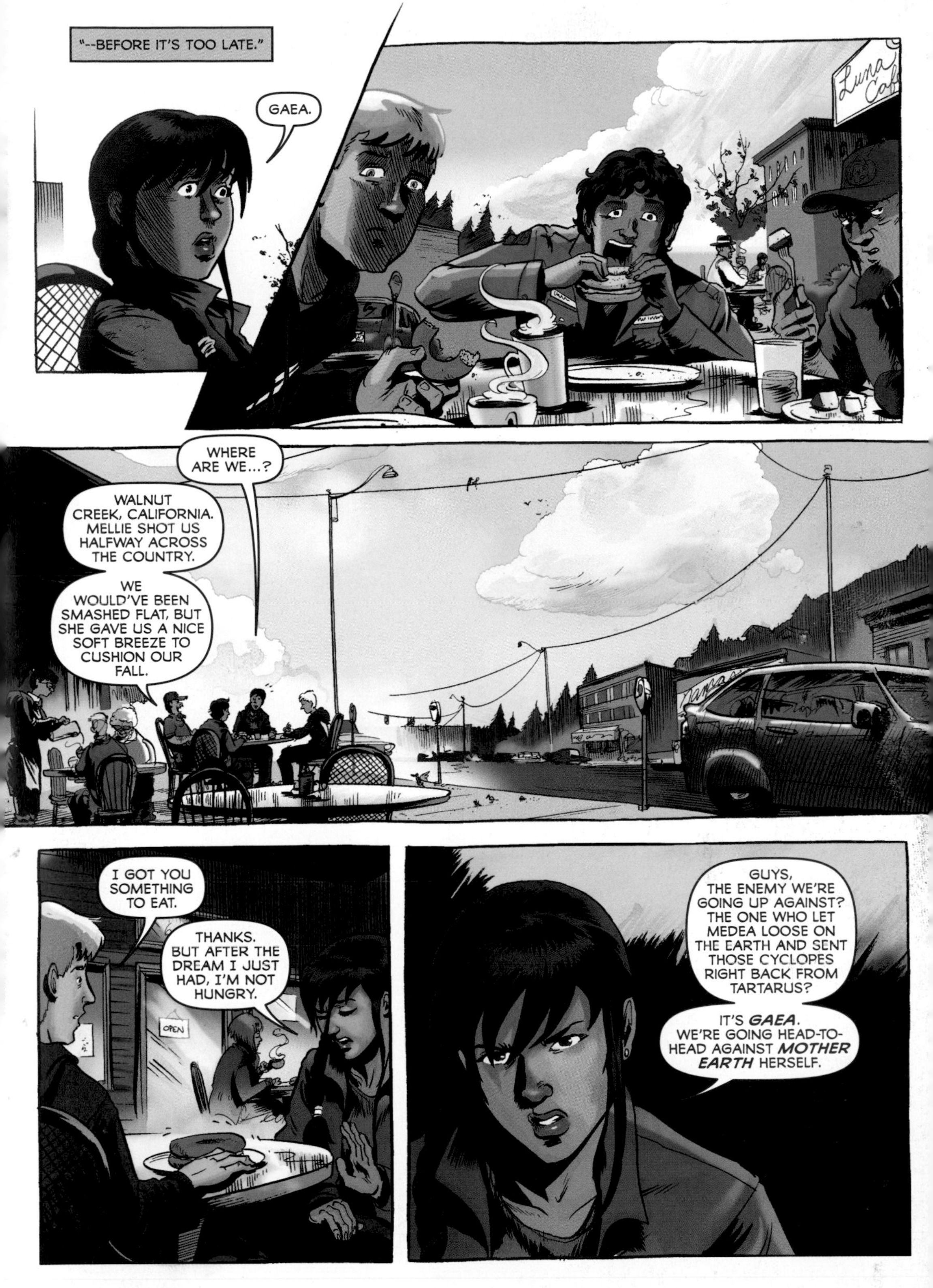
"--BEFORE IT'S TOO LATE."
GAEA.
Luna Cafe
WHERE ARE WE...?
WALNUT CREEK, CALIFORNIA. MELLIE SHOT US HALFWAY ACROSS THE COUNTRY.
WE WOULD'VE BEEN SMASHED FLAT, BUT SHE GAVE US A NICE SOFT BREEZE TO CUSHION OUR FALL.
I GOT YOU SOMETHING TO EAT.
THANKS. BUT AFTER THE DREAM I JUST HAD, I'M NOT HUNGRY.
OPEN
GUYS, THE ENEMY WE'RE GOING UP AGAINST? THE ONE WHO LET MEDEA LOOSE ON THE EARTH AND SENT THOSE CYCLOPES RIGHT BACK FROM TARTARUS?
IT'S *GAEA*. WE'RE GOING HEAD-TO-HEAD AGAINST ***MOTHER EARTH*** HERSELF.

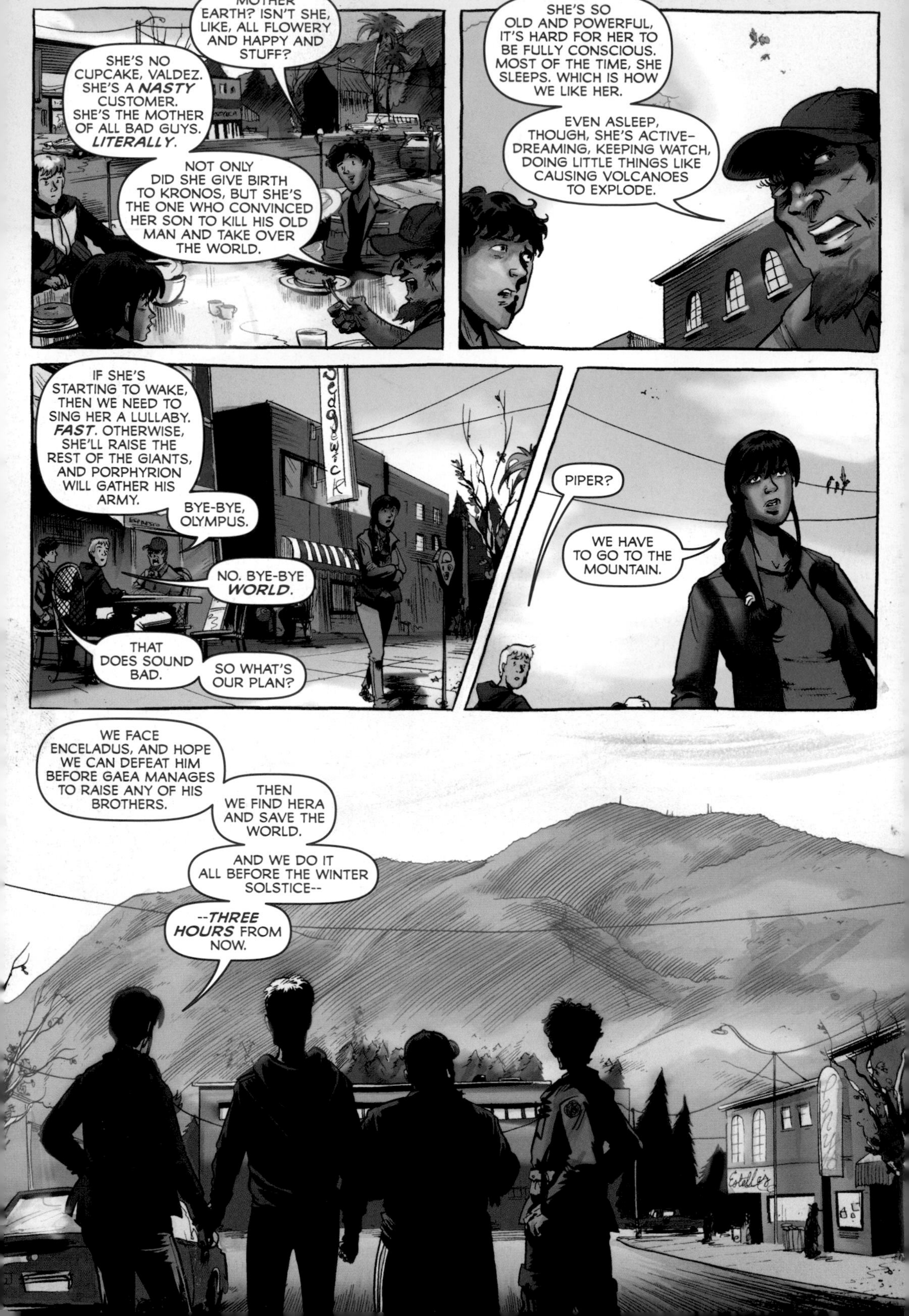

MOTHER EARTH? ISN'T SHE, LIKE, ALL FLOWERY AND HAPPY AND STUFF?
SHE'S NO CUPCAKE, VALDEZ. SHE'S A NASTY CUSTOMER. SHE'S THE MOTHER OF ALL BAD GUYS. LITERALLY.
NOT ONLY DID SHE GIVE BIRTH TO KRONOS, BUT SHE'S THE ONE WHO CONVINCED HER SON TO KILL HIS OLD MAN AND TAKE OVER THE WORLD.
SHE'S SO OLD AND POWERFUL, IT'S HARD FOR HER TO BE FULLY CONSCIOUS. MOST OF THE TIME, SHE SLEEPS. WHICH IS HOW WE LIKE HER.
EVEN ASLEEP, THOUGH, SHE'S ACTIVE–DREAMING, KEEPING WATCH, DOING LITTLE THINGS LIKE CAUSING VOLCANOES TO EXPLODE.
IF SHE'S STARTING TO WAKE, THEN WE NEED TO SING HER A LULLABY. FAST. OTHERWISE, SHE'LL RAISE THE REST OF THE GIANTS, AND PORPHYRION WILL GATHER HIS ARMY.
BYE-BYE, OLYMPUS.
NO. BYE-BYE WORLD.
THAT DOES SOUND BAD.
SO WHAT'S OUR PLAN?
PIPER?
WE HAVE TO GO TO THE MOUNTAIN.
WE FACE ENCELADUS, AND HOPE WE CAN DEFEAT HIM BEFORE GAEA MANAGES TO RAISE ANY OF HIS BROTHERS.
THEN WE FIND HERA AND SAVE THE WORLD.
AND WE DO IT ALL BEFORE THE WINTER SOLSTICE--
--THREE HOURS FROM NOW.

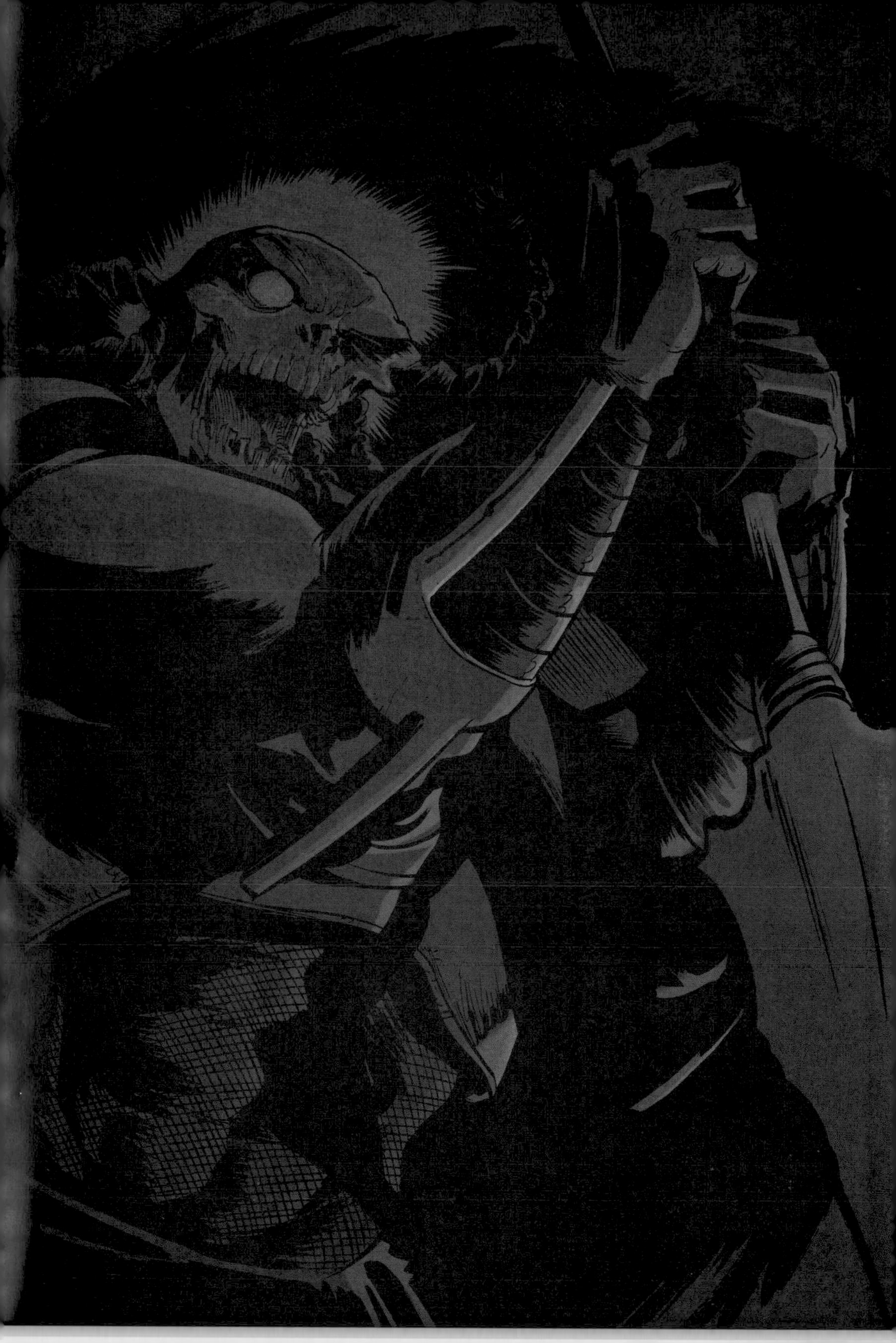

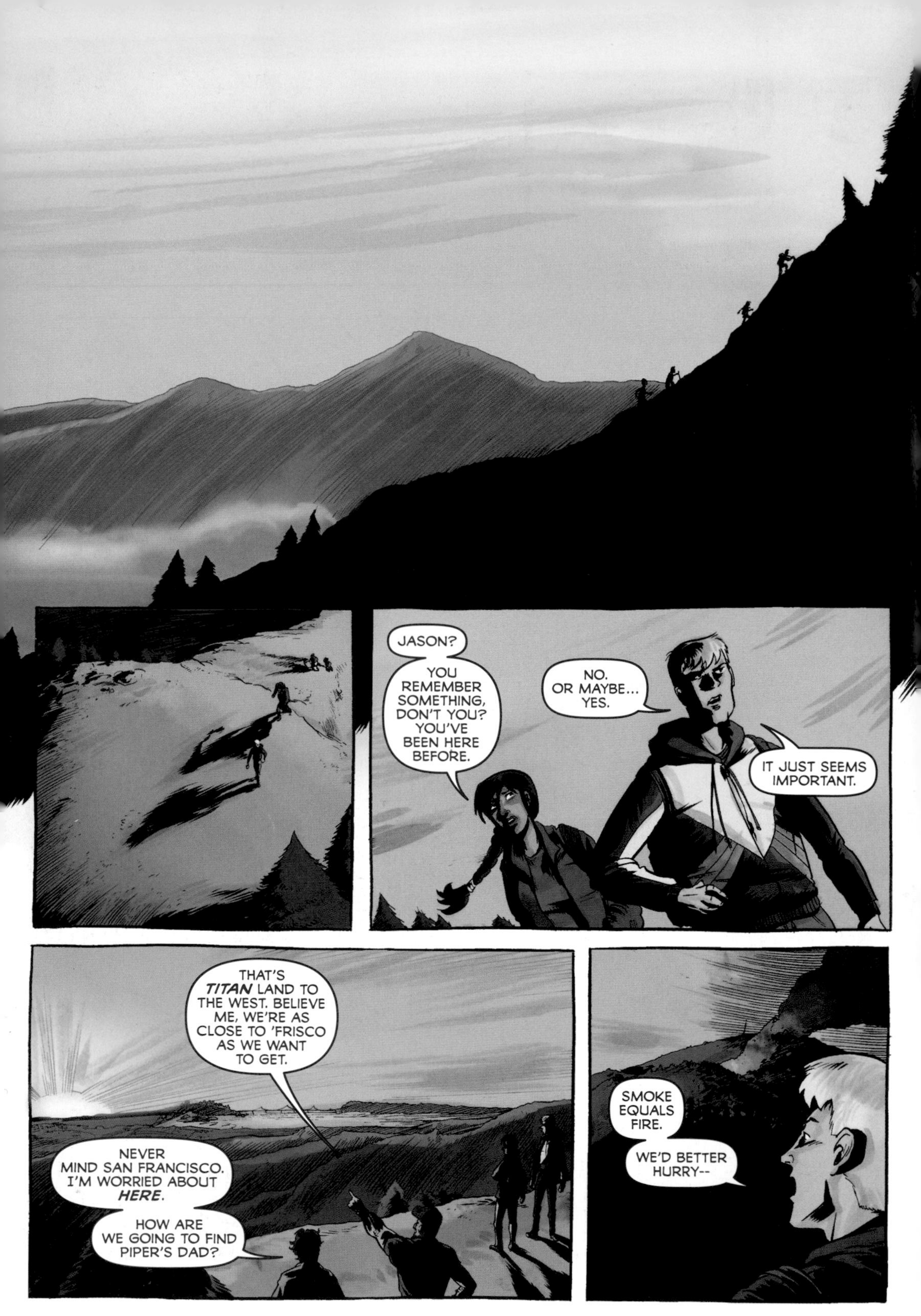
JASON?
YOU REMEMBER SOMETHING, DON'T YOU? YOU'VE BEEN HERE BEFORE.
NO. OR MAYBE... YES.
IT JUST SEEMS IMPORTANT.
THAT'S *TITAN* LAND TO THE WEST. BELIEVE ME, WE'RE AS CLOSE TO 'FRISCO AS WE WANT TO GET.
NEVER MIND SAN FRANCISCO. I'M WORRIED ABOUT ***HERE***.
HOW ARE WE GOING TO FIND PIPER'S DAD?
SMOKE EQUALS FIRE.
WE'D BETTER HURRY--

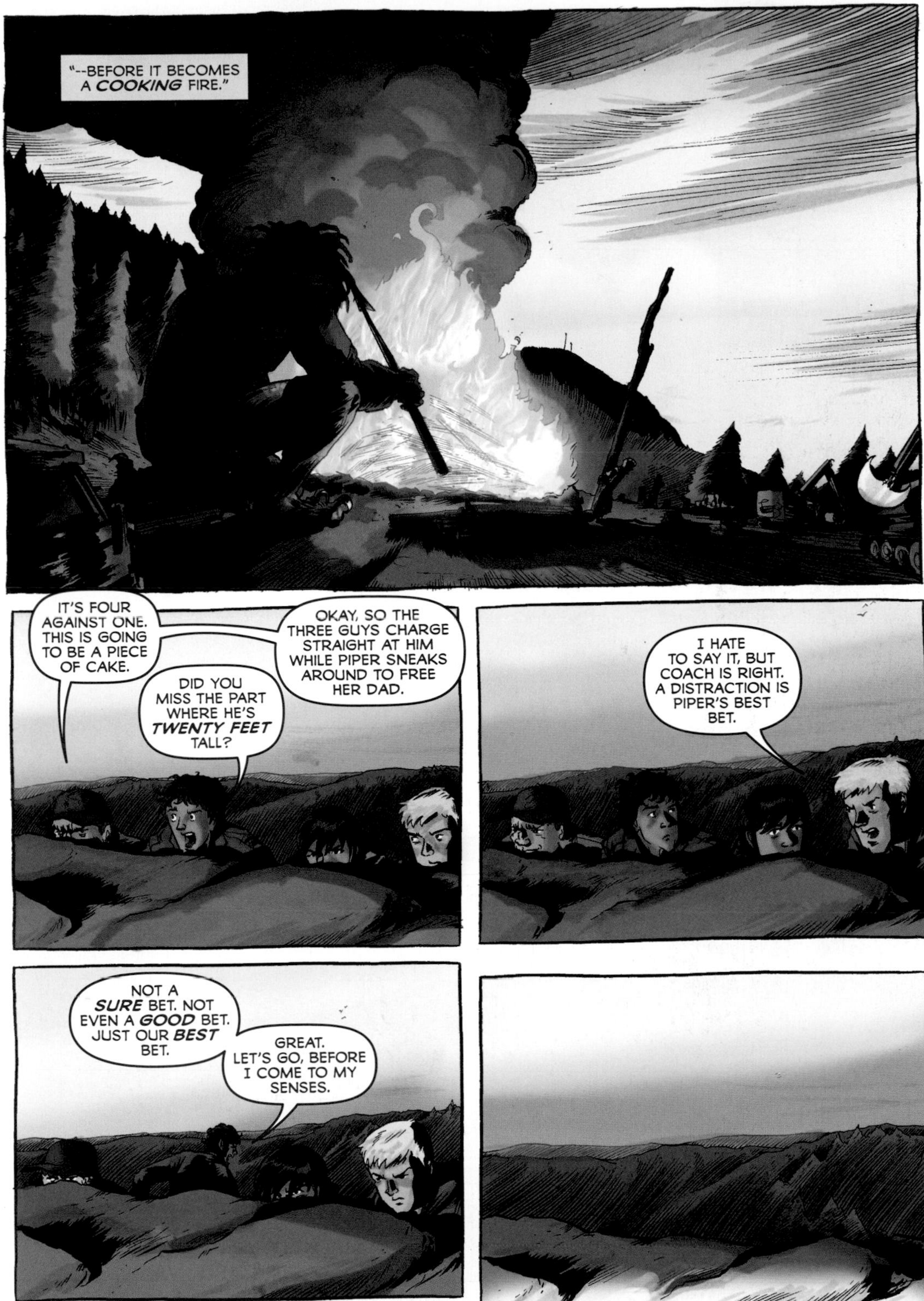
"--BEFORE IT BECOMES A *COOKING* FIRE."
IT'S FOUR AGAINST ONE. THIS IS GOING TO BE A PIECE OF CAKE.
OKAY, SO THE THREE GUYS CHARGE STRAIGHT AT HIM WHILE PIPER SNEAKS AROUND TO FREE HER DAD.
DID YOU MISS THE PART WHERE HE'S *TWENTY FEET* TALL?
I HATE TO SAY IT, BUT COACH IS RIGHT. A DISTRACTION IS PIPER'S BEST BET.
NOT A *SURE* BET. NOT EVEN A *GOOD* BET. JUST OUR *BEST* BET.
GREAT. LET'S GO, BEFORE I COME TO MY SENSES.

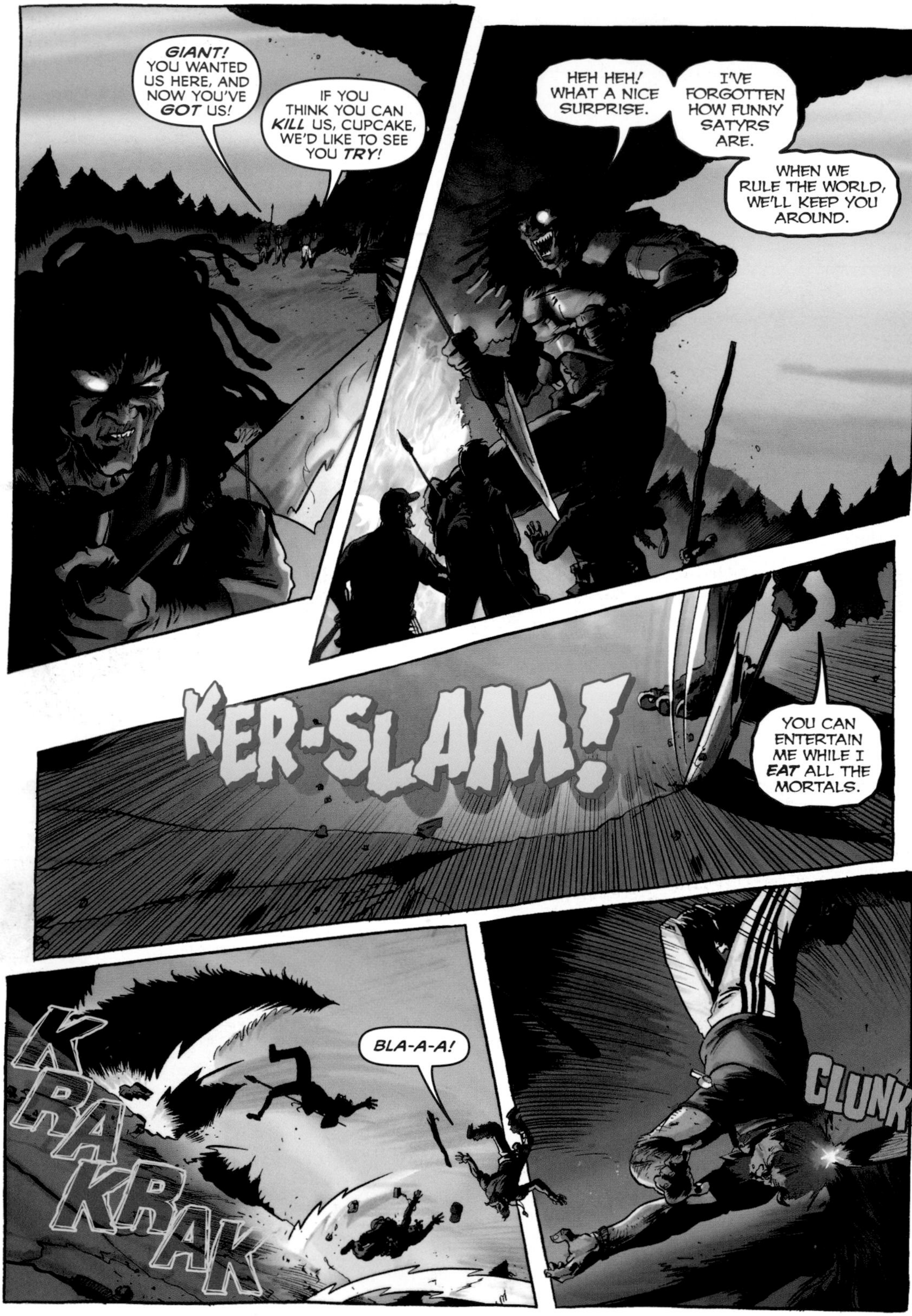
GIANT! YOU WANTED US HERE, AND NOW YOU'VE GOT US!
IF YOU THINK YOU CAN KILL US, CUPCAKE, WE'D LIKE TO SEE YOU TRY!
HEH HEH! WHAT A NICE SURPRISE.
I'VE FORGOTTEN HOW FUNNY SATYRS ARE.
WHEN WE RULE THE WORLD, WE'LL KEEP YOU AROUND.
KER-SLAM!
YOU CAN ENTERTAIN ME WHILE I EAT ALL THE MORTALS.
KRAKRAKRAK
BLA-A-A!
CLUNK

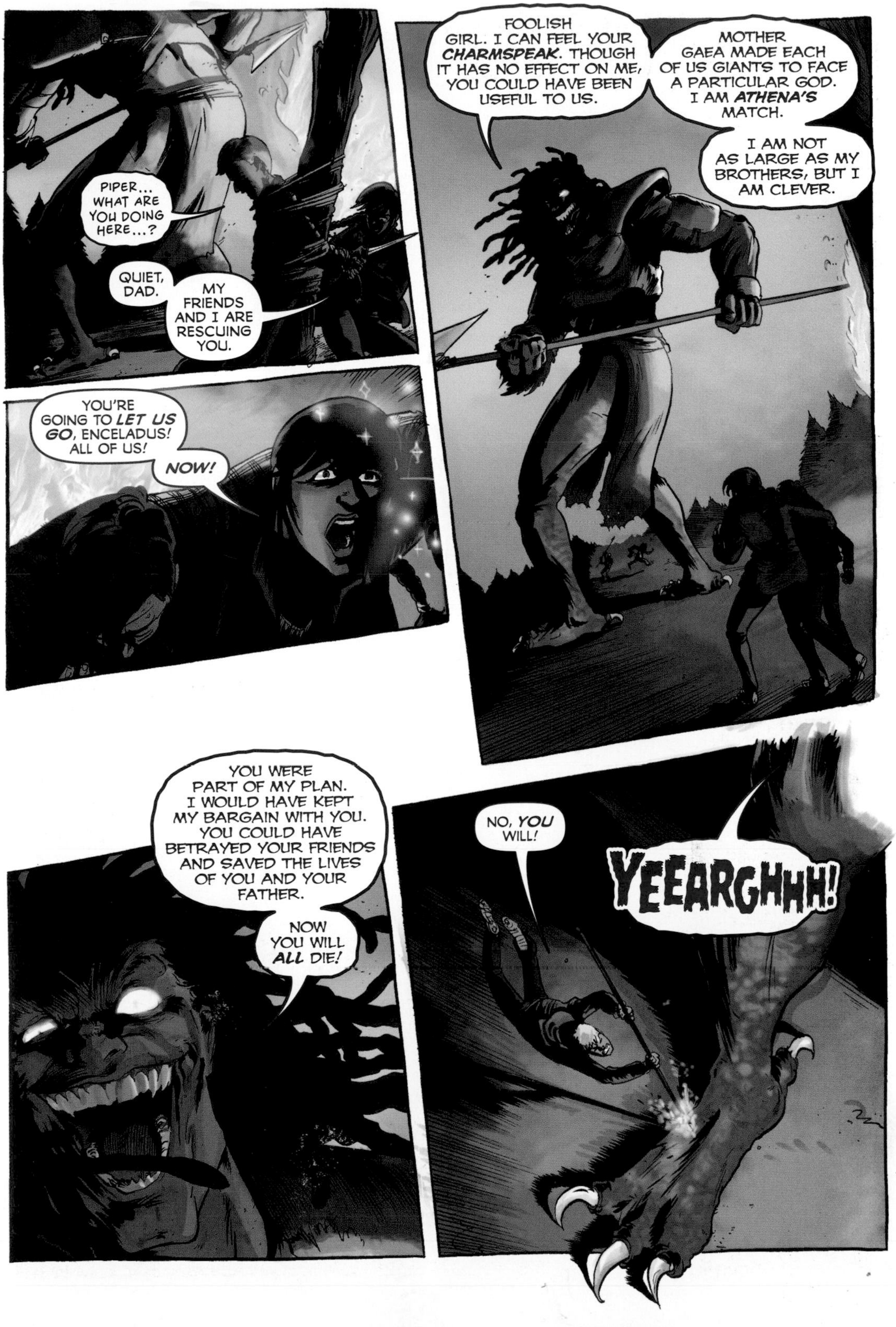
PIPER... WHAT ARE YOU DOING HERE...?
QUIET, DAD.
MY FRIENDS AND I ARE RESCUING YOU.
FOOLISH GIRL. I CAN FEEL YOUR CHARMSPEAK. THOUGH IT HAS NO EFFECT ON ME, YOU COULD HAVE BEEN USEFUL TO US.
MOTHER GAEA MADE EACH OF US GIANTS TO FACE A PARTICULAR GOD. I AM ATHENA'S MATCH.
I AM NOT AS LARGE AS MY BROTHERS, BUT I AM CLEVER.
YOU'RE GOING TO LET US GO, ENCELADUS! ALL OF US!
NOW!
YOU WERE PART OF MY PLAN. I WOULD HAVE KEPT MY BARGAIN WITH YOU. YOU COULD HAVE BETRAYED YOUR FRIENDS AND SAVED THE LIVES OF YOU AND YOUR FATHER.
NOW YOU WILL ALL DIE!
NO, YOU WILL!
YEEARGHHH!

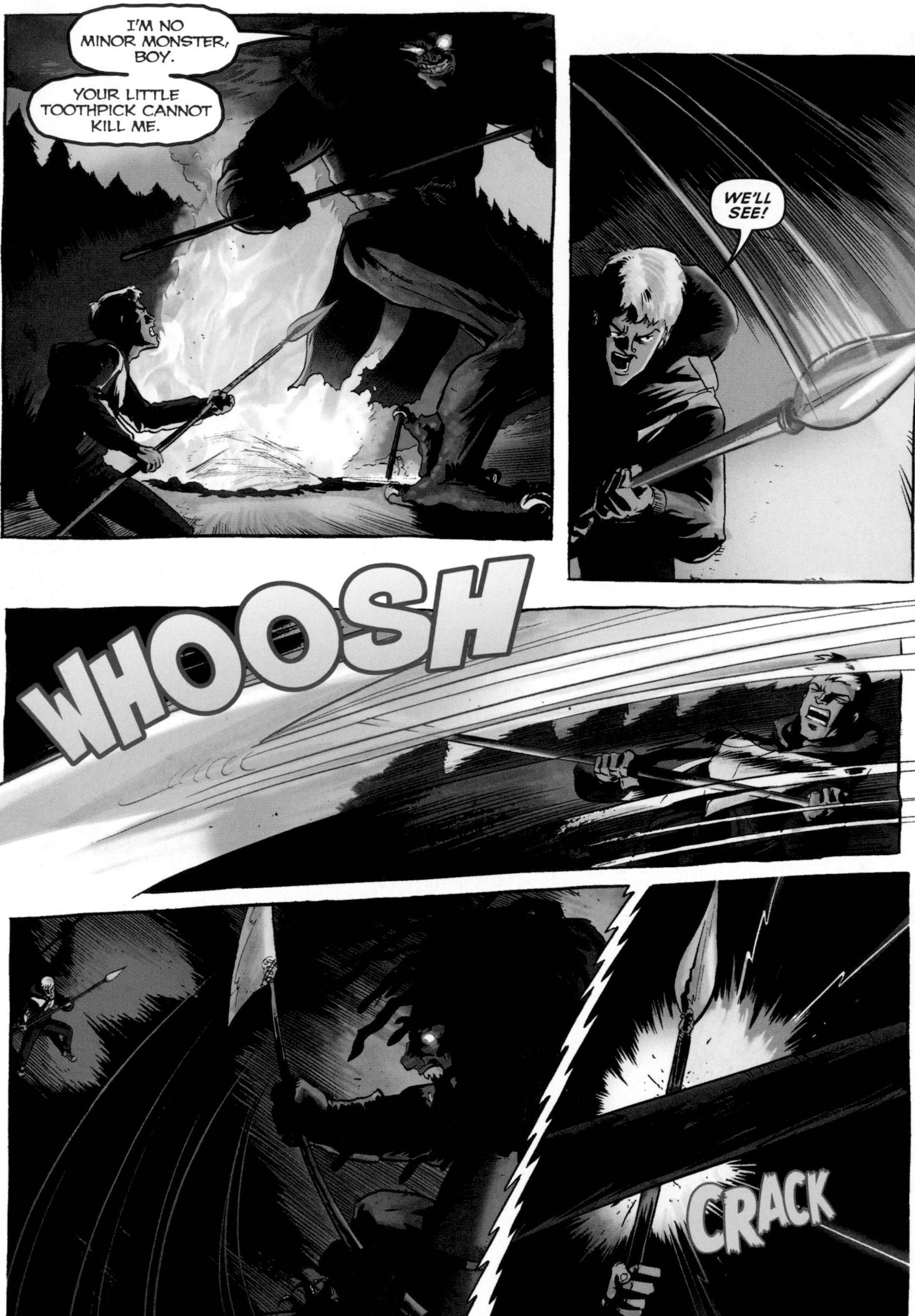
I'M NO MINOR MONSTER, BOY.
YOUR LITTLE TOOTHPICK CANNOT KILL ME.
WE'LL SEE!
WHOOSH
CRACK

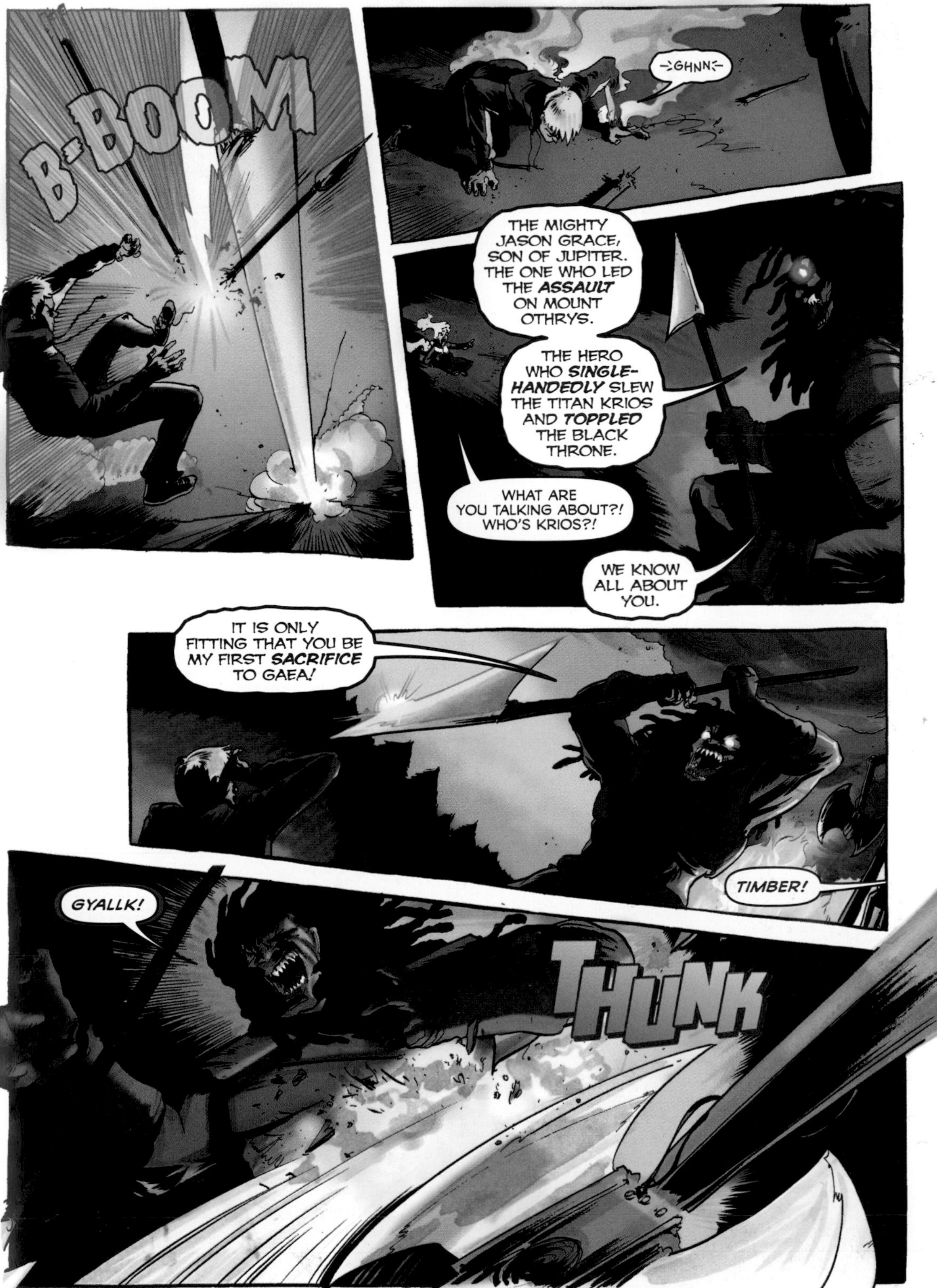
B-BOOM
-GHNN-
THE MIGHTY JASON GRACE, SON OF JUPITER. THE ONE WHO LED THE ASSAULT ON MOUNT OTHRYS.
THE HERO WHO SINGLE-HANDEDLY SLEW THE TITAN KRIOS AND TOPPLED THE BLACK THRONE.
WHAT ARE YOU TALKING ABOUT?! WHO'S KRIOS?!
WE KNOW ALL ABOUT YOU.
IT IS ONLY FITTING THAT YOU BE MY FIRST SACRIFICE TO GAEA!
TIMBER!
GYALLK!
THUNK

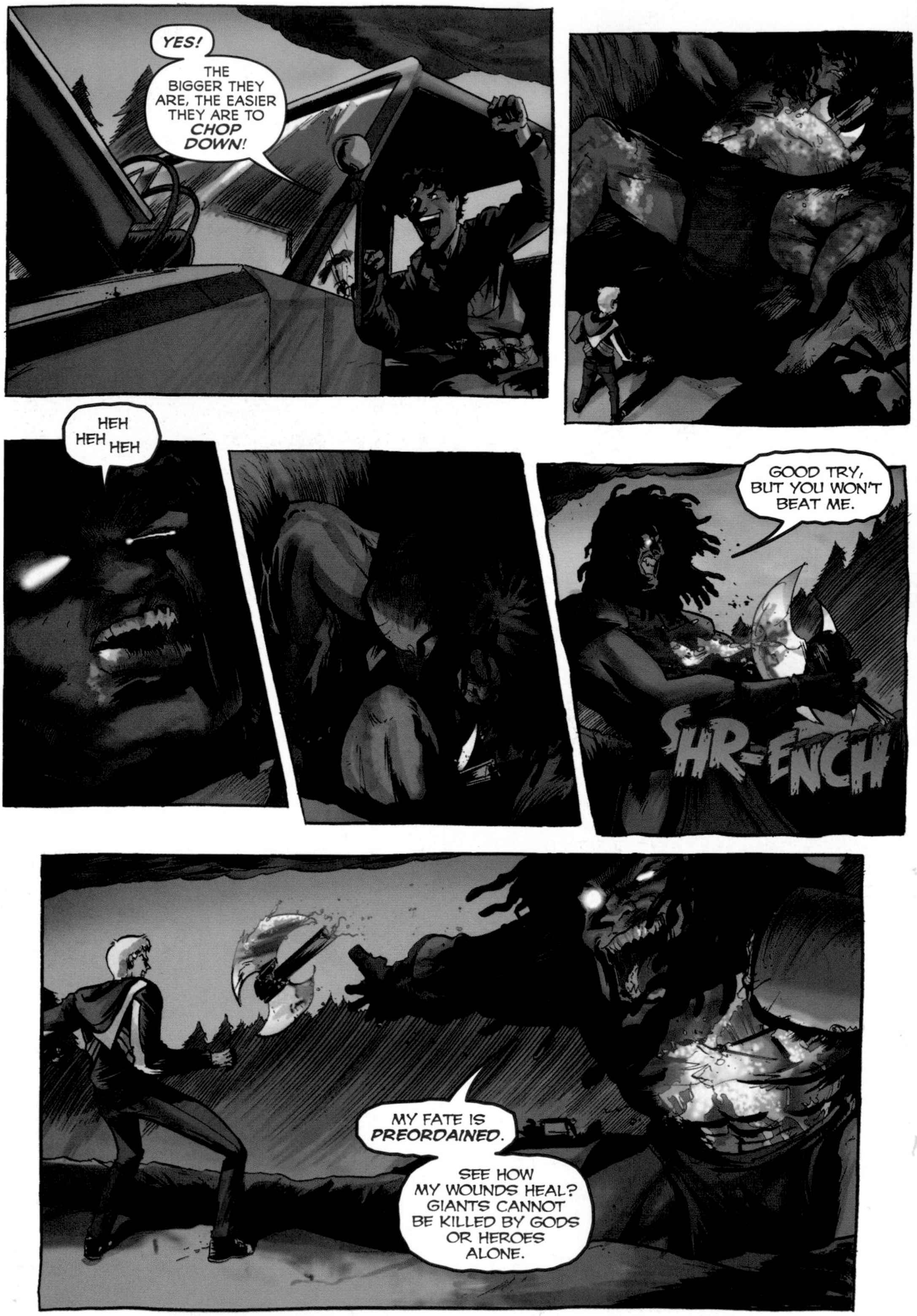
YES!
THE BIGGER THEY ARE, THE EASIER THEY ARE TO CHOP DOWN!
HEH HEH HEH
GOOD TRY, BUT YOU WON'T BEAT ME.
SHR-ENCH
MY FATE IS PREORDAINED.
SEE HOW MY WOUNDS HEAL? GIANTS CANNOT BE KILLED BY GODS OR HEROES ALONE.

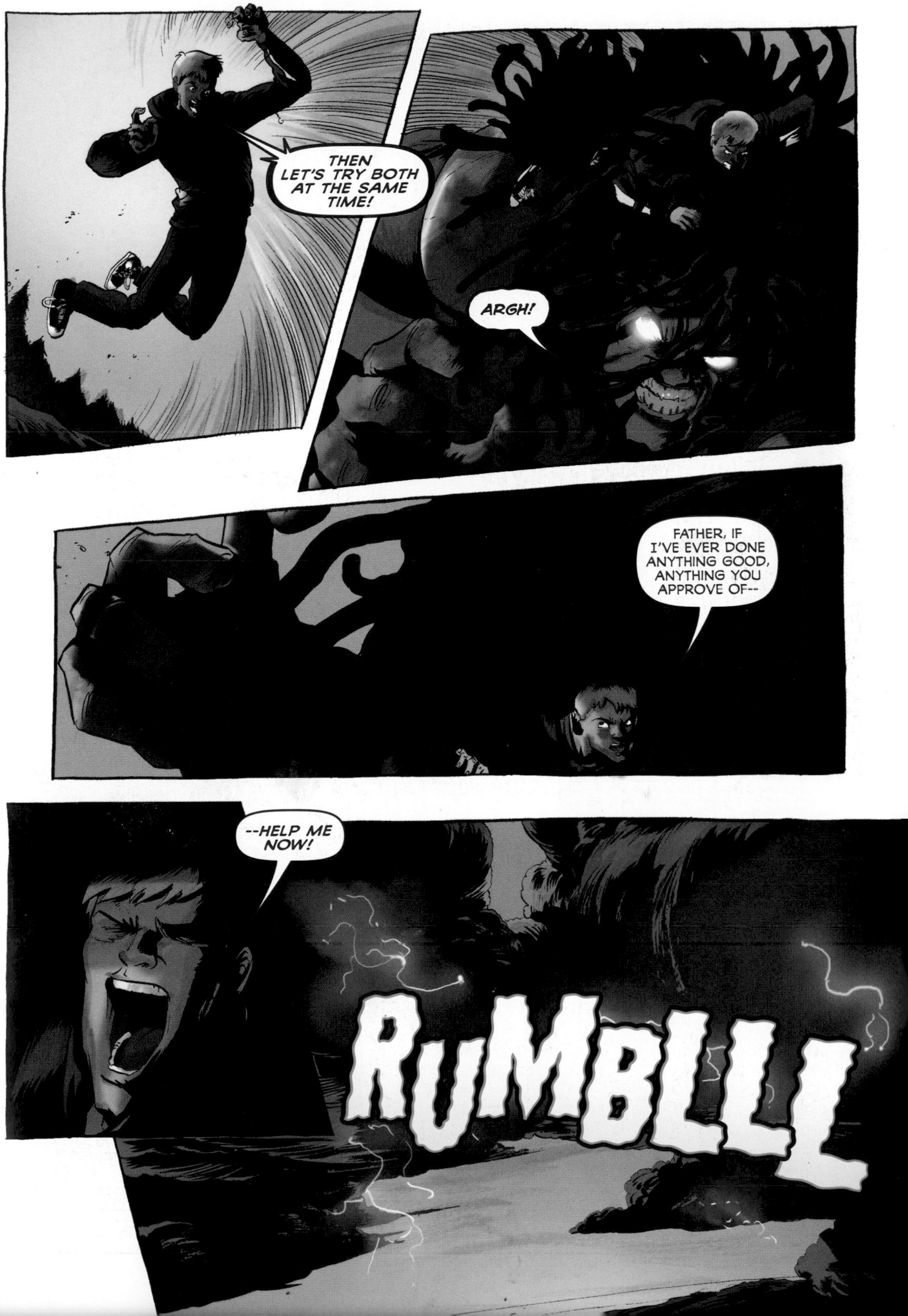
THEN LET'S TRY BOTH AT THE SAME TIME!
ARGH!
FATHER, IF I'VE EVER DONE ANYTHING GOOD, ANYTHING YOU APPROVE OF--
--HELP ME NOW!
RUMBLLL

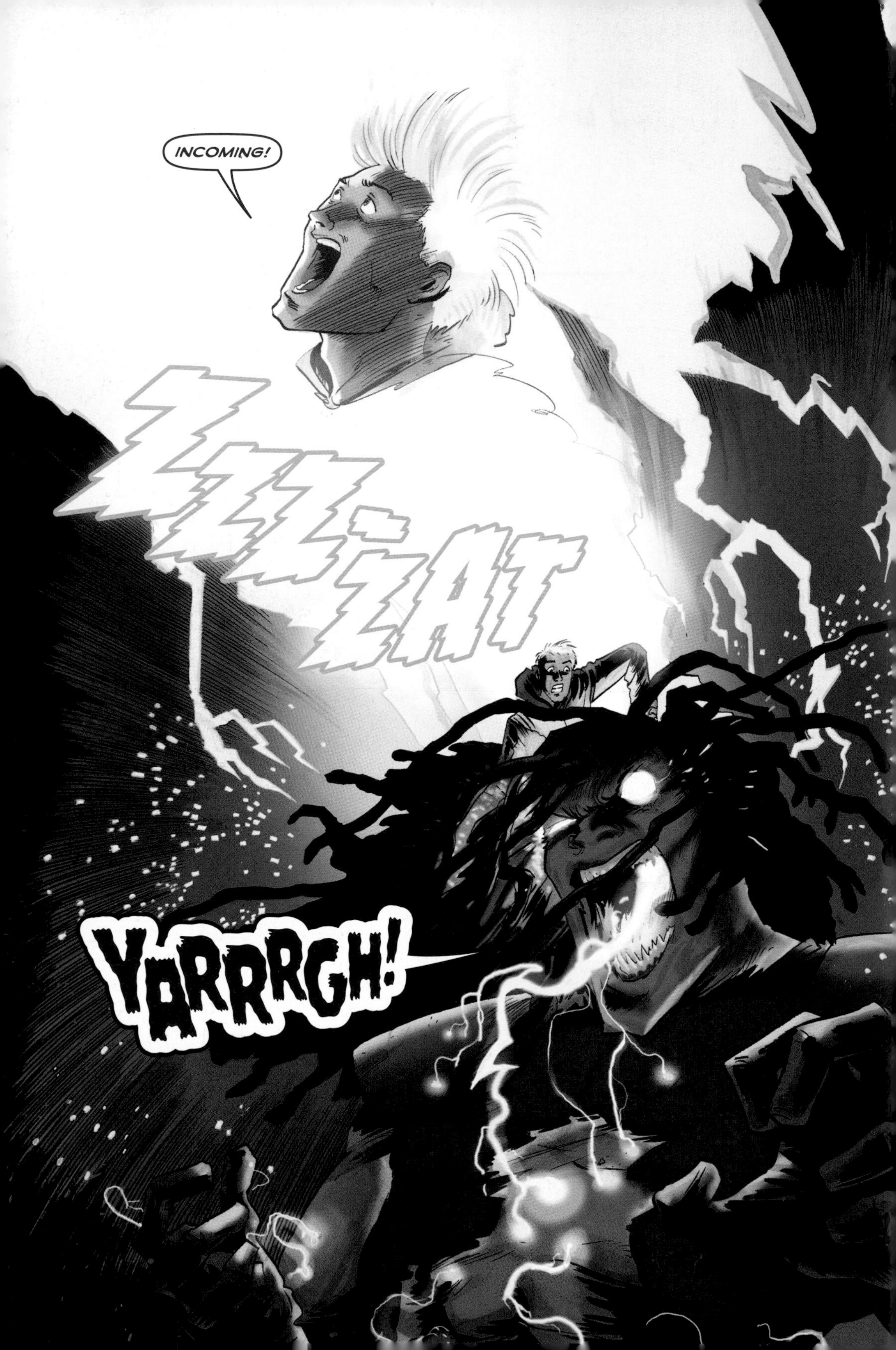
INCOMING!
ZZZZ-ZAT
YARRRGH!

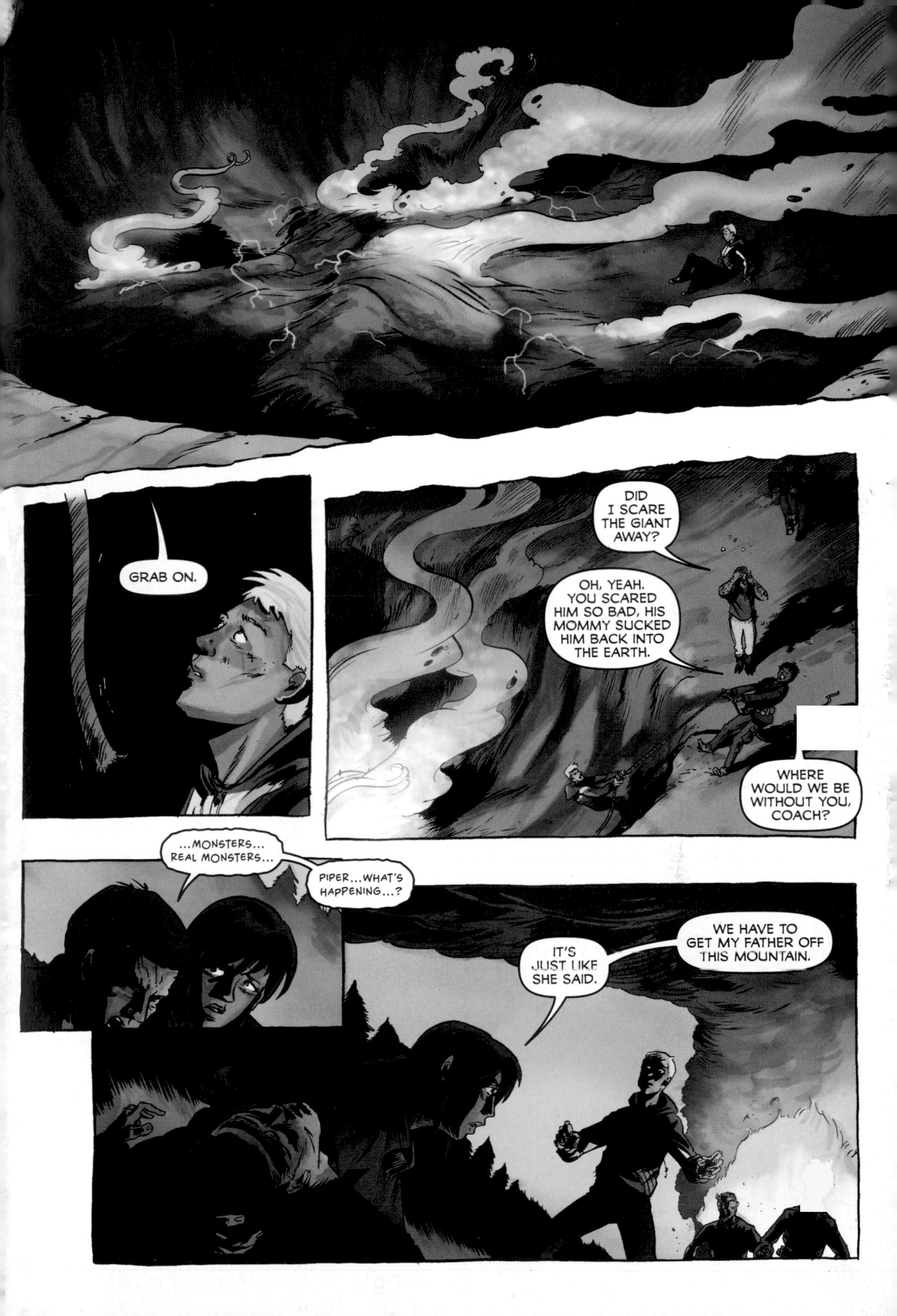
GRAB ON.
DID I SCARE THE GIANT AWAY?
OH, YEAH. YOU SCARED HIM SO BAD, HIS MOMMY SUCKED HIM BACK INTO THE EARTH.
WHERE WOULD WE BE WITHOUT YOU, COACH?
...MONSTERS... REAL MONSTERS...
PIPER...WHAT'S HAPPENING...?
IT'S JUST LIKE SHE SAID.
WE HAVE TO GET MY FATHER OFF THIS MOUNTAIN.

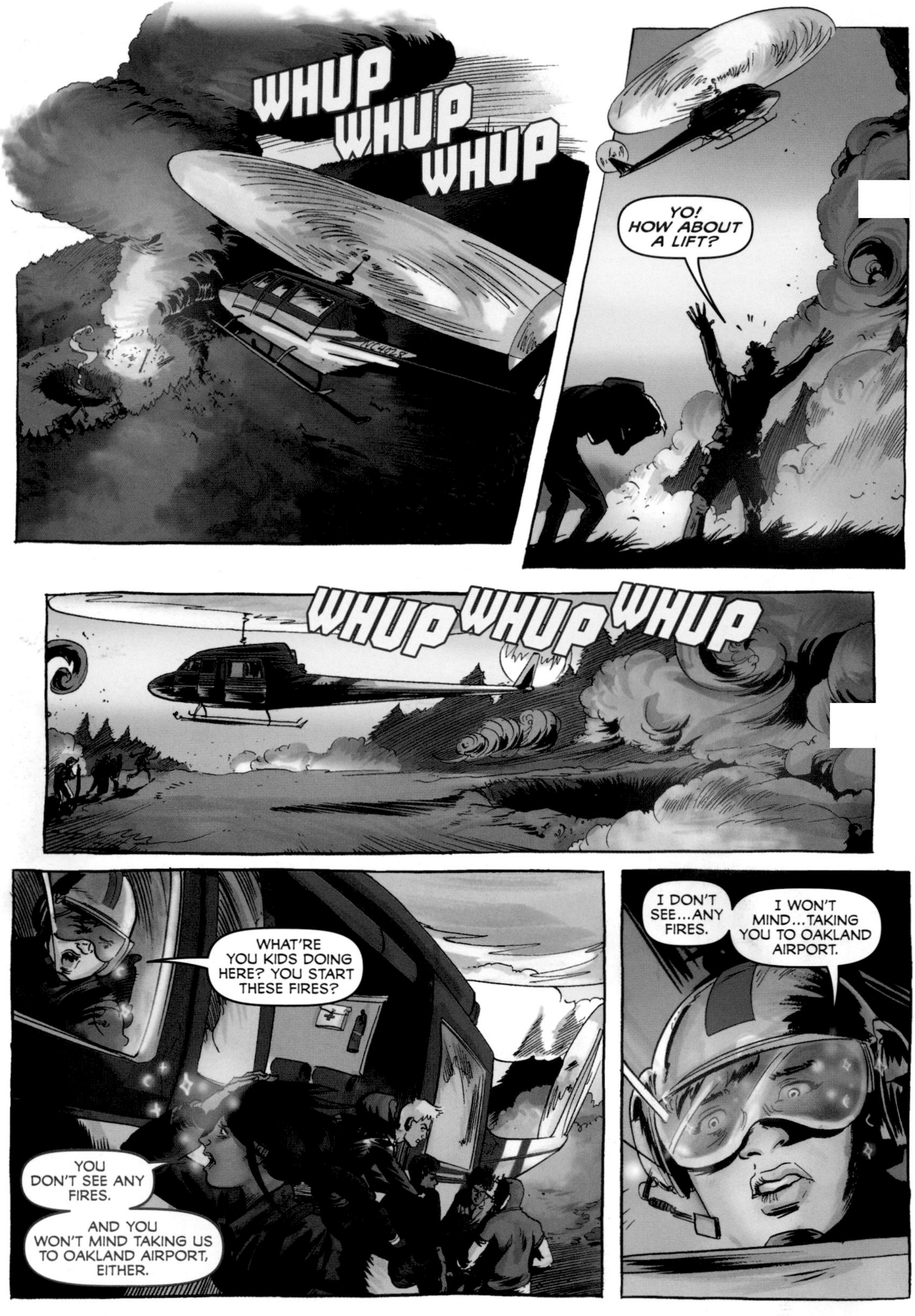
WHUP WHUP WHUP
YO! HOW ABOUT A LIFT?
WHUP WHUP WHUP
WHAT'RE YOU KIDS DOING HERE? YOU START THESE FIRES?
YOU DON'T SEE ANY FIRES.
AND YOU WON'T MIND TAKING US TO OAKLAND AIRPORT, EITHER.
I DON'T SEE...ANY FIRES.
I WON'T MIND...TAKING YOU TO OAKLAND AIRPORT.

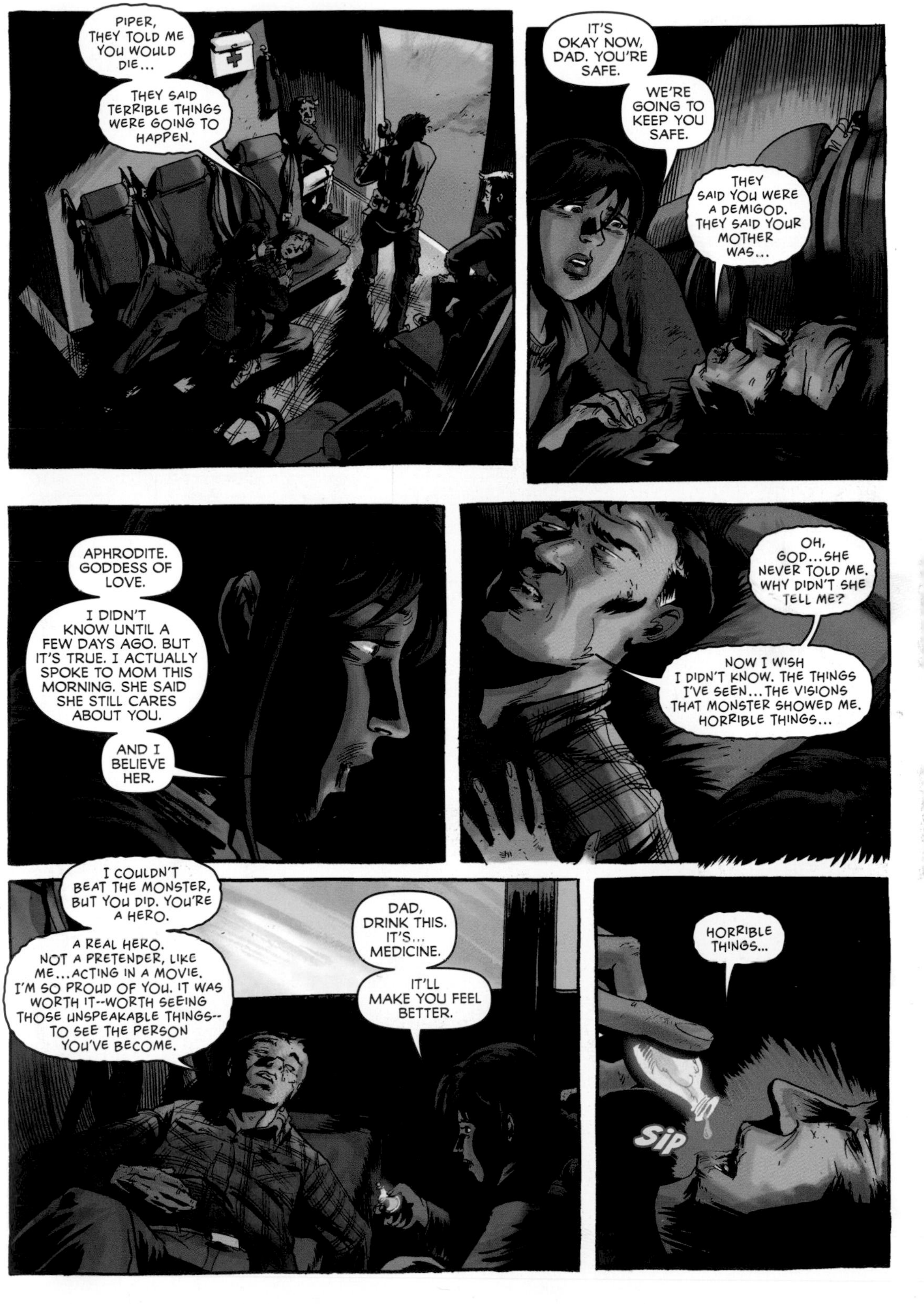
PIPER, THEY TOLD ME YOU WOULD DIE...
THEY SAID TERRIBLE THINGS WERE GOING TO HAPPEN.
IT'S OKAY NOW, DAD. YOU'RE SAFE.
WE'RE GOING TO KEEP YOU SAFE.
THEY SAID YOU WERE A DEMIGOD. THEY SAID YOUR MOTHER WAS...
APHRODITE. GODDESS OF LOVE.
I DIDN'T KNOW UNTIL A FEW DAYS AGO. BUT IT'S TRUE. I ACTUALLY SPOKE TO MOM THIS MORNING. SHE SAID SHE STILL CARES ABOUT YOU.
AND I BELIEVE HER.
OH, GOD...SHE NEVER TOLD ME. WHY DIDN'T SHE TELL ME?
NOW I WISH I DIDN'T KNOW. THE THINGS I'VE SEEN...THE VISIONS THAT MONSTER SHOWED ME. HORRIBLE THINGS...
I COULDN'T BEAT THE MONSTER, BUT YOU DID. YOU'RE A HERO.
A REAL HERO. NOT A PRETENDER, LIKE ME...ACTING IN A MOVIE. I'M SO PROUD OF YOU. IT WAS WORTH IT--WORTH SEEING THOSE UNSPEAKABLE THINGS--TO SEE THE PERSON YOU'VE BECOME.
DAD, DRINK THIS. IT'S... MEDICINE.
IT'LL MAKE YOU FEEL BETTER.
HORRIBLE THINGS...
SIP

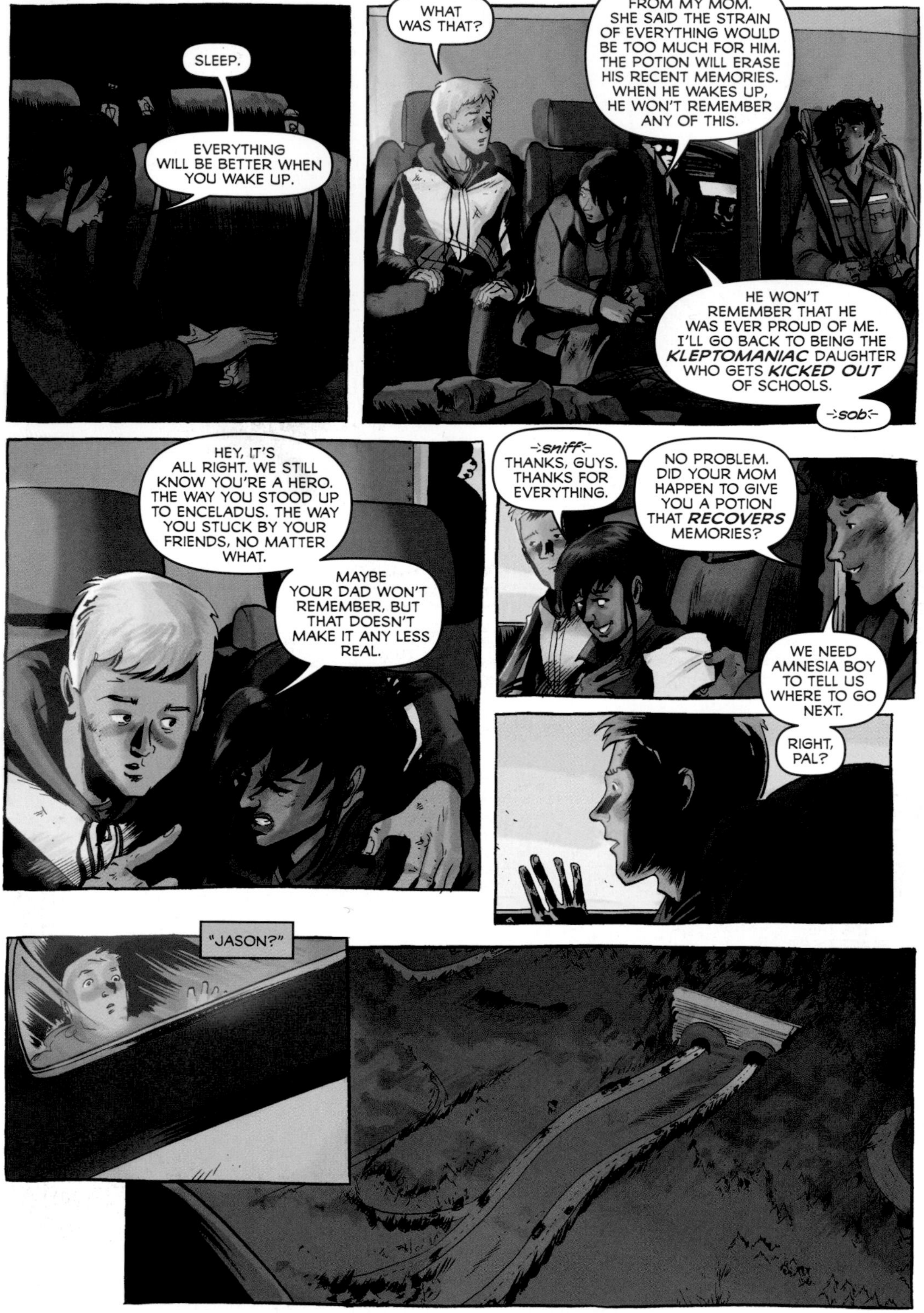
SLEEP.
EVERYTHING WILL BE BETTER WHEN YOU WAKE UP.
WHAT WAS THAT?
I GOT IT FROM MY MOM. SHE SAID THE STRAIN OF EVERYTHING WOULD BE TOO MUCH FOR HIM. THE POTION WILL ERASE HIS RECENT MEMORIES. WHEN HE WAKES UP, HE WON'T REMEMBER ANY OF THIS.
HE WON'T REMEMBER THAT HE WAS EVER PROUD OF ME. I'LL GO BACK TO BEING THE KLEPTOMANIAC DAUGHTER WHO GETS KICKED OUT OF SCHOOLS.
sob
HEY, IT'S ALL RIGHT. WE STILL KNOW YOU'RE A HERO. THE WAY YOU STOOD UP TO ENCELADUS. THE WAY YOU STUCK BY YOUR FRIENDS, NO MATTER WHAT.
MAYBE YOUR DAD WON'T REMEMBER, BUT THAT DOESN'T MAKE IT ANY LESS REAL.
sniff
THANKS, GUYS. THANKS FOR EVERYTHING.
NO PROBLEM. DID YOUR MOM HAPPEN TO GIVE YOU A POTION THAT RECOVERS MEMORIES?
WE NEED AMNESIA BOY TO TELL US WHERE TO GO NEXT.
RIGHT, PAL?
"JASON?"

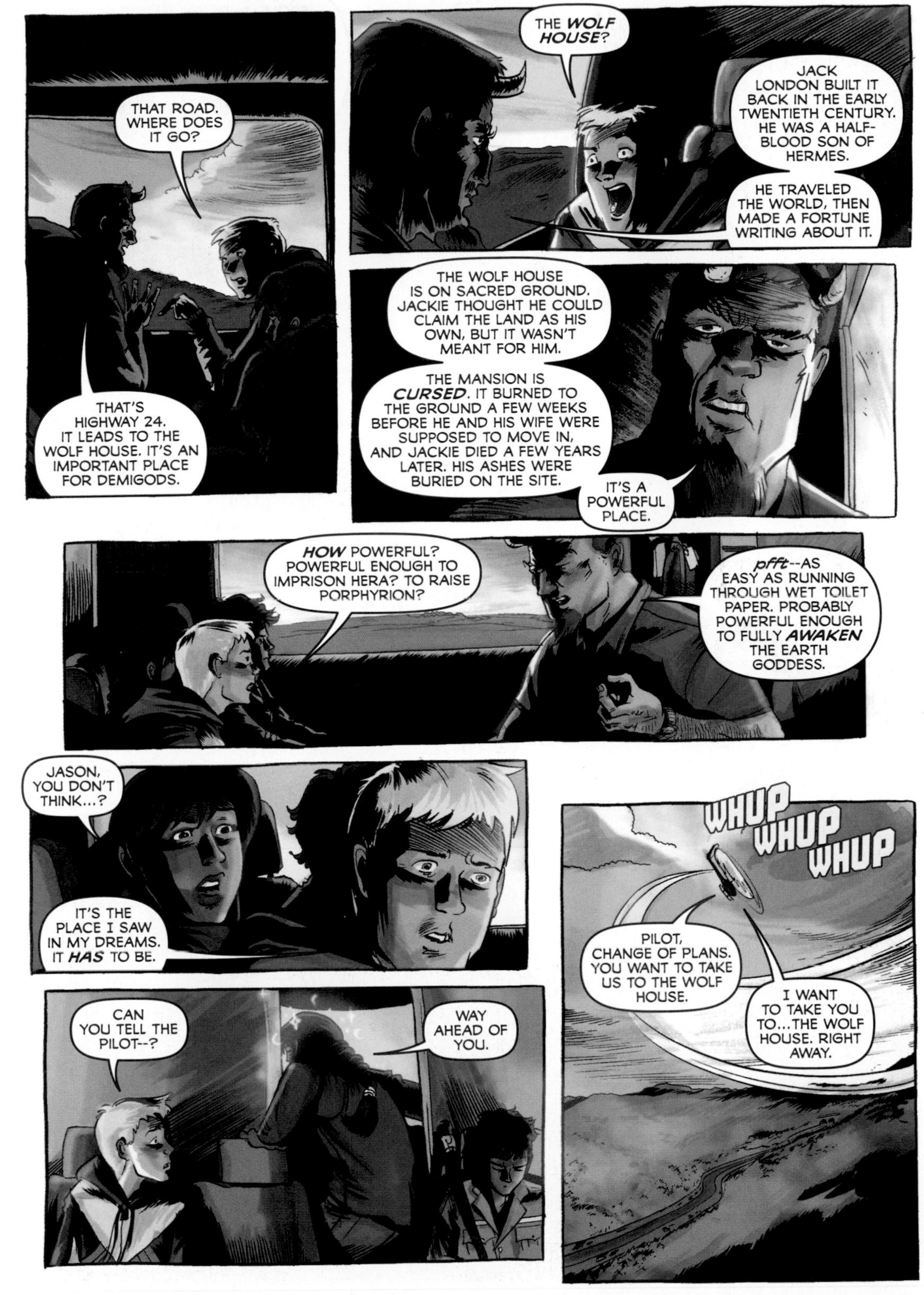
THAT ROAD. WHERE DOES IT GO?
THAT'S HIGHWAY 24. IT LEADS TO THE WOLF HOUSE. IT'S AN IMPORTANT PLACE FOR DEMIGODS.
THE WOLF HOUSE?
JACK LONDON BUILT IT BACK IN THE EARLY TWENTIETH CENTURY. HE WAS A HALF-BLOOD SON OF HERMES.
HE TRAVELED THE WORLD, THEN MADE A FORTUNE WRITING ABOUT IT.
THE WOLF HOUSE IS ON SACRED GROUND. JACKIE THOUGHT HE COULD CLAIM THE LAND AS HIS OWN, BUT IT WASN'T MEANT FOR HIM.
THE MANSION IS CURSED. IT BURNED TO THE GROUND A FEW WEEKS BEFORE HE AND HIS WIFE WERE SUPPOSED TO MOVE IN, AND JACKIE DIED A FEW YEARS LATER. HIS ASHES WERE BURIED ON THE SITE.
IT'S A POWERFUL PLACE.
HOW POWERFUL? POWERFUL ENOUGH TO IMPRISON HERA? TO RAISE PORPHYRION?
pfft--AS EASY AS RUNNING THROUGH WET TOILET PAPER. PROBABLY POWERFUL ENOUGH TO FULLY AWAKEN THE EARTH GODDESS.
JASON, YOU DON'T THINK...?
IT'S THE PLACE I SAW IN MY DREAMS. IT HAS TO BE.
CAN YOU TELL THE PILOT--?
WAY AHEAD OF YOU.
WHUP WHUP WHUP
PILOT, CHANGE OF PLANS. YOU WANT TO TAKE US TO THE WOLF HOUSE.
I WANT TO TAKE YOU TO...THE WOLF HOUSE. RIGHT AWAY.

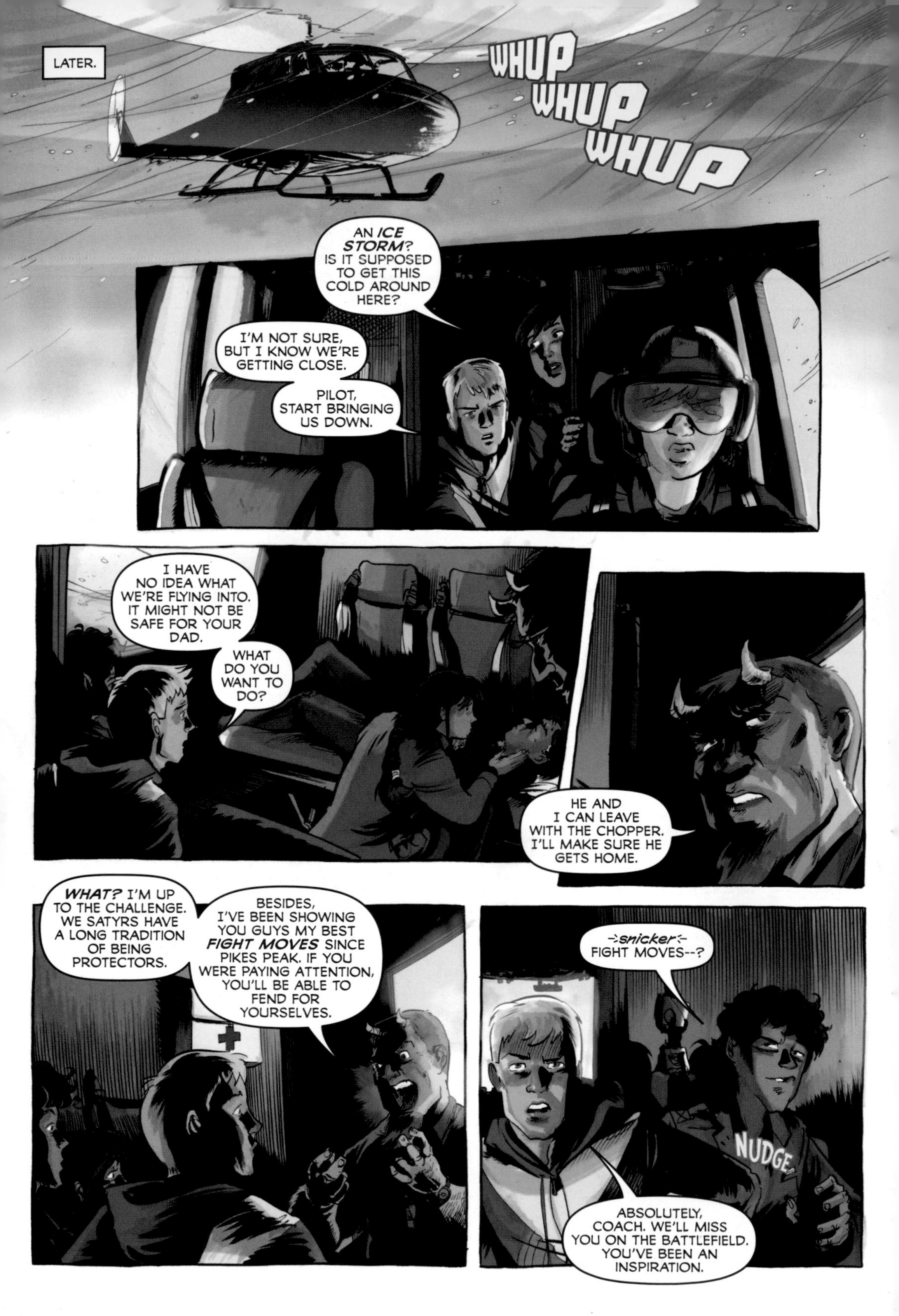
LATER.
WHUP WHUP WHUP
AN *ICE STORM*? IS IT SUPPOSED TO GET THIS COLD AROUND HERE?
I'M NOT SURE, BUT I KNOW WE'RE GETTING CLOSE.
PILOT, START BRINGING US DOWN.
I HAVE NO IDEA WHAT WE'RE FLYING INTO. IT MIGHT NOT BE SAFE FOR YOUR DAD.
WHAT DO YOU WANT TO DO?
HE AND I CAN LEAVE WITH THE CHOPPER. I'LL MAKE SURE HE GETS HOME.
WHAT? I'M UP TO THE CHALLENGE. WE SATYRS HAVE A LONG TRADITION OF BEING PROTECTORS.
BESIDES, I'VE BEEN SHOWING YOU GUYS MY BEST ***FIGHT MOVES*** SINCE PIKES PEAK. IF YOU WERE PAYING ATTENTION, YOU'LL BE ABLE TO FEND FOR YOURSELVES.
snicker FIGHT MOVES--?
NUDGE
ABSOLUTELY, COACH. WE'LL MISS YOU ON THE BATTLEFIELD. YOU'VE BEEN AN INSPIRATION.

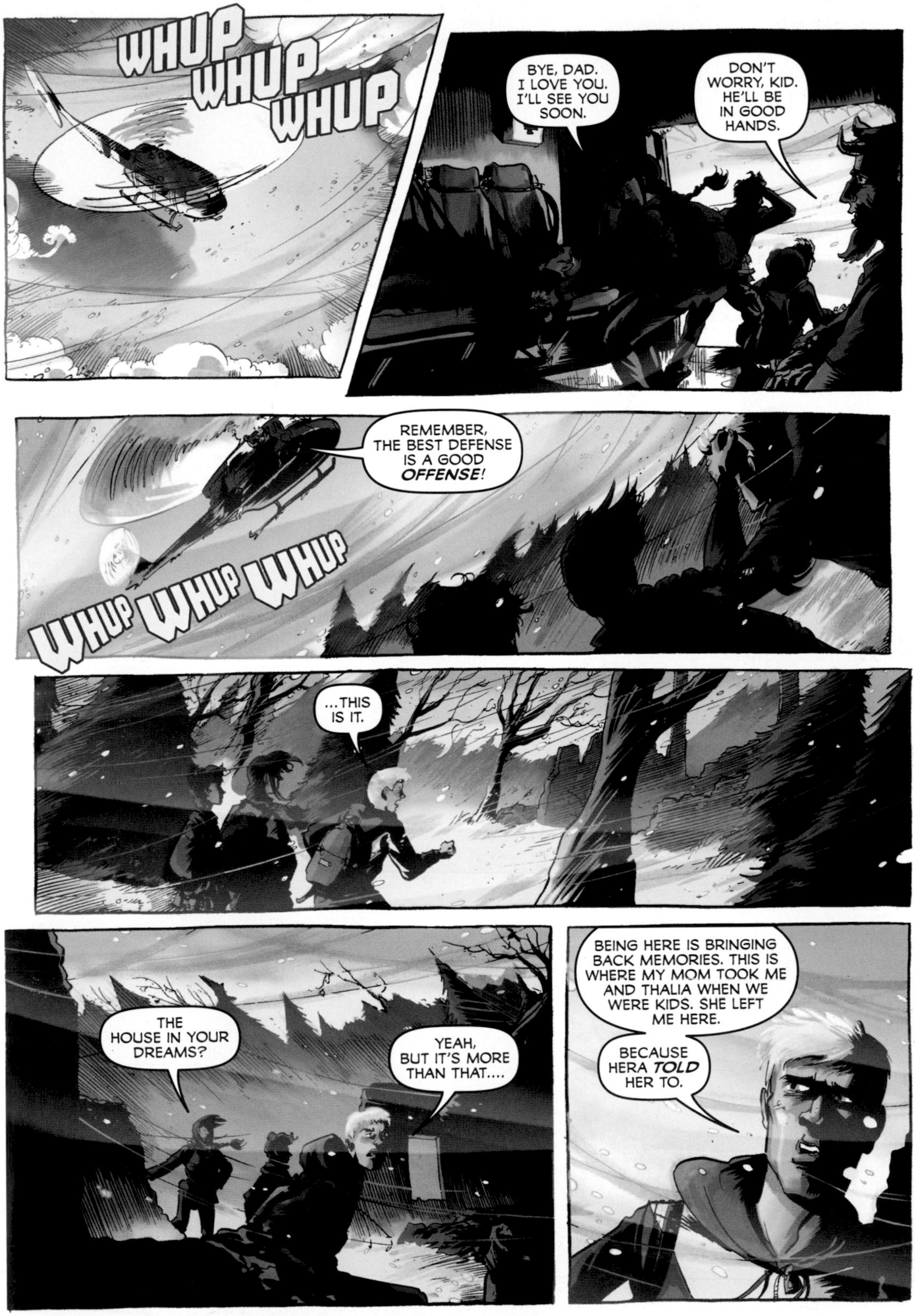
WHUP WHUP WHUP
BYE, DAD. I LOVE YOU. I'LL SEE YOU SOON.
DON'T WORRY, KID. HE'LL BE IN GOOD HANDS.
REMEMBER, THE BEST DEFENSE IS A GOOD OFFENSE!
WHUP WHUP WHUP
...THIS IS IT.
THE HOUSE IN YOUR DREAMS?
YEAH, BUT IT'S MORE THAN THAT....
BEING HERE IS BRINGING BACK MEMORIES. THIS IS WHERE MY MOM TOOK ME AND THALIA WHEN WE WERE KIDS. SHE LEFT ME HERE.
BECAUSE HERA TOLD HER TO.

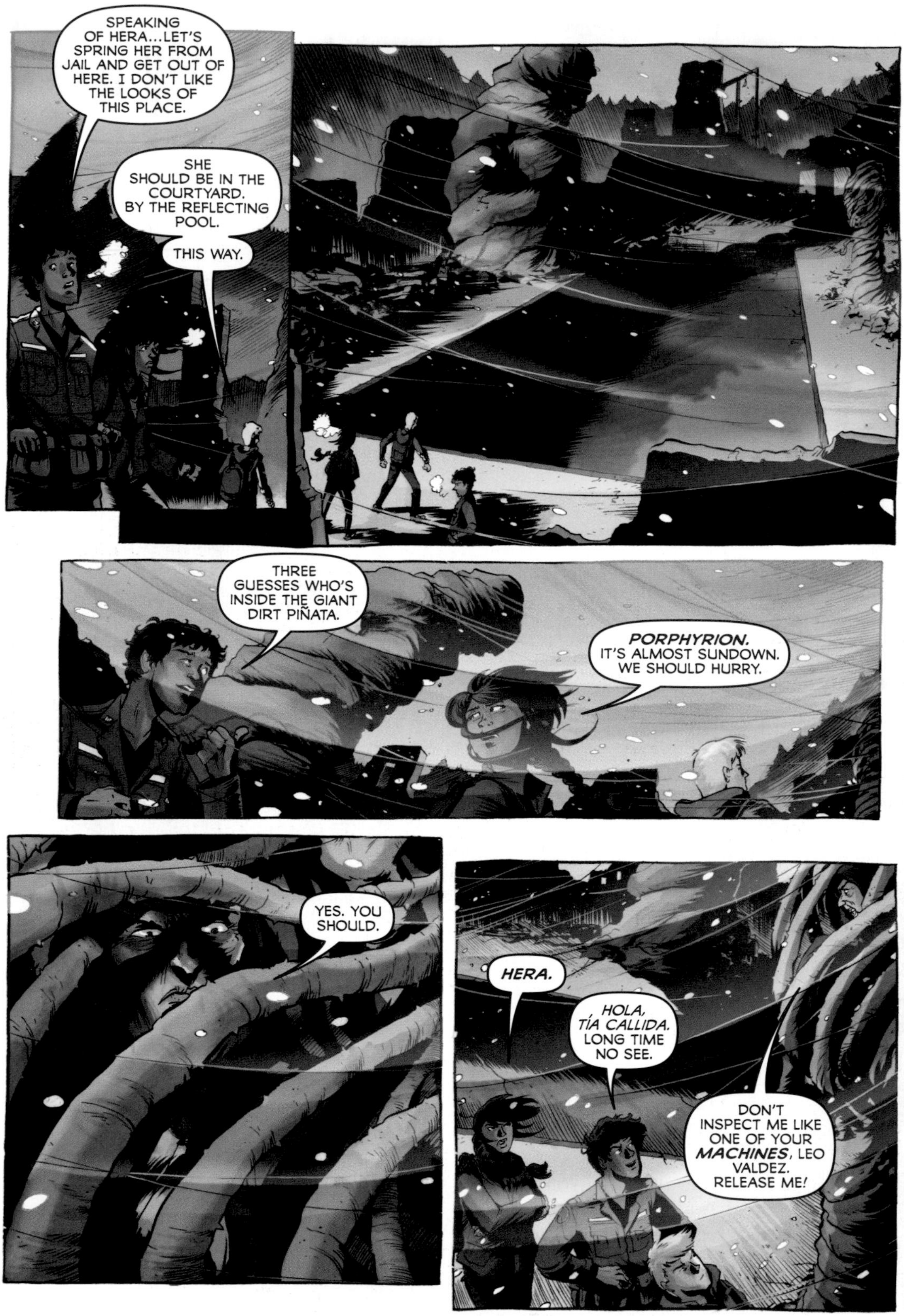
SPEAKING OF HERA...LET'S SPRING HER FROM JAIL AND GET OUT OF HERE. I DON'T LIKE THE LOOKS OF THIS PLACE.
SHE SHOULD BE IN THE COURTYARD. BY THE REFLECTING POOL.
THIS WAY.
THREE GUESSES WHO'S INSIDE THE GIANT DIRT PIÑATA.
PORPHYRION. IT'S ALMOST SUNDOWN. WE SHOULD HURRY.
YES. YOU SHOULD.
HERA.
HOLA, TÍA CALLIDA. LONG TIME NO SEE.
DON'T INSPECT ME LIKE ONE OF YOUR *MACHINES*, LEO VALDEZ. RELEASE ME!

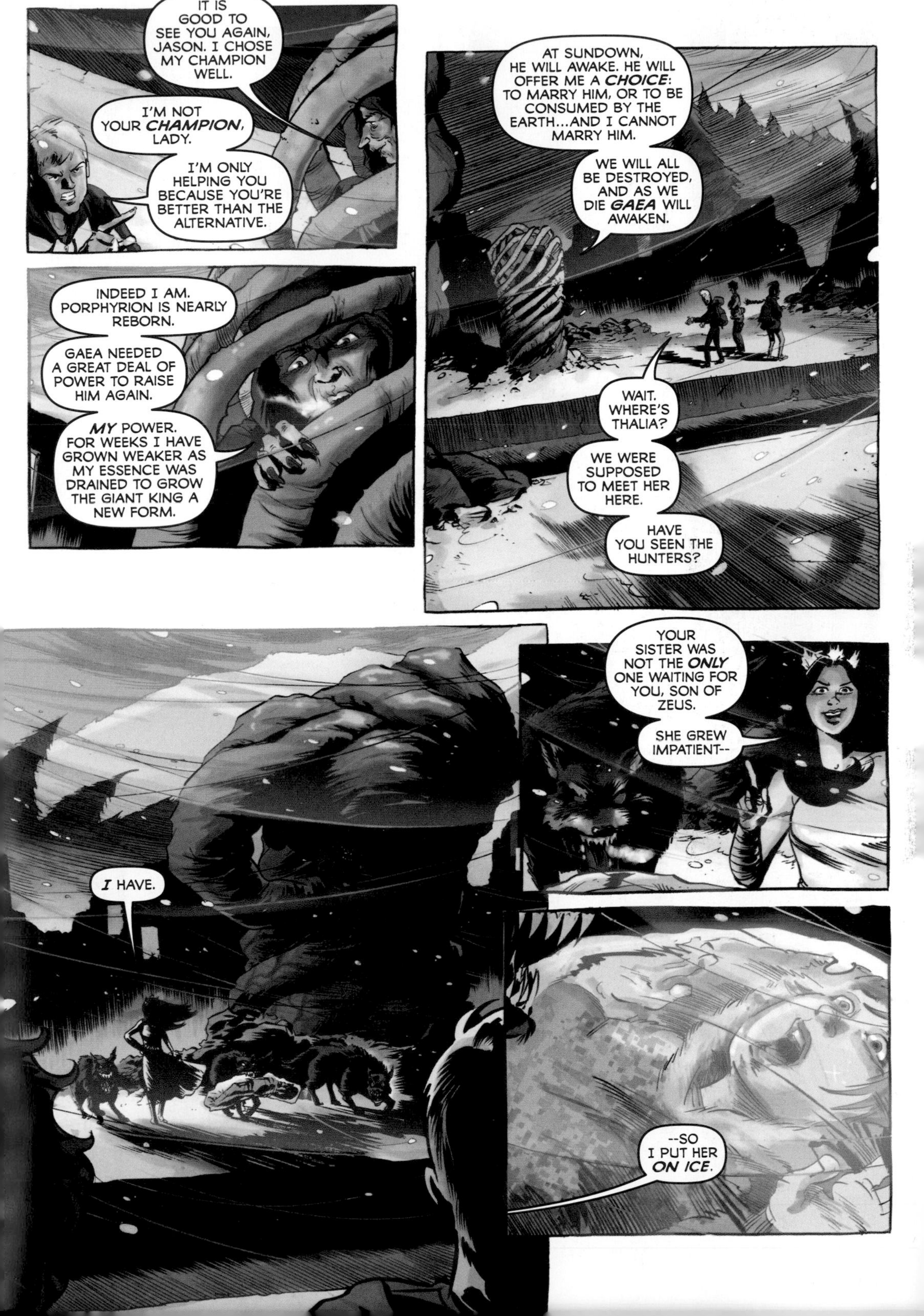
IT IS GOOD TO SEE YOU AGAIN, JASON. I CHOSE MY CHAMPION WELL.
I'M NOT YOUR *CHAMPION*, LADY.
I'M ONLY HELPING YOU BECAUSE YOU'RE BETTER THAN THE ALTERNATIVE.
INDEED I AM. PORPHYRION IS NEARLY REBORN.
GAEA NEEDED A GREAT DEAL OF POWER TO RAISE HIM AGAIN.
MY POWER. FOR WEEKS I HAVE GROWN WEAKER AS MY ESSENCE WAS DRAINED TO GROW THE GIANT KING A NEW FORM.
AT SUNDOWN, HE WILL AWAKE. HE WILL OFFER ME A *CHOICE*: TO MARRY HIM, OR TO BE CONSUMED BY THE EARTH...AND I CANNOT MARRY HIM.
WE WILL ALL BE DESTROYED, AND AS WE DIE *GAEA* WILL AWAKEN.
WAIT. WHERE'S THALIA?
WE WERE SUPPOSED TO MEET HER HERE.
HAVE YOU SEEN THE HUNTERS?
I HAVE.
YOUR SISTER WAS NOT THE *ONLY* ONE WAITING FOR YOU, SON OF ZEUS.
SHE GREW IMPATIENT--
--SO I PUT HER *ON ICE*.

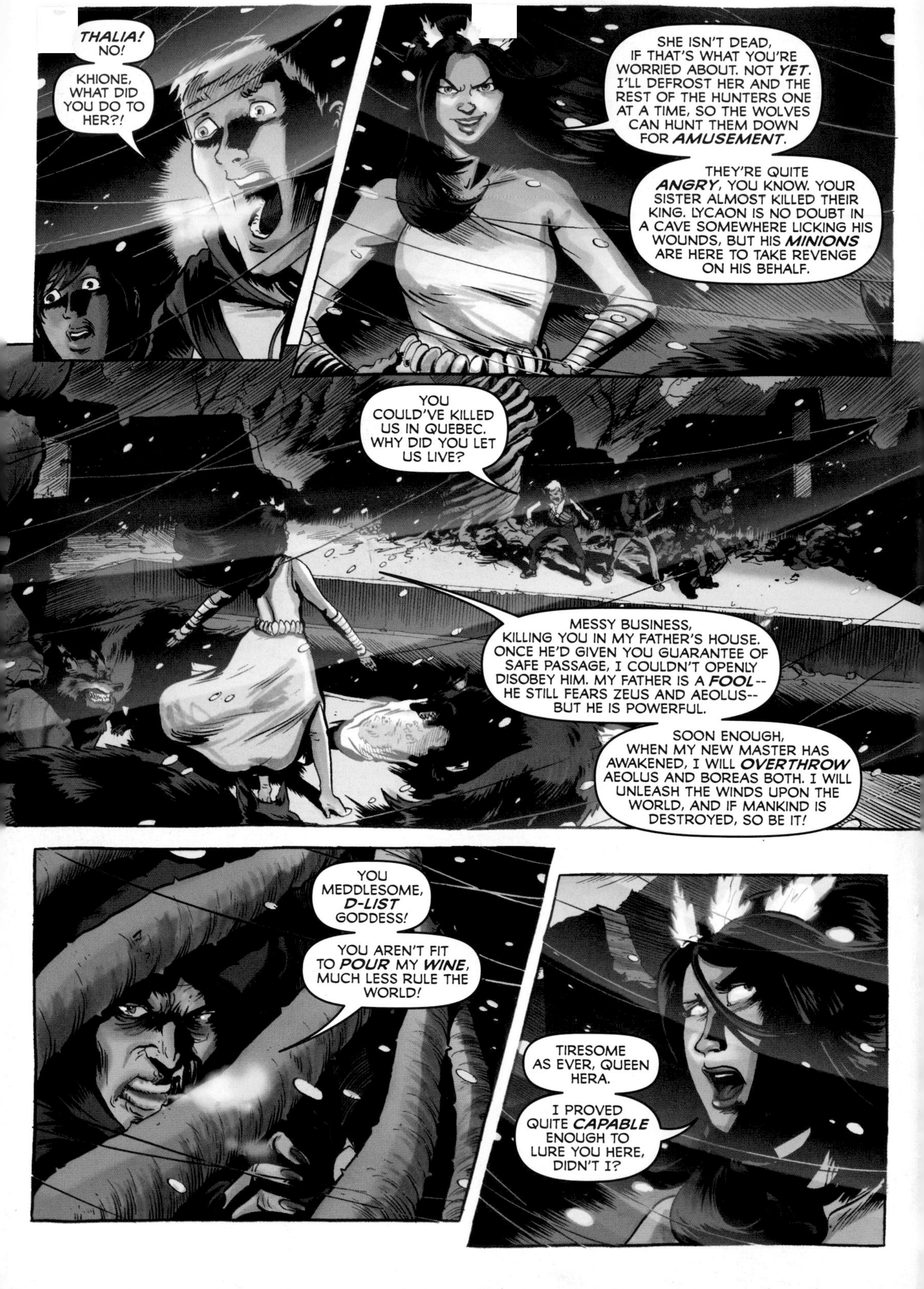
THALIA! NO!
KHIONE, WHAT DID YOU DO TO HER?!
SHE ISN'T DEAD, IF THAT'S WHAT YOU'RE WORRIED ABOUT. NOT YET. I'LL DEFROST HER AND THE REST OF THE HUNTERS ONE AT A TIME, SO THE WOLVES CAN HUNT THEM DOWN FOR AMUSEMENT.
THEY'RE QUITE ANGRY, YOU KNOW. YOUR SISTER ALMOST KILLED THEIR KING. LYCAON IS NO DOUBT IN A CAVE SOMEWHERE LICKING HIS WOUNDS, BUT HIS MINIONS ARE HERE TO TAKE REVENGE ON HIS BEHALF.
YOU COULD'VE KILLED US IN QUEBEC. WHY DID YOU LET US LIVE?
MESSY BUSINESS, KILLING YOU IN MY FATHER'S HOUSE. ONCE HE'D GIVEN YOU GUARANTEE OF SAFE PASSAGE, I COULDN'T OPENLY DISOBEY HIM. MY FATHER IS A FOOL-- HE STILL FEARS ZEUS AND AEOLUS-- BUT HE IS POWERFUL.
SOON ENOUGH, WHEN MY NEW MASTER HAS AWAKENED, I WILL OVERTHROW AEOLUS AND BOREAS BOTH. I WILL UNLEASH THE WINDS UPON THE WORLD, AND IF MANKIND IS DESTROYED, SO BE IT!
YOU MEDDLESOME, D-LIST GODDESS!
YOU AREN'T FIT TO POUR MY WINE, MUCH LESS RULE THE WORLD!
TIRESOME AS EVER, QUEEN HERA.
I PROVED QUITE CAPABLE ENOUGH TO LURE YOU HERE, DIDN'T I?

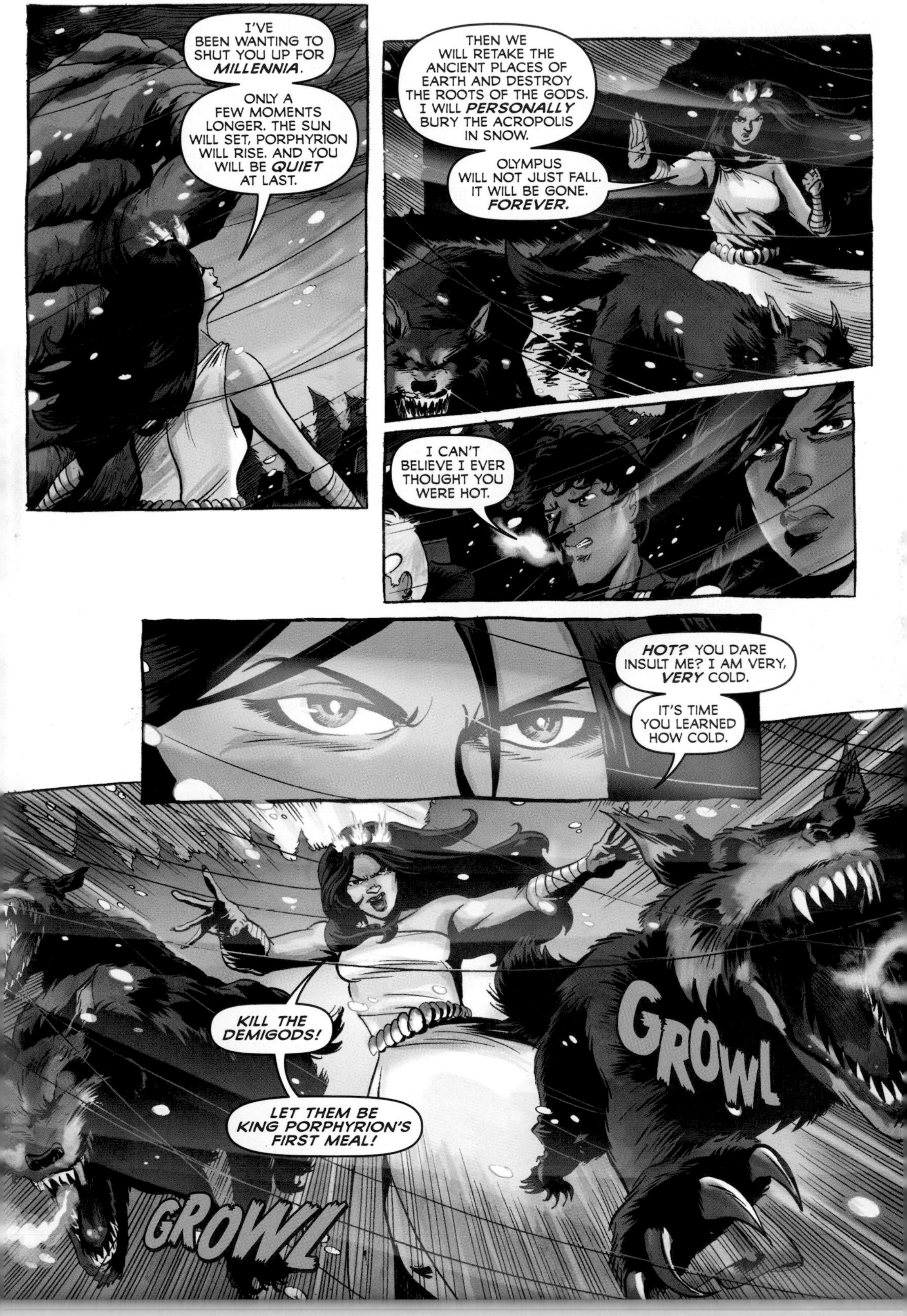
I'VE BEEN WANTING TO SHUT YOU UP FOR *MILLENNIA*.
ONLY A FEW MOMENTS LONGER. THE SUN WILL SET, PORPHYRION WILL RISE. AND YOU WILL BE *QUIET* AT LAST.
THEN WE WILL RETAKE THE ANCIENT PLACES OF EARTH AND DESTROY THE ROOTS OF THE GODS. I WILL *PERSONALLY* BURY THE ACROPOLIS IN SNOW.
OLYMPUS WILL NOT JUST FALL. IT WILL BE GONE. *FOREVER.*
I CAN'T BELIEVE I EVER THOUGHT YOU WERE HOT.
HOT? YOU DARE INSULT ME? I AM VERY, *VERY* COLD.
IT'S TIME YOU LEARNED HOW COLD.
KILL THE DEMIGODS!
LET THEM BE KING PORPHYRION'S FIRST MEAL!
GROWL
GROWL

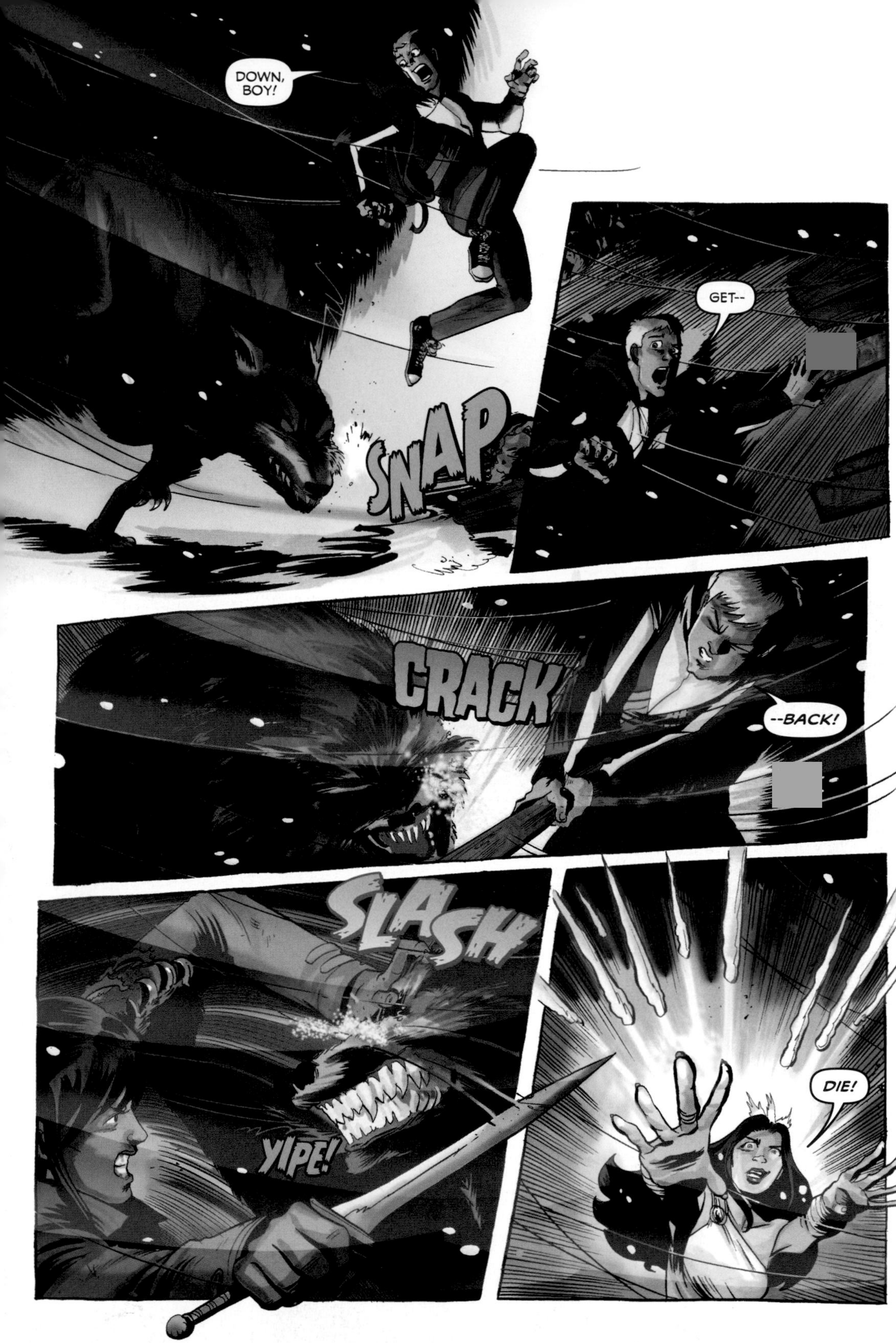
DOWN, BOY!
SNAP
GET--
CRACK
--BACK!
SLASH
YIPE!
DIE!

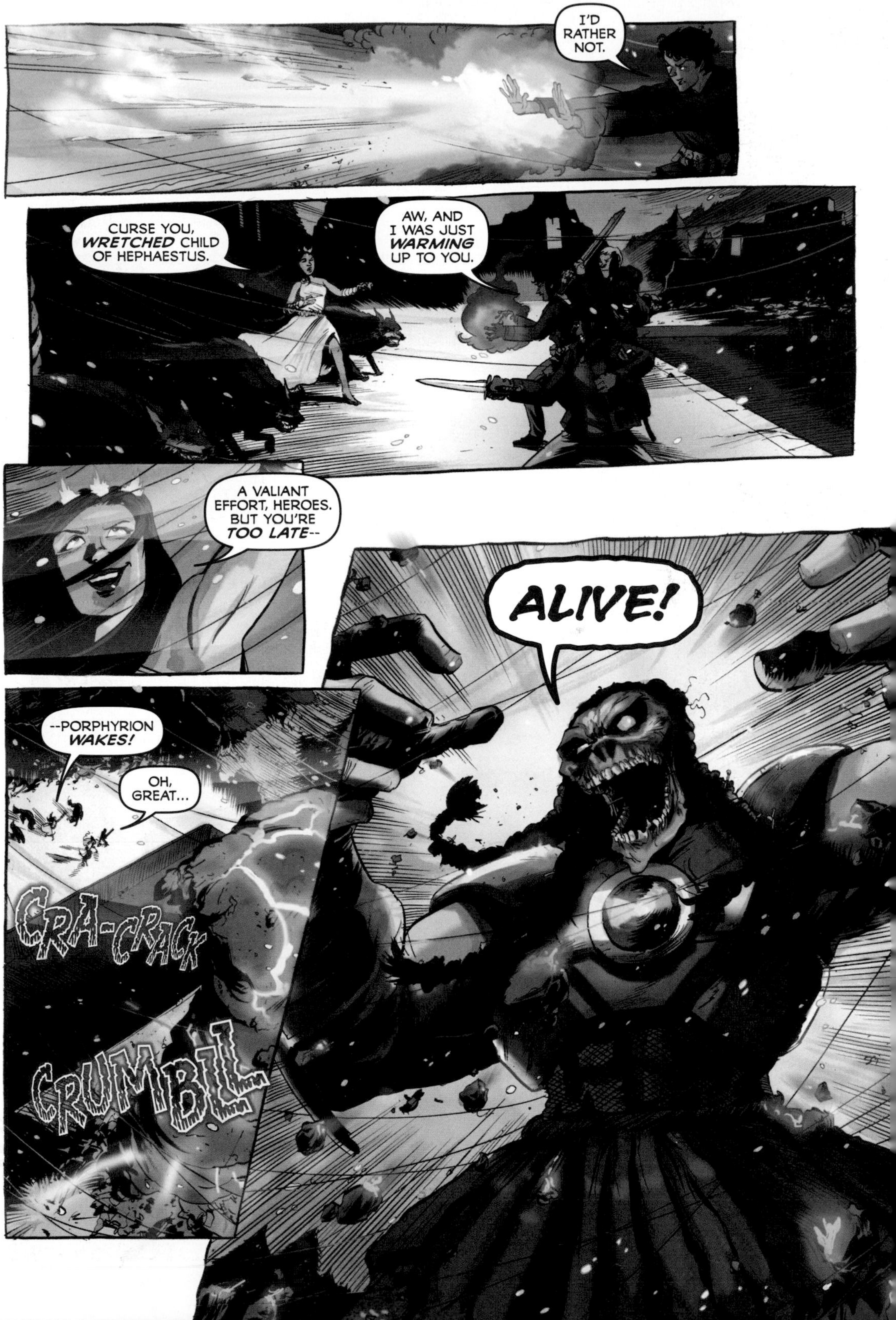
I'D RATHER NOT.
CURSE YOU, WRETCHED CHILD OF HEPHAESTUS.
AW, AND I WAS JUST WARMING UP TO YOU.
A VALIANT EFFORT, HEROES. BUT YOU'RE TOO LATE--
ALIVE!
--PORPHYRION WAKES!
OH, GREAT...
CRA-CRACK
CRUMBLL

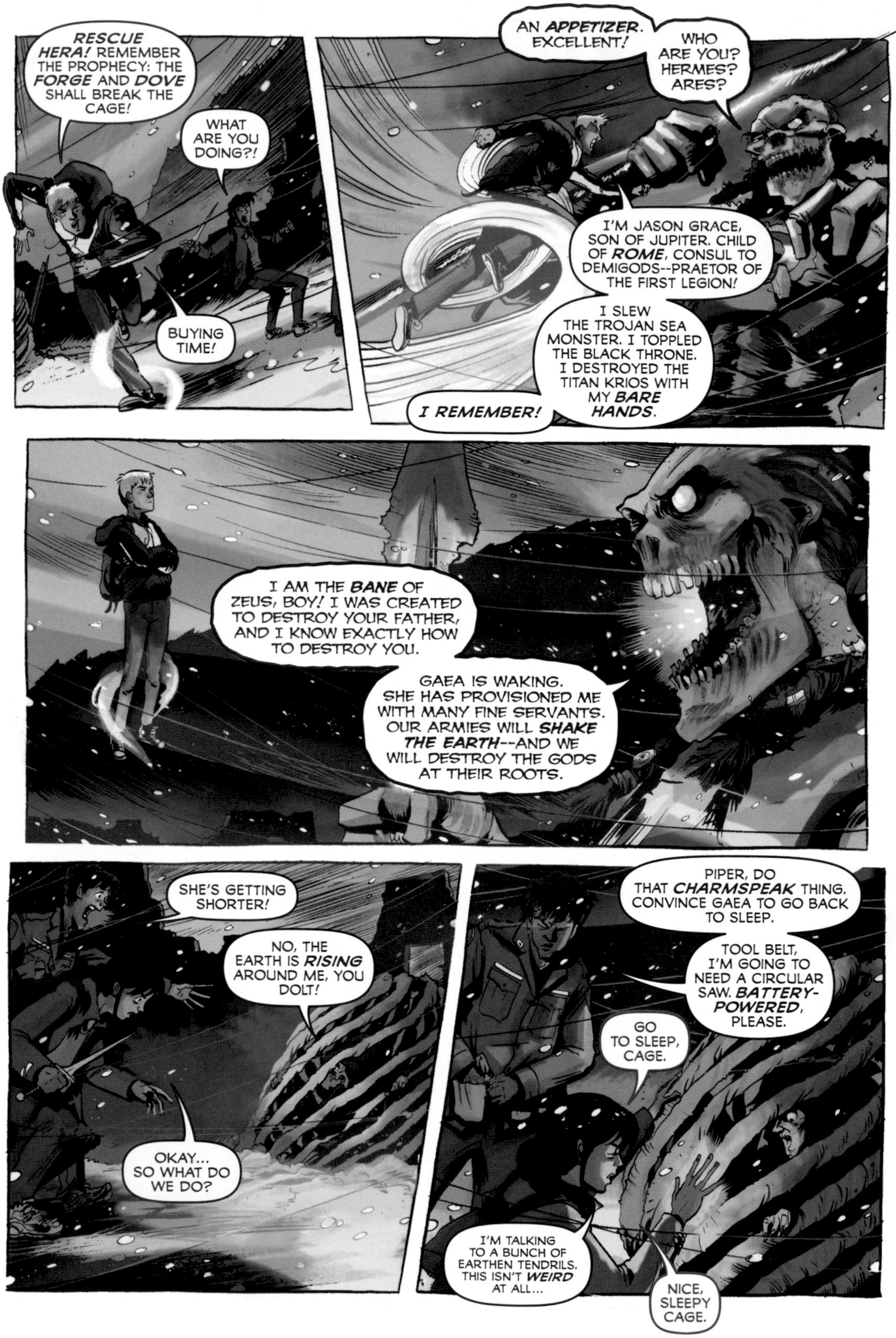
RESCUE HERA! REMEMBER THE PROPHECY: THE FORGE AND DOVE SHALL BREAK THE CAGE!
WHAT ARE YOU DOING?!
BUYING TIME!
AN APPETIZER. EXCELLENT!
WHO ARE YOU? HERMES? ARES?
I'M JASON GRACE, SON OF JUPITER. CHILD OF ROME, CONSUL TO DEMIGODS--PRAETOR OF THE FIRST LEGION!
I SLEW THE TROJAN SEA MONSTER. I TOPPLED THE BLACK THRONE. I DESTROYED THE TITAN KRIOS WITH MY BARE HANDS.
I REMEMBER!
I AM THE BANE OF ZEUS, BOY! I WAS CREATED TO DESTROY YOUR FATHER, AND I KNOW EXACTLY HOW TO DESTROY YOU.
GAEA IS WAKING. SHE HAS PROVISIONED ME WITH MANY FINE SERVANTS. OUR ARMIES WILL SHAKE THE EARTH--AND WE WILL DESTROY THE GODS AT THEIR ROOTS.
SHE'S GETTING SHORTER!
NO, THE EARTH IS RISING AROUND ME, YOU DOLT!
OKAY... SO WHAT DO WE DO?
PIPER, DO THAT CHARMSPEAK THING. CONVINCE GAEA TO GO BACK TO SLEEP.
TOOL BELT, I'M GOING TO NEED A CIRCULAR SAW. BATTERY-POWERED, PLEASE.
GO TO SLEEP, CAGE.
I'M TALKING TO A BUNCH OF EARTHEN TENDRILS. THIS ISN'T WEIRD AT ALL...
NICE, SLEEPY CAGE.

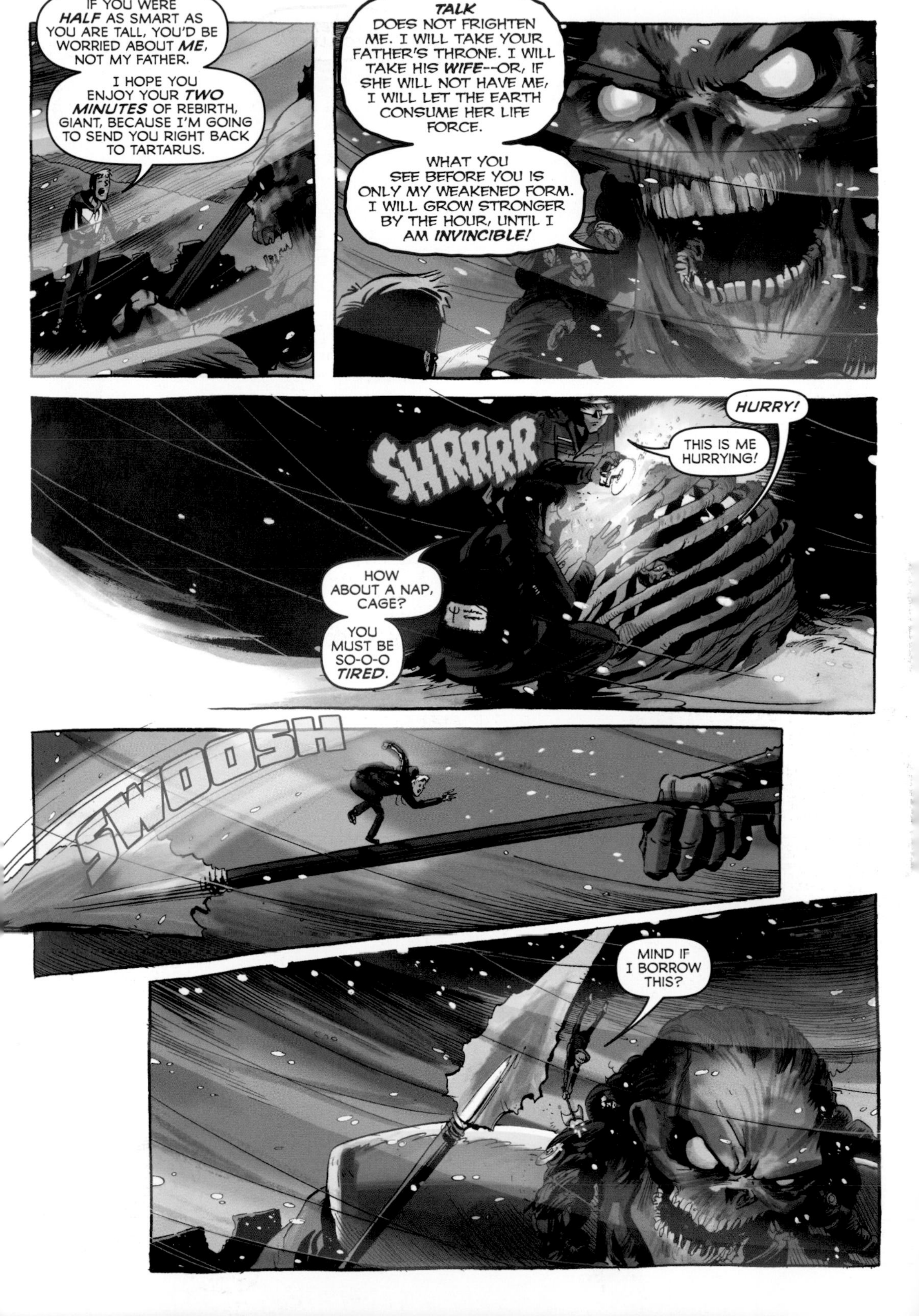

IF YOU WERE HALF AS SMART AS YOU ARE TALL, YOU'D BE WORRIED ABOUT ME, NOT MY FATHER.
I HOPE YOU ENJOY YOUR TWO MINUTES OF REBIRTH, GIANT, BECAUSE I'M GOING TO SEND YOU RIGHT BACK TO TARTARUS.
TALK DOES NOT FRIGHTEN ME. I WILL TAKE YOUR FATHER'S THRONE. I WILL TAKE HIS WIFE--OR, IF SHE WILL NOT HAVE ME, I WILL LET THE EARTH CONSUME HER LIFE FORCE.
WHAT YOU SEE BEFORE YOU IS ONLY MY WEAKENED FORM. I WILL GROW STRONGER BY THE HOUR, UNTIL I AM INVINCIBLE!
SHRRRR
HURRY!
THIS IS ME HURRYING!
HOW ABOUT A NAP, CAGE?
YOU MUST BE SO-O-O TIRED.
SWOOSH
MIND IF I BORROW THIS?

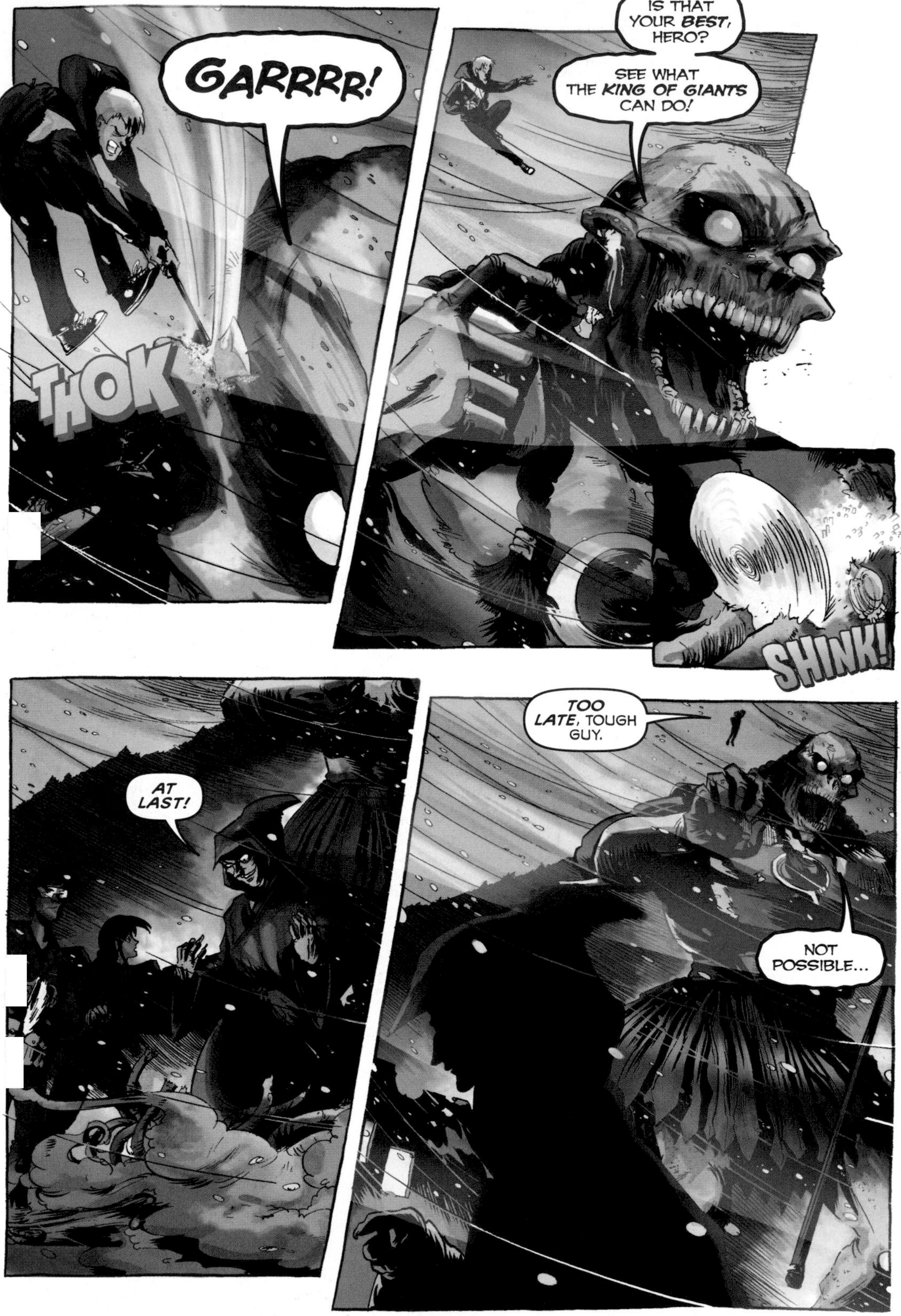
GARRRR!
THOK
IS THAT YOUR BEST, HERO?
SEE WHAT THE KING OF GIANTS CAN DO!
SHINK!
AT LAST!
TOO LATE, TOUGH GUY.
NOT POSSIBLE...

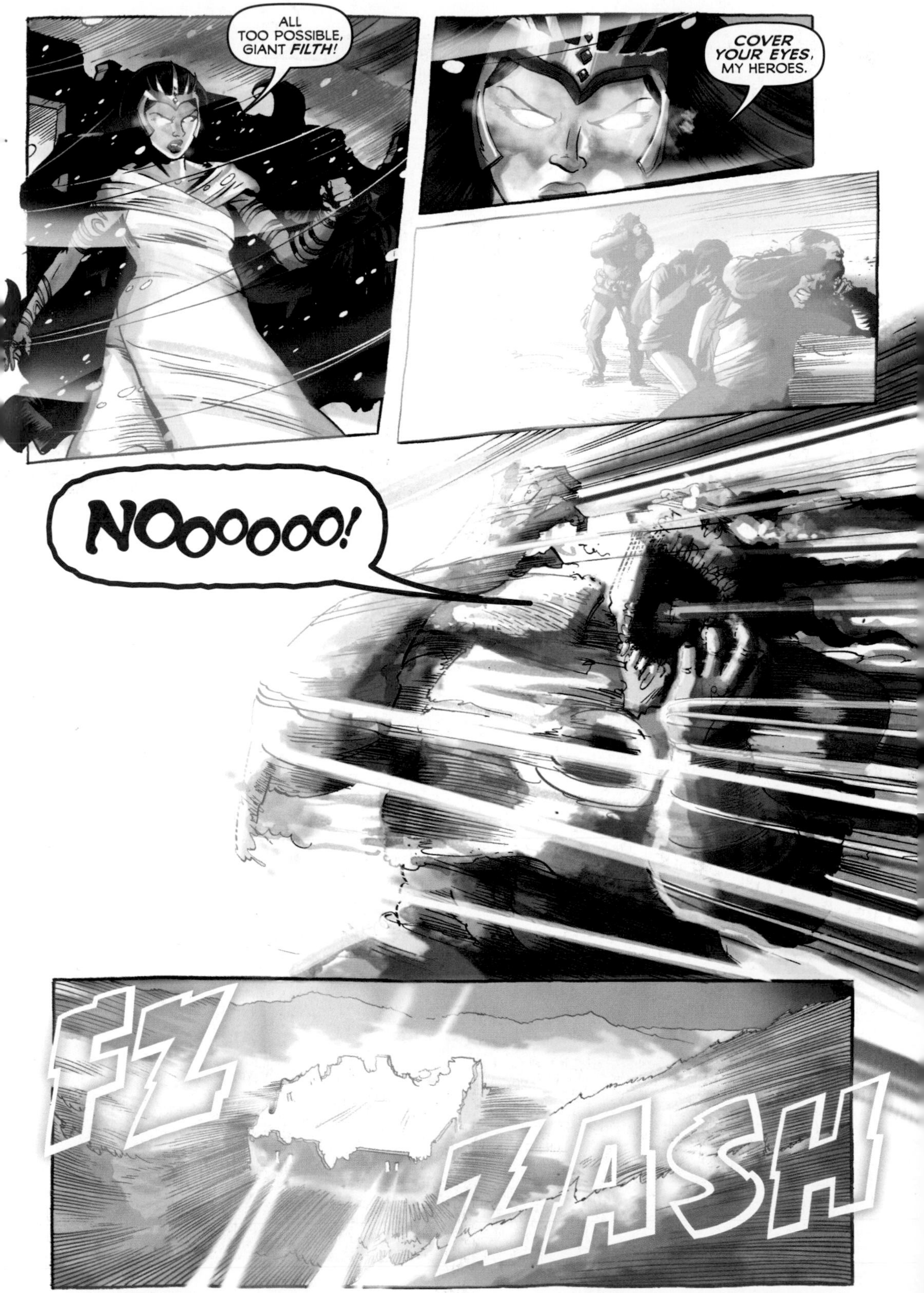
ALL TOO POSSIBLE, GIANT *FILTH*!
COVER YOUR EYES, MY HEROES.
NOOOOOO!
FZ
ZASH

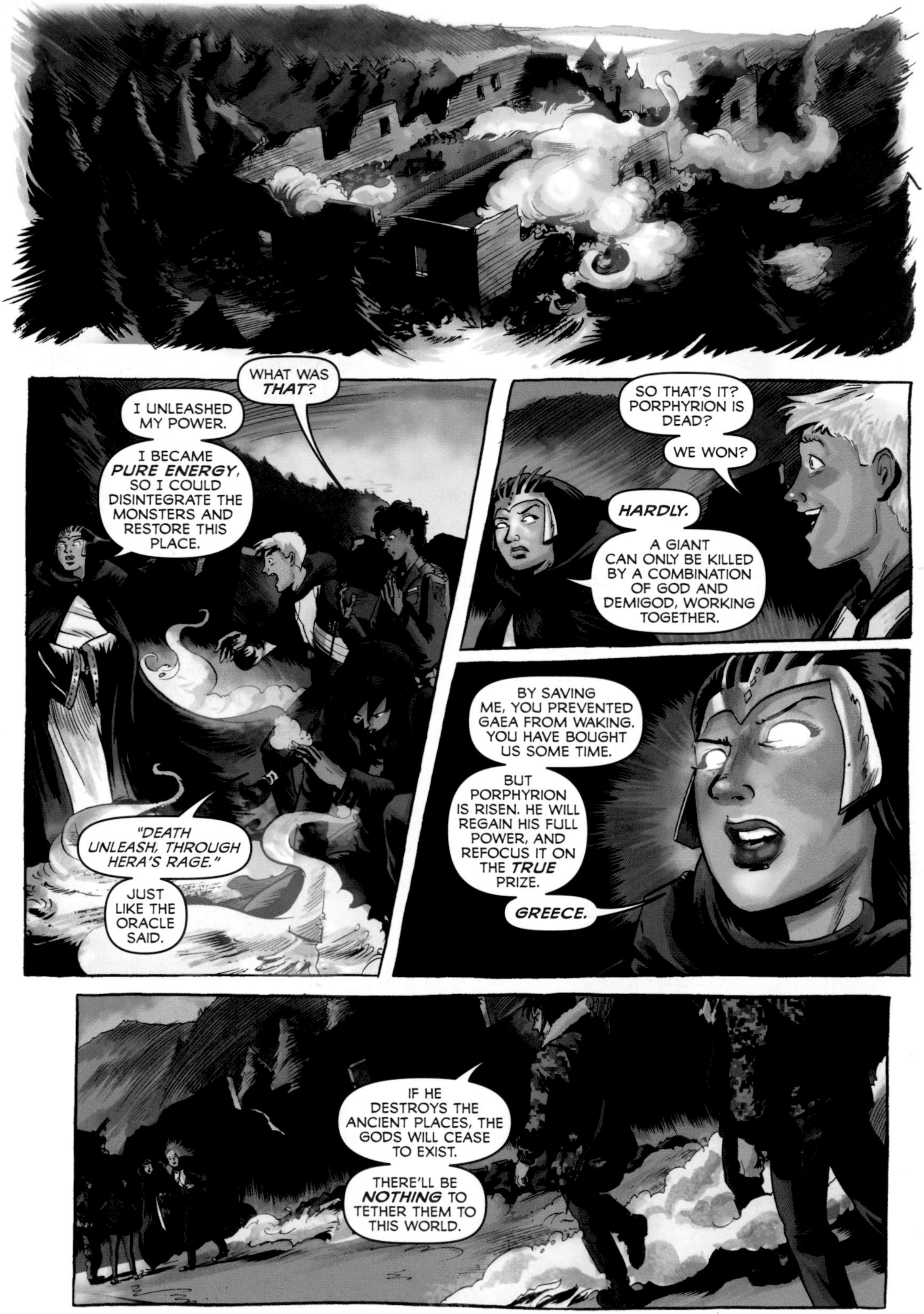
WHAT WAS *THAT*?
I UNLEASHED MY POWER.
I BECAME ***PURE ENERGY***, SO I COULD DISINTEGRATE THE MONSTERS AND RESTORE THIS PLACE.
"DEATH UNLEASH, THROUGH HERA'S RAGE."
JUST LIKE THE ORACLE SAID.
SO THAT'S IT? PORPHYRION IS DEAD?
WE WON?
HARDLY.
A GIANT CAN ONLY BE KILLED BY A COMBINATION OF GOD AND DEMIGOD, WORKING TOGETHER.
BY SAVING ME, YOU PREVENTED GAEA FROM WAKING. YOU HAVE BOUGHT US SOME TIME.
BUT PORPHYRION IS RISEN. HE WILL REGAIN HIS FULL POWER, AND REFOCUS IT ON THE ***TRUE*** PRIZE.
GREECE.
IF HE DESTROYS THE ANCIENT PLACES, THE GODS WILL CEASE TO EXIST.
THERE'LL BE ***NOTHING*** TO TETHER THEM TO THIS WORLD.

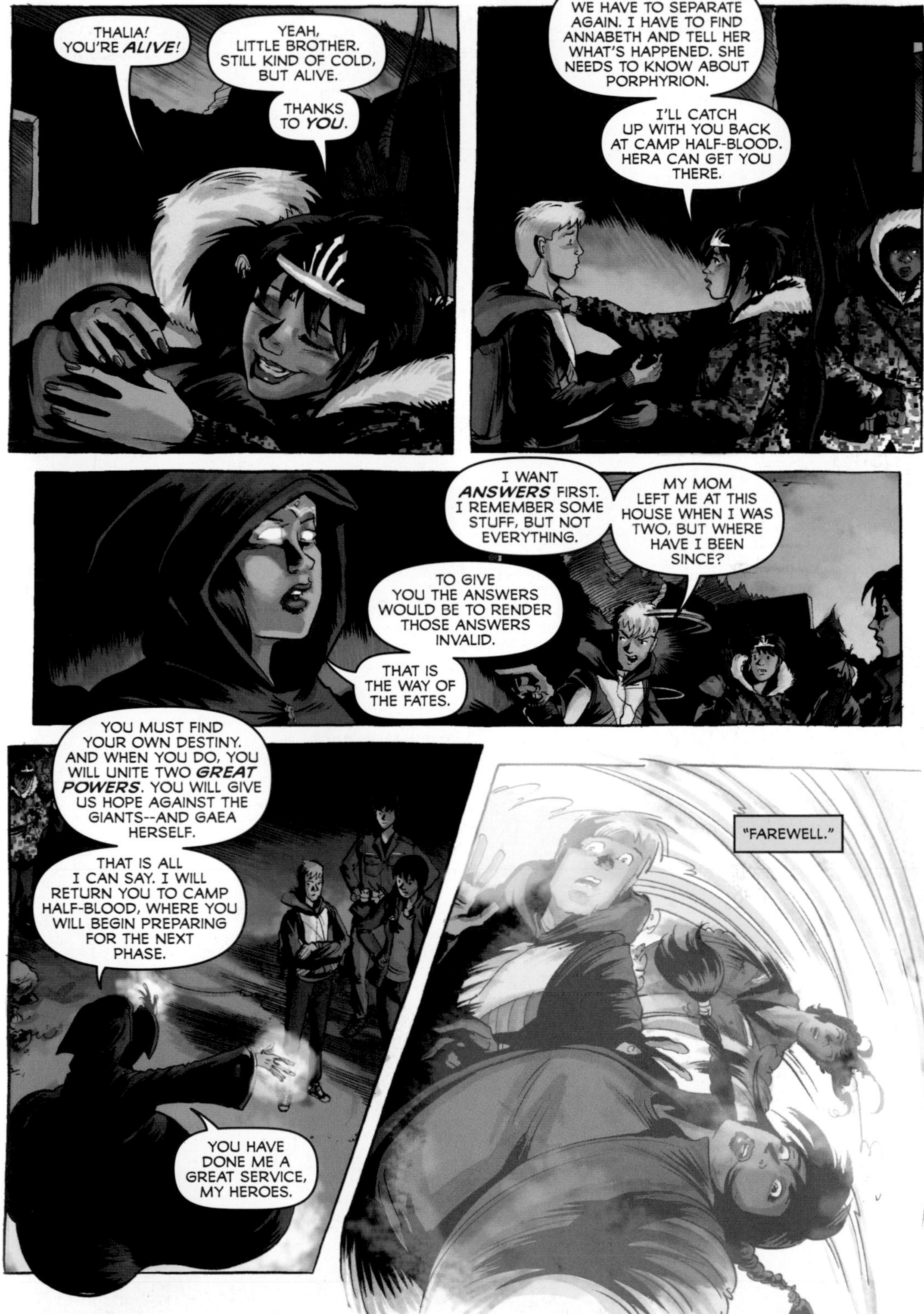
THALIA! YOU'RE *ALIVE*!
YEAH, LITTLE BROTHER. STILL KIND OF COLD, BUT ALIVE.
THANKS TO *YOU*.
AND NOW WE HAVE TO SEPARATE AGAIN. I HAVE TO FIND ANNABETH AND TELL HER WHAT'S HAPPENED. SHE NEEDS TO KNOW ABOUT PORPHYRION.
I'LL CATCH UP WITH YOU BACK AT CAMP HALF-BLOOD. HERA CAN GET YOU THERE.
I WANT *ANSWERS* FIRST. I REMEMBER SOME STUFF, BUT NOT EVERYTHING.
MY MOM LEFT ME AT THIS HOUSE WHEN I WAS TWO, BUT WHERE HAVE I BEEN SINCE?
TO GIVE YOU THE ANSWERS WOULD BE TO RENDER THOSE ANSWERS INVALID.
THAT IS THE WAY OF THE FATES.
YOU MUST FIND YOUR OWN DESTINY. AND WHEN YOU DO, YOU WILL UNITE TWO *GREAT POWERS*. YOU WILL GIVE US HOPE AGAINST THE GIANTS--AND GAEA HERSELF.
THAT IS ALL I CAN SAY. I WILL RETURN YOU TO CAMP HALF-BLOOD, WHERE YOU WILL BEGIN PREPARING FOR THE NEXT PHASE.
YOU HAVE DONE ME A GREAT SERVICE, MY HEROES.
"FAREWELL."

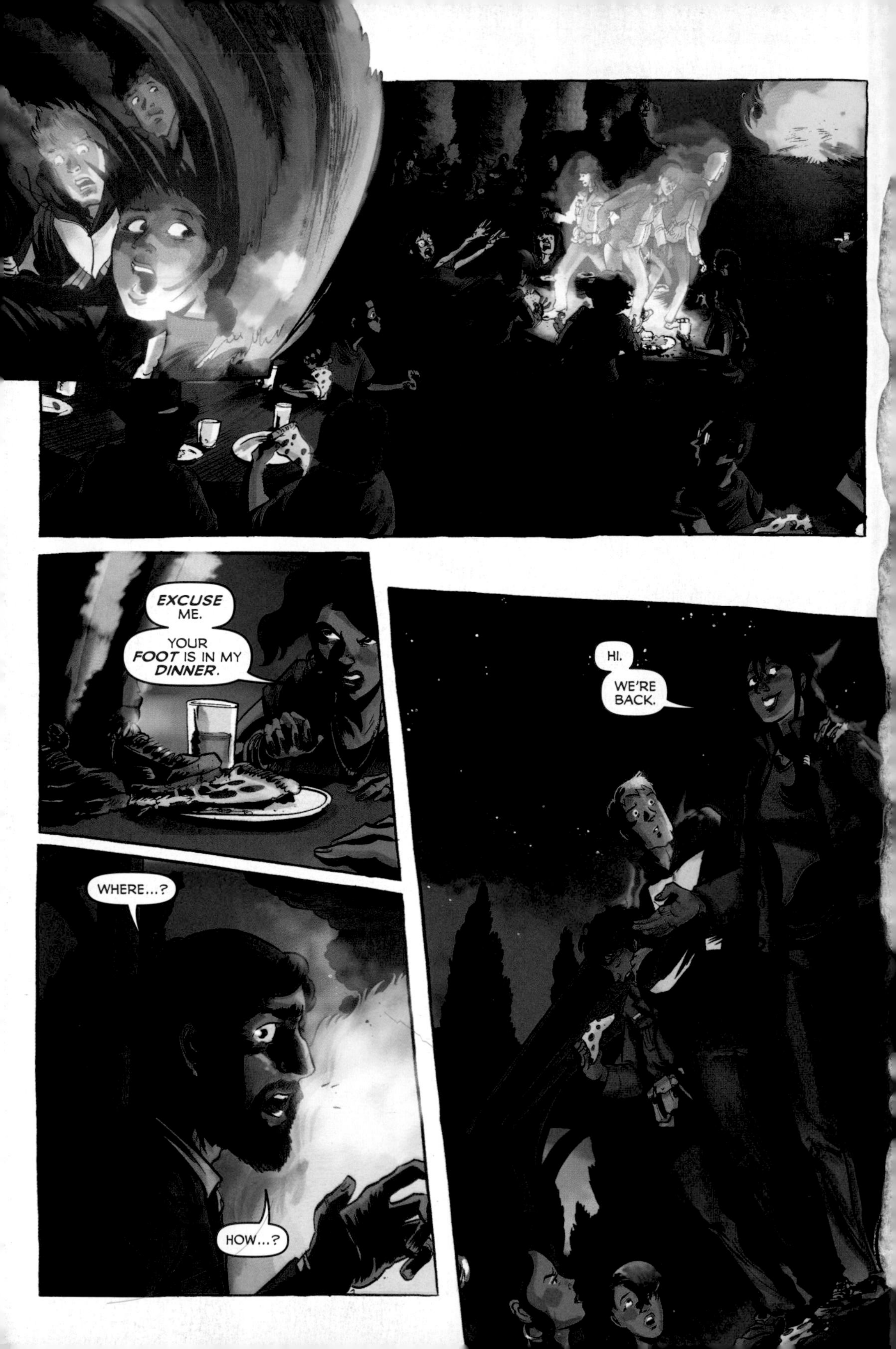
EXCUSE ME.
YOUR FOOT IS IN MY DINNER.
HI.
WE'RE BACK.
WHERE...?
HOW...?

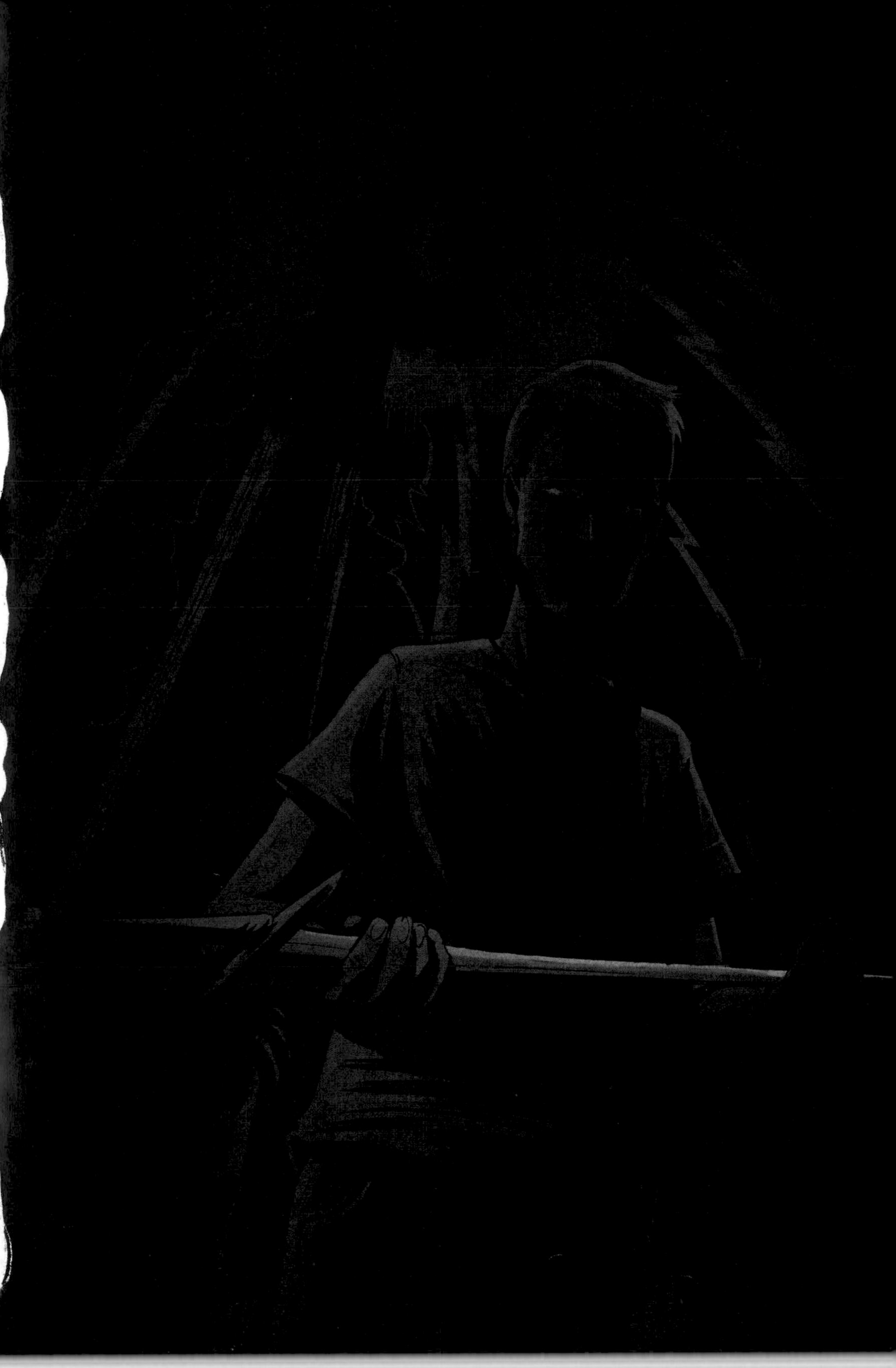

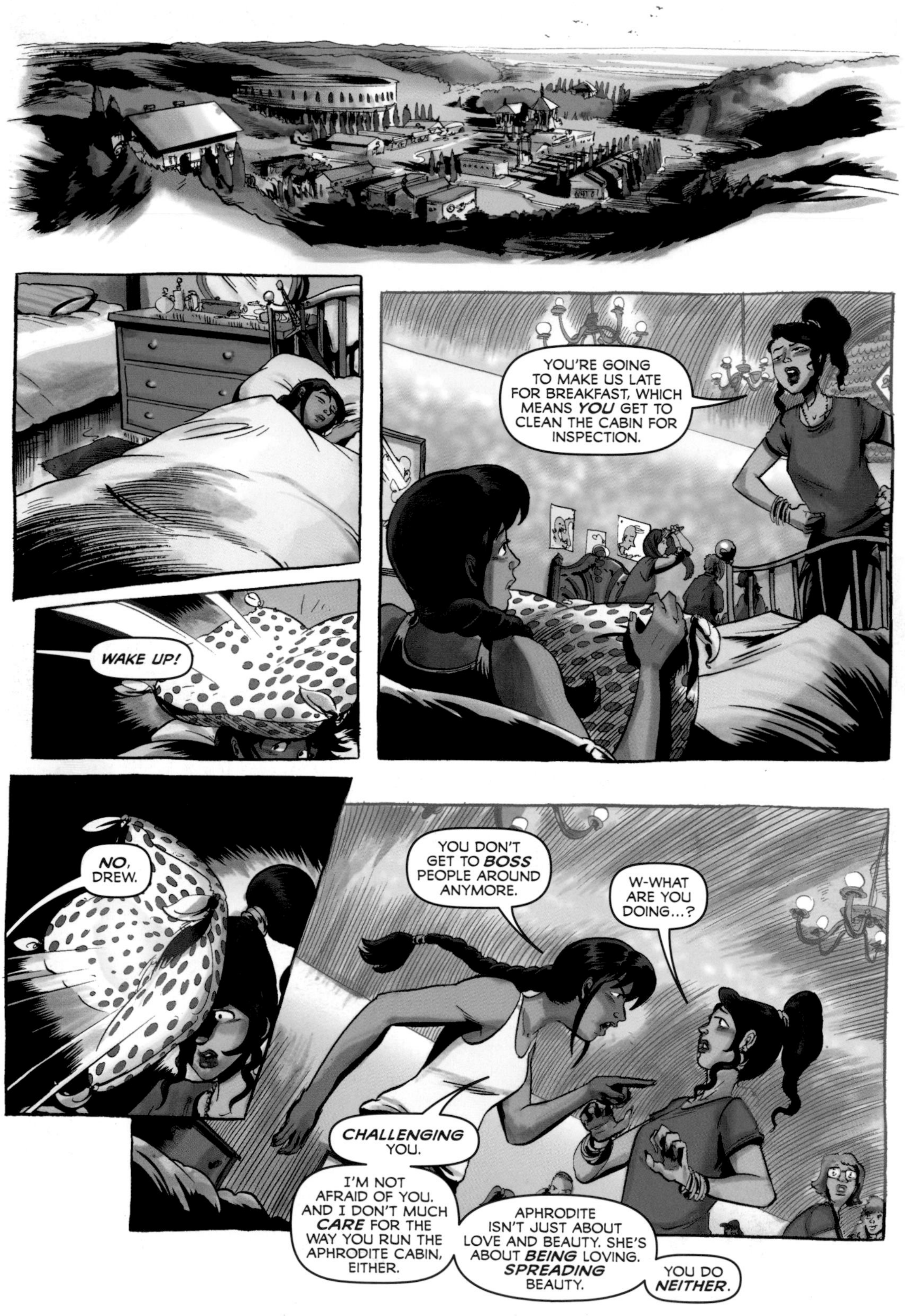
WAKE UP!
YOU'RE GOING TO MAKE US LATE FOR BREAKFAST, WHICH MEANS *YOU* GET TO CLEAN THE CABIN FOR INSPECTION.
NO, DREW.
YOU DON'T GET TO *BOSS* PEOPLE AROUND ANYMORE.
W-WHAT ARE YOU DOING...?
CHALLENGING YOU.
I'M NOT AFRAID OF YOU. AND I DON'T MUCH *CARE* FOR THE WAY YOU RUN THE APHRODITE CABIN, EITHER.
APHRODITE ISN'T JUST ABOUT LOVE AND BEAUTY. SHE'S ABOUT *BEING* LOVING. *SPREADING* BEAUTY.
YOU DO *NEITHER*.

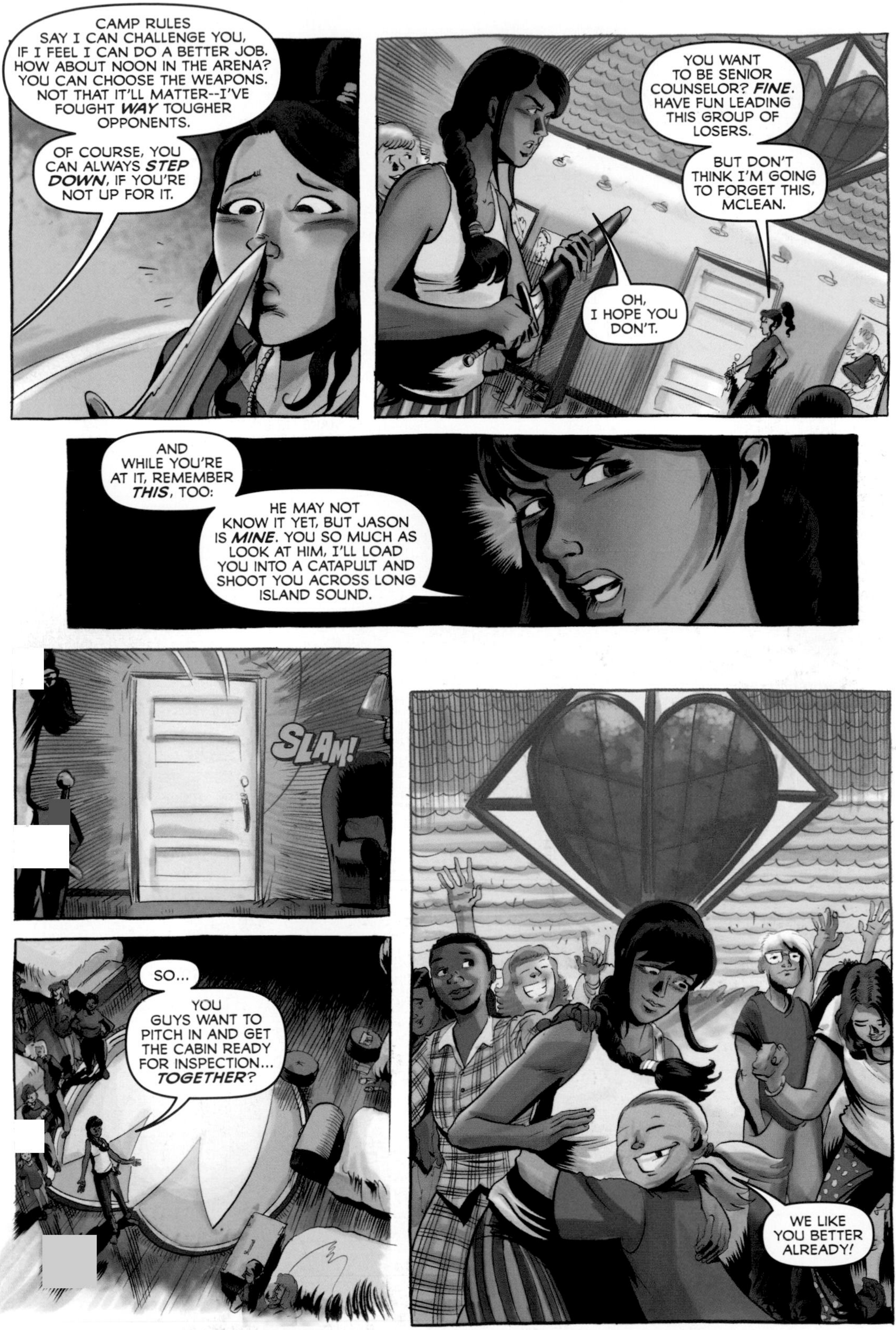
CAMP RULES SAY I CAN CHALLENGE YOU, IF I FEEL I CAN DO A BETTER JOB. HOW ABOUT NOON IN THE ARENA? YOU CAN CHOOSE THE WEAPONS. NOT THAT IT'LL MATTER--I'VE FOUGHT *WAY* TOUGHER OPPONENTS.
OF COURSE, YOU CAN ALWAYS *STEP DOWN*, IF YOU'RE NOT UP FOR IT.
YOU WANT TO BE SENIOR COUNSELOR? *FINE*. HAVE FUN LEADING THIS GROUP OF LOSERS.
BUT DON'T THINK I'M GOING TO FORGET THIS, MCLEAN.
OH, I HOPE YOU DON'T.
AND WHILE YOU'RE AT IT, REMEMBER *THIS*, TOO:
HE MAY NOT KNOW IT YET, BUT JASON IS *MINE*. YOU SO MUCH AS LOOK AT HIM, I'LL LOAD YOU INTO A CATAPULT AND SHOOT YOU ACROSS LONG ISLAND SOUND.
SLAM!
SO...
YOU GUYS WANT TO PITCH IN AND GET THE CABIN READY FOR INSPECTION... *TOGETHER*?
WE LIKE YOU BETTER ALREADY!

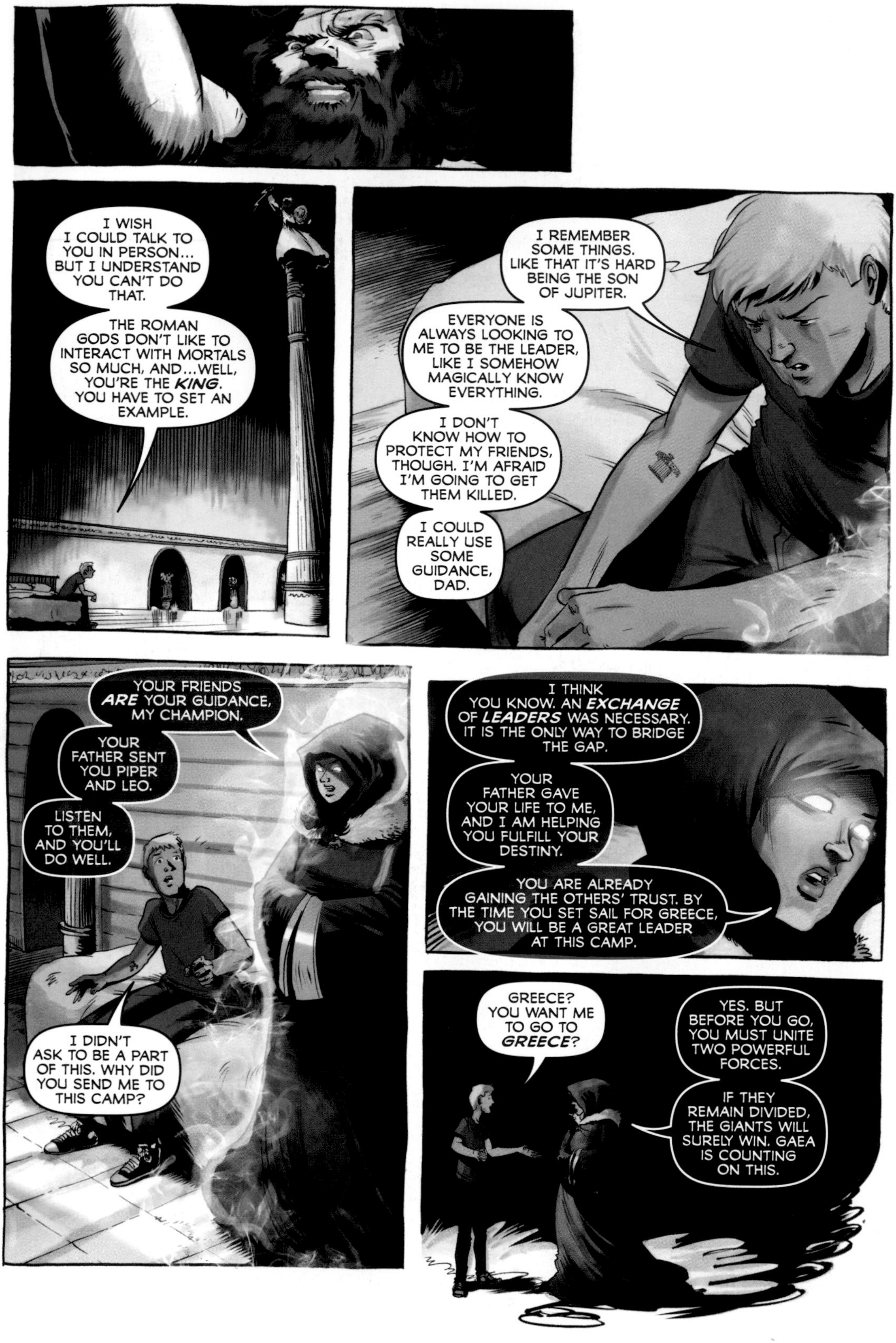
I WISH I COULD TALK TO YOU IN PERSON... BUT I UNDERSTAND YOU CAN'T DO THAT.
THE ROMAN GODS DON'T LIKE TO INTERACT WITH MORTALS SO MUCH, AND...WELL, YOU'RE THE *KING*. YOU HAVE TO SET AN EXAMPLE.
I REMEMBER SOME THINGS. LIKE THAT IT'S HARD BEING THE SON OF JUPITER.
EVERYONE IS ALWAYS LOOKING TO ME TO BE THE LEADER, LIKE I SOMEHOW MAGICALLY KNOW EVERYTHING.
I DON'T KNOW HOW TO PROTECT MY FRIENDS, THOUGH. I'M AFRAID I'M GOING TO GET THEM KILLED.
I COULD REALLY USE SOME GUIDANCE, DAD.
YOUR FRIENDS *ARE* YOUR GUIDANCE, MY CHAMPION.
YOUR FATHER SENT YOU PIPER AND LEO.
LISTEN TO THEM, AND YOU'LL DO WELL.
I DIDN'T ASK TO BE A PART OF THIS. WHY DID YOU SEND ME TO THIS CAMP?
I THINK YOU KNOW. AN *EXCHANGE* OF *LEADERS* WAS NECESSARY. IT IS THE ONLY WAY TO BRIDGE THE GAP.
YOUR FATHER GAVE YOUR LIFE TO ME, AND I AM HELPING YOU FULFILL YOUR DESTINY.
YOU ARE ALREADY GAINING THE OTHERS' TRUST. BY THE TIME YOU SET SAIL FOR GREECE, YOU WILL BE A GREAT LEADER AT THIS CAMP.
GREECE? YOU WANT ME TO GO TO *GREECE*?
YES. BUT BEFORE YOU GO, YOU MUST UNITE TWO POWERFUL FORCES.
IF THEY REMAIN DIVIDED, THE GIANTS WILL SURELY WIN. GAEA IS COUNTING ON THIS.

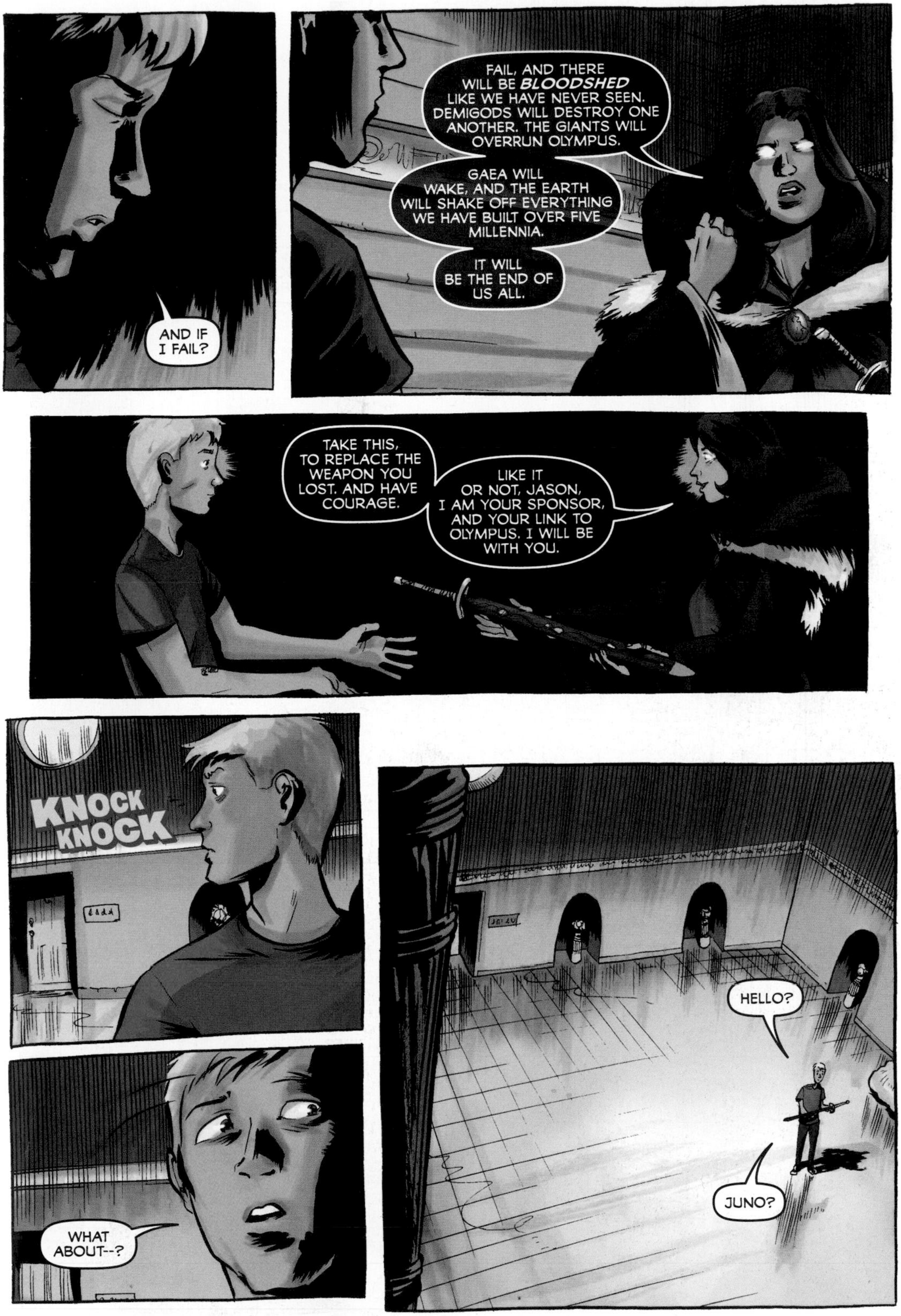
AND IF I FAIL?
FAIL, AND THERE WILL BE *BLOODSHED* LIKE WE HAVE NEVER SEEN. DEMIGODS WILL DESTROY ONE ANOTHER. THE GIANTS WILL OVERRUN OLYMPUS.
GAEA WILL WAKE, AND THE EARTH WILL SHAKE OFF EVERYTHING WE HAVE BUILT OVER FIVE MILLENNIA.
IT WILL BE THE END OF US ALL.
TAKE THIS, TO REPLACE THE WEAPON YOU LOST. AND HAVE COURAGE.
LIKE IT OR NOT, JASON, I AM YOUR SPONSOR, AND YOUR LINK TO OLYMPUS. I WILL BE WITH YOU.
KNOCK KNOCK
WHAT ABOUT--?
HELLO?
JUNO?

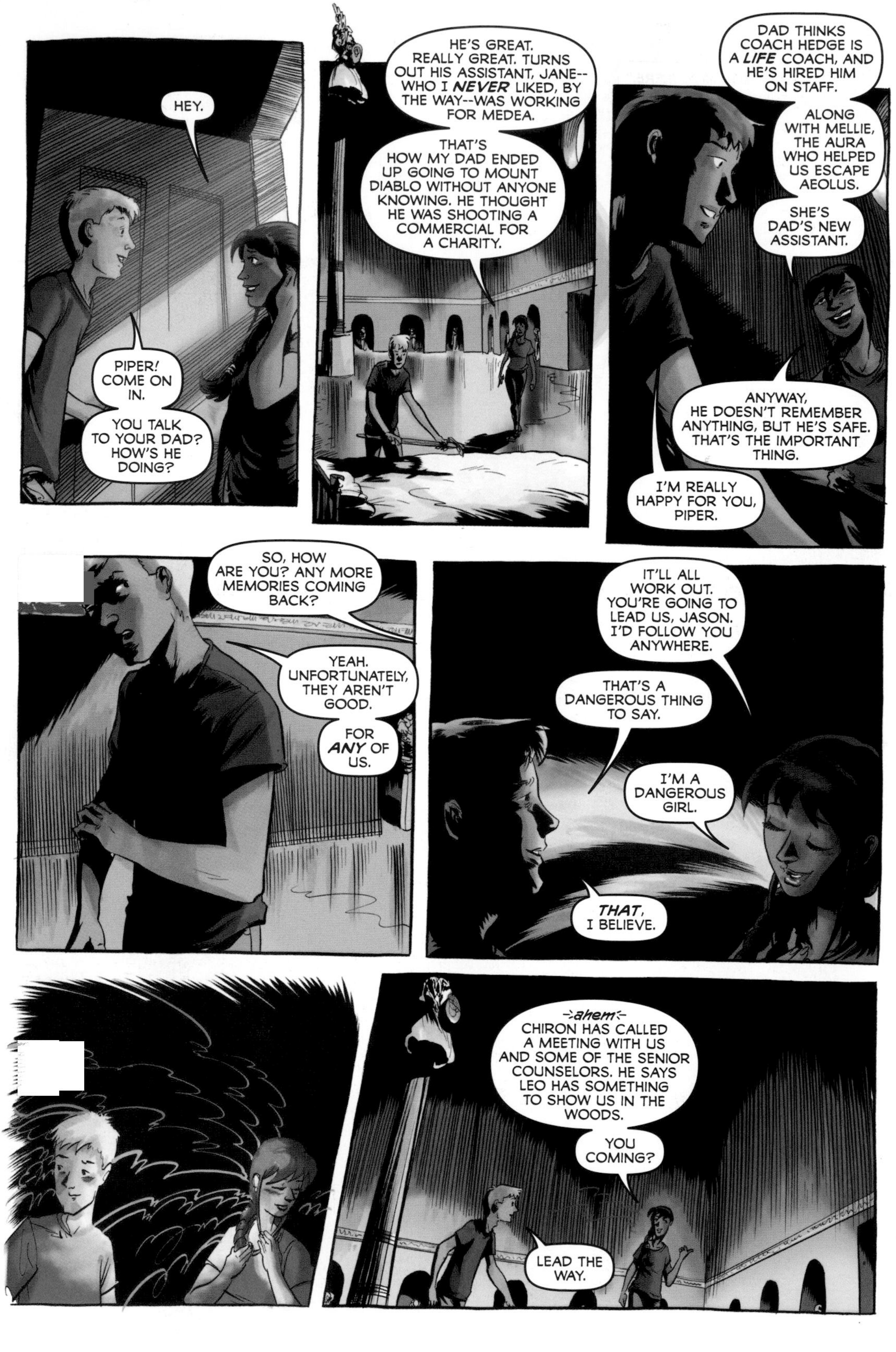
HEY.
PIPER! COME ON IN.
YOU TALK TO YOUR DAD? HOW'S HE DOING?
HE'S GREAT. REALLY GREAT. TURNS OUT HIS ASSISTANT, JANE-- WHO I NEVER LIKED, BY THE WAY--WAS WORKING FOR MEDEA.
THAT'S HOW MY DAD ENDED UP GOING TO MOUNT DIABLO WITHOUT ANYONE KNOWING. HE THOUGHT HE WAS SHOOTING A COMMERCIAL FOR A CHARITY.
DAD THINKS COACH HEDGE IS A LIFE COACH, AND HE'S HIRED HIM ON STAFF.
ALONG WITH MELLIE, THE AURA WHO HELPED US ESCAPE AEOLUS.
SHE'S DAD'S NEW ASSISTANT.
ANYWAY, HE DOESN'T REMEMBER ANYTHING, BUT HE'S SAFE. THAT'S THE IMPORTANT THING.
I'M REALLY HAPPY FOR YOU, PIPER.
SO, HOW ARE YOU? ANY MORE MEMORIES COMING BACK?
YEAH. UNFORTUNATELY, THEY AREN'T GOOD.
FOR ANY OF US.
IT'LL ALL WORK OUT. YOU'RE GOING TO LEAD US, JASON. I'D FOLLOW YOU ANYWHERE.
THAT'S A DANGEROUS THING TO SAY.
I'M A DANGEROUS GIRL.
THAT, I BELIEVE.
ahem
CHIRON HAS CALLED A MEETING WITH US AND SOME OF THE SENIOR COUNSELORS. HE SAYS LEO HAS SOMETHING TO SHOW US IN THE WOODS.
YOU COMING?
LEAD THE WAY.

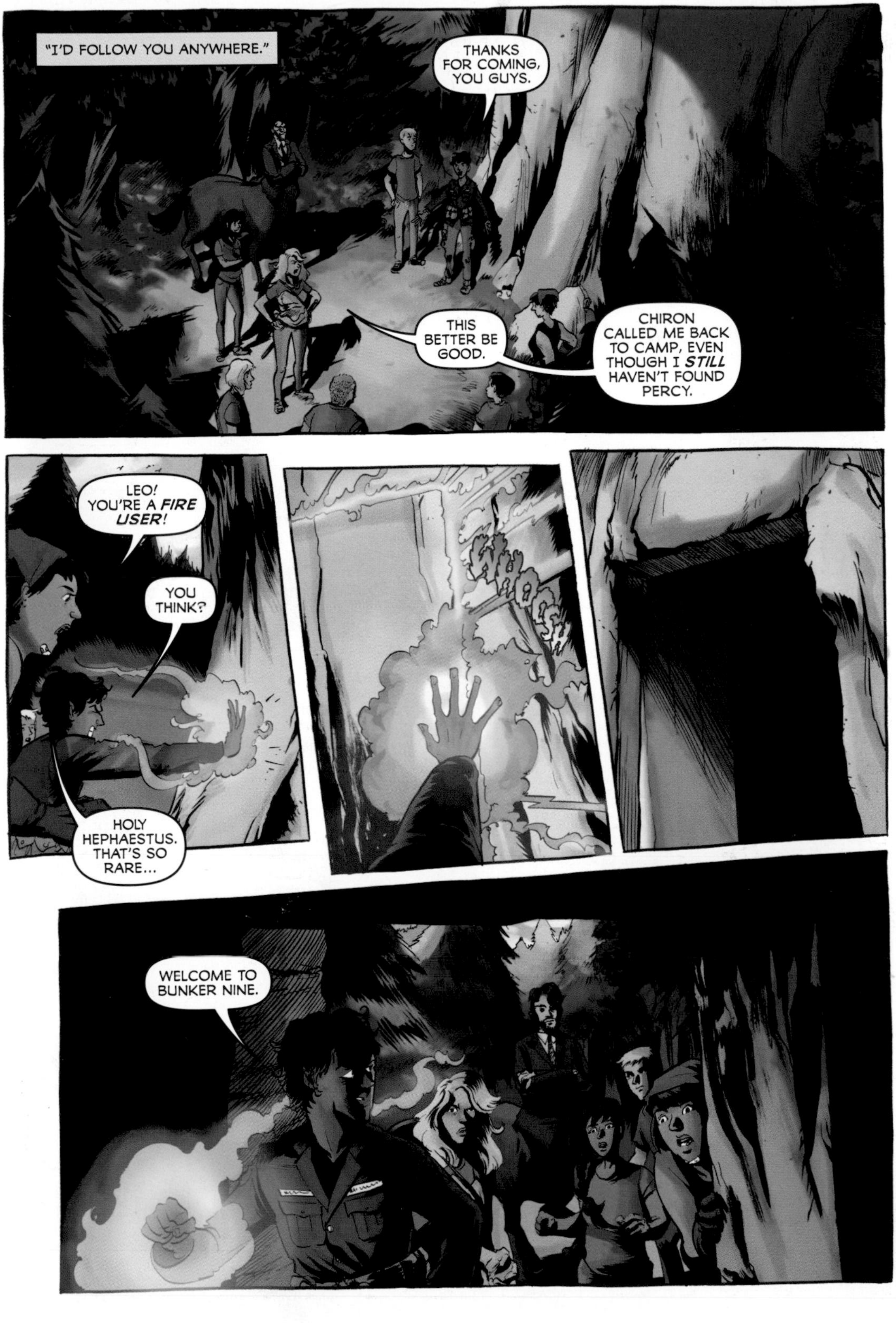
"I'D FOLLOW YOU ANYWHERE."
THANKS FOR COMING, YOU GUYS.
THIS BETTER BE GOOD.
CHIRON CALLED ME BACK TO CAMP, EVEN THOUGH I *STILL* HAVEN'T FOUND PERCY.
LEO! YOU'RE A *FIRE USER*!
YOU THINK?
HOLY HEPHAESTUS. THAT'S SO RARE...
WHOOSH
WELCOME TO BUNKER NINE.

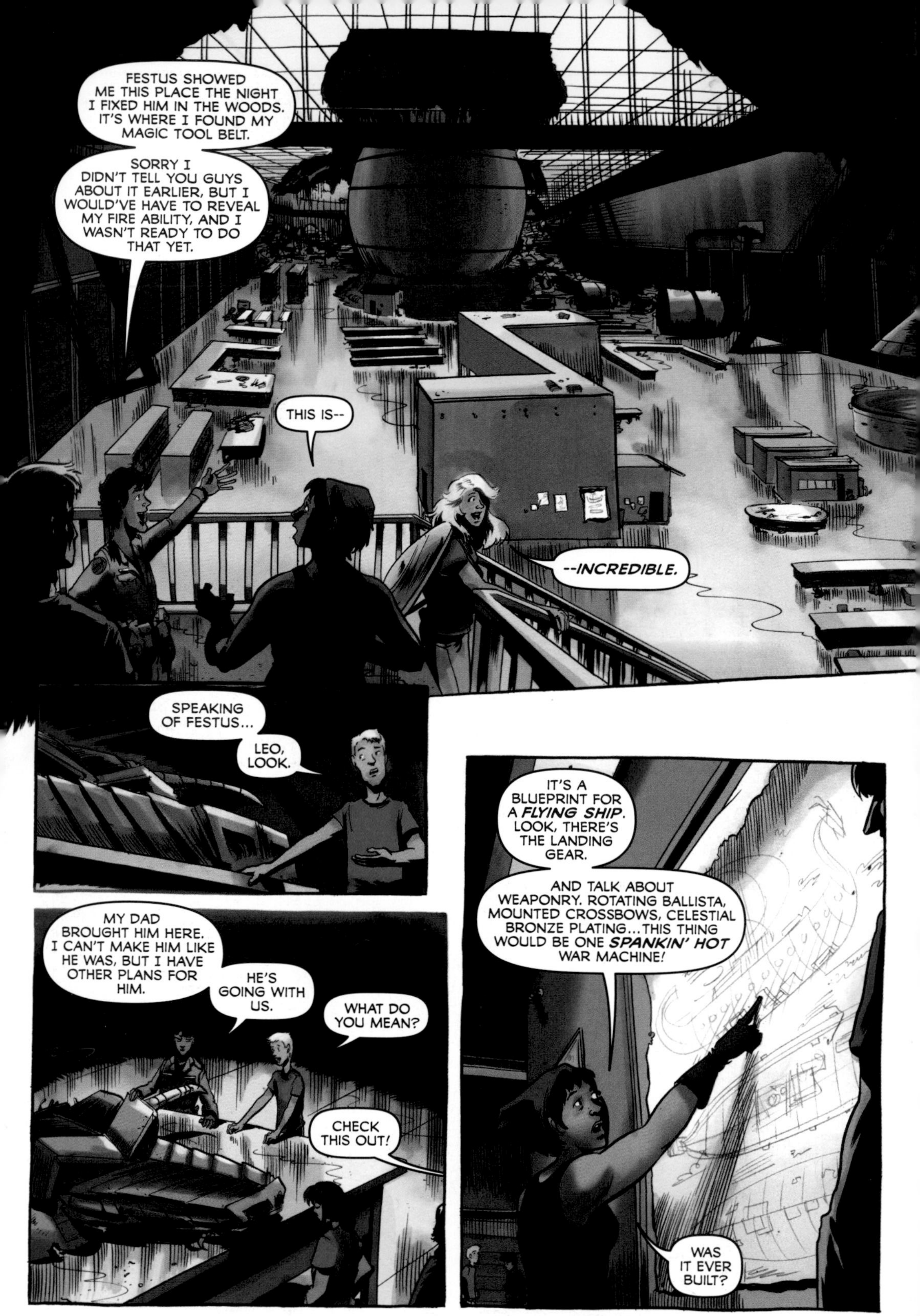
FESTUS SHOWED ME THIS PLACE THE NIGHT I FIXED HIM IN THE WOODS. IT'S WHERE I FOUND MY MAGIC TOOL BELT.
SORRY I DIDN'T TELL YOU GUYS ABOUT IT EARLIER, BUT I WOULD'VE HAVE TO REVEAL MY FIRE ABILITY, AND I WASN'T READY TO DO THAT YET.
THIS IS--
--INCREDIBLE.
SPEAKING OF FESTUS...
LEO, LOOK.
MY DAD BROUGHT HIM HERE. I CAN'T MAKE HIM LIKE HE WAS, BUT I HAVE OTHER PLANS FOR HIM.
HE'S GOING WITH US.
WHAT DO YOU MEAN?
CHECK THIS OUT!
IT'S A BLUEPRINT FOR A *FLYING SHIP*. LOOK, THERE'S THE LANDING GEAR.
AND TALK ABOUT WEAPONRY. ROTATING BALLISTA, MOUNTED CROSSBOWS, CELESTIAL BRONZE PLATING...THIS THING WOULD BE ONE *SPANKIN' HOT* WAR MACHINE!
WAS IT EVER BUILT?

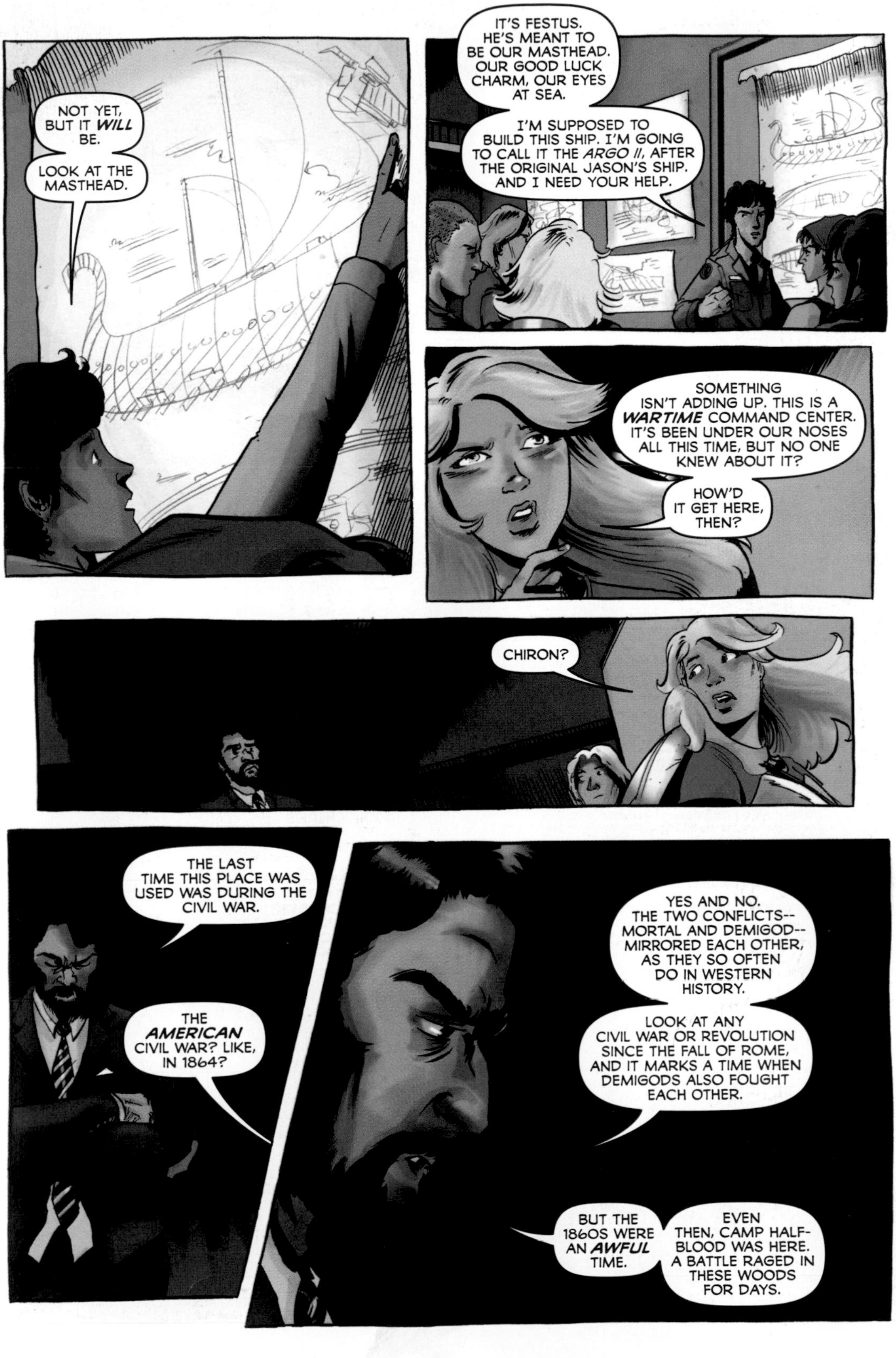
NOT YET, BUT IT *WILL* BE.
LOOK AT THE MASTHEAD.
IT'S FESTUS. HE'S MEANT TO BE OUR MASTHEAD. OUR GOOD LUCK CHARM, OUR EYES AT SEA.
I'M SUPPOSED TO BUILD THIS SHIP. I'M GOING TO CALL IT THE *ARGO II*, AFTER THE ORIGINAL JASON'S SHIP. AND I NEED YOUR HELP.
SOMETHING ISN'T ADDING UP. THIS IS A *WARTIME* COMMAND CENTER. IT'S BEEN UNDER OUR NOSES ALL THIS TIME, BUT NO ONE KNEW ABOUT IT?
HOW'D IT GET HERE, THEN?
CHIRON?
THE LAST TIME THIS PLACE WAS USED WAS DURING THE CIVIL WAR.
THE *AMERICAN* CIVIL WAR? LIKE, IN 1864?
YES AND NO. THE TWO CONFLICTS-- MORTAL AND DEMIGOD-- MIRRORED EACH OTHER, AS THEY SO OFTEN DO IN WESTERN HISTORY.
LOOK AT ANY CIVIL WAR OR REVOLUTION SINCE THE FALL OF ROME, AND IT MARKS A TIME WHEN DEMIGODS ALSO FOUGHT EACH OTHER.
BUT THE 1860S WERE AN *AWFUL* TIME.
EVEN THEN, CAMP HALF-BLOOD WAS HERE. A BATTLE RAGED IN THESE WOODS FOR DAYS.

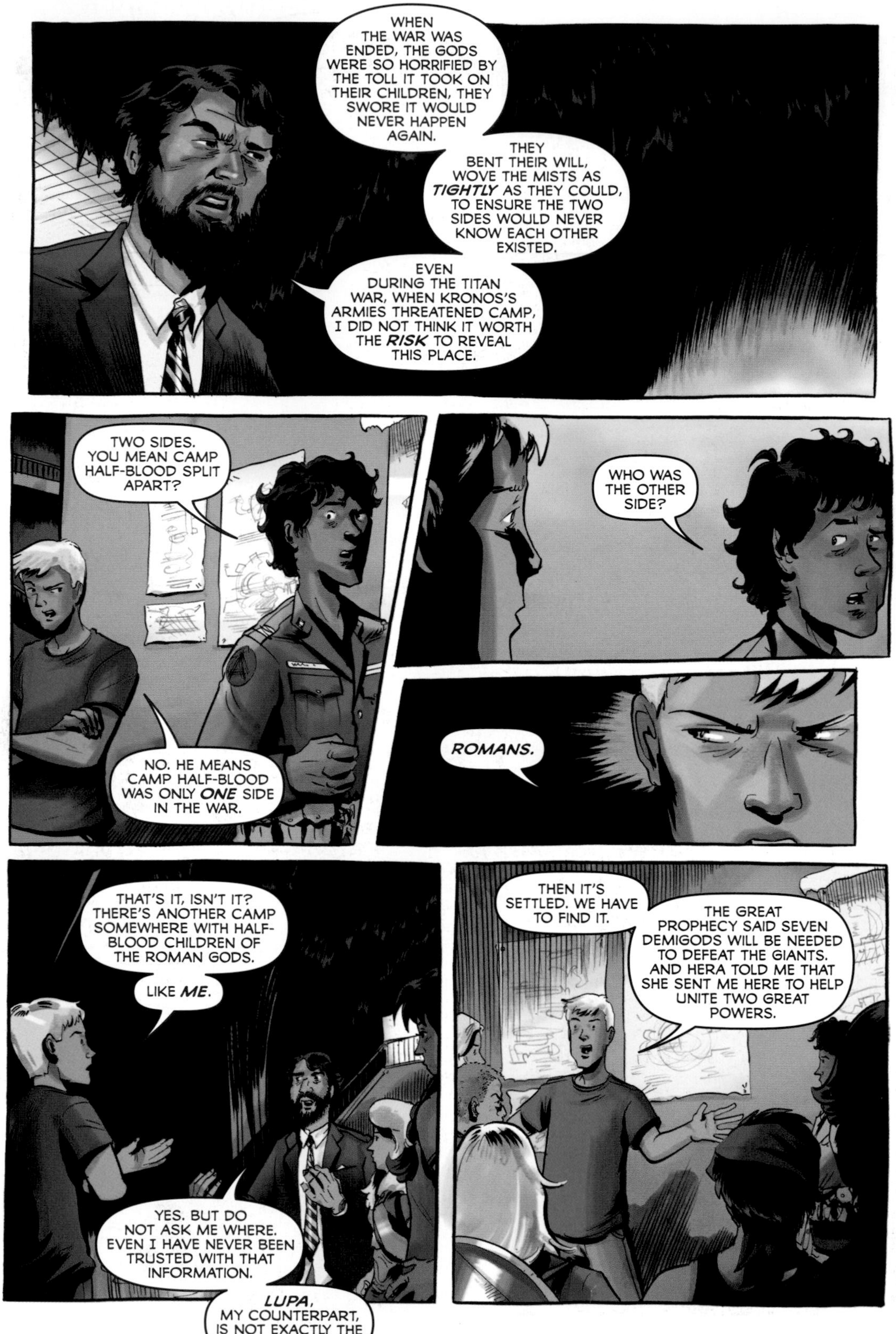
WHEN THE WAR WAS ENDED, THE GODS WERE SO HORRIFIED BY THE TOLL IT TOOK ON THEIR CHILDREN, THEY SWORE IT WOULD NEVER HAPPEN AGAIN.
THEY BENT THEIR WILL, WOVE THE MISTS AS *TIGHTLY* AS THEY COULD, TO ENSURE THE TWO SIDES WOULD NEVER KNOW EACH OTHER EXISTED.
EVEN DURING THE TITAN WAR, WHEN KRONOS'S ARMIES THREATENED CAMP, I DID NOT THINK IT WORTH THE *RISK* TO REVEAL THIS PLACE.
TWO SIDES. YOU MEAN CAMP HALF-BLOOD SPLIT APART?
NO. HE MEANS CAMP HALF-BLOOD WAS ONLY *ONE* SIDE IN THE WAR.
WHO WAS THE OTHER SIDE?
ROMANS.
THAT'S IT, ISN'T IT? THERE'S ANOTHER CAMP SOMEWHERE WITH HALF-BLOOD CHILDREN OF THE ROMAN GODS.
LIKE *ME*.
YES. BUT DO NOT ASK ME WHERE. EVEN I HAVE NEVER BEEN TRUSTED WITH THAT INFORMATION.
LUPA, MY COUNTERPART, IS NOT EXACTLY THE SHARING TYPE.
THEN IT'S SETTLED. WE HAVE TO FIND IT.
THE GREAT PROPHECY SAID SEVEN DEMIGODS WILL BE NEEDED TO DEFEAT THE GIANTS. AND HERA TOLD ME THAT SHE SENT ME HERE TO HELP UNITE TWO GREAT POWERS.

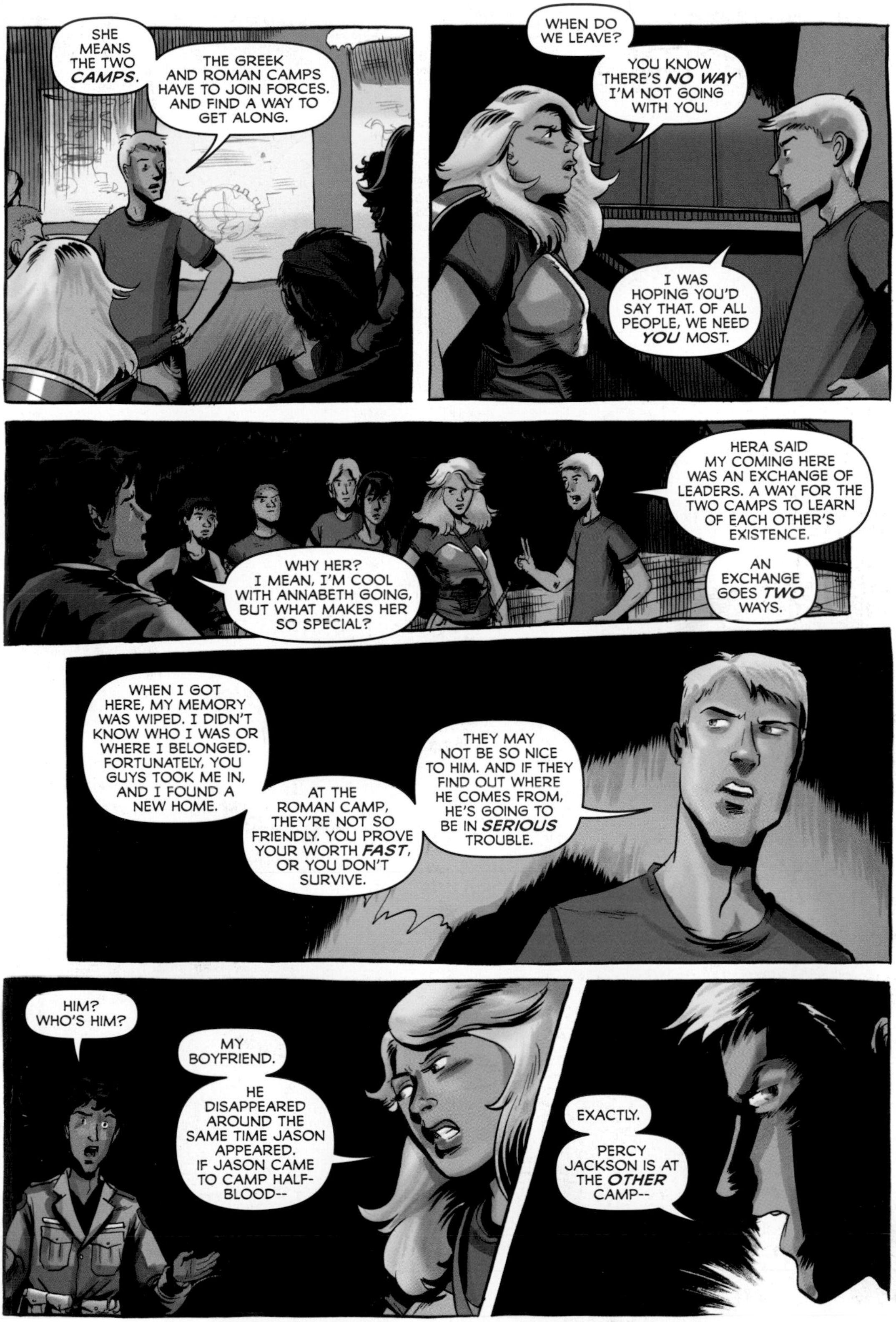
SHE MEANS THE TWO *CAMPS*.
THE GREEK AND ROMAN CAMPS HAVE TO JOIN FORCES. AND FIND A WAY TO GET ALONG.
WHEN DO WE LEAVE?
YOU KNOW THERE'S *NO WAY* I'M NOT GOING WITH YOU.
I WAS HOPING YOU'D SAY THAT. OF ALL PEOPLE, WE NEED *YOU* MOST.
WHY HER? I MEAN, I'M COOL WITH ANNABETH GOING, BUT WHAT MAKES HER SO SPECIAL?
HERA SAID MY COMING HERE WAS AN EXCHANGE OF LEADERS. A WAY FOR THE TWO CAMPS TO LEARN OF EACH OTHER'S EXISTENCE.
AN EXCHANGE GOES *TWO* WAYS.
WHEN I GOT HERE, MY MEMORY WAS WIPED. I DIDN'T KNOW WHO I WAS OR WHERE I BELONGED. FORTUNATELY, YOU GUYS TOOK ME IN, AND I FOUND A NEW HOME.
AT THE ROMAN CAMP, THEY'RE NOT SO FRIENDLY. YOU PROVE YOUR WORTH *FAST*, OR YOU DON'T SURVIVE.
THEY MAY NOT BE SO NICE TO HIM. AND IF THEY FIND OUT WHERE HE COMES FROM, HE'S GOING TO BE IN *SERIOUS* TROUBLE.
HIM? WHO'S HIM?
MY BOYFRIEND.
HE DISAPPEARED AROUND THE SAME TIME JASON APPEARED. IF JASON CAME TO CAMP HALF-BLOOD--
EXACTLY.
PERCY JACKSON IS AT THE *OTHER* CAMP--

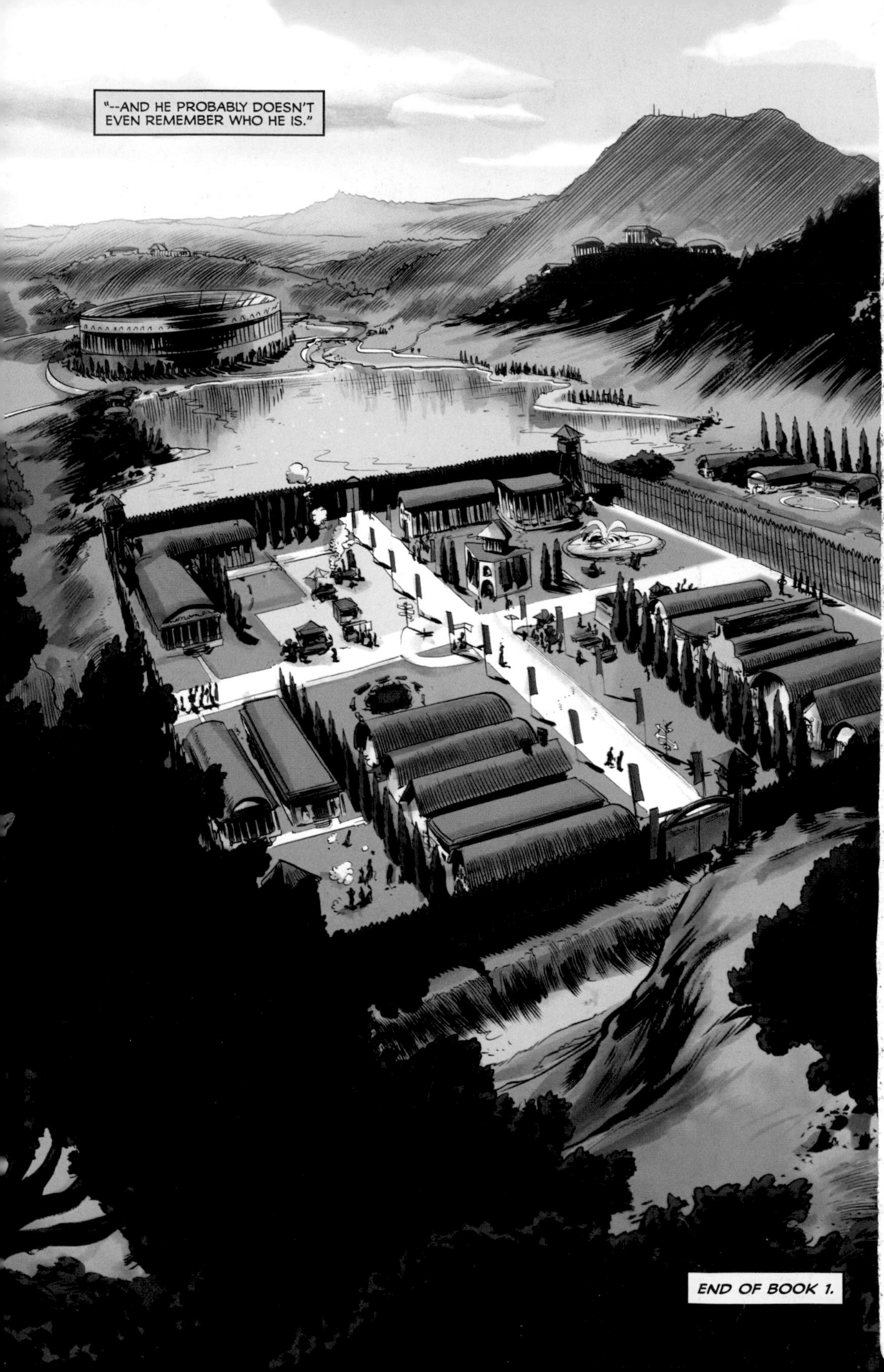
"--AND HE PROBABLY DOESN'T EVEN REMEMBER WHO HE IS."
END OF BOOK 1.